MW00609486

H. P. Lovecraft

H. P. Lovecraft

*Selected Works,
Critical Perspectives and
Interviews on His Influence*

H. P. LOVECRAFT

Edited by LEVERETT BUTTS

McFarland & Company, Inc., Publishers

Jefferson, North Carolina

Works by H.P. Lovecraft used by arrangement
with the Estate of H.P. Lovecraft.

LIBRARY OF CONGRESS CATALOGUING-IN-PUBLICATION DATA

Names: Lovecraft, H. P. (Howard Phillips), 1890–1937, author. |
Butts, Leverett.
Title: H.P. Lovecraft : selected works, critical perspectives and
interviews on his influence / H.P. Lovecraft ; edited by Leverett Butts.
Description: Jefferson, North Carolina : McFarland & Company, Inc.,
Publishers, 2018. | Includes bibliographical references and index.
Identifiers: LCCN 2018022636 | ISBN 9781476670911 (softcover :
acid free paper) ∞
Subjects: LCSH: Lovecraft, H. P. (Howard Phillips), 1890–1937—
Criticism and interpretation.
Classification: LCC PS3523.O833 A6 2018b | DDC 741.5/973—dc23
LC record available at https://lccn.loc.gov/2018022636

BRITISH LIBRARY CATALOGUING DATA ARE AVAILABLE

ISBN (print) 978-1-4766-7091-1
ISBN (ebook) 978-1-4766-3303-9

© 2018 Leverett Butts. All rights reserved

No part of this book may be reproduced or transmitted in any form
or by any means, electronic or mechanical, including photocopying
or recording, or by any information storage and retrieval system,
without permission in writing from the publisher.

Front cover images © 2018 iStock

Printed in the United States of America

McFarland & Company, Inc., Publishers
Box 611, Jefferson, North Carolina 28640
www.mcfarlandpub.com

To Michael Bunch and Christopher Nugent,
who first introduced me
to the works of H.P. Lovecraft,
and who continue to introduce me
to good science fiction and fantasy literature

Acknowledgments

I could not have completed a project of this nature without help. I would first like to thank each of my contributors for agreeing to provide essays. It is, after all, incredibly hard to put together a critical edition without actual criticism. I would also like to thank Brad Strickland, Cherie Priest, Caitlín R. Kiernan, Richard Monaco, and T.E.D. Klein for graciously agreeing to participate in this project by either writing essays or allowing themselves to be interviewed.

In order to determine which historical references and vocabulary needed annotating, I asked two of my former students, a sophomore and a senior, to read the primary texts and highlight anything they found problematic. With this help, I did not have to merely assume what a student may find confusing; I had actual input from college students. I would therefore also like to thank Ann Marie Koehler, Rebekah Terry, and Amanda Adams for their invaluable help. While I'm at it, my stepson, Jake Vinson, deserves credit for "beta testing" the annotations and helping proofread the text.

I would like to thank S.T. Joshi in particular. From the moment I wrote him an unsolicited email asking if he'd be interested in contributing to the project, he has shown as much enthusiasm for it as I felt. In addition to allowing me to reprint an essay he was very shortly to republish himself in a collection, he sent me the most correct text of "Call of Cthulhu" early on to include with the book proposal. When I have reached dead ends in my research, he has consistently provided me with either the answer to my inquiry or a list of sources to consult (seriously, the man knows everything about Lovecraft and everything about what's been written about Lovecraft. Everything. If Joshi doesn't know it, it's not worth knowing). And he has never once over the last few years I have been working on this project seemed irritated or annoyed by my questions. He has never been anything less than encouraging and supportive. I have learned as much or more about Lovecraft through my correspondence with Joshi as I have learned through my own research. Thank you, S.T., and I sincerely hope I have the opportunity to work with you again.

Table of Contents

Preface

Though now considered one of the grandfathers of modern horror, when Howard Phillips Lovecraft died on March 15, 1937, he was all but penniless, having severely undercharged for his ghostwriting and editing work and being relatively unknown as a writer. Unable often to make ends meet, Lovecraft frequently skipped meals, thus suffering from malnutrition, which may well have contributed to the intestinal cancer that took his life.

He left behind more than 60 short stories, novellas, and novels, not counting the more than 30 collaborations (which were often nothing more than Lovecraft's own reworkings of his collaborator's ideas) and ghostwritten tales. While Lovecraft's work saw print in several pulp magazines during his lifetime, none of it was ever widely published in book form (with the exception of a small print run chapbook edition of *The Shadow Over Innsmouth* from 1936). After his death, however, two of his friends, August Derleth and Donald Wandrei, having failed to interest mainstream publishers in his work, created the publishing firm Arkham House with the express intent of producing hardback collections of his fiction and essays.

Virtually unknown during his lifetime, Lovecraft would surely have been surprised to see what became of his literary legacy in the years after his death. Lovecraft's work has inspired countless adaptations in almost every medium: film, comic books, television, stage, and even video games.

Even when not adapting Lovecraft's work specifically, his influence is felt elsewhere: It is hard to find a modern horror writer who doesn't credit Lovecraft as one of their primary influences (and many of the other influences, in turn cite Lovecraft as their influence as well). Stephen King, Caitlín R. Kiernan, Neil Gaiman, Cherie Priest, T.E.D. Klein, and countless others all count Lovecraft as one of their greatest influences.

Several television shows such as *Dark Shadows*, *Buffy the Vampire Slayer*, and *Supernatural* show a decidedly Lovecraftian influence, especially in their employment of what he termed "cosmic horror": a story in which the fear comes from the fatalistic implication of being insignificantly powerless before an indifferent, unknowable, and fundamentally alien universe. There have even been at least three episodes of *Scooby-Doo: Mystery Incorporated* with a decidedly Lovecraftian bent: "The Shrieking Madness," "Pawn of Shadows," and "Come Undone."

Lovecraft's writing has inspired games as well: a popular role-playing game, *The Call of Cthulhu*, is set within Lovecraft country, the blend of fictional and real locales, mostly in New England, in which he set his tales. In addition to the aforementioned game adaptations of Lovecraft's fiction, other video games show a clear tendency towards cosmic horror. *Clive Barker's Undying*, for example, is set in the 1920s and follows the investigations of Patrick Galloway, an Irish paranormal investigator, into mysterious occult activities at the coastal estate of his friend Jeremiah Covenant. *Half-Life* and its sequels, though ostensibly an alternate history science fiction game, include several Lovecraftian elements such as giant, tentacled monsters and alien creatures indifferent to humanity but intent on taking over the planet. More recently, a massively multiplayer online game, *The Secret World*, has been released which involves members of secret societies racing to find a cure for a strange plague and fighting cultists intent on bringing about the end of the world. The first few levels of this game are set in Kingsmouth, a coastal New England town that includes such Lovecraftian locales as Arkham Avenue, Black Goat Woods, and Innsmouth Academy.

Lovecraft is everywhere now: in music, his works have influenced heavy metal bands from Metallica to Black Sabbath. Lovecraft has become a popular fixture in fashion as well, as evidenced by the countless Cthulhu designs on t-shirts, Miskatonic University sweatshirts, and "Cthulhu for President" apparel. A few years ago, a local amusement park, Six Flags Over Georgia, even had a Lovecraft-themed Halloween season. You can buy stuffed Cthulhu plushies, Cthulhu Christmas ornaments, Cthulhu dishwares, and even Cthulhu action figures. In just under 80 years, H.P. Lovecraft has gone from a writer of relative obscurity to the poster-boy of kitsch.

However, as Lovecraft scholar S.T. Joshi rightfully points out in his introduction to *The Evolution of the Weird Tale*, popularity does not necessarily equal quality, and when it comes to critical acceptance, Lovecraft, though he has come a long way since 1947 when noted literary critic Edmond Wilson claimed "the only real horror in most of [Lovecraft's] fictions is the horror of bad taste and bad art," is still often met with blank stares at best and mocking sniggers of derision at worst. This is not to say, however, that Lovecraft doesn't have his literary scholars: Dirk Mosig, S.T. Joshi, and Robert M. Price, for example, spearheaded the drive to bring critical acceptance to Lovecraft during the 1970s, 1980s, and well into the present century. They have in turn inspired a generation of Lovecraft enthusiasts to pursue their own scholarly interests in regards to Lovecraft's oeuvre.

Lovecraft still remains more popularly than critically accepted. Despite his influence on such critically recognized writers as Stephen King, Joyce Carol Oates, Neil Gaiman, and Jorge Luis Borges, and despite his work recently appearing in a Library of America edition, thus implying a place in the American canon, he is still struggling to find acceptance among general literary critics and academics.

Many still consider his work merely pulp, despite the elevation of other "pulp" writers such as Raymond Chandler and Dashiell Hammett to literary respectability. They cite his portentous and overblown prose, his dense and gruesome plots, his sometimes leaden characters. The irony that these same critics also praise such writers as William Faulkner for the exact same qualities, however, is lost on them. Others dismiss Lovecraft's work for its very popularity. Horror, science fiction, and fantasy, they seem to imply, are simply not "literary," whatever that means.

Still others cite Lovecraft's racism. There is no doubt that Lovecraft, especially in his younger years, showed pronounced racist tendencies that did not necessarily abate as he grew older. His most mature fiction is rife, for example, with the idea that "pure" English blood is synonymous with good while evil finds its representation in dark-skinned characters, especially those of mixed race. Admittedly, it's also true that much of Lovecraft's derision is aimed at lower economic classes (a travel agent in *The Shadow Over Innsmouth*, for instance, refers to the denizens of the titular town as "what they call 'white trash' down South—lawless and sly, and full of secret things"). However, one cannot excuse a man's racism on the grounds that he is also a classist.

Some critics have suggested that Lovecraft's racism was more façade than real, an out-ward manifestation of overwhelming Anglophilia. Others point to his marriage to a Jewish woman, Sonia Green, as indication that his vocalized thoughts may have been more for show. However, these defenses ring false given the prevalence of racist/classist attitudes throughout his work. They do, though, show that as with anyone, Lovecraft's racial preju-dices were far more complicated and nuanced than recent critiques portray.

Still others see in his later writings a tempering of his racist tendencies, especially in works such as *At the Mountains of Madness*, where the narrator treats the Elder Things not as aliens to be feared but as compatriots in scientific discovery, and *The Shadow Over Innsmouth*, whose narrator ultimately grows to accept his own mixed blood. These expla-nations, though, may still ring false: while it is true the narrator of *At the Mountains of Madness* finds himself identifying with the Elder Things, the source of that identification is in their perceived mutual disdain for the inferior shoggoths, monsters created by the Elder Things as a slave workforce who eventually rose up in rebellion. Similarly, while the narrator of *The Shadow Over Innsmouth* does come to accept his hidden ancestry, this scene is written to produce fear and disgust on the part of the reader, not acceptance and support.

There's really no point, then, in trying to argue away Lovecraft's racism. It's there; there's no two ways around it. However, his feelings on the matter are not nearly as simplistic as many would have us believe. More importantly, if a writer's perceived racism is one's reason for not considering him literary enough for study, I'm afraid we'll have to throw out several other writers on the grounds of unfettered racism: Herman Melville, Jack London, Rudyard Kipling, Flannery O'Connor, even Dr. Seuss.

Of course this all begs the question of whether or not Lovecraft is even worthy of study. Maybe the man's writing is simply not literary. After all, Stephenie Meyer's *Twilight* saga is extremely popular, but no one is seriously calling for her inclusion in the canon. While E.L. James's *Fifty Shades* books have worked wonders for the social acceptance of whitebread BDSM, she, too, is not considered one of America's shining beacons of literary talent. What makes Lovecraft's densely written, racially charged fiction any better?

Regardless of the problematic aspects of his work, Lovecraft undeniably brought a new genre of fiction into the public eye. While it would take several years after his death and the creation of a publishing house devoted entirely to his work, without Lovecraft's fiction as well as his own literary essays, there is every chance that weird fiction would have disappeared along with the pulp magazines that gave it birth.

Indeed, Lovecraft's work seems to be a normal progression of American naturalism, as expressed by such canonical writers as Stephen Crane. Naturalism presents human beings as mere cogs in the wheel of the natural cycle. The naturalist world is indifferent to the concerns and accomplishments of humanity and one where humanity has little power over its own destiny. Humans' fates are determined largely by chance as well as their environ-ment, heredity, and social status.

Lovecraft's work takes naturalism and applies it cosmically. Where naturalism presents a world unaffected by mankind's influence, Lovecraft's cosmic horror becomes a kind of super-naturalism (pardon the pun) in which the entire cosmos is indifferent to the existence of humanity. In Lovecraft, mankind is not only incapable of affecting the world in any lasting way, but it is also quite literally inconsequential to the universe at large. The "mon-sters" of Lovecraft's work are horrifying not because they represent an "evil" force intent on man's destruction, but because they can bring about man's destruction with neither thought nor malice, in much the same way as the farmer's plow can destroy a mole's warren with absolutely no consideration of the mole. Like the naturalist world, Lovecraft's universe terrifies because it reminds humanity of its own unimportance. Lovecraft's monsters terrify because they remind mankind of its own ignorance and misunderstanding of the laws governing the universe.

Much of Lovecraft's work also lends itself to a study of literary modernism. While Lovecraft himself might have shuddered at the thought, his fiction shows many of the same themes that more traditional modernist writers concerned themselves with: a distrust of religion, the growing prevalence of destruction and chaos, and the inherited guilt of our ancestors' sins. Additionally, Lovecraft's work shares many structural similarities with his modernist contemporaries. Many tales, especially "The Call of Cthulhu," are told nonchronologically, in fragments. Others, such as "The Whisperer in the Darkness" or *The Shadow Over Innsmouth*, subvert narrative authority through the use of possibly insane, and thus woefully unreliable, narrators. The case could even be made that Lovecraft also prefigures post-modernism with his examples of the shortcomings of known science and the dangers of unfettered investigation.

There is, therefore, plenty to study in Lovecraft and his relationship to American letters, and it is for this reason that a critical edition of his work is necessary. The Library of America could issue three more volumes of Lovecraft's tales, but if he isn't taught in the literature classroom, he may as well remain as unknown critically as he was publicly at the time of his death.

A Note on the Text

I use Lovecraft extensively in my own American literature courses for exactly the reasons listed in the Preface, and it is in part these concerns that dictated my choice of primary texts. Each of the selected stories illustrates to a greater or lesser degree Lovecraft's use of naturalist, modernist, and post-modernist themes and techniques. However, narrowing over 60 stories down to a mere 6 was no easy task. As a secondary consideration, I considered how else such a textbook might be used in class. For example, it may perhaps find itself the textbook for a special topics course on horror literature; thus, I next focused only on Lovecraft's most well-known and influential works.

Even this, however, only managed to whittle the number down to just under 30 stories, so I once again considered how else my textbook could be used, and realized that a good many of Lovecraft's work had been translated to feature length films, from Roger Corman's 1963 adaptation of *The Case of Charles Dexter Ward* as *The Haunted Palace* to 2011's *The Whisperer in the Darkness* produced by The H.P. Lovecraft Historical Society. From my new list of stories, then, I chose ones that had been made into feature length films of particular note for possible use in a film studies course.

While "History of the *Necronomicon*" has not, itself, been adapted to film, the *Necronomicon* has appeared in numerous horror films even outside of Lovecraft adaptations, most famously, perhaps, as the catalyst in Sam Raimi's *Evil Dead* films. Besides, it seems appropriate to begin an exploration of Lovecraft's work by looking at what is quite possibly the most famous fictional book in American letters.

In 2005, The H.P. Lovecraft Historical Society adapted "The Call of Cthulhu" into a remarkable silent film using only equipment and filming techniques available during the mid– to late 1920s, the time in which Lovecraft wrote and published the story. It may well be the best and most faithful film adaptation of a Lovecraft story.

"The Colour Out of Space" has been adapted numerous times: in 1965, Daniel Haller directed a Roger Cormanesque adaptation called *Die, Monster, Die!* focusing less on the science fiction aspects of the story and more on the horror. In 1987, it was again adapted, this time more faithfully, in David Keith's *The Curse*. More recently, the story has been adapted twice: in 2008, as the Italian film *The Colour from the Dark*, and in 2010 as the German film *Die Farbe*. The most recent adaptation has been generally well received.

In 1970, "The Dunwich Horror" was adapted as a B-movie starring Dean Stockwell and Sandra Dee. While it begins as a fairly decent adaptation, the film suffers from its more psychedelic aspects, especially during the reveal of Whately's brother. In 2008, the story was again adapted as the straight-to-DVD film *Beyond the Dunwich Horror*. It has received predictably bad reviews. The Syfy channel again adapted the story in 2009 for a poorly received made-for-TV film. All in all, it seems the campy B-movie remains the best adaptation so far.

"The Whisperer in Darkness" has been adapted for film three times: in 1993, it comprised the third act of the anthology film *H.P. Lovecraft's: Necronomicon*. It was also adapted in 2007 by Matt Hundley, who directed this virtually unknown film. As a follow-up to their well-received silent film adaptation of "Call of Cthulhu," in 2011, The H.P. Lovecraft Society produced *The Whisperer in Darkness*. This time, they made a "talkie" film, again using only equipment and techniques available at the time of the story's writing and publication. While some liberties are taken at the end of the film, it is, like its predecessor, an amazing adaptation of Lovecraft's work.

The Shadow Over Innsmouth has been adapted for film at least six times. It was first adapted in 1979 for the Sergio Martino–directed Italian film *Island of the Fishmen*. Chiaki J. Konaka adapted the story in 1992 as *Insmus wo Oou Kage* for Japanese television. In 1999, it appeared as *Return to Innsmouth*, written and adapted by Aaron Vanek. The story also makes up the principal storyline for Stuart Gordon's 2001 film, *Dagon*. Arguably the most critically acclaimed version, though, is 2007's *Cthulhu*, directed and co-written by Dan Gildark.

The poetry section consists of only two poems: "Waste Paper: A Poem of Profound Insignificance" is Lovecraft's parody of T.S. Eliot's *Waste Land* and thus perfectly illustrates Lovecraft's disdain not only for Eliot, but for modernism in general. I chose *Fungi from Yuggoth* in part due to its relationship to several of the stories collected here (including *The Shadow Over Innsmouth*, "The Whisperer in Darkness," and "The Dunwich Horror"). More importantly, though, it presents another example of Lovecraft's blend of classic literary styles (such as the Petrarchan and Shakespearean sonnets) with modern literary sensibilities (these poems may employ the most plain and unadorned speech in Lovecraft's oeuvre, for example). Additionally, if you accept the argument that the sonnets work together to tell a single tale (an argument by no means settled), this is almost certainly the most fractured narrative ever set to verse.

The last of the primary works consists of an abridged version of Lovecraft's seminal work on weird fiction, *Supernatural Horror in Literature*. In this monograph Lovecraft not only elaborates on his definitions of weird fiction and cosmic horror; he presents a fairly in depth history of the genre's development. In several places, however, his discussion of what makes a work "weird" becomes a mere catalog of other authors who essentially do the same thing. In the interest of brevity and clarity for the first-time, student reader, I have deleted such nonessential lists in order to maintain focus on Lovecraft's ideas pertaining to weird fiction as a genre. Similarly, I have abridged several of Lovecraft's plot summaries if they do not contribute directly to a particular quality of cosmic horror under discussion or if they needlessly give away the endings of the stories.

The second section of this critical edition consists of essays and interviews about Lovecraft. I have divided the secondary works into two sections: critical works on Lovecraft make up the first half of this section while essays and interviews with current authors about their opinions of and experiences with Lovecraft's work makeup the second section. Just as in the primary works, I based my selections on how I envisioned the work being used in the classroom.

In the Criticism section, I have tried to include scholars from several areas in order to illustrate that one does not necessarily have to be a specialist in Lovecraft's work (or any field) in order to write intelligently about it. I have included essays by S.T. Joshi and

Robert M. Price, two of the most influential of Lovecraft critics, but I have also included essays from emerging scholars in related fields: Shannon N. Gilstrap of the University of North Georgia, whose primary focus is Victorian literature, provides an essay exploring the Victorian influence on Lovecraft's work, and Tracy Bealer of the Borough of Manhattan Community College, whose focus lies in pop culture, discusses certain modernist tendencies found in Lovecraft's fiction. Poet Joseph Milford gives a close reading of "Waste Paper" and explores its critique of modernism. Finally, I include a more informal essay by Jim Moon, a blogger and podcaster interested in weird fiction, adapted from his online blog that argues *Fungi from Yuggoth* represents a single coherent narrative despite claims to the contrary by other prominent critics.

One of the problems I have found in my composition classes is that many students do not understand the connection between reading and good writing. Therefore, in the Reflections section, I have asked current science fiction, fantasy, horror, and weird fiction authors to contribute essays or participate in interviews discussing their first encounters with Lovecraft's fiction, the nature of their appreciation for his work, and his influence on their own work.

Throughout both sections, I have provided explanatory endnotes. Lovecraft often assumes his readers have a vocabulary and a familiarity with history and literature equal to his own, a daunting task at best for his contemporaries, and an almost impossible one for novice readers. Therefore, I provide annotations for possibly problematic vocabulary, historical figures or events referenced in the story, and references to Lovecraft stories not collected here. In the Criticism section, I denote my annotations with [ed.] in order to differentiate them from those of the articles' authors. All annotations in the Reflections section are my own. All citations of the fiction come from *The Fiction: Complete and Unabridged* published by Barnes & Noble in 2008.

Primary Works

History of the *Necronomicon*

Written in 1927, Lovecraft's "History of the Necronomicon*" was not initially meant to see publication. It was intended simply as an aid to memory in order to prevent continuity errors in future stories. However, shortly after his death in 1937, Wilson Shepherd published the essay in a "Limited Memorial Edition." And later, after his friends David Wandrei and August Derleth created Arkham House Publishing to bring Lovecraft's work to a wider audience, they reprinted it in their second Lovecraft collection,* Beyond the Wall of Sleep. *Since then, it has been reprinted several times.*

While Lovecraft claims that the title, as translated from the Greek language, means "an image of the law of the dead" (nekros–νεκρός meaning "dead," nomos–νόμος meaning "law," and eikon–εικών meaning "image"), the two most prominent Lovecraft scholars disagree. S.T. Joshi claims that Lovecraft's own etymology is flawed because "[t]he last portion of it is […] erroneous, since -ikon is nothing more than a neuter adjectival suffix and has nothing to do with eikōn (image)." Joshi instead translates the title as "Book considering (or classifying) the dead." Robert M. Price notes that the title has been variously translated as "Book of the Names of the Dead," "Book of the Laws of the Dead," "Book of Dead Names," and "Knower of the Laws of the Dead."

Original title *Al Azif*—azif being the word used by Arabs to designate that nocturnal sound (made by insects) suppos'd to be the howling of demons.

Composed by Abdul Alhazred, a mad poet of Sanaá, in Yemen, who is said to have flourished during the period of the Ommiade caliphs, circa AD 700. He visited the ruins of Babylon and the subterranean secrets of Memphis and spent ten years alone in the great southern desert of Arabia—the Roba el Khaliyeh or "Empty Space" of the ancients—and "Dahna" or "Crimson" desert of the modern Arabs, which is held to be inhabited by protective evil spirits and monsters of death. Of this desert many strange and unbelievable marvels are told by those who pretend to have penetrated it. In his last years Alhazred dwelt in Damascus, where the *Necronomicon* (*Al Azif*) was written, and of his final death or disappearance (AD 738) many terrible and conflicting things are told. He is said by Ebn Khallikan[1] (12th cent. biographer) to have been seized by an invisible monster in broad daylight and devoured horribly before a large number of fright-frozen witnesses. Of his madness many things are told. He claimed to have seen fabulous Irem, or City of Pillars,[2] and to have found beneath the ruins of a certain nameless desert town the shocking annals and secrets of a race older than mankind. He was only an indifferent Moslem, worshipping unknown entities whom he called Yog-Sothoth and Cthulhu.[3]

In AD 950 the *Azif*, which had gained a considerable tho' surreptitious circulation amongst the philosophers of the age, was secretly translated into Greek by Theodorus Philetas of Constantinople under the title *Necronomicon*. For a century it impelled certain experimenters to terrible attempts, when it was suppressed and burnt by the patriarch Michael.[4] After this it is only heard of furtively, but (1228) Olaus Wormius[5] made a Latin translation later in the Middle Ages, and the Latin text was printed twice—once in the fifteenth century in black-letter (evidently in Germany) and once in the seventeenth (prob. Spanish)—both editions being without identifying marks, and located as to time and place by internal typographical evidence only. The work both Latin and Greek was banned by Pope Gregory IX in 1232, shortly after its Latin translation, which called attention to it. The Arabic original was lost as early as Wormius' time, as indicated by his prefatory note; and no sight of the Greek copy—which was printed in Italy between 1500 and 1550—has been reported since the burning of a certain Salem man's library in 1692. An English translation made by Dr. Dee[6] was never printed, and exists only in fragments recovered from the original manuscript. Of the Latin texts now existing one (15th cent.) is known to be in the British Museum under lock and key, while another (17th cent.) is in the Bibliothèque Nationale at Paris. A seventeenth-century edition is in the Widener Library at Harvard, and in the library of Miskatonic University at Arkham.[7] Also in the library of the University of Buenos Ayres. Numerous other copies probably exist in secret, and a fifteenth-century one is persistently rumored to form part of the collection of a celebrated American millionaire. A still vaguer rumor credits the preservation of a sixteenth-century Greek text in the Salem family of Pickman; but if it was so preserved, it vanished with the artist R.U. Pickman, who disappeared early in 1926.[8] The book is rigidly suppressed by the authorities of most countries, and by all branches of organized ecclesiasticism. Reading leads to terrible consequences. It was from rumors of this book (of which relatively few of the general public know) that R.W. Chambers is said to have derived the idea of his early novel *The King in Yellow*.[9]

Chronology

Al Azif written circa AD 730 at Damascus by Abdul Alhazred
Tr. to Greek AD 950 as *Necronomicon* by Theodorus Philetas
Burnt by Patriarch Michael 1050 (i.e., Greek text). Arabic text now lost.
Olaus translates Gr. to Latin 1228
1232 Latin ed. (and Gr.) suppr. by Pope Gregory IX
14 … Black-letter printed edition (Germany)
15 … Gr. text printed in Italy
16 … Spanish reprint of Latin text

The Call of Cthulhu

Considered by many scholars to be the definitive Lovecraft story, "The Call of Cthulhu" tells the story of an ancient cult as it prepares for the return of its god, Cthulhu. This story illustrates Lovecraft's developing technical skills as a writer. As S.T. Joshi notes, the narration becomes increasingly removed from the events of the story. For example, the main narrator, Francis Wayland Thurston, never directly experiences the horror of the story. Instead he paraphrases the notes of his great-uncle, a retired linguist professor, who himself paraphrases the reports of a Louisiana police inspector, who is in turn paraphrasing the testimony of a Cthulhu cultist. Lovecraft's skill in maintaining this increasing level of narrative distance is impressive. Most of the time such structural complexity requires a novel length composition for effective execution, and Lovecraft manages to pull it off in a mere 12,000 words.

Of equal importance to the Lovecraft oeuvre, is the story's themes. Kenneth Hite claims that the story's essence lies in humanity's interrelationship between curiosity and fear. For him, the story illustrates mankind's need to satisfy its curiosity despite (or even because of) the often paralyzing fear that results from satisfying curiosity: "The fear of the unknown," claims Hite, "drives us to investigate it, revealing that the truth is even worse." Stefan Dziemianowicz further claims that this story "most clearly articulate[s] Lovecraft's concept of 'cosmic horror,'" the existence of extradimensional beings whose emergence into our world drives mankind mad with an awareness of its utter insignificance in relation to the cosmos. Similarly, Robert M. Price cites the story's ability to build a sense of impending doom for the whole human race as its most effective element of fright.

Thematically, then, the narrative distance Joshi cites also underscores this concept of cosmic horror. Everyone with direct experience of Cthulhu or its cult becomes irrecoverably damaged, physically, mentally, or both. More importantly, however, even though the narrator never directly experiences Cthulhu's awakening, simply knowing of it becomes enough to leave him utterly unnerved and paranoid, seeing potential assassins everywhere and wishing to unlearn what he has discovered through poring over his uncle's manuscripts.

(Found Among the Papers of the
Late Frances Wayland Thurston of Boston)

Of such great powers or beings there may be conceivably a survival ... a survival of a hugely remote period when ... consciousness was manifested, perhaps, in shapes and forms long since withdrawn before the tide of advancing humanity ... forms of which poetry and legend alone have caught a flying memory and called them gods, monsters, mythical beings of all sorts and kinds....
—Algernon Blackwood[1]

I. The Horror in Clay

The most merciful thing in the world, I think, is the inability of the human mind to correlate all its contents. We live on a placid island of ignorance in the midst of black seas of infinity, and it was not meant that we should voyage far. The sciences, each straining in its own direction, have hitherto harmed us little; but some day the piecing together of dissociated knowledge will open up such terrifying vistas of reality, and of our frightful position therein, that we shall either go mad from the revelation or flee from the light into the peace and safety of a new dark age.

Theosophists[2] have guessed at the awesome grandeur of the cosmic cycle wherein our world and human race form transient incidents. They have hinted at strange survivals in terms which would freeze the blood if not masked by a bland optimism. But it is not from them that there came the single glimpse of forbidden eons which chills me when I think of it and maddens me when I dream of it. That glimpse, like all dread glimpses of truth, flashed out from an accidental piecing together of separated things—in this case an old newspaper item and the notes of a dead professor. I hope that no one else will accomplish this piecing out; certainly, if I live, I shall never knowingly supply a link in so hideous a chain. I think that the professor, too intent to keep silent regarding the part he knew, and that he would have destroyed his notes had not sudden death seized him.

My knowledge of the thing began in the winter of 1926–27 with the death of my great-uncle, George Gammell Angell, Professor Emeritus of Semitic Languages in Brown University, Providence, Rhode Island. Professor Angell was widely known as an authority on ancient inscriptions, and had frequently been resorted to by the heads of prominent museums; so that his passing at the age of ninety-two may be recalled by many. Locally, interest was intensified by the obscurity of the cause of death. The professor had been stricken whilst returning from the Newport boat; falling suddenly; as witnesses said, after having been jostled by a nautical-looking negro who had come from one of the queer dark courts on the precipitous hillside which formed a short cut from the waterfront to the deceased's home in Williams Street. Physicians were unable to find any visible disorder, but concluded after perplexed debate that some obscure lesion of the heart, induced by the brisk ascent of so steep a hill by so elderly a man, was responsible for the end. At the time I saw no reason to dissent from this dictum, but latterly I am inclined to wonder—and more than wonder.

As my great-uncle's heir and executor, for he died a childless widower, I was expected to go over his papers with some thoroughness; and for that purpose moved his entire set of files and boxes to my quarters in Boston. Much of the material which I correlated will be later published by the American Archaeological Society, but there was one box which I found exceedingly puzzling, and which I felt much averse from showing to other eyes. It had been locked and I did not find the key till it occurred to me to examine the personal ring which the professor carried in his pocket. Then, indeed, I succeeded in opening it, but when I did so seemed only to be confronted by a greater and more closely locked barrier. For what could be the meaning of the queer clay bas-relief[3] and the disjointed jottings, ramblings, and cuttings which I found? Had my uncle, in his latter years become credulous of the most superficial impostures? I resolved to search out the eccentric sculptor responsible for this apparent disturbance of an old man's peace of mind.

The bas-relief was a rough rectangle less than an inch thick and about five by six inches in area; obviously of modern origin. Its designs, however, were far from modern in atmosphere and suggestion; for, although the vagaries[4] of cubism and futurism[5] are many and wild, they do not often reproduce that cryptic regularity which lurks in prehistoric writing. And writing of some kind the bulk of these designs seemed certainly to be; though my memory, despite much familiarity with the papers and collections of my uncle, failed in any way to identify this particular species, or even hint at its remotest affiliations.

Above these apparent hieroglyphics was a figure of evident pictorial intent, though its impressionistic[6] execution forbade a very clear idea of its nature. It seemed to be a sort of monster, or symbol representing a monster, of a form which only a diseased fancy could conceive. If I say that my somewhat extravagant imagination yielded simultaneous pictures of an octopus, a dragon, and a human caricature, I shall not be unfaithful to the spirit of the thing. A pulpy, tentacled head surmounted a grotesque and scaly body with rudimentary wings; but it was the *general outline* of the whole which made it most shockingly frightful. Behind the figure was a vague suggestions of a Cyclopean[7] architectural background.

The writing accompanying this oddity was, aside from a stack of press cuttings, in Professor Angell's most recent hand; and made no pretense to literary style. What seemed to be the main document was headed "CTHULHU CULT" in characters painstakingly printed to avoid the erroneous reading of a word so unheard-of. This manuscript was divided into two sections, the first of which was headed "1925—Dream and Dream Work of H.A. Wilcox, 7 Thomas St., Providence, R.I.," and the second, "Narrative of Inspector John R. Legrasse, 121 Bienville St., New Orleans, La., at 1908 A.A.S. Mtg.[8]—Notes on Same, & Prof. Webb's Acct." The other manuscript papers were brief notes, some of them accounts of the queer dreams of different persons, some of them citations from theosophical books and magazines (notably W. Scott-Elliot's *Atlantis and the Lost Lemuria*[9]), and the rest comments on long-surviving secret societies and hidden cults, with references to passages in such mythological and anthropological source-books as Frazer's *Golden Bough* and Miss Murray's *Witch-Cult in Western Europe*.[10] The cuttings largely alluded to outré[11] mental illness and outbreaks of group folly or mania in the spring of 1925.

The first half of the principal manuscript told a very particular tale. It appears that on March 1, 1925, a thin, dark young man of neurotic and excited aspect had called upon Professor Angell bearing the singular clay bas-relief, which was then exceedingly damp and fresh. His card bore the name of Henry Anthony Wilcox, and my uncle had recognized him as the youngest son of an excellent family slightly known to him, who had latterly been studying sculpture at the Rhode Island School of Design and living alone at the Fleur-de-Lys Building near that institution. Wilcox was a precocious youth of known genius but great eccentricity, and had from childhood excited attention through the strange stories and odd dreams he was in the habit of relating. He called himself "psychically hypersensitive," but the staid folk of the ancient commercial city dismissed him as merely "queer."

Never mingling much with his kind, he had dropped gradually from social visibility, and was now known only to a small group of esthetes[12] from other towns. Even the Providence Art Club, anxious to preserve its conservatism, had found him quite hopeless.

On the occasion of the visit, ran the professor's manuscript, the sculptor abruptly asked for the benefit of his host's archeological knowledge in identifying the hieroglyphics of the bas-relief. He spoke in a dreamy, stilted manner which suggested pose and alienated sympathy; and my uncle showed some sharpness in replying, for the conspicuous freshness of the tablet implied kinship with anything but archeology. Young Wilcox's rejoinder, which impressed my uncle enough to make him recall and record it verbatim, was of a fantastically poetic cast which must have typified his whole conversation, and which I have since found highly characteristic of him. He said, "It is new, indeed, for I made it last night in a dream of strange cities; and dreams are older than brooding Tyre,[13] or the contemplative Sphinx, or garden-girdled Babylon."

It was then that he began that rambling tale which suddenly played upon a sleeping memory and won the fevered interest of my uncle. There had been a slight earthquake[14] tremor the night before, the most considerable felt in New England for some years; and Wilcox's imagination had been keenly affected. Upon retiring, he had had an unprecedented dream of great Cyclopean cities of Titan blocks and sky-flung monoliths, all dripping with green ooze and sinister with latent horror. Hieroglyphics had covered the walls and pillars, and from some undetermined point below had come a voice that was not a voice; a chaotic sensation which only fancy could transmute into sound, but which he attempted to render by the almost unpronounceable jumble of letters: *"Cthulhu fhtagn."*

This verbal jumble was the key to the recollection which excited and disturbed Professor Angell. He questioned the sculptor with scientific minuteness; and studied with frantic intensity the bas-relief on which the youth had found himself working, chilled and clad only in his night clothes, when waking had stolen bewilderingly over him. My uncle blamed his old age, Wilcox afterwards said, for his slowness in recognizing both hieroglyphics and pictorial design. Many of his questions seemed highly out of place to his visitor, especially those which tried to connect the latter with strange cults or societies; and Wilcox could not understand the repeated promises of silence which he was offered in exchange for an admission of membership in some widespread mystical or paganly religious body. When Professor Angell became convinced that the sculptor was indeed ignorant of any cult or system of cryptic lore, he besieged his visitor with demands for future reports of dreams. This bore regular fruit, for after the first interview the manuscript records daily calls of the young man, during which he related startling fragments of nocturnal imaginary whose burden was always some terrible Cyclopean vista of dark and dripping stone, with a sub-terrene voice or intelligence shouting monotonously in enigmatical sense-impacts uninscribable save as gibberish. The two sounds frequently repeated are those rendered by the letters *"Cthulhu"* and *"R'lyeh."*

On March 23, the manuscript continued, Wilcox failed to appear; and inquiries at his quarters revealed that he had been stricken with an obscure sort of fever and taken to the home of his family in Waterman Street. He had cried out in the night, arousing several other artists in the building, and had manifested since then only alternations of unconsciousness and delirium. My uncle at once telephoned the family, and from that time forward kept close watch of the case; calling often at the Thayer Street office of Dr. Tobey, whom he learned to be in charge. The youth's febrile[15] mind, apparently, was dwelling on strange things; and the doctor shuddered now and then as he spoke of them. They included not only a repetition of what he had formerly dreamed, but touched wildly on a gigantic thing "miles high" which walked or lumbered about.

He at no time fully described this object but occasional frantic words, as repeated by Dr. Tobey, convinced the professor that it must be identical with the nameless monstrosity he had sought to depict in his dream-sculpture. Reference to this object, the doctor added, was invariably a prelude to the young man's subsidence into lethargy. His temperature, oddly enough, was not greatly above normal; but the whole condition was otherwise such as to suggest true fever rather than mental disorder.

On April 2 at about 3 p.m. every trace of Wilcox's malady suddenly ceased. He sat upright in bed, astonished to find himself at home and completely ignorant of what had happened in dream or reality since the night of March 22. Pronounced well by his physician, he returned to his quarters in three days; but to Professor Angell he was of no further assistance. All traces of strange dreaming had vanished with his recovery, and my uncle kept no record of his night-thoughts after a week of pointless and irrelevant accounts of thoroughly usual visions.

Here the first part of the manuscript ended, but references to certain of the scattered notes gave me much material for thought—so much, in fact, that only the ingrained skepticism then forming my philosophy can account for my continued distrust of the artist. The notes in question were those descriptive of the dreams of various persons covering the same period as that in which young Wilcox had had his strange visitations. My uncle, it seems, had quickly instituted a prodigiously[16] far-flung body of inquires amongst nearly all the friends whom he could question without impertinence, asking for nightly reports of their dreams, and the dates of any notable visions for some time past. The reception of his request seems to have varied; but he must, at the very least, have received more responses than any ordinary man could have handled without a secretary. This original correspondence was not preserved, but his notes formed a thorough and really significant digest. Average people in society and business—New England's traditional "salt of the earth"— gave an almost completely negative result, though scattered cases of uneasy but formless nocturnal impressions appear here and there, always between March 23 and April 2—the period of young Wilcox's delirium. Scientific men were little more affected, though four cases of vague description suggest fugitive glimpses of strange landscapes, and in one case there is mentioned a dread of something abnormal.

It was from the artists and poets that the pertinent answers came, and I know that panic would have broken loose had they been able to compare notes. As it was, lacking their original letters, I half suspected the compiler of having asked leading questions, or of having edited the correspondence in corroboration of what he had latently resolved to see. That is why I continued to feel that Wilcox, somehow cognizant of the old data which my uncle had possessed, had been imposing on the veteran scientist. These responses from esthetes told a disturbing tale. From February 28 to April 2 a large proportion of them had dreamed very bizarre things, the intensity of the dreams being immeasurably the stronger during the period of the sculptor's delirium. Over a fourth of those who reported anything, reported scenes and half-sounds not unlike those which Wilcox had described; and some of the dreamers confessed acute fear of the gigantic nameless thing visible toward the last. One case, which the note describes with emphasis, was very sad. The subject, a widely known architect with leanings toward theosophy and occultism, went violently insane on the date of young Wilcox's seizure, and expired several months later after incessant screamings to be saved from some escaped denizen of hell. Had my uncle referred to these cases by name instead of merely by number, I should have attempted some corroboration and personal investigation; but as it was, I succeeded in tracing down only a few. All of these, however, bore out the notes in full. I have often wondered if all the objects of the professor's questioning felt as puzzled as did this fraction. It is well that no explanation shall ever reach them.

The press cuttings, as I have intimated, touched on cases of panic, mania, and eccentricity during the given period. Professor Angell must have employed a cutting bureau, for the number of extracts was tremendous, and the sources scattered throughout the globe. Here was a nocturnal suicide in London, where a lone sleeper had leaped from a window after a shocking cry. Here likewise a rambling letter to the editor of a paper in South America, where a fanatic deduces a dire future from visions he has seen. A dispatch from California describes a theosophist colony as donning white robes en masse for some "glorious fulfilment" which never arrives, whilst items from India speak guardedly of serious native unrest toward the end of March. Voodoo orgies multiply in Haiti, and African outposts report ominous mutterings. American officers in the Philippines find certain tribes bothersome about this time, and New York policemen are mobbed by hysterical Levantines[17] on the night of 22–23 March. The west of Ireland, too, is full of wild rumor and legendry, and a fantastic painter named Ardois-Bonnot hangs a blasphemous *Dream Landscape* in the Paris spring salon of 1926. And so numerous are the recorded troubles in insane asylums that only a miracle can have stopped the medical fraternity from noting strange parallelisms and drawing mystified conclusions. A weird bunch of cuttings, all told; and I can at this date scarcely envisage the callous rationalism with which I set them aside. But I was then convinced that young Wilcox had known of the older matters mentioned by the professor.

II. *The Tale of Inspector Legrasse*

The older matters which had made the sculptor's dream and bas-relief so significant to my uncle formed the subject of the second half of his long manuscript. Once before, it appears, Professor Angell had seen the hellish outlines of the nameless monstrosity, puzzled over the unknown hieroglyphics, and heard the ominous syllables which can be rendered only as *"Cthulhu"*; and all this in so stirring and horrible a connection that it is small wonder he pursued young Wilcox with queries and demands for data.

This earlier experience had come in 1908, seventeen years before, when the American Archaeological Society held its annual meeting in St. Louis. Professor Angell, as befitted one of his authority and attainments, had had a prominent part in all the deliberations; and was one of the first to be approached by the several outsiders who took advantage of the convocation to offer questions for correct answering and problems for expert solution.

The chief of these outsiders, and in a short time the focus of interest for the entire meeting, was a commonplace-looking middle-aged man who had travelled all the way from New Orleans for certain special information unobtainable from any local source. His name was John Raymond Legrasse, and he was by profession an Inspector of Police. With him he bore the subject of his visit, a grotesque, repulsive, and apparently very ancient stone statuette whose origin he was at a loss to determine. It must not be fancied that Inspector Legrasse had the least interest in archaeology. On the contrary, his wish for enlightenment was prompted by purely professional considerations. The statuette, idol, fetish, or whatever it was, had been captured some months before in the wooded swamps south of New Orleans during a raid on a supposed voodoo meeting; and so singular and hideous were the rites connected with it, that the police could not but realize that they had stumbled on a dark cult totally unknown to them, and infinitely more diabolic than even the blackest of the African voodoo circles. Of its origin, apart from the erratic and unbelievable tales extorted from the captured members, absolutely nothing was to be discovered; hence the anxiety of the police for any antiquarian lore which might help them to place the frightful symbol, and through it track down the cult to its fountain-head.

Inspector Legrasse was scarcely prepared for the sensation which his offering created. One sight of the thing had been enough to throw the assembled men of science into a state of tense excitement, and they lost no time in crowding around him to gaze at the diminutive figure whose utter strangeness and air of genuinely abysmal antiquity hinted so potently at unopened and archaic vistas. No recognized school of sculpture had animated this terrible object, yet centuries and even thousands of years seemed recorded in its dim and greenish surface of unplaceable stone.

The figure, which was finally passed slowly from man to man for close and careful study, was between seven and eight inches in height, and of exquisitely artistic workmanship. It represented a monster of vaguely anthropoid outline, but with an octopus-like head whose face was a mass of feelers, a scaly, rubbery-looking body, prodigious claws on hind and fore feet, and long, narrow wings behind. This thing, which seemed instinct with a fearsome and unnatural malignancy, was of a somewhat bloated corpulence, and squatted evilly on a rectangular block or pedestal covered with undecipherable characters. The tips of the wings touched the back edge of the block, the seat occupied the center, whilst the long, curved claws of the doubled-up, crouching hind legs gripped the front edge and extended a quarter of the way clown toward the bottom of the pedestal. The cephalopod[18] head was bent forward, so that the ends of the facial feelers brushed the backs of huge fore paws which clasped the croucher's elevated knees. The aspect of the whole was abnormally life-like, and the more subtly fearful because its source was so totally unknown. Its vast, awesome, and incalculable age was unmistakable; yet not one link did it show with any known type of art belonging to civilization's youth—or indeed to any other time. Totally separate and apart, its very material was a mystery; for the soapy, greenish-black stone with its golden or iridescent flecks and striations resembled nothing familiar to geology or mineralogy. The characters along the base were equally baffling; and no member present, despite a representation of half the world's expert learning in this field, could form the least notion of even their remotest linguistic kinship. They, like the subject and material, belonged to something horribly remote and distinct from mankind as we know it; something frightfully suggestive of old and unhallowed cycles of life in which our world and our conceptions have no part.

And yet, as the members severally shook their heads and confessed defeat at the Inspector's problem, there was one man in that gathering who suspected a touch of bizarre familiarity in the monstrous shape and writing, and who presently told with some diffidence of the odd trifle he knew. This person was the late William Channing Webb, Professor of Anthropology in Princeton University, and an explorer of no slight note. Professor Webb had been engaged, forty-eight years before, in a tour of Greenland and Iceland in search of some Runic inscriptions which he failed to unearth; and whilst high up on the West Greenland coast had encountered a singular tribe or cult of degenerate Esquimaux[19] whose religion, a curious form of devil-worship, chilled him with its deliberate bloodthirstiness and repulsiveness. It was a faith of which other Esquimaux knew little, and which they mentioned only with shudders, saying that it had come down from horribly ancient aeons before ever the world was made. Besides nameless rites and human sacrifices there were certain queer hereditary rituals addressed to a supreme elder devil or *tornasuk*[20]; and of this Professor Webb had taken a careful phonetic copy from an aged *angekok* or wizard-priest, expressing the sounds in Roman letters as best he knew how. But just now of prime significance was the fetish which this cult had cherished, and around which they danced when the aurora[21] leaped high over the ice cliffs. It was, the professor stated, a very crude bas-relief of stone, comprising a hideous picture and some cryptic writing. And so far as he could tell, it was a rough parallel in all essential features of the bestial thing now lying before the meeting.

This data, received with suspense and astonishment by the assembled members, proved doubly exciting to Inspector Legrasse; and he began at once to ply his informant with questions. Having noted and copied an oral ritual among the swamp cult-worshippers his men had arrested, he besought the professor to remember as best he might the syllables taken down amongst the diabolist Esquimaux. There then followed an exhaustive comparison of details, and a moment of really awed silence when both detective and scientist agreed on the virtual identity of the phrase common to two hellish rituals so many worlds of distance apart. What, in substance, both the Esquimaux wizards and the Louisiana swamp-priests had chanted to their kindred idols was something very like this: the word-divisions being guessed at from traditional breaks in the phrase as chanted aloud: *"Ph'nglui mglw'nafh Cthulhu R'lyeh wgah'nagl fhtagn."*

Legrasse had one point in advance of Professor Webb, for several among his mongrel prisoners had repeated to him what older celebrants had told them the words meant. This text, as given, ran something like this: "In his house at R'lyeh dead Cthulhu waits dreaming."

And now, in response to a general and urgent demand, Inspector Legrasse related as fully as possible his experience with the swamp worshippers; telling a story to which I could see my uncle attached profound significance. It savored of the wildest dreams of myth-maker and theosophist, and disclosed an astonishing degree of cosmic imagination among such half-castes and pariahs as might be least expected to possess it.

On November 1, 1907, there had come to the New Orleans police a frantic summons from the swamp and lagoon country to the south. The squatters there, mostly primitive but good-natured descendants of Lafitte's men,[22] were in the grip of stark terror from an unknown thing which had stolen upon them in the night. It was voodoo, apparently, but voodoo of a more terrible sort than they had ever known; and some of their women and children had disappeared since the malevolent tom-tom[23] had begun its incessant beating far within the black haunted woods where no dweller ventured. There were insane shouts and harrowing screams, soul-chilling chants and dancing devil-flames; and, the frightened messenger added, the people could stand it no more.

So a body of twenty police, filling two carriages and an automobile, had set out in the late afternoon with the shivering squatter as a guide. At the end of the passable road they alighted, and for miles splashed on in silence through the terrible cypress woods where day never came. Ugly roots and malignant hanging nooses of Spanish moss beset them, and now and then a pile of dank stones or fragment of a rotting wall intensified by its hint of morbid habitation a depression which every malformed tree and every fungous islet combined to create. At length the squatter settlement, a miserable huddle of huts, hove in sight; and hysterical dwellers ran out to cluster around the group of bobbing lanterns. The muffled beat of tom-toms was now faintly audible far, far ahead; and a curdling shriek came at infrequent intervals when the wind shifted. A reddish glare, too, seemed to filter through pale undergrowth beyond the endless avenues of forest night. Reluctant even to be left alone again, each one of the cowed squatters refused point-blank to advance another inch toward the scene of unholy worship, so Inspector Legrasse and his nineteen colleagues plunged on unguided into black arcades of horror that none of them had ever trod before.

The region now entered by the police was one of traditionally evil repute, substantially unknown and untraversed by white men. There were legends of a hidden lake unglimpsed by mortal sight, in which dwelt a huge, formless white polypous[24] thing with luminous eyes; and squatters whispered that bat-winged devils flew up out of caverns in inner earth to worship it at midnight. They said it had been there before d'Iberville, before La Salle,[25] before the Indians, and before even the wholesome beasts and birds of the woods. It was nightmare itself, and to see it was to die. But it made men dream, and so they knew enough to keep away. The present voodoo orgy was, indeed, on the merest fringe of this abhorred area, but that location was bad enough; hence perhaps the very place of the worship had terrified the squatters more than the shocking sounds and incidents.

Only poetry or madness could do justice to the noises heard by Legrasse's men as they ploughed on through the black morass toward the red glare and muffled tom-toms. There are vocal qualities peculiar to men, and vocal qualities peculiar to beasts; and it is terrible to hear the one when the source should yield the other. Animal fury and orgiastic license here whipped themselves to demoniac heights by howls and squawking ecstasies that tore and reverberated through those nighted woods like pestilential tempests from the gulfs of hell. Now and then the less organized ululation would cease, and from what seemed a well-drilled chorus of hoarse voices would rise in sing-song chant that hideous phrase or ritual: *"Ph'nglui mglw'nafh Cthulhu R'lyeh wgah'nagl fhtagn."*

Then the men, having reached a spot where the trees were thinner, came suddenly in sight of the spectacle itself. Four of them reeled, one fainted, and two were shaken into a frantic cry which the mad cacophony of the orgy fortunately deadened. Legrasse dashed swamp water on the face of the fainting man, and all stood trembling and nearly hypnotized with horror.

In a natural glade of the swamp stood a grassy island of perhaps an acre's extent, clear of trees and tolerably dry. On this now leaped and twisted a more indescribable horde of human abnormality than any but a Sime or an Angarola[26] could paint. Void of clothing, this hybrid spawn were braying, bellowing, and writhing about a monstrous ring-shaped bonfire; in the center of which, revealed by occasional rifts in the curtain of flame, stood a great granite monolith some eight feet in height; on top of which, incongruous in its diminutiveness, rested the noxious carven statuette. From a wide circle of ten scaffolds set up at regular intervals with the flame-girt monolith as a center hung, head downward, the oddly marred bodies of the helpless squatters who had disappeared. It was inside this circle that the ring of worshippers jumped and roared, the general direction of the mass motion being from left to right in endless bacchanale[27] between the ring of bodies and the ring of fire.

It may have been only imagination and it may have been only echoes which induced one of the men, an excitable Spaniard, to fancy he heard antiphonal[28] responses to the ritual from some far and unillumined spot deeper within the wood of ancient legendry and horror. This man, Joseph D. Galvez, I later met and questioned; and he proved distractingly imaginative. He indeed went so far as to hint of the faint beating of great wings, and of a glimpse of shining eyes and a mountainous white bulk beyond the remotest trees but I suppose he had been hearing too much native superstition.

Actually, the horrified pause of the men was of comparatively brief duration. Duty came first; and although there must have been nearly a hundred mongrel celebrants in the throng, the police relied on their firearms and plunged determinedly into the nauseous rout. For five minutes the resultant din and chaos were beyond description. Wild blows were struck, shots were fired, and escapes were made; but in the end Legrasse was able to count some forty-seven sullen prisoners, whom he forced to dress in haste and fall into line between two rows of policemen. Five of the worshippers lay dead, and two severely wounded ones were carried away on improvised stretchers by their fellow-prisoners. The image on the monolith, of course, was carefully removed and carried back by Legrasse.

Examined at headquarters after a trip of intense strain and weariness, the prisoners all proved to be men of a very low, mixed-blooded, and mentally aberrant type. Most were seamen, and a sprinkling of Negroes and mulattoes, largely West Indians or Brava Portuguese from the Cape Verde Islands, gave a coloring of voodooism to the heterogeneous cult. But before many questions were asked, it became manifest that something far deeper and older than Negro fetishism was involved. Degraded and ignorant as they were, the creatures held with surprising consistency to the central idea of their loathsome faith.

They worshipped, so they said, the Great Old Ones who lived ages before there were any men, and who came to the young world out of the sky. Those Old Ones were gone now, inside the earth and under the sea; but their dead bodies had told their secrets in dreams to the first men, who formed a cult which had never died. This was that cult, and the prisoners said it had always existed and always would exist, hidden in distant wastes and dark places all over the world until the time when the great priest Cthulhu, from his dark house in the mighty city of R'lyeh under the waters, should rise and bring the earth again beneath his sway. Some day he would call, when the stars were ready, and the secret cult would always be waiting to liberate him.

Meanwhile no more must be told. There was a secret which even torture could not extract. Mankind was not absolutely alone among the conscious things of earth, for shapes came out of the dark to visit the faithful few. But these were not the Great Old Ones. No man had ever seen the Old Ones. The carven idol was great Cthulhu, but none might say whether or not the others were precisely like him. No one could read the old writing now, but things were told by word of mouth. The chanted ritual was not the secret—that was never spoken aloud, only whispered. The chant meant only this: "In his house at R'lyeh dead Cthulhu waits dreaming."

Only two of the prisoners were found sane enough to be hanged, and the rest were committed to various institutions. All denied a part in the ritual murders, and averred[29] that the killing had been done by Black Winged Ones which had come to them from their immemorial meeting-place in the haunted wood. But of those mysterious allies no coherent account could ever be gained. What the police did extract, came mainly from the immensely aged mestizo[30] named Castro, who claimed to have sailed to strange ports and talked with undying leaders of the cult in the mountains of China.

Old Castro remembered bits of hideous legend that paled the speculations of theosophists and made man and the world seem recent and transient indeed. There had been aeons when other Things ruled on the earth, and They had had great cities. Remains of Them, he said the deathless Chinamen had told him, were still be found as Cyclopean stones on islands in the Pacific. They all died vast epochs of time before men came, but there were arts which could revive Them when the stars had come round again to the right positions in the cycle of eternity. They had, indeed, come themselves from the stars, and brought Their images with Them.

These Great Old Ones, Castro continued, were not composed altogether of flesh and blood. They had shape—for did not this star-fashioned image prove it?—but that shape was not made of matter. When the stars were right, They could plunge from world to world through the sky; but when the stars were wrong, They could not live. But although They no longer lived, They would never really die. They all lay in stone houses in Their great city of R'lyeh, preserved by the spells of mighty Cthulhu for a glorious resurrection when the stars and the earth might once more be ready for Them. But at that time some force from outside must serve to liberate Their bodies. The spells that preserved them intact likewise prevented Them from making an initial move, and They could only lie awake in the dark and think whilst uncounted millions of years rolled by. They knew all that was occurring in the universe, for Their mode of speech was transmitted thought. Even now They talked in Their tombs. When, after infinities of chaos, the first men came, the Great Old Ones spoke to the sensitive among them by molding their dreams; for only thus could Their language reach the fleshly minds of mammals.

Then, whispered Castro, those first men formed the cult around tall idols which the Great Ones shewed[31] them; idols brought in dim eras from dark stars. That cult would never die till the stars came right again, and the secret priests would take great Cthulhu from His tomb to revive His subjects and resume His rule of earth. The time would be easy to know, for then mankind would have become as the Great Old Ones; free and wild and beyond good and evil, with laws and morals thrown aside and all men shouting and killing and reveling in joy. Then the liberated Old Ones would teach them new ways to shout and kill and revel and enjoy themselves, and all the earth would flame with a holocaust of ecstasy and freedom. Meanwhile the cult, by appropriate rites, must keep alive the memory of those ancient ways and shadow forth the prophecy of their return.

In the elder time chosen men had talked with the entombed Old Ones in dreams, but then something happened. The great stone city R'lyeh, with its monoliths and sepulchers, had sunk beneath the waves; and the deep waters, full of the one primal mystery through which not even thought can pass, had cut off the spectral intercourse. But memory never died, and the high-priests said that the city would rise again when the stars were right. Then came out of the earth the black spirits of earth, moldy and shadowy, and full of dim rumors picked up in caverns beneath forgotten sea-bottoms. But of them old Castro dared not speak much. He cut himself off hurriedly, and no amount of persuasion or subtlety could elicit more in this direction. The size of the Old Ones, too, he curiously declined to mention. Of the cult, he said that he thought the center lay amid the pathless desert of Arabia, where Irem, the City of Pillars, dreams hidden and untouched. It was not allied to the European witch-cult, and was virtually unknown beyond its members. No book had ever really hinted of it, though the deathless Chinamen said that there were double meanings in the *Necronomicon* of the mad Arab Abdul Alhazred which the initiated might read as they chose, especially the much-discussed couplet:

> That is not dead which can eternal lie,
> And with strange aeons even death may die.

Legrasse, deeply impressed and not a little bewildered, had inquired in vain concerning the historic affiliations of the cult. Castro, apparently, had told the truth when he said that it was wholly secret. The authorities at Tulane University could shed no light upon either cult or image, and now the detective had come to the highest authorities in the country and met with no more than the Greenland tale of Professor Webb.

The feverish interest aroused at the meeting by Legrasse's tale, corroborated as it was by the statuette, is echoed in the subsequent correspondence of those who attended; although scant mention occurs in the formal publications of the society. Caution is the first care of those accustomed to face occasional charlatanry and imposture. Legrasse for some time lent the image to Professor Webb, but at the latter's death it was returned to him and remains in his possession, where I viewed it not long ago. It is truly a terrible thing, and unmistakably akin to the dream-sculpture of young Wilcox.

That my uncle was excited by the tale of the sculptor I did not wonder, for what thoughts must arise upon hearing, after a knowledge of what Legrasse had learned of the cult, of a sensitive young man who had *dreamed* not only the figure and exact hieroglyphics of the swamp-found image and the Greenland devil tablet, but had come *in his dreams* upon at least three of the precise words of the formula uttered alike by Esquimaux diabolists and mongrel Louisianans? Professor Angell's instant start on an investigation of the utmost thoroughness was eminently natural; though privately I suspected young Wilcox of having heard of the cult in some indirect way, and of having invented a series of dreams to heighten and continue the mystery at my uncle's expense. The dream-narratives and cuttings collected by the professor were, of course, strong corroboration; but the rationalism of my mind and the extravagance of the whole subject led me to adopt what I thought the most sensible conclusions. So, after thoroughly studying the manuscript again and correlating the theosophical and anthropological notes with the cult narrative of Legrasse, I made a trip to Providence to see the sculptor and give him the rebuke I thought proper for so boldly imposing upon a learned and aged man.

Wilcox still lived alone in the Fleur-de-Lys Building in Thomas Street, a hideous Victorian imitation of seventeenth century Breton Architecture which flaunts its stuccoed front amidst the lovely Colonial houses on the ancient hill, and under the very shadow of the finest Georgian steeple in America,[32] I found him at work in his rooms, and at once conceded from the specimens scattered about that his genius is indeed profound and authentic. He will, I believe, some time be heard from as one of the great decadents[33]; for he has crystallized in clay and will one day mirror in marble those nightmares and phantasies which Arthur Machen[34] evokes in prose, and Clark Ashton Smith[35] makes visible in verse and in painting.

Dark, frail, and somewhat unkempt in aspect, he turned languidly at my knock and asked me my business without rising. When I told him who I was, he displayed some interest; for my uncle had excited his curiosity in probing his strange dreams, yet had never explained the reason for the study. I did not enlarge his knowledge in this regard, but sought with some subtlety to draw him out. In a short time I became convinced of his absolute sincerity, for he spoke of the dreams in a manner none could mistake. They and their subconscious residuum had influenced his art profoundly, and he showed me a morbid statue whose contours almost made me shake with the potency of its black suggestion. He could not recall having seen the original of this thing except in his own dream bas-relief, but the outlines had formed themselves insensibly under his hands. It was, no doubt, the giant shape he had raved of in delirium. That he really knew nothing of the hidden cult, save from what my uncle's relentless catechism[36] had let fall, he soon made clear; and again I strove to think of some way in which he could possibly have received the weird impressions.

He talked of his dreams in a strangely poetic fashion; making me see with terrible vividness the damp Cyclopean city of slimy green stone—whose *geometry*, he oddly said, was *all wrong*—and hear with frightened expectancy the ceaseless, half-mental calling from underground: *"Cthulhu fhtagn," "Cthulhu fhtagn."*

These words had formed part of that dread ritual which told of dead Cthulhu's dream-vigil in his stone vault at R'lyeh, and I felt deeply moved despite my rational beliefs. Wilcox, I was sure, had heard of the cult in some casual way, and had soon forgotten it amidst the mass of his equally weird reading and imagining. Later, by virtue of its sheer impressiveness, it had found subconscious expression in dreams, in the bas-relief, and in the terrible statue I now beheld; so that his imposture upon my uncle had been a very innocent one. The youth was of a type, at once slightly affected and slightly ill-mannered, which I could never like, but I was willing enough now to admit both his genius and his honesty. I took leave of him amicably, and wish him all the success his talent promises.

The matter of the cult still remained to fascinate me, and at times I had visions of personal fame from researches into its origin and connections. I visited New Orleans, talked with Legrasse and others of that old-time raiding-party, saw the frightful image, and even questioned such of the mongrel prisoners as still survived. Old Castro, unfortunately, had been dead for some years. What I now heard so graphically at first-hand, though it was really no more than a detailed confirmation of what my uncle had written, excited me afresh; for I felt sure that I was on the track of a very real, very secret, and very ancient religion whose discovery would make me an anthropologist of note. My attitude was still one of absolute materialism,[37] as I wish it still were, and I discounted with almost inexplicable perversity the coincidence of the dream notes and odd cuttings collected by Professor Angell.

One thing I began to suspect, and which I now fear I know, is that my uncle's death was far from natural. He fell on a narrow hill street leading up from an ancient waterfront swarming with foreign mongrels, after a careless push from a Negro sailor. I did not forget the mixed blood and marine pursuits of the cult-members in Louisiana, and would not be surprised to learn of secret methods and rites and beliefs. Legrasse and his men, it is true, have been let alone; but in Norway a certain seaman who saw things is dead. Might not the deeper inquiries of my uncle after encountering the sculptor's data have come to sinister ears? I think Professor Angell died because he knew too much, or because he was likely to learn too much. Whether I shall go as he did remains to be seen, for I have learned much now.

III. *The Madness from the Sea*

If heaven ever wishes to grant me a boon, it will be a total effacing of the results of a mere chance which fixed my eye on a certain stray piece of shelf-paper. It was nothing on which I would naturally have stumbled in the course of my daily round, for it was an old number of an Australian journal, the *Sydney Bulletin* for April 18, 1925. It had escaped even the cutting bureau which had at the time of its issuance been avidly collecting material for my uncle's research.

I had largely given over my inquiries into what Professor Angell called the "Cthulhu Cult," and was visiting a learned friend in Paterson, New Jersey; the curator of a local museum and a mineralogist of note. Examining one day the reserve specimens roughly set on the storage shelves in a rear room of the museum, my eye was caught by an odd picture in one of the old papers spread beneath the stones. It was the *Sydney Bulletin* I have mentioned, for my friend had wide affiliations in all conceivable foreign parts; and the picture was a half-tone cut of a hideous stone image almost identical with that which Legrasse had found in the swamp.

Eagerly clearing the sheet of its precious contents, I scanned the item in detail; and was disappointed to find it of only moderate length. What it suggested, however, was of portentous significance to my flagging quest; and I carefully tore it out for immediate action. It read as follows:

MYSTERY DERELICT FOUND AT SEA

Vigilant Arrives With Helpless Armed New Zealand Yacht in Tow. One Survivor and Dead Man Found Aboard. Tale of Desperate Battle and Deaths at Sea. Rescued Seaman Refuses Particulars of Strange Experience. Odd Idol Found in His Possession. Inquiry to Follow.

The Morrison Co.'s freighter *Vigilant*, bound from Valparaiso,[38] arrived this morning at its wharf in Darling Harbour, having in tow the battled and disabled but heavily armed steam yacht *Alert* of Dunedin, N.Z., which was sighted April 12th in S. Latitude 34°21', W. Longitude 152°17',[39] with one living and one dead man aboard.

The *Vigilant* left Valparaiso March 25th, and on April 2nd was driven considerably south of her course by exceptionally heavy storms and monster waves. On April 12th the derelict was sighted; and though apparently deserted, was found upon boarding to contain one survivor in a half-delirious condition and one man who had evidently been dead for more than a week. The living man was clutching a horrible stone idol of unknown origin, about foot in height, regarding whose nature authorities at Sydney University, the Royal Society, and the Museum in College Street all profess complete bafflement, and which the survivor says he found in the cabin of the yacht, in a small carved shrine of common pattern.

This man, after recovering his senses, told an exceedingly strange story of piracy and slaughter. He is Gustaf Johansen, a Norwegian of some intelligence, and had been second mate of the two-masted schooner *Emma* of Auckland, which sailed for Callao February 20th with a complement of eleven men.

The *Emma*, he says, was delayed and thrown widely south of her course by the great storm of March 1st, and on March 22nd, in S. Latitude 49°51' W. Longitude 128°34',[40] encountered the *Alert*, manned by a queer and evil-looking crew of Kanakas[41] and half-castes. Being ordered peremptorily to turn back, Capt. Collins refused; whereupon the strange crew began to fire savagely and without warning upon the schooner with a peculiarly heavy battery of brass cannon forming part of the yacht's equipment. The *Emma*'s men showed fight, says the survivor, and though the schooner began to sink from shots beneath the water-line they managed to heave alongside their enemy and board her, grappling with the savage crew on the yacht's deck, and being forced to kill them all, the number being slightly superior, because of their particularly abhorrent and desperate though rather clumsy mode of fighting.

Three of the *Emma*'s men, including Capt. Collins and First Mate Green, were killed; and the remaining eight under Second Mate Johansen proceeded to navigate the captured yacht, going ahead in their original direction to see if any reason for their ordering back had existed. The next day, it appears, they raised and landed on a small island, although none is known to exist in that part of the ocean; and six of the men somehow died ashore, though Johansen is queerly reticent about this part of his story, and speaks only of their falling into a rock chasm. Later, it seems, he and one companion boarded the yacht and tried to manage her, but were beaten about by the storm of April 2nd, From that time till his rescue on the 12th the man remembers little, and he does not even recall when William Briden, his companion, died. Briden's death reveals no apparent cause, and was probably due to excitement or exposure. Cable advices from Dunedin report that the *Alert* was well known there as an island trader, and bore an evil reputation along the waterfront. It was owned by a curious group of half-castes whose frequent meetings and night trips to the woods attracted no little curiosity; and it had set sail in great haste just after the storm and earth tremors of March 1st. Our Auckland correspondent gives the *Emma* and her crew an excellent reputation, and Johansen is described as a sober and worthy man. The admiralty will institute an inquiry on the whole matter beginning tomorrow, at which every effort will be made to induce Johansen to speak more freely than he has done hitherto.

This was all, together with the picture of the hellish image; but what a train of ideas it started in my mind! Here were new treasuries of data on the Cthulhu Cult, and evidence that it had strange interests at sea as well as on land. What motive prompted the hybrid crew to order back the *Emma* as they sailed about with their hideous idol? What was the unknown island on which six of the *Emma's* crew had died, and about which the mate Johansen was so secretive? What had the vice-admiralty's investigation brought out, and what was known of the noxious cult in Dunedin? And most marvelous of all, what deep and more than natural linkage of dates was this which gave a malign and now undeniable significance to the various turns of events so carefully noted by my uncle?

March 1st—or February 28th according to the International Date Line—the earthquake and storm had come. From Dunedin the *Alert* and her noisome crew had darted eagerly forth as if imperiously summoned, and on the other side of the earth poets and artists had begun to dream of a strange, dank Cyclopean city whilst a young sculptor had molded in his sleep the form of the dreaded Cthulhu. March 23rd the crew of the *Emma* landed on an unknown island and left six men dead; and on that date the dreams of sensitive men assumed a heightened vividness and darkened with dread of a giant monster's malign pursuit, whilst an architect had gone mad and a sculptor had lapsed suddenly into delirium! And what of this storm of April 2nd—the date on which all dreams of the dank city ceased, and Wilcox emerged unharmed from the bondage of strange fever? What of all this—and of those hints of old Castro about the sunken, star-born Old Ones and their coming reign; their faithful cult *and their mastery of dreams?* Was I tottering on the brink of cosmic horrors beyond man's power to bear? If so, they must be horrors of the mind alone, for in some way the second of April had put a stop to whatever monstrous menace had begun its siege of mankind's soul.

That evening, after a day of hurried cabling and arranging, I bade my host adieu and took a train for San Francisco. In less than a month I was in Dunedin; where, however, I found that little was known of the strange cult-members who had lingered in the old sea-taverns. Waterfront scum was far too common for special mention; though there was vague talk about one inland trip these mongrels had made, during which faint drumming and red flame were noted on the distant hills. In Auckland I learned that Johansen had returned *with yellow hair turned white* after a perfunctory and inconclusive questioning at Sydney, and had thereafter sold his cottage in West Street and sailed with his wife to his old home in Oslo. Of his stirring experience he would tell his friends no more than he had told the admiralty officials, and all they could do was to give me his Oslo address.

After that I went to Sydney and talked profitlessly with seamen and members of the vice-admiralty court. I saw the *Alert*, now sold and in commercial use, at Circular Quay in Sydney Cove, but gained nothing from its non-committal bulk. The crouching image with its cuttlefish head, dragon body, scaly wings, and hieroglyphed pedestal, was preserved in the Museum at Hyde Park; and I studied it long and well, finding it a thing of balefully exquisite workmanship, and with the same utter mystery, terrible antiquity, and unearthly strangeness of material which I had noted in Legrasse's smaller specimen. Geologists, the curator told me, had found it a monstrous puzzle; for they vowed that the world held no rock like it. Then I thought with a shudder of what Old Castro had told Legrasse about the Old Ones; "They had come from the stars, and had brought Their images with Them."

Shaken with such a mental revolution as I had never before known, I now resolved to visit Mate Johansen in Oslo. Sailing for London, I reembarked at once for the Norwegian capital; and one autumn day landed at the trim wharves in the shadow of the Egeberg. Johansen's address, I discovered, lay in the Old Town of King Harold Haardrada, which kept alive the name of Oslo during all the centuries that the greater city masqueraded as "Christiana." I made the brief trip by taxicab, and knocked with palpitant heart at the door of a neat and ancient building with plastered front. A sad-faced woman in black answered my summons, and I was stung the disappointment when she told me in halting English that Gustaf Johansen was no more.

He had not long survived his return, said his wife, for the doings at sea in 1925 had broken him. He had told her no more than he told the public, but had left a long manu-script—of "technical matters" as he said—written in English, evidently in order to guard her from the peril of casual perusal. During a walk rough a narrow lane near the Gothenburg dock, a bundle of papers falling from an attic window had knocked him down. Two Lascar[42] sailors at once helped him to his feet, but before the ambulance could reach him he was dead. Physicians found no adequate cause for the end, and laid it to heart trouble and a weakened constitution. I now felt gnawing at my vitals that dark terror which will never leave me till I, too, am at rest; "accidentally" or otherwise. Persuading the widow that my connection with her husband's "technical matters" was sufficient to entitle me to his man-uscript, I bore the document away and began to read it on the London boat.

It was a simple, rambling thing—a naive sailor's effort at a post-facto[43] diary—and strove to recall day by day that last awful voyage. I cannot attempt to transcribe it verbatim in all its cloudiness and redundance, but I will tell its gist enough to show why the sound of the water against the vessel's sides became so unendurable to me that I stopped my ears with cotton.

Johansen, thank God, did not know quite all, even though he saw the city and the Thing, but I shall never sleep calmly again when I think of the horrors that lurk ceaselessly behind life in time and in space, and of those unhallowed blasphemies from elder stars which dream beneath the sea, known and favored by a nightmare cult ready and eager to loose them upon the world whenever another earthquake shall heave their monstrous stone city again to the sun and air.

Johansen's voyage had begun just as he told it to the vice-admiralty. The *Emma*, in ballast, had cleared Auckland on February 20th, and had felt the full force of that earthquake-born tempest which must have heaved up from the sea-bottom the horrors that filled men's dreams. Once more under control, the ship was making good progress when held up by the *Alert* on March 22nd, and I could feel the mate's regret as he wrote of her bombardment and sinking. Of the swarthy cult-fiends on the *Alert* he speaks with sig-nificant horror. There was some peculiarly abominable quality about them which made their destruction seem almost a duty, and Johansen shows ingenuous wonder at the charge of ruthlessness brought against his party during the proceedings of the court of inquiry. Then, driven ahead by curiosity in their captured yacht under Johansen's command, the men sight a great stone pillar sticking out of the sea, and in S. Latitude 47°9', W. Longitude 126°43',[44] come upon a coastline of mingled mud, ooze, and weedy Cyclopean masonry which can be nothing less than the tangible substance of earth's supreme terror—the night-mare corpse-city of R'lyeh, that was built in measureless aeons behind history by the vast, loathsome shapes that seeped down from the dark stars. There lay great Cthulhu and his hordes, hidden in green slimy vaults and sending out at last, after cycles incalculable, the thoughts that spread fear to the dreams of the sensitive and called imperiously to the faithful to come on a pilgrimage of liberation and restoration. All this Johansen did not suspect, but God knows he soon saw enough!

I suppose that only a single mountain-top, the hideous monolith-crowned citadel whereon great Cthulhu was buried, actually emerged from the waters. When I think of the extent of all that may be brooding down there I almost wish to kill myself forthwith. Johansen and his men were awed by the cosmic majesty of this dripping Babylon of elder demons, and must have guessed without guidance that it was nothing of this or of any sane planet. Awe at the unbelievable size of the greenish stone blocks, at the dizzying height of the great carven monolith, and at the stupefying identity of the colossal statues and bas-reliefs with the queer image found in the shrine on the *Alert*, is poignantly visible in every line of the mate's frightened description.

Without knowing what futurism is like, Johansen achieved something very close to it when he spoke of the city; for instead of describing any definite structure or building, he dwells only on broad impressions of vast angles and stone surfaces—surfaces too great to belong to anything right or proper for this earth, and impious with horrible images and hieroglyphs. I mention his talk about angles because it suggests something Wilcox had told me of his awful dreams. He said that the geometry of the dream-place he saw was abnormal, non–Euclidean, and loathsomely redolent of spheres and dimensions apart from ours. Now an unlettered seaman felt the same thing whilst gazing at the terrible reality.

Johansen and his men landed at a sloping mud-bank on this monstrous acropolis,[45] and clambered slipperily up over titan oozy blocks which could have been no mortal stair-case. The very sun of heaven seemed distorted when viewed through the polarizing miasma welling out from this sea-soaked perversion, and twisted menace and suspense lurked leer-ingly in those crazily elusive angles of carven rock where a second glance showed concavity after the first showed convexity.

Something very like fright had come over all the explorers before anything more defi-nite than rock and ooze and weed was seen. Each would have fled had he not feared the scorn of the others, and it was only half-heartedly that they searched—vainly, as it proved— for some portable souvenir to bear away.

It was Rodriguez the Portuguese who climbed up the foot of the monolith and shouted of what he had found. The rest followed him, and looked curiously at the immense carved door with the now familiar squid-dragon bas-relief. It was, Johansen said, like a great barn-door; and they all felt that it was a door because of the ornate lintel, threshold, and jambs around it, though they could not decide whether it lay flat like a trap-door or slantwise like an outside cellar-door. As Wilcox would have said, the geometry of the place was all wrong. One could not be sure that the sea and the ground were horizontal, hence the relative posi-tion of everything else seemed fantasmally[46] variable.

Briden pushed at the stone in several places without result. Then Donovan felt over it delicately around the edge, pressing each point separately as he went. He climbed inter-minably along the grotesque stone molding—that is, one would call it climbing if the thing was not after all horizontal—and the men wondered how any door in the universe could be so vast. Then, very softly and slowly, the acre-great lintel began to give inward at the top; and they saw that it was balanced.

Donovan slid or somehow propelled himself down or along the jamb and rejoined his fellows, and everyone watched the queer recession of the monstrously carven portal. In this phantasy of prismatic distortion it moved anomalously[47] in a diagonal way, so that all the rules of matter and perspective seemed upset.

The aperture was black with a darkness almost material. That tenebrousness[48] was indeed a *positive quality*; for it obscured such parts of the inner walls as ought to have been revealed, and actually burst forth like smoke from its aeon-long imprisonment, visibly darkening the sun as it slunk away into the shrunken and gibbous[49] sky on flapping membranous wings. The odor rising from the newly opened depths was intolerable, and at length the quick-eared Hawkins thought he heard a nasty, slopping sound down there. Everyone listened, and everyone was listening still when It lumbered slobberingly into sight and gropingly squeezed Its gelatinous green immensity through the black doorway into the tainted outside air of that poison city of madness.

Poor Johansen's handwriting almost gave out when he wrote of this. Of the six men who never reached the ship, he thinks two perished of pure fright in that accursed instant. The Thing cannot be described—there is no language for such abysms of shrieking and immemorial lunacy, such eldritch[50] contradictions of all matter, force, and cosmic order. A mountain walked or stumbled. God! What wonder that across the earth a great architect went mad, and poor Wilcox raved with fever in that telepathic instant? The Thing of the idols, the green, sticky spawn of the stars, had awaked to claim his own. The stars were right again, and what an age-old cult had failed to do by design, a band of innocent sailors had done by accident. After vigintillions[51] of years great Cthulhu was loose again, and ravening for delight.

Three men were swept up by the flabby claws before anybody turned. God rest them, if there be any rest in the universe. They were Donovan, Guerrera, and Angstrom. Parker slipped as the other three were plunging frenziedly over endless vistas of green-crusted rock to the boat, and Johansen swears he was swallowed up by an angle of masonry which shouldn't have been there; an angle which was acute, but behaved as if it were obtuse. So only Briden and Johansen reached the boat, and pulled desperately for the *Alert* as the mountainous monstrosity flopped down the slimy stones and hesitated, floundering at the edge of the water.

Steam had not been suffered to go down entirely, despite the departure of all hands for the shore; and it was the work of only a few moments of feverish rushing up and down between wheel and engines to get the *Alert* under way. Slowly, amidst the distorted horrors of that indescribable scene, she began to churn the lethal waters; whilst on the masonry of that charnel shore that was not of earth the titan Thing from the stars slavered and gibbered like Polypheme[52] cursing the fleeing ship of Odysseus. Then, bolder than the storied Cyclops, great Cthulhu slid greasily into the water and began to pursue with vast wave-raising strokes of cosmic potency. Briden looked back and went mad, laughing shrilly as he kept on laughing at intervals till death found him one night in the cabin whilst Johansen was wandering deliriously.

But Johansen had not given out yet. Knowing that the Thing could surely overtake the *Alert* until steam was fully up, he resolved on a desperate chance; and, setting the engine for full speed, ran lightning-like on deck and reversed the wheel. There was a mighty eddying and foaming in the noisome brine, and as the steam mounted higher and higher the brave Norwegian drove his vessel head on against the pursuing jelly which rose above the unclean froth like the stern of a daemon galleon. The awful squid-head with writhing feelers came nearly up to the bowsprit of the sturdy yacht, but Johansen drove on relentlessly.

There was a bursting as of an exploding bladder, a slushy nastiness as of a cloven sunfish, a stench as of a thousand opened graves, and a sound that the chronicler could not put on paper. For an instant the ship was befouled by an acrid and blinding green cloud, and then there was only a venomous seething astern; where—God in heaven!—the scattered plasticity of that nameless sky-spawn was nebulously[53] *recombining* in its hateful original form, whilst its distance widened every second as the *Alert* gained impetus from its mounting steam.

That was all. After that Johansen only brooded over the idol in the cabin and attended to a few matters of food for himself and the laughing maniac by his side. He did not try to navigate after the first bold flight, for the reaction had taken something out of his soul. Then came the storm of April 2nd, and a gathering of the clouds about his consciousness. There is a sense of spectral whirling through liquid gulfs of infinity, of dizzying rides through reeling universes on a comet's tail, and of hysterical plunges from the pit to the moon and from the moon back again to the pit, all livened by a cachinnating[54] chorus of the distorted, hilarious elder gods and the green, bat-winged mocking imps of Tartarus.[55]

Out of that dream came rescue—the *Vigilant*, the vice-admiralty court, the streets of Dunedin, and the long voyage back home to the old house by the Egeberg. He could not tell—they would think him mad. He would write of what he knew before death came, but his wife must not guess. Death would be a boon if only it could blot out the memories.

That was the document I read, and now I have placed it in the tin box beside the bas-relief and the papers of Professor Angell. With it shall go this record of mine—this test of my own sanity, wherein is pieced together that which I hope may never be pieced together again. I have looked upon all that the universe has to hold of horror, and even the skies of spring and the flowers of summer must ever afterward be poison to me. But I do not think my life will be long. As my uncle went, as poor Johansen went, so I shall go. I know too much, and the cult still lives.

Cthulhu still lives, too, I suppose, again in that chasm of stone which has shielded him since the sun was young. His accursed city is sunken once more, for the Vigilant sailed over the spot after the April storm; but his ministers on earth still bellow and prance and slay around idol-capped monoliths in lonely places. He must have been trapped by the sinking whilst within his black abyss, or else the world would by now be screaming with fright and frenzy. Who knows the end? What has risen may sink, and what has sunk may rise. Loathsomeness waits and dreams in the deep, and decay spreads over the tottering cities of men. A time will come—but I must not and cannot think! Let me pray that, if I do not survive this manuscript, my executors may put caution before audacity and see that it meets no other eye.

The Colour Out of Space

Considered by Lovecraft to be his best story, "The Colour Out of Space" is a significant addition to Lovecraft's oeuvre. Set in the hills just outside Lovecraft's fictional Arkham, MA, this tale describes the tragic fate of a rural family and the surrounding countryside after a strange meteorite falls from the sky.

S.T. Joshi considers it one of Lovecraft's "towering" achievements, referring to it as "a sustained prose-poem" presenting his "most successful portrayal" of a morally ambiguous foe. Though the "colour" ultimately wreaks havoc on its surroundings, Lovecraft gives no indication of its motives, thus implying that the frail human mind is incapable of grasping the purposes of anything so truly alien.

It is this unknowable quality of the colour that prompts Caitlín Kiernan to posit another significant aspect of the story: For her it represents Lovecraft's moving "soundly" from horror into the science fiction genre: "It's one of the best stories of encounters with an alien Other," she explains. "This alien is alien, ultimately incomprehensible, and there's no familiar, reassuring point of reference for the reader to latch onto."

West of Arkham the hills rise wild, and there are valleys with deep woods that no axe has ever cut. There are dark narrow glens where the trees slope fantastically, and where thin brooklets trickle without ever having caught the glint of sunlight. On the gentler slopes there are farms, ancient and rocky, with squat, moss-coated cottages brooding eternally over old New England secrets in the lee of great ledges; but these are all vacant now, the wide chimneys crumbling and the shingled sides bulging perilously beneath low gambrel[1] roofs.

The old folk have gone away, and foreigners do not like to live there. French-Canadians have tried it, Italians have tried it, and the Poles have come and departed. It is not because of anything that can be seen or heard or handled, but because of something that is imagined. The place is not good for the imagination, and does not bring restful dreams at night. It must be this which keeps the foreigners away, for old Ammi Pierce has never told them of anything he recalls from the strange days. Ammi, whose head has been a little queer for years, is the only one who still remains, or who ever talks of the strange days; and he dares to do this because his house is so near the open fields and the travelled roads around Arkham.

There was once a road over the hills and through the valleys, that ran straight where the blasted heath is now; but people ceased to use it and a new road was laid curving far toward the south. Traces of the old one can still be found amidst the weeds of a returning wilderness, and some of them will doubtless linger even when half the hollows are flooded for the new reservoir.[2] Then the dark woods will be cut down and the blasted heath will slumber far below blue waters whose surface will mirror the sky and ripple in the sun. And the secrets of the strange days will be one with the deep's secrets; one with the hidden lore of old ocean, and all the mystery of primal earth.

When I went into the hills and vales to survey for the new reservoir they told me the place was evil. They told me this in Arkham, and because that is a very old town full of witch legends I thought the evil must be something which grandams[3] had whispered to children through centuries. The name "blasted heath" seemed to me very odd and theatrical, and I wondered how it had come into the folklore of a Puritan people. Then I saw that dark westward tangle of glens and slopes for myself, and ceased to wonder at anything besides its own elder mystery. It was morning when I saw it, but shadow lurked always there. The trees grew too thickly, and their trunks were too big for any healthy New England wood. There was too much silence in the dim alleys between them, and the floor was too soft with the dank moss and mattings of infinite years of decay.

In the open spaces, mostly along the line of the old road, there were little hillside farms; sometimes with all the buildings standing, sometimes with only one or two, and sometimes with only a lone chimney or fast-filling cellar. Weeds and briers reigned, and furtive wild things rustled in the undergrowth. Upon everything was a haze of restlessness and oppression; a touch of the unreal and the grotesque, as if some vital element of perspective or chiaroscuro[4] were awry. I did not wonder that the foreigners would not stay, for this was no region to sleep in. It was too much like a landscape of Salvator Rosa[5]; too much like some forbidden woodcut in a tale of terror.

But even all this was not so bad as the blasted heath. I knew it the moment I came upon it at the bottom of a spacious valley; for no other name could fit such a thing, or any other thing fit such a name. It was as if the poet had coined the phrase from having seen this one particular region. It must, I thought as I viewed it, be the outcome of a fire; but why had nothing new ever grown over those five acres of grey desolation that sprawled open to the sky like a great spot eaten by acid in the woods and fields? It lay largely to the north of the ancient road line, but encroached a little on the other side. I felt an odd reluctance about approaching, and did so at last only because my business took me through and past it. There was no vegetation of any kind on that broad expanse, but only a fine grey dust or ash which no wind seemed ever to blow about. The trees near it were sickly and stunted, and many dead trunks stood or lay rotting at the rim. As I walked hurriedly by I saw the tumbled bricks and stones of an old chimney and cellar on my right, and the yawning black maw of an abandoned well whose stagnant vapors played strange tricks with the hues of the sunlight. Even the long, dark woodland climb beyond seemed welcome in contrast, and I marveled no more at the frightened whispers of Arkham people. There had been no house or ruin near; even in the old days the place must have been lonely and remote. And at twilight, dreading to repass that ominous spot, I walked circuitously back to the town by the curving road on the south. I vaguely wished some clouds would gather, for an odd timidity about the deep skyey voids above had crept into my soul.

In the evening I asked old people in Arkham about the blasted heath, and what was meant by that phrase "strange days" which so many evasively muttered. I could not, however, get any good answers, except that all the mystery was much more recent than I had dreamed.

It was not a matter of old legendry at all, but something within the lifetime of those who spoke. It had happened in the eighties, and a family had disappeared or was killed. Speakers would not be exact; and because they all told me to pay no attention to old Ammi Pierce's crazy tales, I sought him out the next morning, having heard that he lived alone in the ancient tottering cottage where the trees first begin to get very thick. It was a fearsomely archaic place, and had begun to exude the faint miasmal odor which clings about houses that have stood too long. Only with persistent knocking could I rouse the aged man, and when he shuffled timidly to the door I could tell he was not glad to see me. He was not so feeble as I had expected; but his eyes drooped in a curious way, and his unkempt clothing and white beard made him seem very worn and dismal. Not knowing just how he could best be launched on his tales, I feigned a matter of business; told him of my surveying, and asked vague questions about the district. He was far brighter and more educated than I had been led to think, and before I knew it had grasped quite as much of the subject as any man I had talked with in Arkham. He was not like other rustics I had known in the sections where reservoirs were to be. From him there were no protests at the miles of old wood and farmland to be blotted out, though perhaps there would have been had not his home lain outside the bounds of the future lake. Relief was all that he showed; relief at the doom of the dark ancient valleys through which he had roamed all his life. They were better under water now—better under water since the strange days. And with this opening his husky voice sank low, while his body leaned forward and his right forefinger began to point shakily and impressively.

It was then that I heard the story, and as the rambling voice scraped and whispered on I shivered again and again despite the summer day. Often I had to recall the speaker from ramblings, piece out scientific points which he knew only by a fading parrot memory of professors' talk, or bridge over gaps where his sense of logic and continuity broke down. When he was done I did not wonder that his mind had snapped a trifle, or that the folk of Arkham would not speak much of the blasted heath. I hurried back before sunset to my hotel, unwilling to have the stars come out above me in the open; and the next day returned to Boston to give up my position. I could not go into that dim chaos of old forest and slope again, or face another time that grey blasted heath where the black well yawned deep beside the tumbled bricks and stones. The reservoir will soon be built now, and all those elder secrets will be safe forever under watery fathoms. But even then I do not believe I would like to visit that country by night—at least, not when the sinister stars are out; and nothing could bribe me to drink the new city water of Arkham.

It all began, old Ammi said, with the meteorite. Before that time there had been no wild legends at all since the witch trials, and even then these western woods were not feared half so much as the small island in the Miskatonic[6] where the devil held court beside a curious stone altar older than the Indians. These were not haunted woods, and their fantastic dusk was never terrible till the strange days. Then there had come that white noontide cloud, that string of explosions in the air, and that pillar of smoke from the valley far in the wood. And by night all Arkham had heard of the great rock that fell out of the sky and bedded itself in the ground beside the well at the Nahum Gardner place. That was the house which had stood where the blasted heath was to come—the trim white Nahum Gardner house amidst its fertile gardens and orchards.

Nahum had come to town to tell people about the stone, and had dropped in at Ammi Pierce's on the way. Ammi was forty then, and all the queer things were fixed very strongly in his mind. He and his wife had gone with the three professors from Miskatonic University who hastened out the next morning to see the weird visitor from unknown stellar space, and had wondered why Nahum had called it so large the day before. It had shrunk, Nahum said as he pointed out the big brownish mound above the ripped earth and charred grass near the archaic well-sweep in his front yard; but the wise men answered that stones do not shrink. Its heat lingered persistently, and Nahum declared it had glowed faintly in the night. The professors tried it with a geologist's hammer and found it was oddly soft. It was, in truth, so soft as to be almost plastic; and they gouged rather than chipped a specimen to take back to the college for testing. They took it in an old pail borrowed from Nahum's kitchen, for even the small piece refused to grow cool. On the trip back they stopped at Ammi's to rest, and seemed thoughtful when Mrs. Pierce remarked that the fragment was growing smaller and burning the bottom of the pail. Truly, it was not large, but perhaps they had taken less than they thought.

The day after that—all this was in June of '82—the professors had trooped out again in a great excitement. As they passed Ammi's they told him what queer things the specimen had done, and how it had faded wholly away when they put it in a glass beaker. The beaker had gone, too, and the wise men talked of the strange stone's affinity for silicon. It had acted quite unbelievably in that well-ordered laboratory; doing nothing at all and showing no occluded gases[7] when heated on charcoal, being wholly negative in the borax bead,[8] and soon proving itself absolutely non-volatile at any producible temperature, including that of the oxy-hydrogen blowpipe.[9] On an anvil it appeared highly malleable, and in the dark its luminosity was very marked. Stubbornly refusing to grow cool, it soon had the college in a state of real excitement; and when upon heating before the spectroscope[10] it displayed shining bands unlike any known colors of the normal spectrum there was much breathless talk of new elements, bizarre optical properties, and other things which puzzled men of science are wont to say when faced by the unknown.

Hot as it was, they tested it in a crucible with all the proper reagents. Water did nothing. Hydrochloric acid was the same. Nitric acid and even aqua regia[11] merely hissed and spattered against its torrid invulnerability. Ammi had difficulty in recalling all these things, but recognized some solvents as I mentioned them in the usual order of use. There were ammonia and caustic soda, alcohol and ether, nauseous carbon disulphide[12] and a dozen others; but although the weight grew steadily less as time passed, and the fragment seemed to be slightly cooling, there was no change in the solvents to show that they had attacked the substance at all. It was a metal, though, beyond a doubt. It was magnetic, for one thing; and after its immersion in the acid solvents there seemed to be faint traces of the Widmannstätten figures[13] found on meteoric iron. When the cooling had grown very considerable, the testing was carried on in glass; and it was in a glass beaker that they left all the chips made of the original fragment during the work. The next morning both chips and beaker were gone without trace, and only a charred spot marked the place on the wooden shelf where they had been.

All this the professors told Ammi as they paused at his door, and once more he went with them to see the stony messenger from the stars, though this time his wife did not accompany him. It had now most certainly shrunk, and even the sober professors could not doubt the truth of what they saw. All around the dwindling brown lump near the well was a vacant space, except where the earth had caved in; and whereas it had been a good seven feet across the day before, it was now scarcely five. It was still hot, and the sages studied its surface curiously as they detached another and larger piece with hammer and chisel. They gouged deeply this time, and as they pried away the smaller mass they saw that the core of the thing was not quite homogeneous.[14]

They had uncovered what seemed to be the side of a large colored globule imbedded in the substance. The color, which resembled some of the bands in the meteor's strange spectrum, was almost impossible to describe; and it was only by analogy that they called it color at all. Its texture was glossy, and upon tapping it appeared to promise both brittleness and hollowness. One of the professors gave it a smart blow with a hammer, and it burst with a nervous little pop. Nothing was emitted, and all trace of the thing vanished with the puncturing. It left behind a hollow spherical space about three inches across, and all thought it probable that others would be discovered as the enclosing substance wasted away.

Conjecture was vain; so after a futile attempt to find additional globules[15] by drilling, the seekers left again with their new specimen—which proved, however, as baffling in the laboratory as its predecessor had been. Aside from being almost plastic, having heat, magnetism, and slight luminosity, cooling slightly in powerful acids, possessing an unknown spectrum, wasting away in air, and attacking silicon compounds with mutual destruction as a result, it presented no identifying features whatsoever; and at the end of the tests the college scientists were forced to own that they could not place it. It was nothing of this earth, but a piece of the great outside; and as such dowered with outside properties and obedient to outside laws.

That night there was a thunderstorm, and when the professors went out to Nahum's the next day they met with a bitter disappointment. The stone, magnetic as it had been, must have had some peculiar electrical property; for it had "drawn the lightning," as Nahum said, with a singular persistence. Six times within an hour the farmer saw the lightning strike the furrow in the front yard, and when the storm was over nothing remained but a ragged pit by the ancient well-sweep, half-choked with caved-in earth. Digging had borne no fruit, and the scientists verified the fact of the utter vanishment. The failure was total; so that nothing was left to do but go back to the laboratory and test again the disappearing fragment left carefully cased in lead. That fragment lasted a week, at the end of which nothing of value had been learned of it. When it had gone, no residue was left behind, and in time the professors felt scarcely sure they had indeed seen with waking eyes that cryptic vestige of the fathomless gulfs outside; that lone, weird message from other universes and other realms of matter, force, and entity.

As was natural, the Arkham papers made much of the incident with its collegiate sponsoring, and sent reporters to talk with Nahum Gardner and his family. At least one Boston daily also sent a scribe, and Nahum quickly became a kind of local celebrity. He was a lean, genial person of about fifty, living with his wife and three sons on the pleasant farmstead in the valley. He and Ammi exchanged visits frequently, as did their wives; and Ammi had nothing but praise for him after all these years. He seemed slightly proud of the notice his place had attracted, and talked often of the meteorite in the succeeding weeks. That July and August were hot, and Nahum worked hard at his haying in the ten-acre pasture across Chapman's Brook; his rattling wain wearing deep ruts in the shadowy lanes between. The labor tired him more than it had in other years, and he felt that age was beginning to tell on him.

Then fell the time of fruit and harvest. The pears and apples slowly ripened, and Nahum vowed that his orchards were prospering as never before. The fruit was growing to phenomenal size and unwonted gloss, and in such abundance that extra barrels were ordered to handle the future crop. But with the ripening came sore disappointment; for of all that gorgeous array of specious lusciousness not one single jot was fit to eat. Into the fine flavor of the pears and apples had crept a stealthy bitterness and sickishness, so that even the smallest of bites induced a lasting disgust. It was the same with the melons and tomatoes, and Nahum sadly saw that his entire crop was lost. Quick to connect events, he declared that the meteorite had poisoned the soil, and thanked heaven that most of the other crops were in the upland lot along the road.

Winter came early, and was very cold. Ammi saw Nahum less often than usual, and observed that he had begun to look worried. The rest of his family, too, seemed to have grown taciturn; and were far from steady in their churchgoing or their attendance at the various social events of the countryside. For this reserve or melancholy no cause could be found, though all the household confessed now and then to poorer health and a feeling of vague disquiet. Nahum himself gave the most definite statement of anyone when he said he was disturbed about certain footprints in the snow. They were the usual winter prints of red squirrels, white rabbits, and foxes, but the brooding farmer professed to see something not quite right about their nature and arrangement. He was never specific, but appeared to think that they were not as characteristic of the anatomy and habits of squirrels and rabbits and foxes as they ought to be. Ammi listened without interest to this talk until one night when he drove past Nahum's house in his sleigh on the way back from Clark's Corners. There had been a moon, and a rabbit had run across the road, and the leaps of that rabbit were longer than either Ammi or his horse liked. The latter, indeed, had almost run away when brought up by a firm rein. Thereafter Ammi gave Nahum's tales more respect, and wondered why the Gardner dogs seemed so cowed and quivering every morning. They had, it developed, nearly lost the spirit to bark.

In February the McGregor boys from Meadow Hill were out shooting woodchucks, and not far from the Gardner place bagged a very peculiar specimen. The proportions of its body seemed slightly altered in a queer way impossible to describe, while its face had taken on an expression which no one ever saw in a woodchuck before. The boys were genuinely frightened, and threw the thing away at once, so that only their grotesque tales of it ever reached the people of the countryside. But the shying of the horses near Nahum's house had now become an acknowledged thing, and all the basis for a cycle of whispered legend was fast taking form.

People vowed that the snow melted faster around Nahum's than it did anywhere else, and early in March there was an awed discussion in Potter's general store at Clark's Corners. Stephen Rice had driven past Gardner's in the morning, and had noticed the skunk-cabbages coming up through the mud by the woods across the road. Never were things of such size seen before, and they held strange colors that could not be put into any words. Their shapes were monstrous, and the horse had snorted at an odor which struck Stephen as wholly unprecedented. That afternoon several persons drove past to see the abnormal growth, and all agreed that plants of that kind ought never to sprout in a healthy world. The bad fruit of the fall before was freely mentioned, and it went from mouth to mouth that there was poison in Nahum's ground. Of course it was the meteorite; and remembering how strange the men from the college had found that stone to be, several farmers spoke about the matter to them.

One day they paid Nahum a visit; but having no love of wild tales and folklore were very conservative in what they inferred. The plants were certainly odd, but all skunk-cabbages are more or less odd in shape and odor and hue. Perhaps some mineral element from the stone had entered the soil, but it would soon be washed away. And as for the footprints and frightened horses—of course this was mere country talk which such a phenomenon as the aërolite[16] would be certain to start. There was really nothing for serious men to do in cases of wild gossip, for superstitious rustics will say and believe anything. And so all through the strange days the professors stayed away in contempt. Only one of them, when given two phials of dust for analysis in a police job over a year and a half later, recalled that the queer color of that skunk-cabbage had been very like one of the anomalous bands of light shown by the meteor fragment in the college spectroscope, and like the brittle globule found imbedded in the stone from the abyss. The samples in this analysis case gave the same odd bands at first, though later they lost the property.

The trees budded prematurely around Nahum's, and at night they swayed ominously in the wind. Nahum's second son Thaddeus, a lad of fifteen, swore that they swayed also when there was no wind; but even the gossips would not credit this. Certainly, however, restlessness was in the air. The entire Gardner family developed the habit of stealthy listening, though not for any sound which they could consciously name. The listening was, indeed, rather a product of moments when consciousness seemed half to slip away. Unfortunately such moments increased week by week, till it became common speech that "something was wrong with all Nahum's folks." When the early saxifrage[17] came out it had another strange color; not quite like that of the skunk-cabbage, but plainly related and equally unknown to anyone who saw it. Nahum took some blossoms to Arkham and showed them to the editor of the Gazette, but that dignitary did no more than write a humorous article about them, in which the dark fears of rustics were held up to polite ridicule. It was a mistake of Nahum's to tell a stolid city man about the way the great, overgrown mourning-cloak butterflies behaved in connection with these saxifrages.

April brought a kind of madness to the country folk, and began that disuse of the road past Nahum's which led to its ultimate abandonment. It was the vegetation. All the orchard trees blossomed forth in strange colors, and through the stony soil of the yard and adjacent pasturage there sprang up a bizarre growth which only a botanist could connect with the proper flora of the region. No sane wholesome colors were anywhere to be seen except in the green grass and leafage; but everywhere those hectic and prismatic variants of some diseased, underlying primary tone without a place among the known tints of earth. The "Dutchman's breeches"[18] became a thing of sinister menace, and the bloodroots[19] grew insolent in their chromatic perversion. Ammi and the Gardners thought that most of the colors had a sort of haunting familiarity, and decided that they reminded one of the brittle globule in the meteor. Nahum ploughed and sowed the ten-acre pasture and the upland lot, but did nothing with the land around the house. He knew it would be of no use, and hoped that the summer's strange growths would draw all the poison from the soil. He was prepared for almost anything now, and had grown used to the sense of something near him waiting to be heard. The shunning of his house by neighbors told on him, of course; but it told on his wife more. The boys were better off, being at school each day; but they could not help being frightened by the gossip. Thaddeus, an especially sensitive youth, suffered the most.

In May the insects came, and Nahum's place became a nightmare of buzzing and crawling. Most of the creatures seemed not quite usual in their aspects and motions, and their nocturnal habits contradicted all former experience. The Gardners took to watching at night—watching in all directions at random for something … they could not tell what. It was then that they all owned that Thaddeus had been right about the trees. Mrs. Gardner was the next to see it from the window as she watched the swollen boughs of a maple against a moonlit sky. The boughs surely moved, and there was no wind. It must be the sap. Strangeness had come into everything growing now. Yet it was none of Nahum's family at all who made the next discovery. Familiarity had dulled them, and what they could not see was glimpsed by a timid windmill salesman from Bolton who drove by one night in ignorance of the country legends. What he told in Arkham was given a short paragraph in the Gazette; and it was there that all the farmers, Nahum included, saw it first. The night had been dark and the buggy-lamps faint, but around a farm in the valley which everyone knew from the account must be Nahum's the darkness had been less thick. A dim though distinct luminosity seemed to inhere in all the vegetation, grass, leaves, and blossoms alike, while at one moment a detached piece of the phosphorescence appeared to stir furtively in the yard near the barn.

The grass had so far seemed untouched, and the cows were freely pastured in the lot near the house, but toward the end of May the milk began to be bad. Then Nahum had the cows driven to the uplands, after which the trouble ceased. Not long after this the change in grass and leaves became apparent to the eye. All the verdure[20] was going grey, and was developing a highly singular quality of brittleness. Ammi was now the only person who ever visited the place, and his visits were becoming fewer and fewer. When school closed the Gardners were virtually cut off from the world, and sometimes let Ammi do their errands in town. They were failing curiously both physically and mentally, and no one was surprised when the news of Mrs. Gardner's madness stole around.

It happened in June, about the anniversary of the meteor's fall, and the poor woman screamed about things in the air which she could not describe. In her raving there was not a single specific noun, but only verbs and pronouns. Things moved and changed and fluttered, and ears tingled to impulses which were not wholly sounds. Something was taken away—she was being drained of something—something was fastening itself on her that ought not to be—someone must make it keep off—nothing was ever still in the night—the walls and windows shifted. Nahum did not send her to the county asylum, but let her wander about the house as long as she was harmless to herself and others. Even when her expression changed he did nothing. But when the boys grew afraid of her, and Thaddeus nearly fainted at the way she made faces at him, he decided to keep her locked in the attic. By July she had ceased to speak and crawled on all fours, and before that month was over Nahum got the mad notion that she was slightly luminous in the dark, as he now clearly saw was the case with the nearby vegetation.

It was a little before this that the horses had stampeded. Something had aroused them in the night, and their neighing and kicking in their stalls had been terrible. There seemed virtually nothing to do to calm them, and when Nahum opened the stable door they all bolted out like frightened woodland deer. It took a week to track all four, and when found they were seen to be quite useless and unmanageable. Something had snapped in their brains, and each one had to be shot for its own good. Nahum borrowed a horse from Ammi for his haying, but found it would not approach the barn. It shied, balked, and whinnied, and in the end he could do nothing but drive it into the yard while the men used their own strength to get the heavy wagon near enough the hayloft for convenient pitching. And all the while the vegetation was turning grey and brittle. Even the flowers whose hues had been so strange were greying now, and the fruit was coming out grey and dwarfed and tasteless. The asters and goldenrod bloomed grey and distorted, and the roses and zinnias and hollyhocks in the front yard were such blasphemous-looking things that Nahum's oldest boy Zenas cut them down. The strangely puffed insects died about that time, even the bees that had left their hives and taken to the woods.

By September all the vegetation was fast crumbling to a greyish powder, and Nahum feared that the trees would die before the poison was out of the soil. His wife now had spells of terrific screaming, and he and the boys were in a constant state of nervous tension. They shunned people now, and when school opened the boys did not go. But it was Ammi, on one of his rare visits, who first realized that the well water was no longer good. It had an evil taste that was not exactly foetid[21] nor exactly salty, and Ammi advised his friend to dig another well on higher ground to use till the soil was good again. Nahum, however, ignored the warning, for he had by that time become calloused to strange and unpleasant things. He and the boys continued to use the tainted supply, drinking it as listlessly and mechanically as they ate their meager and ill-cooked meals and did their thankless and monotonous chores through the aimless days. There was something of stolid resignation about them all, as if they walked half in another world between lines of nameless guards to a certain and familiar doom.

Thaddeus went mad in September after a visit to the well. He had gone with a pail and had come back empty-handed, shrieking and waving his arms, and sometimes lapsing into an inane titter or a whisper about "the moving colours down there." Two in one family was pretty bad, but Nahum was very brave about it. He let the boy run about for a week until he began stumbling and hurting himself, and then he shut him in an attic room across the hall from his mother's. The way they screamed at each other from behind their locked doors was very terrible, especially to little Merwin, who fancied they talked in some terrible language that was not of earth. Merwin was getting frightfully imaginative, and his restlessness was worse after the shutting away of the brother who had been his greatest playmate.

Almost at the same time the mortality among the livestock commenced. Poultry turned greyish and died very quickly, their meat being found dry and noisome upon cutting. Hogs grew inordinately fat, then suddenly began to undergo loathsome changes which no one could explain. Their meat was of course useless, and Nahum was at his wit's end. No rural veterinary would approach his place, and the city veterinary from Arkham was openly baffled. The swine began growing grey and brittle and falling to pieces before they died, and their eyes and muzzles developed singular alterations. It was very inexplicable, for they had never been fed from the tainted vegetation. Then something struck the cows. Certain areas or sometimes the whole body would be uncannily shriveled or compressed, and atrocious collapses or disintegrations were common. In the last stages—and death was always the result—there would be a greying and turning brittle like that which beset the hogs. There could be no question of poison, for all the cases occurred in a locked and undisturbed barn. No bites of prowling things could have brought the virus, for what live beast of earth can pass through solid obstacles? It must be only natural disease—yet what disease could wreak such results was beyond any mind's guessing. When the harvest came there was not an animal surviving on the place, for the stock and poultry were dead and the dogs had run away. These dogs, three in number, had all vanished one night and were never heard of again. The five cats had left some time before, but their going was scarcely noticed since there now seemed to be no mice, and only Mrs. Gardner had made pets of the graceful felines.

On the nineteenth of October Nahum staggered into Ammi's house with hideous news. The death had come to poor Thaddeus in his attic room, and it had come in a way which could not be told. Nahum had dug a grave in the railed family plot behind the farm, and had put therein what he found. There could have been nothing from outside, for the small barred window and locked door were intact; but it was much as it had been in the barn. Ammi and his wife consoled the stricken man as best they could, but shuddered as they did so. Stark terror seemed to cling round the Gardners and all they touched, and the very presence of one in the house was a breath from regions unnamed and unnamable. Ammi accompanied Nahum home with the greatest reluctance, and did what he might to calm the hysterical sobbing of little Merwin. Zenas needed no calming. He had come of late to do nothing but stare into space and obey what his father told him; and Ammi thought that his fate was very merciful. Now and then Merwin's screams were answered faintly from the attic, and in response to an inquiring look Nahum said that his wife was getting very feeble. When night approached, Ammi managed to get away; for not even friendship could make him stay in that spot when the faint glow of the vegetation began and the trees may or may not have swayed without wind. It was really lucky for Ammi that he was not more imaginative. Even as things were, his mind was bent ever so slightly; but had he been able to connect and reflect upon all the portents around him he must inevitably have turned a total maniac. In the twilight he hastened home, the screams of the mad woman and the nervous child ringing horribly in his ears.

Three days later Nahum lurched into Ammi's kitchen in the early morning, and in the absence of his host stammered out a desperate tale once more, while Mrs. Pierce listened in a clutching fright. It was little Merwin this time. He was gone. He had gone out late at night with a lantern and pail for water, and had never come back. He'd been going to pieces for days, and hardly knew what he was about. Screamed at everything. There had been a frantic shriek from the yard then, but before the father could get to the door, the boy was gone. There was no glow from the lantern he had taken, and of the child himself no trace. At the time Nahum thought the lantern and pail were gone too; but when dawn came, and the man had plodded back from his all-night search of the woods and fields, he had found some very curious things near the well. There was a crushed and apparently somewhat melted mass of iron which had certainly been the lantern; while a bent bail and twisted iron hoops beside it, both half-fused, seemed to hint at the remnants of the pail. That was all. Nahum was past imagining, Mrs. Pierce was blank, and Ammi, when he had reached home and heard the tale, could give no guess. Merwin was gone, and there would be no use in telling the people around, who shunned all Gardners now. No use, either, in telling the city people at Arkham who laughed at everything. Thad was gone, and now Merwin was gone. Something was creeping and creeping and waiting to be seen and felt and heard. Nahum would go soon, and he wanted Ammi to look after his wife and Zenas if they survived him. It must all be a judgment of some sort; though he could not fancy what for, since he had always walked uprightly in the Lord's ways so far as he knew.

For over two weeks Ammi saw nothing of Nahum; and then, worried about what might have happened, he overcame his fears and paid the Gardner place a visit. There was no smoke from the great chimney, and for a moment the visitor was apprehensive of the worst. The aspect of the whole farm was shocking—greyish withered grass and leaves on the ground, vines falling in brittle wreckage from archaic walls and gables,[22] and great bare trees clawing up at the grey November sky with a studied malevolence which Ammi could not but feel had come from some subtle change in the tilt of the branches. But Nahum was alive, after all. He was weak, and lying on a couch in the low-ceiled kitchen, but perfectly conscious and able to give simple orders to Zenas. The room was deadly cold; and as Ammi visibly shivered, the host shouted huskily to Zenas for more wood. Wood, indeed, was sorely needed; since the cavernous fireplace was unlit and empty, with a cloud of soot blowing about in the chill wind that came down the chimney. Presently Nahum asked him if the extra wood had made him any more comfortable, and then Ammi saw what had happened. The stoutest cord had broken at last, and the hapless farmer's mind was proof against more sorrow.

Questioning tactfully, Ammi could get no clear data at all about the missing Zenas. "In the well—he lives in the well—" was all that the clouded father would say. Then there flashed across the visitor's mind a sudden thought of the mad wife, and he changed his line of inquiry. "Nabby? Why, here she is!" was the surprised response of poor Nahum, and Ammi soon saw that he must search for himself. Leaving the harmless babbler on the couch, he took the keys from their nail beside the door and climbed the creaking stairs to the attic. It was very close and noisome up there, and no sound could be heard from any direction. Of the four doors in sight, only one was locked, and on this he tried various keys on the ring he had taken. The third key proved the right one, and after some fumbling Ammi threw open the low white door.

It was quite dark inside, for the window was small and half-obscured by the crude wooden bars; and Ammi could see nothing at all on the wide-planked floor. The stench was beyond enduring, and before proceeding further he had to retreat to another room and return with his lungs filled with breathable air. When he did enter he saw something dark in the corner, and upon seeing it more clearly he screamed outright. While he screamed he thought a momentary cloud eclipsed the window, and a second later he felt himself brushed as if by some hateful current of vapor. Strange colors danced before his eyes; and had not a present horror numbed him he would have thought of the globule in the meteor that the geologist's hammer had shattered, and of the morbid vegetation that had sprouted in the spring. As it was he thought only of the blasphemous monstrosity which confronted him, and which all too clearly had shared the nameless fate of young Thaddeus and the livestock. But the terrible thing about this horror was that it very slowly and perceptibly moved as it continued to crumble.

Ammi would give me no added particulars to this scene, but the shape in the corner does not reappear in his tale as a moving object. There are things which cannot be mentioned, and what is done in common humanity is sometimes cruelly judged by the law. I gathered that no moving thing was left in that attic room, and that to leave anything capable of motion there would have been a deed so monstrous as to damn any accountable being to eternal torment. Anyone but a stolid farmer would have fainted or gone mad, but Ammi walked conscious through that low doorway and locked the accursed secret behind him. There would be Nahum to deal with now; he must be fed and tended, and removed to some place where he could be cared for.

Commencing his descent of the dark stairs, Ammi heard a thud below him. He even thought a scream had been suddenly choked off, and recalled nervously the clammy vapor which had brushed by him in that frightful room above. What presence had his cry and entry started up? Halted by some vague fear, he heard still further sounds below. Indubitably there was a sort of heavy dragging, and a most detestably sticky noise as of some fiendish and unclean species of suction. With an associative sense goaded to feverish heights, he thought unaccountably of what he had seen upstairs. Good God! What eldritch dream-world was this into which he had blundered? He dared move neither backward nor forward, but stood there trembling at the black curve of the boxed-in staircase. Every trifle of the scene burned itself into his brain. The sounds, the sense of dread expectancy, the darkness, the steepness of the narrow steps—and merciful heaven! ... The faint but unmistakable luminosity of all the woodwork in sight; steps, sides, exposed laths, and beams alike!

Then there burst forth a frantic whinny from Ammi's horse outside, followed at once by a clatter which told of a frenzied runaway. In another moment horse and buggy had gone beyond earshot, leaving the frightened man on the dark stairs to guess what had sent them. But that was not all. There had been another sound out there. A sort of liquid splash—water—it must have been the well. He had left Hero untied near it, and a buggy-wheel must have brushed the coping and knocked in a stone. And still the pale phosphorescence glowed in that detestably ancient woodwork. God! how old the house was! Most of it built before 1670, and the gambrel roof not later than 1730.

A feeble scratching on the floor downstairs now sounded distinctly, and Ammi's grip tightened on a heavy stick he had picked up in the attic for some purpose. Slowly nerving himself, he finished his descent and walked boldly toward the kitchen. But he did not complete the walk, because what he sought was no longer there. It had come to meet him, and it was still alive after a fashion. Whether it had crawled or whether it had been dragged by any external force, Ammi could not say; but the death had been at it. Everything had happened in the last half-hour, but collapse, greying, and disintegration were already far advanced. There was a horrible brittleness, and dry fragments were scaling off. Ammi could not touch it, but looked horrifiedly into the distorted parody that had been a face. "What was it, Nahum—what was it?" he whispered, and the cleft, bulging lips were just able to crackle out a final answer.

"Nothin' … nothin' … the colour … it burns … cold an' wet … but it burns … it lived in the well…. I seen it … a kind o' smoke … jest like the flowers last spring … the well shone at night…. Thad an' Mernie an' Zenas … everything alive … suckin' the life out of everything … in that stone … it must a' come in that stone … pizened the whole place … dun't know what it wants … that round thing them men from the college dug outen the stone … they smashed it … it was that same colour … jest the same, like the flowers an' plants … must a' ben more of 'em … seeds … seeds … they growed…. I seen it the fust time this week … must a' got strong on Zenas … he was a big boy, full o' life … it beats down your mind an' then gits ye … burns ye up … in the well water … you was right about that … evil water…. Zenas never come back from the well … can't git away … draws ye … ye know summ'at's comin', but 'tain't no use…. I seen it time an' agin senct Zenas was took … whar's Nabby, Ammi? … my head's no good … dun't know how long senct I fed her … it'll git her ef we ain't keerful … jest a colour … her face is gettin' to hev that colour sometimes towards night … an' it burns an' sucks … it come from some place whar things ain't as they is here … one o' them professors said so … he was right … look out, Ammi, it'll do suthin' more … sucks the life out…."

But that was all. That which spoke could speak no more because it had completely caved in. Ammi laid a red checked tablecloth over what was left and reeled out the back door into the fields. He climbed the slope to the ten-acre pasture and stumbled home by the north road and the woods. He could not pass that well from which his horse had run away. He had looked at it through the window, and had seen that no stone was missing from the rim. Then the lurching buggy had not dislodged anything after all—the splash had been something else—something which went into the well after it had done with poor Nahum….

When Ammi reached his house the horse and buggy had arrived before him and thrown his wife into fits of anxiety. Reassuring her without explanations, he set out at once for Arkham and notified the authorities that the Gardner family was no more. He indulged in no details, but merely told of the deaths of Nahum and Nabby, that of Thaddeus being already known, and mentioned that the cause seemed to be the same strange ailment which had killed the livestock. He also stated that Merwin and Zenas had disappeared. There was considerable questioning at the police station, and in the end Ammi was compelled to take three officers to the Gardner farm, together with the coroner, the medical examiner, and the veterinary who had treated the diseased animals. He went much against his will, for the afternoon was advancing and he feared the fall of night over that accursed place, but it was some comfort to have so many people with him.

The six men drove out in a democrat-wagon,[23] following Ammi's buggy, and arrived at the pest-ridden farmhouse about four o'clock. Used as the officers were to gruesome experiences, not one remained unmoved at what was found in the attic and under the red checked tablecloth on the floor below. The whole aspect of the farm with its grey desolation was terrible enough, but those two crumbling objects were beyond all bounds. No one could look long at them, and even the medical examiner admitted that there was very little to examine. Specimens could be analyzed, of course, so he busied himself in obtaining them—and here it develops that a very puzzling aftermath occurred at the college laboratory where the two phials of dust were finally taken. Under the spectroscope both samples gave off an unknown spectrum, in which many of the baffling bands were precisely like those which the strange meteor had yielded in the previous year. The property of emitting this spectrum vanished in a month, the dust thereafter consisting mainly of alkaline phosphates and carbonates.

Ammi would not have told the men about the well if he had thought they meant to do anything then and there. It was getting toward sunset, and he was anxious to be away. But he could not help glancing nervously at the stony curb by the great sweep, and when a detective questioned him he admitted that Nahum had feared something down there—so much so that he had never even thought of searching it for Merwin or Zenas. After that nothing would do but that they empty and explore the well immediately, so Ammi had to wait trembling while pail after pail of rank water was hauled up and splashed on the soaking ground outside. The men sniffed in disgust at the fluid, and toward the last held their noses against the foetor[24] they were uncovering. It was not so long a job as they had feared it would be, since the water was phenomenally low. There is no need to speak too exactly of what they found. Merwin and Zenas were both there, in part, though the vestiges were mainly skeletal. There were also a small deer and a large dog in about the same state, and a number of bones of smaller animals. The ooze and slime at the bottom seemed inexplicably porous and bubbling, and a man who descended on hand-holds with a long pole found that he could sink the wooden shaft to any depth in the mud of the floor without meeting any solid obstruction.

Twilight had now fallen, and lanterns were brought from the house. Then, when it was seen that nothing further could be gained from the well, everyone went indoors and conferred in the ancient sitting-room while the intermittent light of a spectral half-moon played wanly on the grey desolation outside. The men were frankly nonplussed by the entire case, and could find no convincing common element to link the strange vegetable conditions, the unknown disease of livestock and humans, and the unaccountable deaths of Merwin and Zenas in the tainted well. They had heard the common country talk, it is true; but could not believe that anything contrary to natural law had occurred. No doubt the meteor had poisoned the soil, but the illness of persons and animals who had eaten nothing grown in that soil was another matter. Was it the well water? Very possibly. It might be a good idea to analyze it. But what peculiar madness could have made both boys jump into the well? Their deeds were so similar—and the fragments showed that they had both suffered from the grey brittle death. Why was everything so grey and brittle?

It was the coroner, seated near a window overlooking the yard, who first noticed the glow about the well. Night had fully set in, and all the abhorrent grounds seemed faintly luminous with more than the fitful moonbeams; but this new glow was something definite and distinct, and appeared to shoot up from the black pit like a softened ray from a search-light, giving dull reflections in the little ground pools where the water had been emptied. It had a very queer color, and as all the men clustered round the window Ammi gave a violent start. For this strange beam of ghastly miasma was to him of no unfamiliar hue. He had seen that color before, and feared to think what it might mean. He had seen it in the nasty brittle globule in that aërolite two summers ago, had seen it in the crazy vegetation of the springtime, and had thought he had seen it for an instant that very morning against the small barred window of that terrible attic room where nameless things had happened. It had flashed there a second, and a clammy and hateful current of vapor had brushed past him—and then poor Nahum had been taken by something of that color. He had said so at the last—said it was the globule and the plants. After that had come the runaway in the yard and the splash in the well—and now that well was belching forth to the night a pale insidious beam of the same demoniac tint.

It does credit to the alertness of Ammi's mind that he puzzled even at that tense moment over a point which was essentially scientific. He could not but wonder at his gleaning of the same impression from a vapor glimpsed in the daytime, against a window opening on the morning sky, and from a nocturnal exhalation seen as a phosphorescent mist against the black and blasted landscape. It wasn't right—it was against Nature—and he thought of those terrible last words of his stricken friend, "It come from some place whar things ain't as they is here ... one o' them professors said so...."

All three horses outside, tied to a pair of shriveled saplings by the road, were now neighing and pawing frantically. The wagon driver started for the door to do something, but Ammi laid a shaky hand on his shoulder. "Dun't go out thar," he whispered. "They's more to this nor what we know. Nahum said somethin' lived in the well that sucks your life out. He said it must be some'at growed from a round ball like one we all seen in the meteor stone that fell a year ago June. Sucks an' burns, he said, an' is jest a cloud of colour like that light out thar now, that ye can hardly see an' can't tell what it is. Nahum thought it feeds on everything livin' an' gits stronger all the time. He said he seen it this last week. It must be somethin' from away off in the sky like the men from the college last year says the meteor stone was. The way it's made an' the way it works ain't like no way o' God's world. It's some'at from beyond."

So the men paused indecisively as the light from the well grew stronger and the hitched horses pawed and whinnied in increasing frenzy. It was truly an awful moment; with terror in that ancient and accursed house itself, four monstrous sets of fragments—two from the house and two from the well—in the woodshed behind, and that shaft of unknown and unholy iridescence from the slimy depths in front. Ammi had restrained the driver on impulse, forgetting how uninjured he himself was after the clammy brushing of that colored vapor in the attic room, but perhaps it is just as well that he acted as he did. No one will ever know what was abroad that night; and though the blasphemy from beyond had not so far hurt any human of unweakened mind, there is no telling what it might not have done at that last moment, and with its seemingly increased strength and the special signs of purpose it was soon to display beneath the half-clouded moonlit sky.

All at once one of the detectives at the window gave a short, sharp gasp. The others looked at him, and then quickly followed his own gaze upward to the point at which its idle straying had been suddenly arrested. There was no need for words. What had been disputed in country gossip was disputable no longer, and it is because of the thing which every man of that party agreed in whispering later on that the strange days are never talked about in Arkham. It is necessary to premise that there was no wind at that hour of the evening. One did arise not long afterward, but there was absolutely none then. Even the dry tips of the lingering hedge-mustard, grey and blighted, and the fringe on the roof of the standing democrat-wagon were unstirred. And yet amid that tense, godless calm the high bare boughs of all the trees in the yard were moving. They were twitching morbidly and spasmodically, clawing in convulsive and epileptic madness at the moonlit clouds; scratching impotently in the noxious air as if jerked by some alien and bodiless line of linkage with subterrene horrors writhing and struggling below the black roots.

Not a man breathed for several seconds. Then a cloud of darker depth passed over the moon, and the silhouette of clutching branches faded out momentarily. At this there was a general cry; muffled with awe, but husky and almost identical from every throat. For the terror had not faded with the silhouette, and in a fearsome instant of deeper darkness the watchers saw wriggling at that treetop height a thousand tiny points of faint and unhallowed radiance, tipping each bough like the fire of St. Elmo[25] or the flames that came down on the apostles' heads at Pentecost.[26] It was a monstrous constellation of unnatural light, like a glutted swarm of corpse-fed fireflies dancing hellish sarabands[27] over an accursed marsh; and its color was that same nameless intrusion which Ammi had come to recognize and dread. All the while the shaft of phosphorescence from the well was getting brighter and brighter, bringing to the minds of the huddled men a sense of doom and abnormality which far outraced any image their conscious minds could form. It was no longer shining out, it was pouring out; and as the shapeless stream of unplaceable color left the well it seemed to flow directly into the sky.

The veterinary shivered, and walked to the front door to drop the heavy extra bar across it. Ammi shook no less, and had to tug and point for lack of a controllable voice when he wished to draw notice to the growing luminosity of the trees. The neighing and stamping of the horses had become utterly frightful, but not a soul of that group in the old house would have ventured forth for any earthly reward. With the moments the shining of the trees increased, while their restless branches seemed to strain more and more toward verticality. The wood of the well-sweep was shining now, and presently a policeman dumbly pointed to some wooden sheds and bee-hives near the stone wall on the west. They were commencing to shine, too, though the tethered vehicles of the visitors seemed so far unaffected. Then there was a wild commotion and clopping in the road, and as Ammi quenched the lamp for better seeing they realized that the span of frantic greys had broke their sapling and run off with the democrat-wagon.

The shock served to loosen several tongues, and embarrassed whispers were exchanged. "It spreads on everything organic that's been around here," muttered the medical examiner. No one replied, but the man who had been in the well gave a hint that his long pole must have stirred up something intangible. "It was awful," he added. "There was no bottom at all. Just ooze and bubbles and the feeling of something lurking under there." Ammi's horse still pawed and screamed deafeningly in the road outside, and nearly drowned its owner's faint quaver as he mumbled his formless reflections. "It come from that stone … it growed down thar … it got everything livin' … it fed itself on 'em, mind and body.… Thad an' Mernie, Zenas an' Nabby.… Nahum was the last … they all drunk the water … it got strong on 'em … it come from beyond, whar things ain't like they be here … now it's goin' home.…"

At this point, as the column of unknown color flared suddenly stronger and began to weave itself into fantastic suggestions of shape which each spectator later described differently, there came from poor tethered Hero such a sound as no man before or since ever heard from a horse. Every person in that low-pitched sitting room stopped his ears, and Ammi turned away from the window in horror and nausea. Words could not convey it—when Ammi looked out again the hapless beast lay huddled inert on the moonlit ground between the splintered shafts of the buggy. That was the last of Hero till they buried him next day. But the present was no time to mourn, for almost at this instant a detective silently called attention to something terrible in the very room with them. In the absence of the lamplight it was clear that a faint phosphorescence had begun to pervade the entire apartment. It glowed on the broad-planked floor and the fragment of rag carpet, and shimmered over the sashes of the small-paned windows. It ran up and down the exposed corner-posts, coruscated about the shelf and mantel, and infected the very doors and furniture. Each minute saw it strengthen, and at last it was very plain that healthy living things must leave that house.

Ammi showed them the back door and the path up through the fields to the ten-acre pasture. They walked and stumbled as in a dream, and did not dare look back till they were far away on the high ground. They were glad of the path, for they could not have gone the front way, by that well. It was bad enough passing the glowing barn and sheds, and those shining orchard trees with their gnarled, fiendish contours; but thank heaven the branches did their worst twisting high up. The moon went under some very black clouds as they crossed the rustic bridge over Chapman's Brook, and it was blind groping from there to the open meadows.

When they looked back toward the valley and the distant Gardner place at the bottom they saw a fearsome sight. All the farm was shining with the hideous unknown blend of color; trees, buildings, and even such grass and herbage as had not been wholly changed to lethal grey brittleness. The boughs were all straining skyward, tipped with tongues of foul flame, and lambent tricklings of the same monstrous fire were creeping about the ridgepoles of the house, barn, and sheds. It was a scene from a vision of Fuseli, and over all the rest reigned that riot of luminous amorphousness, that alien and undimensioned rainbow of cryptic poison from the well—seething, feeling, lapping, reaching, scintillating, straining, and malignly bubbling in its cosmic and unrecognizable chromaticism.[28]

Then without warning the hideous thing shot vertically up toward the sky like a rocket or meteor, leaving behind no trail and disappearing through a round and curiously regular hole in the clouds before any man could gasp or cry out. No watcher can ever forget that sight, and Ammi stared blankly at the stars of Cygnus, Deneb[29] twinkling above the others, where the unknown color had melted into the Milky Way. But his gaze was the next moment called swiftly to earth by the crackling in the valley. It was just that. Only a wooden ripping and crackling, and not an explosion, as so many others of the party vowed. Yet the outcome was the same, for in one feverish, kaleidoscopic instant there burst up from that doomed and accursed farm a gleamingly eruptive cataclysm of unnatural sparks and substance; blurring the glance of the few who saw it, and sending forth to the zenith a bombarding cloudburst of such colored and fantastic fragments as our universe must needs disown. Through quickly re-closing vapors they followed the great morbidity that had vanished, and in another second they had vanished too. Behind and below was only a darkness to which the men dared not return, and all about was a mounting wind which seemed to sweep down in black, frore[30] gusts from interstellar space. It shrieked and howled, and lashed the fields and distorted woods in a mad cosmic frenzy, till soon the trembling party realized it would be no use waiting for the moon to show what was left down there at Nahum's.

Too awed even to hint theories, the seven shaking men trudged back toward Arkham by the north road. Ammi was worse than his fellows, and begged them to see him inside his own kitchen, instead of keeping straight on to town. He did not wish to cross the nighted, wind-whipped woods alone to his home on the main road. For he had had an added shock that the others were spared, and was crushed forever with a brooding fear he dared not even mention for many years to come. As the rest of the watchers on that tempestuous hill had stolidly set their faces toward the road, Ammi had looked back an instant at the shadowed valley of desolation so lately sheltering his ill-starred friend. And from that stricken, far-away spot he had seen something feebly rise, only to sink down again upon the place from which the great shapeless horror had shot into the sky. It was just a color—but not any color of our earth or heavens. And because Ammi recognized that color, and knew that this last faint remnant must still lurk down there in the well, he has never been quite right since.

Ammi would never go near the place again. It is over half a century now since the horror happened, but he has never been there, and will be glad when the new reservoir blots it out. I shall be glad, too, for I do not like the way the sunlight changed color around the mouth of that abandoned well I passed. I hope the water will always be very deep—but even so, I shall never drink it. I do not think I shall visit the Arkham country hereafter. Three of the men who had been with Ammi returned the next morning to see the ruins by daylight, but there were not any real ruins. Only the bricks of the chimney, the stones of the cellar, some mineral and metallic litter here and there, and the rim of that nefandous[31] well. Save for Ammi's dead horse, which they towed away and buried, and the buggy which they shortly returned to him, everything that had ever been living had gone. Five eldritch acres of dusty grey desert remained, nor has anything ever grown there since. To this day it sprawls open to the sky like a great spot eaten by acid in the woods and fields, and the few who have ever dared glimpse it in spite of the rural tales have named it "the blasted heath."

The rural tales are queer. They might be even queerer if city men and college chemists could be interested enough to analyze the water from that disused well, or the grey dust that no wind seems ever to disperse. Botanists, too, ought to study the stunted flora on the borders of that spot, for they might shed light on the country notion that the blight is spreading—little by little, perhaps an inch a year. People say the color of the neighboring herbage is not quite right in the spring, and that wild things leave queer prints in the light winter snow. Snow never seems quite so heavy on the blasted heath as it is elsewhere. Horses—the few that are left in this motor age—grow skittish in the silent valley; and hunters cannot depend on their dogs too near the splotch of greyish dust.

They say the mental influences are very bad, too. Numbers went queer in the years after Nahum's taking, and always they lacked the power to get away. Then the stronger-minded folk all left the region, and only the foreigners tried to live in the crumbling old homesteads. They could not stay, though; and one sometimes wonders what insight beyond ours their wild, weird stores of whispered magic have given them. Their dreams at night, they protest, are very horrible in that grotesque country; and surely the very look of the dark realm is enough to stir a morbid fancy. No traveller has ever escaped a sense of strangeness in those deep ravines, and artists shiver as they paint thick woods whose mystery is as much of the spirit as of the eye. I myself am curious about the sensation I derived from my one lone walk before Ammi told me his tale. When twilight came I had vaguely wished some clouds would gather, for an odd timidity about the deep skyey voids above had crept into my soul.

Do not ask me for my opinion. I do not know—that is all. There was no one but Ammi to question; for Arkham people will not talk about the strange days, and all three professors who saw the aërolite and its colored globule are dead. There were other globules—depend upon that. One must have fed itself and escaped, and probably there was another which was too late. No doubt it is still down the well—I know there was something wrong with the sunlight I saw above that miasmal brink. The rustics say the blight creeps an inch a year, so perhaps there is a kind of growth or nourishment even now. But whatever daemon hatchling is there, it must be tethered to something or else it would quickly spread. Is it fastened to the roots of those trees that claw the air? One of the current Arkham tales is about fat oaks that shine and move as they ought not to do at night.

What it is, only God knows. In terms of matter I suppose the thing Ammi described would be called a gas, but this gas obeyed laws that are not of our cosmos. This was no fruit of such worlds and suns as shine on the telescopes and photographic plates of our observatories. This was no breath from the skies whose motions and dimensions our astronomers measure or deem too vast to measure. It was just a color out of space—a frightful messenger from unformed realms of infinity beyond all Nature as we know it; from realms whose mere existence stuns the brain and numbs us with the black extra-cosmic gulfs it throws open before our frenzied eyes.

I doubt very much if Ammi consciously lied to me, and I do not think his tale was all a freak of madness as the townsfolk had forewarned. Something terrible came to the hills and valleys on that meteor, and something terrible—though I know not in what proportion—still remains. I shall be glad to see the water come. Meanwhile I hope nothing will happen to Ammi. He saw so much of the thing—and its influence was so insidious. Why has he never been able to move away? How clearly he recalled those dying words of Nahum's—"can't git away ... draws ye ... ye know summ'at's comin,' but 'tain't no use...." Ammi is such a good old man—when the reservoir gang gets to work I must write the chief engineer to keep a sharp watch on him. I would hate to think of him as the grey, twisted, brittle monstrosity which persists more and more in troubling my sleep.

The Dunwich Horror

"The Dunwich Horror" is arguably one of Lovecraft's most popular tales. Relating the events of a rural town's attempt to thwart the plans of a mad cultist as he tries to bring The Old Ones through to this world, this story is unusual for Lovecraft for two reasons: It is one of only a handful of tales in which the heroes successfully defeat their otherworldly foe, and unlike other of Lovecraft's tales (such as "The Colour Out of Space" or At the Mountains of Madness*) that portray the otherworldly antagonist as completely incomprehensible and thus amoral, "The Dunwich Horror" presents a clear dichotomy of "good" protagonists antagonized by "evil" cultists and monsters. For these reasons, S.T. Joshi finds "The Dunwich Horror" to be somewhat flawed.*

Robert M. Price believes the story itself owes much to the writings of Arthur Machen, especially his novella The Great God Pan. *Kenneth Hite goes so far as to call it a pastiche of Machen, and it is there where he finds its value. For Hite, the story involves not so much a dichotomy of good vs. evil as much as a dichotomy of humanism as represented by the character of Professor Armitage vs. religion as represented by the Horror itself: "Armitage is [...] a secular kind of Christ—his purity comes from age, tenure, art [...] and learning, not from God or Heaven. But then, he's a Lovecraftian Christ-figure."*

> "Gorgons, and Hydras, and Chimaeras—dire stories of Celaeno and the Harpies[1]—may reproduce themselves in the brain of superstition—but they were there before. They are transcripts, types—the archetypes are in us, and eternal. How else should the recital of that which we know in a waking sense to be false come to affect us at all? Is it that we naturally conceive terror from such objects, considered in their capacity of being able to inflict upon us bodily injury? O, least of all! These terrors are of older standing. They date beyond body—or without the body, they would have been the same.... That the kind of fear here treated is purely spiritual—that it is strong in proportion as it is objectless on earth, that it predominates in the period of our sinless infancy—are difficulties the solution of which might afford some probable insight into our ante-mundane condition, and a peep at least into the shadowland of pre-existence."
>
> —Charles Lamb: "Witches and Other Night-Fears"[2]

I.

When a traveller in north central Massachusetts takes the wrong fork at the junction of the Aylesbury pike just beyond Dean's Corners[3] he comes upon a lonely and curious country. The ground gets higher, and the brier-bordered stone walls press closer and closer against the ruts of the dusty, curving road. The trees of the frequent forest belts seem too large, and the wild weeds, brambles, and grasses attain a luxuriance not often found in settled regions. At the same time the planted fields appear singularly few and barren; while the sparsely scattered houses wear a surprisingly uniform aspect of age, squalor, and dilapidation. Without knowing why, one hesitates to ask directions from the gnarled, solitary figures spied now and then on crumbling doorsteps or on the sloping, rock-strewn meadows. Those figures are so silent and furtive that one feels somehow confronted by forbidden things, with which it would be better to have nothing to do. When a rise in the road brings the mountains in view above the deep woods, the feeling of strange uneasiness is increased. The summits are too rounded and symmetrical to give a sense of comfort and naturalness, and sometimes the sky silhouettes with especial clearness the queer circles of tall stone pillars with which most of them are crowned.

Gorges and ravines of problematical depth intersect the way, and the crude wooden bridges always seem of dubious safety. When the road dips again there are stretches of marshland that one instinctively dislikes, and indeed almost fears at evening when unseen whippoorwills chatter and the fireflies come out in abnormal profusion to dance to the raucous, creepily insistent rhythms of stridently piping bull-frogs. The thin, shining line of the Miskatonic's upper reaches has an oddly serpent-like suggestion as it winds close to the feet of the domed hills among which it rises.

As the hills draw nearer, one heeds their wooded sides more than their stone-crowned tops. Those sides loom up so darkly and precipitously that one wishes they would keep their distance, but there is no road by which to escape them. Across a covered bridge one sees a small village huddled between the stream and the vertical slope of Round Mountain,[4] and wonders at the cluster of rotting gambrel roofs bespeaking an earlier architectural period than that of the neighboring region. It is not reassuring to see, on a closer glance, that most of the houses are deserted and falling to ruin, and that the broken-steepled church now harbors the one slovenly mercantile establishment of the hamlet. One dreads to trust the tenebrous tunnel of the bridge, yet there is no way to avoid it. Once across, it is hard to prevent the impression of a faint, malign odor about the village street, as of the massed mold and decay of centuries. It is always a relief to get clear of the place, and to follow the narrow road around the base of the hills and across the level country beyond till it rejoins the Aylesbury pike. Afterward one sometimes learns that one has been through Dunwich.

Outsiders visit Dunwich as seldom as possible, and since a certain season of horror all the signboards pointing toward it have been taken down. The scenery, judged by any ordinary aesthetic canon, is more than commonly beautiful; yet there is no influx of artists or summer tourists. Two centuries ago, when talk of witch-blood, Satan-worship, and strange forest presences was not laughed at, it was the custom to give reasons for avoiding the locality. In our sensible age—since the Dunwich horror of 1928 was hushed up by those who had the town's and the world's welfare at heart—people shun it without knowing exactly why. Perhaps one reason—though it cannot apply to uninformed strangers—is that the natives are now repellently decadent, having gone far along that path of retrogression so common in many New England backwaters. They have come to form a race by themselves, with the well-defined mental and physical stigmata of degeneracy and inbreeding. The average of their intelligence is woefully low, whilst their annals[5] reek of overt viciousness and of half-hidden murders, incests, and deeds of almost unnamable violence and perversity. The old gentry, representing the two or three armigerous families[6] which came from Salem in 1692, have kept somewhat above the general level of decay; though many branches are sunk into the sordid populace so deeply that only their names remain as a key to the origin they disgrace. Some of the Whateleys and Bishops still send their eldest sons to Harvard and Miskatonic, though those sons seldom return to the moldering gambrel roofs under which they and their ancestors were born.

No one, even those who have the facts concerning the recent horror, can say just what is the matter with Dunwich; though old legends speak of unhallowed rites and conclaves of the Indians, amidst which they called forbidden shapes of shadow out of the great rounded hills, and made wild orgiastic prayers that were answered by loud crackings and rumblings from the ground below. In 1747 the Rev. Abijah Hoadley, newly come to the Congregational Church at Dunwich Village, preached a memorable sermon on the close presence of Satan and his imps; in which he said:

> It must be allow'd, that these Blasphemies of an infernall Train of Daemons are Matters of too common Knowledge to be deny'd; the cursed Voices of Azazel and Buzrael, of Beelzebub and Belial,[7] being heard now from under Ground by above a Score of credible Witnesses now living. I my self did not more than a Fortnight ago catch a very plain Discourse of evill Powers in the Hill behind my House; wherein there were a Rattling and Rolling, Groaning, Screeching, and Hissing, such as no Things of this Earth cou'd raise up, and which must needs have come from those Caves that only black Magick can discover, and only the Divell unlock.

Mr. Hoadley disappeared soon after delivering this sermon; but the text, printed in Springfield, is still extant. Noises in the hills continued to be reported from year to year, and still form a puzzle to geologists and physiographers.[8]

Other traditions tell of foul odors near the hill-crowning circles of stone pillars, and of rushing airy presences to be heard faintly at certain hours from stated points at the bottom of the great ravines; while still others try to explain the Devil's Hop Yard—a bleak, blasted hillside where no tree, shrub, or grass-blade will grow. Then too, the natives are mortally afraid of the numerous whippoorwills which grow vocal on warm nights. It is vowed that the birds are psychopomps[9] lying in wait for the souls of the dying, and that they time their eerie cries in unison with the sufferer's struggling breath. If they can catch the fleeing soul when it leaves the body, they instantly flutter away chittering in demoniac laughter; but if they fail, they subside gradually into a disappointed silence.

These tales, of course, are obsolete and ridiculous; because they come down from very old times. Dunwich is indeed ridiculously old—older by far than any of the communities within thirty miles of it. South of the village one may still spy the cellar walls and chimney of the ancient Bishop house, which was built before 1700; whilst the ruins of the mill at the falls, built in 1806, form the most modern piece of architecture to be seen. Industry did not flourish here, and the nineteenth-century factory movement proved short-lived. Oldest of all are the great rings of rough-hewn stone columns on the hill-tops, but these are more generally attributed to the Indians than to the settlers. Deposits of skulls and bones, found within these circles and around the sizeable table-like rock on Sentinel Hill, sustain the popular belief that such spots were once the burial-places of the Pocumtucks[10]; even though many ethnologists, disregarding the absurd improbability of such a theory, persist in believing the remains Caucasian.

II.

It was in the township of Dunwich, in a large and partly inhabited farmhouse set against a hillside four miles from the village and a mile and a half from any other dwelling, that Wilbur Whateley was born at 5 AM on Sunday, the second of February 1913. This date was recalled because it was Candlemas,[11] which people in Dunwich curiously observe under another name; and because the noises in the hills had sounded, and all the dogs of the countryside had barked persistently, throughout the night before. Less worthy of notice was the fact that the mother was one of the decadent Whateleys, a somewhat deformed, unattractive albino woman of thirty-five, living with an aged and half-insane father about whom the most frightful tales of wizardry had been whispered in his youth. Lavinia Whateley had no known husband, but according to the custom of the region made no attempt to disavow the child; concerning the other side of whose ancestry the country folk might—and did—speculate as widely as they chose. On the contrary, she seemed strangely proud of the dark, goatish-looking infant who formed such a contrast to her own sickly and pink-eyed albinism, and was heard to mutter many curious prophecies about its unusual powers and tremendous future.

Lavinia was one who would be apt to mutter such things, for she was a lone creature given to wandering amidst thunderstorms in the hills and trying to read the great odorous books which her father had inherited through two centuries of Whateleys, and which were fast falling to pieces with age and worm-holes. She had never been to school, but was filled with disjointed scraps of ancient lore that Old Whateley had taught her. The remote farmhouse had always been feared because of Old Whateley's reputation for black magic, and the unexplained death by violence of Mrs. Whateley when Lavinia was twelve years old had not helped to make the place popular. Isolated among strange influences, Lavinia was fond of wild and grandiose day-dreams and singular occupations; nor was her leisure much taken up by household cares in a home from which all standards of order and cleanliness had long since disappeared.

There was a hideous screaming which echoed above even the hill noises and the dogs' barking on the night Wilbur was born, but no known doctor or midwife presided at his coming. Neighbors knew nothing of him till a week afterward, when Old Whateley drove his sleigh through the snow into Dunwich Village and discoursed incoherently to the group of loungers at Osborn's general store. There seemed to be a change in the old man—an added element of furtiveness in the clouded brain which subtly transformed him from an object to a subject of fear—though he was not one to be perturbed by any common family event. Amidst it all he showed some trace of the pride later noticed in his daughter, and what he said of the child's paternity was remembered by many of his hearers years afterward.

"I dun't keer what folks think—ef Lavinny's boy looked like his pa, he wouldn't look like nothin' ye expeck. Ye needn't think the only folks is the folks hereabaouts. Lavinny's read some, an' has seed some things the most o' ye only tell abaout. I calc'late her man is as good a husban' as ye kin find this side of Aylesbury; an' ef ye knowed as much abaout the hills as I dew, ye wouldn't ast no better church weddin' nor her'n. Let me tell ye suthin'—some day yew folks'll hear a child o' Lavinny's a-callin' its father's name on the top o' Sentinel Hill!"

The only persons who saw Wilbur during the first month of his life were old Zechariah Whateley, of the undecayed Whateleys, and Earl Sawyer's common-law wife, Mamie Bishop.

Mamie's visit was frankly one of curiosity, and her subsequent tales did justice to her observations; but Zechariah came to lead a pair of Alderney cows[12] which Old Whateley had bought of his son Curtis. This marked the beginning of a course of cattle-buying on the part of small Wilbur's family which ended only in 1928, when the Dunwich horror came and went; yet at no time did the ramshackle Whateley barn seem overcrowded with livestock. There came a period when people were curious enough to steal up and count the herd that grazed precariously on the steep hillside above the old farmhouse, and they could never find more than ten or twelve anemic, bloodless-looking specimens. Evidently some blight or distemper, perhaps sprung from the unwholesome pasturage or the diseased fungi and timbers of the filthy barn, caused a heavy mortality amongst the Whateley animals. Odd wounds or sores, having something of the aspect of incisions, seemed to afflict the visible cattle; and once or twice during the earlier months certain callers fancied they could discern similar sores about the throats of the grey, unshaven old man and his slatternly, crinkly-haired albino daughter.

In the spring after Wilbur's birth Lavinia resumed her customary rambles in the hills, bearing in her misproportioned arms the swarthy child. Public interest in the Whateleys subsided after most of the country folk had seen the baby, and no one bothered to comment on the swift development which that newcomer seemed every day to exhibit. Wilbur's growth was indeed phenomenal, for within three months of his birth he had attained a size and muscular power not usually found in infants under a full year of age. His motions and even his vocal sounds showed a restraint and deliberateness highly peculiar in an infant, and no one was really unprepared when, at seven months, he began to walk unassisted, with falterings which another month was sufficient to remove.

It was somewhat after this time—on Hallowe'en—that a great blaze was seen at midnight on the top of Sentinel Hill where the old table-like stone stands amidst its tumulus[13] of ancient bones. Considerable talk was started when Silas Bishop—of the undecayed Bishops—mentioned having seen the boy running sturdily up that hill ahead of his mother about an hour before the blaze was remarked. Silas was rounding up a stray heifer, but he nearly forgot his mission when he fleetingly spied the two figures in the dim light of his lantern. They darted almost noiselessly through the underbrush, and the astonished watcher seemed to think they were entirely unclothed. Afterward he could not be sure about the boy, who may have had some kind of a fringed belt and a pair of dark trunks or trousers on. Wilbur was never subsequently seen alive and conscious without complete and tightly buttoned attire, the disarrangement or threatened disarrangement of which always seemed to fill him with anger and alarm. His contrast with his squalid mother and grandfather in this respect was thought very notable until the horror of 1928 suggested the most valid of reasons.

The next January gossips were mildly interested in the fact that "Lavinny's black brat" had commenced to talk, and at the age of only eleven months. His speech was somewhat remarkable both because of its difference from the ordinary accents of the region, and because it displayed a freedom from infantile lisping of which many children of three or four might well be proud. The boy was not talkative, yet when he spoke he seemed to reflect some elusive element wholly unpossessed by Dunwich and its denizens. The strangeness did not reside in what he said, or even in the simple idioms he used; but seemed vaguely linked with his intonation or with the internal organs that produced the spoken sounds. His facial aspect, too, was remarkable for its maturity; for though he shared his mother's and grandfather's chinlessness, his firm and precociously shaped nose united with the expression of his large, dark, almost Latin eyes to give him an air of quasi-adulthood and well-nigh preternatural intelligence. He was, however, exceedingly ugly despite his appearance of brilliancy; there being something almost goatish or animalistic about his thick lips, large-pored, yellowish skin, coarse crinkly hair, and oddly elongated ears. He was soon disliked even more decidedly than his mother and grandsire, and all conjectures about him were spiced with references to the bygone magic of Old Whateley, and how the hills once shook when he shrieked the dreadful name of Yog-Sothoth in the midst of a circle of stones with a great book open in his arms before him. Dogs abhorred the boy, and he was always obliged to take various defensive measures against their barking menace.

III.

Meanwhile Old Whateley continued to buy cattle without measurably increasing the size of his herd. He also cut timber and began to repair the unused parts of his house—a spacious, peaked-roofed affair whose rear end was buried entirely in the rocky hillside, and whose three least-ruined ground-floor rooms had always been sufficient for himself and his daughter. There must have been prodigious reserves of strength in the old man to enable him to accomplish so much hard labor; and though he still babbled dementedly at times, his carpentry seemed to show the effects of sound calculation. It had already begun as soon as Wilbur was born, when one of the many toolsheds had been put suddenly in order, clapboarded,[14] and fitted with a stout fresh lock. Now, in restoring the abandoned upper story of the house, he was a no less thorough craftsman. His mania showed itself only in his tight boarding-up of all the windows in the reclaimed section—though many declared that it was a crazy thing to bother with the reclamation at all. Less inexplicable was his fitting up of another downstairs room for his new grandson—a room which several callers saw, though no one was ever admitted to the closely boarded upper story. This chamber he lined with tall, firm shelving; along which he began gradually to arrange, in apparently careful order, all the rotting ancient books and parts of books which during his own day had been heaped promiscuously in odd corners of the various rooms.

"I made some use of 'em," he would say as he tried to mend a torn black-letter page with paste prepared on the rusty kitchen stove, "but the boy's fitten to make better use of 'em. He'd orter hev 'em as well sot as he kin, for they're goin' to be all of his larnin'."

When Wilbur was a year and seven months old—in September of 1914—his size and accomplishments were almost alarming. He had grown as large as a child of four, and was a fluent and incredibly intelligent talker. He ran freely about the fields and hills, and accompanied his mother on all her wanderings. At home he would pore diligently over the queer pictures and charts in his grandfather's books, while Old Whateley would instruct and catechise[15] him through long, hushed afternoons. By this time the restoration of the house was finished, and those who watched it wondered why one of the upper windows had been made into a solid plank door. It was a window in the rear of the east gable end, close against the hill; and no one could imagine why a cleated wooden runway was built up to it from the ground. About the period of this work's completion people noticed that the old tool-house, tightly locked and windowlessly clapboarded since Wilbur's birth, had been abandoned again. The door swung listlessly open, and when Earl Sawyer once stepped within after a cattle-selling call on Old Whateley he was quite discomposed by the singular odor he encountered—such a stench, he averred, as he had never before smelt in all his life except near the Indian circles on the hills, and which could not come from anything sane or of this earth. But then, the homes and sheds of Dunwich folk have never been remarkable for olfactory immaculateness.[16]

The following months were void of visible events, save that everyone swore to a slow but steady increase in the mysterious hill noises. On May-Eve of 1915 there were tremors which even the Aylesbury people felt, whilst the following Hallowe'en produced an underground rumbling queerly synchronized with bursts of flame—"them witch Whateleys' doin's"—from the summit of Sentinel Hill. Wilbur was growing up uncannily, so that he looked like a boy of ten as he entered his fourth year. He read avidly by himself now; but talked much less than formerly. A settled taciturnity was absorbing him, and for the first time people began to speak specifically of the dawning look of evil in his goatish face. He would sometimes mutter an unfamiliar jargon, and chant in bizarre rhythms which chilled the listener with a sense of unexplainable terror. The aversion displayed toward him by dogs had now become a matter of wide remark, and he was obliged to carry a pistol in order to traverse the countryside in safety. His occasional use of the weapon did not enhance his popularity amongst the owners of canine guardians.

The few callers at the house would often find Lavinia alone on the ground floor, while odd cries and footsteps resounded in the boarded-up second story. She would never tell what her father and the boy were doing up there, though once she turned pale and displayed an abnormal degree of fear when a jocose[17] fish-peddler tried the locked door leading to the stairway. That peddler told the store loungers at Dunwich Village that he thought he heard a horse stamping on that floor above. The loungers reflected, thinking of the door and runway, and of the cattle that so swiftly disappeared. Then they shuddered as they recalled tales of Old Whateley's youth, and of the strange things that are called out of the earth when a bullock is sacrificed at the proper time to certain heathen gods. It had for some time been noticed that dogs had begun to hate and fear the whole Whateley place as violently as they hated and feared young Wilbur personally.

In 1917 the war came, and Squire Sawyer Whateley, as chairman of the local draft board, had hard work finding a quota of young Dunwich men fit even to be sent to a development camp. The government, alarmed at such signs of wholesale regional decadence, sent several officers and medical experts to investigate; conducting a survey which New England newspaper readers may still recall. It was the publicity attending this investigation which set reporters on the track of the Whateleys, and caused the *Boston Globe* and *Arkham Advertiser* to print flamboyant Sunday stories of young Wilbur's precociousness, Old Whateley's black magic, the shelves of strange books, the sealed second story of the ancient farmhouse, and the weirdness of the whole region and its hill noises. Wilbur was four and a half then, and looked like a lad of fifteen. His lips and cheeks were fuzzy with a coarse dark down, and his voice had begun to break.

Earl Sawyer went out to the Whateley place with both sets of reporters and camera men, and called their attention to the queer stench which now seemed to trickle down from the sealed upper spaces. It was, he said, exactly like a smell he had found in the toolshed abandoned when the house was finally repaired; and like the faint odors which he sometimes thought he caught near the stone circles on the mountains. Dunwich folk read the stories when they appeared, and grinned over the obvious mistakes. They wondered, too, why the writers made so much of the fact that Old Whateley always paid for his cattle in gold pieces of extremely ancient date. The Whateleys had received their visitors with ill-concealed distaste, though they did not dare court further publicity by a violent resistance or refusal to talk.

IV.

For a decade the annals of the Whateleys sink indistinguishably into the general life of a morbid community used to their queer ways and hardened to their May-Eve and All-Hallows orgies. Twice a year they would light fires on the top of Sentinel Hill, at which times the mountain rumblings would recur with greater and greater violence; while at all seasons there were strange and portentous doings at the lonely farmhouse. In the course of time callers professed to hear sounds in the sealed upper story even when all the family were downstairs, and they wondered how swiftly or how lingeringly a cow or bullock was usually sacrificed. There was talk of a complaint to the Society for the Prevention of Cruelty to Animals; but nothing ever came of it, since Dunwich folk are never anxious to call the outside world's attention to themselves.

About 1923, when Wilbur was a boy of ten whose mind, voice, stature, and bearded face gave all the impressions of maturity, a second great siege of carpentry went on at the old house. It was all inside the sealed upper part, and from bits of discarded lumber people concluded that the youth and his grandfather had knocked out all the partitions and even removed the attic floor, leaving only one vast open void between the ground story and the peaked roof. They had torn down the great central chimney, too, and fitted the rusty range with a flimsy outside tin stovepipe.

In the spring after this event Old Whateley noticed the growing number of whippoor-wills that would come out of Cold Spring Glen to chirp under his window at night. He seemed to regard the circumstance as one of great significance, and told the loungers at Osborn's that he thought his time had almost come.[18]

"They whistle jest in tune with my breathin' naow," he said, "an' I guess they're gittin' ready to ketch my soul. They know it's a-goin' aout, an' dun't calc'late to miss it. Yew'll know, boys, arter I'm gone, whether they git me er not. Ef they dew, they'll keep up a-singin' an' laffin' till break o' day. Ef they dun't they'll kinder quiet daown like. I expeck them an' the souls they hunts fer hev some pretty tough tussles sometimes."

On Lammas Night,[19] 1924, Dr. Houghton of Aylesbury was hastily summoned by Wilbur Whateley, who had lashed his one remaining horse through the darkness and telephoned from Osborn's in the village. He found Old Whateley in a very grave state, with a cardiac action and stertorous[20] breathing that told of an end not far off. The shapeless albino daughter and oddly bearded grandson stood by the bedside, whilst from the vacant abyss overhead there came a disquieting suggestion of rhythmical surging or lapping, as of the waves on some level beach. The doctor, though, was chiefly disturbed by the chattering night birds outside; a seemingly limitless legion of whippoorwills that cried their endless message in repetitions timed diabolically to the wheezing gasps of the dying man. It was uncanny and unnatural—too much, thought Dr. Houghton, like the whole of the region he had entered so reluctantly in response to the urgent call.

Toward one o'clock Old Whateley gained consciousness, and interrupted his wheezing to choke out a few words to his grandson.

"More space, Willy, more space soon. Yew grows—an' that grows faster. It'll be ready to sarve ye soon, boy. Open up the gates to Yog-Sothoth with the long chant that ye'll find on page 751 of the complete edition, an' then put a match to the prison. Fire from airth can't burn it nohaow."

He was obviously quite mad. After a pause, during which the flock of whippoorwills outside adjusted their cries to the altered tempo while some indications of the strange hill noises came from afar off, he added another sentence or two.

"Feed it reg'lar, Willy, an' mind the quantity; but dun't let it grow too fast fer the place, fer ef it busts quarters or gits aout afore ye opens to Yog-Sothoth, it's all over an' no use. Only them from beyont kin make it multiply an' work…. Only them, the old uns as wants to come back…."

But speech gave place to gasps again, and Lavinia screamed at the way the whippoor-wills followed the change. It was the same for more than an hour, when the final throaty rattle came. Dr. Houghton drew shrunken lids over the glazing grey eyes as the tumult of birds faded imperceptibly to silence. Lavinia sobbed, but Wilbur only chuckled whilst the hill noises rumbled faintly.

"They didn't git him," he muttered in his heavy bass voice.

Wilbur was by this time a scholar of really tremendous erudition[21] in his one-sided way, and was quietly known by correspondence to many librarians in distant places where rare and forbidden books of old days are kept. He was more and more hated and dreaded around Dunwich because of certain youthful disappearances which suspicion laid vaguely at his door; but was always able to silence inquiry through fear or through use of that fund of old-time gold which still, as in his grandfather's time, went forth regularly and increas-ingly for cattle-buying. He was now tremendously mature of aspect, and his height, having reached the normal adult limit, seemed inclined to wax beyond that figure. In 1925, when a scholarly correspondent from Miskatonic University called upon him one day and departed pale and puzzled, he was fully six and three-quarters feet tall.

Through all the years Wilbur had treated his half-deformed albino mother with a growing contempt, finally forbidding her to go to the hills with him on May-Eve and Hal-lowmass[22]; and in 1926 the poor creature complained to Mamie Bishop of being afraid of him.

"They's more abaout him as I knows than I kin tell ye, Mamie," she said, "an' naowadays they's more nor what I know myself. I vaow afur Gawd, I dun't know what he wants nor what he's a-tryin' to dew."

That Hallowe'en the hill noises sounded louder than ever, and fire burned on Sentinel Hill as usual; but people paid more attention to the rhythmical screaming of vast flocks of unnaturally belated whippoorwills which seemed to be assembled near the unlighted Whateley farmhouse. After midnight their shrill notes burst into a kind of pandemoniac cachinnation[23] which filled all the countryside, and not until dawn did they finally quiet down. Then they vanished, hurrying southward where they were fully a month overdue. What this meant, no one could quite be certain till later. None of the country folk seemed to have died—but poor Lavinia Whateley, the twisted albino, was never seen again.

In the summer of 1927 Wilbur repaired two sheds in the farmyard and began moving his books and effects out to them. Soon afterward Earl Sawyer told the loungers at Osborn's that more carpentry was going on in the Whateley farmhouse. Wilbur was closing all the doors and windows on the ground floor, and seemed to be taking out partitions as he and his grandfather had done upstairs four years before. He was living in one of the sheds, and Sawyer thought he seemed unusually worried and tremulous.[24] People generally suspected him of knowing something about his mother's disappearance, and very few ever approached his neighborhood now. His height had increased to more than seven feet, and showed no signs of ceasing its development.

V.

The following winter brought an event no less strange than Wilbur's first trip outside the Dunwich region. Correspondence with the Widener Library at Harvard, the Bibliothèque Nationale in Paris, the British Museum, the University of Buenos Ayres, and the Library of Miskatonic University of Arkham had failed to get him the loan of a book he desperately wanted; so at length he set out in person, shabby, dirty, bearded, and uncouth of dialect, to consult the copy at Miskatonic, which was the nearest to him geographically. Almost eight feet tall, and carrying a cheap new valise from Osborn's general store, this dark and goatish gargoyle appeared one day in Arkham in quest of the dreaded volume kept under lock and key at the college library—the hideous *Necronomicon* of the mad Arab Abdul Alhazred in Olaus Wormius' Latin version, as printed in Spain in the seventeenth century. He had never seen a city before, but had no thought save to find his way to the university grounds; where, indeed, he passed heedlessly by the great white-fanged watchdog that barked with unnatural fury and enmity, and tugged frantically at its stout chain.

Wilbur had with him the priceless but imperfect copy of Dr. Dee's English version which his grandfather had bequeathed him, and upon receiving access to the Latin copy he at once began to collate the two texts with the aim of discovering a certain passage which would have come on the 751st page of his own defective volume. This much he could not civilly refrain from telling the librarian—the same erudite Henry Armitage (A.M. Miskatonic, Ph.D. Princeton, Litt. D. Johns Hopkins) who had once called at the farm, and who now politely plied him with questions. He was looking, he had to admit, for a kind of formula or incantation containing the frightful name Yog-Sothoth, and it puzzled him to find discrepancies, duplications, and ambiguities which made the matter of determination far from easy. As he copied the formula he finally chose, Dr. Armitage looked involuntarily over his shoulder at the open pages; the left-hand one of which, in the Latin version, contained such monstrous threats to the peace and sanity of the world.

"Nor is it to be thought," ran the text as Armitage mentally translated it, "that man is either the oldest or the last of earth's masters, or that the common bulk of life and substance walks alone. The Old Ones were, the Old Ones are, and the Old Ones shall be. Not in the spaces we know, but between them, They walk serene and primal, undimensioned and to us unseen. Yog-Sothoth knows the gate. Yog-Sothoth is the gate. Yog-Sothoth is the key and guardian of the gate. Past, present, future, all are one in Yog-Sothoth. He knows where the Old Ones broke through of old, and where They shall break through again. He knows where They have trod earth's fields, and where They still tread them, and why no one can behold Them as They tread. By Their smell can men sometimes know Them near, but of Their semblance can no man know, saving only in the features of those They have begotten on mankind; and of those are there many sorts, differing in likeness from man's truest eidolon[25] to that shape without sight or substance which is Them. They walk unseen and foul in lonely places where the Words have been spoken and the Rites howled through at their Seasons. The wind gibbers[26] with Their voices, and the earth mutters with Their consciousness. They bend the forest and crush the city, yet may not forest or city behold the hand that smites. Kadath[27] in the cold waste hath known Them, and what man knows Kadath? The ice desert of the South and the sunken isles of Ocean hold stones whereon Their seal is engraven, but who hath seen the deep frozen city or the sealed tower long garlanded with seaweed and barnacles? Great Cthulhu is Their cousin, yet can he spy Them only dimly. Iä! Shub-Niggurath! As a foulness shall ye know Them. Their hand is at your throats, yet ye see Them not; and Their habitation is even one with your guarded threshold. Yog-Sothoth is the key to the gate, whereby the spheres meet. Man rules now where They ruled once; They shall soon rule where man rules now. After summer is winter, and after winter summer. They wait patient and potent, for here shall They reign again."

Dr. Armitage, associating what he was reading with what he had heard of Dunwich and its brooding presences, and of Wilbur Whateley and his dim, hideous aura that stretched from a dubious birth to a cloud of probable matricide, felt a wave of fright as tangible as a draught of the tomb's cold clamminess. The bent, goatish giant before him seemed like the spawn of another planet or dimension; like something only partly of mankind, and linked to black gulfs of essence and entity that stretch like titan phantasms beyond all spheres of force and matter, space and time. Presently Wilbur raised his head and began speaking in that strange, resonant fashion which hinted at sound-producing organs unlike the run of mankind's.

"Mr. Armitage," he said, "I calc'late I've got to take that book home. They's things in it I've got to try under sarten conditions that I can't git here, an' it 'ud be a mortal sin to let a red-tape rule hold me up. Let me take it along, Sir, an' I'll swar they wun't nobody know the difference. I dun't need to tell ye I'll take good keer of it. It wa'n't me that put this Dee copy in the shape it is...."

He stopped as he saw firm denial on the librarian's face, and his own goatish features grew crafty. Armitage, half-ready to tell him he might make a copy of what parts he needed, thought suddenly of the possible consequences and checked himself. There was too much responsibility in giving such a being the key to such blasphemous outer spheres. Whateley saw how things stood, and tried to answer lightly.

"Wal, all right, ef ye feel that way abaout it. Maybe Harvard wun't be so fussy as yew be." And without saying more he rose and strode out of the building, stooping at each doorway.

Armitage heard the savage yelping of the great watchdog, and studied Whateley's gorilla-like lope as he crossed the bit of campus visible from the window. He thought of the wild tales he had heard, and recalled the old Sunday stories in the Advertiser; these things, and the lore he had picked up from Dunwich rustics and villagers during his one visit there. Unseen things not of earth—or at least not of tri-dimensional earth—rushed fetid and horrible through New England's glens, and brooded obscenely on the mountaintops. Of this he had long felt certain. Now he seemed to sense the close presence of some terrible part of the intruding horror, and to glimpse a hellish advance in the black dominion of the ancient and once passive nightmare. He locked away the *Necronomicon* with a shudder of disgust, but the room still reeked with an unholy and unidentifiable stench. "As a foulness shall ye know them," he quoted. Yes—the odor was the same as that which had sickened him at the Whateley farmhouse less than three years before. He thought of Wilbur, goatish and ominous, once again, and laughed mockingly at the village rumors of his parentage.

"Inbreeding?" Armitage muttered half-aloud to himself. "Great God, what simpletons! Shew them Arthur Machen's Great God Pan[28] and they'll think it a common Dunwich scandal! But what thing—what cursed shapeless influence on or off this three-dimensioned earth—was Wilbur Whateley's father? Born on Candlemas—nine months after May Eve[29] of 1912, when the talk about the queer earth noises reached clear to Arkham—What walked on the mountains that May-Night? What Roodmas[30] horror fastened itself on the world in half-human flesh and blood?"

During the ensuing weeks Dr. Armitage set about to collect all possible data on Wilbur Whateley and the formless presences around Dunwich. He got in communication with Dr. Houghton of Aylesbury, who had attended Old Whateley in his last illness, and found much to ponder over in the grandfather's last words as quoted by the physician. A visit to Dunwich Village failed to bring out much that was new; but a close survey of the *Necronomicon*, in those parts which Wilbur had sought so avidly, seemed to supply new and terrible clues to the nature, methods, and desires of the strange evil so vaguely threatening this planet. Talks with several students of archaic lore in Boston, and letters to many others elsewhere, gave him a growing amazement which passed slowly through varied degrees of alarm to a state of really acute spiritual fear. As the summer drew on he felt dimly that something ought to be done about the lurking terrors of the upper Miskatonic valley, and about the monstrous being known to the human world as Wilbur Whateley.

VI.

The Dunwich horror itself came between Lammas and the equinox[31] in 1928, and Dr. Armitage was among those who witnessed its monstrous prologue. He had heard, meanwhile, of Whateley's grotesque trip to Cambridge, and of his frantic efforts to borrow or copy from the *Necronomicon* at the Widener Library. Those efforts had been in vain, since Armitage had issued warnings of the keenest intensity to all librarians having charge of the dreaded volume. Wilbur had been shockingly nervous at Cambridge; anxious for the book, yet almost equally anxious to get home again, as if he feared the results of being away long.

Early in August the half-expected outcome developed, and in the small hours of the 3d Dr. Armitage was awakened suddenly by the wild, fierce cries of the savage watchdog on the college campus. Deep and terrible, the snarling, half-mad growls and barks continued; always in mounting volume, but with hideously significant pauses. Then there rang out a scream from a wholly different throat—such a scream as roused half the sleepers of Arkham and haunted their dreams ever afterward—such a scream as could come from no being born of earth, or wholly of earth.

Armitage, hastening into some clothing and rushing across the street and lawn to the college buildings, saw that others were ahead of him; and heard the echoes of a burglar-alarm still shrilling from the library. An open window showed black and gaping in the moonlight. What had come had indeed completed its entrance; for the barking and the screaming, now fast fading into a mixed low growling and moaning, proceeded unmistakably from within. Some instinct warned Armitage that what was taking place was not a thing for unfortified eyes to see, so he brushed back the crowd with authority as he unlocked the vestibule[32] door. Among the others he saw Professor Warren Rice and Dr. Francis Morgan, men to whom he had told some of his conjectures and misgivings; and these two he motioned to accompany him inside. The inward sounds, except for a watchful, droning whine from the dog, had by this time quite subsided; but Armitage now perceived with a sudden start that a loud chorus of whippoorwills among the shrubbery had commenced a damnably rhythmical piping, as if in unison with the last breaths of a dying man.

The building was full of a frightful stench which Dr. Armitage knew too well, and the three men rushed across the hall to the small genealogical reading-room whence the low whining came. For a second nobody dared to turn on the light, then Armitage summoned up his courage and snapped the switch. One of the three—it is not certain which—shrieked aloud at what sprawled before them among disordered tables and overturned chairs. Professor Rice declares that he wholly lost consciousness for an instant, though he did not stumble or fall.

The thing that lay half-bent on its side in a fetid pool of greenish-yellow ichor and tarry stickiness was almost nine feet tall, and the dog had torn off all the clothing and some of the skin. It was not quite dead, but twitched silently and spasmodically while its chest heaved in monstrous unison with the mad piping of the expectant whippoorwills outside. Bits of shoe-leather and fragments of apparel were scattered about the room, and just inside the window an empty canvas sack lay where it had evidently been thrown. Near the central desk a revolver had fallen, a dented but undischarged cartridge later explaining why it had not been fired. The thing itself, however, crowded out all other images at the time. It would be trite and not wholly accurate to say that no human pen could describe it, but one may properly say that it could not be vividly visualized by anyone whose ideas of aspect and contour are too closely bound up with the common life-forms of this planet and of the three known dimensions. It was partly human, beyond a doubt, with very man-like hands and head, and the goatish, chinless face had the stamp of the Whateleys upon it. But the torso and lower parts of the body were teratologically[33] fabulous, so that only generous clothing could ever have enabled it to walk on earth unchallenged or uneradicated.

Above the waist it was semi-anthropomorphic; though its chest, where the dog's rending paws still rested watchfully, had the leathery, reticulated[34] hide of a crocodile or alligator. The back was piebald[35] with yellow and black, and dimly suggested the squamous[36] covering of certain snakes. Below the waist, though, it was the worst; for here all human resemblance left off and sheer phantasy began. The skin was thickly covered with coarse black fur, and from the abdomen a score of long greenish-grey tentacles with red sucking mouths protruded limply. Their arrangement was odd, and seemed to follow the symmetries of some cosmic geometry unknown to earth or the solar system. On each of the hips, deep set in a kind of pinkish, ciliated[37] orbit, was what seemed to be a rudimentary eye; whilst in lieu of a tail there depended a kind of trunk or feeler with purple annular[38] markings, and with many evidences of being an undeveloped mouth or throat. The limbs, save for their black fur, roughly resembled the hind legs of prehistoric earth's giant saurians[39]; and terminated in ridgy-veined pads that were neither hooves nor claws. When the thing breathed, its tail and tentacles rhythmically changed color, as if from some circulatory cause normal to the non-human side of its ancestry. In the tentacles this was observable as a deepening of the greenish tinge, whilst in the tail it was manifest as a yellowish appearance which alternated with a sickly greyish-white in the spaces between the purple rings. Of genuine blood there was none; only the fetid greenish-yellow ichor which trickled along the painted floor beyond the radius of the stickiness, and left a curious discoloration behind it.

As the presence of the three men seemed to rouse the dying thing, it began to mumble without turning or raising its head. Dr. Armitage made no written record of its mouthings, but asserts confidently that nothing in English was uttered. At first the syllables defied all correlation with any speech of earth, but toward the last there came some disjointed fragments evidently taken from the *Necronomicon*, that monstrous blasphemy in quest of which the thing had perished. These fragments, as Armitage recalls them, ran something like "N'gai, n'gha'ghaa, bugg-shoggog, y'hah; Yog-Sothoth, Yog-Sothoth...." They trailed off into nothingness as the whippoorwills shrieked in rhythmical crescendos of unholy anticipation.

Then came a halt in the gasping, and the dog raised its head in a long, lugubrious[40] howl. A change came over the yellow, goatish face of the prostrate thing, and the great black eyes fell in appallingly. Outside the window the shrilling of the whippoorwills had suddenly ceased, and above the murmurs of the gathering crowd there came the sound of a panic-struck whirring and fluttering. Against the moon vast clouds of feathery watchers rose and raced from sight, frantic at that which they had sought for prey.

All at once the dog started up abruptly, gave a frightened bark, and leaped nervously out of the window by which it had entered. A cry rose from the crowd, and Dr. Armitage shouted to the men outside that no one must be admitted till the police or medical examiner came. He was thankful that the windows were just too high to permit of peering in, and drew the dark curtains carefully down over each one. By this time two policemen had arrived; and Dr. Morgan, meeting them in the vestibule, was urging them for their own sakes to postpone entrance to the stench-filled reading-room till the examiner came and the prostrate thing could be covered up.

Meanwhile frightful changes were taking place on the floor. One need not describe the kind and rate of shrinkage and disintegration that occurred before the eyes of Dr. Armitage and Professor Rice; but it is permissible to say that, aside from the external appearance of face and hands, the really human element in Wilbur Whateley must have been very small. When the medical examiner came, there was only a sticky whitish mass on the painted boards, and the monstrous odor had nearly disappeared. Apparently Whateley had had no skull or bony skeleton; at least, in any true or stable sense. He had taken somewhat after his unknown father.

VII.

Yet all this was only the prologue of the actual Dunwich horror. Formalities were gone through by bewildered officials, abnormal details were duly kept from press and public, and men were sent to Dunwich and Aylesbury to look up property and notify any who might be heirs of the late Wilbur Whateley. They found the countryside in great agitation, both because of the growing rumblings beneath the domed hills, and because of the unwonted stench and the surging, lapping sounds which came increasingly from the great empty shell formed by Whateley's boarded-up farmhouse. Earl Sawyer, who tended the horse and cattle during Wilbur's absence, had developed a woefully acute case of nerves. The officials devised excuses not to enter the noisome boarded place; and were glad to confine their survey of the deceased's living quarters, the newly mended sheds, to a single visit. They filed a ponderous report at the court-house in Aylesbury, and litigations concerning heirship are said to be still in progress amongst the innumerable Whateleys, decayed and undecayed, of the upper Miskatonic valley.

An almost interminable manuscript in strange characters, written in a huge ledger and adjudged a sort of diary because of the spacing and the variations in ink and penmanship, presented a baffling puzzle to those who found it on the old bureau which served as its owner's desk. After a week of debate it was sent to Miskatonic University, together with the deceased's collection of strange books, for study and possible translation; but even the best linguists soon saw that it was not likely to be unriddled with ease. No trace of the ancient gold with which Wilbur and Old Whateley always paid their debts has yet been discovered.

It was in the dark of September 9th that the horror broke loose. The hill noises had been very pronounced during the evening, and dogs barked frantically all night. Early risers on the 10th noticed a peculiar stench in the air. About seven o'clock Luther Brown, the hired boy at George Corey's, between Cold Spring Glen and the village, rushed frenziedly back from his morning trip to Ten-Acre Meadow with the cows. He was almost convulsed with fright as he stumbled into the kitchen; and in the yard outside the no less frightened herd were pawing and lowing pitifully, having followed the boy back in the panic they shared with him. Between gasps Luther tried to stammer out his tale to Mrs. Corey.

"Up thar in the rud beyont the glen, Mis' Corey—they's suthin' ben thar! It smells like thunder, an' all the bushes an' little trees is pushed back from the rud like they'd a haouse ben moved along of it. An' that ain't the wust, nuther. They's prints in the rud, Mis' Corey—great raound prints as big as barrel-heads, all sunk daown deep like a elephant had ben along, only they's a sight more nor four feet could make! I looked at one or two afore I run, an' I see every one was covered with lines spreadin' aout from one place, like as if big palm-leaf fans—twict or three times as big as any they is—hed of ben paounded daown into the rud. An' the smell was awful, like what it is araound Wizard Whateley's ol' haouse...."

Here he faltered, and seemed to shiver afresh with the fright that had sent him flying home. Mrs. Corey, unable to extract more information, began telephoning the neighbors; thus starting on its rounds the overture of panic that heralded the major terrors. When she got Sally Sawyer, housekeeper at Seth Bishop's, the nearest place to Whateley's, it became her turn to listen instead of transmit; for Sally's boy Chauncey, who slept poorly, had been up on the hill toward Whateley's, and had dashed back in terror after one look at the place, and at the pasturage where Mr. Bishop's cows had been left out all night.

"Yes, Mis' Corey," came Sally's tremulous voice over the party wire,[41] "Cha'ncey he just come back a-postin', an' couldn't haff talk fer bein' scairt! He says Ol' Whateley's haouse is all blowed up, with the timbers scattered raound like they'd ben dynamite inside; only the bottom floor ain't through, but is all covered with a kind o' tar-like stuff that smells awful an' drips daown offen the aidges onto the graoun' whar the side timbers is blown away. An' they's awful kinder marks in the yard, tew—great raound marks bigger raound than a hogshead, an' all sticky with stuff like is on the blowed-up haouse. Cha'ncey he says they leads off into the medders, whar a great swath wider'n a barn is matted daown, an' all the stun walls tumbled every whichway wherever it goes.

"An' he says, says he, Mis' Corey, as haow he sot to look fer Seth's caows, frighted ez he was; an' faound 'em in the upper pasture nigh the Devil's Hop Yard in an awful shape. Haff on 'em's clean gone, an' nigh haff o' them that's left is sucked most dry o' blood, with sores on 'em like they's ben on Whateley's cattle ever senct Lavinny's black brat was born. Seth he's gone aout naow to look at 'em, though I'll vaow he wun't keer ter git very nigh Wizard Whateley's! Cha'ncey didn't look keerful ter see whar the big matted-daown swath led arter it leff the pasturage, but he says he thinks it p'inted towards the glen rud to the village.

"I tell ye, Mis' Corey, they's suthin' abroad as hadn't orter be abroad, an' I for one think that black Wilbur Whateley, as come to the bad eend he desarved, is at the bottom of the breedin' of it. He wa'n't all human hisself, I allus says to everybody; an' I think he an' Ol' Whateley must a raised suthin' in that there nailed-up haouse as ain't even so human as he was. They's allus ben unseen things araound Dunwich—livin' things—as ain't human an' ain't good fer human folks.

"The graoun' was a-talkin' lass night, an' towards mornin' Cha'ncey he heerd the whippoorwills so laoud in Col' Spring Glen he couldn't sleep nun. Then he thought he heerd another faint-like saound over towards Wizard Whateley's—a kinder rippin' or tearin' o' wood, like some big box er crate was bein' opened fur off. What with this an' that, he didn't git to sleep at all till sunup, an' no sooner was he up this mornin', but he's got to go over to Whateley's an' see what's the matter. He see enough, I tell ye, Mis' Corey! This dun't mean no good, an' I think as all the men-folks ought to git up a party an' do suthin'. I know suthin' awful's abaout, an' feel my time is nigh, though only Gawd knows jest what it is.

"Did your Luther take accaount o' whar them big tracks led tew? No? Wal, Mis' Corey, ef they was on the glen rud this side o' the glen, an' ain't got to your haouse yet, I calc'late they must go into the glen itself. They would do that. I allus says Col' Spring Glen ain't no healthy nor decent place. The whippoorwills an' fireflies there never did act like they was creaters o' Gawd, an' they's them as says ye kin hear strange things a-rushin' an' a-talkin' in the air daown thar ef ye stand in the right place, atween the rock falls an' Bear's Den."

By that noon fully three-quarters of the men and boys of Dunwich were trooping over the roads and meadows between the new-made Whateley ruins and Cold Spring Glen, examining in horror the vast, monstrous prints, the maimed Bishop cattle, the strange, noisome wreck of the farmhouse, and the bruised, matted vegetation of the fields and road-sides. Whatever had burst loose upon the world had assuredly gone down into the great sinister ravine; for all the trees on the banks were bent and broken, and a great avenue had been gouged in the precipice-hanging underbrush. It was as though a house, launched by an avalanche, had slid down through the tangled growths of the almost vertical slope. From below no sound came, but only a distant, undefinable fetor; and it is not to be wondered at that the men preferred to stay on the edge and argue, rather than descend and beard the unknown Cyclopean horror in its lair. Three dogs that were with the party had barked furiously at first, but seemed cowed and reluctant when near the glen. Someone telephoned the news to the *Aylesbury Transcript*; but the editor, accustomed to wild tales from Dunwich, did no more than concoct a humorous paragraph about it; an item soon afterward reproduced by the Associated Press.

That night everyone went home, and every house and barn was barricaded as stoutly as possible. Needless to say, no cattle were allowed to remain in open pasturage. About two in the morning a frightful stench and the savage barking of the dogs awakened the household at Elmer Frye's, on the eastern edge of Cold Spring Glen, and all agreed that they could hear a sort of muffled swishing or lapping sound from somewhere outside. Mrs. Frye proposed telephoning the neighbors, and Elmer was about to agree when the noise of splintering wood burst in upon their deliberations. It came, apparently, from the barn; and was quickly followed by a hideous screaming and stamping amongst the cattle. The dogs slavered and crouched close to the feet of the fear-numbed family. Frye lit a lantern through force of habit, but knew it would be death to go out into that black farmyard. The children and the womenfolk whimpered, kept from screaming by some obscure, vestigial instinct of defense which told them their lives depended on silence. At last the noise of the cattle subsided to a pitiful moaning, and a great snapping, crashing, and crackling ensued. The Fryes, huddled together in the sitting-room, did not dare to move until the last echoes died away far down in Cold Spring Glen. Then, amidst the dismal moans from the stable and the demoniac piping of late whippoorwills in the glen, Selina Frye tottered to the telephone and spread what news she could of the second phase of the horror.

The next day all the countryside was in a panic; and cowed, uncommunicative groups came and went where the fiendish thing had occurred. Two titan swaths of destruction stretched from the glen to the Frye farmyard, monstrous prints covered the bare patches of ground, and one side of the old red barn had completely caved in. Of the cattle, only a quarter could be found and identified. Some of these were in curious fragments, and all that survived had to be shot. Earl Sawyer suggested that help be asked from Aylesbury or Arkham, but others maintained it would be of no use. Old Zebulon Whateley, of a branch that hovered about half way between soundness and decadence, made darkly wild suggestions about rites that ought to be practiced on the hill-tops. He came of a line where tradition ran strong, and his memories of chantings in the great stone circles were not altogether connected with Wilbur and his grandfather.

Darkness fell upon a stricken countryside too passive to organize for real defense. In a few cases closely related families would band together and watch in the gloom under one roof; but in general there was only a repetition of the barricading of the night before, and a futile, ineffective gesture of loading muskets and setting pitchforks handily about. Nothing, however, occurred except some hill noises; and when the day came there were many who hoped that the new horror had gone as swiftly as it had come. There were even bold souls who proposed an offensive expedition down in the glen, though they did not venture to set an actual example to the still reluctant majority.

When night came again the barricading was repeated, though there was less huddling together of families. In the morning both the Frye and the Seth Bishop households reported excitement among the dogs and vague sounds and stenches from afar, while early explorers noted with horror a fresh set of the monstrous tracks in the road skirting Sentinel Hill. As before, the sides of the road showed a bruising indicative of the blasphemously stupendous bulk of the horror; whilst the conformation of the tracks seemed to argue a passage in two directions, as if the moving mountain had come from Cold Spring Glen and returned to it along the same path. At the base of the hill a thirty-foot swath of crushed shrubbery saplings led steeply upward, and the seekers gasped when they saw that even the most perpendicular places did not deflect the inexorable[42] trail. Whatever the horror was, it could scale a sheer stony cliff of almost complete verticality; and as the investigators climbed around to the hill's summit by safer routes they saw that the trail ended—or rather, reversed—there.

It was here that the Whateleys used to build their hellish fires and chant their hellish rituals by the table-like stone on May-Eve and Hallowmass. Now that very stone formed the center of a vast space thrashed around by the mountainous horror, whilst upon its slightly concave surface was a thick and fetid deposit of the same tarry stickiness observed on the floor of the ruined Whateley farmhouse when the horror escaped. Men looked at one another and muttered. Then they looked down the hill. Apparently the horror had descended by a route much the same as that of its ascent. To speculate was futile. Reason, logic, and normal ideas of motivation stood confounded. Only old Zebulon, who was not with the group, could have done justice to the situation or suggested a plausible explanation.

Thursday night began much like the others, but it ended less happily. The whippoorwills in the glen had screamed with such unusual persistence that many could not sleep, and about 3 AM all the party telephones rang tremulously. Those who took down their receivers heard a fright-mad voice shriek out, "Help, oh, my Gawd!..." and some thought a crashing sound followed the breaking off of the exclamation. There was nothing more. No one dared do anything, and no one knew till morning whence the call came. Then those who had heard it called everyone on the line, and found that only the Fryes did not reply.

The truth appeared an hour later, when a hastily assembled group of armed men trudged out to the Frye place at the head of the glen. It was horrible, yet hardly a surprise. There were more swaths and monstrous prints, but there was no longer any house. It had caved in like an egg-shell, and amongst the ruins nothing living or dead could be discovered. Only a stench and a tarry stickiness. The Elmer Fryes had been erased from Dunwich.

VIII.

In the meantime a quieter yet even more spiritually poignant phase of the horror had been blackly unwinding itself behind the closed door of a shelf-lined room in Arkham. The curious manuscript record or diary of Wilbur Whateley, delivered to Miskatonic University for translation, had caused much worry and bafflement among the experts in languages both ancient and modern; its very alphabet, notwithstanding a general resemblance to the heavily shaded Arabic used in Mesopotamia, being absolutely unknown to any available authority. The final conclusion of the linguists was that the text represented an artificial alphabet, giving the effect of a cipher; though none of the usual methods of cryptographic solution seemed to furnish any clue, even when applied on the basis of every tongue the writer might conceivably have used. The ancient books taken from Whateley's quarters, while absorbingly interesting and in several cases promising to open up new and terrible lines of research among philosophers and men of science, were of no assistance whatever in this matter. One of them, a heavy tome with an iron clasp, was in another unknown alphabet—this one of a very different cast, and resembling Sanscrit more than anything else. The old ledger was at length given wholly into the charge of Dr. Armitage, both because of his peculiar interest in the Whateley matter, and because of his wide linguistic learning and skill in the mystical formulae of antiquity and the Middle Ages.

Armitage had an idea that the alphabet might be something esoterically used by certain forbidden cults which have come down from old times, and which have inherited many forms and traditions from the wizards of the Saracenic[43] world. That question, however, he did not deem vital; since it would be unnecessary to know the origin of the symbols if, as he suspected, they were used as a cipher in a modern language. It was his belief that, considering the great amount of text involved, the writer would scarcely have wished the trouble of using another speech than his own, save perhaps in certain special formulae and incantations. Accordingly he attacked the manuscript with the preliminary assumption that the bulk of it was in English.

Dr. Armitage knew, from the repeated failures of his colleagues, that the riddle was a deep and complex one; and that no simple mode of solution could merit even a trial. All through late August he fortified himself with the massed lore of cryptography; drawing upon the fullest resources of his own library, and wading night after night amidst the arcana[44] of Trithemius' *Poligraphia*, Giambattista Porta's *De Furtivis Literarum Notis*, De Vigenère's Traité des Chiffres, Falconer's Cryptomenysis Patefacta, Davys' and Thicknesse's eighteenth-century treatises, and such fairly modern authorities as Blair, von Marten, and Klüber's *Kryptographik*.[45] He interspersed his study of the books with attacks on the manuscript itself, and in time became convinced that he had to deal with one of those subtlest and most ingenious of cryptograms, in which many separate lists of corresponding letters are arranged like the multiplication table, and the message built up with arbitrary keywords known only to the initiated. The older authorities seemed rather more helpful than the newer ones, and Armitage concluded that the code of the manuscript was one of great antiquity, no doubt handed down through a long line of mystical experimenters. Several times he seemed near daylight, only to be set back by some unforeseen obstacle. Then, as September approached, the clouds began to clear. Certain letters, as used in certain parts of the manuscript, emerged definitely and unmistakably; and it became obvious that the text was indeed in English.

On the evening of September 2nd the last major barrier gave way, and Dr. Armitage read for the first time a continuous passage of Wilbur Whateley's annals. It was in truth a diary, as all had thought; and it was couched in a style clearly showing the mixed occult erudition and general illiteracy of the strange being who wrote it. Almost the first long passage that Armitage deciphered, an entry dated November 26, 1916, proved highly startling and disquieting. It was written, he remembered, by a child of three and a half who looked like a lad of twelve or thirteen.

> "Today learned the Aklo for the Sabaoth," it ran, "which did not like, it being answerable from the hill and not from the air. That upstairs more ahead of me than I had thought it would be, and is not like to have much earth brain. Shot Elam Hutchins' collie Jack when he went to bite me, and Elam says he would kill me if he dast. I guess he won't. Grandfather kept me saying the Dho formula last night, and I think I saw the inner city at the 2 magnetic poles. I shall go to those poles when the earth is cleared off, if I can't break through with the Dho-Hna formula when I commit it. They from the air told me at Sabbat[46] that it will be years before I can clear off the earth, and I guess grandfather will be dead then, so I shall have to learn all the angles of the planes and all the formulas between the Yr and the Nhhngr. They from outside will help, but they cannot take body without human blood. That upstairs looks it will have the right cast. I can see it a little when I make the Voorish sign or blow the powder of Ibn Ghazi at it, and it is near like them at May-Eve on the Hill. The other face may wear off some. I wonder how I shall look when the earth is cleared and there are no earth beings on it. He that came with the Aklo Sabaoth said I may be transfigured, there being much of outside to work on."

Morning found Dr. Armitage in a cold sweat of terror and a frenzy of wakeful concentration. He had not left the manuscript all night, but sat at his table under the electric light turning page after page with shaking hands as fast as he could decipher the cryptic text. He had nervously telephoned his wife he would not be home, and when she brought him a breakfast from the house he could scarcely dispose of a mouthful. All that day he read on, now and then halted maddeningly as a reapplication of the complex key became necessary. Lunch and dinner were brought him, but he ate only the smallest fraction of either. Toward the middle of the next night he drowsed off in his chair, but soon woke out of a tangle of nightmares almost as hideous as the truths and menaces to man's existence that he had uncovered.

On the morning of September 4th Professor Rice and Dr. Morgan insisted on seeing him for a while, and departed trembling and ashen-grey. That evening he went to bed, but slept only fitfully.[47] Wednesday—the next day—he was back at the manuscript, and began to take copious notes both from the current sections and from those he had already deciphered. In the small hours of that night he slept a little in an easy-chair in his office, but was at the manuscript again before dawn. Some time before noon his physician, Dr. Hartwell, called to see him and insisted that he cease work. He refused; intimating that it was of the most vital importance for him to complete the reading of the diary, and promising an explanation in due course of time.

That evening, just as twilight fell, he finished his terrible perusal and sank back exhausted. His wife, bringing his dinner, found him in a half-comatose state; but he was conscious enough to warn her off with a sharp cry when he saw her eyes wander toward the notes he had taken. Weakly rising, he gathered up the scribbled papers and sealed them all in a great envelope, which he immediately placed in his inside coat pocket. He had sufficient strength to get home, but was so clearly in need of medical aid that Dr. Hartwell was summoned at once. As the doctor put him to bed he could only mutter over and over again, "But what, in God's name, can we do?"

Dr. Armitage slept, but was partly delirious the next day. He made no explanations to Hartwell, but in his calmer moments spoke of the imperative need of a long conference with Rice and Morgan. His wilder wanderings were very startling indeed, including frantic appeals that something in a boarded-up farmhouse be destroyed, and fantastic references to some plan for the extirpation[48] of the entire human race and all animal and vegetable life from the earth by some terrible elder race of beings from another dimension. He would shout that the world was in danger, since the Elder Things[49] wished to strip it and drag it away from the solar system and cosmos of matter into some other plane or phase of entity from which it had once fallen, vigintillions of aeons[50] ago. At other times he would call for the dreaded *Necronomicon* and the *Daemonolatreia of Remigius*,[51] in which he seemed hopeful of finding some formula to check the peril he conjured up.

"Stop them, stop them!" he would shout. "Those Whateleys meant to let them in, and the worst of all is left! Tell Rice and Morgan we must do something—it's a blind business, but I know how to make the powder.... It hasn't been fed since the second of August, when Wilbur came here to his death, and at that rate...."

But Armitage had a sound physique despite his seventy-three years, and slept off his disorder that night without developing any real fever. He woke late Friday, clear of head, though sober with a gnawing fear and tremendous sense of responsibility. Saturday afternoon he felt able to go over to the library and summon Rice and Morgan for a conference, and the rest of that day and evening the three men tortured their brains in the wildest speculation and the most desperate debate. Strange and terrible books were drawn voluminously from the stack shelves and from secure places of storage; and diagrams and formulae were copied with feverish haste and in bewildering abundance. Of skepticism there was none. All three had seen the body of Wilbur Whateley as it lay on the floor in a room of that very building, and after that not one of them could feel even slightly inclined to treat the diary as a madman's raving.

Opinions were divided as to notifying the Massachusetts State Police, and the negative finally won. There were things involved which simply could not be believed by those who had not seen a sample, as indeed was made clear during certain subsequent investigations. Late at night the conference disbanded without having developed a definite plan, but all day Sunday Armitage was busy comparing formulae and mixing chemicals obtained from the college laboratory. The more he reflected on the hellish diary, the more he was inclined to doubt the efficacy[52] of any material agent in stamping out the entity which Wilbur Whateley had left behind him—the earth-threatening entity which, unknown to him, was to burst forth in a few hours and become the memorable Dunwich horror.

Monday was a repetition of Sunday with Dr. Armitage, for the task in hand required an infinity of research and experiment. Further consultations of the monstrous diary brought about various changes of plan, and he knew that even in the end a large amount of uncertainty must remain. By Tuesday he had a definite line of action mapped out, and believed he would try a trip to Dunwich within a week. Then, on Wednesday, the great shock came. Tucked obscurely away in a corner of the *Arkham Advertiser* was a facetious little item from the Associated Press, telling what a record-breaking monster the bootleg whiskey of Dunwich had raised up. Armitage, half stunned, could only telephone for Rice and Morgan. Far into the night they discussed, and the next day was a whirlwind of preparation on the part of them all. Armitage knew he would be meddling with terrible powers, yet saw that there was no other way to annul the deeper and more malign meddling which others had done before him.

IX.

Friday morning Armitage, Rice, and Morgan set out by motor[53] for Dunwich, arriving at the village about one in the afternoon. The day was pleasant, but even in the brightest sunlight a kind of quiet dread and portent seemed to hover about the strangely domed hills and the deep, shadowy ravines of the stricken region. Now and then on some mountaintop a gaunt circle of stones could be glimpsed against the sky. From the air of hushed fright at Osborn's store they knew something hideous had happened, and soon learned of the annihilation of the Elmer Frye house and family. Throughout that afternoon they rode around Dunwich; questioning the natives concerning all that had occurred, and seeing for themselves with rising pangs of horror the drear Frye ruins with their lingering traces of the tarry stickiness, the blasphemous tracks in the Frye yard, the wounded Seth Bishop cattle, and the enormous swaths of disturbed vegetation in various places. The trail up and down Sentinel Hill seemed to Armitage of almost cataclysmic significance, and he looked long at the sinister altar-like stone on the summit.

At length the visitors, apprised of a party of State Police which had come from Aylesbury that morning in response to the first telephone reports of the Frye tragedy, decided to seek out the officers and compare notes as far as practicable. This, however, they found more easily planned than performed; since no sign of the party could be found in any direction. There had been five of them in a car, but now the car stood empty near the ruins in the Frye yard. The natives, all of whom had talked with the policemen, seemed at first as perplexed as Armitage and his companions. Then old Sam Hutchins thought of something and turned pale, nudging Fred Farr and pointing to the dank, deep hollow that yawned close by.

"Gawd," he gasped, "I told 'em not ter go daown into the glen, an' I never thought nobody'd dew it with them tracks an' that smell an' the whippoorwills a-screechin' daown thar in the dark o' noonday...."

A cold shudder ran through natives and visitors alike, and every ear seemed strained in a kind of instinctive, unconscious listening. Armitage, now that he had actually come upon the horror and its monstrous work, trembled with the responsibility he felt to be his. Night would soon fall, and it was then that the mountainous blasphemy lumbered upon its eldritch course. *Negotium perambulans in tenebris.*[54] ... The old librarian rehearsed the formulae he had memorized, and clutched the paper containing the alternative one he had not memorized. He saw that his electric flashlight was in working order. Rice, beside him, took from a valise a metal sprayer of the sort used in combating insects; whilst Morgan uncased the big-game rifle on which he relied despite his colleague's warnings that no material weapon would be of help.

Armitage, having read the hideous diary, knew painfully well what kind of a manifestation to expect; but he did not add to the fright of the Dunwich people by giving any hints or clues. He hoped that it might be conquered without any revelation to the world of the monstrous thing it had escaped. As the shadows gathered, the natives commenced to disperse homeward, anxious to bar themselves indoors despite the present evidence that all human locks and bolts were useless before a force that could bend trees and crush houses when it chose. They shook their heads at the visitors' plan to stand guard at the Frye ruins near the glen; and as they left, had little expectancy of ever seeing the watchers again.

There were rumblings under the hills that night, and the whippoorwills piped threateningly. Once in a while a wind, sweeping up out of Cold Spring Glen, would bring a touch of ineffable fetor to the heavy night air; such a fetor as all three of the watchers had smelled once before, when they stood above a dying thing that had passed for fifteen years and a half as a human being. But the looked-for terror did not appear. Whatever was down there in the glen was biding its time, and Armitage told his colleagues it would be suicidal to try to attack it in the dark.

Morning came wanly, and the night-sounds ceased. It was a grey, bleak day, with now and then a drizzle of rain; and heavier and heavier clouds seemed to be piling themselves up beyond the hills to the northwest. The men from Arkham were undecided what to do. Seeking shelter from the increasing rainfall beneath one of the few undestroyed Frye outbuildings, they debated the wisdom of waiting, or of taking the aggressive and going down into the glen in quest of their nameless, monstrous quarry. The downpour waxed[55] in heaviness, and distant peals of thunder sounded from far horizons. Sheet lightning shimmered, and then a forky bolt flashed near at hand, as if descending into the accursed glen itself. The sky grew very dark, and the watchers hoped that the storm would prove a short, sharp one followed by clear weather.

It was still gruesomely dark when, not much over an hour later, a confused babel of voices sounded down the road. Another moment brought to view a frightened group of more than a dozen men, running, shouting, and even whimpering hysterically. Someone in the lead began sobbing out words, and the Arkham men started violently when those words developed a coherent form.

"Oh, my Gawd, my Gawd," the voice choked out. "It's a-goin' agin, an' this time by day! It's aout—it's aout an' a-movin' this very minute, an' only the Lord knows when it'll be on us all!"

The speaker panted into silence, but another took up his message.

"Nigh on a haour ago Zeb Whateley here heerd the 'phone a-ringin', an' it was Mis' Corey, George's wife, that lives daown by the junction. She says the hired boy Luther was aout drivin' in the caows from the storm arter the big bolt, when he see all the trees a-bendin' at the maouth o' the glen—opposite side ter this—an' smelt the same awful smell like he smelt when he faound the big tracks las' Monday mornin'. An' she says he says they was a swishin', lappin' saound, more nor what the bendin' trees an' bushes could make, an' all on a suddent the trees along the rud begun ter git pushed one side, an' they was a awful stompin' an' splashin' in the mud. But mind ye, Luther he didn't see nothin' at all, only just the bendin' trees an' underbrush.

"Then fur ahead where Bishop's Brook goes under the rud he heerd a awful creakin' an' strainin' on the bridge, an' says he could tell the saound o' wood a-startin' to crack an' split. An' all the whiles he never see a thing, only them trees an' bushes a-bendin'. An' when the swishin' saound got very fur off—on the rud towards Wizard Whateley's an' Sentinel Hill—Luther he had the guts ter step up whar he'd heerd it furst an' look at the graound. It was all mud an' water, an' the sky was dark, an' the rain was wipin' aout all tracks abaout as fast as could be; but beginnin' at the glen maouth, whar the trees had moved, they was still some o' them awful prints big as bar'ls like he seen Monday."

At this point the first excited speaker interrupted.

"But that ain't the trouble naow—that was only the start. Zeb here was callin' folks up an' everybody was a-listenin' in when a call from Seth Bishop's cut in. His haousekeeper Sally was carryin' on fit ter kill—she'd jest seed the trees a-bendin' beside the rud, an' says they was a kind o' mushy saound, like a elephant puffin' an' treadin', a-headin' fer the haouse. Then she up an' spoke suddent of a fearful smell, an' says her boy Cha'ncey was a-screamin' as haow it was jest like what he smelt up to the Whateley rewins Monday mornin.' An' the dogs was all barkin' an' whinin' awful.

"An' then she let aout a turrible yell, an' says the shed daown the rud had jest caved in like the storm hed blowed it over, only the wind wa'n't strong enough to dew that. Everybody was a-listenin,' an' we could hear lots o' folks on the wire a-gaspin.' All to onct Sally she yelled agin, an' says the front yard picket fence hed just crumbled up, though they wa'n't no sign o' what done it. Then everybody on the line could hear Cha'ncey an' ol' Seth Bishop a-yellin' tew, an' Sally was shriekin' aout that suthin' heavy hed struck the haouse—not lightnin' nor nothin,' but suthin' heavy agin the front, that kep' a-launchin' itself agin an' agin, though ye couldn't see nothin' aout the front winders. An' then … an' then…"

Lines of fright deepened on every face; and Armitage, shaken as he was, had barely poise enough to prompt the speaker.

"An' then…. Sally she yelled aout, 'O help, the haouse is a-cavin' in' … an' on the wire we could hear a turrible crashin,' an' a hull flock o' screamin' … jest like when Elmer Frye's place was took, only wuss…"

The man paused, and another of the crowd spoke.

"That's all—not a saound nor squeak over the 'phone arter that. Jest still-like. We that heerd it got aout Fords an' wagons an' raounded up as many able-bodied menfolks as we could git, at Corey's place, an' come up here ter see what yew thought best ter dew. Not but what I think it's the Lord's jedgment fer our iniquities, that no mortal kin ever set aside."

Armitage saw that the time for positive action had come, and spoke decisively to the faltering group of frightened rustics.

"We must follow it, boys." He made his voice as reassuring as possible. "I believe there's a chance of putting it out of business. You men know that those Whateleys were wizards—well, this thing is a thing of wizardry, and must be put down by the same means. I've seen Wilbur Whateley's diary and read some of the strange old books he used to read; and I think I know the right kind of spell to recite to make the thing fade away. Of course, one can't be sure, but we can always take a chance. It's invisible—I knew it would be—but there's a powder in this long-distance sprayer that might make it shew up for a second. Later on we'll try it. It's a frightful thing to have alive, but it isn't as bad as what Wilbur would have let in if he'd lived longer. You'll never know what the world has escaped. Now we've only this one thing to fight, and it can't multiply. It can, though, do a lot of harm; so we mustn't hesitate to rid the community of it.

"We must follow it—and the way to begin is to go to the place that has just been wrecked. Let somebody lead the way—I don't know your roads very well, but I've an idea there might be a shorter cut across lots. How about it?"

The men shuffled about a moment, and then Earl Sawyer spoke softly, pointing with a grimy finger through the steadily lessening rain.

"I guess ye kin git to Seth Bishop's quickest by cuttin' acrost the lower medder here, wadin' the brook at the low place, an' climbin' through Carrier's mowin' and the timber-lot beyont. That comes aout on the upper rud mighty nigh Seth's—a leetle t'other side."

Armitage, with Rice and Morgan, started to walk in the direction indicated; and most of the natives followed slowly. The sky was growing lighter, and there were signs that the storm had worn itself away. When Armitage inadvertently took a wrong direction, Joe Osborn warned him and walked ahead to show the right one. Courage and confidence were mounting; though the twilight of the almost perpendicular wooded hill which lay toward the end of their short cut, and among whose fantastic ancient trees they had to scramble as if up a ladder, put these qualities to a severe test.

At length they emerged on a muddy road to find the sun coming out. They were a little beyond the Seth Bishop place, but bent trees and hideously unmistakable tracks showed what had passed by. Only a few moments were consumed in surveying the ruins just around the bend. It was the Frye incident all over again, and nothing dead or living was found in either of the collapsed shells which had been the Bishop house and barn. No one cared to remain there amidst the stench and tarry stickiness, but all turned instinctively to the line of horrible prints leading on toward the wrecked Whateley farmhouse and the altar-crowned slopes of Sentinel Hill.

As the men passed the site of Wilbur Whateley's abode they shuddered visibly, and seemed again to mix hesitancy with their zeal. It was no joke tracking down something as big as a house that one could not see, but that had all the vicious malevolence of a daemon. Opposite the base of Sentinel Hill the tracks left the road, and there was a fresh bending and matting visible along the broad swath marking the monster's former route to and from the summit.

Armitage produced a pocket telescope of considerable power and scanned the steep green side of the hill. Then he handed the instrument to Morgan, whose sight was keener. After a moment of gazing Morgan cried out sharply, passing the glass to Earl Sawyer and indicating a certain spot on the slope with his finger. Sawyer, as clumsy as most non-users of optical devices are, fumbled a while; but eventually focused the lenses with Armitage's aid. When he did so his cry was less restrained than Morgan's had been.

"Gawd almighty, the grass an' bushes is a-movin'! It's a-goin' up—slow-like—creepin' up ter the top this minute, heaven only knows what fur!"

Then the germ of panic seemed to spread among the seekers. It was one thing to chase the nameless entity, but quite another to find it. Spells might be all right—but suppose they weren't? Voices began questioning Armitage about what he knew of the thing, and no reply seemed quite to satisfy. Everyone seemed to feel himself in close proximity to phases of Nature and of being utterly forbidden, and wholly outside the sane experience of mankind.

X.

In the end the three men from Arkham—old, white-bearded Dr. Armitage, stocky, iron-grey Professor Rice, and lean, youngish Dr. Morgan—ascended the mountain alone. After much patient instruction regarding its focusing and use, they left the telescope with the frightened group that remained in the road; and as they climbed they were watched closely by those among whom the glass was passed around. It was hard going, and Armitage had to be helped more than once. High above the toiling group the great swath trembled as its hellish maker re-passed with snail-like deliberateness. Then it was obvious that the pursuers were gaining.

Curtis Whateley—of the undecayed branch—was holding the telescope when the Arkham party detoured radically from the swath. He told the crowd that the men were evidently trying to get to a subordinate peak which overlooked the swath at a point considerably ahead of where the shrubbery was now bending. This, indeed, proved to be true; and the party were seen to gain the minor elevation only a short time after the invisible blasphemy had passed it.

Then Wesley Corey, who had taken the glass, cried out that Armitage was adjusting the sprayer which Rice held, and that something must be about to happen. The crowd stirred uneasily, recalling that this sprayer was expected to give the unseen horror a moment of visibility. Two or three men shut their eyes, but Curtis Whateley snatched back the telescope and strained his vision to the utmost. He saw that Rice, from the party's point of vantage above and behind the entity, had an excellent chance of spreading the potent powder with marvelous effect.

Those without the telescope saw only an instant's flash of grey cloud—a cloud about the size of a moderately large building—near the top of the mountain. Curtis, who had held the instrument, dropped it with a piercing shriek into the ankle-deep mud of the road. He reeled, and would have crumpled to the ground had not two or three others seized and steadied him. All he could do was moan half-inaudibly, "Oh, oh, great Gawd ... that ... that..."

There was a pandemonium of questioning, and only Henry Wheeler thought to rescue the fallen telescope and wipe it clean of mud. Curtis was past all coherence, and even isolated replies were almost too much for him.

"Bigger'n a barn ... all made o' squirmin' ropes ... hull thing sort o' shaped like a hen's egg bigger'n anything, with dozens o' legs like hogsheads[56] that haff shut up when they step ... nothin' solid abaout it—all like jelly, an' made o' sep'rit wrigglin' ropes pushed clost together ... great bulgin' eyes all over it ... ten or twenty maouths or trunks a-stickin' aout all along the sides, big as stovepipes, an' all a-tossin' an' openin' an' shuttin' ... all grey, with kinder blue or purple rings ... an' Gawd in heaven—that haff face on top!..."

This final memory, whatever it was, proved too much for poor Curtis; and he collapsed completely before he could say more. Fred Farr and Will Hutchins carried him to the roadside and laid him on the damp grass. Henry Wheeler, trembling, turned the rescued telescope on the mountain to see what he might. Through the lenses were discernible three tiny figures, apparently running toward the summit as fast as the steep incline allowed. Only these—nothing more. Then everyone noticed a strangely unseasonable noise in the deep valley behind, and even in the underbrush of Sentinel Hill itself. It was the piping of unnumbered whippoorwills, and in their shrill chorus there seemed to lurk a note of tense and evil expectancy.

Earl Sawyer now took the telescope and reported the three figures as standing on the topmost ridge, virtually level with the altar-stone but at a considerable distance from it. One figure, he said, seemed to be raising its hands above its head at rhythmic intervals; and as Sawyer mentioned the circumstance the crowd seemed to hear a faint, half-musical sound from the distance, as if a loud chant were accompanying the gestures. The weird silhouette on that remote peak must have been a spectacle of infinite grotesqueness and impressiveness, but no observer was in a mood for aesthetic appreciation. "I guess he's sayin' the spell," whispered Wheeler as he snatched back the telescope. The whippoorwills were piping wildly, and in a singularly curious irregular rhythm quite unlike that of the visible ritual.

Suddenly the sunshine seemed to lessen without the intervention of any discernible cloud. It was a very peculiar phenomenon, and was plainly marked by all. A rumbling sound seemed brewing beneath the hills, mixed strangely with a concordant[57] rumbling which clearly came from the sky. Lightning flashed aloft, and the wondering crowd looked in vain for the portents of storm. The chanting of the men from Arkham now became unmistakable, and Wheeler saw through the glass that they were all raising their arms in the rhythmic incantation. From some farmhouse far away came the frantic barking of dogs.

The change in the quality of the daylight increased, and the crowd gazed about the horizon in wonder. A purplish darkness, born of nothing more than a spectral deepening of the sky's blue, pressed down upon the rumbling hills. Then the lightning flashed again, somewhat brighter than before, and the crowd fancied that it had showed a certain mistiness around the altar-stone on the distant height. No one, however, had been using the telescope at that instant. The whippoorwills continued their irregular pulsation, and the men of Dunwich braced themselves tensely against some imponderable menace with which the atmosphere seemed surcharged.

Without warning came those deep, cracked, raucous vocal sounds which will never leave the memory of the stricken group who heard them. Not from any human throat were they born, for the organs of man can yield no such acoustic perversions. Rather would one have said they came from the pit itself, had not their source been so unmistakably the altar-stone on the peak. It is almost erroneous to call them sounds at all, since so much of their ghastly, infra-bass timbre spoke to dim seats of consciousness and terror far subtler than the ear; yet one must do so, since their form was indisputably though vaguely that of half-articulate words. They were loud—loud as the rumblings and the thunder above which they echoed—yet did they come from no visible being. And because imagination might suggest a conjectural source in the world of non-visible beings, the huddled crowd at the mountain's base huddled still closer, and winced as if in expectation of a blow.

"Ygnaiih … ygnaiih … thflthkh'ngha…. Yog-Sothoth…" rang the hideous croaking out of space. "Y'bthnk … h'ehye—n'grkdl'lh…."

The speaking impulse seemed to falter here, as if some frightful psychic struggle were going on. Henry Wheeler strained his eye at the telescope, but saw only the three grotesquely silhouetted human figures on the peak, all moving their arms furiously in strange gestures as their incantation drew near its culmination. From what black wells of Acherontic[58] fear or feeling, from what unplumbed gulfs of extra-cosmic consciousness or obscure, long-latent heredity, were those half-articulate thunder-croakings drawn? Presently they began to gather renewed force and coherence as they grew in stark, utter, ultimate frenzy.

"Eh-ya-ya-ya-yahaah—e'yayayayaaaa … ngh'aaaaa … ngh'aaaa … h'yuh … h'yuh…. HELP! HELP! … ff—ff—ff—FATHER! FATHER! YOG-SOTHOTH!…"

But that was all. The pallid group in the road, still reeling at the indisputably English syllables that had poured thickly and thunderously down from the frantic vacancy beside that shocking altar-stone, were never to hear such syllables again. Instead, they jumped violently at the terrific report which seemed to rend the hills; the deafening, cataclysmic peal whose source, be it inner earth or sky, no hearer was ever able to place. A single lightning-bolt shot from the purple zenith to the altar-stone, and a great tidal wave of viewless force and indescribable stench swept down from the hill to all the countryside. Trees, grass, and underbrush were whipped into a fury; and the frightened crowd at the mountain's base, weakened by the lethal fetor that seemed about to asphyxiate them, were almost hurled off their feet. Dogs howled from the distance, green grass and foliage wilted to a curious, sickly yellow-grey, and over field and forest were scattered the bodies of dead whippoorwills.

The stench left quickly, but the vegetation never came right again. To this day there is something queer and unholy about the growths on and around that fearsome hill. Curtis Whateley was only just regaining consciousness when the Arkham men came slowly down the mountain in the beams of a sunlight once more brilliant and untainted. They were grave and quiet, and seemed shaken by memories and reflections even more terrible than those which had reduced the group of natives to a state of cowed quivering. In reply to a jumble of questions they only shook their heads and reaffirmed one vital fact.

"The thing has gone forever," Armitage said. "It has been split up into what it was originally made of, and can never exist again. It was an impossibility in a normal world. Only the least fraction was really matter in any sense we know. It was like its father—and most of it has gone back to him in some vague realm or dimension outside our material universe; some vague abyss out of which only the most accursed rites of human blasphemy could ever have called him for a moment on the hills."

There was a brief silence, and in that pause the scattered senses of poor Curtis Whateley began to knit back into a sort of continuity; so that he put his hands to his head with a moan. Memory seemed to pick itself up where it had left off, and the horror of the sight that had prostrated him burst in upon him again.

"Oh, oh, my Gawd, that haff face—that haff face on top of it … that face with the red eyes an' crinkly albino hair, an' no chin, like the Whateleys…. It was a octopus, centipede, spider kind o' thing, but they was a haff-shaped man's face on top of it, an' it looked like Wizard Whateley's, only it was yards an' yards acrost…."

He paused exhausted, as the whole group of natives stared in a bewilderment not quite crystallized into fresh terror. Only old Zebulon Whateley, who wonderingly remembered ancient things but who had been silent heretofore, spoke aloud.

"Fifteen year' gone," he rambled, "I heerd Ol' Whateley say as haow some day we'd hear a child o' Lavinny's a-callin' its father's name on the top o' Sentinel Hill…."

But Joe Osborn interrupted him to question the Arkham men anew.

"What was it anyhaow, an' haowever did young Wizard Whateley call it aout o' the air it come from?"

Armitage chose his words very carefully.

"It was—well, it was mostly a kind of force that doesn't belong in our part of space; a kind of force that acts and grows and shapes itself by other laws than those of our sort of Nature. We have no business calling in such things from outside, and only very wicked people and very wicked cults ever try to. There was some of it in Wilbur Whateley him-self—enough to make a devil and a precocious monster of him, and to make his passing out a pretty terrible sight. I'm going to burn his accursed diary, and if you men are wise you'll dynamite that altar-stone up there, and pull down all the rings of standing stones on the other hills. Things like that brought down the beings those Whateleys were so fond of—the beings they were going to let in tangibly to wipe out the human race and drag the earth off to some nameless place for some nameless purpose.

"But as to this thing we've just sent back—the Whateleys raised it for a terrible part in the doings that were to come. It grew fast and big from the same reason that Wilbur grew fast and big—but it beat him because it had a greater share of the outsideness in it. You needn't ask how Wilbur called it out of the air. He didn't call it out. It was his twin brother, but it looked more like the father than he did."

The Whisperer in Darkness

Kenneth Hite sees in "The Whisperer in the Darkness" the paradigm of the Cthulhu Mythos story. It is so well crafted, he claims, that it has, unfortunately, become the template for many hackneyed science fiction or horror writers, thus making the story for some modern readers seem clichéd. The story itself, relating the circumstances of a Miskatonic University professor of folklore investigating reports of strange happenings in rural Vermont, still has much to offer the reader.

"'Whisperer,'" Hite argues, "is about rationality drowned by too much input." Where much of Lovecraft's work relies on a lack of details, this story gives a plethora of exposition about its antagonists, the Mi-Go, and yet they still remain inscrutable. There is far too much information given to be able to collate it all. "If you doubt any of it," Hite continues, "you must doubt all of it—and [...] it vanishes."

Though S.T. Joshi sees many of the same thematic and plotting flaws as found in "The Dunwich Horror," he does not see them as crippling the story. "They are only minor blemishes in an otherwise magnificent tale." While it's true we are given copious amounts of information about the Mi-Go and their disciples, Joshi points out that, as in tales like "The Call of Cthulhu," it is all fragmentary, giving only teasing insinuations of the truth. Thus the tale harkens back to tales such as "The Colour Out of Space" in its ultimate ambivalence towards the Mi-Go's designs.

I.

Bear in mind closely that I did not see any actual visual horror at the end. To say that a mental shock was the cause of what I inferred—that last straw which sent me racing out of the lonely Akeley farmhouse and through the wild domed hills of Vermont in a commandeered motor at night—is to ignore the plainest facts of my final experience. Notwithstanding the deep extent to which I shared the information and speculations of Henry Akeley, the things I saw and heard, and the admitted vividness of the impression produced on me by these things, I cannot prove even now whether I was right or wrong in my hideous inference. For after all, Akeley's disappearance establishes nothing. People found nothing amiss in his house despite the bullet-marks on the outside and inside. It was just as though he had walked out casually for a ramble in the hills and failed to return. There was not even a sign that a guest had been there, or that those horrible cylinders and machines had been stored in the study. That he had mortally feared the crowded green hills and endless trickle of brooks among which he had been born and reared, means nothing at all, either; for thousands are subject to just such morbid fears. Eccentricity, moreover, could easily account for his strange acts and apprehensions toward the last.

The whole matter began, so far as I am concerned, with the historic and unprecedented Vermont floods of November 3, 1927.[1] I was then, as now, an instructor of literature at Miskatonic University in Arkham, Massachusetts, and an enthusiastic amateur student of New England folklore. Shortly after the flood, amidst the varied reports of hardship, suffering, and organized relief which filled the press, there appeared certain odd stories of things found floating in some of the swollen rivers; so that many of my friends embarked on curious discussions and appealed to me to shed what light I could on the subject. I felt flattered at having my folklore study taken so seriously, and did what I could to belittle the wild, vague tales which seemed so clearly an outgrowth of old rustic superstitions. It amused me to find several persons of education who insisted that some stratum[2] of obscure, distorted fact might underlie the rumors.

The tales thus brought to my notice came mostly through newspaper cuttings; though one yarn had an oral source and was repeated to a friend of mine in a letter from his mother in Hardwick, Vermont. The type of thing described was essentially the same in all cases, though there seemed to be three separate instances involved—one connected with the Winooski River near Montpelier, another attached to the West River in Windham County beyond Newfane, and a third centering in the Passumpsic in Caledonia County above Lyndonville.[3] Of course many of the stray items mentioned other instances, but on analysis they all seemed to boil down to these three. In each case country folk reported seeing one or more very bizarre and disturbing objects in the surging waters that poured down from the unfrequented hills, and there was a widespread tendency to connect these sights with a primitive, half-forgotten cycle of whispered legend which old people resurrected for the occasion.

What people thought they saw were organic shapes not quite like any they had ever seen before. Naturally, there were many human bodies washed along by the streams in that tragic period; but those who described these strange shapes felt quite sure that they were not human, despite some superficial resemblances in size and general outline. Nor, said the witnesses, could they have been any kind of animal known to Vermont. They were pinkish things about five feet long; with crustaceous bodies bearing vast pairs of dorsal fins or membranous wings and several sets of articulated limbs, and with a sort of convoluted ellipsoid,[4] covered with multitudes of very short antennae, where a head would ordinarily be. It was really remarkable how closely the reports from different sources tended to coincide; though the wonder was lessened by the fact that the old legends, shared at one time throughout the hill country, furnished a morbidly vivid picture which might well have colored the imaginations of all the witnesses concerned. It was my conclusion that such witnesses—in every case naive and simple backwoods folk—had glimpsed the battered and bloated bodies of human beings or farm animals in the whirling currents; and had allowed the half-remembered folklore to invest these pitiful objects with fantastic attributes.

The ancient folklore, while cloudy, evasive, and largely forgotten by the present generation, was of a highly singular character, and obviously reflected the influence of still earlier Indian tales. I knew it well, though I had never been in Vermont, through the exceedingly rare monograph of Eli Davenport,[5] which embraces material orally obtained prior to 1839 among the oldest people of the state. This material, moreover, closely coincided with tales which I had personally heard from elderly rustics in the mountains of New Hampshire. Briefly summarized, it hinted at a hidden race of monstrous beings which lurked somewhere among the remoter hills—in the deep woods of the highest peaks, and the dark valleys where streams trickle from unknown sources. These beings were seldom glimpsed, but evidences of their presence were reported by those who had ventured farther than usual up the slopes of certain mountains or into certain deep, steep-sided gorges that even the wolves shunned.

There were queer footprints or claw-prints in the mud of brook-margins and barren patches, and curious circles of stones, with the grass around them worn away, which did not seem to have been placed or entirely shaped by Nature. There were, too, certain caves of problematical depth in the sides of the hills; with mouths closed by boulders in a manner scarcely accidental, and with more than an average quota of the queer prints leading both toward and away from them—if indeed the direction of these prints could be justly estimated. And worst of all, there were the things which adventurous people had seen very rarely in the twilight of the remotest valleys and the dense perpendicular woods above the limits of normal hill-climbing.

It would have been less uncomfortable if the stray accounts of these things had not agreed so well. As it was, nearly all the rumors had several points in common; averring that the creatures were a sort of huge, light-red crab with many pairs of legs and with two great bat-like wings in the middle of the back. They sometimes walked on all their legs, and sometimes on the hindmost pair only, using the others to convey large objects of indeterminate nature. On one occasion they were spied in considerable numbers, a detachment of them wading along a shallow woodland watercourse three abreast in evidently disciplined formation. Once a specimen was seen flying—launching itself from the top of a bald, lonely hill at night and vanishing in the sky after its great flapping wings had been silhouetted an instant against the full moon.

These things seemed content, on the whole, to let mankind alone; though they were at times held responsible for the disappearance of venturesome individuals—especially persons who built houses too close to certain valleys or too high up on certain mountains. Many localities came to be known as inadvisable to settle in, the feeling persisting long after the cause was forgotten. People would look up at some of the neighboring mountain-precipices with a shudder, even when not recalling how many settlers had been lost, and how many farmhouses burnt to ashes, on the lower slopes of those grim, green sentinels.

But while according to the earliest legends the creatures would appear to have harmed only those trespassing on their privacy; there were later accounts of their curiosity respecting men, and of their attempts to establish secret outposts in the human world. There were tales of the queer claw-prints seen around farmhouse windows in the morning, and of occasional disappearances in regions outside the obviously haunted areas. Tales, besides, of buzzing voices in imitation of human speech which made surprising offers to lone travellers on roads and cart-paths in the deep woods, and of children frightened out of their wits by things seen or heard where the primal forest pressed close upon their dooryards. In the final layer of legends—the layer just preceding the decline of superstition and the abandonment of close contact with the dreaded places—there are shocked references to hermits and remote farmers who at some period of life appeared to have undergone a repellent mental change, and who were shunned and whispered about as mortals who had sold themselves to the strange beings. In one of the northeastern counties it seemed to be a fashion about 1800 to accuse eccentric and unpopular recluses of being allies or representatives of the abhorred things.

As to what the things were—explanations naturally varied. The common name applied to them was "those ones," or "the old ones," though other terms had a local and transient use. Perhaps the bulk of the Puritan settlers set them down bluntly as familiars of the devil, and made them a basis of awed theological speculation. Those with Celtic legendry in their heritage—mainly the Scotch-Irish element of New Hampshire, and their kindred who had settled in Vermont on Governor Wentworth's[6] colonial grants—linked them vaguely with the malign fairies and "little people" of the bogs and raths, and protected themselves with scraps of incantation handed down through many generations. But the Indians had the most fantastic theories of all. While different tribal legends differed, there was a marked consensus of belief in certain vital particulars; it being unanimously agreed that the creatures were not native to this earth.

The Pennacook[7] myths, which were the most consistent and picturesque, taught that the Winged Ones came from the Great Bear in the sky, and had mines in our earthly hills whence they took a kind of stone they could not get on any other world. They did not live here, said the myths, but merely maintained outposts and flew back with vast cargoes of stone to their own stars in the north. They harmed only those earth-people who got too near them or spied upon them. Animals shunned them through instinctive hatred, not because of being hunted. They could not eat the things and animals of earth, but brought their own food from the stars. It was bad to get near them, and sometimes young hunters who went into their hills never came back. It was not good, either, to listen to what they whispered at night in the forest with voices like a bee's that tried to be like the voices of men. They knew the speech of all kinds of men—Pennacooks, Hurons, men of the Five Nations[8]—but did not seem to have or need any speech of their own. They talked with their heads, which changed color in different ways to mean different things.

All the legendry, of course, white and Indian alike, died down during the nineteenth century, except for occasional atavistical[9] flareups. The ways of the Vermonters became settled; and once their habitual paths and dwellings were established according to a certain fixed plan, they remembered less and less what fears and avoidances had determined that plan, and even that there had been any fears or avoidances. Most people simply knew that certain hilly regions were considered as highly unhealthy, unprofitable, and generally unlucky to live in, and that the farther one kept from them the better off one usually was. In time the ruts of custom and economic interest became so deeply cut in approved places that there was no longer any reason for going outside them, and the haunted hills were left deserted by accident rather than by design. Save during infrequent local scares, only wonder-loving grandmothers and retrospective nonagenarians[10] ever whispered of beings dwelling in those hills; and even such whisperers admitted that there was not much to fear from those things now that they were used to the presence of houses and settlements, and now that human beings let their chosen territory severely alone.

All this I had known from my reading, and from certain folk-tales picked up in New Hampshire; hence when the flood-time rumors began to appear, I could easily guess what imaginative background had evolved them. I took great pains to explain this to my friends, and was correspondingly amused when several contentious souls continued to insist on a possible element of truth in the reports. Such persons tried to point out that the early legends had a significant persistence and uniformity, and that the virtually unexplored nature of the Vermont hills made it unwise to be dogmatic about what might or might not dwell among them; nor could they be silenced by my assurance that all the myths were of a well-known pattern common to most of mankind and determined by early phases of imaginative experience which always produced the same type of delusion.

It was of no use to demonstrate to such opponents that the Vermont myths differed but little in essence from those universal legends of natural personification which filled the ancient world with fauns and dryads and satyrs, suggested the kallikanzari[11] of modern Greece, and gave to wild Wales and Ireland their dark hints of strange, small, and terrible hidden races of troglodytes[12] and burrowers. No use, either, to point out the even more startlingly similar belief of the Nepalese hill tribes in the dreaded Mi-Go or "Abominable Snow-Men"[13] who lurk hideously amidst the ice and rock pinnacles of the Himalayan summits. When I brought up this evidence, my opponents turned it against me by claiming that it must imply some actual historicity for the ancient tales; that it must argue the real existence of some queer elder earth-race, driven to hiding after the advent and dominance of mankind, which might very conceivably have survived in reduced numbers to relatively recent times—or even to the present.

The more I laughed at such theories, the more these stubborn friends asseverated[14] them; adding that even without the heritage of legend the recent reports were too clear, consistent, detailed, and sanely prosaic in manner of telling, to be completely ignored. Two or three fanatical extremists went so far as to hint at possible meanings in the ancient Indian tales which gave the hidden beings a non-terrestrial origin; citing the extravagant books of Charles Fort[15] with their claims that voyagers from other worlds and outer space have often visited earth. Most of my foes, however, were merely romanticists who insisted on trying to transfer to real life the fantastic lore of lurking "little people" made popular by the magnificent horror-fiction of Arthur Machen.

II.

As was only natural under the circumstances, this piquant[16] debating finally got into print in the form of letters to the *Arkham Advertiser*; some of which were copied in the press of those Vermont regions whence the flood-stories came. The *Rutland Herald* gave half a page of extracts from the letters on both sides, while the *Brattleboro Reformer* reprinted one of my long historical and mythological summaries in full, with some accompanying comments in "The Pendrifter's" thoughtful column which supported and applauded my skeptical conclusions. By the spring of 1928 I was almost a well-known figure in Vermont, notwithstanding the fact that I had never set foot in the state. Then came the challenging letters from Henry Akeley which impressed me so profoundly, and which took me for the first and last time to that fascinating realm of crowded green precipices and muttering forest streams.

Most of what I now know of Henry Wentworth Akeley was gathered by correspondence with his neighbors, and with his only son in California, after my experience in his lonely farmhouse. He was, I discovered, the last representative on his home soil of a long, locally distinguished line of jurists, administrators, and gentlemen-agriculturists. In him, however, the family mentally had veered away from practical affairs to pure scholarship; so that he had been a notable student of mathematics, astronomy, biology, anthropology, and folklore at the University of Vermont. I had never previously heard of him, and he did not give many autobiographical details in his communications; but from the first I saw he was a man of character, education, and intelligence, albeit a recluse with very little worldly sophistication.

Despite the incredible nature of what he claimed, I could not help at once taking Akeley more seriously than I had taken any of the other challengers of my views. For one thing, he was really close to the actual phenomena—visible and tangible—that he speculated so grotesquely about; and for another thing, he was amazingly willing to leave his conclusions in a tentative state like a true man of science. He had no personal preferences to advance, and was always guided by what he took to be solid evidence. Of course I began by considering him mistaken, but gave him credit for being intelligently mistaken; and at no time did I emulate some of his friends in attributing his ideas, and his fear of the lonely green hills, to insanity. I could see that there was a great deal to the man, and knew that what he reported must surely come from strange circumstances deserving investigation, however little it might have to do with the fantastic causes he assigned. Later on I received from him certain material proofs which placed the matter on a somewhat different and bewilderingly bizarre basis.

I cannot do better than transcribe in full, so far as is possible, the long letter in which Akeley introduced himself, and which formed such an important landmark in my own intellectual history. It is no longer in my possession, but my memory holds almost every word of its portentous message; and again I affirm my confidence in the sanity of the man who wrote it. Here is the text—a text which reached me in the cramped, archaic-looking scrawl of one who had obviously not mingled much with the world during his sedate, scholarly life.

> R.F.D. #2,
> Townshend, Windham Co.,
> Vermont.
>
> May 5, 1928

Albert N. Wilmarth, Esq.,[17]
118 Saltonstall St.,
Arkham, Mass.,

My dear Sir:—

I have read with great interest the *Brattleboro Reformer*'s reprint (Apr. 23, '28) of your letter on the recent stories of strange bodies seen floating in our flooded streams last fall, and on the curious folklore they so well agree with. It is easy to see why an outlander would take the position you take, and even why "Pendrifter" agrees with you. That is the attitude generally taken by educated persons both in and out of Vermont, and was my own attitude as a young man (I am now 57) before my studies, both general and in Davenport's book, led me to do some exploring in parts of the hills hereabouts not usually visited.

I was directed toward such studies by the queer old tales I used to hear from elderly farmers of the more ignorant sort, but now I wish I had let the whole matter alone. I might say, with all proper modesty, that the subject of anthropology and folklore is by no means strange to me. I took a good deal of it at college, and am familiar with most of the standard authorities such as Tylor, Lubbock, Frazer, Quatrefages, Murray, Osborn, Keith, Boule, G. Elliot Smith, and so on.[18] It is no news to me that tales of hidden races are as old as all mankind. I have seen the reprints of letters from you, and those arguing with you, in the *Rutland Herald*, and guess I know about where your controversy stands at the present time.

What I desire to say now is, that I am afraid your adversaries are nearer right than yourself, even though all reason seems to be on your side. They are nearer right than they realize themselves—for of course they go only by theory, and cannot know what I know. If I knew as little of the matter as they, I would not feel justified in believing as they do. I would be wholly on your side.

You can see that I am having a hard time getting to the point, probably because I really dread getting to the point; but the upshot of the matter is that *I have certain evidence that monstrous things do indeed live in the woods on the high hills which nobody visits.* I have not seen any of the things floating in the rivers, as reported, *but I have seen things like them* under circumstances I dread to repeat. I have seen footprints, and of late have seen them nearer my own home (I live in the old Akeley place south of Townshend Village, on the side of Dark Mountain) than I dare tell you now. And I have overheard voices in the woods at certain points that I will not even begin to describe on paper.

At one place I heard them so much that I took a phonograph there—with a dictaphone attachment and wax blank—and I shall try to arrange to have you hear the record I got. I have run it on the machine for some of the old people up here, and one of the voices had nearly scared them paralyzed by reason of its likeness to a certain voice (that buzzing voice in the woods which Davenport mentions) that their grandmothers have told about and mimicked for them. I know what most people think of a man who tells about "hearing voices"—but before you draw conclusions just listen to this record and ask some of the older backwoods people what they think of it. If you can account for it normally, very well; but there must be something behind it. *Ex nihilo nihil fit,*[19] you know.

Now my object in writing you is not to start an argument, but to give you information which I think a man of your tastes will find deeply interesting. *This is private. Publicly I am on your side*, for certain things show me that it does not do for people to know too much about these matters. My own studies are now wholly private, and I would not think of saying anything to attract people's attention and cause them to visit the places I have explored. It is true—terribly true—that there are *non-human creatures watching us all the time*; with spies among us gathering information. It is from a wretched man who, if he was sane (as I think he was), *was one of those spies*, that I got a large part of my clues to the matter. He later killed himself, but I have reason to think there are others now.

The things come from another planet, being able to live in interstellar space and fly through it on clumsy, powerful wings which have a way of resisting the aether[20] but which are too poor at steering to be of much use in helping them about on earth. I will tell you about this later if you do not dismiss me at once as a madman. They come here to get metals from mines that go deep under the hills, *and I think I know where they come from.* They will not hurt us if we let them alone, but no one can say what will happen if we get too curious about them. Of course a good army of men could wipe out their mining colony. That is what they are afraid of. But if that happened, more would come from *outside*—any number of them. They could easily conquer the earth, but have not tried so far because they have not needed to. They would rather leave things as they are to save bother.

I think they mean to get rid of me because of what I have discovered. There is a great black stone with unknown hieroglyphics half worn away which I found in the woods on Round Hill, east of here; and after I took it home everything became different. If they think I suspect too much they will either kill me *or take me off the earth to where they come from.* They like to take away men of learning once in a while, to keep informed on the state of things in the human world.

This leads me to my secondary purpose in addressing you—namely, to urge you to hush up the present debate rather than give it more publicity. *People must be kept away from these hills*, and in order to effect this, their curiosity ought not to be aroused any further. Heaven knows there is peril enough anyway, with promoters and real estate men flooding Vermont with herds of summer people to overrun the wild places and cover the hills with cheap bungalows.[21]

I shall welcome further communication with you, and shall try to send you that phonograph record and black stone (which is so worn that photographs don't show much) by express if you are willing. I say "try" because I think those creatures have a way of tampering with things around here. There is a sullen, furtive fellow named Brown, on a farm near the village, who I think is their spy. Little by little they are trying to cut me off from our world because I know too much about their world.

They have the most amazing way of finding out what I do. You may not even get this letter. I think I shall have to leave this part of the country and go to live with my son in San Diego, Cal., if things get any worse, but it is not easy to give up the place you were born in, and where your family has lived for six generations. Also, I would hardly dare sell this house to anybody now that the *creatures* have taken notice of it. They seem to be trying to get the black stone back and destroy the phonograph record, but I shall not let them if I can help it. My great police dogs always hold them back, for there are very few here as yet, and they are clumsy in getting about. As I have said, their wings are not much use for short flights on earth. I am on the very brink of deciphering that stone—in a very terrible way—and with your knowledge of folklore you may be able to supply missing links enough to help me. I suppose you know all about the fearful myths antedating the coming of man to the earth—the Yog-Sothoth and Cthulhu cycles—which are hinted at in the *Necronomicon*. I had access to a copy of that once, and hear that you have one in your college library under lock and key.

To conclude, Mr. Wilmarth, I think that with our respective studies we can be very useful to each other. I don't wish to put you in any peril, and suppose I ought to warn you that possession of the stone and the record won't be very safe; but I think you will find any risks worth running for the sake of knowledge. I will drive down to Newfane or Brattleboro to send whatever you authorize me to send, for the express offices there are more to be trusted. I might say that I live quite alone now, since I can't keep hired help any more. They won't stay because of the things that try to get near the house at night, and that keep the dogs barking continually. I am glad I didn't get as deep as this into the business while my wife was alive, for it would have driven her mad.

Hoping that I am not bothering you unduly, and that you will decide to get in touch with me rather than throw this letter into the waste basket as a madman's raving, I am

Yrs. very truly,
Henry W. Akeley

P.S. I am making some extra prints of certain photographs taken by me, which I think will help to prove a number of the points I have touched on. The old people think they are monstrously true. I shall send you these very soon if you are interested.

H.W.A.

It would be difficult to describe my sentiments upon reading this strange document for the first time. By all ordinary rules, I ought to have laughed more loudly at these extravagances than at the far milder theories which had previously moved me to mirth; yet something in the tone of the letter made me take it with paradoxical seriousness. Not that I believed for a moment in the hidden race from the stars which my correspondent spoke of; but that, after some grave preliminary doubts, I grew to feel oddly sure of his sanity and sincerity, and of his confrontation by some genuine though singular and abnormal phenomenon which he could not explain except in this imaginative way. It could not be as he thought it, I reflected, yet on the other hand it could not be otherwise than worthy of investigation. The man seemed unduly excited and alarmed about something, but it was hard to think that all cause was lacking. He was so specific and logical in certain ways—and after all, his yarn did fit in so perplexingly well with some of the old myths—even the wildest Indian legends.

That he had really overheard disturbing voices in the hills, and had really found the black stone he spoke about, was wholly possible despite the crazy inferences he had made—inferences probably suggested by the man who had claimed to be a spy of the outer beings and had later killed himself. It was easy to deduce that this man must have been wholly insane, but that he probably had a streak of perverse outward logic which made the naive Akeley—already prepared for such things by his folklore studies—believe his tale. As for the latest developments—it appeared from his inability to keep hired help that Akeley's humbler rustic neighbors were as convinced as he that his house was besieged by uncanny things at night. The dogs really barked, too.

And then the matter of that phonograph record, which I could not but believe he had obtained in the way he said. It must mean something; whether animal noises deceptively like human speech, or the speech of some hidden, night-haunting human being decayed to a state not much above that of lower animals. From this my thoughts went back to the black hieroglyphed stone, and to speculations upon what it might mean. Then, too, what of the photographs which Akeley said he was about to send, and which the old people had found so convincingly terrible?

As I re-read the cramped handwriting I felt as never before that my credulous opponents might have more on their side than I had conceded. After all, there might be some queer and perhaps hereditarily misshapen outcasts in those shunned hills, even though no such race of star-born monsters as folklore claimed. And if there were, then the presence of strange bodies in the flooded streams would not be wholly beyond belief. Was it too presumptuous to suppose that both the old legends and the recent reports had this much of reality behind them? But even as I harbored these doubts I felt ashamed that so fantastic a piece of bizarrerie[22] as Henry Akeley's wild letter had brought them up.

In the end I answered Akeley's letter, adopting a tone of friendly interest and soliciting further particulars. His reply came almost by return mail; and contained, true to promise, a number of kodak views of scenes and objects illustrating what he had to tell. Glancing at these pictures as I took them from the envelope, I felt a curious sense of fright and nearness to forbidden things; for in spite of the vagueness of most of them, they had a damnably suggestive power which was intensified by the fact of their being genuine photographs—actual optical links with what they portrayed, and the product of an impersonal transmitting process without prejudice, fallibility, or mendacity.[23]

The more I looked at them, the more I saw that my serious estimate of Akeley and his story had not been unjustified. Certainly, these pictures carried conclusive evidence of something in the Vermont hills which was at least vastly outside the radius of our common knowledge and belief. The worst thing of all was the footprint—a view taken where the sun shone on a mud patch somewhere in a deserted upland. This was no cheaply counterfeited thing, I could see at a glance; for the sharply defined pebbles and grass-blades in the field of vision gave a clear index of scale and left no possibility of a tricky double exposure. I have called the thing a "footprint," but "claw-print" would be a better term. Even now I can scarcely describe it save to say that it was hideously crab-like, and that there seemed to be some ambiguity about its direction. It was not a very deep or fresh print, but seemed to be about the size of an average man's foot. From a central pad, pairs of saw-toothed nippers projected in opposite directions—quite baffling as to function, if indeed the whole object were exclusively an organ of locomotion.

Another photograph—evidently a time-exposure taken in deep shadow—was of the mouth of a woodland cave, with a boulder of rounded regularity choking the aperture. On the bare ground in front of it one could just discern a dense network of curious tracks, and when I studied the picture with a magnifier I felt uneasily sure that the tracks were like the one in the other view. A third picture showed a druid-like circle of standing stones on the summit of a wild hill. Around the cryptic circle the grass was very much beaten down and worn away, though I could not detect any footprints even with the glass. The extreme remoteness of the place was apparent from the veritable sea of tenantless mountains which formed the background and stretched away toward a misty horizon.

But if the most disturbing of all the views was that of the footprint, the most curiously suggestive was that of the great black stone found in the Round Hill woods. Akeley had photographed it on what was evidently his study table, for I could see rows of books and a bust of Milton in the background. The thing, as nearly as one might guess, had faced the camera vertically with a somewhat irregularly curved surface of one by two feet; but to say anything definite about that surface, or about the general shape of the whole mass, almost defies the power of language. What outlandish geometrical principles had guided its cutting—for artificially cut it surely was—I could not even begin to guess; and never before had I seen anything which struck me as so strangely and unmistakably alien to this world. Of the hieroglyphics on the surface I could discern very few, but one or two that I did see gave me rather a shock. Of course they might be fraudulent, for others besides myself had read the monstrous and abhorred *Necronomicon* of the mad Arab Abdul Alhazred; but it nevertheless made me shiver to recognize certain ideographs[24] which study had taught me to link with the most blood-curdling and blasphemous whispers of things that had had a kind of mad half-existence before the earth and the other inner worlds of the solar system were made.

Of the five remaining pictures, three were of swamp and hill scenes which seemed to bear traces of hidden and unwholesome tenancy. Another was of a queer mark in the ground very near Akeley's house, which he said he had photographed the morning after a night on which the dogs had barked more violently than usual. It was very blurred, and one could really draw no certain conclusions from it; but it did seem fiendishly like that other mark or claw-print photographed on the deserted upland. The final picture was of the Akeley place itself; a trim white house of two stories and attic, about a century and a quarter old, and with a well-kept lawn and stone-bordered path leading up to a tastefully carved Georgian doorway. There were several huge police dogs on the lawn, squatting near a pleasant-faced man with a close-cropped grey beard whom I took to be Akeley himself—his own photographer, one might infer from the tube-connected bulb in his right hand.

From the pictures I turned to the bulky, closely written letter itself; and for the next three hours was immersed in a gulf of unutterable horror. Where Akeley had given only outlines before, he now entered into minute details; presenting long transcripts of words overheard in the woods at night, long accounts of monstrous pinkish forms spied in thickets at twilight on the hills, and a terrible cosmic narrative derived from the application of profound and varied scholarship to the endless bygone discourses of the mad self-styled spy who had killed himself. I found myself faced by names and terms that I had heard elsewhere in the most hideous of connections—Yuggoth, Great Cthulhu, Tsathoggua, Yog-Sothoth, R'lyeh, Nyarlathotep, Azathoth, Hastur, Yian, Leng, the Lake of Hali, Bethmoora, the Yellow Sign, L'mur-Kathulos, Bran, and the Magnum Innominandum[25]—and was drawn back through nameless aeons and inconceivable dimensions to worlds of elder, outer entity at which the crazed author of the *Necronomicon* had only guessed in the vaguest way. I was told of the pits of primal life, and of the streams that had trickled down therefrom; and finally, of the tiny rivulet from one of those streams which had become entangled with the destinies of our own earth.

My brain whirled; and where before I had attempted to explain things away, I now began to believe in the most abnormal and incredible wonders. The array of vital evidence was damnably vast and overwhelming; and the cool, scientific attitude of Akeley—an attitude removed as far as imaginable from the demented, the fanatical, the hysterical, or even the extravagantly speculative—had a tremendous effect on my thought and judgment. By the time I laid the frightful letter aside I could understand the fears he had come to entertain, and was ready to do anything in my power to keep people away from those wild, haunted hills. Even now, when time has dulled the impression and made me half question my own experience and horrible doubts, there are things in that letter of Akeley's which I would not quote, or even form into words on paper. I am almost glad that the letter and record and photographs are gone now—and I wish, for reasons I shall soon make clear, that the new planet beyond Neptune[26] had not been discovered.

With the reading of that letter my public debating about the Vermont horror permanently ended. Arguments from opponents remained unanswered or put off with promises, and eventually the controversy petered out into oblivion. During late May and June I was in constant correspondence with Akeley; though once in a while a letter would be lost, so that we would have to retrace our ground and perform considerable laborious copying. What we were trying to do, as a whole, was to compare notes in matters of obscure mythological scholarship and arrive at a clearer correlation of the Vermont horrors with the general body of primitive world legend.

For one thing, we virtually decided that these morbidities and the hellish Himalayan Mi-Go were one and the same order of incarnated nightmare. There were also absorbing zoölogical conjectures, which I would have referred to Professor Dexter in my own college but for Akeley's imperative command to tell no one of the matter before us. If I seem to disobey that command now, it is only because I think that at this stage a warning about those farther Vermont hills—and about those Himalayan peaks which bold explorers are more and more determined to ascend—is more conducive to public safety than silence would be. One specific thing we were leading up to was a deciphering of the hieroglyphics on that infamous black stone—a deciphering which might well place us in possession of secrets deeper and more dizzying than any formerly known to man.

III.

Toward the end of June the phonograph record came—shipped from Brattleboro, since Akeley was unwilling to trust conditions on the branch line north of there. He had begun to feel an increased sense of espionage, aggravated by the loss of some of our letters; and said much about the insidious deeds of certain men whom he considered tools and agents of the hidden beings. Most of all he suspected the surly farmer Walter Brown, who lived alone on a run-down hillside place near the deep woods, and who was often seen loafing around corners in Brattleboro, Bellows Falls, Newfane, and South Londonderry in the most inexplicable and seemingly unmotivated way. Brown's voice, he felt convinced, was one of those he had overheard on a certain occasion in a very terrible conversation; and he had once found a footprint or claw-print near Brown's house which might possess the most ominous significance. It had been curiously near some of Brown's own footprints—footprints that faced toward it.

So the record was shipped from Brattleboro, whither Akeley drove in his Ford car along the lonely Vermont back roads. He confessed in an accompanying note that he was beginning to be afraid of those roads, and that he would not even go into Townshend for supplies now except in broad daylight. It did not pay, he repeated again and again, to know too much unless one were very remote from those silent and problematical hills. He would be going to California pretty soon to live with his son, though it was hard to leave a place where all one's memories and ancestral feelings centered.

Before trying the record on the commercial machine which I borrowed from the college administration building I carefully went over all the explanatory matter in Akeley's various letters. This record, he had said, was obtained about 1 a.m. on the first of May 1915, near the closed mouth of a cave where the wooded west slope of Dark Mountain rises out of Lee's Swamp. The place had always been unusually plagued with strange voices, this being the reason he had brought the phonograph, dictaphone, and blank in expectation of results. Former experience had told him that May-Eve—the hideous Sabbat-night of underground European legend—would probably be more fruitful than any other date, and he was not disappointed. It was noteworthy, though, that he never again heard voices at that particular spot.

Unlike most of the overheard forest voices, the substance of the record was quasi-ritualistic, and included one palpably human voice which Akeley had never been able to place. It was not Brown's, but seemed to be that of a man of greater cultivation. The second voice, however, was the real crux of the thing—for this was the accursed buzzing which had no likeness to humanity despite the human words which it uttered in good English grammar and a scholarly accent.

The recording phonograph and dictaphone had not worked uniformly well, and had of course been at a great disadvantage because of the remote and muffled nature of the overheard ritual; so that the actual speech secured was very fragmentary. Akeley had given me a transcript of what he believed the spoken words to be, and I glanced through this again as I prepared the machine for action. The text was darkly mysterious rather than openly horrible, though a knowledge of its origin and manner of gathering gave it all the associative horror which any words could well possess. I will present it here in full as I remember it—and I am fairly confident that I know it correctly by heart, not only from reading the transcript, but from playing the record itself over and over again. It is not a thing which one might readily forget!

(Indistinguishable Sounds)
(A Cultivated Male Human Voice)
…is the Lord of the Woods, even to … and the gifts of the men of Leng … so from the wells of night to the gulfs of space, and from the gulfs of space to the wells of night, ever the praises of Great Cthulhu, of Tsathoggua, and of Him Who is not to be Named. Ever Their praises, and abundance to the Black Goat of the Woods. Iä! Shub-Niggurath! The Goat with a Thousand Young!
(A Buzzing Imitation of Human Speech)
Iä! Shub-Niggurath! The Black Goat of the Woods with a Thousand Young!
(Human Voice)
And it has come to pass that the Lord of the Woods, being … seven and nine, down the onyx steps … (tri)butes to Him in the Gulf, Azathoth, He of Whom Thou hast taught us marv(els) … on the wings of night out beyond space, out beyond th … to That whereof Yuggoth is the youngest child, rolling alone in black aether at the rim….
(Buzzing Voice)
…go out among men and find the ways thereof, that He in the Gulf may know. To Nyarlathotep, Mighty Messenger, must all things be told. And He shall put on the semblance of men, the waxen mask and the robe that hides, and come down from the world of Seven Suns to mock….
(Human Voice)
…(Nyarl)athotep, Great Messenger, bringer of strange joy to Yuggoth through the void, Father of the Million Favoured Ones, Stalker among….
(Speech Cut Off by End of Record)

Such were the words for which I was to listen when I started the phonograph. It was with a trace of genuine dread and reluctance that I pressed the lever and heard the preliminary scratching of the sapphire point, and I was glad that the first faint, fragmentary words were in a human voice—a mellow, educated voice which seemed vaguely Bostonian in accent, and which was certainly not that of any native of the Vermont hills. As I listened to the tantalizingly feeble rendering, I seemed to find the speech identical with Akeley's carefully prepared transcript. On it chanted, in that mellow Bostonian voice ... "Iä! Shub-Niggurath! The Goat with a Thousand Young!..."

And then I heard the other voice. To this hour I shudder retrospectively when I think of how it struck me, prepared though I was by Akeley's accounts. Those to whom I have since described the record profess to find nothing but cheap imposture or madness in it; but could they have heard the accursed thing itself, or read the bulk of Akeley's correspondence (especially that terrible and encyclopedic second letter), I know they would think differently. It is, after all, a tremendous pity that I did not disobey Akeley and play the record for others—a tremendous pity, too, that all of his letters were lost. To me, with my first-hand impression of the actual sounds, and with my knowledge of the background and surrounding circumstances, the voice was a monstrous thing. It swiftly followed the human voice in ritualistic response, but in my imagination it was a morbid echo winging its way across unimaginable abysses from unimaginable outer hells. It is more than two years now since I last ran off that blasphemous waxen cylinder; but at this moment, and at all other moments, I can still hear that feeble, fiendish buzzing as it reached me for the first time.

"Iä! Shub-Niggurath! The Black Goat of the Woods with a Thousand Young!"

But though that voice is always in my ears, I have not even yet been able to analyze it well enough for a graphic description. It was like the drone of some loathsome, gigantic insect ponderously shaped into the articulate speech of an alien species, and I am perfectly certain that the organs producing it can have no resemblance to the vocal organs of man, or indeed to those of any of the mammalia. There were singularities in timbre, range, and overtones which placed this phenomenon wholly outside the sphere of humanity and earth-life. Its sudden advent that first time almost stunned me, and I heard the rest of the record through in a sort of abstracted daze. When the longer passage of buzzing came, there was a sharp intensification of that feeling of blasphemous infinity which had struck me during the shorter and earlier passage. At last the record ended abruptly, during an unusually clear speech of the human and Bostonian voice; but I sat stupidly staring long after the machine had automatically stopped.

I hardly need say that I gave that shocking record many another playing, and that I made exhaustive attempts at analysis and comment in comparing notes with Akeley. It would be both useless and disturbing to repeat here all that we concluded; but I may hint that we agreed in believing we had secured a clue to the source of some of the most repulsive primordial customs in the cryptic elder religions of mankind. It seemed plain to us, also, that there were ancient and elaborate alliances between the hidden outer creatures and certain members of the human race. How extensive these alliances were, and how their state today might compare with their state in earlier ages, we had no means of guessing; yet at best there was room for a limitless amount of horrified speculation. There seemed to be an awful, immemorial linkage in several definite stages betwixt man and nameless infinity. The blasphemies which appeared on earth, it was hinted, came from the dark planet Yuggoth, at the rim of the solar system; but this was itself merely the populous outpost of a frightful interstellar race whose ultimate source must lie far outside even the Einsteinian space-time continuum[27] or greatest known cosmos.

Meanwhile we continued to discuss the black stone and the best way of getting it to Arkham—Akeley deeming it inadvisable to have me visit him at the scene of his nightmare studies. For some reason or other, Akeley was afraid to trust the thing to any ordinary or expected transportation route. His final idea was to take it across county to Bellows Falls and ship it on the Boston and Maine system through Keene and Winchendon and Fitchburg, even though this would necessitate his driving along somewhat lonelier and more forest-traversing hill roads than the main highway to Brattleboro. He said he had noticed a man around the express office at Brattleboro when he had sent the phonograph record, whose actions and expression had been far from reassuring. This man had seemed too anxious to talk with the clerks, and had taken the train on which the record was shipped. Akeley confessed that he had not felt strictly at ease about that record until he heard from me of its safe receipt.

About this time—the second week in July—another letter of mine went astray, as I learned through an anxious communication from Akeley. After that he told me to address him no more at Townshend, but to send all mail in care of the General Delivery at Brattleboro; whither he would make frequent trips either in his car or on the motor-coach line which had lately replaced passenger service on the lagging branch railway.[28] I could see that he was getting more and more anxious, for he went into much detail about the increased barking of the dogs on moonless nights, and about the fresh claw-prints he sometimes found in the road and in the mud at the back of his farmyard when morning came. Once he told about a veritable army of prints drawn up in a line facing an equally thick and resolute line of dog-tracks, and sent a loathsomely disturbing kodak picture to prove it. That was after a night on which the dogs had outdone themselves in barking and howling.

On the morning of Wednesday, July 18, I received a telegram from Bellows Falls, in which Akeley said he was expressing the black stone over the B. & M.[29] on Train No. 5508, leaving Bellows Falls at 12:15 p.m., standard time, and due at the North Station in Boston at 4:12 p.m. It ought, I calculated, to get up to Arkham at least by the next noon; and accordingly I stayed in all Thursday morning to receive it. But noon came and went without its advent, and when I telephoned down to the express office I was informed that no shipment for me had arrived. My next act, performed amidst a growing alarm, was to give a long-distance call to the express agent at the Boston North Station; and I was scarcely surprised to learn that my consignment had not appeared. Train No. 5508 had pulled in only 35 minutes late on the day before, but had contained no box addressed to me. The agent promised, however, to institute a searching inquiry; and I ended the day by sending Akeley a night-letter outlining the situation.

With commendable promptness a report came from the Boston office on the following afternoon, the agent telephoning as soon as he learned the facts. It seemed that the railway express clerk on No. 5508 had been able to recall an incident which might have much bearing on my loss—an argument with a very curious-voiced man, lean, sandy, and rustic-looking, when the train was waiting at Keene, NH, shortly after one o'clock standard time.

The man, he said, was greatly excited about a heavy box which he claimed to expect, but which was neither on the train nor entered on the company's books. He had given the name of Stanley Adams, and had had such a queerly thick droning voice, that it made the clerk abnormally dizzy and sleepy to listen to him. The clerk could not remember quite how the conversation had ended, but recalled starting into a fuller awakeness when the train began to move. The Boston agent added that this clerk was a young man of wholly unquestioned veracity and reliability, of known antecedents and long with the company.

That evening I went to Boston to interview the clerk in person, having obtained his name and address from the office. He was a frank, prepossessing fellow, but I saw that he could add nothing to his original account. Oddly, he was scarcely sure that he could even recognize the strange inquirer again. Realizing that he had no more to tell, I returned to

Arkham and sat up till morning writing letters to Akeley, to the express company, and to the police department and station agent in Keene. I felt that the strange-voiced man who had so queerly affected the clerk must have a pivotal place in the ominous business, and hoped that Keene station employees and telegraph-office records might tell something about him and about how he happened to make his inquiry when and where he did.

I must admit, however, that all my investigations came to nothing. The queer-voiced man had indeed been noticed around the Keene station in the early afternoon of July 18, and one lounger seemed to couple him vaguely with a heavy box; but he was altogether unknown, and had not been seen before or since. He had not visited the telegraph office or received any message so far as could be learned, nor had any message which might justly be considered a notice of the black stone's presence on No. 5508 come through the office for anyone. Naturally Akeley joined with me in conducting these inquiries, and even made a personal trip to Keene to question the people around the station; but his attitude toward the matter was more fatalistic than mine. He seemed to find the loss of the box a portentous and menacing fulfillment of inevitable tendencies, and had no real hope at all of its recovery. He spoke of the undoubted telepathic and hypnotic powers of the hill creatures and their agents, and in one letter hinted that he did not believe the stone was on this earth any longer. For my part, I was duly enraged, for I had felt there was at least a chance of learning profound and astonishing things from the old, blurred hieroglyphs. The matter would have rankled bitterly in my mind had not Akeley's immediate subsequent letters brought up a new phase of the whole horrible hill problem which at once seized all my attention.

IV.

The unknown things, Akeley wrote in a script grown pitifully tremulous, had begun to close in on him with a wholly new degree of determination. The nocturnal barking of the dogs whenever the moon was dim or absent was hideous now, and there had been attempts to molest him on the lonely roads he had to traverse by day. On the second of August, while bound for the village in his car, he had found a tree-trunk laid in his path at a point where the highway ran through a deep patch of woods; while the savage barking of the two great dogs he had with him told all too well of the things which must have been lurking near. What would have happened had the dogs not been there, he did not dare guess—but he never went out now without at least two of his faithful and powerful pack. Other road experiences had occurred on August 5th and 6th; a shot grazing his car on one occasion, and the barking of the dogs telling of unholy woodland presences on the other.

On August 15th I received a frantic letter which disturbed me greatly, and which made me wish Akeley could put aside his lonely reticence and call in the aid of the law. There had been frightful happenings on the night of the 12–13th, bullets flying outside the farm-house, and three of the twelve great dogs being found shot dead in the morning. There were myriads of claw-prints in the road, with the human prints of Walter Brown among them. Akeley had started to telephone to Brattleboro for more dogs, but the wire had gone dead before he had a chance to say much. Later he went to Brattleboro in his car, and learned there that linemen had found the main telephone cable neatly cut at a point where it ran through the deserted hills north of Newfane. But he was about to start home with four fine new dogs, and several cases of ammunition for his big-game repeating rifle. The letter was written at the post office in Brattleboro, and came through to me without delay.

My attitude toward the matter was by this time quickly slipping from a scientific to an alarmedly personal one. I was afraid for Akeley in his remote, lonely farmhouse, and half afraid for myself because of my now definite connection with the strange hill problem. The thing was reaching out so. Would it suck me in and engulf me? In replying to his letter I urged him to seek help, and hinted that I might take action myself if he did not. I spoke of visiting Vermont in person in spite of his wishes, and of helping him explain the situation to the proper authorities. In return, however, I received only a telegram from Bellows Falls which read thus:

APPRECIATE YOUR POSITION BUT CAN DO NOTHING. TAKE NO ACTION YOURSELF FOR IT COULD ONLY HARM BOTH. WAIT FOR EXPLANATION.
HENRY AKELY

But the affair was steadily deepening. Upon my replying to the telegram I received a shaky note from Akeley with the astonishing news that he had not only never sent the wire, but had not received the letter from me to which it was an obvious reply. Hasty inquiries by him at Bellows Falls had brought out that the message was deposited by a strange sandy-haired man with a curiously thick, droning voice, though more than this he could not learn. The clerk showed him the original text as scrawled in pencil by the sender, but the hand-writing was wholly unfamiliar. It was noticeable that the signature was misspelled—A-K-E-L-Y, without the second "E." Certain conjectures were inevitable, but amidst the obvious crisis he did not stop to elaborate upon them.

He spoke of the death of more dogs and the purchase of still others, and of the exchange of gunfire which had become a settled feature each moonless night. Brown's prints, and the prints of at least one or two more shod human figures, were now found regularly among the claw-prints in the road, and at the back of the farmyard. It was, Akeley admitted, a pretty bad business; and before long he would probably have to go to live with his California son whether or not he could sell the old place. But it was not easy to leave the only spot one could really think of as home. He must try to hang on a little longer; perhaps he could scare off the intruders—especially if he openly gave up all further attempts to penetrate their secrets.

Writing Akeley at once, I renewed my offers of aid, and spoke again of visiting him and helping him convince the authorities of his dire peril. In his reply he seemed less set against that plan than his past attitude would have led one to predict, but said he would like to hold off a little while longer—long enough to get his things in order and reconcile himself to the idea of leaving an almost morbidly cherished birthplace. People looked askance at his studies and speculations, and it would be better to get quietly off without setting the countryside in a turmoil and creating widespread doubts of his own sanity. He had had enough, he admitted, but he wanted to make a dignified exit if he could.

This letter reached me on the twenty-eighth of August, and I prepared and mailed as encouraging a reply as I could. Apparently the encouragement had effect, for Akeley had fewer terrors to report when he acknowledged my note. He was not very optimistic, though, and expressed the belief that it was only the full moon season which was holding the crea-tures off. He hoped there would not be many densely cloudy nights, and talked vaguely of boarding in Brattleboro when the moon waned. Again I wrote him encouragingly, but on September 5th there came a fresh communication which had obviously crossed my letter in the mails; and to this I could not give any such hopeful response. In view of its importance I believe I had better give it in full—as best I can do from memory of the shaky script. It ran substantially as follows:

Monday

Dear Wilmarth—

A rather discouraging P.S. to my last. Last night was thickly cloudy—though no rain—and not a bit of moonlight got through. Things were pretty bad, and I think the end is getting near, in spite of all we have hoped. After midnight something landed on the roof of the house, and the dogs all rushed up to see what it was. I could hear them snapping and tearing around, and then one managed to get on the roof by jumping from the low ell. There was a terrible fight up there, and I heard a frightful buzzing which I'll never forget. And then there was a shocking smell. About the same time bullets came through the window and nearly grazed me. I think the main line of the hill creatures had got close to the house when the dogs divided because of the roof business. What was up there I don't know yet, but I'm afraid the creatures are learning to steer better with their space wings. I put out the light and used the windows for loopholes, and raked all around the house with rifle fire aimed just high enough not to hit the dogs. That seemed to end the business, but in the morning I found great pools of blood in the yard, beside pools of a green sticky stuff that had the worst odour I have ever smelled. I climbed up on the roof and found more of the sticky stuff there. Five of the dogs were killed—I'm afraid I hit one by aiming too low, for he was shot in the back. Now I am setting the panes the shots broke, and am going to Brattleboro for more dogs. I guess the men at the kennels think I am crazy. Will drop another note later. Suppose I'll be ready for moving in a week or two, though it nearly kills me to think of it.

Hastily—Akeley

But this was not the only letter from Akeley to cross mine. On the next morning—September 6th—still another came; this time a frantic scrawl which utterly unnerved me and put me at a loss what to say or do next. Again I cannot do better than quote the text as faithfully as memory will let me.

Tuesday

Clouds didn't break, so no moon again—and going into the wane anyhow. I'd have the house wired for electricity and put in a searchlight if I didn't know they'd cut the cables as fast as they could be mended.

I think I am going crazy. It may be that all I have ever written you is a dream or madness. It was bad enough before, but this time it is too much. *They talked to me last night*—talked in that cursed buzzing voice and told me things *that I dare not repeat to you.* I heard them plainly over the barking of the dogs, and once when they were drowned out *a human voice helped them.* Keep out of this, Wilmarth—it is worse than either you or I ever suspected. *They don't mean to let me get to California now—they want to take me off alive, or what theoretically and mentally amounts to alive*—not only to Yuggoth, but beyond that—away outside the galaxy *and possibly beyond the last curved rim of space.* I told them I wouldn't go where they wish*, or in the terrible way they propose to take me,* but I'm afraid it will be no use. My place is so far out that they may come by day as well as by night before long. Six more dogs killed, and I felt presences all along the wooded parts of the road when I drove to Brattleboro today.

It was a mistake for me to try to send you that phonograph record and black stone. Better smash the record before it's too late. Will drop you another line tomorrow if I'm still here. Wish I could arrange to get my books and things to Brattleboro and board there. I would run off without anything if I could, but something inside my mind holds me back. I can slip out to Brattleboro, where I ought to be safe, but I feel just as much a prisoner there as at the house. And I seem to know that I couldn't get much farther even if I dropped everything and tried. It is horrible—don't get mixed up in this.

Yrs—Akeley

I did not sleep at all the night after receiving this terrible thing, and was utterly baffled as to Akeley's remaining degree of sanity. The substance of the note was wholly insane, yet the manner of expression—in view of all that had gone before—had a grimly potent quality of convincingness. I made no attempt to answer it, thinking it better to wait until Akeley might have time to reply to my latest communication. Such a reply indeed came on the following day, though the fresh material in it quite overshadowed any of the points brought up by the letter it nominally answered. Here is what I recall of the text, scrawled and blotted as it was in the course of a plainly frantic and hurried composition.

Wednesday

W—

Yr letter came, but it's no use to discuss anything any more. I am fully resigned. Wonder that I have even enough will power left to fight them off. Can't escape even if I were willing to give up everything and run. They'll get me.

Had a letter from them yesterday—R.F.D. man brought it while I was at Brattleboro. Typed and postmarked Bellows Falls. Tells what they want to do with me—I can't repeat it. Look out for yourself, too! Smash that record. Cloudy nights keep up, and moon waning all the time. Wish I dared to get help—it might brace up my will power—but everyone who would dare to come at all would call me crazy unless there happened to be some proof. Couldn't ask people to come for no reason at all—am all out of touch with everybody and have been for years.

But I haven't told you the worst, Wilmarth. Brace up to read this, for it will give you a shock. I am telling the truth, though. It is this—*I have seen and touched one of the things, or part of one of the things.* God, man, but it's awful! It was dead, of course. One of the dogs had it, and I found it near the kennel this morning. I tried to save it in the woodshed to convince people of the whole thing, but it all evaporated in a few hours. Nothing left. You know, all those things in the rivers were seen only on the first morning after the flood. And here's the worst. I tried to photograph it for you, but when I developed the film *there wasn't anything visible except the woodshed.* What can the thing have been made of? I saw it and felt it, and they all leave footprints. It was surely made of matter—but what kind of matter? The shape can't be described. It was a great crab with a lot of pyramided fleshy rings or knots of thick, ropy stuff covered with feelers where a man's head would be. That green sticky stuff is its blood or juice. And there are more of them due on earth any minute.

Walter Brown is missing—hasn't been seen loafing around any of his usual corners in the villages hereabouts. I must have got him with one of my shots, though the creatures always seem to try to take their dead and wounded away.

Got into town this afternoon without any trouble, but am afraid they're beginning to hold off because they're sure of me. Am writing this in Brattleboro P.O. This may be goodbye—if it is, write my son George Goodenough Akeley, 176 Pleasant St., San Diego, Cal., *but don't come up here.* Write the boy if you don't hear from me in a week, and watch the papers for news.

I'm going to play my last two cards now—if I have the will power left. First to try poison gas on the things (I've got the right chemicals and have fixed up masks for myself and the dogs) and then if that doesn't work, tell the sheriff. They can lock me in a madhouse if they want to—it'll be better than what the *other creatures* would do. Perhaps I can get them to pay attention to the prints around the house—they are faint, but I can find them every morning. Suppose, though, police would say I faked them somehow; for they all think I'm a queer character.

Must try to have a state policeman spend a night here and see for himself—though it would be just like the creatures to learn about it and hold off that night. They cut my wires whenever I try to telephone in the night—the linemen think it is very queer, and may testify for me if they don't go and imagine I cut them myself. I haven't tried to keep them repaired for over a week now.

I could get some of the ignorant people to testify for me about the reality of the horrors, but everybody laughs at what they say, and anyway, they have shunned my place for so long that they don't know any of the new events. You couldn't get one of those run-down farmers to come within a mile of my house for love or money. The mail-carrier hears what they say and jokes me about it—God! If I only dared tell him how real it is! I think I'll try to get him to notice the prints, but he comes in the afternoon and they're usually about gone by that time. If I kept one by setting a box or pan over it, he'd think surely it was a fake or joke.

Wish I hadn't gotten to be such a hermit, so folks don't drop around as they used to. I've never dared shew the black stone or the kodak pictures, or play that record, to anybody but the ignorant people. The others would say I faked the whole business and do nothing but laugh. But I may yet try shewing the pictures. They give those claw-prints clearly, even if the things that made them can't be photographed. What a shame nobody else saw that thing this morning before it went to nothing!

But I don't know as I care. After what I've been through, a madhouse is as good a place as any. The doctors can help me make up my mind to get away from this house, and that is all that will save me.

Write my son George if you don't hear soon. Goodbye, smash that record, and don't mix up in this.

Yrs—Akeley

The letter frankly plunged me into the blackest of terror. I did not know what to say in answer, but scratched off some incoherent words of advice and encouragement and sent them by registered mail. I recall urging Akeley to move to Brattleboro at once, and place himself under the protection of the authorities; adding that I would come to that town with the phonograph record and help convince the courts of his sanity. It was time, too, I think I wrote, to alarm the people generally against this thing in their midst. It will be observed that at this moment of stress my own belief in all Akeley had told and claimed was virtually complete, though I did think his failure to get a picture of the dead monster was due not to any freak of Nature but to some excited slip of his own.

V.

Then, apparently crossing my incoherent note and reaching me Saturday afternoon, September 8th, came that curiously different and calming letter neatly typed on a new machine; that strange letter of reassurance and invitation which must have marked so prodigious a transition in the whole nightmare drama of the lonely hills. Again I will quote from memory—seeking for special reasons to preserve as much of the flavor of the style as I can. It was postmarked Bellows Falls, and the signature as well as the body of the letter was typed—as is frequent with beginners in typing. The text, though, was marvelously accurate for a tyro's[30] work; and I concluded that Akeley must have used a machine at some previous period—perhaps in college. To say that the letter relieved me would be only fair, yet beneath my relief lay a substratum of uneasiness. If Akeley had been sane in his terror, was he now sane in his deliverance? And the sort of "improved rapport" mentioned … what was it? The entire thing implied such a diametrical reversal of Akeley's previous attitude! But here is the substance of the text, carefully transcribed from a memory in which I take some pride.

Townshend, Vermont,
Thursday, Sept. 6, 1928.

My dear Wilmarth:—

It gives me great pleasure to be able to set you at rest regarding all the silly things I've been writing you. I say "silly," although by that I mean my frightened attitude rather than my descriptions of certain phenomena. Those phenomena are real and important enough; my mistake had been in establishing an anomalous attitude toward them.

I think I mentioned that my strange visitors were beginning to communicate with me, and to attempt such communication. Last night this exchange of speech became actual. In response to certain signals I admitted to the house a messenger from those outside—a fellow-human, let me hasten to say. He told me much that neither you nor I had even begun to guess, and shewed clearly how totally we had misjudged and misinterpreted the purpose of the Outer Ones in maintaining their secret colony on this planet.

It seems that the evil legends about what they have offered to men, and what they wish in connexion with the earth, are wholly the result of an ignorant misconception of allegorical speech—speech, of course, moulded by cultural backgrounds and thought-habits vastly different from anything we dream of. My own conjectures, I freely own, shot as widely past the mark as any of the guesses of illiterate farmers and savage Indians. What I had thought morbid and shameful and ignominious[31] is in reality awesome and mind-expanding and even glorious—my previous estimate being merely a phase of man's eternal tendency to hate and fear and shrink from the *utterly different*.

Now I regret the harm I have inflicted upon these alien and incredible beings in the course of our nightly skirmishes. If only I had consented to talk peacefully and reasonably with them in the first place! But they bear me no grudge, their emotions being organised very differently from ours. It is their misfortune to have had as their human agents in Vermont some very inferior specimens—the late Walter Brown, for example. He prejudiced me vastly against them. Actually, they have never knowingly harmed men, but have often been cruelly wronged and spied upon by our species. There is a whole secret cult of evil men (a man of your mystical erudition will understand me when I link them with Hastur and the Yellow Sign) devoted to the purpose of tracking them down and injuring them on behalf of monstrous powers from other dimensions. It is against these aggressors—not against normal humanity—that the drastic precautions of the Outer Ones are directed. Incidentally, I learned that many of our lost letters were stolen not by the Outer Ones but by the emissaries of this malign cult.

All that the Outer Ones wish of man is peace and non-molestation and an increasing intellectual rapport. This latter is absolutely necessary now that our inventions and devices are expanding our knowledge and motions, and making it more and more impossible for the Outer Ones' necessary outposts to exist secretly on this planet. The alien beings desire to know mankind more fully, and to have a few of mankind's philosophic and scientific leaders know more about them. With such an exchange of knowledge all perils will pass, and a satisfactory modus vivendi be established. The very idea of any attempt to enslave or degrade mankind is ridiculous.

As a beginning of this improved rapport, the Outer Ones have naturally chosen me—whose knowledge of them is already so considerable—as their primary interpreter on earth. Much was told me last night—facts of the most stupendous and vista-opening nature—and more will be subsequently communicated to me both orally and in writing. I shall not be called upon to make any trip outside just yet, though I shall probably wish to do so later on—employing special means and transcending everything which we have hitherto been accustomed to regard as human experience. My house will be besieged no longer. Everything has reverted to normal, and the dogs will have no further occupation. In place of terror I have been given a rich boon of knowledge and intellectual adventure which few other mortals have ever shared.

The Outer Beings are perhaps the most marvellous organic things in or beyond all space and time—members of a cosmos-wide race of which all other life-forms are merely degenerate variants. They are more vegetable than animal, if these terms can be applied to the sort of matter composing them, and have a somewhat fungoid structure; though the presence of a chlorophyll-like substance and a very singular nutritive system differentiate them altogether from true cormophytic fungi. Indeed, the type is composed of a form of matter totally alien to our part of space—with electrons having a wholly different vibration-rate. That is why the beings cannot be photographed on the ordinary camera films and plates of our known universe, even though our eyes can see them. With proper knowledge, however, any good chemist could make a photographic emulsion which would record their images.

The genus is unique in its ability to traverse the heatless and airless interstellar void in full corporeal form, and some of its variants cannot do this without mechanical aid or curious surgical transpositions. Only a few species have the ether-resisting wings characteristic of the Vermont variety. Those inhabiting certain remote peaks in the Old World were brought in other ways. Their external resemblance to animal life, and to the sort of structure we understand as material, is a matter of parallel evolution rather than of close kinship. Their brain-capacity exceeds that of any other surviving life-form, although the winged types of our hill country are by no means the most highly developed. Telepathy is their usual means of discourse, though they have rudimentary vocal organs which, after a slight operation (for surgery is an incredibly expert and every-day thing among them), can roughly duplicate the speech of such types of organism as still use speech.

Their main *immediate* abode is a still undiscovered and almost lightless planet at the very edge of our solar system—beyond Neptune, and the ninth in distance from the sun.[32] It is, as we have inferred, the object mystically hinted at as "Yuggoth" in certain ancient and forbidden writings; and it will soon be the scene of a strange focussing of thought upon our world in an effort to facilitate mental rapport. I would not be surprised if astronomers became sufficiently sensitive to these thought-currents to discover Yuggoth when the Outer Ones wish them to do so. But Yuggoth, of course, is only the stepping-stone. The main body of the beings inhabits strangely organised abysses wholly beyond the utmost reach of any human imagination. The space-time globule which we recognise as the totality of all cosmic entity is only an atom in the genuine infinity which is theirs. *And as much of this infinity as any human brain can hold is eventually to be opened up to me, as it has been to not more than fifty other men since the human race has existed.*

You will probably call this raving at first, Wilmarth, but in time you will appreciate the titanic opportunity I have stumbled upon. I want you to share as much of it as is possible, and to that end must tell you thousands of things that won't go on paper. In the past I have warned you not to come to see me. Now that all is safe, I take pleasure in rescinding that warning and inviting you.

Can't you make a trip up here before your college term opens? It would be marvellously delightful if you could. Bring along the phonograph record and all my letters to you as consultative data—we shall need them in piecing together the whole tremendous story. You might bring the kodak prints, too, since I seem to have mislaid the negatives and my own prints in all this recent excitement. But what a wealth of facts I have to add to all this groping and tentative material—*and what a stupendous device I have to supplement my additions!*

Don't hesitate—I am free from espionage now, and you will not meet anything unnatural or disturbing. Just come along and let my car meet you at the Brattleboro station—prepare to stay as long as you can, and expect many an evening of discussion of things beyond all human conjecture. Don't tell anyone about it, of course—for this matter must not get to the promiscuous public.

The train service to Brattleboro is not bad—you can get a time-table in Boston. Take the B. & M. to Greenfield, and then change for the brief remainder of the way. I suggest your taking the convenient 4:10 p.m.—standard—from Boston. This gets into Greenfield at 7:35, and at 9:19 a train leaves there which reaches Brattleboro at 10:01. That is week-days. Let me know the date and I'll have my car on hand at the station.

Pardon this typed letter, but my handwriting has grown shaky of late, as you know, and I don't feel equal to long stretches of script. I got this new Corona in Brattleboro yesterday—it seems to work very well.

Awaiting word, and hoping to see you shortly with the phonograph record and all my letters—and the kodak prints—

I am
Yours in anticipation,
Henry W. Akeley

TO ALBERT N. WILMARTH, ESQ.,
MISKATONIC UNIVERSITY,
ARKHAM, MASS.

The complexity of my emotions upon reading, re-reading, and pondering over this strange and unlooked-for letter is past adequate description. I have said that I was at once relieved and made uneasy, but this expresses only crudely the overtones of diverse and largely subconscious feelings which comprised both the relief and the uneasiness. To begin with, the thing was so antipodally at variance with the whole chain of horrors preceding it—the change of mood from stark terror to cool complacency and even exultation was so unheralded, lightning-like, and complete! I could scarcely believe that a single day could so alter the psychological perspective of one who had written that final frenzied bulletin of Wednesday, no matter what relieving disclosures that day might have brought. At certain moments a sense of conflicting unrealities made me wonder whether this whole distantly reported drama of fantastic forces were not a kind of half-illusory dream created largely within my own mind. Then I thought of the phonograph record and gave way to still greater bewilderment.

The letter seemed so unlike anything which could have been expected! As I analyzed my impression, I saw that it consisted of two distinct phases. First, granting that Akeley had been sane before and was still sane, the indicated change in the situation itself was so swift and unthinkable. And secondly, the change in Akeley's own manner, attitude, and language was so vastly beyond the normal or the predictable. The man's whole personality seemed to have undergone an insidious mutation—a mutation so deep that one could scarcely reconcile his two aspects with the supposition that both represented equal sanity. Word-choice, spelling—all were subtly different. And with my academic sensitiveness to prose style, I could trace profound divergences in his commonest reactions and rhythm-responses. Certainly, the emotional cataclysm or revelation which could produce so radical an overturn must be an extreme one indeed! Yet in another way the letter seemed quite characteristic of Akeley. The same old passion for infinity—the same old scholarly inquis-itiveness. I could not a moment—or more than a moment—credit the idea of spuriousness or malign substitution. Did not the invitation—the willingness to have me test the truth of the letter in person—prove its genuineness?

I did not retire Saturday night, but sat up thinking of the shadows and marvels behind the letter I had received. My mind, aching from the quick succession of monstrous con-ceptions it had been forced to confront during the last four months, worked upon this star-tling new material in a cycle of doubt and acceptance which repeated most of the steps experienced in facing the earlier wonders; till long before dawn a burning interest and curiosity had begun to replace the original storm of perplexity and uneasiness. Mad or sane, metamorphosed or merely relieved, the chances were that Akeley had actually encoun-tered some stupendous change of perspective in his hazardous research; some change at once diminishing his danger—real or fancied—and opening dizzy new vistas of cosmic and superhuman knowledge. My own zeal for the unknown flared up to meet his, and I felt myself touched by the contagion of the morbid barrier-breaking. To shake off the mad-dening and wearying limitations of time and space and natural law—to be linked with the vast outside—to come close to the nighted and abysmal secrets of the infinite and the ulti-mate—surely such a thing was worth the risk of one's life, soul, and sanity! And Akeley had said there was no longer any peril—he had invited me to visit him instead of warning me away as before. I tingled at the thought of what he might now have to tell me—there was an almost paralyzing fascination in the thought of sitting in that lonely and lately belea-guered farmhouse with a man who had talked with actual emissaries from outer space; sit-ting there with the terrible record and the pile of letters in which Akeley had summarized his earlier conclusions.

So late Sunday morning I telegraphed Akeley that I would meet him in Brattleboro on the following Wednesday—September 12th—if that date were convenient for him. In only one respect did I depart from his suggestions, and that concerned the choice of a train. Frankly, I did not feel like arriving in that haunted Vermont region late at night; so instead of accepting the train he chose I telephoned the station and devised another arrangement.

By rising early and taking the 8:07 a.m. (standard) into Boston, I could catch the 9:25 for Greenfield; arriving there at 12:22 noon. This connected exactly with a train reaching Brattleboro at 1:08 p.m.—a much more comfortable hour than 10:01 for meeting Akeley and riding with him into the close-packed, secret-guarding hills.

I mentioned this choice in my telegram, and was glad to learn in the reply which came toward evening that it had met with my prospective host's endorsement. His wire ran thus:

> ARRANGEMENT SATISFACTORY. WILL MEET 1:08 TRAIN WEDNESDAY. DON'T FORGET RECORD AND LETTERS AND PRINTS. KEEP DESTINATION QUIET. EXPECT GREAT REVE-LATIONS.
>
> AKELEY.

Receipt of this message in direct response to one sent to Akeley—and necessarily delivered to his house from the Townshend station either by official messenger or by a restored telephone service—removed any lingering subconscious doubts I may have had about the authorship of the perplexing letter. My relief was marked—indeed, it was greater than I could account for at that time; since all such doubts had been rather deeply buried. But I slept soundly and long that night, and was eagerly busy with preparations during the ensuing two days.

VI.

On Wednesday I started as agreed, taking with me a valise full of simple necessities and scientific data, including the hideous phonograph record, the kodak prints, and the entire file of Akeley's correspondence. As requested, I had told no one where I was going; for I could see that the matter demanded utmost privacy, even allowing for its most favorable turns. The thought of actual mental contact with alien, outside entities was stupefying enough to my trained and somewhat prepared mind; and this being so, what might one think of its effect on the vast masses of uninformed laymen? I do not know whether dread or adventurous expectancy was uppermost in me as I changed trains in Boston and began the long westward run out of familiar regions into those I knew less thoroughly. Waltham—Concord—Ayer—Fitchburg—Gardner—Athol—

My train reached Greenfield seven minutes late, but the northbound connecting express had been held. Transferring in haste, I felt a curious breathlessness as the cars rumbled on through the early afternoon sunlight into territories I had always read of but had never before visited. I knew I was entering an altogether older-fashioned and more primitive New England than the mechanized, urbanized coastal and southern areas where all my life had been spent; an unspoiled, ancestral New England without the foreigners and factory-smoke, billboards and concrete roads, of the sections which modernity has touched. There would be odd survivals of that continuous native life whose deep roots make it the one authentic outgrowth of the landscape—the continuous native life which keeps alive strange ancient memories, and fertilizes the soil for shadowy, marvelous, and seldom-mentioned beliefs.

Now and then I saw the blue Connecticut River gleaming in the sun, and after leaving Northfield we crossed it. Ahead loomed green and cryptical[33] hills, and when the conductor came around I learned that I was at last in Vermont. He told me to set my watch back an hour, since the northern hill country will have no dealings with new-fangled daylight time schemes.[34] As I did so it seemed to me that I was likewise turning the calendar back a century.

The train kept close to the river, and across in New Hampshire I could see the approaching slope of steep Wantastiquet,[35] about which singular old legends cluster. Then streets appeared on my left, and a green island showed in the stream on my right. People rose and filed to the door, and I followed them. The car stopped, and I alighted beneath the long train-shed of the Brattleboro station.

Looking over the line of waiting motors I hesitated a moment to see which one might turn out to be the Akeley Ford, but my identity was divined before I could take the initiative. And yet it was clearly not Akeley himself who advanced to meet me with an outstretched hand and a mellowly phrased query as to whether I was indeed Mr. Albert N. Wilmarth of Arkham. This man bore no resemblance to the bearded, grizzled Akeley of the snapshot; but was a younger and more urban person, fashionably dressed, and wearing only a small, dark moustache. His cultivated voice held an odd and almost disturbing hint of vague familiarity, though I could not definitely place it in my memory.

As I surveyed him I heard him explaining that he was a friend of my prospective host's who had come down from Townshend in his stead. Akeley, he declared, had suffered a sudden attack of some asthmatic trouble, and did not feel equal to making a trip in the outdoor air. It was not serious, however, and there was to be no change in plans regarding my visit. I could not make out just how much this Mr. Noyes—as he announced himself—knew of Akeley's researches and discoveries, though it seemed to me that his casual manner stamped him as a comparative outsider. Remembering what a hermit Akeley had been, I was a trifle surprised at the ready availability of such a friend; but did not let my puzzlement deter me from entering the motor to which he gestured me. It was not the small ancient car I had expected from Akeley's descriptions, but a large and immaculate specimen of recent pattern—apparently Noyes's own, and bearing Massachusetts license plates with the amusing "sacred codfish" device of that year. My guide, I concluded, must be a summer transient in the Townshend region.

Noyes climbed into the car beside me and started it at once. I was glad that he did not overflow with conversation, for some peculiar atmospheric tensity made me feel disinclined to talk. The town seemed very attractive in the afternoon sunlight as we swept up an incline and turned to the right into the main street. It drowsed like the older New England cities which one remembers from boyhood, and something in the collocation of roofs and steeples and chimneys and brick walls formed contours touching deep viol-strings of ancestral emotion. I could tell that I was at the gateway of a region half-bewitched through the piling-up of unbroken time-accumulations; a region where old, strange things have had a chance to grow and linger because they have never been stirred up.

As we passed out of Brattleboro my sense of constraint and foreboding increased, for a vague quality in the hill-crowded countryside with its towering, threatening, close-pressing green and granite slopes hinted at obscure secrets and immemorial survivals which might or might not be hostile to mankind. For a time our course followed a broad, shallow river which flowed down from unknown hills in the north, and I shivered when my companion told me it was the West River. It was in this stream, I recalled from newspaper items, that one of the morbid crab-like beings had been seen floating after the floods.

Gradually the country around us grew wilder and more deserted. Archaic covered bridges lingered fearsomely out of the past in pockets of the hills, and the half-abandoned railway track paralleling the river seemed to exhale a nebulously visible air of desolation.

There were awesome sweeps of vivid valley where great cliffs rose, New England's virgin granite showing grey and austere through the verdure that scaled the crests. There were gorges where untamed streams leaped, bearing down toward the river the unimagined secrets of a thousand pathless peaks. Branching away now and then were narrow, half-concealed roads that bored their way through solid, luxuriant masses of forest among whose primal trees whole armies of elemental spirits might well lurk. As I saw these I thought of how Akeley had been molested by unseen agencies on his drives along this very route, and did not wonder that such things could be.

The quaint, sightly village of Newfane, reached in less than an hour, was our last link with that world which man can definitely call his own by virtue of conquest and complete occupancy. After that we cast off all allegiance to immediate, tangible, and time-touched things, and entered a fantastic world of hushed unreality in which the narrow, ribbon-like road rose and fell and curved with an almost sentient and purposeful caprice[36] amidst the tenantless green peaks and half-deserted valleys. Except for the sound of the motor, and the faint stir of the few lonely farms we passed at infrequent intervals, the only thing that reached my ears was the gurgling, insidious trickle of strange waters from numberless hidden fountains in the shadowy woods.

The nearness and intimacy of the dwarfed, domed hills now became veritably breathtaking. Their steepness and abruptness were even greater than I had imagined from hearsay, and suggested nothing in common with the prosaic objective world we know. The dense, unvisited woods on those inaccessible slopes seemed to harbor alien and incredible things, and I felt that the very outline of the hills themselves held some strange and aeon-forgotten meaning, as if they were vast hieroglyphs left by a rumored titan race whose glories live only in rare, deep dreams. All the legends of the past, and all the stupefying imputations of Henry Akeley's letters and exhibits, welled up in my memory to heighten the atmosphere of tension and growing menace. The purpose of my visit, and the frightful abnormalities it postulated, struck me all at once with a chill sensation that nearly overbalanced my ardor for strange delvings.

My guide must have noticed my disturbed attitude; for as the road grew wilder and more irregular, and our motion slower and more jolting, his occasional pleasant comments expanded into a steadier flow of discourse. He spoke of the beauty and weirdness of the country, and revealed some acquaintance with the folklore studies of my prospective host. From his polite questions it was obvious that he knew I had come for a scientific purpose, and that I was bringing data of some importance; but he gave no sign of appreciating the depth and awfulness of the knowledge which Akeley had finally reached.

His manner was so cheerful, normal, and urbane that his remarks ought to have calmed and reassured me; but oddly enough, I felt only the more disturbed as we bumped and veered onward into the unknown wilderness of hills and woods. At times it seemed as if he were pumping me to see what I knew of the monstrous secrets of the place, and with every fresh utterance that vague, teasing, baffling familiarity in his voice increased. It was not an ordinary or healthy familiarity despite the thoroughly wholesome and cultivated nature of the voice. I somehow linked it with forgotten nightmares, and felt that I might go mad if I recognized it. If any good excuse had existed, I think I would have turned back from my visit. As it was, I could not well do so—and it occurred to me that a cool, scientific conversation with Akeley himself after my arrival would help greatly to pull me together.

Besides, there was a strangely calming element of cosmic beauty in the hypnotic landscape through which we climbed and plunged fantastically. Time had lost itself in the labyrinths behind, and around us stretched only the flowering waves of faery and the recaptured loveliness of vanished centuries—the hoary groves, the untainted pastures edged with gay autumnal blossoms, and at vast intervals the small brown farmsteads nestling amidst huge trees beneath vertical precipices of fragrant brier and meadow-grass. Even the sunlight assumed a supernal glamour, as if some special atmosphere or exhalation mantled the whole region. I had seen nothing like it before save in the magic vistas that sometimes form the backgrounds of Italian primitives. Sodoma[37] and Leonardo[38] conceived such expanses, but only in the distance, and through the vaultings of Renaissance arcades. We were now burrowing bodily through the midst of the picture, and I seemed to find in its necromancy[39] a thing I had innately known or inherited, and for which I had always been vainly searching.

Suddenly, after rounding an obtuse angle at the top of a sharp ascent, the car came to a standstill. On my left, across a well-kept lawn which stretched to the road and flaunted a border of whitewashed stones, rose a white, two-and-a-half-story house of unusual size and elegance for the region, with a congeries[40] of contiguous or arcade-linked barns, sheds, and windmill behind and to the right. I recognized it at once from the snapshot I had received, and was not surprised to see the name of Henry Akeley on the galvanized-iron mail-box near the road. For some distance back of the house a level stretch of marshy and sparsely wooded land extended, beyond which soared a steep, thickly forested hillside ending in a jagged leafy crest. This latter, I knew, was the summit of Dark Mountain, half way up which we must have climbed already.

Alighting from the car and taking my valise, Noyes asked me to wait while he went in and notified Akeley of my advent. He himself, he added, had important business elsewhere, and could not stop for more than a moment. As he briskly walked up the path to the house I climbed out of the car myself, wishing to stretch my legs a little before settling down to a sedentary conversation. My feeling of nervousness and tension had risen to a maximum again now that I was on the actual scene of the morbid beleaguering described so hauntingly in Akeley's letters, and I honestly dreaded the coming discussions which were to link me with such alien and forbidden worlds.

Close contact with the utterly bizarre is often more terrifying than inspiring, and it did not cheer me to think that this very bit of dusty road was the place where those monstrous tracks and that fetid green ichor[41] had been found after moonless nights of fear and death. Idly I noticed that none of Akeley's dogs seemed to be about. Had he sold them all as soon as the Outer Ones made peace with him? Try as I might, I could not have the same confidence in the depth and sincerity of that peace which appeared in Akeley's final and queerly different letter. After all, he was a man of much simplicity and with little worldly experience. Was there not, perhaps, some deep and sinister undercurrent beneath the surface of the new alliance?

Led by my thoughts, my eyes turned downward to the powdery road surface which had held such hideous testimonies. The last few days had been dry, and tracks of all sorts cluttered the rutted, irregular highway despite the unfrequented nature of the district. With a vague curiosity I began to trace the outline of some of the heterogeneous impressions, trying meanwhile to curb the flights of macabre fancy which the place and its memories suggested. There was something menacing and uncomfortable in the funereal stillness, in the muffled, subtle trickle of distant brooks, and in the crowding green peaks and black-wooded precipices that choked the narrow horizon.

And then an image shot into my consciousness which made those vague menaces and flights of fancy seem mild and insignificant indeed. I have said that I was scanning the miscellaneous prints in the road with a kind of idle curiosity—but all at once that curiosity was shockingly snuffed out by a sudden and paralyzing gust of active terror. For though the dust tracks were in general confused and overlapping, and unlikely to arrest any casual gaze, my restless vision had caught certain details near the spot where the path to the house joined the highway; and had recognized beyond doubt or hope the frightful significance of those details. It was not for nothing, alas, that I had pored for hours over the kodak views of the Outer Ones' claw-prints which Akeley had sent. Too well did I know the marks of those loathsome nippers, and that hint of ambiguous direction which stamped the horrors as no creatures of this planet. No chance had been left me for merciful mistake. Here, indeed, in objective form before my own eyes, and surely made not many hours ago, were at least three marks which stood out blasphemously among the surprising plethora of blurred footprints leading to and from the Akeley farmhouse. They were the hellish tracks of the living fungi from Yuggoth.

I pulled myself together in time to stifle a scream. After all, what more was there than I might have expected, assuming that I had really believed Akeley's letters? He had spoken of making peace with the things. Why, then, was it strange that some of them had visited his house? But the terror was stronger than the reassurance. Could any man be expected to look unmoved for the first time upon the claw-marks of animate beings from outer depths of space? Just then I saw Noyes emerge from the door and approach with a brisk step. I must, I reflected, keep command of myself, for the chances were this genial friend knew nothing of Akeley's profoundest and most stupendous probings into the forbidden.

Akeley, Noyes hastened to inform me, was glad and ready to see me; although his sudden attack of asthma would prevent him from being a very competent host for a day or two. These spells hit him hard when they came, and were always accompanied by a debilitating fever and general weakness. He never was good for much while they lasted—had to talk in a whisper, and was very clumsy and feeble in getting about. His feet and ankles swelled, too, so that he had to bandage them like a gouty old beef-eater. Today he was in rather bad shape, so that I would have to attend very largely to my own needs; but he was none the less eager for conversation. I would find him in the study at the left of the front hall—the room where the blinds were shut. He had to keep the sunlight out when he was ill, for his eyes were very sensitive.

As Noyes bade me adieu and rode off northward in his car I began to walk slowly toward the house. The door had been left ajar for me; but before approaching and entering I cast a searching glance around the whole place, trying to decide what had struck me as so intangibly queer about it. The barns and sheds looked trimly prosaic enough, and I noticed Akeley's battered Ford in its capacious, unguarded shelter. Then the secret of the queerness reached me. It was the total silence. Ordinarily a farm is at least moderately murmurous from its various kinds of livestock, but here all signs of life were missing. What of the hens and the hogs? The cows, of which Akeley had said he possessed several, might conceivably be out to pasture, and the dogs might possibly have been sold; but the absence of any trace of cackling or grunting was truly singular.

I did not pause long on the path, but resolutely entered the open house door and closed it behind me. It had cost me a distinct psychological effort to do so, and now that I was shut inside I had a momentary longing for precipitate retreat. Not that the place was in the least sinister in visual suggestion; on the contrary, I thought the graceful late-colonial hallway very tasteful and wholesome, and admired the evident breeding of the man who had furnished it. What made me wish to flee was something very attenuated and indefinable. Perhaps it was a certain odd odor which I thought I noticed—though I well knew how common musty odors are in even the best of ancient farmhouses.

VII.

Refusing to let these cloudy qualms overmaster me, I recalled Noyes's instructions and pushed open the six-paneled, brass-latched white door on my left. The room beyond was darkened, as I had known before; and as I entered it I noticed that the queer odor was stronger there. There likewise appeared to be some faint, half-imaginary rhythm or vibration in the air. For a moment the closed blinds allowed me to see very little, but then a kind of apologetic hacking or whispering sound drew my attention to a great easy-chair in the farther, darker corner of the room. Within its shadowy depths I saw the white blur of a man's face and hands; and in a moment I had crossed to greet the figure who had tried to speak. Dim though the light was, I perceived that this was indeed my host. I had studied the kodak picture repeatedly, and there could be no mistake about this firm, weather-beaten face with the cropped, grizzled beard.

But as I looked again my recognition was mixed with sadness and anxiety; for certainly, this face was that of a very sick man. I felt that there must be something more than asthma behind that strained, rigid, immobile expression and unwinking glassy stare; and realized how terribly the strain of his frightful experiences must have told on him. Was it not enough to break any human being—even a younger man than this intrepid delver into the forbidden? The strange and sudden relief, I feared, had come too late to save him from something like a general breakdown. There was a touch of the pitiful in the limp, lifeless way his lean hands rested in his lap. He had on a loose dressing-gown, and was swathed around the head and high around the neck with a vivid yellow scarf or hood.

And then I saw that he was trying to talk in the same hacking whisper with which he had greeted me. It was a hard whisper to catch at first, since the grey moustache concealed all movements of the lips, and something in its timbre disturbed me greatly; but by concentrating my attention I could soon make out its purport surprisingly well. The accent was by no means a rustic one, and the language was even more polished than correspondence had led me to expect.

"Mr. Wilmarth, I presume? You must pardon my not rising. I am quite ill, as Mr. Noyes must have told you; but I could not resist having you come just the same. You know what I wrote in my last letter—there is so much to tell you tomorrow when I shall feel better. I can't say how glad I am to see you in person after all our many letters. You have the file with you, of course? And the kodak prints and record? Noyes put your valise in the hall—I suppose you saw it. For tonight I fear you'll have to wait on yourself to a great extent. Your room is upstairs—the one over this—and you'll see the bathroom door open at the head of the staircase. There's a meal spread for you in the dining-room—right through this door at your right—which you can take whenever you feel like it. I'll be a better host tomorrow—but just now weakness leaves me helpless.

"Make yourself at home—you might take out the letters and pictures and record and put them on the table here before you go upstairs with your bag. It is here that we shall discuss them—you can see my phonograph on that corner stand.

"No, thanks—there's nothing you can do for me. I know these spells of old. Just come back for a little quiet visiting before night, and then go to bed when you please. I'll rest right here—perhaps sleep here all night as I often do. In the morning I'll be far better able to go into the things we must go into. You realise, of course, the utterly stupendous nature of the matter before us. To us, as to only a few men on this earth, there will be opened up gulfs of time and space and knowledge beyond anything within the conception of human science and philosophy.

"Do you know that Einstein is wrong, and that certain objects and forces can move with a velocity greater than that of light? With proper aid I expect to go backward and forward in time, and actually see and feel the earth of remote past and future epochs. You can't imagine the degree to which those beings have carried science. There is nothing they can't do with the mind and body of living organisms. I expect to visit other planets, and even other stars and galaxies. The first trip will be to Yuggoth, the nearest world fully peopled by the beings. It is a strange dark orb at the very rim of our solar system—unknown to earthly astronomers as yet. But I must have written you about this. At the proper time, you know, the beings there will direct thought-currents toward us and cause it to be discovered—or perhaps let one of their human allies give the scientists a hint.

"There are mighty cities on Yuggoth—great tiers of terraced towers built of black stone like the specimen I tried to send you. That came from Yuggoth. The sun shines there no brighter than a star, but the beings need no light. They have other, subtler senses, and put no windows in their great houses and temples. Light even hurts and hampers and confuses them, for it does not exist at all in the black cosmos outside time and space where they came from originally. To visit Yuggoth would drive any weak man mad—yet I am going there. The black rivers of pitch that flow under those mysterious Cyclopean bridges—things built by some elder race extinct and forgotten before the things came to Yuggoth from the ultimate voids—ought to be enough to make any man a Dante or Poe if he can keep sane long enough to tell what he has seen.

"But remember—that dark world of fungoid gardens and windowless cities isn't really terrible. It is only to us that it would seem so. Probably this world seemed just as terrible to the beings when they first explored it in the primal age. You know they were here long before the fabulous epoch of Cthulhu was over, and remember all about sunken R'lyeh when it was above the waters. They've been inside the earth, too—there are openings which human beings know nothing of—some of them in these very Vermont hills—and great worlds of unknown life down there; blue-litten K'n-yan, red-litten Yoth, and black, lightless N'kai. It's from N'kai that frightful Tsathoggua came—you know, the amorphous, toad-like god-creature mentioned in the *Pnakotic Manuscripts*[42] and the *Necronomicon* and the Commoriom myth-cycle preserved by the Atlantean high-priest Klarkash-Ton.

"But we will talk of all this later on. It must be four or five o'clock by this time. Better bring the stuff from your bag, take a bite, and then come back for a comfortable chat."

Very slowly I turned and began to obey my host; fetching my valise, extracting and depositing the desired articles, and finally ascending to the room designated as mine. With the memory of that roadside claw-print fresh in my mind, Akeley's whispered paragraphs had affected me queerly; and the hints of familiarity with this unknown world of fungous life—forbidden Yuggoth—made my flesh creep more than I cared to own. I was tremendously sorry about Akeley's illness, but had to confess that his hoarse whisper had a hateful as well as pitiful quality. If only he wouldn't gloat so about Yuggoth and its black secrets!

My room proved a very pleasant and well-furnished one, devoid alike of the musty odor and disturbing sense of vibration; and after leaving my valise there I descended again to greet Akeley and take the lunch he had set out for me. The dining-room was just beyond the study, and I saw that a kitchen ell extended still farther in the same direction. On the dining-table an ample array of sandwiches, cake, and cheese awaited me, and a Thermos-bottle beside a cup and saucer testified that hot coffee had not been forgotten. After a well-relished meal I poured myself a liberal cup of coffee, but found that the culinary standard had suffered a lapse in this one detail. My first spoonful revealed a faintly unpleasant acrid taste, so that I did not take more. Throughout the lunch I thought of Akeley sitting silently in the great chair in the darkened next room. Once I went in to beg him to share the repast, but he whispered that he could eat nothing as yet. Later on, just before he slept, he would take some malted milk—all he ought to have that day.

After lunch I insisted on clearing the dishes away and washing them in the kitchen sink—incidentally emptying the coffee which I had not been able to appreciate. Then returning to the darkened study I drew up a chair near my host's corner and prepared for such conversation as he might feel inclined to conduct. The letters, pictures, and record were still on the large center-table, but for the nonce[43] we did not have to draw upon them. Before long I forgot even the bizarre odor and curious suggestions of vibration.

I have said that there were things in some of Akeley's letters—especially the second and most voluminous one—which I would not dare to quote or even form into words on paper. This hesitancy applies with still greater force to the things I heard whispered that evening in the darkened room among the lonely haunted hills. Of the extent of the cosmic horrors unfolded by that raucous voice I cannot even hint. He had known hideous things before, but what he had learned since making his pact with the Outside Things was almost too much for sanity to bear. Even now I absolutely refuse to believe what he implied about the constitution of ultimate infinity, the juxtaposition of dimensions, and the frightful position of our known cosmos of space and time in the unending chain of linked cosmos-atoms which makes up the immediate super-cosmos of curves, angles, and material and semi-material electronic organization.

Never was a sane man more dangerously close to the arcana of basic entity—never was an organic brain nearer to utter annihilation in the chaos that transcends form and force and symmetry. I learned whence Cthulhu first came, and why half the great temporary stars of history had flared forth. I guessed—from hints which made even my informant pause timidly—the secret behind the Magellanic Clouds and globular nebulae, and the black truth veiled by the immemorial allegory of Tao. The nature of the Doels was plainly revealed, and I was told the essence (though not the source) of the Hounds of Tindalos. The legend of Yig, Father of Serpents, remained figurative no longer, and I started with loathing when told of the monstrous nuclear chaos beyond angled space which the *Necronomicon* had mercifully cloaked under the name of Azathoth.[44] It was shocking to have the foulest nightmares of secret myth cleared up in concrete terms whose stark, morbid hatefulness exceeded the boldest hints of ancient and mediaeval mystics. Ineluctably I was led to believe that the first whisperers of these accursed tales must have had discourse with Akeley's Outer Ones, and perhaps have visited outer cosmic realms as Akeley now proposed visiting them.

I was told of the Black Stone and what it implied, and was glad that it had not reached me. My guesses about those hieroglyphics had been all too correct! And yet Akeley now seemed reconciled to the whole fiendish system he had stumbled upon; reconciled and eager to probe farther into the monstrous abyss. I wondered what beings he had talked with since his last letter to me, and whether many of them had been as human as that first emissary he had mentioned. The tension in my head grew insufferable, and I built up all sorts of wild theories about the queer, persistent odor and those insidious hints of vibration in the darkened room.

Night was falling now, and as I recalled what Akeley had written me about those earlier nights I shuddered to think there would be no moon. Nor did I like the way the farmhouse nestled in the lee of that colossal forested slope leading up to Dark Mountain's unvisited crest. With Akeley's permission I lighted a small oil lamp, turned it low, and set it on a distant bookcase beside the ghostly bust of Milton; but afterward I was sorry I had done so, for it made my host's strained, immobile face and listless hands look damnably abnormal and corpse-like. He seemed half-incapable of motion, though I saw him nod stiffly once in a while.

After what he had told, I could scarcely imagine what profounder secrets he was saving for the morrow; but at last it developed that his trip to Yuggoth and beyond—and my own possible participation in it—was to be the next day's topic. He must have been amused by the start of horror I gave at hearing a cosmic voyage on my part proposed, for his head wobbled violently when I showed my fear. Subsequently he spoke very gently of how human beings might accomplish—and several times had accomplished—the seemingly impossible flight across the interstellar void. It seemed that complete human bodies did not indeed make the trip, but that the prodigious surgical, biological, chemical, and mechanical skill of the Outer Ones had found a way to convey human brains without their concomitant physical structure.

There was a harmless way to extract a brain, and a way to keep the organic residue alive during its absence. The bare, compact cerebral matter was then immersed in an occasionally replenished fluid within an ether-tight cylinder of a metal mined in Yuggoth, certain electrodes reaching through and connecting at will with elaborate instruments capable of duplicating the three vital faculties of sight, hearing, and speech. For the winged fungus-beings to carry the brain-cylinders intact through space was an easy matter. Then, on every planet covered by their civilization, they would find plenty of adjustable faculty-instruments capable of being connected with the encased brains; so that after a little fitting these travelling intelligences could be given a full sensory and articulate life—albeit a bodiless and mechanical one—at each stage of their journeying through and beyond the space-time continuum. It was as simple as carrying a phonograph record about and playing it wherever a phonograph of the corresponding make exists. Of its success there could be no question. Akeley was not afraid. Had it not been brilliantly accomplished again and again?

For the first time one of the inert, wasted hands raised itself and pointed to a high shelf on the farther side of the room. There, in a neat row, stood more than a dozen cylinders of a metal I had never seen before—cylinders about a foot high and somewhat less in diameter, with three curious sockets set in an isosceles triangle over the front convex surface of each. One of them was linked at two of the sockets to a pair of singular-looking machines that stood in the background. Of their purport I did not need to be told, and I shivered as with ague.[45] Then I saw the hand point to a much nearer corner where some intricate instruments with attached cords and plugs, several of them much like the two devices on the shelf behind the cylinders, were huddled together.

"There are four kinds of instruments here, Wilmarth," whispered the voice. "Four kinds—three faculties each—makes twelve pieces in all. You see there are four different sorts of beings presented in those cylinders up there. Three humans, six fungoid beings who can't navigate space corporeally, two beings from Neptune (God! if you could see the body this type has on its own planet!), and the rest entities from the central caverns of an especially interesting dark star beyond the galaxy. In the principal outpost inside Round Hill you'll now and then find more cylinders and machines—cylinders of extra-cosmic brains with different senses from any we know—allies and explorers from the uttermost Outside—and special machines for giving them impressions and expression in the several ways suited at once to them and to the comprehensions of different types of listeners. Round Hill, like most of the beings' main outposts all through the various universes, is a very cosmopolitan place! Of course, only the more common types have been lent to me for experiment.

"Here—take the three machines I point to and set them on the table. That tall one with the two glass lenses in front—then the box with the vacuum tubes and sounding-board—and now the one with the metal disc on top. Now for the cylinder with the label 'B-67' pasted on it. Just stand in that Windsor chair to reach the shelf. Heavy? Never mind! Be sure of the number—B-67. Don't bother that fresh, shiny cylinder joined to the two testing instruments—the one with my name on it. Set B-67 on the table near where you've put the machines—and see that the dial switch on all three machines is jammed over to the extreme left.

"Now connect the cord of the lens machine with the upper socket on the cylinder—there! Join the tube machine to the lower left-hand socket, and the disc apparatus to the outer socket. Now move all the dial switches on the machines over to the extreme right—first the lens one, then the disc one, and then the tube one. That's right. I might as well tell you that this is a human being—just like any of us. I'll give you a taste of some of the others tomorrow."

To this day I do not know why I obeyed those whispers so slavishly, or whether I thought Akeley was mad or sane. After what had gone before, I ought to have been prepared for anything; but this mechanical mummery seemed so like the typical vagaries of crazed inventors and scientists that it struck a chord of doubt which even the preceding discourse had not excited. What the whisperer implied was beyond all human belief—yet were not the other things still farther beyond, and less preposterous only because of their remoteness from tangible concrete proof?

As my mind reeled amidst this chaos, I became conscious of a mixed grating and whirring from all three machines lately linked to the cylinder—a grating and whirring which soon subsided into a virtual noiselessness. What was about to happen? Was I to hear a voice? And if so, what proof would I have that it was not some cleverly concocted radio device talked into by a concealed but closely watching speaker? Even now I am unwilling to swear just what I heard, or just what phenomenon really took place before me. But something certainly seemed to take place.

To be brief and plain, the machine with the tubes and sound-box began to speak, and with a point and intelligence which left no doubt that the speaker was actually present and observing us. The voice was loud, metallic, lifeless, and plainly mechanical in every detail of its production. It was incapable of inflection or expressiveness, but scraped and rattled on with a deadly precision and deliberation.

"Mr. Wilmarth," it said, "I hope I do not startle you. I am a human being like yourself, though my body is now resting safely under proper vitalising treatment inside Round Hill, about a mile and a half east of here. I myself am here with you—my brain is in that cylinder and I see, hear, and speak through these electronic vibrators. In a week I am going across the void as I have been many times before, and I expect to have the pleasure of Mr. Akeley's company. I wish I might have yours as well; for I know you by sight and reputation, and have kept close track of your correspondence with our friend. I am, of course, one of the men who have become allied with the outside beings visiting our planet. I met them first in the Himalayas, and have helped them in various ways. In return they have given me experiences such as few men have ever had.

"Do you realise what it means when I say I have been on thirty-seven different celestial bodies—planets, dark stars, and less definable objects—including eight outside our galaxy and two outside the curved cosmos of space and time? All this has not harmed me in the least. My brain has been removed from my body by fissions so adroit that it would be crude to call the operation surgery. The visiting beings have methods which make these extractions easy and almost normal—and one's body never ages when the brain is out of it. The brain, I may add, is virtually immortal with its mechanical faculties and a limited nourishment supplied by occasional changes of the preserving fluid.

"Altogether, I hope most heartily that you will decide to come with Mr. Akeley and me. The visitors are eager to know men of knowledge like yourself, and to shew them the great abysses that most of us have had to dream about in fanciful ignorance. It may seem strange at first to meet them, but I know you will be above minding that. I think Mr. Noyes will go along, too—the man who doubtless brought you up here in his car. He has been one of us for years—I suppose you recognised his voice as one of those on the record Mr. Akeley sent you."

At my violent start the speaker paused a moment before concluding.

"So, Mr. Wilmarth, I will leave the matter to you; merely adding that a man with your love of strangeness and folklore ought never to miss such a chance as this. There is nothing to fear. All transitions are painless, and there is much to enjoy in a wholly mechanised state of sensation. When the electrodes are disconnected, one merely drops off into a sleep of especially vivid and fantastic dreams.

"And now, if you don't mind, we might adjourn our session till tomorrow. Good night—just turn all the switches back to the left; never mind the exact order, though you might let the lens machine be last. Good night, Mr. Akeley—treat our guest well! Ready now with those switches?"

That was all. I obeyed mechanically and shut off all three switches, though dazed with doubt of everything that had occurred. My head was still reeling as I heard Akeley's whispering voice telling me that I might leave all the apparatus on the table just as it was. He did not essay any comment on what had happened, and indeed no comment could have conveyed much to my burdened faculties. I heard him telling me I could take the lamp to use in my room, and deduced that he wished to rest alone in the dark. It was surely time he rested, for his discourse of the afternoon and evening had been such as to exhaust even a vigorous man. Still dazed, I bade my host good night and went upstairs with the lamp, although I had an excellent pocket flashlight with me.

I was glad to be out of that downstairs study with the queer odor and vague suggestions of vibration, yet could not of course escape a hideous sense of dread and peril and cosmic abnormality as I thought of the place I was in and the forces I was meeting. The wild, lonely region, the black, mysteriously forested slope towering so close behind the house, the footprints in the road, the sick, motionless whisperer in the dark, the hellish cylinders and machines, and above all the invitations to strange surgery and stranger voyagings—these things, all so new and in such sudden succession, rushed in on me with a cumulative force which sapped my will and almost undermined my physical strength.

To discover that my guide Noyes was the human celebrant in that monstrous bygone

Sabbat-ritual on the phonograph record was a particular shock, though I had previously sensed a dim, repellent familiarity in his voice. Another special shock came from my own attitude toward my host whenever I paused to analyze it; for much as I had instinctively liked Akeley as revealed in his correspondence, I now found that he filled me with a distinct repulsion. His illness ought to have excited my pity; but instead, it gave me a kind of shudder. He was so rigid and inert and corpse-like—and that incessant whispering was so hateful and unhuman!

It occurred to me that this whispering was different from anything else of the kind I had ever heard; that, despite the curious motionlessness of the speaker's moustache-screened lips, it had a latent strength and carrying-power remarkable for the wheezings of an asthmatic. I had been able to understand the speaker when wholly across the room, and once or twice it had seemed to me that the faint but penetrant sounds represented not so much weakness as deliberate repression—for what reason I could not guess. From the first I had felt a disturbing quality in their timbre. Now, when I tried to weigh the matter, I thought I could trace this impression to a kind of subconscious familiarity like that which had made Noyes's voice so hazily ominous. But when or where I had encountered the thing it hinted at, was more than I could tell.

One thing was certain—I would not spend another night here. My scientific zeal had vanished amidst fear and loathing, and I felt nothing now but a wish to escape from this net of morbidity and unnatural revelation. I knew enough now. It must indeed be true that cosmic linkages do exist—but such things are surely not meant for normal human beings to meddle with.

Blasphemous influences seemed to surround me and press chokingly upon my senses. Sleep, I decided, would be out of the question; so I merely extinguished the lamp and threw myself on the bed fully dressed. No doubt it was absurd, but I kept ready for some unknown emergency; gripping in my right hand the revolver I had brought along, and holding the pocket flashlight in my left. Not a sound came from below, and I could imagine how my host was sitting there with cadaverous stiffness in the dark.

Somewhere I heard a clock ticking, and was vaguely grateful for the normality of the sound. It reminded me, though, of another thing about the region which disturbed me—the total absence of animal life. There were certainly no farm beasts about, and now I realized that even the accustomed night-noises of wild living things were absent. Except for the sinister trickle of distant unseen waters, that stillness was anomalous—interplanetary—and I wondered what star-spawned, intangible blight could be hanging over the region. I recalled from old legends that dogs and other beasts had always hated the Outer Ones, and thought of what those tracks in the road might mean.

VIII.

Do not ask me how long my unexpected lapse into slumber lasted, or how much of what ensued was sheer dream. If I tell you that I awaked at a certain time, and heard and saw certain things, you will merely answer that I did not wake then; and that everything was a dream until the moment when I rushed out of the house, stumbled to the shed where I had seen the old Ford, and seized that ancient vehicle for a mad, aimless race over the haunted hills which at last landed me—after hours of jolting and winding through forest-threatened labyrinths—in a village which turned out to be Townshend.

You will also, of course, discount everything else in my report; and declare that all the pictures, record-sounds, cylinder-and-machine sounds, and kindred evidences were bits of pure deception practiced on me by the missing Henry Akeley. You will even hint that he conspired with other eccentrics to carry out a silly and elaborate hoax—that he had the express shipment removed at Keene, and that he had Noyes make that terrifying wax record. It is odd, though, that Noyes has not even yet been identified; that he was unknown at any of the villages near Akeley's place, though he must have been frequently in the region. I wish I had stopped to memorize the license-number of his car—or perhaps it is better after all that I did not. For I, despite all you can say, and despite all I sometimes try to say to myself, know that loathsome outside influences must be lurking there in the half-unknown hills—and that those influences have spies and emissaries in the world of men. To keep as far as possible from such influences and such emissaries is all that I ask of life in future.

When my frantic story sent a sheriff's posse out to the farmhouse, Akeley was gone without leaving a trace. His loose dressing-gown, yellow scarf, and foot-bandages lay on the study floor near his corner easy-chair, and it could not be decided whether any of his other apparel had vanished with him. The dogs and livestock were indeed missing, and there were some curious bullet-holes both on the house's exterior and on some of the walls within; but beyond this nothing unusual could be detected. No cylinders or machines, none of the evidences I had brought in my valise, no queer odor or vibration-sense, no footprints in the road, and none of the problematical things I glimpsed at the very last.

I stayed a week in Brattleboro after my escape, making inquiries among people of every kind who had known Akeley; and the results convince me that the matter is no figment of dream or delusion. Akeley's queer purchases of dogs and ammunition and chemicals, and the cutting of his telephone wires, are matters of record; while all who knew him—including his son in California—concede that his occasional remarks on strange studies had a certain consistency. Solid citizens believe he was mad, and unhesitatingly pronounce all reported evidences mere hoaxes devised with insane cunning and perhaps abetted by eccentric associates; but the lowlier country folk sustain his statements in every detail. He had showed some of these rustics his photographs and black stone, and had played the hideous record for them; and they all said the footprints and buzzing voice were like those described in ancestral legends.

They said, too, that suspicious sights and sounds had been noticed increasingly around Akeley's house after he found the black stone, and that the place was now avoided by everybody except the mail man and other casual, tough-minded people. Dark Mountain and Round Hill were both notoriously haunted spots, and I could find no one who had ever closely explored either. Occasional disappearances of natives throughout the district's history were well attested, and these now included the semi-vagabond Walter Brown, whom Akeley's letters had mentioned. I even came upon one farmer who thought he had personally glimpsed one of the queer bodies at flood-time in the swollen West River, but his tale was too confused to be really valuable.

When I left Brattleboro I resolved never to go back to Vermont, and I feel quite certain I shall keep my resolution. Those wild hills are surely the outpost of a frightful cosmic race—as I doubt all the less since reading that a new ninth planet has been glimpsed beyond Neptune, just as those influences had said it would be glimpsed. Astronomers, with a hideous appropriateness they little suspect, have named this thing "Pluto." I feel, beyond question, that it is nothing less than nighted Yuggoth—and I shiver when I try to figure out the real reason why its monstrous denizens wish it to be known in this way at this especial time. I vainly try to assure myself that these demoniac creatures are not gradually leading up to some new policy hurtful to the earth and its normal inhabitants.

But I have still to tell of the ending of that terrible night in the farmhouse. As I have said, I did finally drop into a troubled doze; a doze filled with bits of dream which involved monstrous landscape-glimpses. Just what awaked me I cannot yet say, but that I did indeed awake at this given point I feel very certain. My first confused impression was of stealthily creaking floor-boards in the hall outside my door, and of a clumsy, muffled fumbling at the latch. This, however, ceased almost at once; so that my really clear impressions began with the voices heard from the study below. There seemed to be several speakers, and I judged that they were controversially engaged.

By the time I had listened a few seconds I was broad awake, for the nature of the voices was such as to make all thought of sleep ridiculous. The tones were curiously varied, and no one who had listened to that accursed phonograph record could harbor any doubts about the nature of at least two of them. Hideous though the idea was, I knew that I was under the same roof with nameless things from abysmal space; for those two voices were unmistakably the blasphemous buzzings which the Outside Beings used in their communication with men. The two were individually different—different in pitch, accent, and tempo—but they were both of the same damnable general kind.

A third voice was indubitably that of a mechanical utterance-machine connected with one of the detached brains in the cylinders. There was as little doubt about that as about the buzzings; for the loud, metallic, lifeless voice of the previous evening, with its inflectionless, expressionless scraping and rattling, and its impersonal precision and deliberation, had been utterly unforgettable. For a time I did not pause to question whether the intelligence behind the scraping was the identical one which had formerly talked to me; but shortly afterward I reflected that any brain would emit vocal sounds of the same quality if linked to the same mechanical speech-producer; the only possible differences being in language, rhythm, speed, and pronunciation. To complete the eldritch colloquy there were two actually human voices—one the crude speech of an unknown and evidently rustic man, and the other the suave Bostonian tones of my erstwhile guide Noyes.

As I tried to catch the words which the stoutly fashioned floor so bafflingly intercepted, I was also conscious of a great deal of stirring and scratching and shuffling in the room below; so that I could not escape the impression that it was full of living beings—many more than the few whose speech I could single out. The exact nature of this stirring is extremely hard to describe, for very few good bases of comparison exist. Objects seemed now and then to move across the room like conscious entities; the sound of their footfalls having something about it like a loose, hard-surfaced clattering—as of the contact of ill-coördinated surfaces of horn or hard rubber. It was, to use a more concrete but less accurate comparison, as if people with loose, splintery wooden shoes were shambling and rattling about on the polished board floor. On the nature and appearance of those responsible for the sounds, I did not care to speculate.

Before long I saw that it would be impossible to distinguish any connected discourse. Isolated words—including the names of Akeley and myself—now and then floated up, especially when uttered by the mechanical speech-producer; but their true significance was lost for want of continuous context. Today I refuse to form any definite deductions from them, and even their frightful effect on me was one of suggestion rather than of revelation. A terrible and abnormal conclave, I felt certain, was assembled below me; but for what shocking deliberations I could not tell. It was curious how this unquestioned sense of the malign and the blasphemous pervaded me despite Akeley's assurances of the Outsiders' friendliness.

With patient listening I began to distinguish clearly between voices, even though I could not grasp much of what any of the voices said. I seemed to catch certain typical emotions behind some of the speakers. One of the buzzing voices, for example, held an unmistakable note of authority; whilst the mechanical voice, notwithstanding its artificial loudness and regularity, seemed to be in a position of subordination and pleading. Noyes's tones exuded a kind of conciliatory atmosphere. The others I could make no attempt to interpret. I did not hear the familiar whisper of Akeley, but well knew that such a sound could never penetrate the solid flooring of my room.

I will try to set down some of the few disjointed words and other sounds I caught, labeling the speakers of the words as best I know how. It was from the speech-machine that I first picked up a few recognizable phrases.

(*The Speech Machine*)
"...brought it on myself ... sent back the letters and the record ... end on it ... taken in ... seeing and hearing ... damn you ... impersonal force, after all ... fresh, shiny cylinder ... great God...."
(*First Buzzing Voice*)
"...time we stopped ... small and human ... Akeley ... brain ... saying..."
(*Second Buzzing Voice*)
"...Nyarlathotep ... Wilmarth ... records and letters ... cheap imposture...."
(*Noyes*)
"...(an unpronounceable word or name, possibly *N'gah-Kthun*[46]) ... harmless ... peace ... couple of weeks ... theatrical ... told you that before...."
(*First Buzzing Voice*)
"...no reason ... original plan ... effects ... Noyes can watch ... Round Hill ... fresh cylinder ... Noyes's car...."
(*Noyes*)
"...well ... all yours ... down here ... rest ... place...."
(*Several Voices at Once in Indistinguishable Speech*)
(Many Footsteps, Including the Peculiar Loose Stirring or Clattering)
(*A Curious Sort of Flapping Sound*)
(The Sound of an Automobile Starting and Receding)
(Silence)

That is the substance of what my ears brought me as I lay rigid upon that strange upstairs bed in the haunted farmhouse among the demoniac hills—lay there fully dressed, with a revolver clenched in my right hand and a pocket flashlight gripped in my left. I became, as I have said, broad awake; but a kind of obscure paralysis nevertheless kept me inert till long after the last echoes of the sounds had died away. I heard the wooden, deliberate ticking of the ancient Connecticut clock somewhere far below, and at last made out the irregular snoring of a sleeper. Akeley must have dozed off after the strange session, and I could well believe that he needed to do so.

Just what to think or what to do was more than I could decide. After all, what *had* I heard beyond things which previous information might have led me to expect? Had I not known that the nameless Outsiders were now freely admitted to the farmhouse? No doubt Akeley had been surprised by an unexpected visit from them. Yet something in that fragmentary discourse had chilled me immeasurably, raised the most grotesque and horrible doubts, and made me wish fervently that I might wake up and prove everything a dream. I think my subconscious mind must have caught something which my consciousness has not yet recognized. But what of Akeley? Was he not my friend, and would he not have protested if any harm were meant me? The peaceful snoring below seemed to cast ridicule on all my suddenly intensified fears.

Was it possible that Akeley had been imposed upon and used as a lure to draw me into the hills with the letters and pictures and phonograph record? Did those beings mean to engulf us both in a common destruction because we had come to know too much? Again I thought of the abruptness and unnaturalness of that change in the situation which must have occurred between Akeley's penultimate and final letters. Something, my instinct told me, was terribly wrong. All was not as it seemed. That acrid coffee which I refused—had there not been an attempt by some hidden, unknown entity to drug it? I must talk to Akeley at once, and restore his sense of proportion. They had hypnotized him with their promises of cosmic revelations, but now he must listen to reason. We must get out of this before it would be too late. If he lacked the will power to make the break for liberty, I would supply it. Or if I could not persuade him to go, I could at least go myself. Surely he would let me take his Ford and leave it in a garage at Brattleboro. I had noticed it in the shed—the door being left unlocked and open now that peril was deemed past—and I believed there was a good chance of its being ready for instant use. That momentary dislike of Akeley which I had felt during and after the evening's conversation was all gone now. He was in a position much like my own, and we must stick together. Knowing his indisposed condition, I hated to wake him at this juncture, but I knew that I must. I could not stay in this place till morning as matters stood.

At last I felt able to act, and stretched myself vigorously to regain command of my muscles. Arising with a caution more impulsive than deliberate, I found and donned my hat, took my valise, and started downstairs with the flashlight's aid. In my nervousness I kept the revolver clutched in my right hand, being able to take care of both valise and flashlight with my left. Why I exerted these precautions I do not really know, since I was even then on my way to awaken the only other occupant of the house.

As I half tiptoed down the creaking stairs to the lower hall I could hear the sleeper more plainly, and noticed that he must be in the room on my left—the living-room I had not entered. On my right was the gaping blackness of the study in which I had heard the voices. Pushing open the unlatched door of the living-room I traced a path with the flashlight toward the source of the snoring, and finally turned the beams on the sleeper's face. But in the next second I hastily turned them away and commenced a cat-like retreat to the hall, my caution this time springing from reason as well as from instinct. For the sleeper on the couch was not Akeley at all, but my quondam guide Noyes.

Just what the real situation was, I could not guess; but common sense told me that the safest thing was to find out as much as possible before arousing anybody. Regaining the hall, I silently closed and latched the living-room door after me; thereby lessening the chances of awaking Noyes. I now cautiously entered the dark study, where I expected to find Akeley, whether asleep or awake, in the great corner chair which was evidently his favorite resting-place. As I advanced, the beams of my flashlight caught the great center-table, revealing one of the hellish cylinders with sight and hearing machines attached, and with a speech-machine standing close by, ready to be connected at any moment. This, I reflected, must be the encased brain I had heard talking during the frightful conference; and for a second I had a perverse impulse to attach the speech-machine and see what it would say.

It must, I thought, be conscious of my presence even now; since the sight and hearing attachments could not fail to disclose the rays of my flashlight and the faint creaking of the floor beneath my feet. But in the end I did not dare meddle with the thing. I idly saw that it was the fresh, shiny cylinder with Akeley's name on it, which I had noticed on the shelf earlier in the evening and which my host had told me not to bother. Looking back at that moment, I can only regret my timidity and wish that I had boldly caused the apparatus to speak. God knows what mysteries and horrible doubts and questions of identity it might have cleared up! But then, it may be merciful that I let it alone.

From the table I turned my flashlight to the corner where I thought Akeley was, but found to my perplexity that the great easy-chair was empty of any human occupant asleep or awake. From the seat to the floor there trailed voluminously the familiar old dressing-gown, and near it on the floor lay the yellow scarf and the huge foot-bandages I had thought so odd. As I hesitated, striving to conjecture where Akeley might be, and why he had so suddenly discarded his necessary sick-room garments, I observed that the queer odor and sense of vibration were no longer in the room. What had been their cause? Curiously it occurred to me that I had noticed them only in Akeley's vicinity. They had been strongest where he sat, and wholly absent except in the room with him or just outside the doors of that room. I paused, letting the flashlight wander about the dark study and racking my brain for explanations of the turn affairs had taken.

Would to heaven I had quietly left the place before allowing that light to rest again on the vacant chair. As it turned out, I did not leave quietly; but with a muffled shriek which must have disturbed, though it did not quite awake, the sleeping sentinel across the hall. That shriek, and Noyes's still-unbroken snore, are the last sounds I ever heard in that morbidity-choked farmhouse beneath the black-wooded crest of a haunted mountain—that focus of trans-cosmic horror amidst the lonely green hills and curse-muttering brooks of a spectral rustic land.

It is a wonder that I did not drop flashlight, valise, and revolver in my wild scramble, but somehow I failed to lose any of these. I actually managed to get out of that room and that house without making any further noise, to drag myself and my belongings safely into the old Ford in the shed, and to set that archaic vehicle in motion toward some unknown point of safety in the black, moonless night. The ride that followed was a piece of delirium out of Poe or Rimbaud or the drawings of Doré,[47] but finally I reached Townshend. That is all. If my sanity is still unshaken, I am lucky. Sometimes I fear what the years will bring, especially since that new planet Pluto has been so curiously discovered.

As I have implied, I let my flashlight return to the vacant easy-chair after its circuit of the room; then noticing for the first time the presence of certain objects in the seat, made inconspicuous by the adjacent loose folds of the empty dressing-gown. These are the objects, three in number, which the investigators did not find when they came later on. As I said at the outset, there was nothing of actual visual horror about them. The trouble was in what they led one to infer. Even now I have my moments of half-doubt—moments in which I half accept the skepticism of those who attribute my whole experience to dream and nerves and delusion.

The three things were damnably clever constructions of their kind, and were furnished with ingenious metallic clamps to attach them to organic developments of which I dare not form any conjecture. I hope—devoutly hope—that they were the waxen products of a master artist, despite what my inmost fears tell me. Great God! That whisperer in darkness with its morbid odor and vibrations! Sorcerer, emissary, changeling, outsider … that hideous repressed buzzing … and all the time in that fresh, shiny cylinder on the shelf … poor devil … "prodigious surgical, biological, chemical, and mechanical skill."

For the things in the chair, perfect to the last, subtle detail of microscopic resemblance—or identity—were the face and hands of Henry Wentworth Akeley.

The Shadow Over Innsmouth

"The Shadow Over Innsmouth" relates the experiences of young man as he celebrates his coming of age by touring the New England coast. When he visits the decrepit town of Innsmouth, MA (against the advice of virtually everyone he meets), he finds a town in the depths of decay and unearths a secret so heinous, the government, once told of it, raids the city and torpedoes the reef just outside the harbor.

Lovecraft's powers of description are amply represented here. One "can almost taste and smell the stench of fishy decay in a Massachusetts backwater," S.T. Joshi posits. The ending of this tale, however, perfectly illustrates the importance Lovecraft puts on heredity and the past. "For Lovecraft," Joshi writes, "the present […] was nothing but the inevitable result of all […] events of the past, whether we are aware of them or not." For Robert M. Price, however, the ending seems to be the fulfillment of a kind of tribal initiation rite the narrator has unknowingly been participating in throughout the narrative.

Often ranked with "Call of Cthulhu" as one of Lovecraft's best tales, Lovecraft was, according to S.T. Joshi, "profoundly dissatisfied" with the work, considering the prose to be "hackneyed" and the plot pandering "to the demands of markets and the opinions of others." His friend, August Derleth, however, considered it "one of the best" of Mythos tales. Joshi himself claims that the work "may stand at the very pinnacle of Lovecraft's artistic achievement."

I.

During the winter of 1927–28 officials of the Federal government made a strange and secret investigation of certain conditions in the ancient Massachusetts seaport of Innsmouth. The public first learned of it in February, when a vast series of raids and arrests occurred, followed by the deliberate burning and dynamiting—under suitable precautions—of an enormous number of crumbling, worm-eaten, and supposedly empty houses along the abandoned waterfront. Uninquiring souls let this occurrence pass as one of the major clashes in a spasmodic war on liquor.

Keener news-followers, however, wondered at the prodigious number of arrests, the abnormally large force of men used in making them, and the secrecy surrounding the disposal of the prisoners. No trials, or even definite charges were reported; nor were any of the captives seen thereafter in the regular gaols[1] of the nation. There were vague statements about disease and concentration camps, and later about dispersal in various naval and military prisons, but nothing positive ever developed. Innsmouth itself was left almost depopulated, and it is even now only beginning to show signs of a sluggishly revived existence.

Complaints from many liberal organizations were met with long confidential discussions, and representatives were taken on trips to certain camps and prisons. As a result, these societies became surprisingly passive and reticent. Newspaper men were harder to manage, but seemed largely to cooperate with the government in the end. Only one paper—a tabloid always discounted because of its wild policy—mentioned the deep diving submarine that discharged torpedoes downward in the marine abyss just beyond Devil Reef. That item, gathered by chance in a haunt of sailors, seemed indeed rather far-fetched; since the low, black reef lay a full mile and a half out from Innsmouth Harbour.

People around the country and in the nearby towns muttered a great deal among themselves, but said very little to the outer world. They had talked about dying and half-deserted Innsmouth for nearly a century, and nothing new could be wilder or more hideous than what they had whispered and hinted at years before. Many things had taught them secretiveness, and there was no need to exert pressure on them. Besides, they really knew little; for wide salt marshes, desolate and unpeopled, kept neighbors off from Innsmouth on the landward side.

But at last I[2] am going to defy the ban on speech about this thing. Results, I am certain, are so thorough that no public harm save a shock of repulsion could ever accrue from a hinting of what was found by those horrified men at Innsmouth. Besides, what was found might possibly have more than one explanation. I do not know just how much of the whole tale has been told even to me, and I have many reasons for not wishing to probe deeper. For my contact with this affair has been closer than that of any other layman, and I have carried away impressions which are yet to drive me to drastic measures.

It was I who fled frantically out of Innsmouth in the early morning hours of July 16, 1927, and whose frightened appeals for government inquiry and action brought on the whole reported episode. I was willing enough to stay mute while the affair was fresh and uncertain; but now that it is an old story, with public interest and curiosity gone, I have an odd craving to whisper about those few frightful hours in that ill-rumored and evilly-shadowed seaport of death and blasphemous abnormality. The mere telling helps me to restore confidence in my own faculties; to reassure myself that I was not the first to succumb to a contagious nightmare hallucination. It helps me, too, in making up my mind regarding a certain terrible step which lies ahead of me.

I never heard of Innsmouth till the day before I saw it for the first and—so far—last time. I was celebrating my coming of age by a tour of New England—sightseeing, antiquarian, and genealogical—and had planned to go directly from ancient Newburyport[3] to Arkham, whence my mother's family was derived. I had no car, but was travelling by train, trolley and motor-coach, always seeking the cheapest possible route. In Newburyport they told me that the steam train was the thing to take to Arkham; and it was only at the station ticket-office, when I demurred at the high fare, that I learned about Innsmouth. The stout, shrewd-faced agent, whose speech showed him to be no local man, seemed sympathetic toward my efforts at economy, and made a suggestion that none of my other informants had offered.

"You could take that old bus, I suppose," he said with a certain hesitation, "but it ain't thought much of hereabouts. It goes through Innsmouth—you may have heard about that—and so the people don't like it. Run by an Innsmouth fellow—Joe Sargent—but never gets any custom from here, or Arkham either, I guess. Wonder it keeps running at all. I s'pose it's cheap enough, but I never see mor'n two or three people in it—nobody but those Innsmouth folk. Leaves the square—front of Hammond's Drug Store—at 10 a.m. and 7 p.m. unless they've changed lately. Looks like a terrible rattletrap—I've never been on it."

That was the first I ever heard of shadowed Innsmouth. Any reference to a town not shown on common maps or listed in recent guidebooks would have interested me, and the agent's odd manner of allusion roused something like real curiosity. A town able to inspire such dislike in it its neighbors, I thought, must be at least rather unusual, and worthy of a tourist's attention. If it came before Arkham I would stop off there and so I asked the agent to tell me something about it. He was very deliberate, and spoke with an air of feeling slightly superior to what he said.

"Innsmouth? Well, it's a queer kind of a town down at the mouth of the Manuxet.[4] Used to be almost a city—quite a port before the War of 1812—but all gone to pieces in the last hundred years or so. No railroad now—B. and M. never went through, and the branch line from Rowley was given up years ago.

"More empty houses than there are people, I guess, and no business to speak of except fishing and lobstering. Everybody trades mostly either here or in Arkham or Ipswich. Once they had quite a few mills, but nothing's left now except one gold refinery running on the leanest kind of part time.

"That refinery, though, used to be a big thing, and old man Marsh, who owns it, must be richer'n Croesus.[5] Queer old duck, though, and sticks mighty close in his home. He's supposed to have developed some skin disease or deformity late in life that makes him keep out of sight. Grandson of Captain Obed Marsh, who founded the business. His mother seems to've been some kind of foreigner—they say a South Sea islander—so everybody raised Cain when he married an Ipswich girl fifty years ago. They always do that about Innsmouth people, and folks here and hereabouts always try to cover up any Innsmouth blood they have in 'em. But Marsh's children and grandchildren look just like anyone else far's I can see. I've had 'em pointed out to me here—though, come to think of it, the elder children don't seem to be around lately. Never saw the old man.

"And why is everybody so down on Innsmouth? Well, young fellow, you mustn't take too much stock in what people here say. They're hard to get started, but once they do get started they never let up. They've been telling things about Innsmouth—whispering 'em, mostly—for the last hundred years, I guess, and I gather they're more scared than anything else. Some of the stories would make you laugh—about old Captain Marsh driving bargains with the devil and bringing imps out of hell to live in Innsmouth, or about some kind of devil-worship and awful sacrifices in some place near the wharves that people stumbled on around 1845 or thereabouts—but I come from Panton, Vermont, and that kind of story don't go down with me.

"You ought to hear, though, what some of the old-timers tell about the black reef off the coast—Devil Reef, they call it. It's well above water a good part of the time, and never much below it, but at that you could hardly call it an island. The story is that there's a whole legion of devils seen sometimes on that reef—sprawled about, or darting in and out of some kind of caves near the top. It's a rugged, uneven thing, a good bit over a mile out, and toward the end of shipping days sailors used to make big detours just to avoid it.

"That is, sailors that didn't hail from Innsmouth. One of the things they had against old Captain Marsh was that he was supposed to land on it sometimes at night when the tide was right. Maybe he did, for I dare say the rock formation was interesting, and it's just barely possible he was looking for pirate loot and maybe finding it; but there was talk of his dealing with demons there. Fact is, I guess on the whole it was really the Captain that gave the bad reputation to the reef.

"That was before the big epidemic of 1846, when over half the folks in Innsmouth was carried off. They never did quite figure out what the trouble was, but it was probably some foreign kind of disease brought from China or somewhere by the shipping. It surely was bad enough—there was riots over it, and all sorts of ghastly doings that I don't believe ever got outside of town—and it left the place in awful shape. Never came back—there can't be more'n 300 or 400 people living there now.

"But the real thing behind the way folks feel is simply race prejudice—and I don't say I'm blaming those that hold it. I hate those Innsmouth folks myself, and I wouldn't care to go to their town. I s'pose you know—though I can see you're a Westerner by your talk—what a lot our New England ships—used to have to do with queer ports in Africa, Asia, the South Seas, and everywhere else, and what queer kinds of people they sometimes brought back with 'em. You've probably heard about the Salem man that came home with a Chinese wife, and maybe you know there's still a bunch of Fiji Islanders somewhere around Cape Cod.

"Well, there must be something like that back of the Innsmouth people. The place always was badly cut off from the rest of the country by marshes and creeks and we can't be sure about the ins and outs of the matter; but it's pretty clear that old Captain Marsh must have brought home some odd specimens when he had all three of his ships in commission back in the twenties and thirties. There certainly is a strange kind of streak in the Innsmouth folks today—I don't know how to explain it but it sort of makes you crawl. You'll notice a little in Sargent if you take his bus. Some of 'em have queer narrow heads with flat noses and bulgy, starry eyes that never seem to shut, and their skin ain't quite right. Rough and scabby, and the sides of the necks are all shriveled or creased up. Get bald, too, very young. The older fellows look the worst—fact is, I don't believe I've ever seen a very old chap of that kind. Guess they must die of looking in the glass! Animals hate 'em—they used to have lots of horse trouble before the autos came in.

"Nobody around here or in Arkham or Ipswich will have anything to do with 'em, and they act kind of offish themselves when they come to town or when anyone tries to fish on their grounds. Queer how fish are always thick off Innsmouth Harbour when there ain't any anywhere else around—but just try to fish there yourself and see how the folks chase you off! Those people used to come here on the railroad—walking and taking the train at Rowley after the branch was dropped—but now they use that bus.

"Yes, there's a hotel in Innsmouth—called the Gilman House—but I don't believe it can amount to much. I wouldn't advise you to try it. Better stay over here and take the ten o'clock bus tomorrow morning; then you can get an evening bus there for Arkham at eight o'clock. There was a factory inspector who stopped at the Gilman a couple of years ago and he had a lot of unpleasant hints about the place. Seems they get a queer crowd there, for this fellow heard voices in other rooms—though most of 'em was empty—that gave him the shivers. It was foreign talk he thought, but he said the bad thing about it was the kind of voice that sometimes spoke. It sounded so unnatural—slopping like, he said—that he didn't dare undress and go to sleep. Just waited up and lit out the first thing in the morning. The talk went on most all night.

"This fellow—Casey, his name was—had a lot to say about how the Innsmouth folk, watched him and seemed kind of on guard. He found the Marsh refinery a queer place— it's in an old mill on the lower falls of the Manuxet. What he said tallied up with what I'd heard. Books in bad shape, and no clear account of any kind of dealings. You know it's always been a kind of mystery where the Marshes get the gold they refine. They've never seemed to do much buying in that line, but years ago they shipped out an enormous lot of ingots.

"Used to be talk of a queer foreign kind of jewelry that the sailors and refinery men sometimes sold on the sly, or that was seen once or twice on some of the Marsh women- folks. People allowed maybe old Captain Obed traded for it in some heathen port, especially since he always ordered stacks of glass beads and trinkets such as seafaring men used to get for native trade. Others thought and still think he'd found an old pirate cache out on Devil Reef. But here's a funny thing. The old Captain's been dead these sixty years, and there ain't been a good-sized ship out of the place since the Civil War; but just the same the Marshes still keep on buying a few of those native trade things—mostly glass and rubber gewgaws, they tell me. Maybe the Innsmouth folks like 'em to look at themselves—Gawd knows they've gotten to be about as bad as South Sea cannibals and Guinea savages.

"That plague of '46 must have taken off the best blood in the place. Anyway, they're a doubtful lot now, and the Marshes and other rich folks are as bad as any. As I told you, there probably ain't more'n 400 people in the whole town in spite of all the streets they say there are. I guess they're what they call 'white trash' down South—lawless and sly, and full of secret things. They get a lot of fish and lobsters and do exporting by truck. Queer how the fish swarm right there and nowhere else.

"Nobody can ever keep track of these people, and state school officials and census men have a devil of a time. You can bet that prying strangers ain't welcome around Inns- mouth. I've heard personally of more'n one business or government man that's disappeared there, and there's loose talk of one who went crazy and is out at Danvers[6] now. They must have fixed up some awful scare for that fellow.

"That's why I wouldn't go at night if I was you. I've never been there and have no wish to go, but I guess a daytime trip couldn't hurt you—even though the people hereabouts will advise you not to make it. If you're just sightseeing, and looking for old-time stuff, Inns- mouth ought to be quite a place for you."

And so I spent part of that evening at the Newburyport Public Library looking up data about Innsmouth. When I had tried to question the natives in the shops, the lunch- room, the garages, and the fire station, I had found them even harder to get started than the ticket agent had predicted; and realized that I could not spare the time to overcome their first instinctive reticence. They had a kind of obscure suspiciousness, as if there were something amiss with anyone too much interested in Innsmouth. At the Y.M.C.A., where I was stopping, the clerk merely discouraged my going to such a dismal, decadent place; and the people at the library showed much the same attitude. Clearly, in the eyes of the educated, Innsmouth was merely an exaggerated case of civic degeneration.

The Essex County histories on the library shelves had very little to say, except that the town was founded in 1643, noted for shipbuilding before the Revolution, a seat of great marine prosperity in the early 19th century, and later a minor factory center using the Manuxet as power. The epidemic and riots of 1846 were very sparsely treated, as if they formed a discredit to the county.

References to decline were few, though the significance of the later record was unmistakable. After the Civil War all industrial life was confined to the Marsh Refining Company, and the marketing of gold ingots formed the only remaining bit of major commerce aside from the eternal fishing. That fishing paid less and less as the price of the commodity fell and large-scale corporations offered competition, but there was never a dearth of fish around Innsmouth Harbour. Foreigners seldom settled there, and there was some discreetly veiled evidence that a number of Poles and Portuguese who had tried it had been scattered in a peculiarly drastic fashion.

Most interesting of all was a glancing reference to the strange jewelry vaguely associated with Innsmouth. It had evidently impressed the whole countryside more than a little, for mention was made of specimens in the museum of Miskatonic University at Arkham, and in the display room of the Newburyport Historical Society. The fragmentary descriptions of these things were bald and prosaic, but they hinted to me an undercurrent of persistent strangeness. Something about them seemed so odd and provocative that I could not put them out of my mind, and despite the relative lateness of the hour I resolved to see the local sample—said to be a large, queerly-proportioned thing evidently meant for a tiara— if it could possibly be arranged.

The librarian gave me a note of introduction to the curator of the Society, a Miss Anna Tilton, who lived nearby, and after a brief explanation that ancient gentlewoman was kind enough to pilot me into the closed building, since the hour was not outrageously late. The collection was a notable one indeed, but in my present mood I had eyes for nothing but the bizarre object which glistened in a corner cupboard under the electric lights.

It took no excessive sensitiveness to beauty to make me literally gasp at the strange, unearthly splendor of the alien, opulent phantasy that rested there on a purple velvet cushion. Even now I can hardly describe what I saw, though it was clearly enough a sort of tiara, as the description had said. It was tall in front, and with a very large and curiously irregular periphery, as if designed for a head of almost freakishly elliptical outline. The material seemed to be predominantly gold, though a weird lighter lustrousness hinted at some strange alloy with an equally beautiful and scarcely identifiable metal. Its condition was almost perfect, and one could have spent hours in studying the striking and puzzlingly untraditional designs—some simply geometrical, and some plainly marine—chased or molded in high relief on its surface with a craftsmanship of incredible skill and grace.

The longer I looked, the more the thing fascinated me; and in this fascination there was a curiously disturbing element hardly to be classified or accounted for. At first I decided that it was the queer other-worldly quality of the art which made me uneasy. All other art objects I had ever seen either belonged to some known racial or national stream, or else were consciously modernistic defiances of every recognized stream. This tiara was neither. It clearly belonged to some settled technique of infinite maturity and perfection, yet that technique was utterly remote from any—Eastern or Western, ancient or modern—which I had ever heard of or seen exemplified. It was as if the workmanship were that of another planet.

However, I soon saw that my uneasiness had a second and perhaps equally potent source residing in the pictorial and mathematical suggestion of the strange designs. The patterns all hinted of remote secrets and unimaginable abysses in time and space, and the monotonously aquatic nature of the reliefs became almost sinister. Among these reliefs were fabulous monsters of abhorrent grotesqueness and malignity—half ichthyic and half batrachian[7] in suggestion—which one could not dissociate from a certain haunting and uncomfortable sense of pseudomemory, as if they called up some image from deep cells and tissues whose retentive functions are wholly primal and awesomely ancestral. At times I fancied that every contour of these blasphemous fish-frogs was over-flowing with the ultimate quintessence of unknown and inhuman evil.

In odd contrast to the tiara's aspect was its brief and prosy history as related by Miss Tilton. It had been pawned for a ridiculous sum at a shop in State Street in 1873, by a drunken Innsmouth man shortly afterward killed in a brawl. The Society had acquired it directly from the pawnbroker, at once giving it a display worthy of its quality. It was labeled as of probable East-Indian or Indochinese provenance, though the attribution was frankly tentative.

Miss Tilton, comparing all possible hypotheses regarding its origin and its presence in New England, was inclined to believe that it formed part of some exotic pirate hoard discovered by old Captain Obed Marsh. This view was surely not weakened by the insistent offers of purchase at a high price which the Marshes began to make as soon as they knew of its presence, and which they repeated to this day despite the Society's unvarying determination not to sell.

As the good lady showed me out of the building she made it clear that the pirate theory of the Marsh fortune was a popular one among the intelligent people of the region. Her own attitude toward shadowed Innsmouth—which she had never seen—was one of disgust at a community slipping far down the cultural scale, and she assured me that the rumors of devil-worship were partly justified by a peculiar secret cult which had gained force there and engulfed all the orthodox churches.

It was called, she said, "The Esoteric Order of Dagon," and was undoubtedly a debased, quasi-pagan thing imported from the East a century before, at a time when the Innsmouth fisheries seemed to be going barren. Its persistence among a simple people was quite natural in view of the sudden and permanent return of abundantly fine fishing, and it soon came to be the greatest influence in the town, replacing Freemasonry[8] altogether and taking up headquarters in the old Masonic Hall on New Church Green.

All this, to the pious Miss Tilton, formed an excellent reason for shunning the ancient town of decay and desolation; but to me it was merely a fresh incentive. To my architectural and historical anticipations was now added an acute anthropological zeal, and I could scarcely sleep in my small room at the "Y" as the night wore away.

II.

Shortly before ten the next morning I stood with one small valise in front of Hammond's Drug Store in old Market Square waiting for the Innsmouth bus. As the hour for its arrival drew near I noticed a general drift of the loungers to other places up the street, or to the Ideal Lunch across the square. Evidently the ticket-agent had not exaggerated the dislike which local People bore toward Innsmouth and its denizens. In a few moments a small motor-coach of extreme decrepitude and dirty grey color rattled down State Street, made a turn, and drew up at the curb beside me. I felt immediately that it was the right one; a guess which the half-illegible sign on the windshield—Arkham-Innsmouth-Newburyport—soon verified.

There were only three passengers—dark, unkempt men of sullen visage and somewhat youthful cast—and when the vehicle stopped they clumsily shambled out and began walking up State Street in a silent, almost furtive fashion. The driver also alighted, and I watched him as he went into the drug store to make some purchase. This, I reflected, must be the Joe Sargent mentioned by the ticket-agent; and even before I noticed any details there spread over me a wave of spontaneous aversion which could be neither checked nor explained. It suddenly struck me as very natural that the local people should not wish to ride on a bus owned and driven by this man, or to visit any oftener than possible the habitat of such a man and his kinsfolk.

When the driver came out of the store I looked at him more carefully and tried to determine the source of my evil impression. He was a thin, stoop-shouldered man not much under six feet tall, dressed in shabby blue civilian clothes and wearing a frayed golf cap. His age was perhaps thirty-five, but the odd, deep creases in the sides of his neck made him seem older when one did not study his dull, expressionless face. He had a narrow head, bulging, watery-blue eyes that seemed never to wink, a flat nose, a receding forehead and chin, and singularly undeveloped ears. His long thick lip and coarse-pored, greyish cheeks seemed almost beardless except for some sparse yellow hairs that straggled and curled in irregular patches; and in places the surface seemed queerly irregular, as if peeling from some cutaneous[9] disease. His hands were large and heavily veined, and had a very unusual greyish-blue tinge. The fingers were strikingly short in proportion to the rest of the struc-ture, and seemed to have a tendency to curl closely into the huge palm. As he walked toward the bus I observed his peculiarly shambling gait and saw that his feet were inordinately immense. The more I studied them the more I wondered how he could buy any shoes to fit them.

A certain greasiness about the fellow increased my dislike. He was evidently given to working or lounging around the fish docks, and carried with him much of their character-istic smell. Just what foreign blood was in him I could not even guess. His oddities certainly did not look Asiatic, Polynesian, Levantine or negroid, yet I could see why the people found him alien. I myself would have thought of biological degeneration[10] rather than alienage.

I was sorry when I saw there would be no other passengers on the bus. Somehow I did not like the idea of riding alone with this driver. But as leaving time obviously approached I conquered my qualms and followed the man aboard, extending him a dollar bill and murmuring the single word "Innsmouth." He looked curiously at me for a second as he returned forty cents change without speaking. I took a seat far behind him, but on the same side of the bus, since I wished to watch the shore during the journey.

At length the decrepit vehicle stared with a jerk, and rattled noisily past the old brick buildings of State Street amidst a cloud of vapor from the exhaust. Glancing at the people on the sidewalks, I thought I detected in them a curious wish to avoid looking at the bus—or at least a wish to avoid seeming to look at it. Then we turned to the left into High Street, where the going was smoother; flying by stately old mansions of the early republic and still older colonial farmhouses, passing the Lower Green and Parker River, and finally emerging into a long, monotonous stretch of open shore country.

The day was warm and sunny, but the landscape of sand and sedge-grass, and stunted shrubbery became more and desolate as we proceeded. Out the window I could see the blue water and the sandy line of Plum Island,[11] and we presently drew very near the beach as our narrow road veered off from the main highway to Rowley and Ipswich. There were no visible houses, and I could tell by the state of the road that traffic was very light here-abouts. The weather-worn telephone poles carried only two wires. Now and then we crossed crude wooden bridges over tidal creeks that wound far inland and promoted the general isolation of the region.

Once in a while I noticed dead stumps and crumbling foundation-walls above the drifting sand, and recalled the old tradition quoted in one of the histories I had read, that this was once a fertile and thickly-settled countryside. The change, it was said, came simultaneously with the Innsmouth epidemic of 1846, and was thought by simple folk to have a dark connection with hidden forces of evil. Actually, it was caused by the unwise cutting of woodlands near the shore, which robbed the soil of the best protection and opened the way for waves of wind-blown sand.

At last we lost sight of Plum Island and saw the vast expanse of the open Atlantic on our left. Our narrow course began to climb steeply, and I felt a singular sense of disquiet in looking at the lonely crest ahead where the rutted road-way met the sky. It was as if the bus were about to keep on in its ascent, leaving the sane earth altogether and merging with the unknown arcana of upper air and cryptical sky. The smell of the sea took on ominous implications, and the silent driver's bent, rigid back and narrow head became more and more hateful. As I looked at him I saw that the back of his head was almost as hairless as his face, having only a few straggling yellow strands upon a grey scabrous surface.

Then we reached the crest and beheld the outspread valley beyond, where the Manuxet joins the sea just north of the long line of cliffs that culminate in Kingsport Head and veer off toward Cape Ann. On the far misty horizon I could just make out the dizzy profile of the Head, topped by the queer ancient house of which so many legends are told; but for the moment all my attention was captured by the nearer panorama just below me. I had, I realized, come face to face with rumor-shadowed Innsmouth.

It was a town of wide extent and dense construction, yet one with a portentous dearth of visible life. From the tangle of chimney-pots scarcely a wisp of smoke came, and the three tall steeples loomed stark and unpainted against the seaward horizon. One of them was crumbling down at the top, and in that and another there were only black gaping holes where clock-dials should have been. The vast huddle of sagging gambrel roofs and peaked gables conveyed with offensive clearness the idea of wormy decay, and as we approached along the now descending road I could see that many roofs had wholly caved in. There were some large square Georgian houses, too, with hipped roofs, cupolas, and railed "widow's walks."[12] These were mostly well back from the water, and one or two seemed to be in moderately sound condition. Stretching inland from among them I saw the rusted, grass-grown line of the abandoned railway, with leaning telegraph-poles now devoid of wires, and the half-obscured lines of the old carriage roads to Rowley and Ipswich.

The decay was worst close to the waterfront, though in its very midst I could spy the white belfry[13] of a fairly well preserved brick structure which looked like a small factory. The harbor, long clogged with sand, was enclosed by an ancient stone breakwater; on which I could begin to discern the minute forms of a few seated fishermen, and at whose end were what looked like the foundations of a bygone lighthouse. A sandy tongue had formed inside this barrier and upon it I saw a few decrepit cabins, moored dories,[14] and scattered lobster-pots. The only deep water seemed to be where the river poured out past the belfried structure and turned southward to join the ocean at the breakwater's end.

Here and there the ruins of wharves jutted out from the shore to end in indeterminate rottenness, those farthest south seeming the most decayed. And far out at sea, despite a high tide, I glimpsed a long, black line scarcely rising above the water yet carrying a suggestion of odd latent malignancy. This, I knew, must be Devil Reef. As I looked, a subtle, curious sense of beckoning seemed superadded to the grim repulsion; and oddly enough, I found this overtone more disturbing than the primary impression.

We met no one on the road, but presently began to pass deserted farms in varying stages of ruin. Then I noticed a few inhabited houses with rags stuffed in the broken windows and shells and dead fish lying about the littered yards. Once or twice I saw listless-looking people working in barren gardens or digging clams on the fishy-smelling beach below, and groups of dirty, simian-visaged[15] children playing around weed-grown doorsteps. Somehow these people seemed more disquieting than the dismal buildings, for almost every one had certain peculiarities of face and motions which I instinctively disliked without being able to define or comprehend them. For a second I thought this typical physique suggested some picture I had seen, perhaps in a book, under circumstances of particular horror or melancholy; but this pseudo-recollection passed very quickly.

As the bus reached a lower level I began to catch the steady note of a waterfall through the unnatural stillness, The leaning, unpainted houses grew thicker, lined both sides of the road, and displayed more urban tendencies than did those we were leaving behind, The panorama ahead had contracted to a street scene, and in spots I could see where a cobblestone pavement and stretches of brick sidewalk had formerly existed. All the houses were apparently deserted, and there were occasional gaps where tumbledown chimneys and cellar walls told of buildings that had collapsed. Pervading everything was the most nauseous fishy odor imaginable.

Soon cross streets and junctions began to appear; those on the left leading to shoreward realms of unpaved squalor and decay, while those on the right showed vistas of departed grandeur. So far I had seen no people in the town, but there now came signs of a sparse habitation—curtained windows here and there, and an occasional battered motorcar at the curb. Pavement and sidewalks were increasingly well-defined, and though most of the houses were quite old—wood and brick structures of the early 19th century—they were obviously kept fit for habitation. As an amateur antiquarian I almost lost my olfactory disgust and my feeling of menace and repulsion amidst this rich, unaltered survival from the past.

But I was not to reach my destination without one very strong impression of poignantly disagreeable quality. The bus had come to a sort of open concourse or radial point with churches on two sides and the bedraggled remains of a circular green in the center, and I was looking at a large pillared hall on the right-hand junction ahead. The structure's once white paint was now gray and peeling and the black and gold sign on the pediment was so faded that I could only with difficulty make out the words "Esoteric Order of Dagon." This, then was the former Masonic Hall now given over to a degraded cult. As I strained to decipher this inscription my notice was distracted by the raucous tones of a cracked bell across the street, and I quickly turned to look out the window on my side of the coach.

The sound came from a squat stone church of manifestly later date than most of the houses, built in a clumsy Gothic fashion and having a disproportionately high basement with shuttered windows. Though the hands of its clock were missing on the side I glimpsed, I knew that those hoarse strokes were tolling the hour of eleven. Then suddenly all thoughts of time were blotted out by an onrushing image of sharp intensity and unaccountable horror which had seized me before I knew what it really was. The door of the church basement was open, revealing a rectangle of blackness inside. And as I looked, a certain object crossed or seemed to cross that dark rectangle; burning into my brain a momentary conception of nightmare which was all the more maddening because analysis could not show a single nightmarish quality in it.

It was a living object—the first except the driver that I had seen since entering the compact part of the town—and had I been in a steadier mood I would have found nothing whatever of terror in it. Clearly, as I realized a moment later, it was the pastor; clad in some peculiar vestments doubtless introduced since the Order of Dagon had modified the ritual of the local churches. The thing which had probably caught my first subconscious glance and supplied the touch of bizarre horror was the tall tiara he wore; an almost exact duplicate of the one Miss Tilton had shown me the previous evening. This, acting on my imagination, had supplied namelessly sinister qualities to the indeterminate face and robed, shambling form beneath it. There was not, I soon decided, any reason why I should have felt that shuddering touch of evil pseudo-memory. Was it not natural that a local mystery cult should adopt among its regimentals an unique type of head-dress made familiar to the community in some strange way—perhaps as treasure-trove?

A very thin sprinkling of repellent-looking youngish people now became visible on the sidewalks—lone individuals, and silent knots of two or three. The lower floors of the crumbling houses sometimes harbored small shops with dingy signs, and I noticed a parked truck or two as we rattled along. The sound of waterfalls became more and more distinct, and presently I saw a fairly deep river-gorge ahead, spanned by a wide, iron-railed highway bridge beyond which a large square opened out. As we clanked over the bridge I looked out on both sides and observed some factory buildings on the edge of the grassy bluff or part way down. The water far below was very abundant, and I could see two vigorous sets of falls upstream on my right and at least one downstream on my left. From this point the noise was quite deafening. Then we rolled into the large semicircular square across the river and drew up on the right-hand side in front of a tall, cupola crowned building with remnants of yellow paint and with a half-effaced sign proclaiming it to be the Gilman House.

I was glad to get out of that bus, and at once proceeded to check my valise in the shabby hotel lobby. There was only one person in sight—an elderly man without what I had come to call the "Innsmouth look"—and I decided not to ask him any of the questions which bothered me; remembering that odd things had been noticed in this hotel. Instead, I strolled out on the square, from which the bus had already gone, and studied the scene minutely and appraisingly.

One side of the cobblestoned open space was the straight line of the river; the other was a semicircle of slant-roofed brick buildings of about the 1800 period, from which several streets radiated away to the southeast, south, and southwest. Lamps were depressingly few and small—all low-powered incandescents—and I was glad that my plans called for departure before dark, even though I knew the moon would be bright. The buildings were all in fair condition, and included perhaps a dozen shops in current operation; of which one was a grocery of the First National chain, others a dismal restaurant, a drug store, and a wholesale fish-dealer's office, and still another, at the eastward extremity of the square near the river an office of the town's only industry—the Marsh Refining Company. There were perhaps ten people visible, and four or five automobiles and motor trucks stood scattered about. I did not need to be told that this was the civic center of Innsmouth. Eastward I could catch blue glimpses of the harbor, against which rose the decaying remains of three once beautiful Georgian steeples. And toward the shore on the opposite bank of the river I saw the white belfry surmounting what I took to be the Marsh refinery.

For some reason or other I chose to make my first inquiries at the chain grocery, whose personnel was not likely to be native to Innsmouth. I found a solitary boy of about seventeen in charge, and was pleased to note the brightness and affability which promised cheerful information. He seemed exceptionally eager to talk, and I soon gathered that he did not like the place, its fishy smell, or its furtive people. A word with any outsider was a relief to him. He hailed from Arkham, boarded with a family who came from Ipswich, and went back whenever he got a moment off. His family did not like him to work in Innsmouth, but the chain had transferred him there and he did not wish to give up his job.

There was, he said, no public library or chamber of commerce in Innsmouth, but I could probably find my way about. The street I had come down was Federal. West of that were the fine old residence streets—Broad, Washington, Lafayette, and Adams—and east of it were the shoreward slums. It was in these slums—along Main Street—that I would find the old Georgian churches, but they were all long abandoned. It would be well not to make oneself too conspicuous in such neighborhoods—especially north of the river since the people were sullen and hostile. Some strangers had even disappeared.

Certain spots were almost forbidden territory, as he had learned at considerable cost. One must not, for example, linger much around the Marsh refinery, or around any of the still used churches, or around the pillared Order of Dagon Hall at New Church Green. Those churches were very odd—all violently disavowed by their respective denominations elsewhere, and apparently using the queerest kind of ceremonials and clerical vestments. Their creeds were heterodox and mysterious, involving hints of certain marvelous trans-formations leading to bodily immorality—of a sort—on this earth. The youth's own pas-tor—Dr. Wallace of Asbury M.E. Church in Arkham—had gravely urged him not to join any church in Innsmouth.

As for the Innsmouth people—the youth hardly knew what to make of them. They were as furtive and seldom seen as animals that live in burrows, and one could hardly imag-ine how they passed the time apart from their desultory fishing. Perhaps—judging from the quantities of bootleg liquor they consumed—they lay for most of the daylight hours in an alcoholic stupor. They seemed sullenly banded together in some sort of fellowship and understanding—despising the world as if they had access to other and preferable spheres of entity. Their appearance—especially those staring, unwinking eyes which one never saw shut—was certainly shocking enough; and their voices were disgusting. It was awful to hear them chanting in their churches at night, and especially during their main festivals or revivals, which fell twice a year on April 30th and October 31st.[16]

They were very fond of the water, and swam a great deal in both river and harbor. Swimming races out to Devil Reef were very common, and everyone in sight seemed well able to share in this arduous sport. When one came to think of it, it was generally only rather young people who were seen about in public, and of these the oldest were apt to be the most tainted-looking. When exceptions did occur, they were mostly persons with no trace of aberrancy, like the old clerk at the hotel. One wondered what became of the bulk of the older folk, and whether the "Innsmouth look" were not a strange and insidious disease-phenomenon which increased its hold as years advanced.

Only a very rare affliction, of course, could bring about such vast and radical anatom-ical changes in a single individual after maturity—changes invoking osseous factors as basic as the shape of the skull—but then, even this aspect was no more baffling and unheard-of than the visible features of the malady as a whole. It would be hard, the youth implied, to form any real conclusions regarding such a matter; since one never came to know the natives personally no matter how long one might live in Innsmouth.

The youth was certain that many specimens even worse than the worst visible ones were kept locked indoors in some places. People sometimes heard the queerest kind of sounds. The tottering waterfront hovels north of the river were reputedly connected by hidden tunnels, being thus a veritable warren of unseen abnormalities. What kind of foreign blood—if any—these beings had, it was impossible to tell. They sometimes kept certain especially repulsive characters out of sight when government and others from the outside world came to town.

It would be of no use, my informant said, to ask the natives anything about the place. The only one who would talk was a very aged but normal looking man who lived at the poorhouse on the north rim of the town and spent his time walking about or lounging around the fire station. This hoary character, Zadok Allen, was 96 years old and somewhat touched in the head, besides being the town drunkard. He was a strange, furtive creature who constantly looked over his shoulder as if afraid of something, and when sober could not be persuaded to talk at all with strangers. He was, however, unable to resist any offer of his favorite poison; and once drunk would furnish the most astonishing fragments of whispered reminiscence.

After all, though, little useful data could be gained from him; since his stories were all insane, incomplete hints of impossible marvels and horrors which could have no source save in his own disordered fancy. Nobody ever believed him, but the natives did not like him to drink and talk with strangers; and it was not always safe to be seen questioning him. It was probably from him that some of the wildest popular whispers and delusions were derived.

Several non-native residents had reported monstrous glimpses from time to time, but between old Zadok's tales and the malformed inhabitants it was no wonder such illusions were current. None of the non-natives ever stayed out late at night, there being a widespread impression that it was not wise to do so. Besides, the streets were loathsomely dark.

As for business—the abundance of fish was certainly almost uncanny, but the natives were taking less and less advantage of it. Moreover, prices were falling and competition was growing. Of course the town's real business was the refinery, whose commercial office was on the square only a few doors east of where we stood. Old Man Marsh was never seen, but sometimes went to the works in a closed, curtained car.

There were all sorts of rumors about how Marsh had come to look. He had once been a great dandy; and people said he still wore the frock-coated finery of the Edwardian age curiously adapted to certain deformities. His son had formerly conducted the office in the square, but latterly they had been keeping out of sight a good deal and leaving the brunt of affairs to the younger generation. The sons and their sisters had come to look very queer, especially the elder ones; and it was said that their health was failing.

One of the Marsh daughters was a repellent, reptilian-looking woman who wore an excess of weird jewelry clearly of the same exotic tradition as that to which the strange tiara belonged. My informant had noticed it many times, and had heard it spoken of as coming from some secret hoard, either of pirates or of demons. The clergymen—or priests, or whatever they were called nowadays—also wore this kind of ornament as a headdress; but one seldom caught glimpses of them. Other specimens the youth had not seen, though many were rumored to exist around Innsmouth.

The Marshes, together with the other three gently bred families of the town—the Waites, the Gilmans, and the Eliots—were all very retiring. They lived in immense houses along Washington Street, and several were reputed to harbor in concealment certain living kinsfolk whose personal aspect forbade public view, and whose deaths had been reported and recorded.

Warning me that many of the street signs were down, the youth drew for my benefit a rough but ample and painstaking sketch map of the town's salient features. After a moment's study I felt sure that it would be of great help, and pocketed it with profuse thanks. Disliking the dinginess of the single restaurant I had seen, I bought a fair supply of cheese crackers and ginger wafers to serve as a lunch later on. My program, I decided, would be to thread the principal streets, talk with any non-natives I might encounter, and catch the eight o'clock coach for Arkham. The town, I could see, formed a significant and exaggerated example of communal decay; but being no sociologist I would limit my serious observations to the field of architecture.

Thus I began my systematic though half-bewildered tour of Innsmouth's narrow, shadow-blighted ways. Crossing the bridge and turning toward the roar of the lower falls, I passed close to the Marsh refinery, which seemed to be oddly free from the noise of industry. The building stood on the steep river bluff near a bridge and an open confluence of streets which I took to be the earliest civic center, displaced after the Revolution by the present Town Square.

Re-crossing the gorge on the Main Street bridge, I struck a region of utter desertion which somehow made me shudder. Collapsing huddles of gambrel roofs formed a jagged and fantastic skyline, above which rose the ghoulish, decapitated steeple of an ancient church. Some houses along Main Street were tenanted, but most were tightly boarded up. Down unpaved side streets I saw the black, gaping windows of deserted hovels, many of which leaned at perilous and incredible angles through the sinking of part of the foundations. Those windows stared so spectrally that it took courage to turn eastward toward the water-front. Certainly, the terror of a deserted house swells in geometrical rather than arithmetical progression as houses multiply to form a city of stark desolation. The sight of such endless avenues of fishy-eyed vacancy and death, and the thought of such linked infinities of black, brooding compartments given over to cob-webs and memories and the conqueror worm,[17] start up vestigial fears and aversions that not even the stoutest philosophy can disperse.

Fish Street was as deserted as Main, though it differed in having many brick and stone warehouses still in excellent shape. Water Street was almost its duplicate, save that there were great seaward gaps where wharves had been. Not a living thing did I see except for the scattered fishermen on the distant break-water, and not a sound did I hear save the lapping of the harbor tides and the roar of the falls in the Manuxet. The town was getting more and more on my nerves, and I looked behind me furtively as I picked my way back over the tottering Water Street bridge. The Fish Street bridge, according to the sketch, was in ruins.

North of the river there were traces of squalid life—active fish-packing houses in Water Street, smoking chimneys and patched roofs here and there, occasional sounds from indeterminate sources, and infrequent shambling forms in the dismal streets and unpaved lanes—but I seemed to find this even more oppressive than the southerly desertion. For one thing, the people were more hideous and abnormal than those near the center of the town; so that I was several times evilly reminded of something utterly fantastic which I could not quite place. Undoubtedly the alien strain in the Innsmouth folk was stronger here than farther inland—unless, indeed, the "Innsmouth look" were a disease rather than a blood stain, in which case this district might be held to harbor the more advanced cases.

One detail that annoyed me was the distribution of the few faint sounds I heard. They ought naturally to have come wholly from the visibly inhabited houses, yet in reality were often strongest inside the most rigidly boarded-up facades. There were creakings, scurryings, and hoarse doubtful noises; and I thought uncomfortably about the hidden tunnels suggested by the grocery boy. Suddenly I found myself wondering what the voices of those denizens would be like. I had heard no speech so far in this quarter, and was unaccountably anxious not to do so.

Pausing only long enough to look at two fine but ruinous old churches at Main and Church Streets, I hastened out of that vile waterfront slum. My next logical goal was New Church Green, but somehow or other I could not bear to repass the church in whose basement I had glimpsed the inexplicably frightening form of that strangely diademed priest or pastor. Besides, the grocery youth had told me that churches, as well as the Order of Dagon Hall, were not advisable neighborhoods for strangers.

Accordingly I kept north along Main to Martin, then turning inland, crossing Federal Street safely north of the Green, and entering the decayed patrician[18] neighborhood of northern Broad, Washington, Lafayette, and Adams Streets. Though these stately old avenues were ill-surfaced and unkempt, their elm-shaded dignity had not entirely departed. Mansion after mansion claimed my gaze, most of them decrepit and boarded up amidst neglected grounds, but one or two in each street showing signs of occupancy. In Washington Street there was a row of four or five in excellent repair and with finely-tended lawns and gardens. The most sumptuous of these—with wide terraced parterres[19] extending back the whole way to Lafayette Street—I took to be the home of Old Man Marsh, the afflicted refinery owner.

In all these streets no living thing was visible, and I wondered at the complete absence of cats and dogs from Innsmouth. Another thing which puzzled and disturbed me, even in some of the best-preserved mansions, was the tightly shuttered condition of many third-story and attic windows. Furtiveness and secretiveness seemed universal in this hushed city of alienage and death, and I could not escape the sensation of being watched from ambush on every hand by sly, staring eyes that never shut.

I shivered as the cracked stroke of three sounded from a belfry on my left. Too well did I recall the squat church from which those notes came. Following Washington Street toward the river, I now faced a new zone of former industry and commerce; noting the ruins of a factory ahead, and seeing others, with the traces of an old railway station and covered railway bridge beyond, up the gorge on my right.

The uncertain bridge now before me was posted with a warning sign, but I took the risk and crossed again to the south bank where traces of life reappeared. Furtive, shambling creatures stared cryptically in my direction, and more normal faces eyed me coldly and curiously. Innsmouth was rapidly becoming intolerable, and I turned down Paine Street toward the Square in the hope of getting some vehicle to take me to Arkham before the still-distant starting-time of that sinister bus.

It was then that I saw the tumbledown fire station on my left, and noticed the red faced, bushy-bearded, watery eyed old man in nondescript rags who sat on a bench in front of it talking with a pair of unkempt but not abnormal looking firemen. This, of course, must be Zadok Allen, the half-crazed, liquorish nonagenarian whose tales of old Innsmouth and its shadow were so hideous and incredible.

III.

It must have been some imp of the perverse[20]—or some sardonic pull from dark, hidden sources—which made me change my plans as I did. I had long before resolved to limit my observations to architecture alone, and I was even then hurrying toward the Square in an effort to get quick transportation out of this festering city of death and decay; but the sight of old Zadok Allen set up new currents in my mind and made me slacken my pace uncertainly.

I had been assured that the old man could do nothing but hint at wild, disjointed, and incredible legends, and I had been warned that the natives made it unsafe to be seen talking with him; yet the thought of this aged witness to the town's decay, with memories going back to the early days of ships and factories, was a lure that no amount of reason could make me resist. After all, the strangest and maddest of myths are often merely symbols or allegories based upon truth—and old Zadok must have seen everything which went on around Innsmouth for the last ninety years. Curiosity flared up beyond sense and caution, and in my youthful egotism I fancied I might be able to sift a nucleus of real history from the confused, extravagant outpouring I would probably extract with the aid of raw whiskey.

I knew that I could not accost him then and there, for the firemen would surely notice and object. Instead, I reflected, I would prepare by getting some bootleg liquor at a place where the grocery boy had told me it was plentiful. Then I would loaf near the fire station in apparent casualness, and fall in with old Zadok after he had started on one of his frequent rambles. The youth had said that he was very restless, seldom sitting around the station for more than an hour or two at a time.

A quart bottle of whiskey was easily, though not cheaply, obtained in the rear of a dingy variety-store just off the Square in Eliot Street. The dirty-looking fellow who waited on me had a touch of the staring "Innsmouth look," but was quite civil in his way; being perhaps used to the custom of such convivial strangers—truckmen, gold-buyers, and the like—as were occasionally in town.

Reentering the Square I saw that luck was with me; for—shuffling out of Paine street around the corner of the Gilman House—I glimpsed nothing less than the tall, lean, tattered form of old Zadok Allen himself. In accordance with my plan, I attracted his attention by brandishing my newly-purchased bottle: and soon realized that he had begun to shuffle wistfully after me as I turned into Waite Street on my way to the most deserted region I could think of.

I was steering my course by the map the grocery boy had prepared, and was aiming for the wholly abandoned stretch of southern waterfront which I had previously visited. The only people in sight there had been the fishermen on the distant breakwater; and by going a few squares south I could get beyond the range of these, finding a pair of seats on some abandoned wharf and being free to question old Zadok unobserved for an indefinite time. Before I reached Main Street I could hear a faint and wheezy "Hey, Mister!" behind me and I presently allowed the old man to catch up and take copious pulls from the quart bottle.

I began putting out feelers as we walked amidst the omnipresent desolation and crazily tilted ruins, but found that the aged tongue did not loosen as quickly as I had expected. At length I saw a grass-grown opening toward the sea between crumbling brick walls, with the weedy length of an earth-and-masonry wharf projecting beyond. Piles of moss-covered stones near the water promised tolerable seats, and the scene was sheltered from all possible view by a ruined warehouse on the north. Here, I thought was the ideal place for a long secret colloquy; so I guided my companion down the lane and picked out spots to sit in among the mossy stones. The air of death and desertion was ghoulish, and the smell of fish almost insufferable; but I was resolved to let nothing deter me.

About four hours remained for conversation if I were to catch the eight o'clock coach for Arkham, and I began to dole out more liquor to the ancient tippler; meanwhile eating my own frugal lunch. In my donations I was careful not to overshoot the mark, for I did not wish Zadok's vinous garrulousness[21] to pass into a stupor. After an hour his furtive taciturnity showed signs of disappearing, but much to my disappointment he still sidetracked my questions about Innsmouth and its shadow-haunted past. He would babble of current topics, revealing a wide acquaintance with newspapers and a great tendency to philosophize in a sententious[22] village fashion.

Toward the end of the second hour I feared my quart of whiskey would not be enough to produce results, and was wondering whether I had better leave old Zadok and go back for more. Just then, however, chance made the opening which my questions had been unable to make; and the wheezing ancient's rambling took a turn that caused me to lean forward and listen alertly. My back was toward the fishy-smelling sea, but he was facing it and something or other had caused his wandering gaze to light on the low, distant line of Devil Reef, then showing plainly and almost fascinatingly above the waves. The sight seemed to displease him, for he began a series of weak curses which ended in a confidential whisper and a knowing leer. He bent toward me, took hold of my coat lapel, and hissed out some hints that could not be mistaken.

"Thar's whar it all begun—that cursed place of all wickedness whar the deep water starts. Gate o' hell—sheer drop daown to a bottom no saoundin'-line kin tech. Ol' Cap'n Obed done it—him that faound aout more'n was good fer him in the Saouth Sea islands.

"Everybody was in a bad way them days. Trade fallin' off, mills losin' business—even the new ones—an' the best of our menfolks kilt aprivateerin' in the War of 1812 or lost with the Elizy brig an' the Ranger scow—both on 'em Gilman venters. Obed Marsh he had three ships afloat—brigantine Columby, brig Hefty, an' barque Sumatry Queen. He was the only one as kep' on with the East-Injy an' Pacific trade, though Esdras Martin's barkentine Malay Bride made a venter as late as twenty-eight.

"Never was nobody like Cap'n Obed—old limb o' Satan! Heh, heh! I kin mind him a-tellin' abaout furren parts, an' callin' all the folks stupid for goin' to Christian meetin' an' bearin' their burdns meek an' lowly. Says they'd orter git better gods like some o' the folks in the Injies—gods as ud bring 'em good fishin' in return for their sacrifices, an' ud reely answer folks's prayers.

"Matt Eliot his fust mate, talked a lot too, only he was again' folks's doin' any heathen things. Told abaout an island east of Othaheite whar they was a lot o' stone ruins older'n anybody knew anything abaout, kind o' like them on Ponape, in the Carolines, but with carven's of faces that looked like the big statues on Easter Island.[23] Thar was a little volcanic island near thar, too, whar they was other ruins with diff'rent carvin'—ruins all wore away like they'd ben under the sea onct, an' with picters of awful monsters all over 'em.

"Wal, Sir, Matt he says the natives around thar had all the fish they cud ketch, an' sported bracelets an' armlets an' head rigs made aout o' a queer kind o' gold an' covered with picters o' monsters jest like the ones carved over the ruins on the little island—sorter fish-like frogs or froglike fishes that was drawed in all kinds o' positions likes they was human bein's. Nobody cud get aout o' them whar they got all the stuff, an' all the other natives wondered haow they managed to find fish in plenty even when the very next island had lean pickin's. Matt he got to wonderon' too an' so did Cap'n Obed. Obed he notices, besides, that lots of the hn'some young folks ud drop aout o' sight fer good from year to year, an' that they wan't many old folks around. Also, he thinks some of the folks looked dinned queer even for Kanakys.[24]

"It took Obed to git the truth aout o' them heathen. I dun't know haow he done it, but he begun by tradin' fer the gold-like things they wore. Ast 'em whar they come from, an' ef they cud git more, an' finally wormed the story aout o' the old chief—Walakea, they called him. Nobody but Obed ud ever a believed the old yeller devil, but the Cap'n cud read folks like they was books. Heh, heh! Nobody never believes me naow when I tell 'em, an' I dun't s'pose you will, young feller—though come to look at ye, ye hev kind o' got them sharp-readin' eyes like Obed had."

The old man's whisper grew fainter, and I found myself shuddering at the terrible and sincere portentousness of his intonation, even though I knew his tale could be nothing but drunken phantasy.

"Wal, Sir, Obed he 'lart that they's things on this arth as most folks never heerd about—an' wouldn't believe ef they did hear. lt seems these Kanakys was sacrificin' heaps o' their young men an' maidens to some kind o' god-things that lived under the sea, an' gittin' all kinds o' favour in return. They met the things on the little islet with the queer ruins, an' it seems them awful picters o' frog-fish monsters was supposed to be picters o' these things. Mebbe they was the kind o' critters as got all the mermaid stories an' sech started.

"They had all kinds a' cities on the sea-bottom, an' this island was heaved up from thar. Seems they was some of the things alive in the stone buildin's when the island come up sudden to the surface, That's how the Kanakys got wind they was daown thar. Made sign-talk as soon as they got over bein' skeert, an' pieced up a bargain afore long.

"Them things liked human sacrifices. Had had 'em ages afore, but lost track o' the upper world after a time. What they done to the victims it ain't fer me to say, an' I guess Obed was'n't none too sharp abaout askin.' But it was all right with the heathens, because they'd ben havin' a hard time an' was desp'rate abaout everything. They give a sarten number o' young folks to the sea-things twice every year—May-Eve an' Hallawe'en—reg'lar as cud be. Also give some a' the carved knick-knacks they made. What the things agreed to give in return was plenty a' fish—they druv 'em in from all over the sea—an' a few gold like things naow an' then.

"Wal, as I says, the natives met the things on the little volcanic islet—goin' thar in canoes with the sacrifices et cet'ry, and bringin' back any of the gold-like jools as was comin' to 'em. At fust the things didn't never go onto the main island, but arter a time they come to want to. Seems they hankered arter mixin' with the folks, an' havin' j'int ceremonies on the big days—May-Eve an' Hallowe'en. Ye see, they was able to live both in ant aout o' water—what they call amphibians, I guess. The Kanakys told 'em as haow folks from the other islands might wanta wipe 'em out if they got wind o' their bein' thar, but they says they dun't keer much, because they cud wipe aout the hull brood o' humans ef they was willin' to bother—that is, any as didn't have, sarten signs sech as was used onct by the lost Old Ones, whoever they was. But not wantin' to bother, they'd lay low when anybody visited the island.

"When it come to matin' with them toad-lookin' fishes, the Kanakys kind o' balked, but finally they larnt something as put a new face on the matter. Seems that human folks has got a kind a' relation to sech water-beasts—that everything alive come aout o' the water onct an' only needs a little change to go back agin. Them things told the Kanakys that ef they mixed bloods there'd be children as ud look human at fust, but later turn more'n more like the things, till finally they'd take to the water an' jine the main lot o' things daown har. An' this is the important part, young feller—them as turned into fish things an' went into the water wouldn't never die. Them things never died excep' they was kilt violent.

"Wal, Sir, it seems by the time Obed knowed them islanders they was all full o' fish blood from them deep water things. When they got old an' begun to shew it, they was kep' hid until they felt like takin' to the water an' quittin' the place. Some was more teched than others, an' some never did change quite enough to take to the water; but mostly they turned out jest the way them things said. Them as was born more like the things changed arly, but them as was nearly human sometimes stayed on the island till they was past seventy, though they'd usually go daown under for trial trips afore that. Folks as had took to the water gen'rally come back a good deal to visit, so's a man ud often be a'talkin' to his own five-times-great-grandfather who'd left the dry land a couple o' hundred years or so afore.

"Everybody got aout o' the idee o' dyin'—excep' in canoe wars with the other islanders, or as sacrifices to the sea-gods daown below, or from snakebite or plague or sharp gallopin' ailments or somethin' afore they cud take to the water—but simply looked forrad to a kind o' change that wa'n't a bit horrible arter a while. They thought what they'd got was well wuth all they'd had to give up—an' I guess Obed kind o' come to think the same hisself when he'd chewed over old Walakea's story a bit. Walakea, though, was one of the few as hadn't got none of the fish blood—bein' of a royal line that intermarried with royal lines on other islands.

"Walakea he shewed Obed a lot o' rites an' incantations as had to do with the sea things, an' let him see some o' the folks in the village as had changed a lot from human shape. Somehaow or other, though, he never would let him see one of the reg'lar things from right aout o' the water. In the end he give him a funny kind o' thingumajig made aout o' lead or something, that he said ud bring up the fish things from any place in the water whar they might be a nest o' 'em. The idee was to drop it daown with the right kind o' prayers an' sech. Walakea allowed as the things was scattered all over the world, so's anybody that looked abaout cud find a nest an' bring 'em up ef they was wanted.

"Matt he didn't like this business at all, an' wanted Obed shud keep away from the island; but the Cap'n was sharp fer gain, an' faound he cud get them gold-like things so cheap it ud pay him to make a specialty of them. Things went on that way for years an' Obed got enough o' that gold-like stuff to make him start the refinery in Waite's old run-daown fullin' mill.[25] He didn't dass sell the pieces like they was, for folks ud be all the time askin' questions. All the same his crews ud get a piece an' dispose of it naow and then, even though they was swore to keep quiet; an' he let his women-folks wear some o' the pieces as was more human-like than most.

"Well, come abaout thutty-eight—when I was seven year' old—Obed he faound the island people all wiped aout between v'yages. Seems the other islanders had got wind o' what was goin' on, and had took matters into their own hands. S'pose they must a had, after all, them old magic signs as the sea things says was the only things they was afeard of. No tellin' what any o' them Kanakys will chance to git a holt of when the sea-bottom throws up some island with ruins older'n the deluge. Pious cusses, these was—they didn't leave nothin' standin' on either the main island or the little volcanic islet excep' what parts of the ruins was too big to knock daown. In some places they was little stones strewed abaout—like charms—with somethin' on 'em like what ye call a swastika naowadays. Prob'ly them was the Old Ones' signs. Folks all wiped aout no trace o' no gold-like things an' none the nearby Kanakys ud breathe a word abaout the matter. Wouldn't even admit they'd ever ben any people on that island.

"That naturally hit Obed pretty hard, seein' as his normal trade was doin' very poor. It hit the whole of Innsmouth, too, because in seafarint days what profited the master of a ship gen'lly profited the crew proportionate. Most of the folks araound the taown took the hard times kind o' sheep-like an' resigned, but they was in bad shape because the fishin' was peterin' aout an' the mills wan't doin' none too well.

"Then's the time Obed he begun a-cursin' at the folks fer bein' dull sheep an' prayin' to a Christian heaven as didn't help 'em none. He told 'em he'd knowed o' folks as prayed to gods that give somethin' ye reely need, an' says ef a good bunch o' men ud stand by him, he cud mebbe get a holt o' sarten paowers as ud bring plenty o' fish an' quite a bit of gold. O' course them as sarved on the Sumatry Queen, an' seed the island knowed what he meant, an' wa'n't none too anxious to get clost to sea-things like they'd heard tell on, but them as didn't know what 'twas all abaout got kind o' swayed by what Obed had to say, and begun to ast him what he cud do to sit 'em on the way to the faith as ud bring 'em results."

Here the old man faltered, mumbled, and lapsed into a moody and apprehensive silence; glancing nervously over his shoulder and then turning back to stare fascinatedly at the distant black reef. When I spoke to him he did not answer, so I knew I would have to let him finish the bottle. The insane yarn I was hearing interested me profoundly, for I fancied there was contained within it a sort of crude allegory based upon the strangeness of Innsmouth and elaborated by an imagination at once creative and full of scraps of exotic legend. Not for a moment did I believe that the tale had any really substantial foundation; but none the less the account held a hint of genuine terror if only because it brought in references to strange jewels clearly akin to the malign tiara I had seen at Newburyport. Perhaps the ornaments had, after all, come from some strange island; and possibly the wild stories were lies of the bygone Obed himself rather than of this antique toper.[26]

I handed Zadok the bottle, and he drained it to the last drop. It was curious how he could stand so much whiskey, for not even a trace of thickness had come into his high, wheezy voice. He licked the nose of the bottle and slipped it into his pocket, then beginning to nod and whisper softly to himself. I bent close to catch any articulate words he might utter, and thought I saw a sardonic smile behind the stained bushy whiskers. Yes—he was really forming words, and I could grasp a fair proportion of them.

"Poor Matt—Matt he allus was agin it—tried to line up the folks on his side, an' had long talks with the preachers—no use—they run the Congregational parson aout o' taown, an' the Methodist feller quit—never did see Resolved Babcock, the Baptist parson, agin—Wrath o' Jehovy—I was a mightly little critter, but I heerd what I heerd an, seen what I seen—Dagon an' Ashtoreth—Belial an' Beelzebub—Golden Caff an' the idols o' Canaan an' the Philistines—Babylonish abominations—*Mene, mene, tekel, upharisn*[27]—."

He stopped again, and from the look in his watery blue eyes I feared he was close to a stupor after all. But when I gently shook his shoulder he turned on me with astonishing alertness and snapped out some more obscure phrases.

"Dun't believe me, hey? Hey, heh, heh—then jest tell me, young feller, why Cap'n Obed an' twenty odd other folks used to row aout to Devil Reef in the dead o' night an' chant things so laoud ye cud hear 'em all over taown when the wind was right? Tell me that, hey? An' tell me why Obed was allus droppin' heavy things daown into the deep water t'other side o' the reef whar the bottom shoots daown like a cliff lower'n ye kin saound? Tell me what he done with that funny-shaped lead thingumajig as Walakea give him? Hey, boy? An' what did they all haowl on May-Eve, an, agin the next Hallowe'en? An' why'd the new church parsons—fellers as used to be sailors—wear them queer robes an' cover their-selves with them gold-like things Obed brung? Hey?"

The watery blue eyes were almost savage and maniacal now, and the dirty white beard bristled electrically. Old Zadok probably saw me shrink back, for he began to cackle evilly.

"Heh, heh, heh, heh! Beginni'n to see hey? Mebbe ye'd like to a ben me in them days, when I seed things at night aout to sea from the cupalo top o' my haouse. Oh, I kin tell ye' little pitchers hev big ears, an' I wa'n't missin' nothin' o' what was gossiped abaout Cap'n Obed an' the folks aout to the reef! Heh, heh, heh! Haow abaout the night I took my pa's ship's glass up to the cupalo an' seed the reef a-bristlin' thick with shapes that dove off quick soon's the moon riz?

"Obed an' the folks was in a dory, but them shapes dove off the far side into the deep water an' never come up...

"Haow'd ye like to be a little shaver alone up in a cupola a-watchin' shapes *as wa'n't human shapes*? ... Heh? ... Heh, heh, heh..."

The old man was getting hysterical, and I began to shiver with a nameless alarm. He laid a gnarled claw on my shoulder, and it seemed to me that its shaking was not altogether that of mirth.

"S'pose one night ye seed somethin' heavy heaved offen Obed's dory beyond the reef, and then learned next day a young feller was missin' from home. Hey! Did anybody ever see hide or hair o' Hiram Gilman agin. Did they? An' Nick Pierce, an' Luelly Waite, an' Adoniram Saouthwick, an' Henry Garrison Hey? Heh, heh, heh, heh.... Shapes talkin' sign language with their hands ... them as had reel hands...

"Wal, Sir, that was the time Obed begun to git on his feet agin. Folks see his three darters a-wearin' gold-like things as nobody'd never see on 'em afore, an' smoke started comin' aout o' the refin'ry chimbly. Other folks was prosp'rin', too—fish begun to swarm into the harbour fit to kill' an' heaven knows what sized cargoes we begun to ship aout to Newb'ryport, Arkham, an' Boston. T'was then Obed got the ol' branch railrud put through. Some Kingsport fishermen heerd abaout the ketch an' come up in sloops, but they was all lost. Nobody never see 'em agin. An' jest then our folk organised the Esoteric Order o' Dagon, an' bought Masonic Hall offen Calvary Commandery[28] for it ... heh, heh, heh! Matt Eliot was a Mason an' agin' the sellin', but he dropped aout o' sight jest then.

"Remember, I ain't sayin' Obed was set on hevin' things jest like they was on that Kanaky isle. I dun't think he aimed at fust to do no mixin', nor raise no younguns to take to the water an' turn into fishes with eternal life. He wanted them gold things, an' was willin' to pay heavy, an' I guess the others was satisfied fer a while...

"Come in' forty-six the taown done some lookin' an' thinkin' fer itself. Too many folks missin'—too much wild preachin' at meetin' of a Sunday—too much talk abaout that reef. I guess I done a bit by tellin' Selectman Mowry what I see from the cupalo. They was a party one night as follered Obed's craowd aout to the reef, an' I heerd shots betwixt the dories. Nex' day Obed and thutty-two others was in gaol, with everybody a-wonderin' jest what was afoot and jest what charge agin 'em cud be got to holt. God, ef anybody'd look'd ahead ... a couple o' weeks later, when nothin' had ben throwed into the sea fer thet long..."

Zadok was shewing sings of fright and exhaustion, and I let him keep silence for a while, though glancing apprehensively at my watch. The tide had turned and was coming in now, and the sound of the waves seemed to arouse him. I was glad of that tide, for at high water the fishy smell might not be so bad. Again I strained to catch his whispers.

"That awful night ... I seed 'em. I was up in the cupalo ... hordes of 'em ... swarms of 'em ... all over the reef an' swimmin' up the harbour into the Manuxet.... God, what happened in the streets of Innsmouth that night ... they rattled our door, but pa wouldn't open ...

then he clumb aout the kitchen winder with his musket to find Selectman Mowry an' see what he cud do…. Maounds o' the dead an' the dyin' … shots and screams … shaoutin' in Ol Squar an' Taown Squar an' New Church Green—gaol throwed open—proclamation … treason … called it the plague when folks come in an' faoud haff our people missin' … nobody left but them as ud jine in with Obed an' them things or else keep quiet … never heard o' my pa no more…"

The old man was panting and perspiring profusely. His grip on my shoulder tightened.

"Everything cleaned up in the mornin'—but they was traces…. Obed he kinder takes charge an' says things is goin' to be changed … others'll worship with us at meetin'-time, an' sarten haouses hez got to entertain guests … they wanted to mix like they done with the Kanakys, an' he for one didn't feel baound to stop 'em. Far gone, was Obed … jest like a crazy man on the subjeck. He says they brung us fish an' treasure, an' shud hev what they hankered after…"

"Nothin' was to be diff'runt on the outside, only we was to keep shy o' strangers ef we knowed what was good fer us.

"We all hed to take the Oath o' Dagon, an' later on they was secon' an' third oaths that some o' us took. Them as ud help special, ud git special rewards—gold an' sech—No use balkin', fer they was millions of 'em daown thar. They'd ruther not start risin' an' wipin' aout human-kind, but ef they was gave away an' forced to, they cud do a lot toward jest that. We didn't hev them old charms to cut 'em off like folks in the Saouth Sea did, an' them Kanakys wudn't never give away their secrets.

"Yield up enough sacrifices an' savage knick-knacks an' harbourage in the taown when they wanted it, an' they'd let well enough alone. Wudn't bother no strangers as might bear tales aoutside—that is, withaout they got pryin.' All in the band of the faithful—Order o' Dagon—an' the children shud never die, but go back to the Mother Hydra an' Father Dagon[29] what we all come from onct…. *Iä! Iä! Cthulhu fhtagn! Ph'nglui mglw'nafh Cthulhu R'lyeh wgah-nagl fhtaga-*"[30]

Old Zadok was fast lapsing into stark raving, and I held my breath. Poor old soul—to what pitiful depths of hallucination had his liquor, plus his hatred of the decay, alienage, and disease around him, brought that fertile, imaginative brain? He began to moan now, and tears were coursing down his channelled checks into the depths of his beard.

"God, what I seen senct I was fifteen year' old—*Mene, mene, tekel, upharsin!*—the folks as was missin,' and them as kilt theirselves—them as told things in Arkham or Ipswich or sech places was all called crazy, like you're callin' me right naow—but God, what I seen—They'd a kilt me long ago fer' what I know, only I'd took the fust an' secon' Oaths o' Dagon offen Obed, so was pertected unlessen a jury of 'em proved I told things knowin' an' delib'rit … but I wudn't take the third Oath—I'd a died ruther'n take that—

"It got wuss araound Civil War time, *when children born senct 'forty-six begun to grow up*—some 'em, that is. I was afeared—never did no pryin' arter that awful night, an' never see one o' them—clost to in all my life. That is, never no full-blooded one. I went to the war, an' ef I'd a had any guts or sense I'd a never come back, but settled away from here. But folks wrote me things wa'n't so bad. That, I s'pose, was because gov'munt draft men was in taown arter 'sixty-three. Arter the war it was jest as bad agin. People begun to fall off—mills an' shops shet daown—shippin' stopped an' the harbour choked up—railrud give up—but they … they never stopped swimmin' in an' aout o' the river from that cursed reef o' Satan—an' more an' more attic winders got a-boarded up, an' more an' more noises was heerd in haouses as wa'n't s'posed to hev nobody in 'em…

"Folks aoutside hev their stories abaout us—s'pose you've heerd a plenty on 'em, seein' what questions ye ast—stories abaout things they've seed naow an' then, an' abaout that queer joolry as still comes in from somewhars an' ain't quite all melted up—but nothin' never gits def'nite. Nobody'll believe nothin.' They call them gold-like things pirate loot, an' allaow the Innsmouth folks hez furren blood or is dis-tempered or somethin.' Beside, them that lives here shoo off as many strangers as they kin, an' encourage the rest not to git very cur'ous, specially raound night time. Beasts balk at the critters—hosses wuss'n mules—but when they got autos that was all right.

"In 'forty-six Cap'n Obed took a second wife *that nobody in the taown never see—*some says he didn't want to, but was made to by them as he'd called in—had three children by her—two as disappeared young, but one gal as looked like anybody else an' was eddicated in Europe. Obed finally got her married off by a trick to an Arkham feller as didn't suspect nothin.' But nobody aoutside'll hav nothin' to do with Innsmouth folks naow. Barnabas Marsh that runs the refin'ry now is Obed's grandson by his fust wife—son of Onesiphorus, his eldest son, *but his mother was another o' them as wa'n't never seen aoutdoors.*

"Right naow Barnabas is abaout changed. Can't shet his eyes no more, an' is all aout o' shape. They say he still wears clothes, but he'll take to the water soon. Mebbe he's tried it already—they do sometimes go daown for little spells afore they go daown for good. Ain't ben seed abaout in public fer nigh on ten year.' Dun't know haow his poor wife kin feel—she come from Ipswich, an' they nigh lynched Barnabas when he courted her fifty odd year' ago. Obed he died in 'seventy-eight an' all the next gen'ration is gone naow—the fust wife's children dead, and the rest…. God knows…."

The sound of the incoming tide was now very insistent, and little by little it seemed to change the old man's mood from maudlin tearfulness to watchful fear. He would pause now and then to renew those nervous glances over his shoulder or out toward the reef, and despite the wild absurdity of his tale, I could not help beginning to share his apprehensiveness. Zadok now grew shriller, seemed to be trying to whip up his courage with louder speech.

"Hey, yew, why dun't ye say somethin'? Haow'd ye like to be livin' in a taown like this, with everything a-rottin' an' dyin,' an' boarded-up monsters crawlin' an' bleatin' an' barkin' an' hoppin' araoun' black cellars an' attics every way ye turn? Hey? Haow'd ye like to hear the haowlin' night arter night from the churches an' Order o' Dagon Hall, *an' know what's doin' part o' the haowlin'?* Haow'd ye like to hear what comes from that awful reef every May-Eve an' Hallowmass? Hey? Think the old man's crazy, eh? Wal, Sir, let me tell ye *that ain't the wust!*"

Zadok was really screaming now, and the mad frenzy of his voice disturbed me more than I care to own.

"Curse ye, dun't set thar a'starin' at me with them eyes—I tell Obed Marsh he's in hell, an, hez got to stay thar! Heh, heh … in hell, I says! Can't git me—I hain't done nothin' nor told nobody nothin'—

"Oh, you, young feller? Wal, even ef I hain't told nobody nothin' yet, I'm a'goin' to naow! Yew jest set still an' listen to me, boy—this is what I ain't never told nobody…. I says I didn't get to do pryin' arter that night—*but I faound things aout jest the same!*"

"Yew want to know what the reel horror is, hey? Wal, it's this—it ain't what them fish devils *hez done, but what they're a-goin' to do!* They're a-bringin' things up aout o' whar they come from into the taown—been doin' it fer years, an' slackenin' up lately. Them haouses north o' the river be-twixt Water an' Main Streets is full of 'em—them devils *an' what they brung*—an' when they git ready.... I say, *when they git ready* ... ever hear tell of a *shoggoth*?

"Hey, d'ye hear me? I tell ye *I know what them things be—I seen 'em one night when ...* eh-ahhh-ah! e'yahhh..."

The hideous suddenness and inhuman frightfulness of the old man's shriek almost made me faint. His eyes, looking past me toward the malodorous sea, were positively starting from his head; while his face was a mask of fear worthy of Greek tragedy. His bony claw dug monstrously into my shoulder, and he made no motion as I turned my head to look at whatever he had glimpsed.

There was nothing that I could see. Only the incoming tide, with perhaps one set of ripples more local than the long-flung line of breakers. But now Zadok was shaking me, and I turned back to watch the melting of that fear-frozen face into a chaos of twitching eyelids and mumbling gums. Presently his voice came back—albeit as a trembling whisper.

"*Git aout o' here!* Get aout o' here! *They seen us*—git aout fer your life! Dun't wait fer nothin'—*they know naow*—Run fer it—quick—*aout o' this taown*—"

Another heavy wave dashed against the loosing masonry of the bygone wharf, and changed the mad ancient's whisper to another inhuman and blood-curdling scream. "E-yaahhhh! ... Yheaaaaa!..."

Before I could recover my scattered wits he had relaxed his clutch on my shoulder and dashed wildly inland toward the street, reeling northward around the ruined warehouse wall.

I glanced back at the sea, but there was nothing there. And when I reached Water Street and looked along it toward the north there was no remaining trace of Zadok Allen.

IV.

I can hardly describe the mood in which I was left by this harrowing episode—an episode at once mad and pitiful, grotesque and terrifying. The grocery boy had prepared me for it, yet the reality left me none the less bewildered and disturbed. Puerile though the story was, old Zadok's insane earnestness and horror had communicated to me a mounting unrest which joined with my earlier sense of loathing for the town and its blight of intangible shadow.

Later I might sift the tale and extract some nucleus of historic allegory; just now I wished to put it out of my head. The hour grown perilously late—my watch said 7:15, and the Arkham bus left Town Square at eight—so I tried to give my thoughts as neutral and practical a cast as possible, meanwhile walking rapidly through the deserted streets of gaping roofs and leaning houses toward the hotel where I had checked my valise and would find my bus.

Though the golden light of late afternoon gave the ancient roofs and decrepit chimneys an air of mystic loveliness and peace, I could not help glancing over my shoulder now and then. I would surely be very glad to get out of malodorous and fear-shadowed Innsmouth, and wished there were some other vehicle than the bus driven by that sinister-looking fellow Sargent. Yet I did not hurry too precipitately, for there were architectural details worth viewing at every silent corner; and I could easily, I calculated, cover the necessary distance in a half-hour.

Studying the grocery youth's map and seeking a route I had not traversed before, I chose Marsh Street instead of State for my approach to Town Square. Near the corner of Fall Street I began to see scattered groups of furtive whisperers, and when I finally reached the Square I saw that almost all the loiterers were congregated around the door of the Gilman House. It seemed as if many bulging, watery, unwinking eyes looked oddly at me as I claimed my valise in the lobby, and I hoped that none of these unpleasant creatures would be my fellow-passengers on the coach.

The bus, rather early, rattled in with three passengers somewhat before eight, and an evil-looking fellow on the sidewalk muttered a few indistinguishable words to the driver. Sargent threw out a mail-bag and a roll of newspapers, and entered the hotel; while the passengers—the same men whom I had seen arriving in Newburyport that morning—shambled to the sidewalk and exchanged some faint guttural words with a loafer in a language I could have sworn was not English. I boarded the empty coach and took the seat I had taken before, but was hardly settled before Sargent re-appeared and began mumbling in a throaty voice of peculiar repulsiveness.

I was, it appeared, in very bad luck. There had been something wrong with the engine, despite the excellent time made from Newburyport, and the bus could not complete the journey to Arkham. No, it could not possibly be repaired that night, nor was there any other way of getting transportation out of Innsmouth either to Arkham or elsewhere. Sargent was sorry, but I would have to stop over at the Gilman. Probably the clerk would make the price easy for me, but there was nothing else to do. Almost dazed by this sudden obstacle, and violently dreading the fall of night in this decaying and half-unlighted town, I left the bus and reentered the hotel lobby; where the sullen queer-looking night clerk told me I could have Room 428 on next the top floor—large, but without running water—for a dollar.

Despite what I had heard of this hotel in Newburyport, I signed the register, paid my dollar, let the clerk take my valise, and followed that sour, solitary attendant up three creaking flights of stairs past dusty corridors which seemed wholly devoid of life. My room was a dismal rear one with two windows and bare, cheap furnishings, overlooked a dingy court-yard otherwise hemmed in by low, deserted brick blocks, and commanded a view of decrepit westward-stretching roofs with a marshy countryside beyond. At the end of the corridor was a bathroom—a discouraging relic with ancient marble bowl, tin tub, faint electric light, and musty wooded paneling around all the plumbing fixtures.

It being still daylight, I descended to the Square and looked around for a dinner of some sort; noticing as I did so the strange glances I received from the unwholesome loafers. Since the grocery was closed, I was forced to patronize the restaurant I had shunned before; a stooped, narrow-headed man with staring, unwinking eyes, and a flat-nosed wench with unbelievably thick, clumsy hands being in attendance. The service was all of the counter type, and it relieved me to find that much was evidently served from cans and packages. A bowl of vegetable soup with crackers was enough for me, and I soon headed back for my cheerless room at the Gilman; getting a evening paper and a fly-specked magazine from the evil-visaged clerk at the rickety stand beside his desk.

As twilight deepened I turned on the one feeble electric bulb over the cheap, iron-framed bed, and tried as best I could to continue the reading I had begun. I felt it advisable to keep my mind wholesomely occupied, for it would not do to brood over the abnormalities of this ancient, blight-shadowed town while I was still within its borders. The insane yarn I had heard from the aged drunkard did not promise very pleasant dreams, and I felt I must keep the image of his wild, watery eyes as far as possible from my imagination.

Also, I must not dwell on what that factory inspector had told the Newburyport ticket-agent about the Gilman House and the voices of its nocturnal tenants—not on that, nor on the face beneath the tiara in the black church doorway; the face for whose horror my conscious mind could not account. It would perhaps have been easier to keep my thoughts from disturbing topics had the room not been so gruesomely musty. As it was, the lethal mustiness blended hideously with the town's general fishy odor and persistently focused one's fancy on death and decay.

Another thing that disturbed me was the absence of a bolt on the door of my room. One had been there, as marks clearly showed, but there were signs of recent removal. No doubt it had been out of order, like so many other things in this decrepit edifice. In my nervousness I looked around and discovered a bolt on the clothes press which seemed to be of the same size, judging from the marks, as the one formerly on the door. To gain a partial relief from the general tension I busied myself by transferring this hardware to the vacant place with the aid of a handy three-in-one device including a screwdriver which I kept on my key-ring. The bolt fitted perfectly, and I was somewhat relieved when I knew that I could shoot it firmly upon retiring. Not that I had any real apprehension of its need, but that any symbol of security was welcome in an environment of this kind. There were adequate bolts on the two lateral doors to connecting rooms, and these I proceeded to fasten.

I did not undress, but decided to read till I was sleepy and then lie down with only my coat, collar, and shoes off. Taking a pocket flash light from my valise, I placed it in my trousers, so that I could read my watch if I woke up later in the dark. Drowsiness, however, did not come; and when I stopped to analyze my thoughts I found to my disquiet that I was really unconsciously listening for something—listening for something which I dreaded but could not name. That inspector's story must have worked on my imagination more deeply than I had suspected. Again I tried to read, but found that I made no progress.

After a time I seemed to hear the stairs and corridors creak at intervals as if with footsteps, and wondered if the other rooms were beginning to fill up. There were no voices, however, and it struck me that there was something subtly furtive about the creaking. I did not like it, and debated whether I had better try to sleep at all. This town had some queer people, and there had undoubtedly been several disappearances. Was this one of those inns where travelers were slain for their money? Surely I had no look of excessive prosperity. Or were the towns folk really so resentful about curious visitors? Had my obvious sight-seeing, with its frequent map-consultations, aroused unfavorable notice. It occurred to me that I must be in a highly nervous state to let a few random creakings set me off speculating in this fashion—but I regretted none the less that I was unarmed.

At length, feeling a fatigue which had nothing of drowsiness in it, I bolted the newly outfitted hall door, turned off the light, and threw myself down on the hard, uneven bed—coat, collar, shoes, and all. In the darkness every faint noise of the night seemed magnified, and a flood of doubly unpleasant thoughts swept over me. I was sorry I had put out the light, yet was too tired to rise and turn it on again. Then, after a long, dreary interval, and prefaced by a fresh creaking of stairs and corridor, there came that soft, damnably unmistakable sound which seemed like a malign fulfillment of all my apprehensions. Without the least shadow of a doubt, the lock of my door was being tried—cautiously, furtively, tentatively—with a key.

My sensations upon recognizing this sign of actual peril were perhaps less rather than more tumultuous because of my previous vague fears. I had been, albeit without definite reason, instinctively on my guard—and that was to my advantage in the new and real crisis, whatever it might turn out to be. Nevertheless the change in the menace from vague pre-monition to immediate reality was a profound shock, and fell upon me with the force of a genuine blow. It never once occurred to me that the fumbling might be a mere mistake. Malign purpose was all I could think of, and I kept deathly quiet, awaiting the would-be intruder's next move.

After a time the cautious rattling ceased, and I heard the room to the north entered with a pass key. Then the lock of the connecting door to my room was softly tried. The bolt held, of course, and I heard the floor creak as the prowler left the room. After a moment there came another soft rattling, and I knew that the room to the south of me was being entered. Again a furtive trying of a bolted connecting door, and again a receding creaking. This time the creaking went along the hall and down the stairs, so I knew that the prowler had realized the bolted condition of my doors and was giving up his attempt for a greater or lesser time, as the future would show.

The readiness with which I fell into a plan of action proves that I must have been sub-consciously fearing some menace and considering possible avenues of escape for hours. From the first I felt that the unseen fumbler meant a danger not to be met or dealt with, but only to be fled from as precipitately as possible. The one thing to do was to get out of that hotel alive as quickly as I could, and through some channel other than the front stairs and lobby.

Rising softly and throwing my flashlight on the switch, I sought to light the bulb over my bed in order to choose and pocket some belongings for a swift, valiseless flight. Nothing, however, happened; and I saw that the power had been cut off. Clearly, some cryptic, evil movement was afoot on a large scale—just what, I could not say. As I stood pondering with my hand on the now useless switch I heard a muffled creaking on the floor below, and thought I could barely distinguish voices in conversation. A moment later I felt less sure that the deeper sounds were voices, since the apparent hoarse barkings and loose-syllabled croakings bore so little resemblance to recognized human speech. Then I thought with renewed force of what the factory inspector had heard in the night in this moldering and pestilential building.

Having filled my pockets with the flashlight's aid, I put on my hat and tiptoed to the windows to consider chances of descent. Despite the state's safety regulations there was no fire escape on this side of the hotel, and I saw that my windows commanded only a sheer three story drop to the cobbled courtyard. On the right and left, however, some ancient brick business blocks abutted on the hotel; their slant roofs coming up to a reasonable jumping distance from my fourth-story level. To reach either of these lines of buildings I would have to be in a room two from my own—in one case on the north and in the other case on the south—and my mind instantly set to work what chances I had of making the transfer.

I could not, I decided, risk an emergence into the corridor; where my footsteps would surely be heard, and where the difficulties of entering the desired room would be insuper-able. My progress, if it was to be made at all, would have to be through the less solidly-built connecting doors of the rooms; the locks and bolts of which I would have to force violently, using my shoulder as a battering-ram whenever they were set against me. This, I thought, would be possible owing to the rickety nature of the house and its fixtures; but I realized I could not do it noiselessly. I would have to count on sheer speed, and the chance of getting to a window before any hostile forces became coordinated enough to open the right door toward me with a pass-key. My own outer door I reinforced by pushing the bureau against it—little by little, in order to make a minimum of sound.

I perceived that my chances were very slender, and was fully prepared for any calamity. Even getting to another roof would not solve the problem for there would then remain the task of reaching the ground and escaping from the town. One thing in my favor was the deserted and ruinous state of the abutting building and the number of skylights gaping blackly open in each row.

Gathering from the grocery boy's map that the best route out of town was southward, I glanced first at the connecting door on the south side of the room. It was designed to open in my direction, hence I saw—after drawing the bolt and finding other fastenings in place—it was not a favorable one for forcing. Accordingly abandoning it as a route, I cautiously moved the bedstead against it to hamper any attack which might be made on it later from the next room. The door on the north was hung to open away from me, and this—though a test proved it to be locked or bolted from the other side—I knew must be my route. If I could gain the roofs of the buildings in Paine Street and descend successfully to the ground level, I might perhaps dart through the courtyard and the adjacent or opposite building to Washington or Bates—or else emerge in Paine and edge around southward into Washington. In any case, I would aim to strike Washington somehow and get quickly out of the Town Square region. My preference would be to avoid Paine, since the fire station there might be open all night.

As I thought of these things I looked out over the squalid sea of decaying roofs below me, now brightened by the beams of a moon not much past full. On the right the black gash of the river-gorge clove the panorama; abandoned factories and railway station clinging barnacle-like to its sides. Beyond it the rusted railway and the Rowley road led off through a flat marshy terrain dotted with islets of higher and dryer scrub-grown land. On the left the creek-threaded country-side was nearer, the narrow road to Ipswich gleaming white in the moonlight. I could not see from my side of the hotel the southward route toward Arkham which I had determined to take.

I was irresolutely speculating on when I had better attack the northward door, and on how I could least audibly manage it, when I noticed that the vague noises underfoot had given place to a fresh and heavier creaking of the stairs. A wavering flicker of light showed through my transom, and the boards of the corridor began to groan with a ponderous load. Muffled sounds of possible vocal origin approached, and at length a firm knock came at my outer door.

For a moment I simply held my breath and waited. Eternities seemed to elapse, and the nauseous fishy odor of my environment seemed to mount suddenly and spectacularly. Then the knocking was repeated—continuously, and with growing insistence. I knew that the time for action had come, and forthwith drew the bolt of the northward connecting door, bracing myself for the task of battering it open. The knocking waxed louder, and I hoped that its volume would cover the sound of my efforts. At last beginning my attempt, I lunged again and again at the thin paneling with my left shoulder, heedless of shock or pain. The door resisted even more than I expected, but I did not give in. And all the while the clamor at the outer door increased.

Finally the connecting door gave, but with such a crash that I knew those outside must have heard. Instantly the outside knocking became a violent battering, while keys sounded ominously in the hall doors of the rooms on both sides of me. Rushing through the newly opened connection, I succeeded in bolting the northerly hall door before the lock could he turned; but even as I did so I heard the hall door of the third room—the one from whose window I had hoped to reach the roof below—being tried with a pass key.

For an instant I felt absolute despair, since my trapping in a chamber with no window egress seemed complete. A wave of almost abnormal horror swept over me, and invested with a terrible but unexplainable singularity the flashlight-glimpsed dust prints made by the intruder who had lately tried my door from this room. Then, with a dazed automatism which persisted despite hopelessness, I made for the next connecting door and performed the blind motion of pushing at it in an effort to get through and—granting that fastenings might be as providentially intact as in this second room—bolt the hall door beyond before the lock could be turned from outside.

Sheer fortunate chance gave me my reprieve—for the connecting door before me was not only unlocked but actually ajar. In a second I was through, and had my right knee and shoulder against a hall door which was visibly opening inward. My pressure took the opener off guard, for the thing shut as I pushed, so that I could slip the well-conditioned bolt as I had done with the other door. As I gained this respite I heard the battering at the two other doors abate, while a confused clatter came from the connecting door I had shielded with the bedstead. Evidently the bulk of my assailants had entered the southerly room and were massing in a lateral attack. But at the same moment a pass key sounded in the next door to the north, and I knew that a nearer peril was at hand.

The northward connecting door was wide open, but there was no time to think about checking the already turning lock in the hall. All I could do was to shut and bolt the open connecting door, as well as its mate on the opposite side—pushing a bedstead against the one and a bureau against the other, and moving a washstand in front of the hall door. I must, I saw, trust to such makeshift barriers to shield me till I could get out the window and on the roof of the Paine Street block. But even in this acute moment my chief horror was something apart from the immediate weakness of my defenses. I was shuddering because not one of my pursuers, despite some hideous panting, grunting, and subdued barkings at odd intervals, was uttering an unmuffled or intelligible vocal sound.

As I moved the furniture and rushed toward the windows I heard a frightful scurrying along the corridor toward the room north of me, and perceived that the southward battering had ceased. Plainly, most of my opponents were about to concentrate against the feeble connecting door which they knew must open directly on me. Outside, the moon played on the ridgepole of the block below, and I saw that the jump would be desperately hazardous because of the steep surface on which I must land.

Surveying the conditions, I chose the more southerly of the two windows as my avenue of escape; planning to land on the inner slope of the roof and make for the nearest sky-light. Once inside one of the decrepit brick structures I would have to reckon with pursuit; but I hoped to descend and dodge in and out of yawning doorways along the shadowed courtyard, eventually getting to Washington Street and slipping out of town toward the south.

The clatter at the northerly connecting door was now terrific, and I saw that the weak paneling was beginning to splinter. Obviously, the besiegers had brought some ponderous object into play as a battering-ram. The bedstead, however, still held firm; so that I had at least a faint chance of making good my escape. As I opened the window I noticed that it was flanked by heavy velour draperies suspended from a pole by brass rings, and also that there was a large projecting catch for the shutters on the exterior. Seeing a possible means of avoiding the dangerous jump, I yanked at the hangings and brought them down, pole and all; then quickly hooking two of the rings in the shutter catch and flinging the drapery outside. The heavy folds reached fully to the abutting roof, and I saw that the rings and catch would be likely to bear my weight. So, climbing out of the window and down the improvised rope ladder, I left behind me forever the morbid and horror-infested fabric of the Gilman House.

I landed safely on the loose slates of the steep roof, and succeeded in gaining the gaping black skylight without a slip. Glancing up at the window I had left, I observed it was still dark, though far across the crumbling chimneys to the north I could see lights ominously blazing in the Order of Dagon Hall, the Baptist church, and the Congregational church which I recalled so shiveringly. There had seemed to be no one in the courtyard below, and I hoped there would be a chance to get away before the spreading of a general alarm. Flashing my pocket lamp into the skylight, I saw that there were no steps down. The distance was slight, however, so I clambered over the brink and dropped; striking a dusty floor littered with crumbling boxes and barrels.

The place was ghoulish-looking, but I was past minding such impressions and made at once for the staircase revealed by my flashlight—after a hasty glance at my watch, which showed the hour to be 2 a.m. The steps creaked, but seemed tolerably sound; and I raced down past a barnlike second storey to the ground floor. The desolation was complete, and only echoes answered my footfalls. At length I reached the lower hall at the end of which I saw a faint luminous rectangle marking the ruined Paine Street doorway. Heading the other way, I found the back door also open; and darted out and down five stone steps to the grass-grown cobblestones of the courtyard.

The moonbeams did not reach down here, but I could just see my way about without using the flashlight. Some of the windows on the Gilman House side were faintly glowing, and I thought I heard confused sounds within. Walking softly over to the Washington Street side I perceived several open doorways, and chose the nearest as my route out. The hallway inside was black, and when I reached the opposite end I saw that the street door was wedged immovably shut. Resolved to try another building, I groped my way back toward the courtyard, but stopped short when close to the doorway.

For out of an opened door in the Gilman House a large crowd of doubtful shapes was pouring—lanterns bobbing in the darkness, and horrible croaking voices exchanging low cries in what was certainly not English. The figures moved uncertainly, and I realized to my relief that they did not know where I had gone; but for all that they sent a shiver of horror through my frame. Their features were indistinguishable, but their crouching, shambling gait was abominably repellent. And worst of all, I perceived that one figure was strangely robed, and unmistakably surmounted by a tall tiara of a design altogether too familiar. As the figures spread throughout the courtyard, I felt my fears increase. Suppose I could find no egress from this building on the street side? The fishy odor was detestable, and I wondered I could stand it without fainting. Again groping toward the street, I opened a door off the hall and came upon an empty room with closely shuttered but sashless windows. Fumbling in the rays of my flashlight, I found I could open the shutters; and in another moment had climbed outside and was fully closing the aperture in its original manner.

I was now in Washington Street, and for the moment saw no living thing nor any light save that of the moon. From several directions in the distance, however, I could hear the sound of hoarse voices, of footsteps, and of a curious kind of pattering which did not sound quite like footsteps. Plainly I had no time to lose. The points of the compass were clear to me, and I was glad that all the street lights were turned off, as is often the custom on strongly moonlit nights in prosperous rural regions. Some of the sounds came from the south, yet I retained my design of escaping in that direction. There would, I knew, be plenty of deserted doorways to shelter me in case I met any person or group who looked like pursuers.

I walked rapidly, softly, and close to the ruined houses. While hatless and disheveled after my arduous climb, I did not look especially noticeable; and stood a good chance of passing unheeded if forced to encounter any casual wayfarer.

At Bates Street I drew into a yawning vestibule while two shambling figures crossed in front of me, but was soon on my way again and approaching the open space where Eliot Street obliquely crosses Washington at the intersection of South. Though I had never seen this space, it had looked dangerous to me on the grocery youth's map; since the moonlight would have free play there. There was no use trying to evade it, for any alternative course would involve detours of possibly disastrous visibility and delaying effect. The only thing to do was to cross it boldly and openly; imitating the typical shamble of the Innsmouth folk as best I could, and trusting that no one—or at least no pursuer of mine—would be there.

Just how fully the pursuit was organized—and indeed, just what its purpose might be—I could form no idea. There seemed to be unusual activity in the town, but I judged that the news of my escape from the Gilman had not yet spread. I would, of course, soon have to shift from Washington to some other southward street; for that party from the hotel would doubtless be after me. I must have left dust prints in that last old building, revealing how I had gained the street.

The open space was, as I had expected, strongly moonlit; and I saw the remains of a parklike, iron-railed green in its center. Fortunately no one was about though a curious sort of buzz or roar seemed to be increasing in the direction of Town Square. South Street was very wide, leading directly down a slight declivity to the waterfront and commanding a long view out a sea; and I hoped that no one would be glancing up it from afar as I crossed in the bright moonlight.

My progress was unimpeded, and no fresh sound arose to hint that I had been spied. Glancing about me, I involuntarily let my pace slacken for a second to take in the sight of the sea, gorgeous in the burning moonlight at the street's end. Far out beyond the breakwater was the dim, dark line of Devil Reef, and as I glimpsed it I could not help thinking of all the hideous legends I had heard in the last twenty-four hours—legends which portrayed this ragged rock as a veritable gateway to realms of unfathomed horror and inconceivable abnormality.

Then, without warning, I saw the intermittent flashes of light on the distant reef. They were definite and unmistakable, and awaked in my mind a blind horror beyond all rational proportion. My muscles tightened for panic flight, held in only by a certain unconscious caution and half-hypnotic fascination. And to make matters worse, there now flashed forth from the lofty cupola of the Gilman House, which loomed up to the northeast behind me, a series of analogous though differently spaced gleams which could be nothing less than an answering signal.

Controlling my muscles, and realizing afresh—how plainly visible I was, I resumed my brisker and feignedly shambling pace; though keeping my eyes on that hellish and ominous reef as long as the opening of South Street gave me a seaward view. What the whole proceeding meant, I could not imagine; unless it involved some strange rite connected with

Devil Reef, or unless some party had landed from a ship on that sinister rock. I now bent to the left around the ruinous green; still gazing toward the ocean as it blazed in the spectral summer moonlight, and watching the cryptical flashing of those nameless, unexplainable beacons.

It was then that the most horrible impression of all was borne in upon me—the impression which destroyed my last vestige of self-control and sent me running frantically southward past the yawning black doorways and fishily staring windows of that deserted nightmare street. For at a closer glance I saw that the moonlit waters between the reef and the shore were far from empty. They were alive with a teeming horde of shapes swimming inward toward the town; and even at my vast distance and in my single moment of perception I could tell that the bobbing heads and flailing arms were alien and aberrant in a way scarcely to be expressed or consciously formulated.

My frantic running ceased before I had covered a block, for at my left I began to hear something like the hue and cry of organized pursuit. There were footsteps and guttural sounds, and a rattling motor wheezed south along Federal Street. In a second all my plans were utterly changed—for if the southward highway were blocked ahead of me, I must clearly find another egress from Innsmouth. I paused and drew into a gaping doorway, reflecting how lucky I was to have left the moonlit open space before these pursuers came down the parallel street.

A second reflection was less comforting. Since the pursuit was down another street, it was plain that the party was not following me directly. It had not seen me, but was simply obeying a general plan of cutting off my escape. This, however, implied that all roads leading out of Innsmouth were similarly patrolled; for the people could not have known what route I intended to take. If this were so, I would have to make my retreat across country away from any road; but how could I do that in view of the marshy and creek-riddled nature of all the surrounding region? For a moment my brain reeled—both from sheer hopelessness and from a rapid increase in the omnipresent fishy odor.

Then I thought of the abandoned railway to Rowley, whose solid line of ballasted, weed-grown earth still stretched off to the northwest from the crumbling station on the edge at the river-gorge. There was just a chance that the townsfolk would not think of that; since its briar-choked desertion made it half-impassable, and the unlikeliest of all avenues for a fugitive to choose. I had seen it clearly from my hotel window and knew about how it lay. Most of its earlier length was uncomfortably visible from the Rowley road, and from high places in the town itself; but one could perhaps crawl inconspicuously through the undergrowth. At any rate, it would form my only chance of deliverance, and there was nothing to do but try it.

Drawing inside the hall of my deserted shelter, I once more consulted the grocery boy's map with the aid of the flashlight. The immediate problem was how to reach the ancient railway; and I now saw that the safest course was ahead to Babson Street; then west to Lafayette—there edging around but not crossing an open space homologous to the one I had traversed—and subsequently back northward and westward in a zigzagging line through Lafayette, Bates, Adam, and Bank streets—the latter skirting the river gorge—to the abandoned and dilapidated station I had seen from my window. My reason for going ahead to Babson was that I wished neither to recross the earlier open space nor to begin my westward course along a cross street as broad as South.

Starting once more, I crossed the street to the right-hand side in order to edge around into Babson as inconspicuously as possible. Noises still continued in Federal Street, and as

I glanced behind me I thought I saw a gleam of light near the building through which I had escaped. Anxious to leave Washington Street, I broke into a quiet dogtrot, trusting to luck not to encounter any observing eye. Next the corner of Babson Street I saw to my alarm that one of the houses was still inhabited, as attested by curtains at the window; but there were no lights within, and I passed it without disaster.

In Babson Street, which crossed Federal and might thus reveal me to the searchers, I clung as closely as possible to the sagging, uneven buildings; twice pausing in a doorway as the noises behind me momentarily increased. The open space ahead shone wide and desolate under the moon, but my route would not force me to cross it. During my second pause I began to detect a fresh distribution of vague sounds; and upon looking cautiously out from cover beheld a motor car darting across the open space, bound outward along Eliot Street, which there intersects both Babson and Lafayette.

As I watched—choked by a sudden rise in the fishy odor after a short abatement—I saw a band of uncouth, crouching shapes loping and shambling in the same direction; and knew that this must be the party guarding the Ipswich road, since that highway forms an extension of Eliot Street. Two of the figures I glimpsed were in voluminous robes, and one wore a peaked diadem which glistened whitely in the moonlight. The gait of this figure was so odd that it sent a chill through me—for it seemed to me the creature was almost hopping.

When the last of the band was out of sight I resumed my progress; darting around the corner into Lafayette Street, and crossing Eliot very hurriedly lest stragglers of the party be still advancing along that thoroughfare. I did hear some croaking and clattering sounds far off toward Town Square, but accomplished the passage without disaster. My greatest dread was in re-crossing broad and moonlit South Street—with its seaward view—and I had to nerve myself for the ordeal. Someone might easily be looking, and possible Eliot Street stragglers could not fail to glimpse me from either of two points. At the last moment I decided I had better slacken my trot and make the crossing as before in the shambling gait of an average Innsmouth native.

When the view of the water again opened out—this time on my right—I was half-determined not to look at it at all. I could not however, resist; but cast a sidelong glance as I carefully and imitatively shambled toward the protecting shadows ahead. There was no ship visible, as I had half-expected there would be. Instead, the first thing which caught my eye was a small rowboat pulling in toward the abandoned wharves and laden with some bulky, tarpaulin-covered object. Its rowers, though distantly and indistinctly seen, were of an especially repellent aspect. Several swimmers were still discernible; while on the far black reef I could see a faint, steady glow unlike the winking beacon visible before, and of a curious color which I could not precisely identify. Above the slant roofs ahead and to the right there loomed the tall cupola of the Gilman House, but it was completely dark. The fishy odor, dispelled for a moment by some merciful breeze, now closed in again with maddening intensity.

I had not quite crossed the street when I heard a muttering band advancing along Washington from the north. As they reached the broad open space where I had had my first disquieting glimpse of the moonlit water I could see them plainly only a block away—and was horrified by the bestial abnormality of their faces and the doglike sub-humanness of their crouching gait. One man moved in a positively simian way, with long arms frequently touching the ground; while another figure—robed and tiaraed—seemed to progress in an almost hopping fashion. I judged this party to be the one I had seen in the Gilman's courtyard—the one, therefore, most closely on my trail. As some of the figures turned to look in my direction I was transfixed with fright, yet managed to preserve the casual, shambling gait I had assumed. To this day I do not know whether they saw me or not. If they did, my stratagem must have deceived them, for they passed on across the moonlit space without varying their course—meanwhile croaking and jabbering in some hateful guttural patois I could not identify.

Once more in shadow, I resumed my former dog-trot past the leaning and decrepit houses that stared blankly into the night. Having crossed to the western sidewalk I rounded the nearest corner into Bates Street where I kept close to the buildings on the southern side. I passed two houses showing signs of habitation, one of which had faint lights in upper rooms, yet met with no obstacle. As I tuned into Adams Street I felt measurably safer, but received a shock when a man reeled out of a black doorway directly in front of me. He proved, however, too hopelessly drunk to be a menace; so that I reached the dismal ruins of the Bank Street warehouses in safety.

No one was stirring in that dead street beside the river-gorge, and the roar of the waterfalls quite drowned my foot steps. It was a long dog-trot to the ruined station, and the great brick warehouse walls around me seemed somehow more terrifying than the fronts of private houses. At last I saw the ancient arcaded station—or what was left of it—and made directly for the tracks that started from its farther end.

The rails were rusty but mainly intact, and not more than half the ties had rotted away. Walking or running on such a surface was very difficult; but I did my best, and on the whole made very fair time. For some distance the line kept on along the gorge's brink, but at length I reached the long covered bridge where it crossed the chasm at a dizzying height. The condition of this bridge would determine my next step. If humanly possible, I would use it; if not, I would have to risk more street wandering and take the nearest intact highway bridge.

The vast, barnlike length of the old bridge gleamed spectrally in the moonlight, and I saw that the ties were safe for at least a few feet within. Entering, I began to use my flashlight, and was almost knocked down by the cloud of bats that flapped past me. About halfway across there was a perilous gap in the ties which I feared for a moment would halt me; but in the end I risked a desperate jump which fortunately succeeded.

I was glad to see the moonlight again when I emerged from that macabre tunnel. The old tracks crossed River Street at grade, and at once veered off into a region increasingly rural and with less and less of Innsmouth's abhorrent fishy odor. Here the dense growth of weeds and briers hindered me and cruelly tore at my clothes, but I was none the less glad that they were there to give me concealment in case of peril. I knew that much of my route must be visible from the Rowley road.

The marshy region began very abruptly, with the single track on a low, grassy embankment where the weedy growth was somewhat thinner. Then came a sort of island of higher ground, where the line passed through a shallow open cut choked with bushes and brambles. I was very glad of this partial shelter, since at this point the Rowley road was uncomfortably near according to my window view. At the end of the cut it would cross the track and swerve off to a safer distance; but meanwhile I must be exceedingly careful. I was by this time thankfully certain that the railway itself was not patrolled.

Just before entering the cut I glanced behind me, but saw no pursuer. The ancient spires and roofs of decaying Innsmouth gleamed lovely and ethereal in the magic yellow moonlight, and I thought of how they must have looked in the old days before the shadow fell. Then, as my gaze circled inland from the town, something less tranquil arrested my notice and held me immobile for a second.

What I saw—or fancied I saw—was a disturbing suggestion of undulant motion far to the south; a suggestion which made me conclude that a very large horde must be pouring out of the city along the level Ipswich road. The distance was great and I could distinguish nothing in detail; but I did not at all like the look of that moving column. It undulated too much, and glistened too brightly in the rays of the now westering moon. There was a suggestion of sound, too, though the wind was blowing the other way—a suggestion of bestial scraping and bellowing even worse than the muttering of the parties I had lately overheard.

All sorts of unpleasant conjectures crossed my mind. I thought of those very extreme Innsmouth types said to be hidden in crumbling, centuried warrens near the waterfront; I thought, too, of those nameless swimmers I had seen. Counting the parties so far glimpsed, as well as those presumably covering other roads, the number of my pursuers must be strangely large for a town as depopulated as Innsmouth.

Whence could come the dense personnel of such a column as I now beheld? Did those ancient, unplumbed warrens teem with a twisted, uncatalogued, and unsuspected life? Or had some unseen ship indeed landed a legion of unknown outsiders on that hellish reef? Who were they? Why were they here? And if such a column of them was scouring the Ipswich road, would the patrols on the other roads be likewise augmented?

I had entered the brush-grown cut and was struggling along at a very slow pace when that damnable fishy odor again waxed dominant. Had the wind suddenly changed eastward, so that it blew in from the sea and over the town? It must have, I concluded, since I now began to hear shocking guttural murmurs from that hitherto silent direction. There was another sound, too—a kind of wholesale, colossal flopping or pattering which somehow called up images of the most detestable sort. It made me think illogically of that unpleasantly undulating column on the far-off Ipswich road.

And then both stench and sounds grew stronger, so that I paused shivering and grateful for the cut's protection. It was here, I recalled, that the Rowley road drew so close to the old railway before crossing westward and diverging. Something was coming along that road, and I must lie low till its passage and vanishment in the distance. Thank heaven these creatures employed no dogs for tracking—though perhaps that would have been impossible amidst the omnipresent regional odor. Crouched in the bushes of that sandy cleft I felt reasonably safe, even though I knew the searchers would have to cross the track in front of me not much more than a hundred yards away. I would be able to see them, but they could not, except by a malign miracle, see me.

All at once I began dreading to look at them as they passed. I saw the close moonlit space where they would surge by, and had curious thoughts about the irredeemable pollution of that space. They would perhaps be the worst of all Innsmouth types—something one would not care to remember.

The stench waxed overpowering, and the noises swelled to a bestial babel of croaking, baying and barking without the least suggestion of human speech. Were these indeed the voices of my pursuers? Did they have dogs after all? So far I had seen none of the lower animals in Innsmouth. That flopping or pattering was monstrous—I could not look upon the degenerate creatures responsible for it. I would keep my eyes shut till the sound receded toward the west. The horde was very close now—air foul with their hoarse snarlings, and the ground almost shaking with their alien-rhythmed footfalls. My breath nearly ceased to come, and I put every ounce of will-power into the task of holding my eyelids down.

I am not even yet willing to say whether what followed was a hideous actuality or only a nightmare hallucination. The later action of the government, after my frantic appeals, would tend to confirm it as a monstrous truth; but could not an hallucination have been repeated under the quasi-hypnotic spell of that ancient, haunted, and shadowed town? Such places have strange properties, and the legacy of insane legend might well have acted on more than one human imagination amidst those dead, stench-cursed streets and huddles of rotting roofs and crumbling steeples. Is it not possible that the germ of an actual contagious madness lurks in the depths of that shadow over Innsmouth? Who can be sure of reality after hearing things like the tale of old Zadok Allen? The government men never found poor Zadok, and have no conjectures to make as to what became of him. Where does madness leave off and reality begin? Is it possible that even my latest fear is sheer delusion?

But I must try to tell what I thought I saw that night under the mocking yellow moon—saw surging and hopping down the Rowley road in plain sight in front of me as I crouched among the wild brambles of that desolate railway cut. Of course my resolution to keep my eyes shut had failed. It was foredoomed to failure—for who could crouch blindly while a legion of croaking, baying entities of unknown source flopped noisomely past, scarcely more than a hundred yards away?

I thought I was prepared for the worst, and I really ought to have been prepared considering what I had seen before.

My other pursuers had been accursedly abnormal—so should I not have been ready to face a strengthening of the abnormal element; to look upon forms in which there was no mixture of the normal at all? I did not open my eyes until the raucous clamor came loudly from a point obviously straight ahead. Then I knew that a long section of them must be plainly in sight where the sides of the cut flattened out and the road crossed the track—and I could no longer keep myself from sampling whatever honor that leering yellow moon might have to show.

It was the end, for whatever remains to me of life on the surface of this earth, of every vestige of mental peace and confidence in the integrity of nature and of the human mind. Nothing that I could have imagined—nothing, even, that I could have gathered had I credited old Zadok's crazy tale in the most literal way—would be in any way comparable to the demoniac, blasphemous reality that I saw—or believe I saw. I have tried to hint what it was in order to postpone the horror of writing it down baldly. Can it be possible that this planet has actually spawned such things; that human eyes have truly seen, as objective flesh, what man has hitherto known only in febrile phantasy and tenuous legend?

And yet I saw them in a limitless stream—flopping, hopping, croaking, bleating—urging inhumanly through the spectral moonlight in a grotesque, malignant saraband of fantastic nightmare. And some of them had tall tiaras of that nameless whitish-gold metal … and some were strangely robed … and one, who led the way, was clad in a ghoulishly humped black coat and striped trousers, and had a man's felt hat perched on the shapeless thing that answered for a head.

I think their predominant color was a greyish-green, though they had white bellies. They were mostly shiny and slippery, but the ridges of their backs were scaly. Their forms vaguely suggested the anthropoid, while their heads were the heads of fish, with prodigious bulging eyes that never closed. At the sides of their necks were palpitating gills, and their long paws were webbed. They hopped irregularly, sometimes on two legs and sometimes on four. I was somehow glad that they had no more than four limbs. Their croaking, baying voices, clearly used for articulate speech, held all the dark shades of expression which their staring faces lacked.

But for all of their monstrousness they were not unfamiliar to me. I knew too well what they must be—for was not the memory of the evil tiara at Newburyport still fresh? They were the blasphemous fish-frogs of the nameless design—living and horrible—and as I saw them I knew also of what that humped, tiaraed priest in the black church basement had fearsomely reminded me. Their number was past guessing. It seemed to me that there were limitless swarms of them and certainly my momentary glimpse could have shown only the least fraction. In another instant everything was blotted out by a merciful fit of fainting; the first I had ever had.

V.

It was a gentle daylight rain that awaked me front my stupor in the brush-grown railway cut, and when I staggered out to the roadway ahead I saw no trace of any prints in the fresh mud. The fishy odor, too, was gone, Innsmouth's ruined roofs and toppling steeples loomed up greyly toward the southeast, but not a living creature did I spy in all the desolate salt marshes around. My watch was still going, and told me that the hour was past noon.

The reality of what I had been through was highly uncertain in my mind, but I felt that something hideous lay in the background. I must get away from evil-shadowed Innsmouth—and accordingly I began to test my cramped, wearied powers of locomotion. Despite weakness hunger, horror, and bewilderment I found myself after a time able to walk; so started slowly along the muddy road to Rowley. Before evening I was in the village, getting a meal and providing myself with presentable clothes. I caught the night train to Arkham, and the next day talked long and earnestly with government officials there; a process I later repeated in Boston. With the main result of these colloquies the public is now familiar—and I wish, for normality's sake, there were nothing more to tell. Perhaps it is madness that is overtaking me—yet perhaps a greater horror—or a greater marvel—is reaching out.

As may well be imagined, I gave up most of the foreplanned features of the rest of my tour—the scenic, architectural, and antiquarian diversions on which I had counted so heavily. Nor did I dare look for that piece of strange jewelry said to be in the Miskatonic University Museum. I did, however, improve my stay in Arkham by collecting some genealogical notes I had long wished to possess; very rough and hasty data, it is true, but capable of good use later on when I might have time to collate and codify them. The curator of the historical society there—Mr. B. Lapham Peabody—was very courteous about assisting me, and expressed unusual interest when I told him I was a grandson of Eliza Orne of Arkham, who was born in 1867 and had married James Williamson of Ohio at the age of seventeen.

It seemed that a material uncle of mine had been there many years before on a quest much like my own; and that my grandmother's family was a topic of some local curiosity. There had, Mr. Peabody said, been considerable discussion about the marriage of her father, Benjamin Orne, just after the Civil War; since the ancestry of the bride was peculiarly puzzling. That bride was understood to have been an orphaned Marsh of New Hampshire—a cousin of the Essex County Marshes—but her education had been in France and she knew very little of her family. A guardian had deposited funds in a Boston bank to maintain her and her French governess; but that guardian's name was unfamiliar to Arkham people, and in time he dropped out of sight, so that the governess assumed the role by court appointment. The Frenchwoman—now long dead—was very taciturn, and there were those who said she would have told more than she did.

But the most baffling thing was the inability of anyone to place the recorded parents of the young woman—Enoch and Lydia (Meserve) Marsh—among the known families of New Hampshire. Possibly, many suggested, she was the natural daughter of some Marsh of prominence—she certainly had the true Marsh eyes. Most of the puzzling was done after her early death, which took place at the birth of my grandmother—her only child. Having formed some disagreeable impressions connected with the name of Marsh, I did not welcome the news that it belonged on my own ancestral tree; nor was I pleased by Mr. Peabody's suggestion that I had the true Marsh eyes myself. However, I was grateful for data which I knew would prove valuable; and took copious notes and lists of book references regarding the well-documented Orne family.

I went directly home to Toledo from Boston, and later spent a month at Maumee[31] recuperating from my ordeal. In September I entered Oberlin[32] for my final year, and from then till the next June was busy with studies and other wholesome activities—reminded of the bygone terror only by occasional official visits from government men in connection with the campaign which my pleas and evidence had started. Around the middle of July—just a year after the Innsmouth experience—I spent a week with my late mother's family in Cleveland; checking some of my new genealogical data with the various notes, traditions, and bits of heirloom material in existence there, and seeing what kind of a connected chart I could construct.

I did not exactly relish this task, for the atmosphere of the Williamson home had always depressed me. There was a strain of morbidity there, and my mother had never encouraged my visiting her parents as a child, although she always welcomed her father when he came to Toledo. My Arkham-born grandmother had seemed strange and almost terrifying to me, and I do not think I grieved when she disappeared. I was eight years old then, and it was said that she had wandered off in grief after the suicide of my Uncle Douglas, her eldest son. He had shot himself after a trip to New England—the same trip, no doubt, which had caused him to be recalled at the Arkham Historical Society.

This uncle had resembled her, and I had never liked him either. Something about the staring, unwinking expression of both of them had given me a vague, unaccountable uneasiness. My mother and Uncle Walter had not looked like that. They were like their father, though poor little cousin Lawrence—Walter's son—had been almost perfect duplicate of his grandmother before his condition took him to the permanent seclusion of a sanitarium at Canton. I had not seen him in four years, but my uncle once implied that his state, both mental and physical, was very bad. This worry had probably been a major cause of his mother's death two years before.

My grandfather and his widowed son Walter now comprised the Cleveland household, but the memory of older times hung thickly over it. I still disliked the place, and tried to get my researches done as quickly as possible. Williamson records and traditions were supplied in abundance by my grandfather; though for Orne material I had to depend on my uncle Walter, who put at my disposal the contents of all his files, including notes, letters, cuttings, heirlooms, photographs, and miniatures.

It was in going over the letters and pictures on the Orne side that I began to acquire a kind of terror of my own ancestry. As I have said, my grandmother and Uncle Douglas had always disturbed me. Now, years after their passing, I gazed at their pictured faces with a measurably heightened feeling of repulsion and alienation. I could not at first understand the change, but gradually a horrible sort of comparison began to obtrude itself on my unconscious mind despite the steady refusal of my consciousness to admit even the least suspicion of it. It was clear that the typical expression of these faces now suggested something it had not suggested before—something which would bring stark panic if too openly thought of.

But the worst shock came when my uncle showed me the Orne jewelry in a downtown safe deposit vault. Some of the items were delicate and inspiring enough, but there was one box of strange old pieces descended from my mysterious great-grandmother which my uncle was almost reluctant to produce. They were, he said, of very grotesque and almost repulsive design, and had never to his knowledge been publicly worn; though my grandmother used to enjoy looking at them. Vague legends of bad luck clustered around them, and my great-grandmother's French governess had said they ought not to be worn in New England, though it would be quite safe to wear them in Europe.

As my uncle began slowly and grudgingly to unwrap the things he urged me not to be shocked by the strangeness and frequent hideousness of the designs. Artists and archaeologists who had seen them pronounced their workmanship superlatively and exotically exquisite, though no one seemed able to define their exact material or assign them to any specific art tradition. There were two armlets, a tiara, and a kind of pectoral; the latter having in high relief certain figures of almost unbearable extravagance.

During this description I had kept a tight rein on my emotions, but my face must have betrayed my mounting fears. My uncle looked concerned, and paused in his unwrapping to study my countenance. I motioned to him to continue, which he did with renewed signs of reluctance. He seemed to expect some demonstration when the first piece—the tiara—became visible, but I doubt if he expected quite what actually happened. I did not expect it, either, for I thought I was thoroughly forewarned regarding what the jewelry would turn out to be. What I did was to faint silently away, just as I had done in that brier choked railway cut a year before.

From that day on my life has been a nightmare of brooding and apprehension nor do I know how much is hideous truth and how much madness. My great-grandmother had been a Marsh of unknown source whose husband lived in Arkham—and did not old Zadok say that the daughter of Obed Marsh by a monstrous mother was married to an Arkham man through a trick? What was it the ancient toper had muttered about the line of my eyes to Captain Obed's? In Arkham, too, the curator had told me I had the true Marsh eyes. Was Obed Marsh my own great-great-grandfather? Who—or what—then, was my great-great-grandmother? But perhaps this was all madness. Those whitish-gold ornaments might easily have been bought from some Innsmouth sailor by the father of my great-grandmother, whoever he was. And that look in the staring-eyed faces of my grandmother and self-slain uncle might be sheer fancy on my part—sheer fancy, bolstered up by the Innsmouth shadow which had so darkly colored my imagination. But why had my uncle killed himself after an ancestral quest in New England?

For more than two years I fought off these reflections with partial success. My father secured me a place in an insurance office, and I buried myself in routine as deeply as possible. In the winter of 1930–31, however, the dreams began. They were very sparse and insidious at first, but increased in frequency and vividness as the weeks went by. Great watery spaces opened out before me, and I seemed to wander through titanic sunken porticos and labyrinths of weedy cyclopean walls with grotesque fishes as my companions. Then the other shapes began to appear, filling me with nameless horror the moment I awoke. But during the dreams they did not horrify me at all—I was one with them; wearing their unhuman trappings, treading their aqueous ways, and praying monstrously at their evil sea-bottom temples.

There was much more than I could remember, but even what I did remember each morning would be enough to stamp me as a madman or a genius if ever I dared write it down. Some frightful influence, I felt, was seeking gradually to drag me out of the sane world of wholesome life into unnamable abysses of blackness and alienage; and the process told heavily on me. My health and appearance grew steadily worse, till finally I was forced to give up my position and adopt the static, secluded life of an invalid. Some odd nervous affliction had me in its grip, and I found myself at times almost unable to shut my eyes.

It was then that I began to study the mirror with mounting alarm. The slow ravages of disease are not pleasant to watch, but in my case there was something subtler and more puzzling in the background. My father seemed to notice it, too, for he began looking at me curiously and almost affrightedly. What was taking place in me? Could it be that I was coming to resemble my grandmother and uncle Douglas?

One night I had a frightful dream in which I met my grandmother under the sea. She lived in a phosphorescent palace of many terraces, with gardens of strange leprous corals and grotesque brachiate efflorescences,[33] and welcomed me with a warmth that may have been sardonic. She had changed—as those who take to the water change—and told me she had never died. Instead, she had gone to a spot her dead son had learned about, and had leaped to a realm whose wonders—destined for him as well—he had spurned with a smoking pistol. This was to be my realm, too—I could not escape it. I would never die, but would live with those who had lived since before man ever walked the earth.

I met also that which had been her grandmother. For eighty thousand years Pth'thya-l'yi[34] had lived in Y'ha-nthlei, and thither she had gone back after Obed Marsh was dead. Y'ha-nthlei was not destroyed when the upper-earth men shot death into the sea. It was hurt, but not destroyed. The Deep Ones could never be destroyed, even though the palaeogean[35] magic of the forgotten Old Ones might sometimes check them. For the present they would rest; but some day, if they remembered, they would rise again for the tribute Great Cthulhu craved. It would be a city greater than Innsmouth next time. They had planned to spread, and had brought up that which would help them, but now they must wait once more. For bringing the upper-earth men's death I must do a penance, but that would not be heavy. This was the dream in which I saw a shoggoth for the first time, and the sight set me awake in a frenzy of screaming. That morning the mirror definitely told me I had acquired *the Innsmouth look*.

So far I have not shot myself as my uncle Douglas did. I bought an automatic and almost took the step, but certain dreams deterred me. The tense extremes of horror are lessening, and I feel queerly drawn toward the unknown sea-deeps instead of fearing them. I hear and do strange things in sleep, and awake with a kind of exaltation instead of terror. I do not believe I need to wait for the full change as most have waited. If I did, my father would probably shut me up in a sanitarium as my poor little cousin is shut up. Stupendous and unheard-of splendors await me below, and I shall seek them soon. *Iä -R'lyeh! Cthulhu fhtagn! Iä! Iä!*[36] No, I shall not shoot myself—I cannot be made to shoot myself!

I shall plan my cousin's escape from that Canton mad-house, and together we shall go to marvel-shadowed Innsmouth. We shall swim out to that brooding reef in the sea and dive down through black abysses to Cyclopean and many-columned Y'ha-nthlei, and in that lair of the Deep Ones we shall dwell amidst wonder and glory for ever.

Waste Paper

It is safe to say that Lovecraft was no fan of T.S. Eliot, or at least of his seminal work The Waste Land, *referring to it as "a practically meaning-less collection of phrases, learned allusions, quotations, slang, and scraps in general." He even went so far as to take a jab at the poem in* The Case of Charles Dexter Ward *when Dr. Willett begins muttering the Lord's Prayer, "eventually trailing off into a mnemonic hodge-podge like the modernistic* Waste Land *of Mr. T.S. Eliot." It is unknown when Lovecraft's parody of Eliot's poem was written, only that it was printed "in the news-paper" at some point, probably, according to S.T. Joshi, either* Providence Journal *or the* Providence Evening Bulletin.

Regardless of when or where it was published, "Waste Paper: A Poem of Profound Insignificance" is, to use Joshi's description, "an exquisite par-ody" of Eliot's poem, filled with near absurd examples of the aspects of The Waste Land *Lovecraft finds objectionable: pointless allusions (in this case to popular songs of the day), quotations from his own poetry and that of his influences, slang, and scraps of personal details only under-stood by his own circle of acquaintances. Even the subtitle itself reflects Lovecraft's disdain for Eliot's original poem, described by its fans as "a poem of profound significance." However, this subtitle is false, as Joshi affirms, "this is [Lovecraft's] best satiric poem."*

A Poem of Profound Insignificance

Πάντα γέλως καί πάντα κόνις καί πάντα τό μηδὲν[1]

Out of the reaches of illimitable light
The blazing planet grew, and forc'd to life
Unending cycles of progressive strife
And strange mutations of undying light
And boresome books, than hell's own self more trite
And thoughts repeated and become a blight,
And cheap rum-hounds with moonshine hootch made tight,
And quite contrite to see the flight of fright so bright
I used to ride my bicycle in the night
With a dandy acetylene lantern that cost $3.00
In the evening, by the moonlight, you can hear those darkies singing
Meet me tonight in dreamland ... BAH
I used to sit on the stairs of the house where I was born
After we left it but before it was sold

And play on a zobo[2] with two other boys.
We called ourselves the Blackstone Military Band
Won't you come home, Bill Bailey, won't you come home?[3]
In the spring of the year, in the silver rain
When petal by petal the blossoms fall
And the mocking birds call
And the whippoorwill sings, Marguerite.[4]
The first cinema show in our town opened in 1906
At the old Olympic, which was then call'd Park,
And moving beams shot weirdly thro' the dark
And spit tobacco seldom hit the mark.
Have you read Dickens' *American Notes*[5]?
My great-great-grandfather[6] was born in a white house
Under green trees in the country
And he used to believe in religion and the weather.
"Shantih, shantih, shantih"[7] … *Shanty House*[8]
Was the name of a novel by I forget whom
Published serially in the *All-Story Weekly*[9]
Before it was a weekly. Advt.
Disillusion is wonderful, I've been told,
And I take quinine to stop a cold
But it makes my ears ring … always ring…
Always ringing in my ears…
It is the ghost of the Jew I murdered that Christmas day
Because he played "Three O'Clock in the Morning"[10] in the flat above me.
Three O'Clock in the morning, I've danc'd the whole night through,
Dancing on the graves in the graveyard
Where life is buried; life and beauty
Life and art and love and duty
Ah, there, sweet cutie.
Stung!
Out of the night that covers me
Black as the pit from pole to pole
I never quote things straight except by accident.
Sophistication! Sophistication!
You are the idol of our nation
Each fellow has
Fallen for jazz
And we'll give the past a merry razz
Thro' the ghoul-guarded gateways of slumber[11]
And fellow-guestship with the glutless worm.
Next stop is 57th St.—57th St. the next stop.
Achilles' wrath, to Greece the direful spring,[12]
And the Governor-General of Canada is Lord Byng[13]
Whose ancestor was shot or hung,
I forget which, the good die young.
Here's to your ripe old age,
Copyright, 1847, by Joseph Miller,[14]
Entered according to act of Congress
In the office of the librarian of Congress
America was discovered in 1492
This way out.
No, lady, you gotta change at Washington St. to the Everett train.

Out in the rain on the elevated
Crated, sated, all mismated.
Twelve seats on this bench,
How quaint.
In a shady nook, beside a brook, two lovers stroll along.
Express to Park Ave., Car Following.
No, we had it cleaned with the sand blast.
I know it ought to be torn down.
Before the bar of a saloon there stood a reckless crew,
When one said to another, "Jack, this message came for you."
"It may be from a sweetheart, boys," said someone in the crowd,
And here the words are missing ... but Jack cried out aloud:
    "It's only a message from home, sweet home,
      From loved ones down on the farm
      Fond wife and mother, sister and brother...."
    Bootleggers all and you're another
In the shade of the old apple tree
'Neath the old cherry tree sweet Marie
The Conchologist's First Book
By Edgar Allan Poe[15]
Stubbed his toe
On a broken brick that didn't shew
Or a banana peel
In the fifth reel
By George Creel[16]
It is to laugh
And quaff
It makes you stout and hale,
And all my days I'll sing the praise
Of Ivory Soap
Have you a little T.S. Eliot[17] in your home?
The stag at eve had drunk his fill
The thirsty hart look'd up the hill
And craned his neck just as a feeler
To advertise the Double-Dealer.
William Congreve[18] was a gentleman
O art what sins are committed in thy name
For tawdry fame and fleeting flame
And everything, ain't dat a shame?
Mah Creole Belle, ah lubs yo' well;
Aroun' mah heart you hab cast a spell
But I can't learn to spell pseudocracy[19]
Because there ain't no such word.
And I says to Lizzie, if Joe was my feller
I'd teach him to go to dances with that
Rat, bat, cat, hat, flat, plat, fat
Fry the fat, fat the fry
You'll be a drug-store by and by.
Get the hook!
Above the lines of brooding hills
Rose spires that reeked of nameless ills,
And ghastly shone upon the sight
In ev'ry flash of lurid light

To be continued.
No smoking.
Smoking on four rear seats.
Fare will return to 5¢ after August 1st
Except outside the Cleveland city limits.
In the ghoul-haunted woodland of Weir[20]
Strangers pause to shed a tear;
Henry Fielding wrote *Tom Jones*.[21]
And cursed be he that moves my bones.
Good night, good night, the stars are bright
I saw the Leonard-Tendler fight[22]
Farewell, farewell, O go to hell.
Nobody home
In the shantih.

Fungi from Yuggoth

Many critics consider Fungi from Yuggoth, *Lovecraft's collection of 36 sonnets, his most enduring piece of weird verse. Written from 1929–1930, this collection presents several plots, themes, and imagery that appear later in Lovecraft's own prose. For this reason, S.T. Joshi claims that the cycle represents a "collection of sonnets […] with little order or sequence" that allowed Lovecraft "an opportunity to crystallise various conceptions, types of imagery, and fragments of dreams that could not have found creative expression in fiction."*

Other critics disagree. For example, while not in complete disagreement with Joshi's position, Robert M. Price does posit that the cycle (sonnets XIII, XIV, XXVIII, XXX, and XXXVI in particular) reflects "Lovecraft's mysticism of place and past." Jim Moon, however, disagrees completely with Joshi's assertion, claiming that the poem details the visions or encounters the narrator experiences after stealing a mysterious book in the first three sonnets. The connections between sonnets, Moon claims are more complex than plot, however. "While some sonnets echo their predecessors' dominant concepts or continue a theme," he explains, "others share a location or similar geography with their predecessors."

I. The Book

The place was dark and dusty and half-lost
In tangles of old alleys near the quays,
Reeking of strange things brought in from the seas,
And with queer curls of fog that west winds tossed.
Small lozenge[1] panes, obscured by smoke and frost,
Just shewed the books, in piles like twisted trees,
Rotting from floor to roof—congeries[2]
Of crumbling elder lore at little cost.

I entered, charmed, and from a cobwebbed heap
Took up the nearest tome[3] and thumbed it through,
Trembling at curious words that seemed to keep
Some secret, monstrous if one only knew.
Then, looking for some seller old in craft,
I could find nothing but a voice that laughed.

II. Pursuit

I held the book beneath my coat, at pains
To hide the thing from sight in such a place;

Hurrying through the ancient harbor lanes
With often-turning head and nervous pace.
Dull, furtive windows in old tottering brick
Peered at me oddly as I hastened by,
And thinking what they sheltered, I grew sick
For a redeeming glimpse of clean blue sky.

No one had seen me take the thing—but still
A blank laugh echoed in my whirling head,
And I could guess what nighted worlds of ill
Lurked in that volume I had coveted.
The way grew strange—the walls alike and madding—
And far behind me, unseen feet were padding.

III. The Key

I do not know what windings in the waste
Of those strange sea-lanes brought me home once more,
But on my porch I trembled, white with haste
To get inside and bolt the heavy door.
I had the book that told the hidden way
Across the void and through the space-hung screens
That hold the undimensioned worlds at bay,
And keep lost aeons to their own demesnes.[4]

At last the key was mine to those vague visions
Of sunset spires and twilight woods that brood
Dim in the gulfs beyond this earth's precisions,
Lurking as memories of infinitude.
The key was mine, but as I sat there mumbling,
The attic window shook with a faint fumbling.

IV. Recognition

The day had come again, when as a child
I saw—just once—that hollow of old oaks,
Grey with a ground-mist that enfolds and chokes
The slinking shapes which madness has defiled.
It was the same—an herbage rank and wild
Clings round an altar whose carved sign invokes
That Nameless One to whom a thousand smokes
Rose, aeons gone, from unclean towers up-piled.
I saw the body spread on that dank stone,
And knew those things which feasted were not men;
I knew this strange, grey world was not my own,
But Yuggoth, past the starry voids—and then
The body shrieked at me with a dead cry,
And all too late I knew that it was I!

V. Homecoming

The daemon said that he would take me home
To the pale, shadowy land I half recalled
As a high place of stair and terrace, walled
With marble balustrades that sky-winds comb,
While miles below a maze of dome on dome
And tower on tower beside a sea lies sprawled.
Once more, he told me, I would stand enthralled
On those old heights, and hear the far-off foam.

All this he promised, and through sunset's gate
He swept me, past the lapping lakes of flame,
And red-gold thrones of gods without a name
Who shriek in fear at some impending fate.
Then a black gulf with sea-sounds in the night:
"Here was your home," he mocked, "when you had sight!"

VI. *The Lamp*

We found the lamp inside those hollow cliffs
Whose chiseled sign no priest in Thebes[5] could read,
And from whose caverns frightened hieroglyphs
Warned every creature of earth's breed.
No more was there—just that one brazen bowl
With traces of a curious oil within;
Fretted with some obscurely patterned scroll,
And symbols hinting vaguely of strange sin.

Little the fears of forty centuries meant
To us as we bore off our slender spoil,
And when we scanned it in our darkened tent
We struck a match to test the ancient oil.
It blazed—great God! … But the vast shapes we saw
In that mad flash have seared our lives with awe.

VII. *Zaman's Hill*

The great hill hung close over the old town,
A precipice against the main street's end;
Green, tall, and wooded, looking darkly down
Upon the steeple at the highway bend.
Two hundred years the whispers had been heard
About what happened on the man-shunned slope—
Tales of an oddly mangled deer or bird,
Or of lost boys whose kin had ceased to hope.

One day the mail-man found no village there,
Nor were its folk or houses seen again;
People came out from Aylesbury to stare—
Yet they all told the mail-man it was plain
That he was mad for saying he had spied
The great hill's gluttonous eyes, and jaws stretched wide.

VIII. *The Port*

Ten miles from Arkham I had struck the trail
That rides the cliff-edge over Boynton Beach,
And hoped that just at sunset I could reach
The crest that looks on Innsmouth[6] in the vale.
Far out at sea was a retreating sail,
White as hard years of ancient winds could bleach,
But evil with some portent beyond speech,
So that I did not wave my hand or hail.

Sails out of lnnsmouth! echoing old renown
Of long-dead times. But now a too-swift night
Is closing in, and I have reached the height
Whence I so often scan the distant town.
The spires and roofs are there—but look! The gloom
Sinks on dark lanes, as lightless as the tomb!

IX. The Courtyard

It was the city I had known before;
The ancient, leprous[7] town where mongrel throngs[8]
Chant to strange gods, and beat unhallowed gongs
In crypts beneath foul alleys near the shore.
The rotting, fish-eyed houses leered at me
From where they leaned, drunk and half-animate,
As edging through the filth I passed the gate
To the black courtyard where the man would be.

The dark walls closed me in, and loud I cursed
That ever I had come to such a den,
When suddenly a score of windows burst
Into wild light, and swarmed with dancing men:
Mad, soundless revels of the dragging dead—
And not a corpse had either hands or head!

X. The Pigeon-Flyers

They took me slumming, where gaunt walls of brick
Bulge outward with a viscous stored-up evil,
And twisted faces, thronging foul and thick,
Wink messages to alien god and devil.
A million fires were blazing in the streets,
And from flat roofs a furtive few would fly
Bedraggled birds into the yawning sky
While hidden drums droned on with measured beats.

I knew those fires were brewing monstrous things,
And that those birds of space had been *Outside*—
I guessed to what dark planet's crypts they plied,
And what they brought from Thog[9] beneath their wings.
The others laughed—till struck too mute to speak
By what they glimpsed in one bird's evil beak.

XI. The Well

Farmer Seth Atwood was past eighty when
He tried to sink that deep well by his door,
With only Eb to help him bore and bore.
We laughed, and hoped he'd soon be sane again.
And yet, instead, young Eb went crazy, too,
So that they shipped him to the county farm.[10]
Seth bricked the well-mouth up as tight as glue—
Then hacked an artery in his gnarled left arm.

After the funeral we felt bound to get
Out to that well and rip the bricks away,
But all we saw were iron hand-holds set
Down a black hole deeper than we could say.
And yet we put the bricks back—for we found
The hole too deep for any line to sound.

XII. The Howler

They told me not to take the Briggs' Hill path
That used to be the highroad through to Zoar,[11]
For Goody Watkins, hanged in seventeen-four,
Had left a certain monstrous aftermath.

Yet when I disobeyed, and had in view
The vine-hung cottage by the great rock slope,
I could not think of elms or hempen rope,
But wondered why the house still seemed so new.

Stopping a while to watch the fading day,
I heard faint howls, as from a room upstairs,
When through the ivied panes one sunset ray
Struck in, and caught the howler unawares.
I glimpsed—and ran in frenzy from the place,
And from a four-pawed thing with human face.

XIII. Hesperia[12]

The winter sunset, flaming beyond spires
And chimneys half-detached from this dull sphere,
Opens great gates to some forgotten year
Of elder splendours and divine desires.
Expectant wonders burn in those rich fires,
Adventure-fraught, and not untinged with fear;
A row of sphinxes where the way leads clear
Toward walls and turrets quivering to far lyres.

It is the land where beauty's meaning flowers;
Where every unplaced memory has a source;
Where the great river Time begins its course
Down the vast void in starlit streams of hours.
Dreams bring us close—but ancient lore repeats
That human tread has never soiled these streets.

XIV. Star-Winds

It is a certain hour of twilight glooms,
Mostly in autumn, when the star-wind pours
Down hilltop streets, deserted out-of-doors,
But shewing early lamplight from snug rooms.
The dead leaves rush in strange, fantastic twists,
And chimney-smoke whirls round with alien grace,
Heeding geometries of outer space,
While Fomalhaut[13] peers in through southward mists.

This is the hour when moonstruck poets know
What fungi sprout in Yuggoth, and what scents
And tints of flowers fill Nithon's[14] continents,
Such as in no poor earthly garden blow.
Yet for each dream these winds to us convey,
A dozen more of ours they sweep away!

XV. Antarktos[15]

Deep in my dream the great bird whispered queerly
Of the black cone amid the polar waste;
Pushing above the ice-sheet lone and drearly,
By storm-crazed aeons battered and defaced.
Hither no living earth-shapes take their courses,
And only pale auroras and faint suns
Glow on that pitted rock, whose primal sources
Are guessed at dimly by the Elder Ones.

If men should glimpse it, they would merely wonder
What tricky mound of Nature's build they spied;
But the bird told of vaster parts, that under
The mile-deep ice-shroud crouch and brood and bide.
God help the dreamer whose mad visions shew
Those dead eyes set in crystal gulfs below!

XVI. *The Window*

The house was old, with tangled wings outthrown,
Of which no one could ever half keep track,
And in a small room somewhat near the back
Was an odd window sealed with ancient stone.
There, in a dream-plagued childhood, quite alone
I used to go, where night reigned vague and black;
Parting the cobwebs with a curious lack
Of fear, and with a wonder each time grown.
One later day I brought the masons there
To find what view my dim forbears had shunned,
But as they pierced the stone, a rush of air
Burst from the alien voids that yawned beyond.
They fled—but I peered through and found unrolled
All the wild worlds of which my dreams had told.

XVII. *A Memory*

There were great steppes, and rocky table-lands[16]
Stretching half-limitless in starlit night,
With alien campfires shedding feeble light
On beasts with tinkling bells, in shaggy bands.
Far to the south the plain sloped low and wide
To a dark zigzag line of wall that lay
Like a huge python of some primal day
Which endless time had chilled and petrified.

I shivered oddly in the cold, thin air,
And wondered where I was and how I came,
When a cloaked form against a campfire's glare
Rose and approached, and called me by my name.
Staring at that dead face beneath the hood,
I ceased to hope—because I understood.

XVIII. *The Gardens of Yin*

Beyond that wall, whose ancient masonry
Reached almost to the sky in moss-thick towers,
There would be terraced gardens, rich with flowers,
And flutter of bird and butterfly and bee.
There would be walks, and bridges arching over
Warm lotos-pools reflecting temple eaves,
And cherry-trees with delicate boughs and leaves
Against a pink sky where the herons hover.

All would be there, for had not old dreams flung
Open the gate to that stone-lanterned maze
Where drowsy streams spin out their winding ways,
Trailed by green vines from bending branches hung?
I hurried—but when the wall rose, grim and great,
I found there was no longer any gate.

XIX. The Bells

Year after year I heard that faint, far ringing
Of deep-toned bells on the black midnight wind;
Peals from no steeple I could ever find,
But strange, as if across some great void winging.
I searched my dreams and memories for a clue,
And thought of all the chimes my visions carried;
Of quiet Innsmouth, where the white gulls tarried
Around an ancient spire that once I knew.

Always perplexed I heard those far notes falling,
Till one March night the bleak rain splashing cold
Beckoned me back through gateways of recalling
To elder towers where the mad clappers[17] tolled.
They tolled—but from the sunless tides that pour
Through sunken valleys on the sea's dead floor.

XX. Night-Gaunts

Out of what crypt they crawl, I cannot tell,
But every night I see the rubbery things,
Black, horned, and slender, with membraneous wings,
And tails that bear the bifid[18] barb of hell.
They come in legions on the north wind's swell,
With obscene clutch that titillates and stings,
Snatching me off on monstrous voyagings
To grey worlds hidden deep in nightmare's well.

Over the jagged peaks of Thok[19] they sweep,
Heedless of all the cries I try to make,
And down the nether pits to that foul lake
Where the puffed shoggoths splash in doubtful sleep.
But oh! If only they would make some sound,
Or wear a face where faces should be found!

XXI. Nyarlathotep

And at the last from inner Egypt came
The strange dark One to whom the fellahs[20] bowed;
Silent and lean and cryptically proud,
And wrapped in fabrics red as sunset flame.
Throngs pressed around, frantic for his commands,
But leaving, could not tell what they had heard;
While through the nations spread the awestruck word
That wild beasts followed him and licked his hands.
Soon from the sea a noxious birth began;
Forgotten lands with weedy spires of gold;
The ground was cleft, and mad auroras rolled
Down on the quaking citadels of man.
Then, crushing what he chanced to mould in play,
The idiot Chaos[21] blew Earth's dust away.

XXII. Azathoth

Out in the mindless void the daemon bore me,
Past the bright clusters of dimensioned space,
Till neither time nor matter stretched before me,
But only Chaos, without form or place.

Here the vast Lord of All in darkness muttered
Things he had dreamed but could not understand,
While near him shapeless bat-things flopped and fluttered
In idiot vortices that ray-streams fanned.

They danced insanely to the high, thin whining
Of a cracked flute clutched in a monstrous paw,
Whence flow the aimless waves whose chance combining
Gives each frail cosmos its eternal law.
"I am His Messenger," the daemon said,
As in contempt he struck his Master's head.

XXIII. Mirage

I do not know if ever it existed—
That lost world floating dimly on Time's stream—
And yet I see it often, violet-misted,
And shimmering at the back of some vague dream.
There were strange towers and curious lapping rivers,
Labyrinths of wonder, and low vaults of light,
And bough-crossed skies of flame, like that which quivers
Wistfully just before a winter's night.

Great moors led off to sedgy shores unpeopled,
Where vast birds wheeled, while on a windswept hill
There was a village, ancient and white-steepled,
With evening chimes for which I listen still.
I do not know what land it is—or dare
Ask when or why I was, or will be, there.

XXIV. The Canal

Somewhere in dream there is an evil place
Where tall, deserted buildings crowd along
A deep, black, narrow channel, reeking strong
Of frightful things whence oily currents race.
Lanes with old walls half meeting overhead
Wind off to streets one may or may not know,
And feeble moonlight sheds a spectral glow
Over long rows of windows, dark and dead.

There are no footfalls, and the one soft sound
Is of the oily water as it glides
Under stone bridges, and along the sides
Of its deep flume, to some vague ocean bound.
None lives to tell when that stream washed away
Its dream-lost region from the world of clay.

XXV. St. Toad's

"Beware St. Toad's cracked chimes!" I heard him scream
As I plunged into those mad lanes that wind
In labyrinths obscure and undefined
South of the river where old centuries dream.
He was a furtive figure, bent and ragged,
And in a flash had staggered out of sight,
So still I burrowed onward in the night
Toward where more roof-lines rose, malign and jagged.

No guide-book told of what was lurking here—
But now I heard another old man shriek:
"Beware St. Toad's cracked chimes!" And growing weak,
I paused, when a third greybeard croaked in fear:
"Beware St. Toad's cracked chimes!" Aghast, I fled—
Till suddenly that black spire loomed ahead.

XXVI. *The Familiars*

John Whateley lived about a mile from town,
Up where the hills began to huddle thick;
We never thought his wits were very quick,
Seeing the way he let his farm run down.
He used to waste his time on some queer books
He'd found around the attic of his place,
Till funny lines got creased into his face,
And folks all said they didn't like his looks.

When he began those night-howls we declared
He'd better be locked up away from harm,
So three men from the Aylesbury town farm
Went for him—but came back alone and scared.
They'd found him talking to two crouching things
That at their step flew off on great black wings.

XXVII. *The Elder Pharos*

From Leng, where rocky peaks climb bleak and bare
Under cold stars obscure to human sight,
There shoots at dusk a single beam of light
Whose far blue rays make shepherds whine in prayer.
They say (though none has been there) that it comes
Out of a pharos in a tower of stone,
Where the last Elder One lives on alone,
Talking to Chaos with the beat of drums.

The Thing, they whisper, wears a silken mask
Of yellow, whose queer folds appear to hide
A face not of this earth, though none dares ask
Just what those features are, which bulge inside.
Many, in man's first youth, sought out that glow,
But what they found, no one will ever know.

XXVIII. *Expectancy*

I cannot tell why some things hold for me
A sense of unplumbed marvels to befall,
Or of a rift in the horizon's wall
Opening to worlds where only gods can be.
There is a breathless, vague expectancy,
As of vast ancient pomps[22] I half recall,
Or wild adventures, uncorporeal,[23]
Ecstasy-fraught, and as a day-dream free.

It is in sunsets and strange city spires,
Old villages and woods and misty downs,
South winds, the sea, low hills, and lighted towns,
Old gardens, half-heard songs, and the moon's fires.
But though its lure alone makes life worth living,
None gains or guesses what it hints at giving.

XXIX Nostalgia

Once every year, in autumn's wistful glow,
The birds fly out over an ocean waste,
Calling and chattering in a joyous haste
To reach some land their inner memories know.
Great terraced gardens where bright blossoms blow,
And lines of mangoes luscious to the taste,
And temple-groves with branches interlaced
Over cool paths—all these their vague dreams shew.

They search the sea for marks of their old shore—
For the tall city, white and turreted—
But only empty waters stretch ahead,
So that at last they turn away once more.
Yet sunken deep where alien polyps throng,
The old towers miss their lost, remembered song.

XXX. Background

I never can be tied to raw, new things,
For I first saw the light in an old town,
Where from my window huddled roofs sloped down
To a quaint harbour rich with visionings.
Streets with carved doorways where the sunset beams
Flooded old fanlights and small window-panes,
And Georgian steeples topped with gilded vanes—
These were the sights that shaped my childhood dreams.

Such treasures, left from times of cautious leaven,
Cannot but loose the hold of flimsier wraiths
That flit with shifting ways and muddled faiths
Across the changeless walls of earth and heaven.
They cut the moment's thongs and leave me free
To stand alone before eternity.

XXXI. The Dweller

It had been old when Babylon was new;
None knows how long it slept beneath that mound,
Where in the end our questing shovels found
Its granite blocks and brought it back to view.
There were vast pavements and foundation-walls,
And crumbling slabs and statues, carved to shew
Fantastic beings of some long ago
Past anything the world of man recalls.
And then we saw those stone steps leading down
Through a choked gate of graven dolomite[24]
To some black haven of eternal night
Where elder signs and primal secrets frown.
We cleared a path—but raced in mad retreat
When from below we heard those clumping feet.

XXXII. Alienation

His solid flesh had never been away,
For each dawn found him in his usual place,
But every night his spirit loved to race
Through gulfs and worlds remote from common day.

He had seen Yaddith,[25] yet retained his mind,
And come back safely from the Ghooric zone,[26]
When one still night across curved space was thrown
That beckoning piping from the voids behind.

He waked that morning as an older man,
And nothing since has looked the same to him.
Objects around float nebulous and dim—
False, phantom trifles of some vaster plan.
His folk and friends are now an alien throng
To which he struggles vainly to belong.

XXXIII. *Harbour Whistles*

Over old roofs and past decaying spires
The harbour whistles chant all through the night;
Throats from strange ports, and beaches far and white,
And fabulous oceans, ranged in motley choirs.
Each to the other alien and unknown,
Yet all, by some obscurely focussed force
From brooding gulfs beyond the Zodiac's course,
Fused into one mysterious cosmic drone.

Through shadowy dreams they send a marching line
Of still more shadowy shapes and hints and views;
Echoes from outer voids, and subtle clues
To things which they themselves cannot define.
And always in that chorus, faintly blent,[27]
We catch some notes no earth-ship ever sent.

XXXIV. *Recapture*

The way led down a dark, half-wooded heath
Where moss-grey boulders humped above the mould,
And curious drops, disquieting and cold,
Sprayed up from unseen streams in gulfs beneath.
There was no wind, nor any trace of sound
In puzzling shrub, or alien-featured tree,
Nor any view before—till suddenly,
Straight in my path, I saw a monstrous mound.

Half to the sky those steep sides loomed upspread,
Rank-grassed, and cluttered by a crumbling flight
Of lava stairs that scaled the fear-topped height
In steps too vast for any human tread.
I shrieked—and *knew* what primal star and year
Had sucked me back from man's dream-transient sphere!

XXXV. *Evening Star*

I saw it from that hidden, silent place
Where the old wood half shuts the meadow in.
It shone through all the sunset's glories—thin
At first, but with a slowly brightening face.
Night came, and that lone beacon, amber-hued,
Beat on my sight as never it did of old;
The evening star—but grown a thousandfold
More haunting in this hush and solitude.

It traced strange pictures on the quivering air—
Half-memories that had always filled my eyes—
Vast towers and gardens; curious seas and skies
Of some dim life—I never could tell where.
But now I knew that through the cosmic dome
Those rays were calling from my far, lost home.

XXXVI. *Continuity*

There is in certain ancient things a trace
Of some dim essence—more than form or weight;
A tenuous aether, indeterminate,
Yet linked with all the laws of time and space.
A faint, veiled sign of continuities
That outward eyes can never quite descry[28];
Of locked dimensions harbouring years gone by,
And out of reach except for hidden keys.
It moves me most when slanting sunbeams glow
On old farm buildings set against a hill,
And paint with life the shapes which linger still
From centuries less a dream than this we know.
In that strange light I feel I am not far
From the fixt mass whose sides the ages are.

Supernatural Horror
in Literature

By and large, critics disagree to greater or lesser degrees on what weird fiction means. It has been equated with such other genres as horror, dark fantasy, or Gothic, all of which share some overlap but are not really synonymous. While Lovecraft did not coin the term, he presents, perhaps, the best (though still problematic) definition: a weird tale contains "a certain atmosphere of breathless and unexplainable dread of outer, unknown forces" which bring with them an unnerving failure of natural laws, "our only safeguard against the assaults of chaos and the daemons of unplumbed space."

"Lovecraft," writes S.T. Joshi, "is, in many senses, the linchpin of the twentieth-century weird tale." This is true not only because of his direct contributions to the form through his own fiction, nor even because of his nurturing other writers such as Robert E. Howard and Robert Bloch in their own development of the form: Perhaps his greatest contribution lies in his essay Supernatural Horror in Literature, the first full-length discussion of the genre as a genre.

I. Introduction

The oldest and strongest emotion of mankind is fear, and the oldest and strongest kind of fear is fear of the unknown. These facts few psychologists will dispute, and their admitted truth must establish for all time the genuineness and dignity of the weirdly horrible tale as a literary form. Against it are discharged all the shafts of a materialistic sophistication which clings to frequently felt emotions and external events, and of a naively insipid idealism which deprecates[1] the aesthetic motive and calls for a didactic literature to uplift the reader toward a suitable degree of smirking optimism. But in spite of all this opposition the weird tale has survived, developed, and attained remarkable heights of perfection; founded as it is on a profound and elementary principle whose appeal, if not always universal, must necessarily be poignant and permanent to minds of the requisite sensitiveness.

The appeal of the spectrally macabre is generally narrow because it demands from the reader a certain degree of imagination and a capacity for detachment from every-day life. Relatively few are free enough from the spell of the daily routine to respond to rappings from outside, and tales of ordinary feelings and events, or of common sentimental distortions of such feelings and events, will always take first place in the taste of the majority; rightly, perhaps, since of course these ordinary matters make up the greater part of human experience. But the sensitive are always with us, and sometimes a curious streak of fancy invades an obscure corner of the very hardest head; so that no amount of rationalization, reform, or Freudian analysis[2] can quite annul the thrill of the chimney-corner whisper or the lonely wood. There is here involved a psychological pattern or tradition as real and as deeply grounded in mental experience as any other pattern or tradition of mankind; coeval[3] with the religious feeling and closely related to many aspects of it, and too much a part of our inmost biological heritage to lose keen potency over a very important, though not numerically great, minority of our species.

Man's first instincts and emotions formed his response to the environment in which he found himself. Definite feelings based on pleasure and pain grew up around the phenomena whose causes and effects he understood, whilst around those which he did not understand—and the universe teemed with them in the early days—were naturally woven such personifications, marvelous interpretations, and sensations of awe and fear as would be hit upon by a race having few and simple ideas and limited experience. The unknown, being likewise the unpredictable, became for our primitive forefathers a terrible and omnipotent source of boons and calamities visited upon mankind for cryptic and wholly extra-terrestrial reasons, and thus clearly belonging to spheres of existence whereof we know nothing and wherein we have no part. The phenomenon of dreaming likewise helped to build up the notion of an unreal or spiritual world; and in general, all the conditions of savage dawn-life so strongly conduced toward a feeling of the supernatural, that we need not wonder at the thoroughness with which man's very hereditary essence has become saturated with religion and superstition. That saturation must, as a matter of plain scientific fact, be regarded as virtually permanent so far as the subconscious mind and inner instincts are concerned; for though the area of the unknown has been steadily contracting for thousands of years, an infinite reservoir of mystery still engulfs most of the outer cosmos, whilst a vast residuum of powerful inherited associations clings around all the objects and processes that were once mysterious, however well they may now be explained. And more than this, there is an actual physiological fixation of the old instincts in our nervous tissue, which would make them obscurely operative even were the conscious mind to be purged of all sources of wonder.

Because we remember pain and the menace of death more vividly than pleasure, and because our feelings toward the beneficent aspects of the unknown have from the first been captured and formalized by conventional religious rituals, it has fallen to the lot of the darker and more maleficent[4] side of cosmic mystery to figure chiefly in our popular supernatural folklore. This tendency, too, is naturally enhanced by the fact that uncertainty and danger are always closely allied; thus making any kind of an unknown world a world of peril and evil possibilities. When to this sense of fear and evil the inevitable fascination of wonder and curiosity is superadded, there is born a composite body of keen emotion and imaginative provocation whose vitality must of necessity endure as long as the human race itself. Children will always be afraid of the dark, and men with minds sensitive to hereditary impulse will always tremble at the thought of the hidden and fathomless worlds of strange life which may pulsate in the gulfs beyond the stars, or press hideously upon our own globe in unholy dimensions which only the dead and the moonstruck can glimpse.

With this foundation, no one need wonder at the existence of a literature of cosmic fear. It has always existed, and always will exist; and no better evidence of its tenacious vigor can be cited than the impulse which now and then drives writers of totally opposite leanings to try their hands at it in isolated tales, as if to discharge from their minds certain phantasmal shapes which would otherwise haunt them. Thus Dickens wrote several eerie narratives; Browning, the hideous poem "Childe Roland"; Henry James, *The Turn of the Screw*; Dr. Holmes, the subtle novel *Elsie Venner*; F. Marion Crawford, "The Upper Berth" and a number of other examples; Mrs. Charlotte Perkins Gilman, social worker, "The Yellow Wall Paper"; whilst the humorist W.W. Jacobs produced that able melodramatic bit called "The Monkey's Paw."[5]

This type of fear-literature must not be confounded with a type externally similar but psychologically widely different; the literature of mere physical fear and the mundanely gruesome. Such writing, to be sure, has its place, as has the conventional or even whimsical or humorous ghost story where formalism or the author's knowing wink removes the true sense of the morbidly unnatural; but these things are not the literature of cosmic fear in its purest sense. The true weird tale has something more than secret murder, bloody bones, or a sheeted form clanking chains according to rule. A certain atmosphere of breathless and unexplainable dread of outer, unknown forces must be present; and there must be a hint, expressed with a seriousness and portentousness becoming its subject, of that most terrible conception of the human brain—a malign and particular suspension or defeat of those fixed laws of Nature which are our only safeguard against the assaults of chaos and the demons of unplumbed space.

Naturally we cannot expect all weird tales to conform absolutely to any theoretical model. Creative minds are uneven, and the best of fabrics have their dull spots. Moreover, much of the choicest weird work is unconscious; appearing in memorable fragments scattered through material whose massed effect may be of a very different cast. Atmosphere is the all-important thing, for the final criterion of authenticity is not the dovetailing of a plot but the creation of a given sensation. We may say, as a general thing, that a weird story whose intent is to teach or produce a social effect, or one in which the horrors are finally explained away by natural means, is not a genuine tale of cosmic fear; but it remains a fact that such narratives often possess, in isolated sections, atmospheric touches which fulfill every condition of true supernatural horror-literature. Therefore we must judge a weird tale not by the author's intent, or by the mere mechanics of the plot; but by the emotional level which it attains at its least mundane point. If the proper sensations are excited, such a "high spot" must be admitted on its own merits as weird literature, no matter how prosaically it is later dragged down. The one test of the really weird is simply this—whether or not there be excited in the reader a profound sense of dread, and of contact with unknown spheres and powers; a subtle attitude of awed listening, as if for the beating of black wings or the scratching of outside shapes and entities on the known universe's utmost rim. And of course, the more completely and unifiedly a story conveys this atmosphere, the better it is as a work of art in the given medium.

II. *The Dawn of the Horror-Tale*

As may naturally be expected of a form so closely connected with primal emotion, the horror-tale is as old as human thought and speech themselves.

Cosmic terror appears as an ingredient of the earliest folklore of all races, and is crystallized in the most archaic ballads, chronicles, and sacred writings. It was, indeed, a prominent feature of the elaborate ceremonial magic, with its rituals for the evocation of daemons and specters, which flourished from prehistoric times, and which reached its highest development in Egypt and the Semitic nations. Fragments like the Book of Enoch and the Claviculae of Solomon[6] well illustrate the power of the weird over the ancient Eastern mind, and upon such things were based enduring systems and traditions whose echoes extend obscurely even to the present time. Touches of this transcendental fear are seen in classic literature, and there is evidence of its still greater emphasis in a ballad literature which paralleled the classic stream but vanished for lack of a written medium. The Middle Ages, steeped in fanciful darkness, gave it an enormous impulse toward expression; and East and West alike were busy preserving and amplifying the dark heritage, both of random folklore and of academically formulated magic and cabbalism,[7] which had descended to them. Witch, werewolf, vampire, and ghoul brooded ominously on the lips of bard and grandam, and needed but little encouragement to take the final step across the boundary that divides the chanted tale or song from the formal literary composition. In the Orient, the weird tale tended to assume a gorgeous coloring and sprightliness which almost transmuted it into sheer phantasy. In the West, where the mystical Teuton[8] had come down from his black Boreal[9] forests and the Celt remembered strange sacrifices in Druidic groves, it assumed a terrible intensity and convincing seriousness of atmosphere which doubled the force of its half-told, half-hinted horrors.

Much of the power of Western horror-lore was undoubtedly due to the hidden but often suspected presence of a hideous cult of nocturnal worshippers whose strange customs—descended from pre–Aryan[10] and pre-agricultural times when a squat race of Mongoloids[11] roved over Europe with their flocks and herds—were rooted in the most revolting fertility-rites of immemorial antiquity. This secret religion, stealthily handed down amongst peasants for thousands of years despite the outward reign of the Druidic, Graeco-Roman, and Christian faiths in the regions involved, was marked by wild "Witches' Sabbaths" in lonely woods and atop distant hills on Walpurgis-Night and Hallowe'en, the traditional breeding-seasons of the goats and sheep and cattle; and became the source of vast riches of sorcery-legend, besides provoking extensive witchcraft- prosecutions of which the Salem affair forms the chief American example. Akin to it in essence, and perhaps connected with it in fact, was the frightful secret system of inverted theology or Satan-worship which produced such horrors as the famous "Black Mass"[12]; whilst operating toward the same end we may note the activities of those whose aims were somewhat more scientific or philosophical—the astrologers, cabbalists, and alchemists of the Albertus Magnus or Raymond Lully[13] type, with whom such rude ages invariably abound. The prevalence and depth of the mediaeval horror-spirit in Europe, intensified by the dark despair which waves of pestilence brought, may be fairly gauged by the grotesque carvings slyly introduced into much of the finest later Gothic ecclesiastical work of the time; the demoniac gargoyles of Notre Dame and Mont St. Michel being among the most famous specimens. And throughout the period, it must be remembered, there existed amongst educated and uneducated alike a most unquestioning faith in every form of the supernatural; from the gentlest of Christian doctrines to the most monstrous morbidities of witchcraft and black magic. It was from no empty background that the Renaissance magicians and alchemists—Nostradamus, Trithemius, Dr. John Dee, Robert Fludd,[14] and the like—were born.

In this fertile soil were nourished types and characters of somber myth and legend which persist in weird literature to this day, more or less disguised or altered by modern technique. Many of them were taken from the earliest oral sources, and form part of mankind's permanent heritage. The shade which appears and demands the burial of its bones, the daemon lover who comes to bear away his still living bride, the death-fiend[15] or psychopomp riding the night-wind, the man-wolf, the sealed chamber, the deathless sorcerer—all these may be found in that curious body of mediaeval lore which the late Mr. Baring-Gould[16] so effectively assembled in book form. Wherever the mystic Northern blood was strongest, the atmosphere of the popular tales became most intense; for in the Latin races there is a touch of basic rationality which denies to even their strangest superstitions many of the overtones of glamour so characteristic of our own forest-born and ice-fostered whisperings.

Just as all fiction first found extensive embodiment in poetry, so is it in poetry that we first encounter the permanent entry of the weird into standard literature. Most of the ancient instances, curiously enough, are in prose; as the werewolf incident in Petronius, the gruesome passages in Apuleius, the brief but celebrated letter of Pliny the Younger to Sura, and the odd compilation *On Wonderful Events* by the Emperor Hadrian's Greek freedman, Phlegon.[17] It is in Phlegon that we first find that hideous tale of the corpse-bride, "Philinnion and Machates," later related by Proclus and in modern times forming the inspiration of Goethe's "Bride of Corinth" and Washington Irving's "German Student." But by the time the old Northern myths take literary form, and in that later time when the weird appears as a steady element in the literature of the day, we find it mostly in metrical dress; as indeed we find the greater part of the strictly imaginative writing of the Middle Ages and Renaissance. The Scandinavian Eddas and Sagas thunder with cosmic horror, and shake with the stark fear of Ymir and his shapeless spawn; whilst our own Anglo-Saxon *Beowulf* and the later Continental Nibelung tales are full of eldritch weirdness. Dante is a pioneer in the classic capture of macabre atmosphere, and in Spenser's stately stanzas will be seen more than a few touches of fantastic terror in landscape, incident, and character. Prose literature gives us Malory's *Morte d'Arthur,* in which are presented many ghastly situations taken from early ballad sources—the theft of the sword and silk from the corpse in Chapel Perilous by Sir Launcelot, the ghost of Sir Gawaine, and the tomb-fiend seen by Sir Galahad—whilst other and cruder specimens were doubtless set forth in the cheap and sensational "chapbooks" vulgarly hawked about and devoured by the ignorant. In Elizabethan drama, with its *Dr. Faustus,* the witches in *Macbeth,* the ghost in *Hamlet,* and the horrible gruesomeness of Webster, we may easily discern the strong hold of the demoniac on the public mind; a hold intensified by the very real fear of living witchcraft, whose terrors, first wildest on the Continent, begin to echo loudly in English ears as the witch-hunting crusades of James the First[18] gain headway. To the lurking mystical prose of the ages is added a long line of treatises on witchcraft and demonology which aid in exciting the imagination of the reading world.

Through the seventeenth and into the eighteenth century we behold a growing mass of fugitive legendry and balladry of darksome cast; still, however, held down beneath the surface of polite and accepted literature. Chapbooks of horror and weirdness multiplied, and we glimpse the eager interest of the people through fragments like Defoe's[19] "Apparition of Mrs. Veal," a homely tale of a dead woman's spectral visit to a distant friend, written to advertise covertly a badly selling theological disquisition on death. The upper orders of society were now losing faith in the supernatural, and indulging in a period of classic rationalism. Then, beginning with the translations of Eastern tales in Queen Anne's reign and taking definite form toward the middle of the century, comes the revival of romantic feeling—the era of new joy in Nature, and in the radiance of past times, strange scenes, bold deeds, and incredible marvels. We feel it first in the poets, whose utterances take on new qualities of wonder, strangeness, and shuddering. And finally, after the timid appearance of a few weird scenes in the novels of the day—such as Smollett's *Adventures of Ferdinand, Count Fathom*[20]—the released instinct precipitates itself in the birth of a new school of writing; the "Gothic" school of horrible and fantastic prose fiction, long and short, whose literary posterity is destined to become so numerous, and in many cases so resplendent in artistic merit. It is, when one reflects upon it, genuinely remarkable that weird narration as a fixed and academically recognized literary form should have been so late of final birth. The impulse and atmosphere are as old as man, but the typical weird tale of standard literature is a child of the eighteenth century.

III. The Early Gothic Novel

The shadow-haunted landscapes of "Ossian,"[21] the chaotic visions of William Blake, the grotesque witch-dances in Burns's "Tam O'Shanter,"[22] the sinister demonism of Coleridge's *Christabel* and *Ancient Mariner,* the ghostly charm of James Hogg's "Kilmeny,"[23] and the more restrained approaches to cosmic horror in *Lamia* and many of Keats's other poems, are typical British illustrations of the advent of the weird to formal literature. Our Teutonic cousins of the Continent were equally receptive to the rising flood, and Bürger's "Wild Huntsman" and the even more famous daemon-bridegroom ballad of "Lenore"[24]— both imitated in English by Scott,[25] whose respect for the supernatural was always great— are only a taste of the eerie wealth which German song had commenced to provide. [...]

But it remained for a very sprightly and worldly Englishman—none other than Horace Walpole[26] himself—to give the growing impulse definite shape and become the actual founder of the literary horror-story as a permanent form. Fond of mediaeval romance and mystery as a dilettante's diversion, and with a quaintly imitated Gothic castle as his abode at Strawberry Hill, Walpole in 1764 published *The Castle of Otranto;* a tale of the supernatural which, though thoroughly unconvincing and mediocre in itself, was destined to exert an almost unparalleled influence on the literature of the weird. First venturing it only as a translation by one "William Marshal, Gent." from the Italian of a mythical "Onuphrio Muralto," the author later acknowledged his connection with the book and took pleasure in its wide and instantaneous popularity—a popularity which extended to many editions, early dramatization, and wholesale imitation both in England and in Germany. [...]

Such is the tale; flat, stilted, and altogether devoid of the true cosmic horror which makes weird literature. Yet such was the thirst of the age for those touches of strangeness and spectral antiquity which it reflects, that it was seriously received by the soundest readers and raised in spite of its intrinsic ineptness to a pedestal of lofty importance in literary history. What it did above all else was to create a novel type of scene, puppet-characters, and incidents; which, handled to better advantage by writers more naturally adapted to weird creation, stimulated the growth of an imitative Gothic school which in turn inspired the real weavers of cosmic terror—the line of actual artists beginning with Poe. This novel dramatic paraphernalia consisted first of all of the Gothic castle, with its awesome antiquity, vast distances and ramblings, deserted or ruined wings, damp corridors, unwholesome hidden catacombs, and galaxy of ghosts and appalling legends, as a nucleus of suspense and demoniac fright. In addition, it included the tyrannical and malevolent nobleman as villain; the saintly, long persecuted, and generally insipid heroine who undergoes the major terrors and serves as a point of view and focus for the reader's sympathies; the valorous and immaculate hero, always of high birth but often in humble disguise; the convention of high-sounding foreign names, mostly Italian, for the characters; and the infinite array of stage properties which includes strange lights, damp trap-doors, extinguished lamps, moldy hidden manuscripts, creaking hinges, shaking arras, and the like. All this paraphernalia reappears with amusing sameness, yet sometimes with tremendous effect, throughout the history of the Gothic novel; and is by no means extinct even today, though subtler technique now forces it to assume a less naive and obvious form. An harmonious milieu for a new school had been found, and the writing world was not slow to grasp the opportunity.

German romance at once responded to the Walpole influence, and soon became a byword for the weird and ghastly. In England one of the first imitators was the celebrated Mrs. Barbauld, then Miss Aikin, who in 1773 published an unfinished fragment called "Sir Bertrand,"[27] in which the strings of genuine terror were truly touched with no clumsy hand. A nobleman on a dark and lonely moor, attracted by a tolling bell and distant light, enters a strange and ancient turreted castle whose doors open and close and whose bluish will-o'-the-wisps lead up mysterious staircases toward dead hands and animated black statues. A coffin with a dead lady, whom Sir Bertrand kisses, is finally reached; and upon the kiss the scene dissolves to give place to a splendid apartment where the lady, restored to life, holds a banquet in honor of her rescuer. Walpole admired this tale, though he accorded less respect to an even more prominent offspring of his *Otranto—The Old English Baron,* by Clara Reeve,[28] published in 1777. Truly enough, this tale lacks the real vibration to the note of outer darkness and mystery which distinguishes Mrs. Barbauld's fragment; and though less crude than Walpole's novel, and more artistically economical of horror in its possession of only one spectral figure, it is nevertheless too definitely insipid for greatness. Here again we have the virtuous heir to the castle disguised as a peasant and restored to his heritage through the ghost of his father; and here again we have a case of wide popularity leading to many editions, dramatization, and ultimate translation into French. Miss Reeve wrote another weird novel, unfortunately unpublished and lost.

The Gothic novel was now settled as a literary form, and instances multiply bewilderingly as the eighteenth century draws toward its close. […] [In 1790,] all existing lamps are paled by the rising of a fresh luminary of wholly superior order—Mrs. Ann Radcliffe (1764–1823),[29] whose famous novels made terror and suspense a fashion, and who set new and higher standards in the domain of macabre and fear-inspiring atmosphere despite a provoking custom of destroying her own phantoms at the last through labored mechanical explanations. To the familiar Gothic trappings of her predecessors Mrs. Radcliffe added a genuine sense of the unearthly in scene and incident which closely approached genius; every touch of setting and action contributing artistically to the impression of illimitable frightfulness which she wished to convey. A few sinister details like a track of blood on castle stairs, a groan from a distant vault, or a weird song in a nocturnal forest can with her conjure up the most powerful images of imminent horror; surpassing by far the extravagant and toilsome elaborations of others. Nor are these images in themselves any the less potent because they are explained away before the end of the novel. Mrs. Radcliffe's visual imagination was very strong, and appears as much in her delightful landscape touches—always in broad, glamorously pictorial outline, and never in close detail—as in her weird phantasies. Her prime weaknesses, aside from the habit of prosaic disillusionment, are a tendency toward erroneous geography and history and a fatal predilection for bestrewing her novels with insipid little poems, attributed to one or another of the characters.

Mrs. Radcliffe wrote six novels. […] Of these *Udolpho* is by far the most famous, and may be taken as a type of the early Gothic tale at its best. It is the chronicle of Emily, a young Frenchwoman transplanted to an ancient and portentous castle in the Apennines through the death of her parents and the marriage of her aunt to the lord of the castle—the scheming nobleman Montoni. Mysterious sounds, opened doors, frightful legends, and a nameless horror in a niche behind a black veil all operate in quick succession to unnerve the heroine and her faithful attendant Annette. […] Mrs. Radcliffe's characters are puppets, but they are less markedly so than those of her forerunners. And in atmospheric creation she stands preëminent among those of her time.

Of Mrs. Radcliffe's countless imitators, the American novelist Charles Brockden Brown[30] stands the closest in spirit and method. Like her, he injured his creations by natural explanations; but also like her, he had an uncanny atmospheric power which gives his horrors a frightful vitality as long as they remain unexplained. He differed from her in contemptuously discarding the external Gothic paraphernalia and properties and choosing modern American scenes for his mysteries; but this repudiation did not extend to the Gothic spirit and type of incident. Brown's novels involve some memorably frightful scenes, and excel even Mrs. Radcliffe's in describing the operations of the perturbed mind. […] But Brown's most famous book is *Wieland; or, The Transformation* (1798), in which a Pennsylvania German, engulfed by a wave of religious fanaticism, hears voices and slays his wife and children as a sacrifice. His sister Clara, who tells the story, narrowly escapes. The scene, laid at the woodland estate of Mittingen on the Schuylkill's remote reaches, is drawn with extreme vividness; and the terrors of Clara, beset by spectral tones, gathering fears, and the sound of strange footsteps in the lonely house, are all shaped with truly artistic force. In the end a lame ventriloquial explanation is offered, but the atmosphere is genuine while it lasts. […]

IV. *The Apex of Gothic Romance*

Horror in literature attains a new malignity in the work of Matthew Gregory Lewis[31] (1775–1818), whose novel *The Monk* (1796) achieved marvelous popularity and earned him the nickname of "Monk" Lewis. This young author, educated in Germany and saturated with a body of wild Teuton lore unknown to Mrs. Radcliffe, turned to terror in forms more violent than his gentle predecessor had ever dared to think of; and produced as a result a masterpiece of active nightmare whose general Gothic cast is spiced with added stores of ghoulishness. The story is one of a Spanish monk, Ambrosio, who from a state of overproud virtue is tempted to the very nadir of evil by a fiend in the guise of the maiden Matilda; and who is finally, when awaiting death at the Inquisition's hands, induced to purchase escape at the price of his soul from the Devil, because he deems both body and soul already lost. […] The novel contains some appalling descriptions such as the incantation in the vaults beneath the convent cemetery, the burning of the convent, and the final end of the wretched abbot. In the sub-plot where the Marquis de las Cisternas meets the specter of his erring ancestress, The Bleeding Nun, there are many enormously potent strokes; notably the visit of the animated corpse to the Marquis's bedside, and the cabbalistic ritual whereby the Wandering Jew helps him to fathom and banish his dead tormentor. Nevertheless *The*

Monk drags sadly when read as a whole. It is too long and too diffuse, and much of its potency is marred by flippancy and by an awkwardly excessive reaction against those canons of decorum which Lewis at first despised as prudish. [...]

Gothic romances, both English and German, now appeared in multitudinous and mediocre profusion. Most of them were merely ridiculous in the light of mature taste. [...] This particular school was petering out, but before its final subordination there arose its last and greatest figure in the person of Charles Robert Maturin (1782–1824), an obscure and eccentric Irish clergyman. Out of an ample body of miscellaneous writing which includes one confused Radcliffian imitation called *Fatal Revenge; or, The Family of Montorio* (1807), Maturin at length evolved the vivid horror-masterpiece of *Melmoth the Wanderer* (1820), in which the Gothic tale climbed to altitudes of sheer spiritual fright which it had never known before.

Melmoth is the tale of an Irish gentleman who, in the seventeenth century, obtained a preternaturally extended life from the Devil at the price of his soul. If he can persuade another to take the bargain off his hands, and assume his existing state, he can be saved; but this he can never manage to effect, no matter how assiduously he haunts those whom despair has made reckless and frantic. The framework of the story is very clumsy; involving tedious length, digressive episodes, narratives within narratives, and labored dovetailing and coincidences; but at various points in the endless rambling there is felt a pulse of power undiscoverable in any previous work of this kind—a kinship to the essential truth of human nature, an understanding of the profoundest sources of actual cosmic fear, and a white heat of sympathetic passion on the writer's part which makes the book a true document of aesthetic self-expression rather than a mere clever compound of artifice. No unbiased reader can doubt that with *Melmoth* an enormous stride in the evolution of the horror-tale is represented. Fear is taken out of the realm of the conventional and exalted into a hideous cloud over mankind's very destiny. Maturin's shudders, the work of one capable of shuddering himself, are of the sort that convince. Mrs. Radcliffe and Lewis are fair game for the parodist, but it would be difficult to find a false note in the feverishly intensified action and high atmospheric tension of the Irishman whose less sophisticated emotions and strain of Celtic mysticism gave him the finest possible natural equipment for his task. [...]

None can fail to notice the difference between this modulated, suggestive, and artistically molded horror and—to use the words of Professor George Saintsbury[32]—"the artful but rather jejune rationalism of Mrs. Radcliffe, and the too often puerile extravagance, the bad taste, and the sometimes slipshod style of Lewis." Maturin's style in itself deserves particular praise, for its forcible directness and vitality lift it altogether above the pompous artificialities of which his predecessors are guilty. Professor Edith Birkhead, in her history of the Gothic novel,[33] justly observes that with all his faults Maturin was the greatest as well as the last of the Goths. *Melmoth* was widely read and eventually dramatized, but its late date in the evolution of the Gothic tale deprived it of the tumultuous popularity of *Udolpho* and *The Monk*.

V. *The Aftermath of Gothic Fiction*

Meanwhile other hands had not been idle, so that above the dreary plethora of trash [...] there arose many memorable weird works both in English and German. Classic in merit, and markedly different from its fellows because of its foundation in the Oriental tale rather than the Walpolesque Gothic novel, is the celebrated *History of the Caliph Vathek* by the wealthy dilettante William Beckford,[34] first written in the French language but published in an English translation before the appearance of the original. Eastern tales, introduced to European literature early in the eighteenth century through Galland's[35] French translation of the inexhaustibly opulent *Arabian Nights,* had become a reigning fashion; being used both for allegory and for amusement. The sly humor which only the Eastern mind knows how to mix with weirdness had captivated a sophisticated generation, till Bagdad and Damascus names became as freely strewn through popular literature as dashing Italian and Spanish ones were soon to be. Beckford, well read in Eastern romance, caught the atmosphere with unusual receptivity; and in his fantastic volume reflected very potently the haughty luxury, sly disillusion, bland cruelty, urbane treachery, and shadowy spectral horror of the Saracen spirit. His seasoning of the ridiculous seldom mars the force of his sinister theme, and the tale marches onward with a phantasmagoric pomp in which the laughter is that of skeletons feasting under Arabesque domes. *Vathek* is a tale of the grandson of the Caliph Haroun, who, tormented by that ambition for super-terrestrial power, pleasure, and learning which animates the average Gothic villain or Byronic hero (essentially cognate types), is lured by an evil genius to seek the subterranean throne of the mighty and fabulous pre–Adamite sultans in the fiery halls of Eblis, the Mahometan Devil. The descriptions of Vathek's palaces and diversions, of his scheming sorceress-mother Carathis and her witch-tower with the fifty one-eyed negresses, of his pilgrimage to the haunted ruins of Istakhar (Persepolis) and of the impish bride Nouronihar whom he treacherously acquired on the way, of Istakhar's primordial towers and terraces in the burning moonlight of the waste, and of the terrible Cyclopean halls of Eblis, where, lured by glittering promises, each victim is compelled to wander in anguish for ever, his right hand upon his blazingly ignited and eternally burning heart, are triumphs of weird coloring which raise the book to a permanent place in English letters. [...] Beckford, however, lacks the essential mysticism which marks the acutest form of the weird; so that his tales have a certain knowing Latin hardness and clearness preclusive of sheer panic fright.

But Beckford remained alone in his devotion to the Orient. Other writers, closer to the Gothic tradition and to European life in general, were content to follow more faithfully in the lead of Walpole. Among the countless producers of terror-literature in these times may be mentioned the Utopian economic theorist William Godwin,[36] who followed his famous but non-supernatural *Caleb Williams* (1794) with the intendedly weird *St. Leon* (1799), in which the theme of the elixir of life, as developed by the imaginary secret order of "Rosicrucians," is handled with ingeniousness if not with atmospheric convincingness. This element of Rosicrucianism, fostered by a wave of popular magical interest exemplified in the vogue of the charlatan Cagliostro and the publication of Francis Barrett's *The Magus* (1801), a curious and compendious treatise on occult principles and ceremonies, of which a reprint was made as lately as 1896, figures in Bulwer-Lytton[37] and in many late Gothic novels, especially that remote and enfeebled posterity which straggled far down into the nineteenth century and was represented by George W.M. Reynolds' *Faust and the Demon* and *Wagner, the Wehr-wolf.*[38] [...]

His daughter, the wife of Shelley,[39] was much more successful; and her inimitable *Frankenstein; or, The Modern Prometheus* (1818) is one of the horror-classics of all time. Composed in competition with her husband, Lord Byron, and Dr. John William Polidori in an effort to prove supremacy in horror-making, Mrs. Shelley's *Frankenstein* was the only one of the rival narratives to be brought to an elaborate completion; and criticism has failed to prove that the best parts are due to Shelley rather than to her. The novel, somewhat tinged but scarcely marred by moral didacticism, tells of the artificial human being molded from charnel fragments by Victor Frankenstein, a young Swiss medical student. Created by its designer "in the mad pride of intellectuality," the monster possesses full intelligence but owns a hideously loathsome form. It is rejected by mankind, becomes embittered, and at length begins the successive murder of all whom young Frankenstein loves best, friends and family. [...] Mrs. Shelley wrote other novels, including the fairly notable *Last Man;* but never duplicated the success of her first effort. It has the true touch of cosmic fear, no matter how much the movement may lag in places. [...]

Dickens now rises with occasional weird bits like "The Signalman," a tale of ghostly warning conforming to a very common pattern and touched with a verisimilitude which allies it as much with the coming psychological school as with the dying Gothic school. At this time a wave of interest in spiritualistic charlatanry, mediumism, Hindoo theosophy, and such matters, much like that of the present day, was flourishing; so that the number of weird tales with a "psychic" or pseudo-scientific basis became very considerable. For a number of these the prolific and popular Lord Edward Bulwer-Lytton was responsible; and despite the large doses of turgid rhetoric and empty romanticism in his products, his success in the weaving of a certain kind of bizarre charm cannot be denied.

"The House and the Brain," which hints of Rosicrucianism and at a malign and death-less figure perhaps suggested by Louis XV's mysterious courtier St. Germain, yet survives as one of the best short haunted-house tales ever written. The novel *Zanoni* (1842) contains similar elements more elaborately handled, and introduces a vast unknown sphere of being pressing on our own world and guarded by a horrible "Dweller of the Threshold" who haunts those who try to enter and fail. Here we have a benign brotherhood kept alive from age to age till finally reduced to a single member, and as a hero an ancient Chaldaean sor-cerer surviving in the pristine bloom of youth to perish on the guillotine of the French Revolution. Though full of the conventional spirit of romance, marred by a ponderous net-work of symbolic and didactic meanings, and left unconvincing through lack of perfect atmospheric realization of the situations hinging on the spectral world, *Zanoni* is really an excellent performance as a romantic novel; and can be read with genuine interest today by the not too sophisticated reader. It is amusing to note that in describing an attempted ini-tiation into the ancient brotherhood the author cannot escape using the stock Gothic castle of Walpolian lineage.

In *A Strange Story* (1862) Bulwer-Lytton shows a marked improvement in the creation of weird images and moods. The novel, despite enormous length, a highly artificial plot bolstered up by opportune coincidences, and an atmosphere of homiletic pseudo-science designed to please the matter-of-fact and purposeful Victorian reader, is exceedingly effec-tive as a narrative; evoking instantaneous and unflagging interest, and furnishing many potent—if somewhat melodramatic—tableaux and climaxes. Again we have the mysterious user of life's elixir in the person of the soulless magician Margrave, whose dark exploits stand out with dramatic vividness against the modern background of a quiet English town and of the Australian bush; and again we have shadowy intimations of a vast spectral world of the unknown in the very air about us—this time handled with much greater power and vitality than in *Zanoni.* One of the two great incantation passages, where the hero is driven by a luminous evil spirit to rise at night in his sleep, take a strange Egyptian wand, and evoke nameless presences in the haunted and mausoleum-facing pavilion of a famous Ren-aissance alchemist, truly stands among the major terror scenes of literature. Just enough is suggested, and just little enough is told. Unknown words are twice dictated to the sleep-walker, and as he repeats them the ground trembles, and all the dogs of the countryside begin to bay at half-seen amorphous shadows that stalk athwart the moonlight. When a third set of unknown words is prompted, the sleep-walker's spirit suddenly rebels at uttering them, as if the soul could recognize ultimate abysmal horrors concealed from the mind; and at last an apparition of an absent sweetheart and good angel breaks the malign spell. This fragment well illustrates how far Lord Lytton was capable of progressing beyond his usual pomp and stock romance toward that crystalline essence of artistic fear which belongs to the domain of poetry. In describing certain details of incantations, Lytton was greatly indebted to his amusingly serious occult studies, in the course of which he came in touch with that odd French scholar and cabbalist Alphonse-Louis Constant ("Eliphas Lévi"),[40] who claimed to possess the secrets of ancient magic, and to have evoked the specter of the old Grecian wizard Apollonius of Tyana,[41] who lived in Nero's time.

The romantic, semi-Gothic, quasi-moral tradition here represented was carried far down the nineteenth century by such authors as Joseph Sheridan LeFanu, Thomas Preskett Prest with his famous *Varney, the Vampyre* (1847), Wilkie Collins, the late Sir H. Rider Haggard (whose *She* is really remarkably good), Sir A. Conan Doyle, H.G. Wells, and Robert Louis Stevenson[42]—the latter of whom, despite an atrocious tendency toward jaunty mannerisms, created permanent classics in "Markheim," "The Body-Snatcher," and *Dr. Jekyll and Mr. Hyde.* Indeed, we may say that this school still survives; for to it clearly belong such of our contemporary horror-tales as specialize in events rather than atmospheric details, address the intellect rather than the impressionistic imagination, cultivate a luminous glamour rather than a malign tensity or psychological verisimilitude, and take a definite stand in sympathy with mankind and its welfare. It has its undeniable strength, and because of its "human element" commands a wider audience than does the sheer artistic nightmare. If not quite so potent as the latter, it is because a diluted product can never achieve the intensity of a concentrated essence.

Quite alone both as a novel and as a piece of terror-literature stands the famous *Wuthering Heights* (1847) by Emily Brontë, with its mad vista of bleak, windswept Yorkshire moors and the violent, distorted lives they foster. Though primarily a tale of life, and of human passions in agony and conflict, its epically cosmic setting affords room for horror of the most spiritual sort. Heathcliff, the modified Byronic villain-hero, is a strange dark waif found in the streets as a small child and speaking only a strange gibberish till adopted by the family he ultimately ruins. That he is in truth a diabolic spirit rather than a human being is more than once suggested, and the unreal is further approached in the experience of the visitor who encounters a plaintive child-ghost at a bough-brushed upper window. Between Heathcliff and Catherine Earnshaw is a tie deeper and more terrible than human love. After her death he twice disturbs her grave, and is haunted by an impalpable presence which can be nothing less than her spirit. The spirit enters his life more and more, and at last he becomes confident of some imminent mystical reunion. He says he feels a strange change approaching, and ceases to take nourishment. At night he either walks abroad or opens the casement by his bed. When he dies the casement is still swinging open to the pouring rain, and a queer smile pervades the stiffened face. They bury him in a grave beside the mound he has haunted for eighteen years, and small shepherd boys say that he yet walks with his Catherine in the churchyard and on the moor when it rains. Their faces, too, are sometimes seen on rainy nights behind that upper casement at Wuthering Heights. Miss Brontë's eerie terror is no mere Gothic echo, but a tense expression of man's shuddering reaction to the unknown. In this respect, *Wuthering Heights* becomes the symbol of a literary transition, and marks the growth of a new and sounder school.

VI. *Spectral Literature on the Continent*

On the Continent literary horror fared well. The celebrated short tales and novels of Ernst Theodor Wilhelm Hoffmann[43] (1776–1822) are a byword for mellowness of background and maturity of form, though they incline to levity and extravagance, and lack the exalted moments of stark, breathless terror which a less sophisticated writer might have achieved. Generally they convey the grotesque rather than the terrible. Most artistic of all the Continental weird tales is the German classic *Undine* (1811), by Friedrich Heinrich Karl, Baron de la Motte Fouqué.[44] In this story of a water-spirit who married a mortal and gained a human soul there is a delicate fineness of craftsmanship which makes it notable in any department of literature, and an easy naturalness which places it close to the genuine folkmyth. It is, in fact, derived from a tale told by the Renaissance physician and alchemist Paracelsus[45] in his *Treatise on Elemental Sprites.*

[…] Many passages and atmospheric touches in this tale reveal Fouqué as an accomplished artist in the field of the macabre; especially the descriptions of the haunted wood with its gigantic snow-white man and various unnamed terrors, which occur early in the narrative.

Not so well known as *Undine,* but remarkable for its convincing realism and freedom from Gothic stock devices, is the *Amber Witch* of Wilhelm Meinhold,[46] another product of the German fantastic genius of the earlier nineteenth century. This tale, which is laid in the time of the Thirty Years' War, purports to be a clergyman's manuscript found in an old church at Coserow, and centers round the writer's daughter, Maria Schweidler, who is wrongly accused of witchcraft. […] Meinhold's great strength is in his air of casual and realistic verisimilitude, which intensifies our suspense and sense of the unseen by half persuading us that the menacing events must somehow be either the truth or very close to the truth. Indeed, so thorough is this realism that a popular magazine once published the main points of *The Amber Witch* as an actual occurrence of the seventeenth century! […]

It is in Théophile Gautier[47] that we first seem to find an authentic French sense of the unreal world, and here there appears a spectral mastery which, though not continuously used, is recognizable at once as something alike genuine and profound. Short tales like "Avatar," "The Foot of the Mummy," and "Clarimonde"[48] display glimpses of forbidden visits that allure, tantalize, and sometimes horrify; whilst the Egyptian visions evoked in "One of Cleopatra's Nights"[49] are of the keenest and most expressive potency. Gautier captured the inmost soul of aeon-weighted Egypt, with its cryptic life and Cyclopean architecture, and uttered once and for all the eternal horror of its nether world of catacombs, where to the end of time millions of stiff, spiced corpses will stare up in the blackness with glassy eyes, awaiting some awesome and unrelateable summons. […] Later on we see the stream divide, producing strange poets and fantasists of the Symbolist and Decadent schools whose dark interests really center more in abnormalities of human thought and instinct than in the actual supernatural, and subtle story-tellers whose thrills are quite directly derived from the night-black wells of cosmic unreality. Of the former class of "artists in sin" the illustrious poet Baudelaire, influenced vastly by Poe, is the supreme type; whilst the psychological novelist Joris-Karl Huysmans,[50] a true child of the eighteen-nineties, is at once the summation and finale. The latter and purely narrative class is continued by Prosper Mérimée, whose "Venus of Ille"[51] presents in terse and convincing prose the same ancient statue-bride theme which Thomas Moore cast in ballad form in "The Ring."[52]

The horror-tales of the powerful and cynical Guy de Maupassant, written as his final madness gradually overtook him, present individualities of their own; being rather the morbid outpourings of a realistic mind in a pathological state than the healthy imaginative products of a vision naturally disposed toward phantasy and sensitive to the normal illusions of the unseen. Nevertheless they are of the keenest interest and poignancy; suggesting with marvelous force the imminence of nameless terrors, and the relentless dogging of an ill-starred individual by hideous and menacing representatives of the outer blackness. Of these stories "The Horla" is generally regarded as the masterpiece. Relating the advent to France of an invisible being who lives on water and milk, sways the minds of others, and seems to be the vanguard of a horde of extra-terrestrial organisms arrived on earth to subjugate and overwhelm mankind, this tense narrative is perhaps without a peer in its particular department; notwithstanding its indebtedness to a tale by the American Fitz-James O'Brien[53] for details in describing the actual presence of the unseen monster. [...]

The collaborators Erckmann-Chatrian[54] enriched French literature with many spectral fancies like *The Man-Wolf,* in which a transmitted curse works toward its end in a traditional Gothic-castle setting. Their power of creating a shuddering midnight atmosphere was tremendous despite a tendency toward natural explanations and scientific wonders; and few short tales contain greater horror than "The Invisible Eye," where a malignant old hag weaves nocturnal hypnotic spells which induce the successive occupants of a certain inn chamber to hang themselves on a cross-beam. "The Owl's Ear" and "The Waters of Death" are full of engulfing darkness and mystery, the latter embodying the familiar overgrown-spider theme so frequently employed by weird fictionists. Villiers de l'Isle-Adam[55] likewise followed the macabre school; his "Torture by Hope," the tale of a stake-condemned prisoner permitted to escape in order to feel the pangs of recapture, being held by some to constitute the most harrowing short story in literature. This type, however, is less a part of the weird tradition than a class peculiar to itself—the so-called *conte cruel,* in which the wrenching of the emotions is accomplished through dramatic tantalizations, frustrations, and grue-some physical horrors. Almost wholly devoted to this form is the living writer Maurice Level,[56] whose very brief episodes have lent themselves so readily to theatrical adaptation in the "thrillers" of the Grand Guignol. As a matter of fact, the French genius is more nat-urally suited to this dark realism than to the suggestion of the unseen; since the latter process requires, for its best and most sympathetic development on a large scale, the inher-ent mysticism of the Northern mind.

A very flourishing, though till recently quite hidden, branch of weird literature is that of the Jews, kept alive and nourished in obscurity by the somber heritage of early Eastern magic, apocalyptic literature, and cabbalism. The Semitic mind, like the Celtic and Teutonic, seems to possess marked mystical inclinations; and the wealth of underground horror-lore surviving in ghettoes and synagogues must be much more considerable than is generally imagined. Cabbalism itself, so prominent during the Middle Ages, is a system of philosophy explaining the universe as emanations of the Deity, and involving the existence of strange spiritual realms and beings apart from the visible world, of which dark glimpses may be obtained through certain secret incantations. Its ritual is bound up with mystical interpre-tations of the Old Testament, and attributes an esoteric significance to each letter of the Hebrew alphabet—a circumstance which has imparted to Hebrew letters a sort of spectral glamour and potency in the popular literature of magic. Jewish folklore has preserved much of the terror and mystery of the past, and when more thoroughly studied is likely to exert considerable influence on weird fiction. The best examples of its literary use so far are the German novel *The Golem,* by Gustav Meyrink, and the drama *The Dybbuk,* by the Jewish writer using the pseudonym "Ansky."[57] The former, with its haunting shadowy suggestions of marvels and horrors just beyond reach, is laid in Prague, and describes with singular mastery that city's ancient ghetto with its spectral, peaked gables. The name is derived from a fabulous artificial giant supposed to be made and animated by mediaeval rabbis according to a certain cryptic formula. *The Dybbuk,* translated and produced in America in 1925, and more recently produced as an opera, describes with singular power the possession of a living body by the evil soul of a dead man. Both golems and dybbuks are fixed types, and serve as frequent ingredients of later Jewish tradition.

VII. *Edgar Allan Poe*

In the eighteen-thirties occurred a literary dawn directly affecting not only the history of the weird tale, but that of short fiction as a whole; and indirectly molding the trends and fortunes of a great European aesthetic school. It is our good fortune as Americans to be able to claim that dawn as our own, for it came in the person of our illustrious and unfortunate fellow-countryman Edgar Allan Poe. Poe's fame has been subject to curious undulations, and it is now a fashion amongst the "advanced intelligentsia" to minimize his importance both as an artist and as an influence; but it would be hard for any mature and reflective critic to deny the tremendous value of his work and the pervasive potency of his mind as an opener of artistic vistas. True, his type of outlook may have been anticipated; but it was he who first realized its possibilities and gave it supreme form and systematic expression. True also, that subsequent writers may have produced greater single tales than his; but again we must comprehend that it was only he who taught them by example and precept the art which they, having the way cleared for them and given an explicit guide, were perhaps able to carry to greater lengths. Whatever his limitations, Poe did that which no one else ever did or could have done; and to him we owe the modern horror-story in its final and perfected state.

Before Poe the bulk of weird writers had worked largely in the dark; without an understanding of the psychological basis of the horror appeal, and hampered by more or less of conformity to certain empty literary conventions such as the happy ending, virtue rewarded, and in general a hollow moral didacticism, acceptance of popular standards and values, and striving of the author to obtrude his own emotions into the story and take sides with the partisans of the majority's artificial ideas. Poe, on the other hand, perceived the essential impersonality of the real artist; and knew that the function of creative fiction is merely to express and interpret events and sensations as they are, regardless of how they tend or what they prove—good or evil, attractive or repulsive, stimulating or depressing—with the author always acting as a vivid and detached chronicler rather than as a teacher, sympathizer, or vendor of opinion. He saw clearly that all phases of life and thought are equally eligible as subject-matter for the artist, and being inclined by temperament to strangeness and gloom, decided to be the interpreter of those powerful feeling, and frequent happenings which attend pain rather than pleasure, decay rather than growth, terror rather than tranquility, and which are fundamentally either adverse or indifferent to the tastes and traditional outward sentiments of mankind, and to the health, sanity, and normal expansive welfare of the species.

Poe's specters thus acquired a convincing malignity possessed by none of their predecessors, and established a new standard of realism in the annals of literary horror. The impersonal and artistic intent, moreover, was aided by a scientific attitude not often found before; whereby Poe studied the human mind rather than the usages of Gothic fiction, and worked with an analytical knowledge of terror's true sources which doubled the force of his narratives and emancipated him from all the absurdities inherent in merely conventional shudder-coining. This example having been set, later authors were naturally forced to conform to it in order to compete at all; so that in this way a definite change began to affect the main stream of macabre writing. Poe, too, set a fashion in consummate craftsmanship; and although today some of his own work seems slightly melodramatic and unsophisticated, we can constantly trace his influence in such things as the maintenance of a single mood and achievement of a single impression in a tale, and the rigorous paring down of incidents to such as have a direct bearing on the plot and will figure prominently in the climax. Truly may it be said that Poe invented the short story in its present form. His elevation of disease, perversity, and decay to the level of artistically expressible themes was likewise infinitely far-reaching in effect; for avidly seized, sponsored, and intensified by his eminent French admirer Charles Pierre Baudelaire,[58] it became the nucleus of the principal aesthetic movements in France, thus making Poe in a sense the father of the Decadents and the Symbolists.[59]

Poet and critic by nature and supreme attainment, logician and philosopher by taste and mannerism, Poe was by no means immune from defects and affectations. His pretense to profound and obscure scholarship, his blundering ventures in stilted and labored pseudo-humor, and his often vitriolic outbursts of critical prejudice must all be recognized and forgiven. Beyond and above them, and dwarfing them to insignificance, was a master's vision of the terror that stalks about and within us, and the worm that writhes and slavers in the hideously close abyss. Penetrating to every festering horror in the gaily painted mockery called existence, and in the solemn masquerade called human thought and feelings that vision had power to project itself in blackly magical crystallizations and transmutations; till there bloomed in the sterile America of the thirties and forties such a moon-nourished garden of gorgeous poison fungi as not even the nether slope of Saturn might boast. Verses and tales alike sustain the burthen of cosmic panic. The raven whose noisome beak pierces the heart, the ghouls that toll iron bells in pestilential steeples, the vault of Ulalume in the black October night, the shocking spires and domes under the sea, the "wild, weird clime that lieth, sublime, out of Space—out of Time"—all these things and more leer at us amidst maniacal rattlings in the seething nightmare of the poetry. And in the prose there yawn open for us the very jaws of the pit—inconceivable abnormalities slyly hinted into a horrible half-knowledge by words whose innocence we scarcely doubt till the cracked tension of the speaker's hollow voice bids us fear their nameless implications; demoniac patterns and presences slumbering noxiously till waked for one phobic instant into a shrieking revelation that cackles itself to sudden madness or explodes in memorable and cataclysmic echoes. A Witches' Sabbath of horror flinging off decorous robes is flashed before us—a sight the more monstrous because of the scientific skill with which every particular is marshaled and brought into an easy apparent relation to the known gruesomeness of material life.

Poe's tales, of course, fall into several classes; some of which contain a purer essence of spiritual horror than others. The tales of logic and ratiocination,[60] forerunners of the modern detective story, are not to be included at all in weird literature; whilst certain others, probably influenced considerably by Hoffmann,[61] possess an extravagance which relegates them to the borderline of the grotesque. Still a third group deal with abnormal psychology and monomania[62] in such a way as to express terror but not weirdness. A substantial residuum, however, represent the literature of supernatural horror in its acutest form; and give their author a permanent and unassailable place as deity and fountain-head of all modern diabolic fiction. Who can forget the terrible swollen ship poised on the billow-chasm's edge in "MS. Found in a Bottle"—the dark intimations of her unhallowed age and monstrous growth, her sinister crew of unseeing greybeards, and her frightful southward rush under full sail through the ice of the Antarctic night, sucked onward by some resistless devil-current toward a vortex of eldritch enlightenment which must end in destruction?

Then there is the unutterable "M. Valdemar," kept together by hypnotism for seven months after his death, and uttering frantic sounds but a moment before the breaking of the spell leaves him "a nearly liquid mass of loathsome—of detestable putrescence." In the *Narrative of A. Gordon Pym* the voyagers reach first a strange south polar land of murderous savages where nothing is white and where vast rocky ravines have the form of titanic Egyptian letters spelling terrible primal arcana of earth; and thereafter a still more mysterious realm where everything is white, and where shrouded giants and snowy-plumed birds guard a cryptic cataract of mist which empties from immeasurable celestial heights into a torrid milky sea. [...] Poe's mind was never far from terror and decay, and we see in every tale, poem, and philosophical dialogue a tense eagerness to fathom unplumbed wells of night, to pierce the veil of death, and to reign in fancy as lord of the frightful mysteries of time and space.

Certain of Poe's tales possess an almost absolute perfection of artistic form which makes them veritable beacon-lights in the province of the short story. Poe could, when he wished, give to his prose a richly poetic cast; employing that archaic and Orientalized style with jeweled phrase, quasi-Biblical repetition, and recurrent burthen so successfully used by later writers like Oscar Wilde and Lord Dunsany[63]; and in the cases where he has done this we have an effect of lyrical phantasy almost narcotic in essence—an opium pageant of dream in the language of dream, with every unnatural color and grotesque image bodied forth in a symphony of corresponding sound. "The Masque of the Red Death," "Silence— A Fable," and "Shadow—A Parable" are assuredly poems in every sense of the word save the metrical one, and owe as much of their power to aural cadence as to visual imagery. But it is in two of the less openly poetic tales, "Ligeia" and "The Fall of the House of Usher"—especially the latter—that one finds those very summits of artistry whereby Poe takes his place at the head of fictional miniaturists. Simple and straightforward in plot, both of these tales owe their supreme magic to the cunning development which appears in the selection and collocation of every least incident. [...]

These bizarre conceptions, so awkward in unskillful hands, become under Poe's spell living and convincing terrors to haunt our nights; and all because the author understood so perfectly the very mechanics and physiology of fear and strangeness—the essential details to emphasize, the precise incongruities and conceits to select as preliminaries or concomitants to horror, the exact incidents and allusions to throw out innocently in advance as symbols or prefigurings of each major step toward the hideous denouement to come, the nice adjustments of cumulative force and the unerring accuracy in linkage of parts which make for faultless unity throughout and thunderous effectiveness at the climactic moment, the delicate nuances of scenic and landscape value to select in establishing and sustaining the desired mood and vitalizing the desired illusion—principles of this kind, and dozens of obscurer ones too elusive to be described or even fully comprehended by any ordinary commentator. Melodrama and unsophistication there may be—we are told of one fastidious Frenchman who could not bear to read Poe except in Baudelaire's urbane and Gallically modulated translation[64]—but all traces of such things are wholly overshadowed by a potent and inborn sense of the spectral, the morbid, and the horrible which gushed forth from every cell of the artist's creative mentality and stamped his macabre work with the ineffaceable mark of supreme genius. Poe's weird tales are *alive* in a manner that few others can ever hope to be.

Like most fantasists, Poe excels in incidents and broad narrative effects rather than in character drawing. His typical protagonist is generally a dark, handsome, proud, melancholy, intellectual, highly sensitive, capricious, introspective, isolated, and sometimes slightly mad gentleman of ancient family and opulent circumstances; usually deeply learned in strange lore, and darkly ambitious of penetrating to forbidden secrets of the universe. Aside from a high-sounding name, this character obviously derives little from the early Gothic novel; for he is clearly neither the wooden hero nor the diabolical villain of Radcliffian or Ludovician[65] romance. Indirectly, however, he does possess a sort of genealogical connection; since his gloomy, ambitious, and anti-social qualities savor strongly of the typical Byronic hero,[66] who in turn is definitely an offspring of the Gothic Manfreds,[67] Montonis, and Ambrosios. More particular qualities appear to be derived from the psychology of Poe himself, who certainly possessed much of the depression, sensitiveness, mad aspiration, loneliness, and extravagant freakishness which he attributes to his haughty and solitary victims of Fate.

VIII. The Weird Tradition in America

The public for whom Poe wrote, though grossly unappreciative of his art, was by no means unaccustomed to the horrors with which he dealt. America, besides inheriting the usual dark folklore of Europe, had an additional fund of weird associations to draw upon; so that spectral legends had already been recognized as fruitful subject-matter for literature. Charles Brockden Brown had achieved phenomenal fame with his Radcliffian romances, and Washington Irving's lighter treatment of eerie themes had quickly become classic. This additional fund proceeded, as Paul Elmer More[68] has pointed out, from the keen spiritual and theological interests of the first colonists, plus the strange and forbidding nature of the scene into which they were plunged. The vast and gloomy virgin forests in whose perpetual twilight all terrors might well lurk; the hordes of coppery Indians whose strange, saturnine visages and violent customs hinted strongly at traces of infernal origin; the free rein given under the influence of Puritan theocracy to all manner of notions respecting man's relation to the stern and vengeful God of the Calvinists, and to the sulphureous Adversary of that God, about whom so much was thundered in the pulpits each Sunday; and the morbid introspection developed by an isolated backwoods life devoid of normal amusements and of the recreational mood, harassed by commands for theological self-examination, keyed to unnatural emotional repression, and forming above all a mere grim struggle for survival—all these things conspired to produce an environment in which the black whisperings of sinister grandams were heard far beyond the chimney corner, and in which tales of witchcraft and unbelievable secret monstrosities lingered long after the dread days of the Salem nightmare.

Poe represents the newer, more disillusioned, and more technically finished of the weird schools that rose out of this propitious milieu. Another school—the tradition of moral values, gentle restraint, and mild, leisurely phantasy tinged more or less with the whimsical—was represented by another famous, misunderstood, and lonely figure in American letters—the shy and sensitive Nathaniel Hawthorne, scion of antique Salem and great-grandson of one of the bloodiest of the old witchcraft judges. In Hawthorne we have none of the violence, the daring, the high coloring, the intense dramatic sense, the cosmic malignity, and the undivided and impersonal artistry of Poe. Here, instead, is a gentle soul cramped by the Puritanism of early New England; shadowed and wistful, and grieved at an unmoral universe which everywhere transcends the conventional patterns thought by our forefathers to represent divine and immutable law. Evil, a very real force to Hawthorne, appears on every hand as a lurking and conquering adversary; and the visible world becomes in his fancy a theatre of infinite tragedy and woe, with unseen half-existent influences hovering over it and through it, battling for supremacy and molding the destinies of the hapless mortals who form its vain and self-deluded population. The heritage of American weirdness was his to a most intense degree, and he saw a dismal throng of vague specters behind the common phenomena of life; but he was not disinterested enough to value impressions, sensations, and beauties of narration for their own sake. He must needs weave his phantasy into some quietly melancholy fabric of didactic or allegorical cast, in which his meekly resigned cynicism may display with naive moral appraisal the perfidy of a human race which he cannot cease to cherish and mourn despite his insight into its hypocrisy. Supernatural horror, then, is never a primary object with Hawthorne; though its impulses were so deeply woven into his personality that he cannot help suggesting it with the force of genius when he calls upon the unreal world to illustrate the pensive sermon he wishes to preach.

Hawthorne's intimations of the weird, always gentle, elusive, and restrained, may be traced throughout his work. The mood that produced them found one delightful vent in the Teutonised retelling of classic myths for children contained in *A Wonder Book* and *Tanglewood Tales,* and at other times exercised itself in casting a certain strangeness and intangible witchery or malevolence over events not meant to be actually supernatural; as in the macabre posthumous novel *Dr. Grimshawe's Secret,* which invests with a peculiar sort of repulsion a house existing to this day in Salem, and abutting on the ancient Charter Street Burying Ground. In *The Marble Faun,* whose design was sketched out in an Italian villa reputed to be haunted, a tremendous background of genuine phantasy and mystery palpitates just beyond the common reader's sight; and glimpses of fabulous blood in mortal veins are hinted at during the course of a romance which cannot help being interesting despite the persistent incubus of moral allegory, anti–Popery propaganda, and a Puritan prudery which has caused the late D.H. Lawrence to express a longing to treat the author in a highly undignified manner. *Septimius Felton,* a posthumous novel whose idea was to have been elaborated and incorporated into the unfinished *Dolliver Romance,* touches on the Elixir of Life in a more or less capable fashion; whilst the notes for a never-written tale to be called "The Ancestral Footstep" show what Hawthorne would have done with an intensive treatment of an old English superstition—that of an ancient and accursed line whose members left footprints of blood as they walked—which appears incidentally in both *Septimius Felton* and *Dr. Grimshawe's Secret.* […]

But foremost as a finished, artistic unit among all our author's weird material is the famous and exquisitely wrought novel, *The House of the Seven Gables,* in which the relentless working out of an ancestral curse is developed with astonishing power against the sinister background of a very ancient Salem house—one of those peaked Gothic affairs which formed the first regular building-up of our New England coast towns. [...]

From this setting came the immortal tale—New England's greatest contribution to weird literature—and we can feel in an instant the authenticity of the atmosphere presented to us. Stealthy horror and disease lurk within the weather-blackened, moss-crusted, and elm-shadowed walls of the archaic dwelling so vividly displayed, and we grasp the brooding malignity of the place when we read that its builder—old Colonel Pyncheon—snatched the land with peculiar ruthlessness from its original settler, Matthew Maule, whom he condemned to the gallows as a wizard in the year of the panic. Maule died cursing old Pyncheon—"God will give him blood to drink"—and the waters of the old well on the seized land turned bitter. Maule's carpenter son consented to build the great gabled house for his father's triumphant enemy, but the old Colonel died strangely on the day of its dedication. Then followed generations of odd vicissitudes, with queer whispers about the dark powers of the Maules, and peculiar and sometimes terrible ends befalling the Pyncheons.

The overshadowing malevolence of the ancient house—almost as alive as Poe's House of Usher, though in a subtler way—pervades the tale as a recurrent motif pervades an operatic tragedy; and when the main story is reached, we behold the modern Pyncheons in a pitiable state of decay. Poor old Hepzibah, the eccentric reduced gentlewoman; child-like, unfortunate Clifford, just released from undeserved imprisonment; sly and treacherous Judge Pyncheon, who is the old Colonel all over again—all these figures are tremendous symbols, and are well matched by the stunted vegetation and anemic fowls in the garden. It was almost a pity to supply a fairly happy ending, with a union of sprightly Phoebe, cousin and last scion of the Pyncheons, to the prepossessing young man who turns out to be the last of the Maules. This union, presumably, ends the curse. Hawthorne avoids all violence of diction or movement, and keeps his implications of terror well in the background; but occasional glimpses amply serve to sustain the mood and redeem the work from pure allegorical aridity. Incidents like the bewitching of Alice Pyncheon in the early eighteenth century, and the spectral music of her harpsichord which precedes a death in the family—the latter a variant of an immemorial type of Aryan myth—link the action directly with the supernatural; whilst the dead nocturnal vigil of old Judge Pyncheon in the ancient parlor, with his frightfully ticking watch, is stark horror of the most poignant and genuine sort. The way in which the Judge's death is first adumbrated by the motions and sniffing of a strange cat outside the window, long before the fact is suspected either by the reader or by any of the characters, is a stroke of genius which Poe could not have surpassed. Later the strange cat watches intently outside that same window in the night and on the next day, for—something. It is clearly the psychopomp of primeval myth, fitted and adapted with infinite deftness to its latter-day setting.

But Hawthorne left no well-defined literary posterity. His mood and attitude belonged to the age which closed with him, and it is the spirit of Poe—who so clearly and realistically understood the natural basis of the horror-appeal and the correct mechanics of its achievement—which survived and blossomed. Among the earliest of Poe's disciples may be reckoned the brilliant young Irishman Fitz-James O'Brien (1828–1862), who became naturalized as an American and perished honorably in the Civil War. It is he who gave us "What Was It?," the first well-shaped short story of a tangible but invisible being, and the prototype of de Maupassant's "Horla"; he also who created the inimitable "Diamond Lens," in which a young microscopist falls in love with a maiden of an infinitesimal world which he has discovered in a drop of water. O'Brien's early death undoubtedly deprived us of some masterful tales of strangeness and terror, though his genius was not, properly speaking, of the same titan quality which characterized Poe and Hawthorne.

Closer to real greatness was the eccentric and saturnine journalist Ambrose Bierce, born in 1842; who likewise entered the Civil War, but survived to write some immortal tales and to disappear in 1913 in as great a cloud of mystery as any he ever evoked from his nightmare fancy. Bierce was a satirist and pamphleteer of note, but the bulk of his artistic reputation must rest upon his grim and savage short stories; a large number of which deal with the Civil War and form the most vivid and realistic expression which that conflict has yet received in fiction. Virtually all of Bierce's tales are tales of horror; and whilst many of them treat only of the physical and psychological horrors within Nature, a substantial proportion admit the malignly supernatural and form a leading element in America's fund of weird literature. Mr. Samuel Loveman,[69] a living poet and critic who was personally acquainted with Bierce, thus sums up the genius of the great shadow-maker in the preface to some of his letters:

"In Bierce, the evocation of horror becomes for the first time, not so much the prescription or perversion of Poe and Maupassant, but an atmosphere definite and uncannily precise. Words, so simple that one would be prone to ascribe them to the limitations of a literary hack, take on an unholy horror, a new and unguessed transformation. In Poe one finds it a *tour de force,* in Maupassant a nervous engagement of the flagellated climax. To Bierce, simply and sincerely, diabolism held in its tormented depth, a legitimate and reliant means to the end. Yet a tacit confirmation with Nature is in every instance insisted upon.

"In 'The Death of Halpin Frayser,' flowers, verdure, and the boughs and leaves of trees are magnificently placed as an opposing foil to unnatural malignity. Not the accustomed golden world, but a world pervaded with the mystery of blue and the breathless recalcitrance of dreams, is Bierce's. Yet, curiously, inhumanity is not altogether absent."

The "inhumanity" mentioned by Mr. Loveman finds vent in a rare strain of sardonic comedy and graveyard humor, and a kind of delight in images of cruelty and tantalizing disappointment. The former quality is well illustrated by some of the subtitles in the darker narratives; such as "One does not always eat what is on the table," describing a body laid out for a coroner's inquest, and "A man though naked may be in rags," referring to a frightfully mangled corpse.

Bierce's work is in general somewhat uneven. Many of the stories are obviously mechanical, and marred by a jaunty and commonplacely artificial style derived from journalistic models; but the grim malevolence stalking through all of them is unmistakable, and several stand out as permanent mountain-peaks of American weird writing. "The Death of Halpin Frayser," called by Frederic Taber Cooper[70] the most fiendishly ghastly tale in the literature of the Anglo-Saxon race, tells of a body skulking by night without a soul in a weird and horribly ensanguined wood, and of a man beset by ancestral memories who met death at the claws of that which had been his fervently loved mother. "The Damned Thing," frequently copied in popular anthologies, chronicles the hideous devastations of an invisible entity that waddles and flounders on the hills and in the wheatfields by night and day. [...]

Bierce seldom realizes the atmospheric possibilities of his themes as vividly as Poe; and much of his work contains a certain touch of naiveté, prosaic angularity, or early-American provincialism which contrasts somewhat with the efforts of later horror-masters. Nevertheless the genuineness and artistry of his dark intimations are always unmistakable, so that his greatness is in no danger of eclipse. As arranged in his definitively collected works, Bierce's weird tales occur mainly in two volumes, *Can Such Things Be?* and *In the Midst of Life.* The former, indeed, is almost wholly given over to the supernatural.

Much of the best in American horror-literature has come from pens not mainly devoted to that medium. Oliver Wendell Holmes's historic *Elsie Venner* suggests with admirable restraint an unnatural ophidian element in a young woman prenatally influenced, and sustains the atmosphere with finely discriminating landscape touches. In *The Turn of the Screw* Henry James triumphs over his inevitable pomposity and prolixity sufficiently well to create a truly potent air of sinister menace; depicting the hideous influence of two dead and evil servants, Peter Quint and the governess Miss Jessel, over a small boy and girl who had been under their care. James is perhaps too diffuse, too unctuously urbane, and too much addicted to subtleties of speech to realize fully all the wild and devastating horror in his situations; but for all that there is a rare and mounting tide of fright, culminating in the death of the little boy, which gives the novelette a permanent place in its special class.

F. Marion Crawford produced several weird tales of varying quality, now collected in a volume entitled *Wandering Ghosts.* [...] *The Upper Berth*, however, is Crawford's weird masterpiece; and is one of the most tremendous horror-stories in all literature. In this tale of a suicide-haunted stateroom such things as the spectral salt-water dampness, the strangely open porthole, and the nightmare struggle with the nameless object are handled with incomparable dexterity.

Very genuine, though not without the typical mannered extravagance of the eighteen-nineties, is the strain of horror in the early work of Robert W. Chambers,[71] since renowned for products of a very different quality. *The King in Yellow,* a series of vaguely connected short stories having as a background a monstrous and suppressed book whose perusal brings fright, madness, and spectral tragedy, really achieves notable heights of cosmic fear in spite of uneven interest and a somewhat trivial and affected cultivation of the Gallic studio atmosphere made popular by Du Maurier's *Trilby.*[72] [...]

It is worth observing that the author derives most of the names and allusions connected with his eldritch land of primal memory from the tales of Ambrose Bierce. Other early works of Mr. Chambers displaying the outré and macabre element are *The Maker of Moons* and *In Search of the Unknown.* One cannot help regretting that he did not further develop a vein in which he could so easily have become a recognized master.

Horror material of authentic force may be found in the work of the New England realist Mary E. Wilkins[73]; whose volume of short tales, *The Wind in the Rose-Bush,* contains a number of noteworthy achievements. In "The Shadows on the Wall" we are shown with consummate skill the response of a staid New England household to uncanny tragedy; and the sourceless shadow of the poisoned brother well prepares us for the climactic moment when the shadow of the secret murderer, who has killed himself in a neighboring city, suddenly appears beside it. Charlotte Perkins Gilman, in "The Yellow Wall Paper," rises to a classic level in subtly delineating the madness which crawls over a woman dwelling in the hideously papered room where a madwoman was once confined. [...]

Still further carrying on our spectral tradition is the gifted and versatile humorist Irvin S. Cobb,[74] whose work both early and recent contains some finely weird specimens. "Fishhead," an early achievement, is banefully effective in its portrayal of unnatural affinities between a hybrid idiot and the strange fish of an isolated lake, which at the last avenge their biped kinsman's murder. Later work of Mr. Cobb introduces an element of possible science, as in the tale of hereditary memory where a modern man with a negroid strain utters words in African jungle speech when run down by a train under visual and aural circumstances recalling the maiming of his black ancestor by a rhinoceros a century before.

Extremely high in artistic stature is the novel *The Dark Chamber* (1927), by the late Leonard Cline.[75] This is the tale of a man who—with the characteristic ambition of the Gothic or Byronic hero-villain—seeks to defy Nature and recapture every moment of his past life through the abnormal stimulation of memory. To this end he employs endless notes, records, mnemonic objects, and pictures—and finally odors, music, and exotic drugs. At last his ambition goes beyond his personal life and reaches toward the black abysses of *hereditary* memory—even back to pre-human days amidst the steaming swamps of the Carboniferous age, and to still more unimaginable deeps of primal time and entity. He calls for madder music and takes stronger drugs, and finally his great dog grows oddly afraid of him. A noxious animal stench encompasses him, and he grows vacant-faced and sub-human. In the end he takes to the woods, howling at night beneath windows. He is finally found in a thicket, mangled to death. Beside him is the mangled corpse of his dog. They have killed each other. The atmosphere of this novel is malevolently potent, much attention being paid to the central figure's sinister home and household.

A less subtle and well-balanced but nevertheless highly effective creation is Herbert S. Gorman's novel, *The Place Called Dagon*,[76] which relates the dark history of a western Massachusetts backwater where the descendants of refugees from the Salem witchcraft still keep alive the morbid and degenerate horrors of the Black Sabbat. [...]

Of younger Americans, none strikes the note of cosmic terror so well as the California poet, artist, and fictionist Clark Ashton Smith, whose bizarre writings, drawings, paintings, and stories are the delight of a sensitive few. Mr. Smith has for his background a universe of remote and paralyzing fright—jungles of poisonous and iridescent blossoms on the moons of Saturn, evil and grotesque temples in Atlantis, Lemuria, and forgotten elder worlds, and dank morasses of spotted death-fungi in spectral countries beyond earth's rim. His longest and most ambitious poem, *The Hashish-Eater,* is in pentameter blank verse; and opens up chaotic and incredible vistas of kaleidoscopic nightmare in the spaces between the stars. In sheer daemonic strangeness and fertility of conception, Mr. Smith is perhaps unexcelled by any other writer dead or living. Who else has seen such gorgeous, luxuriant, and feverishly distorted visions of infinite spheres and multiple dimensions and lived to tell the tale? His short stories deal powerfully with other galaxies, worlds, and dimensions, as well as with strange regions and aeons on the earth. He tells of primal Hyperborea and its black amorphous god Tsathoggua; of the lost continent Zothique, and of the fabulous, vampire-curst land of Averoigne in mediaeval France. Some of Mr. Smith's best work can be found in the brochure entitled *The Double Shadow and Other Fantasies* (1933).

IX. *The Weird Tradition in the British Isles*

Recent British literature, besides including the three or four greatest fantasists of the present age, has been gratifyingly fertile in the element of the weird. Rudyard Kipling has often approached it; and has, despite the omnipresent mannerisms, handled it with indubitable mastery in such tales as "The Phantom Rickshaw," "The Finest Story in the World,'" "The Recrudescence of Imray," and "The Mark of the Beast." This latter is of particular poignancy; the pictures of the naked leper-priest who mewed like an otter, of the spots which appeared on the chest of the man that priest cursed, of the growing carnivorousness of the victim and of the fear which horses began to display toward him, and of the eventually half-accomplished transformation of that victim into a leopard, being things which no reader is ever likely to forget. The final defeat of the malignant sorcery does not impair the force of the tale or the validity of its mystery.

Lafcadio Hearn,[77] strange, wandering, and exotic, departs still farther from the realm of the real; and with the supreme artistry of a sensitive poet weaves phantasies impossible to an author of the solid roast-beef type. His *Fantastics,* written in America, contains some of the most impressive ghoulishness in all literature; whilst his *Kwaidan,* written in Japan, crystallizes with matchless skill and delicacy the eerie lore and whispered legends of that richly colorful nation. Still more of Hearn's weird wizardry of language is shown in some of his translations from the French, especially from Gautier and Flaubert. His version of the latter's *Temptation of St. Anthony* is a classic of fevered and riotous imagery clad in the magic of singing words.

Oscar Wilde may likewise be given a place amongst weird writers, both for certain of his exquisite fairy tales, and for his vivid *Picture of Dorian Gray,* in which a marvelous portrait for years assumes the duty of ageing and coarsening instead of its original, who meanwhile plunges into every excess of vice and crime without the outward loss of youth, beauty, and freshness. [...]

Matthew Phipps Shiel,[78] author of many weird, grotesque, and adventurous novels and tales, occasionally attains a high level of horrific magic. "Xélucha" is a noxiously hideous fragment, but is excelled by Mr. Shiel's undoubted masterpiece, "The House of Sounds," floridly written in the "yellow 'nineties," and re-cast with more artistic restraint in the early twentieth century. This story, in final form, deserves a place among the foremost things of its kind. It tells of a creeping horror and menace trickling down the centuries on a subarctic island off the coast of Norway; where, amidst the sweep of daemon winds and the ceaseless din of hellish waves and cataracts, a vengeful dead man built a brazen tower of terror. It is vaguely like, yet infinitely unlike, Poe's "Fall of the House of Usher." In the novel *The Purple Cloud* Mr. Shiel describes with tremendous power a curse which came out of the arctic to destroy mankind, and which for a time appears to have left but a single inhabitant on our planet. The sensations of this lone survivor as he realizes his position, and roams through the corpse-littered and treasure-strewn cities of the world as their absolute master, are delivered with a skill and artistry falling little short of actual majesty. Unfortunately the second half of the book, with its conventionally romantic element, involves a distinct "letdown."

Better known than Shiel is the ingenious Bram Stoker, who created many starkly horrific conceptions in a series of novels whose poor technique sadly impairs their net effect. *The Lair of the White Worm,* dealing with a gigantic primitive entity that lurks in a vault beneath an ancient castle, utterly ruins a magnificent idea by a development almost infantile. *The Jewel of Seven Stars,* touching on a strange Egyptian resurrection, is less crudely written. But best of all is the famous *Dracula,* which has become almost the standard modern exploitation of the frightful vampire myth. Count Dracula, a vampire, dwells in a horrible castle in the Carpathians; but finally migrates to England with the design of populating the country with fellow vampires. How an Englishman fares within Dracula's stronghold of terrors, and how the dead fiend's plot for domination is at last defeated, are elements which unite to form a tale now justly assigned a permanent place in English letters. [...] Much subtler and more artistic, and told with singular skill through the juxtaposed narratives of the several characters, is the novel *Cold Harbour,* by Francis Brett Young,[79] in which an ancient house of strange malignancy is powerfully delineated. The mocking and well-nigh omnipotent fiend Humphrey Furnival holds echoes of the Manfred- Montoni type of early Gothic "villain," but is redeemed from triteness by many clever individualities. Only the slight diffuseness of explanation at the close, and the somewhat too free use of divination as a plot factor, keep this tale from approaching absolute perfection.

In the novel *Witch Wood* John Buchan depicts with tremendous force a survival of the evil Sabbat in a lonely district of Scotland. The description of the black forest with the evil stone, and of the terrible cosmic adumbrations when the horror is finally extirpated, will repay one for wading through the very gradual action and plethora of Scottish dialect. [...]

Deserving of distinguished notice as a forceful craftsman to whom an unseen mystic world is ever a close and vital reality is the poet Walter de la Mare,[80] whose haunting verse and exquisite prose alike bear consistent traces of a strange vision reaching deeply into veiled spheres of beauty and terrible and forbidden dimensions of being. In the novel *The Return* we see the soul of a dead man reach out of its grave of two centuries and fasten itself upon the flesh of the living, so that even the face of the victim becomes that which had long ago returned to dust. Of the shorter tales, of which several volumes exist, many are unforgettable for their command of fear's and sorcery's darkest ramifications; notably "Seaton's Aunt," in which there lowers a noxious background of malignant vampirism; "The Tree," which tells of a frightful vegetable growth in the yard of a starving artist; "Out of the Deep," wherein we are given leave to imagine what thing answered the summons of a dying wastrel in a dark lonely house when he pulled a long-feared bell-cord in the attic chamber of his dread-haunted boyhood; "A Recluse," which hints at what sent a chance guest flying from a house in the night; "Mr. Kempe," which shows us a mad clerical hermit in quest of the human soul, dwelling in a frightful sea-cliff region beside an archaic abandoned chapel; and "All-Hallows," a glimpse of demoniac forces besieging a lonely mediaeval church and miraculously restoring the rotting masonry. De la Mare does not make fear the sole or even the dominant element of most of his tales, being apparently more interested in the subtleties of character involved. Occasionally he sinks to sheer whimsical phantasy of the Barrie order. Still, he is among the very few to whom unreality is a vivid, living presence; and as such he is able to put into his occasional fear-studies a keen potency which only a rare master can achieve. His poem "The Listeners" restores the Gothic shudder to modern verse.

The weird short story has fared well of late, an important contributor being the versatile E.F. Benson,[81] whose "The Man Who Went Too Far" breathes whisperingly of a house at the edge of a dark wood, and of Pan's hoof-mark on the breast of a dead man. Mr. Benson's volume, *Visible and Invisible,* contains several stories of singular power; notably "*Negotium Perambulans,*" whose unfolding reveals an abnormal monster from an ancient ecclesiastical panel which performs an act of miraculous vengeance in a lonely village on the Cornish coast, and "The Horror-Horn," through which lopes a terrible half-human survival dwelling on unvisited Alpine peaks. "The Face," in another collection, is lethally potent in its relentless aura of doom. H.R. Wakefield,[82] in his collections *They Return at Evening* and *Others Who Return,* manages now and then to achieve great heights of horror despite a vitiating air of sophistication. The most notable stories are "The Red Lodge" with its slimy aqueous evil, "He Cometh and He Passeth By," "And He Shall Sing...," "The Cairn," "Look Up There!," "Blind Man's Buff," and that bit of lurking millennial horror, "The Seventeenth Hole at Duncaster." Mention has been made of the weird work of H.G. Wells and A. Conan Doyle. The former, in "The Ghost of Fear," reaches a very high level; while all the items in *Thirty Strange Stories* have strong fantastic implications. Doyle now and then struck a powerfully spectral note, as in "The Captain of the 'Pole-Star,'" a tale of arctic ghostliness, and "Lot No. 249," wherein the reanimated mummy theme is used with more than ordinary skill. [...] May Sinclair's *Uncanny Stories* contain more of traditional occultism than of that creative treatment of fear which marks mastery in this field, and are inclined to lay more stress on human emotions and psychological delving than upon the stark phenomena of a cosmos utterly unreal. It may be well to remark here that occult believers are probably less effective than materialists in delineating the spectral and the fantastic, since to them the phantom world is so commonplace a reality that they tend to refer to it with less awe, remoteness, and impressiveness than do those who see in it an absolute and stupendous violation of the natural order.

Of rather uneven stylistic quality, but vast occasional power in its suggestion of lurking worlds and beings behind the ordinary surface of life, is the work of William Hope Hodgson,[83] known today far less than it deserves to be. Despite a tendency toward conventionally sentimental conceptions of the universe, and of man's relation to it and to his fellows, Mr. Hodgson is perhaps second only to Algernon Blackwood in his serious treatment of unreality. Few can equal him in adumbrating the nearness of nameless forces and monstrous besieging entities through casual hints and insignificant details, or in conveying feelings of the spectral and the abnormal in connection with regions or buildings. [...]

The House on the Borderland (1908)—perhaps the greatest of all Mr. Hodgson's works— tells of a lonely and evilly regarded house in Ireland which forms a focus for hideous other-world forces and sustains a siege by blasphemous hybrid anomalies from a hidden abyss below. The wanderings of the narrator's spirit through limitless light-years of cosmic space and kalpas of eternity, and its witnessing of the solar system's final destruction, constitute something almost unique in standard literature. And everywhere there is manifest the author's power to suggest vague, ambushed horrors in natural scenery. But for a few touches of commonplace sentimentality this book would be a classic of the first water. [...]

The Night Land (1912) is a long-extended (583 pp.) tale of the earth's infinitely remote future—billions of billions of years ahead, after the death of the sun. [...]

Allowing for all its faults, it is yet one of the most potent pieces of macabre imagination ever written. The picture of a night-black, dead planet, with the remains of the human race concentrated in a stupendously vast metal pyramid and besieged by monstrous, hybrid, and altogether unknown forces of the darkness, is something that no reader can ever forget. Shapes and entities of an altogether non-human and inconceivable sort—the prowlers of the black, man-forsaken, and unexplored world outside the pyramid—are *suggested* and *partly* described with ineffable potency; while the night-bound landscape with its chasms and slopes and dying volcanism takes on an almost sentient terror beneath the author's touch.

Midway in the book the central figure ventures outside the pyramid on a quest through death-haunted realms untrod by man for millions of years—and in his slow, minutely described, day-by-day progress over unthinkable leagues of immemorial blackness there is a sense of cosmic alienage, breathless mystery, and terrified expectancy unrivalled in the whole range of literature. The last quarter of the book drags woefully, but fails to spoil the tremendous power of the whole. [...]

Naturally it is impossible in a brief sketch to trace out all the classic modern uses of the terror element. The ingredient must of necessity enter into all work both prose and verse treating broadly of life; and we are therefore not surprised to find a share in such writers as the poet Browning, whose "Childe Roland to the Dark Tower Came" is instinct with hideous menace, or the novelist Joseph Conrad, who often wrote of the dark secrets within the sea, and of the demoniac driving power of Fate as influencing the lives of lonely and maniacally resolute men. Its trail is one of infinite ramifications; but we must here confine ourselves to its appearance in a relatively unmixed state, where it determines and dominates the work of art containing it.

Somewhat separate from the main British stream is that current of weirdness in Irish literature which came to the fore in the Celtic Renaissance of the later nineteenth and early twentieth centuries. Ghost and fairy lore have always been of great prominence in Ireland, and for over an hundred years have been recorded by a line of such faithful transcribers and translators as William Carleton, T. Crofton Croker, Lady Wilde—mother of Oscar Wilde—Douglas Hyde, and W.B. Yeats.[84] Brought to notice by the modern movement, this body of myth has been carefully collected and studied; and its salient features reproduced in the work of later figures like Yeats, J.M. Synge, "A.E.," Lady Gregory, Padraic Colum, James Stephens, and their colleagues.[85]

Whilst on the whole more whimsically fantastic than terrible, such folklore and its consciously artistic counterparts contain much that falls truly within the domain of cosmic horror. Tales of burials in sunken churches beneath haunted lakes, accounts of death-heralding banshees and sinister changelings, ballads of specters and "the unholy creatures of the raths"[86]—all these have their poignant and definite shivers, and mark a strong and distinctive element in weird literature. Despite homely grotesqueness and absolute naiveté, there is genuine nightmare in the class of narrative represented by the yarn of Teig O'Kane, who in punishment for his wild life was ridden all night by a hideous corpse that demanded burial and drove him from churchyard to churchyard as the dead rose up loathsomely in each one and refused to accommodate the newcomer with a berth. Yeats, undoubtedly the greatest figure of the Irish revival if not the greatest of all living poets, has accomplished notable things both in original work and in the codification of old legends.

X. *The Modern Masters*

The best horror-tales of today, profiting by the long evolution of the type, possess a naturalness, convincingness, artistic smoothness, and skillful intensity of appeal quite beyond comparison with anything in the Gothic work of a century or more ago. Technique, craftsmanship, experience, and psychological knowledge have advanced tremendously with the passing years, so that much of the older work seems naive and artificial; redeemed, when redeemed at all, only by a genius which conquers heavy limitations. The tone of jaunty and inflated romance, full of false motivation and investing every conceivable event with a counterfeit significance and carelessly inclusive glamour, is now confined to lighter and more whimsical phases of supernatural writing. Serious weird stories are either made realistically intense by close consistency and perfect fidelity to Nature except in the one supernatural direction which the author allows himself, or else cast altogether in the realm of phantasy, with atmosphere cunningly adapted to the visualization of a delicately exotic world of unreality beyond space and time, in which almost anything may happen if it but happen in true accord with certain types of imagination and illusion normal to the sensitive human brain. This, at least, is the dominant tendency; though of course many great contemporary writers slip occasionally into some of the flashy postures of immature romanticism, or into bits of the equally empty and absurd jargon of pseudo-scientific "occultism," now at one of its periodic high tides.

Of living creators of cosmic fear raised to its most artistic pitch, few if any can hope to equal the versatile Arthur Machen; author of some dozen tales long and short, in which the elements of hidden horror and brooding fright attain an almost incomparable substance and realistic acuteness. Mr. Machen, a general man of letters and master of an exquisitely lyrical and expressive prose style, has perhaps put more conscious effort into his picaresque *Chronicle of Clemendy,* his refreshing essays, his vivid autobiographical volumes, his fresh and spirited translations, and above all his memorable epic of the sensitive aesthetic mind, *The Hill of Dreams,* in which the youthful hero responds to the magic of that ancient Welsh environment which is the author's own, and lives a dream-life in the Roman city of Isca Silurum, now shrunk to the relic-strewn village of Caerleon-on-Usk. But the fact remains that his powerful horror-material of the nineties and earlier nineteen-hundreds stands alone in its class, and marks a distinct epoch in the history of this literary form.

Mr. Machen, with an impressionable Celtic heritage linked to keen youthful memories of the wild domed hills, archaic forests, and cryptical Roman ruins of the Gwent country-side, has developed an imaginative life of rare beauty, intensity, and historic background. He has absorbed the mediaeval mystery of dark woods and ancient customs, and is a champion of the Middle Ages in all things—including the Catholic faith. He has yielded, likewise, to the spell of the Britanno-Roman life which once surged over his native region; and finds strange magic in the fortified camps, tessellated pavements, fragments of statues, and kindred things which tell of the day when classicism reigned and Latin was the language of the country. [...]

Of Mr. Machen's horror-tales the most famous is perhaps "The Great God Pan" (1894), which tells of a singular and terrible experiment and its consequences. [...]

But the charm of the tale is in the telling. No one could begin to describe the cumulative suspense and ultimate horror with which every paragraph abounds without following fully the precise order in which Mr. Machen unfolds his gradual hints and revelations. Melodrama is undeniably present, and coincidence is stretched to a length which appears absurd upon analysis; but in the malign witchery of the tale as a whole these trifles are forgotten, and the sensitive reader reaches the end with only an appreciative shudder and a tendency to repeat the words of one of the characters: "It is too incredible, too monstrous; such things can never be in this quiet world.... Why, man, if such a case were possible, our earth would be a nightmare."

Less famous and less complex in plot than "The Great God Pan," but definitely finer in atmosphere and general artistic value, is the curious and dimly disquieting chronicle called "The White People," whose central portion purports to be the diary or notes of a little girl whose nurse has introduced her to some of the forbidden magic and soul-blasting traditions of the noxious witch-cult—the cult whose whispered lore was handed down long lines of peasantry throughout Western Europe, and whose members sometimes stole forth at night, one by one, to meet in black woods and lonely places for the revolting orgies of the Witches' Sabbath. Mr. Machen's narrative, a triumph of skillful selectiveness and restraint, accumulates enormous power as it flows on in a stream of innocent childish prattle; introducing allusions to strange "nymphs," "Dôls," "voolas," "White, Green, and Scarlet Ceremonies," "Aklo letters," "Chian language," "Mao games," and the like. [...]

In the episodic novel of *The Three Impostors,* a work whose merit as a whole is somewhat marred by an imitation of the jaunty Stevenson manner, occur certain tales which perhaps represent the high-water mark of Machen's skill as a terror-weaver. Here we find in its most artistic form a favorite weird conception of the author's; the notion that beneath the mounds and rocks of the wild Welsh hills dwell subterraneously that squat primitive race whose vestiges gave rise to our common folk legends of fairies, elves, and the "little people," and whose acts are even now responsible for certain unexplained disappearances, and occasional substitutions of strange dark "changelings" for normal infants. This theme receives its finest treatment in the episode entitled "The Novel of the Black Seal"; where a professor, having discovered a singular identity between certain characters scrawled on Welsh limestone rocks and those existing in a prehistoric black seal from Babylon, sets out on a course of discovery which leads him to unknown and terrible things. [...]

Also in *The Three Impostors* is the "Novel of the White Powder," which approaches the absolute culmination of loathsome fright. Francis Leicester, a young law student nervously worn out by seclusion and overwork, has a prescription filled by an old apothecary none too careful about the state of his drugs. The substance, it later turns out, is an unusual salt which time and varying temperature have accidentally changed to something very strange and terrible; nothing less, in short, than the mediaeval *Vinum Sabbati*,[87] whose consumption at the horrible orgies of the Witches' Sabbath gave rise to shocking transformations and—if injudiciously used—to unutterable consequences. [...]

Less intense than Mr. Machen in delineating the extremes of stark fear, yet infinitely more closely wedded to the idea of an unreal world constantly pressing upon ours, is the inspired and prolific Algernon Blackwood, amidst whose voluminous and uneven work may be found some of the finest spectral literature of this or any age. Of the quality of Mr. Blackwood's genius there can be no dispute; for no one has even approached the skill, seriousness, and minute fidelity with which he records the overtones of strangeness in ordinary things and experiences, or the preternatural insight with which he builds up detail by detail the complete sensations and perceptions leading from reality into supernormal life or vision. Without notable command of the poetic witchery of mere words, he is the one absolute and unquestioned master of weird atmosphere; and can evoke what amounts almost to a story from a simple fragment of humorless psychological description. Above all others he understands how fully some sensitive minds dwell forever on the borderland of dream, and how relatively slight is the distinction betwixt those images formed from actual objects and those excited by the play of the imagination.

Mr. Blackwood's lesser work is marred by several defects such as ethical didacticism, occasional insipid whimsicality, the flatness of benignant supernaturalism, and a too free use of the trade jargon of modern "occultism." A fault of his more serious efforts is that diffuseness and long-windedness which results from an excessively elaborate attempt, under the handicap of a somewhat bald and journalistic style devoid of intrinsic magic, color, and vitality, to visualize precise sensations and nuances of uncanny suggestion. But in spite of all this, the major products of Mr. Blackwood attain a genuinely classic level, and evoke as does nothing else in literature an awed and convinced sense of the immanence of strange spiritual spheres or entities.

The well-nigh endless array of Mr. Blackwood's fiction includes both novels and shorter tales, the latter sometimes independent and sometimes arrayed in series. Foremost of all must be reckoned "The Willows," in which the nameless presences on a desolate Danube island are horribly felt and recognized by a pair of idle voyagers. Here art and restraint in narrative reach their very highest development, and an impression of lasting poignancy is produced without a single strained passage or a single false note. Another amazingly potent though less artistically finished tale is "The Wendigo," where we are confronted by horrible evidences of a vast forest daemon about which North Woods lumbermen whisper at evening. The manner in which certain footprints tell certain unbelievable things is really a marked triumph in craftsmanship. In "An Episode in a Lodging House" we behold frightful presences summoned out of black space by a sorcerer, and "The Listener" tells of the awful psychic residuum creeping about an old house where a leper died. In the volume titled *Incredible Adventures* occur some of the finest tales which the author has yet produced, leading the fancy to wild rites on nocturnal hills, to secret and terrible aspects lurking behind stolid scenes, and to unimaginable vaults of mystery below the sands and pyramids of Egypt; all with a serious finesse and delicacy that convince where a cruder or lighter treatment would merely amuse. Some of these accounts are hardly stories at all, but rather studies in elusive impressions and half-remembered snatches of dream. Plot is everywhere negligible, and atmosphere reigns untrammelled.

John Silence—Physician Extraordinary is a book of five related tales, through which a single character runs his triumphant course. Marred only by traces of the popular and conventional detective-story atmosphere—for Dr. Silence is one of those benevolent geniuses who employ their remarkable powers to aid worthy fellow-men in difficulty—these narratives contain some of the author's best work, and produce an illusion at once emphatic and lasting. The opening tale, "A Psychical Invasion," relates what befell a sensitive author in a house once the scene of dark deeds, and how a legion of fiends was exorcised. "Ancient Sorceries," perhaps the finest tale in the book, gives an almost hypnotically vivid account of an old French town where once the unholy Sabbath was kept by all the people in the form of cats. In "The Nemesis of Fire" a hideous elemental is evoked by new-spilt blood, whilst "Secret Worship" tells of a German school where Satanism held sway, and where long afterward an evil aura remained. "The Camp of the Dog" is a werewolf tale, but is weakened by moralization and professional "occultism."

Too subtle, perhaps, for definite classification as horror-tales, yet possibly more truly artistic in an absolute sense, are such delicate phantasies as *Jimbo* or *The Centaur*. Mr. Blackwood achieves in these novels a close and palpitant approach to the inmost substance of dream, and works enormous havoc with the conventional barriers between reality and imagination.

Unexcelled in the sorcery of crystalline singing prose, and supreme in the creation of a gorgeous and languorous world of iridescently exotic vision, is Edward John Moreton Drax Plunkett, Eighteenth Baron Dunsany, whose tales and short plays form an almost unique element in our literature. Inventor of a new mythology and weaver of surprising folklore, Lord Dunsany stands dedicated to a strange world of fantastic beauty, and pledged to eternal warfare against the coarseness and ugliness of diurnal reality. His point of view is the most truly cosmic of any held in the literature of any period. As sensitive as Poe to dramatic values and the significance of isolated words and details, and far better equipped rhetorically through a simple lyric style based on the prose of the King James Bible, this author draws with tremendous effectiveness on nearly every body of myth and legend within the circle of European culture; producing a composite or eclectic cycle of phantasy in which Eastern color, Hellenic form, Teutonic somberness, and Celtic wistfulness are so superbly blended that each sustains and supplements the rest without sacrifice of perfect congruity and homogeneity. In most cases Dunsany's lands are fabulous—"beyond the East," or "at the edge of the world." His system of original personal and place names, with roots drawn from classical, Oriental, and other sources, is a marvel of versatile inventiveness and poetic discrimination; as one may see from such specimens as "Argimēnēs," "Bethmoora," "Poltarnees," "Camorak," "Illuriel," or "Sardathrion."

Beauty rather than terror is the keynote of Dunsany's work. He loves the vivid green of jade and of copper domes, and the delicate flush of sunset on the ivory minarets of impossible dream-cities. Humor and irony, too, are often present to impart a gentle cynicism and modify what might otherwise possess a naive intensity. Nevertheless, as is inevitable in a master of triumphant unreality, there are occasional touches of cosmic fright which come well within the authentic tradition. Dunsany loves to hint slyly and adroitly of monstrous things and incredible dooms, as one hints in a fairy tale. In *The Book of Wonder* we read of Hlo-hlo, the gigantic spider-idol which does not always stay at home; of what the Sphinx feared in the forest; of Slith, the thief who jumps over the edge of the world after seeing a certain light lit and knowing *who* lit it; of the anthropophagous Gibbelins, who inhabit an evil tower and guard a treasure; of the Gnoles, who live in the forest and from whom it is not well to steal; of the City of Never, and the eyes that watch in the Under Pits; and of kindred things of darkness. *A Dreamer's Tales* tells of the mystery that sent forth all men from Bethmoora in the desert; of the vast gate of Perdóndaris, that was carved from a *single piece* of ivory; and of the voyage of poor old Bill, whose captain cursed the crew and paid calls on nasty-looking isles new-risen from the sea, with low thatched cottages having evil, obscure windows. [...]

But no amount of mere description can convey more than a fraction of Lord Dunsany's pervasive charm. His prismatic cities and unheard-of rites are touched with a sureness which only mastery can engender, and we thrill with a sense of actual participation in his secret mysteries. To the truly imaginative he is a talisman and a key unlocking rich storehouses of dream and fragmentary memory; so that we may think of him not only as a poet, but as one who makes each reader a poet as well.

At the opposite pole of genius from Lord Dunsany, and gifted with an almost diabolic power of calling horror by gentle steps from the midst of prosaic daily life, is the scholarly Montague Rhodes James,[88] Provost of Eton College, antiquary of note, and recognized authority on mediaeval manuscripts and cathedral history. Dr. James, long fond of telling spectral tales at Christmastide, has become by slow degrees a literary weird fictionist of the very first rank; and has developed a distinctive style and method likely to serve as models for an enduring line of disciples.

The art of Dr. James is by no means haphazard, and in the preface to one of his collections he has formulated three very sound rules for macabre composition. A ghost story, he believes, should have a familiar setting in the modern period, in order to approach closely the reader's sphere of experience. Its spectral phenomena, moreover, should be malevolent rather than beneficent; since *fear* is the emotion primarily to be excited. And finally, the technical patois of "occultism" or pseudo-science ought carefully to be avoided; lest the charm of casual verisimilitude be smothered in unconvincing pedantry.

Dr. James, practicing what he preaches, approaches his themes in a light and often conversational way. Creating the illusion of every-day events, he introduces his abnormal phenomena cautiously and gradually; relieved at every turn by touches of homely and prosaic detail, and sometimes spiced with a snatch or two of antiquarian scholarship. Conscious of the close relation between present weirdness and accumulated tradition, he generally provides remote historical antecedents for his incidents; thus being able to utilize very aptly his exhaustive knowledge of the past, and his ready and convincing command of archaic diction and coloring. A favorite scene for a James tale is some centuried cathedral, which the author can describe with all the familiar minuteness of a specialist in that field.

Sly humorous vignettes and bits of life-like genre portraiture and characterization are often to be found in Dr. James's narratives, and serve in his skilled hands to augment the general effect rather than to spoil it, as the same qualities would tend to do with a lesser craftsman. In inventing a new type of ghost, he has departed considerably from the conventional Gothic tradition; for where the older stock ghosts were pale and stately, and apprehended chiefly through the sense of sight, the average James ghost is lean, dwarfish, and hairy—a sluggish, hellish night-abomination midway betwixt beast and man—and usually *touched* before it is *seen.* Sometimes the specter is of still more eccentric composition; a roll of flannel with spidery eyes, or an invisible entity which molds itself in bedding and shows *a face of crumpled linen.* Dr. James has, it is clear, an intelligent and scientific knowledge of human nerves and feelings; and knows just how to apportion statement, imagery, and subtle suggestions in order to secure the best results with his readers. He is an artist in incident and arrangement rather than in atmosphere, and reaches the emotions more often through the intellect than directly. This method, of course, with its occasional absences of sharp climax, has its drawbacks as well as its advantages; and many will miss the thorough atmospheric tension which writers like Machen are careful to build up with words and scenes. But only a few of the tales are open to the charge of tameness. Generally the laconic unfolding of abnormal events in adroit order is amply sufficient to produce the desired effect of cumulative horror.

The short stories of Dr. James are contained in four small collections, entitled respectively *Ghost-Stories of an Antiquary, More Ghost Stories of an Antiquary, A Thin Ghost and Others,* and *A Warning to the Curious.* There is also a delightful juvenile phantasy, *The Five Jars,* which has its spectral adumbrations. Amidst this wealth of material it is hard to select a favorite or especially typical tale, though each reader will no doubt have such preferences as his temperament may determine. [...]

Dr. James, for all his light touch, evokes fright and hideousness in their most shocking forms; and will certainly stand as one of the few really creative masters in his darksome province.

For those who relish speculation regarding the future, the tale of supernatural horror provides an interesting field. Combated by a mounting wave of plodding realism, cynical flippancy, and sophisticated disillusionment, it is yet encouraged by a parallel tide of growing mysticism, as developed both through the fatigued reaction of "occultists" and religious fundamentalists against materialistic discovery and through the stimulation of wonder and fancy by such enlarged vistas and broken barriers as modern science has given us with its intra-atomic chemistry, advancing astrophysics, doctrines of relativity, and probings into biology and human thought. At the present moment the favoring forces would appear to have somewhat of an advantage; since there is unquestionably more cordiality shown toward weird writings than when, thirty years ago, the best of Arthur Machen's work fell on the stony ground of the smart and cocksure nineties. Ambrose Bierce, almost unknown in his own time, has now reached something like general recognition.

Startling mutations, however, are not to be looked for in either direction. In any case an approximate balance of tendencies will continue to exist; and while we may justly expect a further subtilization of technique, we have no reason to think that the general position of the spectral in literature will be altered. It is a narrow though essential branch of human expression, and will chiefly appeal as always to a limited audience with keen special sensibilities. Whatever universal masterpiece of tomorrow may be wrought from phantasm or terror will owe its acceptance rather to a supreme workmanship than to a sympathetic theme. Yet who shall declare the dark theme a positive handicap? Radiant with beauty, the Cup of the Ptolemies[89] was carven of onyx.

Secondary Works

The Structure of Lovecraft's Longer Narratives

S.T. JOSHI

Abbreviations

HM   *The Horror at the Museum and Other Revisions* (Del Rey, 2007)
SHL   *Supernatural Horror in Literature* (Annotated, Hippocampus Press, 2012)
SL   *Selected Letters* (Arkahm House, 1965–76, 5 vols.)

As early as 1952 Peter Penzoldt, in *The Supernatural in Fiction*, remarked that Lovecraft's tales are "nearly always perfect in structure"[1]; but neither Penzoldt himself nor subsequent scholars have actually made a detailed examination of this structural perfection. Lovecraft is, indeed, a master almost unrivalled in the writing of novelettes, novellas, and short novels; and his best tales are almost without exception his longer narratives. It may, then, be well to give closer attention to the structural devices employed by Lovecraft in his longer works.

We can, I think, distinguish four structural patterns in Lovecraft's novelettes, although a given tale may happen to employ, in differing degrees, two or even three of the patterns. The four patterns can be enumerated as 1. strict chronology (i.e., where the incidents of a tale are narrated without a break in chronological sequence); 2. flashback; 3. double or multiple climax; and 4. narrative within narrative. Let us examine these four methods in greater detail.

The tales that are narrated without any interruption or rearrangement of chronological time are usually the simplest in structure; and are, in a sense, mere outgrowths of the short story. It may, then, be significant that Lovecraft's first true novelette (excluding the two serials "Herbert West—Reanimator" and "The Lurking Fear"), "The Rats in the Walls" (1923), employs this structure; indeed, the tale is hardly much longer than a short story itself. The opening of the tale has become celebrated: "On July 16, 1923, I moved into Exham Priory after the last workman had finished his labours" ("Rats" 240). The tale can actually be regarded as a huge flashback, since in the last paragraph we are finally told of the present state of the narrator: "Now they have blown up Exham Priory, taken my Nigger-Man[2] away from me, and shut me into this barred room at Hanwell…" (240). Indeed, there is a certain deception in the narration of this tale (as with several other of the flashback type in Lovecraft); since the narrator, although fully aware of the horrific events he is telling, nevertheless expounds his tale quite rationally at the beginning, as if he is unaware of what is to be. (One supposes that Lovecraft might have justified this device by implying that the narrator, as he begins relating the increasingly horrible events of the tale, gradually loses his self-control and descends to the gibbering of the penultimate paragraph.) This tale cannot strictly qualify as a flashback as I propose to define it, since we are not aware that it is a flashback until the end of the narrative; moreover, although the tale involves a brief exposition of the history of Exham Priory and of the narrator's ancestry (hence perhaps belonging to the class of narrative within narrative), the narrator clearly and emphatically brings us back to present time by concluding his digression with the words: "As I have said, I moved in on July 16, 1923..." (244).

More purely adhering to strict chronology is, surprisingly, Lovecraft's first novel, *The Dream-Quest of Unknown Kadath* (1926–27)—surprisingly because a strictly chronological framework is difficult to manage in a very long work without the danger of tedium. Lovecraft, however, clearly intended such a structure for his work, since he could thus achieve that sense of wonder and amazement at the successive encounters with odd beings and events which is typical of works embodying the "Odyssey theme"—a theme which we find in Lovecraft's earlier tale "The White Ship" (1919). (The *Odyssey*, of course, is of vastly intricate construction in its plot structure alone, to say nothing of subtle thematic parallels.)[3] Lovecraft declared, indeed, that "This tale is one of picaresque adventure—a quest for the gods through varied and incredible scenes and perils—and is written continuously like *Vathek* without any subdivision into chapters" (*SL* II.94); a passage which recalls Lovecraft's description of his inchoate novel *Azathoth* ("The weird Vathek-like novel *Azathoth*" [*SL* I.185]), which appears to have been similarly designed in a strict chronological framework, as the opening lines reveal: "When age fell upon the world, and wonder went out of the minds of men; ... there was a man who travelled out of life on a quest into the spaces whither the world's dreams had fled" ("Azathoth" 214). That *Azathoth* is thus an adumbration or precursor to *The Dream-Quest* (whose "moral" seems to have been based on the earlier "Celephais" [1920]) is very likely.

The flashbacks or narratives within narratives in *The Dream-Quest* are all very brief, and usually involve allusions to previous works by Lovecraft whose incidents he is attempting subtly to tie into the thread of his novel. Thus we find hints of such tales as "The White Ship," "Celephais," "Pickman's Model," "The Other Gods," and the like, but the time spent in recounting the plots of these tales is scant, as can be seen in the summary of "The White Ship":

> He [Carter] saw slip past him the glorious lands and cities of which a fellow-dreamer of earth—a lighthouse-keeper in ancient Kingsport—had often discoursed in the old days, and recognized the templed terraces of Zak, abode of forgotten dreams; the spires of infamous Thalarion, that daemon-city of a thousand wonders where the eidolon Lathi reigns; the charnel gardens of Xura, land of pleasures unattained, and the twin head-lands of crystal, meeting above in a resplendent arch, which guard the harbour of Sona-Nyl, blessed land of fancy. ("Dream Quest" 418).

The description of the "Basalt Pillars of the West, beyond which simple folk say splendid Cathuria lies," takes only another paragraph. The whole point of the novel, then, is the almost kaleidoscopic display of bizarre scenes one upon the other, and to the accomplishment of this design the simple narrative structure of strict chronology is clearly the best suited. That Lovecraft employed this simple technique deliberately and not through any incompetency in structural design can be seen in *The Case of Charles Dexter Ward*, one of the most structurally complex of Lovecraft's works, written directly after *The Dream-Quest*.

"The Dreams in the Witch House" (1932) presents a deceptively simple pattern; for although ostensibly a strictly chronological narrative (proceeding from the moment Gilman enters the Witch House to his eventual death), the tale actually becomes a quasi-"narrative within a narrative" (i.e., Gilman's "dreams" of hyperspace), although in both "narratives" Gilman is the central figure. The tale is thus somewhat akin to "The Shadow out of Time," where the narrator similarly "dreams" of himself in a wholly different environment; but here the two "narratives"—Gilman's "real life" existence in Arkham and his dream-journeys—are so intricately knit together and alternate so rapidly back and forth (unlike "The Shadow out of Time," which, because of the extended description of the narrator's experiences as a member of the Great Race, qualifies as a true narrative within a narrative) that the tale becomes—fascinatingly and brilliantly—a structural anomaly.[4] Ultimately the two "narratives" cannot be separated, in spite of the fact that Gilman himself tries to make a distinction between his "real" and his "dream" existence—a distinction difficult to maintain when certain concrete particulars from the "dream" world (e.g., the spiky image from the dream-balustrade) obtrude upon his "real" world. The employment of these two simultaneous narratives was the only means by which Lovecraft could imply that Gilman was actually living on two planes of reality—i.e., three dimensional space and hyperspace—at the same time. This is only one of several examples where the philosophical bases of a tale has actually inspired or necessitated a specific narrative technique.

The second narrative structure—the flashback—has been used by Lovecraft in varying degrees in many tales, long and short. Indeed, this is perhaps the most common type of structure employed by Lovecraft. On a minor level we find it in many short tales; note the opening of "Dagon" (1917): "I am writing this under an appreciable mental strain, since by tonight I shall be no more" ("Dagon" 23). Or "The Tomb" (1917): "In relating the circumstances which have led to my confinement within this refuge for the demented, I am aware that my present position will create a natural doubt to the authenticity of my narrative" ("The Tomb" 14). Often the flashback method opens with a grand and almost philosophical series of reflections impelled by the events through which the narrator has passed; note "Beyond the Wall of Sleep" (1919): "I have frequently wondered if the majority of mankind ever pause to reflect upon the occasionally titanic significance of dreams…" ("Beyond the Wall" 37). Or "Under the Pyramids" (1924): "Mystery attracts mystery" ("Pyramids" 270). Or the very famous opening of "The Call of Cthulhu" (1926): "The most merciful thing in the world, I think, is the inability of the human mind to correlate all its contents" ("Cthulhu" 355).

At its simplest, the flashback technique becomes little more than the strict chronological technique with a brief introduction where the narrator reflects upon his experiences; note that in "The Tomb" the narrative proceeds directly after a paragraph where the narrator speculates that "there is no sharp distinction betwixt the real and the unreal" ("The Tomb" 14). Almost all Lovecraft's shorter tales are of this very simple type.

In other cases, however, the flashback becomes a rather more significant device; and in the longer tales we are given a proportionally longer introduction to the tale proper—an introduction full of reflections about the incidents about to be, told from the standpoint of the chronological end of the events. The first adumbration of this device we find in "The Horror at Red Hook" (1925), where the whole first chapter is given over to a description and analysis of Thomas Malone's curious "lapse of behavior" ("Red Hook" 314) in the village of Pascoag, where he loses control of himself after seeing some tall buildings. In this opening chapter—which in the chronology of the tale occurs some times after the events narrated in the bulk of the story—Lovecraft can arouse our curiosity first by the seeming psychological absurdity of the event, and then by hints of the causes for Malone's lapse—"There had been a collapse of several old brick buildings [in New York] during a raid in which he had shared, and something about the whole-sale loss of life, both of prisoners and of his companions, has peculiarly appalled him" (315). Here again, as with all the tales of the flashback type, we encounter a certain deception in the narration; for the omniscient third-person narrator of the tale obviously knows the real reason for Malone's collapse, but fails to record it at this time.

In "The Colour out of Space" (1927) and "The Dunwich Horror" (1928) the flashback technique is slightly altered. Here we are, at that tales' beginning, presented with an essentially "timeless" description of the unhealthy environment of the respective regions: "When a traveller in north central Massachusetts takes the wrong fork at the junction of the Aylesbury pike beyond Dean's Corners he comes upon a lonely and curious country" ("Dunwich" 633). In both tales reference is made—almost in passing—to the horrific events about to be described (in "The Dunwich Horror": "In our sensible age—since the Dunwich horror of 1928 was hushed up by those who had the town's and the world's welfare at heart—people shun it without knowing exactly why" [634]), but this flashback is not central to the description. Indeed, in the "Dunwich Horror" reference is made not merely to the "Dunwich horror of 1928" but to the Salem witch trials and to the Reverend Hoadley's sermon of 1747. The difference between the flashback openings here and that of "The Horror at Red Hook" is that in the former tales the description is general, timeless, and does not involve any of the central characters of the tale proper. "The Whisperer in the Darkness" (1930), with its very brief flashback opening, is thus more similar to "The Horror at Red Hook" or even to Lovecraft's shorter tales.

"Through the Gates of the Silver Key" (1932–33) presents a combination of the flashback and the narrative within a narrative; the opening scene (in the New Orleans home of de Marigny) is not set chronologically after all the incidents of the tale, but only some of them (i.e., those describing Carter's odd adventures through space and time); the opening is in fact somewhat clumsy, as it must (like the successive episodes of "Herbert West—Reanimator") initially describe the events of "The Silver Key" of which the story is a sequel. The New Orleans setting thus recurs after the "Swami Chandraputra" narrates Carter's adventures. (It is interesting to note that Price's original version of the sequel similarly opens with a two-paragraph recounting of the events of "The Silver Key," although without any New Orleans scene.) It is difficult to see how this structural clumsiness—perhaps inherent in sequels could have been avoided, and it is thus not difficult to understand Lovecraft's displeasure at completing this forced collaboration.

As for the double or multiple climax, we naturally find it initially in the two serial tales "Herbert West—Reanimator" (1921–22) and "The Lurking Fear" (1922); Lovecraft, indeed, remarking of the former that "To write to order, and to drag one figure through a series of artificial episodes, involves the violation of all that spontaneity and singleness of impression which should characterize short story work" (*SL* I.158). There are several important points in this statement: first, it reveals that Lovecraft was at this time (1921) still exclusively concerned with writing short stories which had "singleness of impression" (we are reminded of Lovecraft's later remark of Poe's "maintenance of a single mood and achievement of a single impression in a tale" (*SHL* 56); and secondly, we learn that Lovecraft was not certain as to the aesthetic value of multiple climaxes in a single tale—particularly when the respective climaxes were of *equal importance or power*. Indeed, although Lovecraft was, for "The Lurking Fear," forced to tack on a climax at the end of each of the four sections, it is significant that here the final climax is much more potent than the three subsidiary ones; the tale in effect reveals Lovecraft's growing mastery of structure in the employment of several subsidiary climaxes but only one major climax at the conclusion, thus preserving—after a fashion—the "singleness of impression" he desired. "The Lurking Fear" is notably lacking in the redundant synopses of previous episodes which makes "Herbert West—Reanimator" so tedious, and maintains a unity far more than its predecessor. Significantly, Lovecraft's first true novelette—"The Rats in the Walls"—was written less than a year after the writing of "The Lurking Fear."

"The Call of the Cthulhu" (1926) is built somewhat on the same pattern (although this is more probably one of a narrative—or, rather, two narratives—within a narrative), but there is only one real climax—the actual encountering of Cthulhu by Johansen's ship. The end of the first chapter—that impressive listing of bizarre happenings all over the world as culled from Prof. Angell's "press cuttings" ("Cthulhu" 360)—is not a climax in the strictest sense, for it merely causes a certain perturbation and wonderment in the reader, who is at a loss to account for so many odd occurrences at a single time. The conclusion of the second chapter provides still less of a climax, since the function of the chapter is to provide the clue for the strange incidents of Chapter I and to supply information on the Old Ones. Only with the actual sight of Cthulhu do we encounter a true climax; and even here Lovecraft is striving to escape from any sensationalism or floridity—we here find no italicized last sentence, but after the narrator's calm conclusion of Johansen's experience ("that was all" [378]), he continues for four paragraphs with some general remarks which serve to conclude the tale tranquilly. For in fact the true climax of the tale is *not* the emergence of Cthulhu (who in any case vanishes after a few moments), but the *implication* of the narrative—the implication that hideous, vastly powerful entities lurk just behind our consciousness. This is the point of the narrator's offhand remark "Cthulhu still lives, I suppose," and his much more harried thought that "Loathsomeness awaits and dreams in the deep, and decay spreads over the tottering cities of men. A time will come—but I must not and cannot think!..." (379). Although in a certain sense employing the multiple climax technique, Lovecraft has here escaped the need of making any overt climax at all.

The double climax is authentically employed in "The Dunwich Horror," a tale whose structure—like that of "The Shadow Over Innsmouth" (1931)—has frequently been misunderstood. Drake Douglas, commenting on Lovecraft's detailed description of the death of Wilbur Whateley, wrote: "One wonders why, in this particular instance, Lovecraft decided to go to so much trouble to provide an exact description which, in truth, is not very satisfying. A rather vaguely defined horror is often more terrifying than the one which is clearly outlined for us."[5] The last sentence is, of course, a truism of fantasy literature; but Douglas finds the description here unsatisfying precisely because he seems to conceive it as the major climax, when in fact it is only a subsidiary climax and the first real indication of the "non-human side of [Whateley's] ancestry" ("Dunwich 649). Lovecraft was perfectly aware of the importance of mere suggestion as opposed to overt description in a tale; of Blackwood's "The Willows" he remarked that "the *lack of anything concrete* is the *great asset* of the story" (*SL* III.429). (We may add that this is likewise the great asset of Lovecraft's last work, "The Night Ocean.") Indeed, Lovecraft may have employed such a detailed, almost clinical description of Whateley's death precisely as an indication of the greater horror of his brother. The fact that this first climax occurs precisely half way through the narrative may confirm this view.

The situation is the same with "The Shadow Over Innsmouth" (1931). Far from believing

L. Sprague de Camp's remarkable statement of "Lovecraft's blunder of putting the climax [i.e., the narrator's pursuit by the Innsmouth denizens] in the middle,"[6] we must understand that this subsidiary climax is only a preparation for the enormously greater climax of the narrator's gradual awareness that he has gained "the Innsmouth look." Here we note Lovecraft's preference for climaxes of a deceptively quiet or mental nature, in contrast to those of an "action" or physical sort.

Two tales with double climaxes somewhat similar to those of "The Dunwich Horror" are *At the Mountains of Madness* (1931) and "The Shadow out of Time" (1934–35). In the broadest terms, the first "climax" in both tales (although it is really not presented as such) is the encounter with the *first* genus of extra-terrestrial beings—i.e., the Old Ones and the Great Race. These beings are both initially portrayed as horrifying from a human perspective; but in the course of the narrative we actually come to gain a certain sympathy with them, and the real horror (the "second" climax) emerges with the appearance of the shoggoth and the Blind Beings. Fritz Leiber brilliantly characterized this pattern by speaking (in reference to *At the Mountains of Madness*) of the "transition whereby the feared entities [i.e., the Old Ones] become the fearing; the author shows us horrors and then pulls back the curtain a little farther, letting us glimpse the horrors of which even the horrors are afraid!"[7] Precisely as in "The Dunwich Horror" with the description of Wilbur Whateley, the first "horrors" (Old Ones and Great Race) are described in some detail, whereas the second or real horrors are merely adumbrated; indeed, the Blind Beings never make an actual appearance in "The Shadow out of Time," while in *At the Mountains of Madness* the climax—the witnessing of the shoggoth—is prepared by an elaborated series of subclimaxes: the narrators first stumble across the material from Lake's camp transported by the Old Ones, then the three sledges and the body of Gedney, then the gigantic albino penguins (actually a deliberate anticlimax), then the decapitated bodies of the Old Ones, and then finally the shoggoth itself, The real climaxes to both stories are prepared with almost excessive care and detail : in *At the Mountains of Madness* the narrators' "glance backward" (*Mountains* 800) is described in five excruciatingly long paragraphs (a remarkable example of the "freezing" of time), while in "The Shadow out of Time" the narrator's descent into the primal ruins fills nearly a third of the narrative, and the narrator's hesitation actually to tell the horrible truth (that he saw the record he himself had written millions of years ago) is emphasized by the thrice-repeated anaphoric utterance "Had I…?" toward the close of the tale. Indeed, the very fact that the Old Ones and Great Race are described in such a calm and rational manner, whereas the real horrors are narrated feverishly and almost poetically, ought to inform us of Lovecraft's true climactic intentions.

The revision "Medusa's Coil" also contains several climaxes (the deaths of Marsh and Denis, the emergence of Marceline's hair from its grave after the narrator shoots the picture, the discovery that the mansion had actually burned down five or six years before the narrator's visit, and finally the discovery that Marceline had been a negress), but there are actually too many of them, and they do not fit together into a coherent whole. Indeed, the revelation of the mansion's razing five years before the narrators' arrival seems particularly gratuitous, and is difficult to explain even by supernatural means. Clearly Lovecraft did not take much trouble in working out the plot for this tale—or perhaps this part of the plot was the nucleus by Mrs. Bishop upon which he based the rest of the story.

In the case of the narrative within a narrative technique, we may subdivide it into two types: the indirect narrative (i.e., where the narrator himself has not pieced together the subsidiary narrative) and its converse, the direct narrative. The former is a cruder form, and sometimes entails structural difficulties, while the latter creates a much more unified effect. In no instance, however, ought the employment of the narrative within a narrative device be considered in itself a structural defect. We are, of course, reminded of Lovecraft's criticism of Melmoth the Wanderer, where the subsidiary narrative of John and Moncada "takes up the bulk of Maturin's four-volume book; this disproportion being considered one of the chief technical faults of the composition" (*SHL* 41). Lovecraft avoided this structural flaw even in his worst-constructed tales by sufficiently integrating the subsidiary narrative with the principal one. Thus in "Medusa's Coil," the bulk of the work is given over to de Russy's tale of his son, Marceline, and the portrait by Marsh; but his narrative is followed by actions based upon it leading to the (presumably) major climax—the destruction of the mansion. There is, nonetheless, a certain awkwardness in the whole procedure, and this tale is clearly the crudest example of Lovecraft's use of character actually to tell the subordinate narrative (another example, causing equal structural clumsiness, is "Through the Gates of the Silver Key"); we are usually presented with the main narrator's discovery of a document which represents the subsidiary narrative (as in "The Mound"), and rarely is this document quoted directly; rather it undergoes constant interpretation by the narrator (the best example is *At the Mountains of Madness*, where the narrator constantly comments upon the bas-reliefs being examined) and as a result the narrator is constantly kept before our eyes. Lovecraft's failure to adopt this subtler device in "Medusa's Coil" (one presumes that the narrator could have found some document in the house—a diary, perhaps —which could have told him the gist of de Russy's narrative) again indicates his lack of concern in the refinement of this tale.

"Medusa's Coil" nonetheless indicates an important trait inherent in Lovecraft's use of the indirect narrative within a narrative: in the subsidiary narrative one character gradually emerges with a personality of his own, and the reader comes to identify with him. This happens in a trilogy of stories—"The Horror at Red Hook," "The Whisperer in Darkness," and "The Thing on the Doorstep"—whose subsidiary narratives are so intricately woven into the central narrative that we can hardly speak of two narratives at all. In "The Horror at Red Hook," the central narrative ostensibly concerns Malone's attempts to purge Red Hook of its sinister horrors; but through Malone's eyes and through his gradual accumulation of data another narrative emerges—the tale of Robert Suydam, who is initially portrayed as unpleasant and vaguely horrific but who ultimately becomes a subordinate "hero" by nullifying the black magic being performed at the underground waterfront. It cannot, of course, be said that the two narratives are distinct; in fact, they are intimately connected. But the process of expounding the Suydam narrative is indirect —i.e., through Malone—hence can be considered subordinate. Similarly, in "The Whisperer in Darkness" Akeley emerges as a separate character—in spite of the fact that Wilmarth is the narrator and ostensibly the central figure—but here again the means is indirect: it is accomplished wholly through the correspondence between Akeley and Wilmarth. In "The Thing on the Doorstep" the narrator is not the central character at all, but it is he who tells the story of Edward Derby and Asenath Waite—for reasons obviously essential to the plot (although it might have been fascinating had Lovecraft attempted to narrate the tale from Derby's point of view[8]; Derby's intermittent possession by Asenath might have been conveyed by the employment of a radically different style—note Wilmarth's detecting the psychological difference between Akeley's letters and the final letter from the aliens ["Word-choice, spelling—all were subtly different" ("Whisperer" 698)]—while Derby's emergence from the grave in the rotting corpse of Asenath might have brought forth a scene similar to the conclusion of "The Outsider"). All these tales and other of Lovecraft's longer stories reveal the care with which Lovecraft devoted on the best narrative point of view and structure to employ for a given tale. The use of correspondence to expound Akeley's involvement with the Winged Ones keeps these horrific events at a proper narrative "distance," similar perhaps to the use of the messenger to narrate the climax of Greek tragedies (one thinks especially of the Medea of Euripides, where the Messenger tells the grisly tale of the deaths of Glauke and her father Kreon).[9]

This creation of a narrative "distance" is most emphatically displayed in "The Call of Cthulhu," the last of the indirect narrative-within-a-narrative tales to be studied here. This tale is remarkable in having not merely one but as many as three narratives within the basic narrative. An outline might more clearly depict the structure:

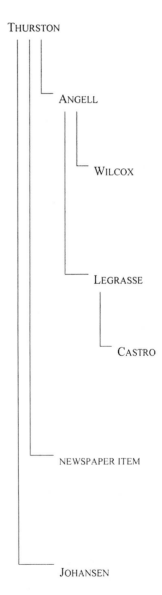

Narrative voices in "The Call of Cthulhu."

I. Narrative of Francis Wayland Thurston
   A. Narrative of Prof. Angell's discussions with Henry Wilcox
   B. Narrative of Prof. Angell's account of the account of Inspector Legrasse
      1. Inspector Legrasse's cross-examination of Castro (information about Old Ones)
   C. Narrator's discovery of newspaper article telling of Johansen's ship
   D. Narrator's discovery and recital of Johansen's manuscript

In this elaborate structure we may note several things: first, the number of characters or elements required to tell the entire narrative (Thurston, Angell, Wilcox, Legrasse, Castro, the newspaper article, Johansen); and secondly, the fact that the most sensational parts of the narrative—the explanation of the Old Ones by Castro and the encountering of Cthulhu—are told in an extremely circumspect way; indeed, the Castro narrative is three times removed from the central one: Thurston-Angell-Legrasse-Castro. This can be depicted by the following chart of the narrative voices:

This structure, however, never becomes clumsy, since we always keep the principal narrator in view, as he continually interprets the evidence and brings himself forward; at one point he actually interviews Wilcox again after reading his uncle's papers, charmingly concluding: "I took leave of him amicably, and wish him all the success his talent promises" ("Cthulhu" 370).

"The Call of the Cthulhu" provides a transition to what I have called the direct narrative within a narrative for in that tale the narrator himself has pieced together some of the information representing the subsidiary narratives (i.e., his discovery of the newspaper item and the Johansen narrative). It is this device—one much more conducive to unity, in spite of the much greater length of the judiciary narratives which we generally find in this group—which Lovecraft has employed in some of his most impressive roles; namely, "The Shunned House," The Case of Charles Dexter Ward, "The Mound," *At the Mountains of Madness*, "The Shadow out of Time," and "The Haunter of the Dark."

For the direct narrative within a narrative the earliest example on an extended scale seems to be "The Lurking Fear" (1922), where the narrator, in order to understand why "Fear had lurked on Tempest Mountain for more than a century" ("Lurking" 224), must do much research into the history of the Martense family. Indeed, the narrator remarks with a certain poignancy that "History … Was all I had after everything else ended in mocking Satanism"[10]—a remark which makes us realize that all the narrative within narratives in this group involve a reaching backward through time—a technique frequent in Lovecraft even in tales technically outside this specific group (e.g., "The Rats in the Walls," "Facts Concerning the Late Arthur Jermyn and His Family," even so early a tale as "The Alchemist"). In any case, the whole historical research in this tale is performed by the narrator; and through his direct exposition of his findings the tale gains a unity lacking in such a tale as "Medusa's Coil." The exigencies of the serial form of "The Lurking Fear" forced Lovecraft to confine the subsidiary narrative of the Martenses to a single chapter (the third); in later tales he greatly expands the narrative, to the point that (e.g., in "The Mound") it occupies more than half the length of the whole tale.

In "The Shunned House" (1924) the technique of employing a subsidiary narrative is subtilized; for not only is the history of the shunned house not told all at one time—the narrator's discovery of the "French element" ("Shunned" 302) (i.e., the tale of Etienne Roulet) being delayed after the preliminary exposition of the house's history—but the narrator is constantly kept in our view: Chapter II begins: "Not till my adult years did my uncle set before me the notes and data which he had collected concerning the shunned house"; Chapter III opens: "It may well be imagined how powerfully I was affected by the annals of the Harrises"; and finally the narrator begins his own researches, carrying forward his uncle's work.

This same device is found in *The Case of Charles Dexter Ward* (1927), upon whose rich complexity we can here only touch. The subsidiary narrative—the tale of Joseph Curwen's doings in the seventeenth and eighteenth centuries—is ostensibly limited to part II ("An Antecedent and a Horror"), and throughout this section we find Ward intruding as the information is being presented: "Charles Ward told his father, when they discussed Curwen one winter morning…"; "The collection of Durfee-Arnold letters, discovered by Charles Ward…"; "Parts of [a letter], copied and preserved in the private archives of the family where Charles Ward found it…"; "Charles Ward, however, discovered another vague sidelight in some Fenner correspondence…" (*Charles Dexrter Ward* , 500, 505, 514); and the like. But this intrusion of a twentieth-century character into an eighteenth-century world then reverses, as the hoary Curwen, as it were, bursts out of his narrative and comes more and more to dominate Ward. In Part III, we find Ward still accumulating data, coming across more letters written in the crabbed archaism of the seventeenth century; and throughout the rest of the novel, which is supposed to be set in the contemporary age, we constantly encounter intrusions of archaism: Curwen's diary, letters written to Curwen/Ward so late as 1928 (letters contrasting harshly with Ward's own epistle to Willett of March 8, 1928), and finally Curwen's complete replacement of Ward, conveyed—as in "The Whisperer in Darkness" and "The Thing on the Doorstep"—through a tell-tale stylistic difference; this time a difference of speech, as Curwen reveals his age with such terms as "bigness," "phthisical," and the like (555). (Lovecraft's omnivorous reading of eighteenth-century literature held him in good stead here.) As in "The Call of Cthulhu," the use of many types of documents—letters, diaries, newspaper articles, even the scrap of eight-century Latin minuscule—serves to "distance" the narrative and subtilize it; indeed, we must pay enormously close attention to ascertain exactly when Curwen finally kills Ward and supplants him permanently (hence the constant debates by the alienists as to the precise commencement of Ward's "madness" [i.e., replacement], which help not only to clarify the structure of the novel but to provide clues as to when we are to understand that the final transition has occurred). As in many of Lovecraft's tales, the "subsidiary" historical narrative comes ultimately to dominate the rest of the narrative; a technique which can be interpreted philosophically as indicating Lovecraft's belief in the deathlessness of the past and its power over the present.

"The Mound" (1929–30) is not so sound structurally as some of Lovecraft's original narratives, for here the narrative of Zamacona—an actual parchment found by the narrator, and presented in a paraphrase—occupies the whole of Chapters III to VI, and this great length forces us almost to lose track of the central, contemporary narrative: indeed, when, at the opening of Chapter VII, we read "When I looked up from my half-stupefied reading and note-making…" (*HM* 155), we have almost forgotten that the narrative is in the first person. Nonetheless, the tale is indicative of Lovecraft's interest in increasingly alien civilizations: the tale, though apparently reporting a fifteenth-century Spaniard's narrative, actually tells an incalculably older tale—the settlement and civilization of the underground race that came from the stars; the tale thus becomes a triple narrative within a narrative within a narrative (modern times—Zamacona—mound civilization), and reaches farther back in time than any of Lovecraft's previous historical interludes.

This temporally distant sub-narrative is employed in two of Lovecraft's most brilliant tales, *At the Mountains of Madness* and "The Shadow out of Time." In both tales the means for expounding the alternative civilizations here presented (Old Ones and Great Race) is no mere manuscript, but, in the first case, the bas-reliefs of the Old Ones' city, and in the second case, the narrator's "dreams" of his experiences in the Great Race's city. In *At the Mountains of Madness* we again note the enormously subtle device of using style or aesthetics to tell an historical narrative; a technique carried still further here, when the narrator encounters—well after the exposition of the basic historical segment in Chapters VII and VIII—the "new and degenerate work [which] was coarse, bold, and wholly lacking in delicacy of detail" (*Mountains* 795); the work, of course, of the shoggoths. The historical segment does not, as in "The Mound," dominate the novel: instead, enormously elaborate descriptions of the voyage to the Antarctic, Lake's sub-expedition, and the protagonists' exploration of the Old One's dead city preface the subsidiary talk, so that we never lose track of the central story line. In "The Shadow out of Time" similar restraint is used: we learn the whole history and civilization of the Great Race gradually and sporadically through the successive dreams of the narrator; and we have seen how the last third of the tale is wholly occupied with the narrator's maniacal trip through the ruined city.

Some general remarks about Lovecraft's varied structural patterns can now be made. In regard to the strictly chronological or flashback technique, we have noted how the majority of Lovecraft's shorter tales and some of this longer works fall into this pattern; indeed, the pattern is almost mandatory for stories narrated in the first person (and it is to be noted that the majority of Lovecraft's tales that are not narrated in the first person—e.g., "The Dreams in the Witch House"—still center so much around one character that the distinction becomes nominal). We must actually commend Lovecraft for his ability to incorporate the narrative within a narrative technique in to a first-person account—successfully in *At the Mountains of Madness* and "The Shadow out of Time" and perhaps less so in "The Mound." The double or multiple climax can be handled either in first- or third-person narrative (e.g., "The Shadow Over Innsmouth" and "The Dunwich Horror").

We have already cited Lovecraft's criticism of Maturin's Melmoth in its use of the narrative within a narrative; and we may well ask how Lovecraft managed generally to escape such a flaw in construction when he used the device. The answer appears to lie in the fact that in nearly all cases the narrator or central character (e.g., Ward) either tells the facts of the case himself (and has usually assembled or collected them) or paraphrases the account of someone else (e.g., "The Call of Cthulhu," "The Mound"). Moreover, the "subsidiary" narrative which frames it is the really subsidiary narrative. In "The Mound," for example, the central plot of the narrative is the fate Zamacona in the underground world; the actual narrator has merely unearthed the data and, at the end, comes upon a definite confirmation[11] of Zamacona's fate. Similarly, in "The Call of Cthulhu" the actual narrator has acted merely as an industrious detective in unearthing the facts about the Cthulhu cult and of Johansen's encounter with the being. In several instances, however, the "subsidiary" historical narrative reaches out of the plot and has an effect upon the future: in "The Shunned House" and *The Case of Charles Dexter Ward*, the horror is averted and the tales end "happily"; in others— e.g., "The Haunter of the Dark"—the reverse is the case.

That Lovecraft himself was fully aware of the importance of structure in fiction can be fully observed in some of his essays, notably "Notes on Writing Weird Fiction," where he recommends the preparation of two synopses for a tale, one explaining the events in order of chronological occurrence, and the second in order of narration in the story. That these two synopses could be widely different (indeed, the degree of their difference may point to the structural complexity of a given tale) can be seen if we attempt to form two synopses of "The Call of Cthulhu":

1. Order of Occurrence	*2. Order of Narration*
History of arrival of Old Ones	Death of Prof. Angell—narrator begins examination of papers
American Archaeological Society meeting of 1908	American Archaeological Society meeting—Castro's narrative of Old Ones
Dreams of Henry Wilcox (1925)	
Johansen's encounter with Cthulhu (1925)	Johansen's encounter with Cthulhu (after narrator discovers newspaper item and locates Johansen's narrative)
Death of Prof. Angell (late 1926)	
Narrator begins examination of Prof. Angell's papers—discovers truth	

An even more intricate design can be formed for, e.g., *The Case of Charles Dexter Ward* or for "The Shadow out of Time," where Leiber has pointed out that the use of the "terminal climax" necessitates an elaborately convoluted structure.[12]

We may tread on shaky ground when we attempt to find any literary influences for the structural complexity of Lovecraft's longer tales: narrative structure does not lend itself to influence as do images or phraseology or themes, since each tale normally requires a structure peculiar to it because of the exigencies of the plot and the author's philosophical goal; and in Lovecraft's case we can find several early tales which prefigure the profound complexity of his later tales—in "The Nameless City" (1921) we find a device for narrating the history of alien civilizations repeated in much elaborated form in *At the Mountains of Madness*; in "Beyond the Wall of Sleep (1919) "dreams" are used to convey fragments of an alternate reality, as was done much more extensively in "The Dreams in the Witch House" and "The Shadow out of Time." We may in any case hazard some speculations on particular authors or works which may have suggested structural patterns. Lovecraft probably derived little from the Gothic novelists, while Poe's short tales fall almost wholly into the strictly chronological or modest flashback type. Some of Ambrose Bierce's longer narratives—notably "The Death of Halpin Frayser" and "The Damned Thing"—have what Maurice Levy called an "architectural framework"[13] which may have impressed Lovecraft. I think, however, that Lovecraft learned most about narrative structure from two fantasists whose output consists largely of novelettes or novels—Arthur Machen and especially M.R. James. Of "The Great God Pan" Lovecraft wrote: "But the charm is in the telling. No one could begin to describe the cumulative suspense and ultimate horror with which every paragraph abounds without following fully the precise order in which Mr. Machen unfolds his gradual hints and revelations" (*SHL* 83)—a remark which tells us how faithfully Lovecraft studied Machen's construction. Indeed, we may suppose that the structure of "The Call of Cthulhu"—the gradual piecing together of widely disparate data of equally disparate form (a bas-relief, newspaper cuttings, the results of an archaeological meeting, documents, and narratives by various individuals) may have been triggered by similar amassing of evidence found in Machen's "Novel of the Black Seal." M.R. James, however, was the great master of structure—something which Lovecraft confirms by his almost disproportionately long plot description of "Count Magnus" in "Supernatural Horror in Literature." Here Lovecraft has done nothing but tell the story *in order of chronological occurrence*, since the James tale is so intricately convoluted in its construction that such a thing is necessary in order to explain the story at all. One may wonder whether even Lovecraft carried structural complexity to this level. But we must remember that the tracing of an influence in narrative structure is an exceedingly tenuous and tentative business; and at best Machen, James, and others only provided analogies which Lovecraft used in his own unique way.

We may, then, agree with Peter Penzoldt as to the structural perfection of most of Lovecraft's narratives; always—save perhaps in revisions or ghost-written tales where he may have been less concerned about the excellence, structural or otherwise, of a tale—do we note Lovecraft's extreme care about such elements as the arrangement and order of incidents, the selection of a narrative voice, the incorporation of subsidiary or coordinate narratives or of multiple climaxes, and countless other subtler techniques. We have attempted here only the broadest of structural analyses; and a study of each of Lovecraft's longer tales could in truth fill the space of this essay. In the end we must agree with Lovecraft when he wrote that "the synopsis is the real heart of the story"[14]; and it is unfortunate the we have the notes and synopses for so few of his finished tales. Lovecraft's prose style, his use of images, the philosophical depth of this tales, all have been commended by critics; and it is time that readers and scholars alike found an almost architectural beauty in the structure of Lovecraft's narratives.

S.T. Joshi is the author of The Weird Tale, The Modern Weird Tale, *and* Unutterable Horror. *His award-winning biography* H.P. Lovecraft *was later expanded and updated as* I Am Providence. *He has prepared annotated editions of works by H.P. Lovecraft and other weird writers. He has won the Bram Stoker Award and the British Fantasy Award, among others. This essay originally appeared in abridgement in the 1986* Candlemas *issue of* Crypt of Cthulhu *before appearing in full text in* Selected Papers on Lovecraft (*Necronomicon Press, 1989*).

Cosmic Fear and the Fear of the Lord

Lovecraft's Religious Vision

ROBERT M. PRICE

In my opinion the greatest and most penetrating exposition of Lovecraft's work is that of Fritz Leiber in a small series of essays including "A Literary Copernicus" and "Through Hyperspace with Brown Jenkin."[1] Among the many excellent thoughts to be found in these essays is the pivotal insight that Lovecraft had furnished a new fulcrum on which to hoist the weight of literary horror. Though perhaps not quite the first to employ it, he was certainly the one to perfect the aesthetic of "cosmic horror" or "cosmic fear." That is, it was the universe and its vastness, indifferent and unfriendly toward man, that Lovecraft made into the chief horror. It was no longer the threat of an untimely death, not the possible visitation of vampires and specters, nor even the destruction of the world, that was to provide the chillest shudders, but the destruction of the comfortably human-centered worldview that had prevailed until the discoveries of Copernicus, Darwin and Freud. These thinkers had effectively dethroned homo sapiens from his imagined lordship over space and time. And this was a revelation homo sapiens by no means welcomed!

The now-famous epigram to "The Call of Cthulhu" predicted that if the revelations of modern science continued unabated in their tendency to minimize and marginalize human significance, reducing us to mere flotsam and jetsam in the vast scheme of things, then sooner or later, insecure humanity, its delusions of self-importance forever threatened, would surely take up again the self-blinded perspective of primitivism and superstition.

That the prospect of science's impact on the human self-estimate was a real and terrible threat, and no mere fancy of Lovecraft's, is clearly evident from the history of ecclesiastical opposition to science. What discoverer did the Church not attempt to silence at the stake or in the dungeon in order to preserve the illusion that God had created the tidy little universe as an ideal habitat for humanity, indeed that God spent his time occupied with little else than the bliss and advantage of humanity? The quixotic crusades of today's "scientific creationists" demonstrate that the "new dark age" is already well-advanced.

So for Lovecraft the element of cosmic fear was the distaste of facing the truth of a boundless universe in which humanity has but a minimal and insignificant temporary role. The universe itself becomes, as Maurice Levy correctly sees, a terrible abyss of potential horrors "too deep for any line to sound." The starry heaven has become hell, for its stars have turned out to be, not angels watching over man, but rather immense fire-balls burning for no one in particular to see, and ever threatening to extinguish us in an unfelt ecstasy of supernova.

Yet I am convinced that in this scenario we have but half the story. And the remainder of the tale is surprising indeed. As implied above, the cosmic vision Lovecraft espoused was perceived as a threat to conventional religion (though the degree to which even Victorian Evangelicalism rejected Darwinism has been much overestimated). It was certainly the anti-science obscurantism of many in the religious establishment that fueled the fires of Lovecraft's contempt for religion. Yet I am going to argue that Lovecraft's own experience of "cosmic fear" produced in him what we would readily recognize as an essentially religious and mystical worldview if we were not led off track by his various fulminations against traditional theism.

We must begin with a second look at his "cosmicism." Here is a typical statement on the matter. "The true function of phantasy is to give the imagination a ground for limitless expansion, and to satisfy aesthetically the sincere and burning curiosity and sense of awe which a sensitive minority of mankind feel toward the alluring and provocative abysses of unplumbed space and unguessed entity which press in upon the known world from unknown infinities and in unknown relationships of time, space, matter, force, dimensionality, and consciousness. I know that my most poignant emotional experiences are those which concern the lure of unplumbed space, the terror of the encroaching outer void, and the struggle to transcend the known and established order" (from a letter to Clark Ashton Smith, October 17, 1930).

Anyone familiar with Rudolf Otto's classic treatment of religious phenomenology, *The Idea of the Holy*, will recognize in this passage a perfect example of the core religious experience, the numinous experience, the encounter with the Holy. Otto scrutinized the archives of visionary and worship experiences through history and across cultures and found that when one penetrated beneath differing dogmatic formulae and varying names for the Divine, one found a broad commonality of underlying pre-rational, pre-conceptual religious experience. It all proceeds from the encounter with the Wholly Other, the Infinite, the Eternal, the Absolute, and that encounter calls forth a double-edged reaction, both of holy terror and of enthralling fascination.

Otto spoke first of the encounter with the Holy perceived as the *Mysterium Tremendum*, the great Mystery at which we tremble. We shudder with consuming fear at that which is utterly alien, weird and uncanny, defying all worldly categories and inexpressible in worldly terms. The *Mysterium* is, as Otto put it, overpowering, full of awe, and full of being. Before it we feel we are the merest shadows. The fear we experience is not that of a concrete threat to life and safety, but rather that "oldest emotion of mankind," by Lovecraft's reckoning, spectral fear, fear of the great Unknown, now about to be terribly unveiled. We shrink before it in a kind of shame, yet it is not so much moral guilt we feel as ontological deficiency. We are nothing. Otto called it "creature feeling."

What Lovecraft derided and rejected religion for, ironically, was its humanistic hubris. A self-arrogating Church had set mankind in the center of the cosmic scheme, but if Otto is correct, as I believe he is, the essential religious experience is precisely that of the great ontological shock of apprehending the insignificance of man in the face of the infinity of "elder, outer entity." As the Psalmist put it, "When I consider the heavens, the work of thy hands, the moon and the stars which thou hast ordained, what is man that thou art mindful of him?" (Psalm 8:3–4). It is not ageless, dreaming Cthulhu, but Yahweh who is addressed this way: "A thousand years in thy sight are but as yesterday when it is past, or as a watch in the night. Thou dost sweep men away; they are like a dream" (Psalm 90:4–5). When still another Psalmist laments, "How they are destroyed in a moment, swept away utterly by terrors! They are like a dream when one awakes; on awaking, you despise their phantoms" (Psalm 73:19–20), we might first think we are hearing a Lovecraft protagonist bemoaning humanity's eventual fate at the hands of the blind forces of cosmic indifferentism! But it is the infinitude of God which serves nicely to annihilate man's smug pretensions.

At the same time man experiences the siren-call of the Holy perceived as the *Mysterium Fascinans*, that Mystery which enthralls even as it repels. How can it do both? Simply because what we cringe from is exactly what promises us fulfillment: we are pathetically finite. The Holy is gloriously and bogglingly infinite. Its uncanny Otherness frightens, yet its Otherness is what we know we require, what would fill up that ontological deficiency which makes us cringe!

And Lovecraft's words ring loudly with the magnetic fascination exerted by that very same universe which, as an immeasurable abyss, thwarts and dwarfs us! It is equally clear that the cosmic revelation so unwelcome to "self-blinded earth-gazers" is the very fulfillment (albeit imaginary for the purposes of fiction) that would satisfy that burning curiosity of the "sensitive minority." Lovecraft's fascination with cosmic fear was an experience of the central religious awareness.

But, the reader may object, the fact remains that Lovecraft, consistently or inconsistently, did not go on to conclude that God exists. But this objection misses the point. As Otto indicates, the parallels between various Eastern and Western religions make clear that personalistic theism is but one possible theoretical model with which some traditions have thought to articulate the experience of the Holy. It is by no means a necessary one, or one demanded by the numinous experience itself. The Buddhist Sunyata, the Vedanta Hindu Nirguna Brahman, are by no means personal Gods, but they articulate the same set of experiences. It is a commonplace among scholars of comparative religion that religion need not imply theism. I am arguing not that Loveccraft was a theist (of course he was not), but rather that he was religious in vision and outlook, even though his own tendency to equate (to confuse?) religion with theism prevented him from using the term "religious" to describe himself.

But to recognize this is but the beginning. Another aspect of HPL's unnamed religiosity becomes manifest once we consider the work of another great comparative religions scholar, Mircea Eliade, the author of many fine works of which *The Sacred and the Profane* is exemplary. In this volume Eliade develops and documents the universal religio-cultural apprehension of "sacred time" and "sacred space." Eliade explained that, as perceived by universal religious instinct (and most clearly visible to us in primitive societies and archaic religious practices), there are two kinds of time. Profane, or ordinary, time runs on drearily like Old Man River, with neither end nor goal in view. In the stream of profane time one can do naught but mark time. But profane time is given meaning by the periodic inbreaking of sacred time. This latter is not linear but cyclical. It is the primordial time of creation, when all things received their due allotment of reality. But as the year goes on, all things grow old and wear down. Thus there is a need for rejuvenation. Every new year, it was believed, the sacred time of origins spirals back and intersects the line of profane time, imparting a new dose of reality to the world.

Of course the origin of this whole schema is the cycle of the seasons, but it came to color all aspects of ancient life. Whenever one sought medical care, the shaman would chant of the sacred time of creation, so as to invoke it anew in a special case. If you sewed up the holes in your fish net or mended your axe, you hummed the song about when the ancestors or culture heroes taught these arts, so as to reinvoke their creative power and make the repair successful. Sacred time, then, is an imagined ancient time of greater reality that can intrude into our own profane time to lend it a greater semblance of eternal reality.

Similarly, says Eliade, human beings experience both sacred space and profane space. Sacred space is a higher, primordial, and invisible realm. It is the source of reality, itself realer than the shadowy world of mundane, ordinary, profane space in which we live. Profane space would be utterly undistinguished but for its sporadic penetration by sacred space. Where such epiphanies of the sacred have occurred the mythical imagination has erected "*axes mundi*," vertical links connecting heaven and earth (Mount Olympus, Jacob's Ladder, Yggdrasil, Sentinel Hill). These are places where some of the holiness/reality of sacred space has blazed forth to suffuse just a bit of profane space, lending it a derived holiness, as when Moses is told he has chanced upon holy ground, hence he must take off his sandals and leave them; having touched sacred space they have themselves become holy relics. These are the places where temples are sooner or later built, where oracles set up shop, where one can catch a glimpse of the Other Reality already here on the hither shore. Their presence lends meaning to the surrounding waste of profane space. The holy sites become the coordinates of the culture's map of reality, centers of government and pilgrimage.

Though one can find traces of it elsewhere, e.g., the final revelatory speech of Nyarlathotep in *The Dream Quest of Unknown Kadath*, I believe it is in the sonnet-cycle *Fungi from Yuggoth* that we find a rich deposit of what I would call Lovecraft's mysticism of place and past:

XIII. Hesperia

The winter sunset, flaming beyond spires
And chimneys half-detached from this dull sphere,
Open great gates to some forgotten year
Of elder splendours and divine desires.
Expectant wonders burn in those rich fires,
Adventure-fraught, and not untinged with fear;
A row of sphinxes where the way leads clear
Toward walls and turrets quivering to far lyres.

It is the land where beauty's meaning flowers;
Where every unplaced memory has a source;
Where the great river Time begins its course
Down the vast void in starlit streams of hours.
Dreams bring us close—but ancient lore repeats
That human tread has never soiled these streets.

XIV. Star-Winds

It is a certain hour of twilight glooms,
Mostly in autumn, when the star-wind pours
Down hill-top streets, deserted out of doors,
But showing early lamplight from snug rooms.
The dead leaves rush in strange, fantastic twists,
And chimney-smoke whirls round with alien grace
Heeding geometries of outer space,
While Fomalhaut peers in through southward mists.

This is the hour when moonstruck poets know
What fungi sprout on Yuggoth, and what scents

And tints fill Nithon's continents,
Such as in no poor earthly garden blow.
Yet for each dream these winds to us convey,
A dozen more of ours they sweep away!

XXVIII. Expectancy

I cannot tell why some things hold for me
A sense of unplumbed marvels to befall,
Or of a rift in the horizon's wall
Opening to worlds where only gods can be.
There is a breathless, vague expectancy,
As of vast, ancient pomps I half recall,
Or wild adventures, uncorporeal,
Ecstasy-fraught, and as a daydream free.

It is in sunsets and strange city spires,
Old villages and woods and misty downs,
South winds, the sea, low hills, and lighted towns,
Old gardens, half-heard songs, and the moon's fires.
But though its lure alone makes life worth living,
None gains or guesses what it hints at giving.

XXX. Background

I never can be tied to raw, new things,
For I first saw the light in an old town,
Where from my window huddled roofs sloped down
To a quaint harbour rich with visionings.
Streets with carved doorways where the sunset beams
Flooded old fanlights and small window-panes,
And Georgian Steeples topped with gilded vanes -
These were the sights that shaped my childhood dreams.

Such treasures, left from times of cautious leaven,
Cannot but loose the hold of flimsier wraiths
That flit with shifting ways and muddled faiths
Across the changeless walls of earth and heaven.
They cut the moment's thongs and leave me free
To stand alone before eternity.

XXXVI. Continuity

There is in certain ancient things a trace
Of some dim essence—more than form or weight;
A tenuous aether, indeterminate,
Yet linked with all the laws of time and space.
A faint, veiled sign of continuities
That outward eyes can never quite descry;
Of locked dimensions harbouring years gone by,
And out of reach except for hidden keys.

It moves me most when slanting sunbeams glow
On old farm buildings set against a hill,
And paint with life the shapes which linger still
From centuries less a dream than this we know.
In that strange light I feel I am not far
From that fixt mass whose sides the ages are.

Can any reader miss here the aching of the mystic for the Eternal, the Real, hidden in the twin realms of sacred space and primordial past, made known in will-o-the-wisp epiphanies in certain evocative seasons and surroundings? I say this is a religious mysticism, even if the word "religion" was rejected by Lovecraft because of past associations or too-narrow definitions. The mysticism of place and past we see in these poems certainly has little in common with "the correct doctrines of theology—preferably those of the Congregationalists" ("The Unnamable" 256).

But Lovecraft's religious vision does indeed have more than a little in common with an entirely different religious tradition: that of Mahayana Buddhism. Here I am thinking primarily of his approach to ethics in a morally neutral universe. As is well known to Lovecraft scholars, HPL rejected the classical attempt to derive ethics from ontology or metaphysics. That is, he thought Plato and his followers in error when they argued that the very nature of reality implied a "right" way to behave, that in being a "good" person, one was acting in accord with the pattern of Being itself. Implicitly, Lovecraft also rejected any connection between aesthetics and ontology, since he chose to make ethics simply a branch of aesthetics, whereas classically philosophers had made both ethics and aesthetics twin branches of axiology (the question of value-judgments), itself derived from the ultimate order of Being. In short, as with modern Existentialists, Lovecraft believed that morality was a human projection onto a neutral universe, not a human discernment of a pre-existent moral order inherent in the universe. Perhaps he derived this doctrine from the ancient Sophists contemporary with Socrates and Plato, for like the Sophists, Lovecraft believed that even though one had undermined moral norms by showing their relativity, one ought to abide by them nonetheless. The alternative is distasteful chaos. One ought to act the role of the Gentleman because things were more pleasant that way.

Though of course he derived none of this from Buddhism, the system of Lovecraft has a parallel in Buddhism. Nagarjuna, one of the greatest Mahayana mystics in the Madhyamika tradition, formulated a dialectic by which one might transcend the sterile alternatives of seeing the phenomenal world as truly real, and of seeing it as nothing but illusion (*maya*). Nagarjuna reasoned that if the phenomenal world were not ultimately real, one need not deny its penultimate reality. It might be naught but a thin film on top of a stream of water, but once one admitted how low a grade of reality it possessed, it was by no means to be despised. Thus a "healthy" view of everyday reality became possible for the world-denying mystic. His denial need not be absolute.

Ethics would fit in right at this point: ultimately the One is Void (*Sunyata*) of good/evil distinctions, but insofar as we are involved with the penultimate realm, the not-quite-real science of morality has its proper place. And ethics seem to occupy the same relative place in Lovecraft's ontology. There is no moral structure inherent in the nature of things. Morality has but the tenuous existence of a shared convention. It is a human projection onto life. Yet knowing that it is merely that does not invalidate it. I am not trying to paint HPL as a Buddhist, but rather to show that a moral outlook such as his is by no means incompatible with a religious sensitivity.

In the parlance of the Yogacara school of the Mahayana, all objects in the phenomenal world are *maya* in the sense that none has any true *dharma*, or nature. All is Emptiness. The proper attitude of the bodhisattva (one striving for Buddhahood) toward this realm is not one of loathing, but rather of indifference, detachment. He is quite happy to exist in this world so as to assist all beings toward enlightenment. But nothing in it any longer tempts him. And since he has no axe to grind, nothing to prove, no one to impress, the enlightened one comes to view all beings equally with an eye of compassion (*karuna*). He can do so since he has no reason to prefer one to another. No selfish striving or self-defensiveness enters into it.

I would like to suggest that though Lovecraft certainly did have likes and dislikes (his racism, for example, is notorious), insofar as he did have marked compassion on others it was based neither on self-interest nor on Western religious moralism, but rather on a Buddhist-style compassion of disinterest based on an understanding of Emptiness or no-*dharmas*. My evidence here is anecdotal.

Samuel Loveman, in one of his valuable reminiscences of his friend Lovecraft, recalls that "His pity for the peccadillos of his friends or acquaintances was unswerving. I remember a particular instance where one of our friends whose predominating characteristic was that of insincerity, became involved in an incriminating, ghastly episode. Lovecraft's remark, made with a negative gesture of both hands: 'Well, only another collection of molecules!' Adding: 'I pass no judgements on anyone. I take no one too seriously. Disillusion has its disadvantages, but therein lies safety'" (35). How ironic that a radically dim view of human nature, namely that there is no such thing, can produce greater rather than less compassion for one's fellows—just as it does in Buddhism! (And for that matter, remember the words of Psalm 103:13–14: "As a father pities his children, so Yahweh pities those who fear him. For he knows our frame; he remembers that we are dust"—i.e., just another collection of molecules!)

Would Lovecraft have considered himself a religious man? Of course not. His many published remarks make it clear he would have laughed at the thought. But I believe we may press his disavowal no farther than denoting his repudiation of obscurantist creeds and denominations. I suggest that his letters, fiction, and poetry all reveal a strong religious sense, a mysticism of Eternity and its epiphanies in sacred time ("centuries less a dream than this we know") and sacred space ("worlds where only gods can be"), clothed by his imagination in literary symbolism fully as evocative as the mythic symbols of any known religion.

Robert M. Price is the editor of Crypt of Cthulhu *and a series of Cthulhu Mythos anthologies. He traces the origins of Lovecraft's entities, motifs, and literary style. His theological background informs his Mythos criticism, detecting gnostic themes in Lovecraft's fictional god Azathoth. His annotated collection of Lovecraft's fiction, juvenilia, and revisions is forthcoming. He received the Robert Bloch Award for contributions to Lovecraft scholarship. This article originally appeared in* Tekeli-li #2 *(Summer 1991) and was reprinted in* Black Forbidden Things *(Borgo Press, 1992).*

The Victorian Era's Influence on H.P. Lovecraft

SHANNON N. GILSTRAP

Howard Phillips Lovecraft lived his entire life in the United States, principally in Providence, Rhode Island. Every work included in the present collection takes place in America, and Lovecraft wrote them all in the 20th century. He does not, therefore, immediately strike one as an appropriate subject in whom to explore the influence of the 19th century period in Britain known as the Victorian Era.[1] Lovecraft's fiction and his literary philosophy, however, are remarkably influenced by Victorian thought and worldview; therefore, taking time to trace Lovecraft's indebtedness to the Victorians not only clarifies some of his work's prevailing themes and their genealogy, but also points out avenues for further research into his connections with the Victorians.

To begin, if one wants to explore the 19th century's literary influence on Lovecraft, one can do no better than thumb through his long essay *Supernatural Horror in Literature*. There, Lovecraft gives his British and European literary genealogy, his 19th century predecessors. Among others, a reader will find Charles Robert Maturin, William Beckford, Friedrich Heinrich Karl, Mary Shelley, Sir Walter Scott, Charles Dickens, Robert Browning, Edward Bulwer-Lytton, Sheridan LeFanu, Wilkie Collins, Emily Brontë, Theophile Gautier, Charles Baudelaire, Guy de Maupassant, and Joris-Karl Huysmans. A Lovecraft student should read and be familiar with his catalogue of literary influences for, according to Lovecraft himself, these writers have contributed to his vision of "cosmic horror." These predecessors' artistry and style, stock characters and situations, literary and philosophical theories, and content are the foundation upon which Lovecraft built his vision of the terror lurking just beyond the penumbra of human experience and reason. As many of the essays in the present collection affirm, these 19th century writers continue shaping the horror genre in both style and substance.

The Victorian Era, though, gave to Lovecraft more than literary exemplars; he is heir to an entire worldview, or—to use a word popular in the 19th century—an entire *weltanschauung*. Poised as Lovecraft was between two centuries—he was born in the last decade of the 19th century and died in 1937—his culture was, though American, greatly influenced by Victorian Britain and, more generally, 19th century Europe. Although America had been testing and asserting its own literary voice through the persons of Mark Twain, Ralph Waldo Emerson, Emily Dickinson, Edgar Allan Poe, and Walt Whitman during the 19th century, Britain was still a literary powerhouse in the 19th century. Americans flocked to theaters to hear eminent Victorians such as Charles Dickens, Matthew Arnold, and Oscar Wilde as they engaged in long speaking tours through the States. Additionally, many of the major voices of 19th century American fiction—excepting Edgar Allan Poe—were not always praised by Lovecraft. When writing of Nathaniel Hawthorne, Lovecraft allows him "genius" but laments that "Supernatural horror … is never a primary object with Hawthorne; though … he cannot help suggesting it with the force of genius when he calls upon the unreal world to illustrate the pensive sermon he wishes to preach," and Hawthorne subsequently "left no well-defined literary posterity" (*Supernatural* 62, 65). Another great American novelist, Henry James, succumbs to "pomposity and prolixity" too much to "create a truly potent air of sinister menace" (*Supernatural* 68). Moreover, when Lovecraft was maturing, America had, slightly less than a generation before, weathered its first identity crisis in the form of the American Civil War, and the first World War occurred during Lovecraft's young adulthood, further fracturing the world. England and Europe, in the 19th century, were the centers of the industrial and intellectual worlds; America had not solidified the position in world affairs it currently believes it holds.

What follows is an exploration of how Lovecraft engages in his works two distinctly Victorian ideas: Aestheticism and optimism. Even though H.P. Lovecraft is a 20th century American author, he is continually engaging, positively and negatively, the Victorian worldview in his literary productions.

I. *H.P. Lovecraft's Poetics of Horror and the Aesthetic Movement*

> "…the final criterion of authenticity is … the creation of a given sensation."
> —H.P. Lovecraft, *Supernatural Horror in Literature*

Aestheticism was a social, philosophical, and artistic movement whose development spanned much of the 19th century in Britain and Europe. It appeared in many guises over the course of the century, and H.P. Lovecraft's reaction to and incorporation of a few of its tenets make it an important touchstone for understanding some of his literary ideals, or his poetics. Chiefly, Aestheticism contributed to Lovecraft's elitism, his emphasis on the connection between form and sensation, and his rejection of moral didacticism as a literary aim.

However, Aestheticism was not a completely unified philosophy, for it evolved throughout the 19th century in both Britain and on the Continent, and understanding this evolution is essential for understanding how and why Lovecraft embraced and rejected different Aesthetic tenets. Early Aesthetes reacted to what they felt was the increasing ugliness of Victorian England. Although many towns in England were feeling an economic boom from different industries, including coal, iron, and textile manufacturing, that money was concentrated in a very few and was acquired at the expense of many who lived in squalor. This economic disparity contributed to the ugliness of the world. What was more, the up-and-coming middle class despite their money, were not living beautiful lives. Matthew Arnold captured many Aesthetes' attitudes towards the upper-middle class:

> Consider these people, then, their way of life, their habits, their manners, the very tones of their voice; look at them attentively; observe the literature they read, the things which give them pleasure,

the words which come forth out of their mouths, the thoughts which make the furniture of their minds; would any amount of wealth be worth having with the condition that one was to become just like these people by having it? [*Culture and Anarchy* 36].

Arnold even termed the aristocracy "Barbarians," and the rising middle class he termed "Philistines," neither epithet carrying positive connotations. In a world ruled by economy—in business, religion, architecture, manufacturing, and morality—all sense of beauty had been carved out of life as extraneous, thus maximizing profit and utility. Into such a world entered the first of Aestheticism's three stages. Early Aesthetes emphasized the role of art (broadly defined to include craftsmanship, architecture, and the visual arts) in unifying a society fractured by the factory system, Social Darwinism, capitalism, and Utilitarianism into one whose citizens experienced in all their work "the spontaneous joy of creativity ... derived from [their] everyday occupation" (Altick 283). Such an early Aesthetic philosophy was popularized by John Ruskin and William Morris, among others.

As the 19th century progressed, however, Aesthetes began believing that beauty was something removed from the increasingly industrialized social world. Art, rather than working on and in the world, became a vehicle for creating a "second world" beyond mundane life. Rather than a moral imperative, the cultivation of beauty for beauty's sake became an Aesthetic imperative. "Beauty must be sought in the privacy of one's own imagination," writes Richard Altick, and expressed through one's living a beautiful life, however defined (288).

This movement towards the individualistic expression and cultivation of beauty, in art and lifestyle, initiated the final phase of the Aesthetic movement, a time period also called the "Yellow Nineties," and the Decadent movement that followed. During this time, living a beautiful life included living a life characterized by intense experiences, the imperative to "abandon [one's] delicately responsive sensibility to the constant play of sensations and impressions—sight, sound, odor, touch, taste" (Altick 292). Only a finely tuned receptivity could hope to "drink life to the lees" as Alfred Tennyson's Ulysses desired, and only an Aesthetic temperament could abandon conventional morality in order to realize that beauty existed apart from socially or traditionally defined standards of "good." As such, "Aesthetes devoted themselves to exploring the mystery of human consciousness and emotion as they beheld it on the screen of their own vivid sensibilities" (Altick 294). Ultimately, during the Decadent movement of the 1890s, those who possessed such delicate sensibilities "extended the Aesthetes' cultivation of the senses to the realm of the abnormal and perverse...: sexual aberrations, drug-taking, absinthe-drinking—an array of vices sufficient to rend the whole massive monolith of Victorian morality" as they searched "for new sensations ... a preoccupation with morbid and exotic experience" (Altick 297). This three-part development of the Aesthetic philosophy shows how the movement's conclusion differed from its origins, especially the move from the social to the subjective. Each phase, however, uniquely contributed to Lovecraft's art and philosophy.

Lovecraft embraces Aestheticism firstly through his constant references, in *Supernatural Horror in Literature*, to the mind of his reader, the cultivated imagination and sensitivity of one who can both write and appreciate the profound effects of what he terms "cosmic horror." According to an early Aesthete, Walter Pater, the purpose of literature was "to withdraw the thoughts for a little while from the mere machinery of life, to fix them ... 'on the great and universal passions of men'" (qtd. Houghton 281). Correspondingly, for Lovecraft, "The oldest and strongest emotion of mankind is fear" (*Supernatural* 25). Lovecraft insists that in horror literature "there be excited in the reader a profound sense of dread, and of contact with unknown spheres and powers," but such an effect can only be produced if both artist and reader are capable of "a subtle attitude of awed listening" (*Supernatural* 28). In order to cultivate a sense of cosmic horror, Lovecraft believed that the artist's mind had to be capable of producing "healthy imaginative products of a vision naturally disposed toward phantasy and sensitive to the normal illusions of the unseen" (*Supernatural* 52). This temperament is an integral part of the character Henry Anthony Wilcox in "The Call of Cthulhu." From our first introduction to him, we know that he as the temperament of the Aesthete, for he was "of known genius but great eccentricity," who defines himself as being "psychically hypersensitive" ("Cthulhu" 357). When the narrator goes to visit Wilcox later in the story, Wilcox is described as "one of the great decadents" because he has "crystallized in clay and will one day mirror in marble those nightmares and fantasies" (369). Clearly, Lovecraft believed that the production and appreciation of horror literature, or "weird literature" as he frequently termed it, was the province of an elite group of select individuals whose minds were subtly tuned.

Such elitism particularly characterized the later Aesthetes and Decadents during what was termed the "Yellow Nineties," so-called because of the publication *The Yellow Book*, in which many "decadent" works were published in the early and mid-1890s.[2] Although such scurrilous works contributed negatively to the image of these late Aesthetes, the artist's removal of him/herself from the necessities of moral obligation (characteristic, as we saw, of early Aestheticism) allowed the artist to focus intensely on art's form and the effect it produced. Lovecraft shared such an emphasis on form, recognizing that art's sole purpose was to, as the epigraph for this section suggests, produce a given sensation, and often in *Supernatural Horror in Literature* that sensation is one of "illimitable frightfulness" (36). Although the American writer Edgar Allan Poe is the subject of Lovecraft's praise in the following quote, Poe's work was highly prized by the Aesthetes, particularly the Decadents, and Lovecraft deftly describes how an emphasis on form can convey a given sensation to a reader:

> Poe could, when he wished, give to his prose a richly poetic cast; employing that archaic and Orientalised style with jeweled phrase, quasi-Biblical repetition, and recurrent burthen so successfully used by later writers like Oscar Wilde and Lord Dunsany; and in the cases where he has done this we have an effect of lyrical phantasy almost narcotic in essence—an opium pageant of dream in the language of dream, with every unnatural colour and grotesque image bodied forth in a symphony of corresponding sound [*Supernatural* 58].

Linking Poe to the Aesthetes Oscar Wilde and Lord Dunsany, as well as Lovecraft's recognition that language, the form of the work, connected sensation with a corresponding sound, clearly shows how Aestheticism's emphasis on form influenced Lovecraft's own ideas about how to communicate horror to the reader.

Such a cultivation of sensation through artificial means (language is, after all, artificial) is characteristic of Decadent writing and characters such as the narrator Des Essientes in J.K. Huysman's *A Rebours (Against Nature)*. In a particularly famous scene in chapter 10, Des Essientes, using perfumes, creates for himself an entire imaginative journey in his home simply by infusing the air around him with different expertly blended scents. In fact, Des Essientes confirms paradoxically that since "the essence obtained by distillation from the flower itself cannot possibly offer more than a very distant, very vulgar analogy with the real aroma of the living flower … all the flowers in existence are represented to perfection by combinations of alcoholates and essences" (Huysmans 119).[3] With the help of his essences, Des Essientes infuses his room with the smell of a meadow where "linden trees swayed in the wind, shedding on the ground about them their pale emanations, counterfeited by the London extract of tilia." Next, "he sprayed the room with a light rain of essences that were half-human, half-feline, smacking of the petticoat, indicating the presence of woman in her paint and powder." Soon, "the horizon was filled with factories, whose fearsome chimneys belched fire and flame like so many bowls of punch. A breath of industry, a whiff of chemical products now floated on the breeze he raised by fanning the air..." (Huysmans 124). As with perfumes, so with words for both the Victorian Aesthetes and H.P. Lovecraft.

A third inheritance Lovecraft claimed from the Aesthetes is his belief that literature should not instill any particular social or moral value in its reader. In fact, when criticizing the horror tales produced by many Victorians, Lovecraft remarks that they were often marred by a tendency to "please the matter-of-fact and purposeful Victorian reader" (*Supernatural* 47). This is markedly different from Aestheticism's early emphasis on art's moral role; however, it is in line with later trends that moved art away from moral obligation. In fact, Oscar Wilde's "Preface to *The Picture of Dorian Gray*" famously asserts, "there is no such thing as a moral or an immoral book. Books are well written or badly written. That is all.... All art is quite useless" (3). Generally misunderstood by his contemporaries but embraced by such Aesthetes as Charles Baudelaire, Edgar Allan Poe is praised by Lovecraft for recognizing "that all phases of life and thought are equally eligible as subject matter for the artist ... strangeness and gloom ... pain ... decay ... terror ... which are fundamentally either adverse or indifferent to the tastes and traditional outward sentiments of mankind, and to the health, sanity, and normal expansive welfare of the species" (*Supernatural* 55). Poe's "elevation of disease, perversity, and decay to the level of artistically expressible themes was ... infinitely far-reaching in effect" (*Supernatural* 56). As mentioned earlier, although Poe was generally misunderstood in America, many Aesthetes across the Atlantic, especially the Decadents, were influenced by his work. Lovecraft even writes of the "strange poets and fantasies of the symbolic and decadent schools whose dark interests really center more in abnormalities of human thought and instinct than in the actual supernatural, and subtle story-tellers whose thrills are quite directly derived from the night-black wells of cosmic unreality" (*Supernatural* 52). Such a move away from any concern with accepted or traditional obligations to morality and good taste characterizes much later Aesthetic works, and Lovecraft approves of this, even going so far as to cite "ethical didacticism" as a flaw in any work desiring inclusion in the horror genre (*Supernatural* 88).

As can be seen, Aestheticism, broadly defined and in its many guises in Britain and on the Continent, provided a foundation for several of Lovecraft's ideas about literature, specifically horror literature. His elitism, his belief in the power of form to affect a sensation in an elite reader, and his conviction that evoking horror as sensation rises above any claims of morality all have their roots in the Aesthetic movement in 19th century Britain.

II. H.P. Lovecraft's Distrust of Victorian Optimism

> "We live on a placid island of ignorance in the midst of black seas
> of infinity, and it was not meant that we should voyage far."
> —H.P. Lovecraft, "The Call of Cthulhu"

Perhaps the signal characteristic of the Victorian period was its optimism. Nineteenth century literature captured it often, but it was best symbolized by the Great Exhibition

Hall, also known as the Crystal Palace, built and designed with characteristic Victorian earnestness by Joseph Paxton. Historian Bill Bryson describes it and implies its symbolic value:

> The finished building was precisely 1,851 feet long (in celebration of the year), 408 feet across, and almost 110 feet high along its central spine ... 293,655 panes of glass, 33,000 iron trusses, and tens of thousands of feet of wooden flooring.... The Crystal Palace was at once the world's largest building and its lightest, most ethereal one. Today we are used to encountering glass in volume, but to someone living in 1851 the idea of strolling through cubit acres of airy light *inside* a building was dazzling.... The arriving visitor's first sight of the Exhibition Hall from afar, glinting and transparent, is really beyond our imagining. It would have seemed as delicate and evanescent, as miraculously improbable as a soap bubble [12–13].

This miraculously improbable structure, though, *was* present, and the vigor with which Paxton pursued the project indicates the level of self-confidence underpinning Victorian optimism. The Crystal Palace was better than a soap bubble, though, for it was supported, and it stood as a testament to this optimism until 1936.[4]

The Crystal Palace, though, and all its technical innovations was only one point on a trajectory traceable to the very wellsprings of the Enlightenment. However, one can safely say that the Victorians saw themselves as the culmination of the Enlightenment project, set into motion during the 17th century by Sir Francis Bacon, among others, with his celebration of rationalism and scientific method. Bacon summarized his project as one that would open a way for humanity to understand the world around it, and allow that "the mind may exercise over the nature of things the authority which properly belongs to it" (Bacon 7). Bacon's belief that the human mind could control the nature of things had also a spiritual dimension, for by increased understanding of the natural world, humans could rationalize the space God occupied, thus they "may give to faith that which is faith" (15). Of course, believing that he could make a place for God through reason shows a level of hubris in Bacon that some Victorians would accept as their rightful inheritance.

The Victorians kept the Enlightenment torch burning, and with it lighting the way believed that "by the control of environment human life might be vastly improved" (Houghton 28). The belief in science's ability to control the physical environment extended to the whole life of humankind. The emerging fields of economics, psychology, and sociology each sought scientific approaches to improving life and society, all supported by an unflagging optimism in human reason's ability to do so. Frederic Harrison wrote, appropriating a phrase made famous by a Charles Dickens novel, "We all feel a-tiptoe with hope and confidence. We *are* on the threshold of a great time, even if our time is not great itself. In science, in religion, in social organization, we all know what great things are in the air.... It is the age of great expectation and unwearied striving after better things" (qtd. Houghton 32–33).

Lovecraft, though, demonstrates—in both his non-fiction and fiction—an intense distrust of the Enlightenment project and the "bland optimism" it produced in the Victorians ("Cthulhu" 355). Into the 19th century's vision of mankind doing God's work better than God, Lovecraft introduces a world beyond rationalism's reach. Lovecraft seems, despite his staunch atheism, to take even Friedrich Nietzsche to task for deigning to proclaim in *Thus Spake Zarathustra*, "GOD IS DEAD" (1.2). To Nietzsche and others, Lovecraft's Cthulhu mythos and his idea of cosmic horror ridicule the notion that humankind has thought its way out of its own understanding of God. Cosmic horror dwarfs this sense of confidence and optimism, even Nietzsche's confidence that he had upended millennia of philosophical enquiry and spirituality. In fact, the narrator of "The Call of Cthulhu," Francis Wayland Thurston, frequently calls the reader's attention to the "rationalism of my mind" which led him to "the most sensible," albeit *false*, conclusions ("Cthulhu" 369). The narrator of *At the Mountains of Madness* echoes Thurston, writing that his fateful trip to Antarctica "marked [his] loss, at the age of fifty-four, of all that peace and balance which the normal mind possesses through its accustomed conception of external nature and nature's laws" (*Mountains* 744). Clearly, materialism and rationalism are insufficient in the face of the Great Old Ones.

In response to the Victorians, Lovecraft writes at the beginning of "The Call of Cthulhu," "The sciences, each straining in its own direction, have hitherto harmed us little: but some day the piecing together of dissociated knowledge will open up such terrifying vistas of reality, and of our frightful position therein, that we shall either go mad from the revelation or flee from the deadly light into the peace and safety of a new dark age" (355). The idea that scientific understanding could push humanity further away from understanding, into a new dark age, is certainly antithetical to Victorian optimism. In a specifically scientific sense, several stories within the present collection highlight the advance of science and technology into the realm of what Lovecraft calls the Great Old Ones, the race of beings and gods—and their minions—who came from the stars and ruled the cosmos, including Earth, long before humankind was even a thought. Science's advance makes it more difficult for those humans who *have* seen into the Old Ones' dark hearts to keep these figures occult, or for the Old Ones themselves to have secret places. Lovecraft's vision, therefore, works inversely from Bacon's project: the more we encroach on the Old Ones' territory the less we understand them, and they become more powerful as our puny powers of science and rationalism wane in their presence. It is for this reason that the narrator of *At the Mountains of Madness* consistently implores his auditors to not engage in "any rash and over-ambitious programme into the reign of these mountains of madness" (723). In "The Whisperer in Darkness," Henry Akeley comments that the tide of scientific advancement is decreasing the area in which the Great Old Ones and their minions live: "All that the Outer Ones wish of man is peace and non-molestation and an increasing intellectual rapport. This latter is absolutely necessary now that our inventions and devices are expanding our knowledge and motions, and making it more and more impossible for the Outer Ones' necessary outposts to exist *secretly* on this planet" (695). Although Akeley's comment appears to support the Victorians' belief in the beneficent tide of progress, Lovecraft balances that vision with another description, this time of the narrator Wilmarth going to see Akeley: "I knew I was entering an altogether older-fashioned and more primitive New England than the *mechanised, urbanised* coastal and southern areas where all my life had been spent; an unspoiled ancestral New England without the *foreigners,* and *factory-smoke*, billboards and concrete roads of the sections which *modernity* has touched" (700, emphasis mine). The italicized words emphasize only a fleeting sense of safety; we feel the fear that will always reside just outside the technological and urbanized bubble—free from foreign invasion—that humankind has used to lull itself into a feeling of safety and superiority. Such a landscape is also evoked by the descriptions of Dunwich and its natives in "The Dunwich Horror."

Likewise, Lovecraft's presentation of technological progress reminds the reader that science could very well be leading humanity away from clarity and understanding. In fact, technology is presented in "The Whisperer in Darkness" as a tool for deception that mocks humanity's perceived confidence in its self-understanding. Akeley tells Wilmarth that space travel is possible by extracting human brains and placing them in "an occasionally replenished fluid within an ether-tight cylinder of metal" from which wires could connect with elaborate instruments capable of duplicating the three vital faculties of sight, hearing and speech.... Then, on every planet covered by [the Outer Ones'] civilisation, they would find plenty of adjustable faculty-instruments capable of being connected within the encased brains; so that after a little fitting these travelling intelligences could be given a full sensory and articulate life—albeit a bodiless and mechanical one [710].

The closing images of this story, to be saved for the reader of this collection to enjoy, drive home this technology's ability to mock humanity.

Lovecraft's understanding of fear and his ideal of cosmic horror depend upon, in some ways, the Enlightenment's *failure*. Humanity's scientific impulse is so strong because "Against [fear] are discharged all the shafts of materialistic sophistication," and those "fixed laws of Nature" that Sir Francis Bacon sought "are our only safeguard against the assaults of chaos and the daemons of unplumbed space" (*Supernatural* 25, 28). Inverting Bacon's optimism about the end of his "great instauration," especially as it pertains to faith, Lovecraft reminds us, "for though the area of the unknown has been steadily contracting for thousands of years, an infinite reservoir of mystery still engulfs most of the outer cosmos, while a vast residuum of powerful inherited associations clings round all the objects and processes that were once mysterious, however well they might be explained" (*Supernatural* 26). Lovecraft echoes this sentiment in *At the Mountains of Madness* when the narrator laments that the sight of the city beyond the mountains "held ineffable suggestions of a vague, ethereal beyondness far more than terrestrially spatial, and gave appalling reminders of the utter remoteness, separateness, desolation, and aeon-long death of this untrodden and unfathomed austral world" (745). As can be seen, in Lovecraft's estimation, fear anchors the Enlightenment project, and the scientific community from Bacon to the Victorians put its entire weight behind methodically decreasing the space in which humans believed irrational fear could hide. Lovecraft's purpose is to undermine that hubris, presenting his readers with a cosmos in which human reason does not make sense or is at the very best a poor weapon. Against Cthulhu and the other Great Old Ones, Lovecraft insists humankind has brought a paperclip to a gunfight.

Reason's failure, and the cosmic horror that follows, is well demonstrated in the short story "The Colour Out of Space." Into the languid New England countryside comes a literally cosmic visitor—a meteorite. After visiting Nahum Gardner's farm to take samples of the meteorite, the scientists return with strange tales of the sample's behavior. Tellingly, Lovecraft writes that the sample "had acted quite unbelievably in that well-ordered laboratory" (597). By contrasting the sample's erratic behavior with the image of the laboratory as a controlled environment, under the watchful supervision of scientists, Lovecraft evokes fear in his reader. To drive the point home, Lovecraft writes that the sample "was nothing of this earth, but a piece of the great outside; and as such dowered with outside properties *and obedient to outside laws*" (599, emphasis mine). Here, then is an item, a force, undermining centuries of scientific progress and law-giving, reminding the reader that there are depths to experience that human reason cannot fathom. When Lake, in *At the Mountains of Madness*, tries to tell his fellow researchers what the alien bodies look like, he recognizes that "its habits could not be predicted from any existing analogy" (741). In such instances, Lovecraft pokes fun at human attempts to control the universe through science, reason, and progress. The Victorian writer Winwood Reade's comments in *The Martyrdom of Man* (1872) throw Lovecraft's jibes into further relief: "Finally, men will master the forces of Nature; they will become themselves architects of systems, manufacturers of worlds, Man then will be perfect; he will then be a Creator; he will therefore be what the vulgar worship as a God" (qtd. Houghton 36). Lovecraft rejects Reade's comments, and many like them from other eminent Victorians, throughout his stories, and rewards such pride with a terrifying fall.

Another excellent example comes in "The Call of Cthulhu." During the Victorian Era, Utilitarians and Economists approached many human ethical and moral dilemmas through mathematics, an approach that, though popular, was often caricatured through such figures as Thomas Gradgrind in Charles Dickens's *Hard Times*: "Thomas Gradgrind. With a rule and a pair of scales, and the multiplication table always in his pocket, Sir, ready to weigh and measure any parcel of human nature, and tell you exactly what it comes to. It is a mere question of figures, a case of simple arithmetic" (6). Lovecraft, to great effect, exposes the limits of mathematics in his world. As Thurston, the narrator of "The Call of Cthulhu," recounts the tale of Johansen, we see how his explanation of his vision violates mathematics and geometry, those most rational of rational approaches to the world:

> instead of describing any definite structure or building, he dwells only on the broad impressions of vast angles and stone surfaces—surfaces too big to belong to any thing right or proper for this earth…. I mention his talk about angles because it suggests something Wilcox [an earlier character] had told me of his awful dreams. He had said that the *geometry* of the dream-place he saw was abnormal, non–Euclidian … crazily elusive angles of carven rock where a second glance shewed concavity after the first shewed convexity…. One could not be sure that the sea and the ground were horizontal, hence the relative position of everything else seemed phantasmally variable [376].

Later, as Johansen runs from Cthulhu, he writes that the experience showed "such eldritch contradictions of all matter, force, and cosmic order" and that "he was swallowed up by an angle of masonry which shouldn't have been there; an angle which was acute, but behaved as if it were obtuse" (377). Such mathematical contradictions arise in *At the Mountains of Madness*, too, when the city is found to be "embodying monstrous perversions of geometrical laws" and containing "geometrical forms for which an Euclid could scarcely find a name" (746, 762). Clearly, Lovecraft, through his language and imagery, calls the reader's attention to human understanding's failure, symbolized by irrational mathematics and geometry, to grasp the world lying outside humanity's very small place in the cosmos. One wonders, what could be more horrifying than realizing that the "laws" of mathematics are complete fantasies? The fact that one of the characters who go mad in "The Call of Cthulhu" is an architect is of no small importance in light of such notions (see 360, 373, 377). The confidence characterized by the Crystal Palace is undermined when mathematics no longer make sense.

The technological advances experienced by the Victorians helped propel the industrial revolution and solidify Victorian optimism and faith in science. However, this faith was antithetical to the horror Lovecraft wanted to convey. Moreover, it was antithetical to his poetics. Several instances in *Supernatural Horror in Literature*, for instance, cite the presence of science and rationalism as deficiencies in works of horror that otherwise would have earned his praise. He writes of a "touch of basic rationality which denies to even their strangest superstitions many of the overtones of glamour so characteristic of our own forest-born and ice-fostered whisperings" (31). *Vathek*, a 19th century production, loses some of its power because of a "hardness and clearness preclusive of sheer panic fright" (44). The detective novel, initiated by Wilkie Collins's *The Moonstone*, honed by Lovecraft's idol Edgar Allan Poe, and popularized by Sir Arthur Conan Doyle (all during the 19th century), are "not to be included at all in weird literature" because of their "logic and ratiocination" (*Supernatural* 57). As can be seen, the best in weird literature, and the best expressions of cosmic horror, are works that demonstrate the shortcomings of the Enlightenment project, concluded by the Victorians. Lovecraft reacted against Victorian confidence and optimism, shared by much of Europe during the 19th century, in his best fiction. Only by referencing in his works the failure of the assumptions about human reason that the Victorians took as Gospel could Lovecraft hope to suggest to his readers the very real horror that lurks just beyond humankind's hubris.

III. *Conclusion*

As can be seen, Lovecraft's relationship to the Victorians was multifaceted and complex. He recognized that, as a writer and thinker, he stood on the shoulders of giants. He embraced some Victorian ideals while rejecting others. His belief about the Victorian influence on his contemporaries is best summed up in the following quote from *Supernatural Horror in Literature*:

> Indeed, we may say that this school still survives; for to it clearly belong such of our contemporary horror-tales as specialize in events rather than atmospheric details, address the intellect rather than the impressionistic imagination, cultivate a luminous glamour rather than a malign tensity or psychological verisimilitude, and take a definite stand in sympathy with mankind and its welfare. It has its undeniable strength, and because of its 'human element' commands a wider audience than does the sheer artistic nightmare [48].

Although it may command a wider audience, in true Aesthetic elitist fashion Lovecraft believes such writing is not *true* horror. In those lines are echoed many points elaborated on throughout this essay. The sympathy with mankind and its welfare parallels Lovecraft's rejection of Victorian optimism and its faith in the Enlightenment project, while his praise of the "impressionistic imagination" over the "intellect" demonstrates his fidelity to an Aesthetic credo.

Interestingly, though, Lovecraft embraced a different sort of science, a science that in the 21st century is gaining pop-culture status for its ability to evoke the very strangeness and uncertainty that cosmic horror is supposed to unleash on its reader. He writes, at the close of *Supernatural Horror in Literature*:

> [Weird literature] is yet encouraged by a … tide of growing mysticism, as developed both through the fatigued reaction of 'occultists' and religious fundamentalists against the materialistic discovery and through the stimulation of wonder and fancy by such enlarged vistas and broken barriers as modern science has given us with its intra-atomic chemistry, advancing astro-physics, doctrines of relativity, and probings into biology and human thought [96].

Lovecraft here comments on the beginnings of Quantum Physics. More than anything, Quantum Physics reacts against Newtonian Physics. Here is a science of the horrifying, giving us a world filled with parallel universes, wormholes, Higgs-Boson particles and—what H.P. Lovecraft would have loved the most—Dark Energy.

Perhaps in the 21st century we have pushed beyond the Victorian optimism and faith in the Enlightenment project to embrace a world that makes room for Lovecraft's vision of horror. In doing so, though, in accommodating that, are we fooling ourselves into complacency?

Shannon N. Gilstrap earned his Ph.D. in literary studies from Georgia State University and is an associate professor of English at the University of North Georgia. He has published on Matthew Arnold's prose and poetry in Victorians *and* Victorian Review *and maintains the scholarly website arnoldian.com.*

The Shadow Also Rises
H.P. Lovecraft's Ambivalent Modernism
Tracy Bealer

H.P. Lovecraft's apologia for the inclusion of horror fiction in the literary canon, entitled "Supernatural Horror in Literature," concludes with an argument that this particular genre is a particularly appropriate aesthetic response to the monumental advances in science, technology, and psychology that shaped modern America:

> Combated by a mounting wave of plodding realism, cynical flippancy, and sophisticated disillusionment, [horror writing] is yet encouraged by a parallel tide of growing mysticism … and through the stimulation of wonder and fancy by such enlarged vistas and broken barriers as modern science has given us with its intra-atomic chemistry, advancing astrophysics, doctrines of relativity, and probings into biology and human thought. At the present moment the favouring forces would appear to have somewhat of an advantage; since there is unquestionably more cordiality shown toward weird writings than when, thirty years ago [the best horror fiction] fell on the stony ground of the smart and cocksure 'nineties [96].

Lovecraft suggests that the radical reformulation of common conceptions about human beings and their environment occurring in the early twentieth century prompted a concurrent reinvigoration of popular interest in horror writing because these new advancements rendered the known world strange. Psychoanalysts posited that there were parts of the human mind that could never be fully integrated into conscious thought. Scientific discoveries were revealing a universe incomprehensible in its vastness and seemingly infinite in its subatomic complexity. According to Lovecraft, these developments provoked an affective response of "wonder and fancy" in American writers and readers which attracted them to fiction that reflected the disorienting and chaotic world modern scientists and philosophers were uncovering.

The rapid and irrevocable restructuring of the way people understood themselves and their place in the world during this period produced not only "wonder and fancy," but also disillusionment, alienation, and anxiety. Industrialization opened the cities and the public sphere to women and racial and ethnic minorities to a previously unprecedented degree. The shift from a principally rural to urban economy dislodged people from familiar social systems and environments. For many Americans, by expanding and transforming the social landscape, modernity simultaneously rendered their place in that landscape unstable and unfamiliar. Philosopher Marshall Berman posits that ambivalence is endemic to living in a modern setting which "promises us adventure, power, joy, growth, transformation of ourselves and the world—and, at the same time … threatens to destroy everything we have, everything we know, everything we are" (15). As Timothy Evans notes in his discussion of tradition in Lovecraft, "Much horror literature is predicated upon feelings of insecurity brought about by cultural change, by the idea that our families and communities, our familiar beliefs and cultural forms, are increasingly under assault by forces beyond our control" (100). Therefore, modernist ambivalence can be read productively through horror literature, and Lovecraft in particular.

"Supernatural Horror in Literature" was written in 1925–26, published in 1927, and extensively revised and republished in 1935—a time span that roughly corresponds to the flourishing of canonical literary modernism in America. During these years, writers like Ernest Hemingway, William Faulkner, and T.S. Eliot were producing fiction and poetry that explicitly engaged with the "enlarged vistas and broken barriers" that Lovecraft identifies as producing both amazement and alarm, particularly in men of Western European descent. This ambivalence more often than not manifests in the fiction of canonical modernists as either a pose of nostalgic despair (think of Quentin Compson's suicidal regret at his failure to fulfill the anachronistic masculinity of pre-bellum Southern gentility in *The Sound and the Fury*) or one of ironic detachment (for example, Jake Barnes's cutting rejoinder to Brett Ashley's disappointment that circumstance has thwarted what would be a fulfilling relationship between them: "Isn't it pretty to think so"). These fictional moves betray a corresponding ethical and aesthetic position that privileges hardness, solipsism and anti-sentimentalism in response to the existential threats posed by modernity. However, Lovecraft's theory and practice of "weird fiction" offers a counternarrative to such aesthetic coping mechanisms as irony and abstraction. As Michael Saler argues, "one of the most important legacies of Lovecraft's life and fiction is how he came to terms, not just with disenchantment, but also with difference" (16–17). Lovecraft's 1931 short story "The Shadow Over Innsmouth" literalizes the racial anxieties activated by modernist social change into a horror plot, and, through the resolution of that plot, reveals a writer working through and considering an empathetic, though still deeply ambivalent, aesthetic response to racial difference.

The story's account of where Innsmouth's otherness comes from, though paranormal in content, nonetheless engages a complex of anxieties about modernity shared by many of Lovecraft's more canonical contemporaries. The unnamed protagonist of "Shadow" is a young traveler who becomes fascinated with the mysterious town of Innsmouth. The knowledge he eventually uncovers threatens a stable understanding of the human condition, including his own. Through interviewing residents, exploring the decaying city, and observing the secretive inhabitants of Innsmouth, the protagonist comes to realize that the townspeople have been inter-breeding with an aquatic alien race, resulting in a population of half-human "fish-frogs" that eventually grow grotesquely amphibian in appearance and return to the ocean. The foreignness of the aliens themselves, both in terms of their extra-terrestrial origin and their previous residence in the Indies renders their interactions with humans a neat encapsulation of interracial contact. They are, for all intents and purposes, racially marked immigrants overtaking and, according to the initial response of the narrator, polluting and degrading Innsmouth's Anglo Saxon stock, sapping the citizenry's humanity in both appearance and behavior.

As Evans acknowledges, Lovecraft's own "horror at the disintegration of American culture in the face of moral, racial, and scientific chaos" (101) mirrors the initial revulsion of his narrator. The xenophobia and racism that undergird the representation of the aliens in "Innsmouth" is both unique to Lovecraft's psycho-biographical makeup and another intensification of contemporary cultural discourse. Lovecraft's mistrust of and distaste for the way the mass immigration of the period was changing the cultural makeup of America is evident in his personal correspondence as well as his fiction, and is a particularly odious aspect of his life and work that critics must confront. Saler, referencing "Innsmouth" in particular, explains:

> Lovecraft clung anxiously to Anglo-Saxon culture because he believed culture remained the only source of stability amidst the flux of modernity. Like many conservatives, he turned to the continuity of tradition as a refuge against the forces of change; borders and boundaries must be enforced to counteract modern anomie, isolation, and homogenization. Hybridity of any sort terrified him: most of the horrors in his fictions are described as 'hybrid' or 'fluid,' lacking boundaries or clear definitions [26].

In part because of this unavoidable biographical connection, the most unfavorable readings of "Innsmouth" interpret the devolution of the citizens and narrator due to unfavorable breeding as Lovecraft's support for eugenics. However, this impulse to reject and dehumanize the racially marked other is complicated by the conclusion of the story, when the narrator's further research reveals that he is the product of such miscegenation, and is destined to transform into a marine creature and join his great-grandmother underwater for eternity. Evans references the "considerable debate about whether the end of ["The Shadow Over Innsmouth"] is meant to dramatize a corruption of the narrator, or whether it constitutes a humanizing of the Deep Ones, a recognition that 'alien' traditions may be as valid as New England traditions." As Evans goes on to explain, this debate often hinges on biographical details, using evidence that Lovecraft did present aliens sympathetically in several of his late stories, a

> movement which paralleled the abandonment of much of the racism and anti-immigrant xenophobia that marked his upbringing. It is worth noting that Lovecraft, who for much of his life was anti–Semitic and horrified by miscegenation, married a Ukrainian Jewish immigrant. It may be that the ambiguous ending of this story is deliberate; Lovecraft is acknowledging the presence of conflicting emotions in the face of change. In this story he mourns the loss of New England traditions while at the same time he is learning to accept new cultures, acknowledging a future in which hybrid people and cultural forms may be recognized as the norm [125].

I propose to read the narrator's "ambiguous" interaction with the aliens in "Innsmouth" and his own extra-terrestrial ontology as indicative of modernist ambivalence towards the racial other, and therefore impossible to situate conclusively on a scale between racist and progressive.

The narrator's description of the "Innsmouth look" and his phenomenological response to it, reveal a pervasive suspicion on the part of the narrator that racial otherness cannot be safely objectified or contained. Reinforcing this point at the level of plot, Lovecraft's description of the inhabitants of Innsmouth and their response to the narrator's exploration of their community offers an account of othering and otherness that complicates the distance from and domination of racially marked subjects that the narrator strives to establish and maintain. Prior to his encounter with Innsmouth and its inhabitants, the narrator assumes the ethos of a scientific researcher. The purpose of his New England journey is to examine and record the history and architecture of the area. After learning about Innsmouth and the fearful disgust its inhabitants inspire in a neighboring town, the narrator is compelled to explore it precisely because it has not yet been incorporated into the official discourse of modern America: "Any reference to a town not shewn on common maps or listed in recent guide-books would have interested me, and the agent's odd manner of allusion roused something like real curiosity" (809). The narrator experiences a sense of "acute anthropological zeal" (814–825) at the prospect of exploring Innsmouth. By assuming the pose of an anthropologist, he imagines himself to be a person capable of unearthing and codifying the social system and culture of Innsmouth, presumably from the position of a detached observer. The narrator's fixation on the "Innsmouth look" simultaneously reveals both an obsession to categorize and degrade difference *and* the unsettling realization that the racialized other is always already looking back.

Before the narrator encounters an actual citizen of Innsmouth, he hears a variety of theories attempting to account for the nature of their difference. The Innsmouthians are variously described as "foreign" (811); "what they call 'white trash' down South" (812); and "quasi-pagan" (814). These explanations all include an impulse on the part of the citizens of neighboring towns to establish a stable ontological distinction between themselves and people they find intolerably unlike them. A ticket agent best articulates the way the appearance of the citizens is conflated with a debased and inexplicable otherness:

> But the real thing behind the way the folks feel is simply race prejudice—and I don't say I'm blaming those that hold it. I hate those Innsmouth folks myself, and I wouldn't care to go to their town. I s'pose you know—though I can see you're a Westerner by your talk—what a lot our New England ships used to have to do with queer ports in Africa, Asia, the South Seas, and everywhere else, and what queer kinds of people they sometimes brought back with 'em…. There certainly is a strange kind of streak in the Innsmouth folks today—I don't know how to explain it, but it sort of makes you crawl…. Some of 'em have queer narrow heads with flat noses and bulgy, stary eyes that never seem to shut, and their skin ain't quite right. Rough and scabby, and the sides of the necks are all shrivelled or creased up. Get bald, too, very young. The older fellows look the worst—fact is, I don't believe I've ever seen a very old chap of that kind. Guess they must die of looking in the glass! [810–811].

What's interesting about Lovecraft's construction of the human/alien hybrids is not merely their ugliness—their "flat noses" and their "rough and scabby" bald heads—but the nature of that ugliness and the response this physical deformity inspires in those who see it. The "Innsmouth look" provokes hatred, mistrust, and physical revulsion even in a person who recognizes his response as "race prejudice" unhinged from any real offense committed by a person with this type of face and body. The look itself is jokingly imagined to be lethal—an ugliness so profound that it threatens those who encounter it in the mirror with death. This speculation, though, betrays a profound anxiety about physical difference that racial hatred and discrimination seeks to contain. Here, the "bulgy, stary eyes that never seem to shut" are crucial to explicating the implications of the Innsmouth look for modernist politics. If those eyes encounter themselves in the mirror the effect is imagined as suicidal, but what happens when the gaze turns outward? What does it mean for a normative observer to encounter an othered object that has the potential to kill? By acknowledging the shared humanity of those marked as racially other, their ability to look back, does a part of the privileged self have to die? As the narrator descends into Innsmouth, this existential threat is precisely what he encounters, struggles to manage, and fails to maintain on a literal and conceptual level.

To contextualize the way the Innsmouth look defies and dismantles a racist gaze, it is helpful to look at Frantz Fanon's phenomenological analysis of his own experience of being the object of such a look. According to *Black Skin, White Masks*, personal interaction is crucial to producing racism because of the visually apparent physical difference. Following Freud's account of the sensitivity and immediacy of the sense organs' connection to the psyche, Fanon stresses that the sight of a black body is especially provocative to the white gaze:

> "Mama, see the Negro! I'm frightened!" Frightened! Frightened! Now they were beginning to be afraid of me. I made up my mind to laugh myself to tears, but laughter had become impossible. [...] In the train it was no longer a question of being aware of my body in the third person but in a triple person. In the train I was given not one but two, three places. I had already stopped being amused. It was not that I was finding febrile coordinates in the world. I existed triply: I occupied space. I moved toward the other ... and the evanescent other, hostile but not opaque, transparent, not there, disappeared. Nausea ... I was responsible at the same time for my body, for my race, for my ancestors. I subjected myself to an objective examination [112; ellipses Fanon's, bracketed ellipses, mine].

According to Fanon, his black body inspires fear when apprehended by a white child, and his own affective defense, laughter, is unsustainable. The white child recoils in fear and horror immediately upon *seeing* black skin. The *white* response to the racial other, whether engagement or retraction, governs the interaction, and Fanon is objectified not only in the eyes of the white child, but also in his own. He "occupie[s] space" as an object available for "examination," while the subject of the gaze "disappear[s]," exempt from objectification by Fanon by virtue of his racial privilege. Encountering the racial other reduces Fanon to merely surface: "the corporeal schema crumbled, its place taken by a racial epidermal schema." A corporeal schema allows a psyche to perceive and respond to the world as a whole, cohesive being. Racism replaces the corpus with the epidermis: any and all connection with others is mediated by Fanon's black skin.

The behavior of those who have the Innsmouth look provides a counterpoint to Fanon's description of the objectification and diminishment provoked by the racist gaze. In one connotation, the story's reference to the Innsmouth look encapsulates the way outsiders attempt to categorize the citizens of Innsmouth by a "racial epidermal schema": The "queer narrow heads with flat noses and bulgy, stary eyes that never seem to shut" and skin that "ain't quite right" skin (810–811). However, the "stary eyes" also point towards the Innsmouth citizens' resistance to such objectification. Fanon writes that the objectification of the racist gaze is felt as a sense of physical and psychic *confinement*. The "glances of the other" "seal" Fanon into a "crushing objecthood" that renders him "fixed ... in the sense in which a chemical solution is fixed by a dye" (109). The Innsmouth residents, on the other hand, are not immobilized by the gaze of the other, but rather exhibit a masterful and threatening authority by and through the primary marker of their racial difference: eyes that never seem to shut. "The staring 'Innsmouth look'" (826) creates an atmosphere of ominous omnipresence, leading the *narrator* to feel the confinement Fanon describes: "I could not escape the sensation of being watched from ambush on every hand by sly, staring eyes that never shut" (825).

The narrator feels increasingly overwhelmed in and by Innsmouth until he abandons his scientific detachment completely, deciding that, "Later I might sift the tale and extract some nucleus of historic allegory; just now I wished to put it out of my head" (837). The narrator's anxiety stems both literally and conceptually from the refusal of the Innsmouth residents to submit to his intrusion into their community and its accompanying objectifying gaze. His attempt to categorize the Innsmouth look is frustrated by his realization that he is not primarily the subject but rather the object of the others' gaze. The recognition of the Innsmouth citizens' capacity to return the narrator's gaze utterly dismantles the objective (and objectifying) pose. He acknowledges both the power and the abiding mystery of the town, questioning, "Did those ancient, unplumbed warrens teem with a twisted, uncatalogued, and unsuspected life?" (851). This feeling of ocular menace and inscrutable authority soon progresses into an actual attempt on the narrator's life, as the inhabitants chase the narrator out of town.

Returning to the question I posed above, what does it mean, for this narrator, to be the object of a gaze imagined to be lethal in its ugliness and otherness? The final twist of the story, meant to be both horrifying and provocative, is that the narrator is, in fact, the great-grandson of Obed Marsh, and after his terrifying ordeal in Innsmouth, his alien great-grandmother begins to beckon to him in his dreams. However, the development of the protagonist's response to the realization that the otherness that terrified and revolted him in Innsmouth also comprises his being offers space for a reading of Lovecraft's story that challenges the rejection of otherness and privileging of impenetrability found in other canonical modernist texts. He does not surrender to suicidal despair at the knowledge that he contains within him the degraded and racialized other, nor does he withdraw into irony because the terms of the plot demand that he cannot absent himself from the situation through language or posturing. Instead, he accepts and embraces his connection to the aliens, and the conclusion of the story finds him planning to join his great-grandmother and live beneath the sea.

I do not mean to argue that "Innsmouth" depicts a progressive and politically operable model for anti-racist or feminist politics. The narrator does not expand his definition of the human to include the aliens; rather, he surrenders his humanity (and, incidentally, his "place in an insurance office" [857]—a quintessential example of the enervating work derided by contemporary social critics), conceptually affirming the ticket clerk's supposition that the "Innsmouth look" can "kill." But he frames the transformation as a liberation, not a degradation: "I … awake with a kind of exaltation instead of terror.… Stupendous and unheard-of splendours await me below, and I shall seek them soon" (858). The narrator's acquiescence to his alien heritage is here an extension of his modernist quest for knowledge: he will discover and witness the "unheard-of splendours" of an unknown world. An earlier story, "Facts Concerning the Late Arthur Jermyn and His Family" (1920), offers a helpful point of comparison. Jermyn, after learning that the wife of his distant ancestor was a white Congolese ape, kills all his children and sets himself on fire ("Arthur Jermyn" 108–109). The decision made by the protagonist of "Innsmouth" to acknowledge and cultivate the unknowable elements of his interiority gesture towards a less violent and self-loathing and more empathetic response to the racial otherness modern life invites and fosters.

The narrator opens his retrospective account by confessing, "I have an odd craving to whisper about those few frightful hours in that ill-rumoured and evilly shadowed seaport of death and blasphemous abnormality. The mere telling helps me to restore confidence in my own faculties" (808). Evident in this introduction are not only the narrator's ambivalence about his experience in Innsmouth and the subsequent discovery about himself, but also his pleasure in sharing his story. Lovecraft's own articulation of his aesthetic also emphasizes the connection between speaker and listener; story and reader: "The one test of the really weird is simply this—whether or not there by excited in the reader a profound sense of attitude of awed listening ("Supernatural" 5). Lovecraft's insistence upon the experiential quality of reading models an encounter with and mutual negotiation of difference that "Innsmouth" rehearses on the level of plot. However, as García Augustín articulates, an ambivalence lurks even within this denial of irony and abstraction:

And as a result [of reading "Innsmouth"], s/he feels as frightened as the character was at the beginning of his journey, because what is most horrible and repulsive is not what s/he has been told, but the way in which s/he feels identified with monstrosity. Lovecraft's tale manages to uncover in its readers the monstrous element which is lurking within each of them; it makes people read with Innsmouth eyes, which are fixedly-looking and never closed [29].

It is this impulse in Lovecraft, and in modernist horror fiction as a genre, that a space for ambivalent connection between writer and reader can be mapped.

Whitworth writes that "Modernist writers distinguish between abstraction and empathy, often claiming to prefer the former" (14), and this supposed preference often manifests itself in the impersonal and "hard" postures of the canonical modernists like Eliot and Hemingway. *Because* Lovecraft writes genre fiction, and *because* the conventions of the genre demand a degree of sensitivity to and consideration of the emotional response of an other outside the author and text, I contend that modernist genre fiction might be a place to discover, even in the canonical authors, an empathetic and progressive strain that comprises a counternarrative to nostalgic despair and detached irony. Neil Gaiman said that "horror is very often the lie that tells the truth about our lives—and in that sense, it's ultimately an optimistic genre" (qtd. by Gilmore 2). In Lovecraft, that optimism expresses itself through the desire not to despise but to embrace the unknown, whether it be found in a mysterious town, an alien race, or in the writer and reader's own self.

Tracy Bealer earned her Ph.D. from the University of South Carolina and teaches literature and composition at Borough of Manhattan Community College, specializing in 20th century American novels. She has published on various authors and filmmakers, as well as the Harry Potter *and* Twilight *series, and coedited* Neil Gaiman and Philosophy. *This essay was first published in the Fall 2010 issue of* Journal of Philosophy.

Shantih Versus Shanty
Lovecraft's Parody of Eliot's Utopian Anxiety

Joseph Milford

No anthology of modern Western poetry would be complete without T.S. Eliot's epic quest poem, "The Waste Land," among its pages. This poem was Eliot's (and Ezra Pound's) most recognizable and quoted work in the Western Canon, and its attempt to conceptualize the psyche of the Western world after World War I was commendable, complex, and ambitious. Eliot embraced modernist tropes of abstract expressionism, French Symbolism, fragmentation, pop-culture references, shifting narratives, scattered literary references, and free verse which could meander through huge cognitive leaps for the audience. Eliot also, while writing in a Modernist style and ethos, expresses the angst, apathy, and alienation which the Modern age brings along with it. As a young English major, ten years before the beginning of the 21st century, my professors often referred to "The Waste Land" as the quintessential Modernist poem—an exemplar of the form.

H.P. Lovecraft's parody of this poem, "Waste Paper," with its crude reference to refuse and toiletries, approaches metapoetics, post-war utopian society, and Modernism in a much different, and humorous noir vein—Lovecraft's poem actually approaches the postmodern and post-avant in its pastiche. Eliot's epic poem was an attempt to restore order after chaos with its questing or remembering voices bent upon surviving the infertility of the industrial war machine and the oncoming technocracy and fascism, which would lend itself to World War II. As the speaker of Lovecraft's poem asserts, "Disillusion is wonderful, I've been told" (line 34); we can observe the double-entendre of the chagrin of Modernism's influence and the need to embrace the irony of it. Post World War I Western thought was rapidly evolving, for better or worse, beyond the transparency which conventional religion or conventional economies could provide the average subway passenger. As Eliot's (Christian) idealism led him to the restoration of "Camelot," or an idea of what Europa could have been or could become in his Fisher King freneticism, Lovecraft's poem, "Waste Paper," embraced the postmodern sense of humor and "pseudocracy" (line 104) which the poet most likely saw as the ridiculous outcome of a new world order based on multi-conglomerate war machines with little regard for the sustenance or spirituality of the individual.

In section V. of Eliot's "The Waste Land," "What The Thunder Said," the poet ends the long poem with the chant, "Shantih shantih shantih" (line 433). According to Eliot's notes on his own poem, the word "shantih" is translated, in English or in the Western sensibility, as "the peace which passeth all understanding" (North 26). In Sanskrit, shanti (Eliot spells it with an "h") is the state of pure bliss which follows knowledge and understanding—a state of bliss which can transport one through duress—a total state of inner peace. Eliot ends his poem with this Hindu chant of spiritual and mental peace; however, has the Fisher King been restored? Has the grail been found? Is Eliot implying that, even after the post-war destruction, that a "peace beyond understanding" has been acquired? This type of "peace" represents a complete contradiction to the machinery of the Modern era and its progressive technology and industrialism. Also, even though this poem invites the use of widespread sampling, from various literary and religious sources, its primary impetus relies on Christianity, and the paganism which Christianity enveloped, when it absorbed the Green Man, Celtic and Druidic traditions, and Arthurian legends, for instance.

Lovecraft, a lifelong atheist, would understandably be skeptical of sampling from religious traditions in such an ambitious epic poem. Eliot also references the Tarot in his poem, but he admits in his own notes on the poem that he uses a card "arbitrarily" and for his own purposes, in "The Waste Land," and he is not really familiar with the Tarot itself (North 6). Lovecraft would also be skeptical of such an "arbitrary" use of mysticism, without irony and humor anyway, to tackle issues of history, religion, the human psyche, and aesthetics. Lovecraft's speaker in his poem admits to a "ringing in his ears" being the "ghost of [a] Jew [he] murdered that Christmas day" (lines 36–37), and even though his tone is ironic and sarcastic throughout the poem, knowing the poem is a parody of Eliot adds even more vitriol to the lines. There are many moments of what Eliot, or other followers of the Anglican Church, might find sacrilegious or blasphemous in Lovecraft's "Waste Paper," and whether these lines are there to mock Eliot directly or to mock a certain vein of Modernism is not completely clear (but both can be assumed). Consequently, Lovecraft's poem does not depend upon an obscuration of literary and religious texts to provide mosaic materials for the construction of higher meaning, or higher levels of peace beyond understanding. "Waste Paper," rather, has the tone and delivery of a street-crier or carny barker, not of the supremely-educated Classical Brit scholar who is contending with the likes of Yeats, Pound, and Joyce in a post Alexander Pope, John Milton, William Blake English lyrical and poetic waste land while also attempting to bring a certain religious tradition into the Modern era through collage and multiple fractured narratives.

It emerges here that Lovecraft does not believe the earnestness of the dramatic monologues of "The Waste Land's" voices. Part V of "The Waste Land" finds us in an almost postapocalyptic desert where no water (no rebirth or fertility) can be found, and the speaker of the poem laments "Falling towers/ Jerusalem Athens Alexandria/ Vienna London" (lines 373–376). These fallen cities represent religion, philosophy and democracy, knowledge and library, art and architecture, commerce and industry, respectively. In contrast, Lovecraft's poem is concerned with references to pop songs, the Cleveland city limits, references to alcohol consumption, and the Leonard-Tendler boxing match. The references in Lovecraft's poem are (purposefully) not of the high mimetic or of the quester allegory—Lovecraft states, in the last two lines of the poem, that nobody is home in the "shantih." No one is to be found in the peace that transcends when there is no peace that ultimately transcends war and the falling of the towers of civilization. Eliot's attempts to tackle the fragmentation of Modernism, using fragments himself of mysticism, myth, religion, and Eastern spirituality, only provide Lovecraft with plenty of fodder for ridicule and criticism. "Waste Paper" avoids all that is "holy" or lofty in the literary sense quite purposefully to demonstrate the folly of writing such an elitist epic in a time when popular culture was binding, for better or worse, the common men of Western culture way more than reading Dickens or Homer was. The "shanty," by another translation, is a lower-class, or poverty-stricken, makeshift shelter, thrown together with post-war, post-colonial, or lowest caste materials. You would be hard-pressed, most likely, to find a copy of "The Waste Land" in a third world shanty-town, ghetto, or barrio home—Lovecraft even asks, in line 93 of "Waste Paper," "Have you a little T.S. Eliot in your home?" This brand of skepticism and sarcasm is so prominent in Lovecraft's parody of Eliot that an obvious statement of class struggle resonates.

The speaker in Lovecraft's poem is not referencing games of chess or speaking of Philomel—he is talking about playing a "zobo" (a cheap kazoo-like instrument) (line 15), riding his bike (line 9), drinking "moonshine hootch" (line 7), and listening to those "darkies singing" (line 17). These images are concentric with the lower classes of the British Empire and the "conquered" "darkies" who are products of British imperialism and colonialism. Colonization creates the shantytown; prejudice creates the shantytown; the aftermath of war creates the shantytown; and economic tyranny creates the shantytown. A quick analysis of British foreign policy in Africa, India, and Asia, circa 1922, when "The Waste Land" was published in its entirety, yields a history of economic violence (and many other forms of violence, of course) towards other nationalities—this, when you consider the British Empire's history in India, makes Eliot's use of a Sanskrit religious phrase in his poem almost atrocious and in poor taste. Once again, in lines 127–129 of "Waste Paper," Lovecraft's speaker ends the poem with "Farewell, farewell, O go to hell/ Nobody home/ In the shantih." This is, of course, another double-entendre. No one has found inner peace, or home, in Modernity or post World War culture, and no one can find meaning or peace in the shan-tytown beyond the basic modes of poverty-stricken survival. Obviously, Lovecraft's con-clusion to his poem is a direct attack on Eliot's presumed idea of replenishment or rebirth—or of how we should enter the Modern era itself. We find ourselves with shantih as prayer versus shanty as the outcome of colonial economic policy, and both of these worlds are colliding in the Modern British milieu. Lovecraft, in "Waste Paper," embraces the common, the pop-culture, the lowbrow, and the accessible quite intentionally in his poem to provide a contrast to Eliot's Classical, literary, Biblical, and esoteric allusions and samplings. Another salt-of-the-earth interpretation of the word shanty is its translation into traditional shipboard working songs. Shanties, or chanteys, were sung onboard ships, primarily in British, American, and Canadian traditions, to pass the time and to create a rhythm for hard labor (Smith). They also were full of folklore, code, humor, warning, and allegory. I find it ironic that Eliot's voice, in "The Waste Land," is searching for water, or the blood of the Grail, when one who sings a shanty would be upon the desert, or waste land, of the ocean itself. Coleridge comes to mind, in "Rime of the Ancient Mariner," when he writes, "Water, water everywhere and not a drop to drink" (lines 121–122). The home of the common man, the shanty, or the song of the common man, the shanty, are quite different from the shantih of the final prayer in "The Waste Land."

Lovecraft, in lines 30–33 of "Waste Paper," mentions a novel titled *Shanty House*; he writes: "...*Shanty House*/ Was the name of a novel by I forget whom/ Published serially in the *All-Story Weekly*." Lovecraft is referring to a literary journal, the *All-Story Weekly*, which published the likes of Edgar Rice Burroughs (of whom Lovecraft was an immense fan) and other British writers of Lovecraft's time. Lovecraft, in a letter of praise and criticism, wrote to the *All-Story Weekly* describing what he considered good and bad choices of publication regarding British literature. In his letter to the editor, he wrote, "William Loren Curtiss tells a homely yet exciting sort of tale which exerts upon the reader a curious fascination. 'Shanty House' seems to me the better of the two he has contributed to The All-Story"

(Hillman). I was unable to find a copy of this story, which Lovecraft references in "Waste Paper," but I found something of interest in his letter to the *All-Story Weekly*, which can possibly further inform his philosophy regarding literature, and why a poem like "The Waste Land" would be so contentious to him. Lovecraft wrote,

> In the present age of vulgar taste and sordid realism it is a relief to peruse a publication such as *The All-Story*, which has ever been and still remains under the influence of the imaginative school of Poe and Verne.
>
> For such materialistic readers as your North-British correspondent, Mr. G.W.P. of Dundee, there are only too many periodicals containing "probable" stories; let *The All-Story* continue to hold its unique position as purveyor of literature to those whose minds cannot be confined within the narrow circle of probability, or dulled into a passive acceptance of the tedious round of things as they are.
>
> If, in fact, man is unable to create living beings out of inorganic matter, to hypnotize the beasts of the forests to do his will, to swing from tree to tree with apes of the African jungle, to restore to life the mummified corpses of the Pharaohs and the Incas, or to explore the atmosphere of Venus and the deserts of Mars, permit us, at least in fancy, to witness these miracles and to satisfy that craving for the unknown, the weird, and the impossible which exists in every active human brain.
>
> Particularly professors and sober Scotch men may denounce it as childish the desire for imaginative fiction; nay, I am not sure but that such a desire is childish, and rightly so, for are not many of man's noblest attributes but the remnants of his young nature? He who can retain in his older years the untainted mind, the lively imagination, and the artless curiosity of his infancy, is rather blessed than cursed; such men as those are our authors, scientists and inventors [Hillman].

This excerpt delineates Lovecraft's affinity towards imaginative flights of fancy and child-like wonder. He draws a distinction between himself and the "professors and sober Scotch men" who have their own idea of what literature should or has to be. Perhaps he would rather be exploring the fantastic wastelands of Mars rather than the metaphysical wastelands of Eliot? This is not to say that Lovecraft is not serious about contributing to the literary tradition of fiction in American and British arts and letters; his and Eliot's interpretation of Poe's influences simply went in different directions, and this is a good thing. Modernism and postmodernism have plenty of room for both of these schools of thought and myriad more.

In all fairness to Eliot and his literary accomplishments, this critic did obsess over one word from his epic poem, the word "shantih," and this reader did so with a hostile influence towards Eliot in mind, one H.P. Lovecraft. Lovecraft, however, demonstrates that this comparison and discussion can provide a useful and interesting window into how British literature was entering and interpreting the Modern era and its burgeoning literature and poetry. Just as there is much more to mine and appreciate in the works of Lovecraft, there is much more to be embraced in the poetry of Eliot, and in "The Waste Land" itself. Eliot's poem was ultimately concerned with how Western culture could avoid losing its humanity in the wake of Modernism, and this question still remains an unresolved one. Lovecraft, also concerned with what British literature was becoming and was to become, as evidenced in his letter to *The All-Story*, wanted there to be room for a significant appreciation of horror, science fiction, stories of the common man and Realism, and the grotesque and arabesque (following Poe in a different way than did Eliot). Obviously, time has shown us that Lovecraft is much more accessible and popular than Eliot, in Western culture, so maybe he was right in his critique and approach all along.

Joseph Milford studied English and philosophy at the University of West Georgia and then received his MFA in poetry at the Iowa Writers' Workshop. His first collection of poetry, Cracked Altimeter, *was published in 2010 and a second collection is forthcoming. He is an English professor for eCore and is working on his doctorate in education while also hosting* The Joe Milford Poetry Show.

The Internal Continuity
of Lovecraft's
Fungi from Yuggoth

JIM MOON

Part I. The Verse of HP Lovecraft

When considering the question of who was the most influential author of weird fiction in the 20th century, HP Lovecraft is a strong contender for the title although during his lifetime he was only appreciated by the readers of pulp magazines such as *Weird Tales*. However despite this limited exposure HPL was soon forging friendships and corresponding with the likes of Robert Bloch, Robert E. Howard, Fritz Leiber, Henry Kuttner, Clark Ashton Smith, Carl Jacobi and Frank Belknap Long—a veritable who's who of the fantastic fiction of the day.

After his death in 1937, his works were reissued in a series of volumes by Arkham House, a small press set up by his friends August Derleth and Donald Wandrei with the express purpose of publishing Lovecraft in book form. Throughout the '40s and '50s, Lovecraft began regularly appearing in anthologies of weird fiction, and the '60s saw his tales being issued in mass market paperbacks. Much like Tolkien, HPL's fiction was keenly embraced by the blossoming counter culture; the Cthulhu mythos proving as equally alluring as the legends of Middle Earth, but also his vein of cosmic horror, filled with sanity stretching visions of the infinite struck a chord with the generation who had discovered mind expanding drugs and esoteric practices.

And he has never been out of print since, with many big names; Stephen King, Clive Barker, Ramsey Campbell, Guillermo del Toro, HR Giger, Neil Gaiman and Alan Moore to name but a few, citing Lovecraft as major influence and inspiration. And Lovecraft's creations are everywhere these days, having inspired countless books, comics, films, records and games. Cthulhu and his kin are seemingly manifesting with increased regularity here, there and anywhere—you can even buy cuddly elder gods now. And even if you've never heard his name, if you are into genre fiction then you have certainly seen his influence somewhere, usually in the form of tentacled beasts, malign elder gods being reawakened to wreak havoc, or tales of aliens influencing early man.

What is less well known is Lovecraft's work as a poet. And in fairness this is largely due to the fact that his poetry lacks the individual flair and imagination that has ensured his stories continue to win ever greater numbers of admirers with each passing year. Indeed much of his poetry has little to do with the strange and fantastic; instead we have political satires, seasonal verses, odes to friends, and poems written adopting classical styles—only occasionally did he pen verse that falls under shadow of the weird. And as the Old Gentleman himself observed in later life, poetry was not his true metier; like many of us, he often wrote poetry for his personal reasons rather than to create great art, and in Lovecraft's case this was to recreate for himself the atmosphere and ethos of the Georgian period—a time in which he felt he would have been more at home than the early decades of the 20th century. As he wrote in 1929—

> Language, vocabulary, ideas, imagery—everything succumbed to my own intense purpose of thinking & dreaming myself back into the world of periwigs and long s's which for some odd reason seemed to me the normal world [Selected Letters 1925–29 p.314–315].

Although increasingly modern readers do not realize that Lovecraft's prose was actually somewhat antiquarian in construction for the '20s and '30s, the bulk of his poetry is clearly archaic, written in forms and styles from the Augustan age, mimicking the verses of Georgian luminaries such as Pope, Goldsmith, and Addison.[1] Of the poems he produced that don't hark back to the 18th century, much of the remainder reflect Lovecraft's other great passion—Edgar Allan Poe. Much of his poetry that may be considered weird verse, echoes of the gothic poetry Poe produced.

However rather tellingly, as his career in prose progresses the less poetry he writes— over three quarters of his poetic output dates from before 1919. Looking at chronologies of his writing, it is very clear that as he embraces the short story as a mode of creative expression his poetic output declines sharply. Seemingly as Lovecraft found his own distinctive voice in prose fiction, the need to conjure up in verse the atmosphere of England in the reign of Queen Anne diminishes. And in his stories he was to find a command of imagery and language that his forays into verse rarely achieved. Although his early works clearly show the influence of Poe and another of his favorites, Lord Dunsany, he soon develops his own distinctive voice and iconic creations.

But he never entirely gave up on poetry, and was still producing occasional verse and poems for friends up until his final years. And while I generally concur with Stephen King's remark in *Danse Macabre* that "the best we can say about his poetry is that he was a competent enough versifier"—damning with faint praise indeed—it must be said that Lovecraft did produce one epic work of verse that deserves to be remembered and more widely appreciated.

Between December 27th 1929 and January 4th 1930, Lovecraft penned a staggering thirty six sonnets, which he arranged into a cycle which he entitled *Fungi from Yuggoth*— which can be read here. And this was to be his last major poetical work; the handful of poems he produced in the remaining years of his life are largely brief verses and odes for friends. It would appear that Lovecraft hit something of poetic peak with this great torrent of sonnets. And unlike much of his other poetry, he throws away the Augustan rulebooks and sees him adopt a variety of differing styles and voices. Unusually for a man somewhat obsessed with classical forms, his sonnets don't follow either of the usual sonnet structures, the Shakespearian and the Petrarchan. Equally unusually, unlike a lot of his other weird verse, *Fungi from Yuggoth* doesn't read like echoes of Poe; these sonnets are pure Lovecraft in tone and theme.

To begin with I should to clear up some confusions about the title. Firstly it has nothing to do with the trans-Plutonian entities, the Mi-go, detailed in his classic tale "The Whisperer in the Darkness" written later in 1930. Although the Mi-go are also referred to as 'fungi from Yuggoth,' the title of this cycle comes from lines in Sonnet XIV "Star Winds":

> This is the hour when moon struck poets know
> What fungi sprout in Yuggoth, and what scents
> And tints of flowers fill Nithon's continents

Several commentators have alleged that these lines appear to be referring to a place or region, rather than as the Cthulhu Mythos name for Pluto which is how Yuggoth is employed in "The Whisperer in Darkness." And this has been held up as evidence of the way that Lovecraft would use the same or similar terms in differing contexts and seemingly to refer to different things in several stories—deliberately building in confusions in his own mythology that mirror the contradictions in real world myth and legend.

And undoubtedly, Lovecraft did play these games with the reader—for example the different references and contexts he attaches to the term 'Old Ones' in several of his tales. However in this case, scholars making the case for the reference in Star Winds to be a Yuggoth that is a place rather than a planet, are forgetting that an earlier entry in the poem cycle, Sonnet IV—Recognition, clearly states that "I knew this strange grey world was not my own,/But Yuggoth, past the starry void," which would suggest that Lovecraft was clearly and consistently thinking of Yuggoth as a world in its own right while writing these poems. So having addressed the issues of the title, what of the actual cycle itself?

The first three sonnets form a distinct narrative which tells of a man who discovers a curious tome in an old bookstore, a volume of forgotten lore that details how to open "the hidden way" to experience visions and/or travel to through the interstellar void to other worlds and into other dimensions and times. However after this opening trilogy in verse, the narrative stops and the remaining thirty three poems all stand alone.

We get a variety of styles and tones; many are miniature stories. Some like Sonnets XI—The Well and XXVI—The Familiars, are told in a poetic approximation of colloquial speech, spinning tales redolent of New England folk lore, others employ the same vivid poetic phrasing as his Dreamlands tales (XIII—Hesperia and XVIII -The Gardens of Yin), and of course some invoke the creeping horrors of the Cthulhu Mythos canon (XV—Antarktos and XX—Night-Gaunts).

But also among this exercises in micro weird fiction, we have verses detailing strange visions; some revisit lost dreams (XXIII Mirage) and others melancholy whimsy (XXIX—Nostalgia). And also thrown into the mix are verses of a more philosophical bent; for example sonnets like XXVIII—Expectancy and XXX—Background illustrate Lovecraft's own reasons for writing.

In the introductions and forewords of many collections and anthologies, the following quote appears—

> All my stories, unconnected as they may be, are based on the fundamental lore of legend that this world was at one time inhabited by another race who, in practicing black magic, lost their foothold and were expelled, yet live on outside ever ready to take possession of this earth.

However, scholars have been unable to find a source for this alleged quote, and currently it is believed that this sound bite was actually created by August Derleth, who incidentally also coined the term 'Cthulhu Mythos' to describe the shared background lore of places, books and entities that populate many of Lovecraft's fictions.

Indeed the above quote is hardly accurate of Lovecraft's canon, and not even apt for his Mythos stories alone. It's very applicable for "The Dunwich Horror" but not so much for *At the Mountains of Madness* where the eldritch threats come from beyond the stars. And although best known for his Cthulhu Mythos tales, not all of his canon fits under this umbrella, for example his Dreamlands tales, are concerned with a fantastical world inspired by the work of Lord Dunsany and although some are horror tales, few feature the usual elder gods arising from an aeons long sleep.

As Ramsey Campbell points out in his introduction to his own collection of Lovecraft-inspired tales "Cold Print," a better description comes from one of Lovecraft's own letters. In 1935, HPL remarked that

> Nothing is really typical of my efforts…. I'm simply casting about for better ways to crystallise and capture certain strong impressions (involving the elements of time, the unknown, cause and effect, fear, scenic and architectural beauty and other ill assorted things) which persist in clamouring for expression."

Not only is this a more helpful and indeed more accurate overview of the premises that underlie all his works, Cthulhu Mythos or not, but it is also a good summary of the themes and motifs presented in *Fungi from Yuggoth*.

In many ways, this sonnet cycle is like a tour through the different aspects of Lovecraft's fiction, visiting the varied aesthetics and concepts underpinning his stories. As a whole the cycle is like condensed Lovecraft, and although some of his most famous creations, Cthulhu and Yog Sothoth don't get a name check, the verses do reflect the core ideas and atmosphere of the stories that do feature them.

Structurally the cycle as a whole is often interpreted as a series of visions or encounters the unnamed narrator of the first three sonnets unleashes from the stolen tome. And this approach does make a certain sense; as *Fungi from Yuggoth* begins as a narrative, it is only natural that readers expect there is some scheme stretching through the rest of the cycle. Others, however, see the opening linked verses merely as an introduction or framing device for a random selection of poems lumped together as they were written in the same burst of creativity, or alternatively that Lovecraft had begun the cycle with an idea of a narrative thread that he quickly abandoned.

Indeed in *A Subtle Magick—The Writings and Philosophy of HP Lovecraft* (Wildside Press, 1996) the high priest of Lovecraft scholarship, ST Joshi claims that "it seems difficult to deny that the dominant feature of this sonnet cycle is utter randomness of tone, mood and import" (p.234). He considers the series of visions approach as a "very implausible interpretation" and furthermore discounts any claims to a thematic continuity, arguing that there is no real system to the cycle as just because they share common tropes, as the presence of the same shared elements in his stories do not connect all the stories and novels in his canon into one uber-work. Joshi's concluding assessment is that *Fungi from Yuggoth* was an attempt to crystallize a plethora of story seeds and fragments in poetic form as "an imaginative house cleaning" and "a versified commonplace book."

However I have several problems with this conclusion. Firstly, many writers keep a commonplace book—a tome where stray ideas, quotes and other inspirations are noted down—as indeed Lovecraft did. Furthermore HPL's commonplace books have the origins of many of the sonnets in them. So quite why he would feel the need to note them again in verse form seems a little perplexing. While it may be argued the cycle was an attempt to give these unused ideas some form of creative expression, I find it difficult to believe that Lovecraft would have no other artistic purpose in mind other than releasing some imaginative pressure.

Secondly Lovecraft paid very close attention to the form and structure of his works. He was a master stylist; choice of spelling, length of phrasing and even the placement of every punctuation mark mattered a great deal to him. He was often greatly annoyed by the edits imposed by the pulp magazine editors; seeing the glosses to his texts as ruining his carefully crafted prose. And somewhat unfortunately until ST Joshi began examining the original manuscripts, no one had realized that the texts printed by Arkham House and subsequent publishers were in fact quite corrupt.

Therefore, I find it difficult to credit that such a meticulous literary craftsman as Lovecraft would just collect together thirty six sonnets without any thought to structural arrangement. Personally I have always favored the interpretation that after the opening trilogy the rest of the cycle is a kaleidoscope of visions from beyond conjured by the cobwebbed tome. Furthermore I believe there is a definite scheme of links in the arrangement of the verses. If one looks closely at the order of the poems and carefully examine their content—the tone, imagery, and themes featured, it would appear that this trip through Lovecraft's universe is not quite as random as many have thought.

But while the scholars of weird fiction have much debated the orchestration of *Fungi from Yuggoth*, it would appear that there is something to this arrangement of sonnets that appeals to musicians. As early as 1932, Harold E Farnese, dean of the Los Angeles Institute of Musical Art, wrote to Lovecraft proposing they collaborate on a one act Cthulhoid operetta to be named *Fen River* and set on Yuggoth. *Fungi from Yuggoth* had apparently inspired this proposed project, and Farnese had already set two of the sonnets, Mirage (XXIII) and The Elder Pharos (XXVII) to music. Unfortunately this collaboration never happened, and sadly the two compositions Farnese's wrote appear to have vanished into the ether too.

With the boom of interest in Lovecraft in the '60s and '70s, unsurprisingly Lovecraft inspired songs and titles began to regularly appear, with even folk/psychedelic outfit naming themselves HP Lovecraft. However it wasn't until the late '80s that any of the sonnets from *Fungi from Yuggoth* appeared in musical form. In 1989, small press publishers Fedogan & Bremer issued a cassette of the complete cycle set to music, and this version of the cycle is easily my favorite of all the many readings of this work available. The narrator John Arthur gives a fantastic performance, adopting different voices and intonations for the readings and the music by Mike Olsen is atmospheric, eerie and beautiful. Although reissued on CD some years later, sadly this work is now out of print, and as Fedogan and Bremer seem to be lost in some administrative limbo it seems unlikely we'll see it released again any time soon. However you can hear the complete cycle in several parts on YouTube.

Jim Clark has also recorded a reading of the cycle set to music. Again this can be found on YouTube with some quite strange animations of Lovecraft 'performing' the vocals. Also Colin Timothy Gagnon has done a reading set to his own compositions which is available for download. Plus Greek composer Dionysis Boukouvalas has an ongoing project to set the cycle to music.

More recently, though, Rhea Tucanae (one of the aliases of electronic artist Dan Söderqvist) has teamed up with Pixyblink to adapt eleven of the sonnets into musical pieces. And the results are quite stunning—after many years the Arthur/Olsen version finally has a rival for my affections. Dark and very evocative, this is a superb LP which had me reaching for the credit card as soon as I heard it. The only downside is that it only comprises a small portion of the cycle and naturally some favorites aren't included. But nevertheless this is a fine piece of work, and I can only hope a second volume will appear at some point.

I think one of the reasons *Fungi from Yuggoth* has proved to be so popular with musicians and readers is that there is great variety in the sonnets themselves; they other a diversity of voices and language which inspires performances. Of course there is also the fact that the cycle is a marvelous piece of writing.

And while it's unlikely anyone is going rank *Fungi from Yuggoth* above classic works by Keats or T.S. Eliot, it is a very pleasurable read. The simplicity of many of the verses echoes in the mind and its gentler verses show a lighter, less doom-laden side to Lovecraft. He may have never had the talent to be regarded a great poet but with *Fungi from Yuggoth*, he did produce a remarkable work of verse. Poetically speaking, the sonnets may be simply, even naively, constructed but that does not detract from the beauty, imagination, and atmosphere they conjure.

Part II. A Tour of Yuggoth

The question of whether there is actually any form of continuity in HP Lovecraft's sonnet cycle, *Fungi from Yuggoth* is one that has perplexed both scholars and readers for many years. After the opening three sonnets, which form a linked narrative, the cycle plunges from location to location, through different worlds and times, and crosses a plethora of genres. And as mentioned earlier, while some have argued that there is a thematic thread linking the poems, others, such as noted Lovecraft expert ST Joshi, firmly believes there is not. The sonnets, such critics assume, are simply a kind of anthology of story seed fragments in verse form.

However, there are some problems with such an assumption. Lovecraft had not previously assembled any of his poetry in a grab-bag manner; three poems written in 1918 'Oceanus,' 'Clouds' and 'Mother Earth' were entitled *A Cycle of Verse*. Similarly the only other collection of verse in his poetic career was *Poemata Minora Vol. II* written in 1902, and was a collection on five poems about Roman times which, as the dedication makes clear, are intended to be read as a series. Therefore there is no reason to assume that Lovecraft was merely anthologizing disparate verses with *Fungi from Yuggoth*; this approach is simply too slapdash for the Old Gentleman. If he united these thirty sonnets under a single banner, then he most likely had some design for this arrangement.

But the question remains—what form does this continuity take? A major stumbling block and what perplexes many readers and critics is the way the cycle shifts through different genres; sonnets like XII—"The Howler" recalls Lovecraft's New England horror tales such as "The Picture in the House" and "In The Vault," others like XVIII—"The Gardens of Yin" feel like his Dreamlands tales such as "Celephais" and "The White Ship," while yet others clearly belong to the Cthulhu Mythos.

Perhaps, though, approaching the cycle in terms of the genres Lovecraft wrote in is the problem. Generally, readers know Lovecraft through his stories first and then discover his other literary works such as his poetry and his letters, thus coming to *Fungi from Yuggoth* with categories based upon his fiction in mind.

Typically, a new reader coming to the Lovecraft canon will be reading his Cthulhu Mythos tales first, and given the tantalizing nature of this created mythology the novice will then be scouring all his works for further references and allusions. And as readers progress though his body of work or delve into the work of Lovecraft criticism, they soon begin to assume that different tales must fit into different schools of stories: Cthulhu mythos, Dreamlands, etc.

It should be noted, though, that Lovecraft himself did not acknowledge any such distinctions. While in hindsight we may discern evolving trends in his fiction career, reading his fiction chronologically allows us to witness such influences come and go and see Lovecraft's own style developing. Lovecraft himself was merely trying with each successive work to create the perfect weird tale, and the creation of what we now refer to as the Cthulhu Mythos was just one of the literary devices he employed to evoke the feelings of fear and cosmic awe he was striving for.

Therefore when we read *Fungi from Yuggoth* and begin slotting the sonnets into different categories, we are in fact creating artificial divisions, building critical walls that obscure whatever continuity may be there in the complete cycle. And if we dispense with these literary classifications and concentrate on the content, tone and atmosphere of the verses, *Fungi from Yuggoth* begins to appear far more coherent.

To begin, if we survey the placement of the different varieties of verse, although the content and style may seem to be randomly jumping around, there is a distinct flow. It is telling that the more philosophical vignettes cluster around the close of the cycle, seeming to serve as conclusions to the motifs explored. Similarly, other themes are found nestling close to each other.

The arrangement is a bit more complex than Lovecraft merely organizing around recurring themes, though. Each verse follows up on a specific element from its immediate predecessor. While some sonnets echo their predecessors' dominant concepts or continue a theme, others share a location or similar geography with their predecessors.

Admittedly, this interpretation is just a tentative theory, I make no claims that the continuity I have found is the correct reading Lovecraft intended. And indeed there aren't perfect links between all the sonnets, but the following detailed examination does show that *Fungi from Yuggoth* is far from being as utterly random as some believe it is.

After the first three sonnets, whose links are explicit, Sonnet IV can be read as continuing the narrative. Sonnet III—"The Key" refers to visions the narrator has had of "sunset spires and twilight woods that brood/beyond this earth's precisions," while Sonnet IV—"Recognition" is set in a "hollow of old oaks" on the grey world of Yuggoth. It is not too much of a stretch to suggest that this first vision from the book is of the afore mentioned "twilight woods," which "The Key" implies have been haunting the narrator for years. Also it is worth noting at this point that Sonnet XXXIV—"Recapture" could well be a sequel to "Recognition"—featuring as it does a similar strange wilderness and ancient ruins—certainly it would explain the closing lines of "Recapture":

> I shrieked—and *knew* what primal star and year
> Had sucked me back from man's dream-transient sphere!

Sonnet V—"Homecoming" has the narrator, having been horrified by the trip to Yuggoth, "the daemon"—a figure that arguably reappears later—whisks him away to another time and place. And the next scene shows a panorama of a fantastic city—the "sunset spires" alluded to in The Key. Again we may infer from The Key that Sonnets III and IV are the book and its daemon revealing to the narrator the origin of these twin visions that have been haunting him.

The closing lines of IV come from the daemon "'here was your home' he mocked 'when you had sight.'" Fittingly, the next three entries in the cycle are themed around vision and perplexing sights—VI—"The Lamp" closes with "vast shapes" seen in "a mad flash," and these maddening glimpses are echoed by the insane sight the mailman experiences in IV—"Zaman's Hill." This 'sight' trilogy concludes with VIII—"The Port," where the verse's narrator is troubled by the sight of darkness swallowing the streets of Innsmouth.

The next sonnet, IX—"The Courtyard" also takes place in an "ancient, leprous" city by the sea, with the narrator wandering through the dark lanes and alleys. The transition between the sonnets works very cinematically: from the hill top view of Innsmouth, the imaginary camera zooms in and dissolves into the similar seaside location of "The Courtyard." It concludes with the narrator surrounded by a strange ritual throng. It is also worth mentioning that 'the man' the narrator is going to meet may in fact be the previously mentioned daemon.

Sonnet X—"The Pigeon-Flyers" again takes place in a strange dark city, opening with the lines 'They took me slumming,' and again, I don't think we are stretching a narrative point to interpret this as the narrator being swept away to darker places by "the mad revels of the dragging dead" of the previous verse.

Admittedly, a greater leap of faith is required to connect the next sonnet. The horrors of "The Pigeon-Flyers" concludes upon certain things being unearthed from alien crypts, whereas XI—"The Well" has New England farmers delving deep into the bowels of the earth and discovering madness and death. While this link may be subtle to the point of tenuousness, there is a faint accord here.[2]

The next sonnet fits more comfortably: XII—"The Howler" is another micro weird tale set New England. It is almost as if the guiding force behind the visions is saying "and further down the road from Seth Atwood's farm this happened." Many commentators identify "the four pawed thing with human face" as a precursor to Brown Jenkin in "Dreams in the Witch-House," which Lovecraft would write two years later. But it could well be a reference to the ghasts featured in Zealia Bishop's "The Mound" which HPL "revised" (heavily rewrote) in the same period as penning *Fungi from Yuggoth*. Alternatively, and more likely in my opinion, this mystery beast is a call back to "Pickman's Model" which features Lovecraft's conception of the legendary ghoul.[3] And this tale explicitly states these bestial beings can evolve from humans and have strong ties to the old witch cults: "One canvas shewed a ring of them baying about a hanged witch on Gallows Hill, whose dead face held a close kinship to theirs."

"The Howler" takes places at sunset, and the next verse, XIII—"Hesperia," follows this with a truly cosmic vision inspired by "the winter sunset, flaming beyond spires/and chimneys." Again this is another cinematic dissolve with one sunset bleeding into another. Lovecraft continues with another image-based link, for after sunset comes twilight and according to Sonnet XIV—"The Star Winds," this is the time that the star winds blow, breathing strange dreams across the land.

Next Sonnet XV—"Antarktos" begins with what may be one of these dreams: "Deep in my dream the great bird whispered queerly" of a strange structure jutting from the ice that entombs an ancient demon.[4]

In contrast to horrors buried beneath centuries of glaciers, Sonnet XVI—"The Window" brings us more benign visions. While the two poems may seem unconnected, Lovecraft extends his motifs of hidden secrets and revealing dreams by presenting a contrast—after all, not all dreams are nightmares. "Antarktos" deals with dream visions that blast the sanity, whereas the curious aperture in "The Window" reveals wonders; it is a portal to "all the wild worlds of which my dreams had told."

If we once again imagine the cycle in cinematic terms, the exotic landscape of Sonnet

XVII—"A Memory" conceivably is one of the "wild worlds" we reach by travelling through the window of the previous sonnet. On more certain ground however is XVIII—"The Gardens of Yin," a dream vision of a wondrous garden viewed through gates "flung open" by "old dreams," concluding this quartet of dream related verse.

Overlapping into the next sonnet, XIX—"The Bells," is the theme of questing for revelations (as seen in XVII and XVIII)—the narrator in this verse scours his "dreams and memories for a clue" to the persistent phantom peals. However "The Bells" also begins a quartet that explores the Cthulhu Mythos—beginning with Innsmouth and once again this benighted town leads to alien locations in the nether world, hinting of the undersea horrors Lovecraft would later detail in "The Shadow Over Innsmouth."

Next, the narrator of Sonnet XX—"Night-Gaunts" is swept away by the titular beings to encounter other aquatic horrors. The location of the Peaks of Thok is somewhat obscure; in his early fantasy novel *The Dream-Quest of Unknown Kadath*, Lovecraft locates these titanic mountains in the Underworld of his Dreamlands; however, other sources and writers have identified Thok as one of the moons of Yuggoth.

This particular verse was inspired by HPL's childhood nightmares and previously the Night-Gaunts had appeared in *Dream-Quest*, one of his tales centering on his recurring Randolph Carter who in the novel sets out to find a sunset city seen in his dreams...

...And the main adversary in that curious tome is the star of Sonnet XXI—"Nyarlathotep." Also like its predecessor this verse is based on a nightmare Lovecraft had, which he had previously attempted to turn into a short story back in 1920. This vision of the apocalypse closes with the line "the idiot Chaos[5] blew earth's dust away" and the next sonnet details this entity, the daemon sultan Azathoth, who also appears in *Dream-Quest* and the afore mentioned Peaks of Thok are colloquially named "Azathoth's Teeth." As Mythos scholars will know, Nyarlathotep serves the Other Gods, of whom Azathoth is chief, and hence "the daemon" mentioned in XXII is indubitably the same entity and, I'd argue, is the same daemon we met earlier in V- "Homecoming."

"Azathoth" claims that this being, bubbling in the center of all infinity, creates all worlds and dimensions in the cosmos. Appropriately, the next two poems concern strange worlds in hidden dimensions. XXIII—"Mirage" concerns a lost realm "floating dimly on Time's stream" and XXIV—"The Canal" features an evil place "somewhere, in dream." Now this isn't as much as a stretch as it first seems as in Lovecraft's fiction dreams are often visits to other dimensions. With its tolling bells and uncertain placement in time and space, "Mirage" echoes both sonnets XIX and XVII. The world of "The Canal" appears to be a dark counter part of the realm detailed in XIII, but also recalls the grim dead cities of IX and X.

And in a similar shift between IX and X, the dark deserted streets of The Canal dissolve into "the mad lanes" "south of the river" where the great black spire of St Toad's lurks in Sonnet XXV. As Lovecraft scholar Robert M. Price points out in his article "St. Toad's Hagiography," this sonnet possibly inspired the scene in "The Shadow Over Innsmouth" when the protagonist, Robert Olmstead, stumbles across a not dissimilar church. Considering we have twice returned to this benighted town in the cycle, it is not difficult to believe that Innsmouth is the home to St Toad's. Certainly it would appear we are back in our world, somewhere in Lovecraft's haunted New England.

Both the geographical setting and the theme of blasphemous worship are continued in Sonnet XXVI—"The Familiars." Another of the New England horrors, this sonnet tells of an isolated farmer who becomes obsessed with hidden lore and after "he began those night howls"—presumably some form of ritual or worship—his neighbors who fear for his sanity discover him "talking to two crouching things / That at their step flew off on great black wings."[6] And this leads in neatly to XXVIII—"The Elder Pharos," where another hermit, this time in Lovecraft's mythical region Leng, talks "to chaos with the beat of drums."[7]

As well as communication with eldritch entities, "The Elder Pharos" also features a mysterious light that shines out from the fantastic vistas of Leng, whose origin many "in man's first youth" have sought out but have never returned. And the next verse, XXVIII—"Expectancy," echoes this theme of questing into mysteries that can never be unraveled. Again this is a contrasting pair—"The Elder Pharos" contains a sinister mystery that dooms all who seek to unravel it, whereas "Expectancy" is about never quite grasped yet rewarding transcendent hints that some things inspire in us. Like "Antarktos" and "The Window," this pair highlights the fact that awe and terror are two sides of the same revelatory coin.

XXIX—"Nostalgia" also addresses the questing theme, and in this case we have both a lost legendary location, echoing "The Elder Pharos" and the mysterious inner hints of "Expectancy." Here the birds fly out looking for a city "in some land their inner memories know" but which is now vanished beneath the waves. And aside from continuing a theme, tonally this sonnet has the same air of what I would term "magical melancholy" as the preceding sonnet.

And this air, evoking nostalgia in its truest sense, continues in the next sonnet which explores a similar bonding with landscape and architecture. However in XXX—"Background," the narrator has discovered the key to his own transcendent visions—the historic townscape of his youth. Unfortunately, not all such ancient buildings offer such delightful reveries, as the next sonnet reveals.

XXXI—"The Dweller" is another micro tale, telling of an expedition to excavate some curious ruins that were "old when Babylon was new." And rather than a treasure left "from times of cautious leaven," these antediluvian ruins hold a frightening secret that has the archaeologists (a Miskatonic University party I'd wager) fleeing in terror. While providing a contrast to XXX, "The Dweller" also reintroduces the theme of strange revelations which is picked up in the next verse.

XXXII—"Alienation" deals with the price of gaining outré knowledge. Like Gulliver in Swift's famous novel, the narrator here discovered that his mystic voyages have destroyed his connections to his family and his ordinary life—indeed the final two lines of this sonnet are an apt epigraph for the finale of Gulliver's Travels. Incidentally the Ghooric Zone is a region located on Yuggoth's moon, Thog which we heard about in X- "The Pigeon-Flyers," and later Cthulhu Mythos tales have identified as the location of the "foul lake where the puffed shoggoths splash in doubtful sleep" in XX—"Night-Gaunts." The "piping from the voids beyond" is a reference to XXII—evidently the dreamer in this verse unwittingly found his way to the center of all infinity and beholding the blind nuclear madness of Azathoth "giv[ing] each frail cosmos its eternal law" has destroyed all perception of meaning in his life.

And the piping from the Daemon sultan's court can be heard again in XXXIII—"Harbour Whistles." Here notes from the ship's whistles are "fused into one cosmic drone" that "echoes outer voids." But also this naturally evolving sound recalls the transcendent hints contained in the "half-heard songs" of XXVIII and the occult keys to other realms the stolen book of I–III contains.

Fittingly (if somewhat tenuously) XXXIV—"Recapture" appears to be almost a replay of the first vision from the stolen book, IV- "Recognition." As I remarked earlier, the imagery and setting is remarkably similar and the final lines would imply that the narrator has found himself once more in "that hollow of old oaks." And if we interpret this sonnet as a return to that wooded altar on Yuggoth, then we could assume that this visit takes place before IV—note that the narrator claims he realizes "what primal star and year" has brought him back here. Combined with the title itself, "Recapture," the implication appears to be that this is how the narrator ends up a "body spread on that dank stone," an unclean feast for things that "were not men."

And the cycle could have ended there; however, two more sonnets remain. Throughout this series of verse, as we have seen Lovecraft has been alternately delivering poems that evoke terror and awe; for every dark benighted city where eldritch horrors dwell there is a fantastical place laden with beauty and inspiration. Hence XXXV is a bright reflection of "Recapture"—instead of the sinister dark woods and ruins, "Evening Star" has a rural meadow. And instead of some nameless fate in the hands of horrors from outside the stars, we have visions of the sunlit realms and magical landscapes evoked in earlier poems, such as the world beyond "The Window," "the land where beauties meaning flowers" or "The Gardens of Yin." And similar to its predecessor, this penultimate verse echoes an early vision from the stolen book, V—"Homecoming." However, here we have the narrator himself experiencing the revelation rather than being informed by the mocking daemon, and reaching this inner knowledge provides an optimistic conclusion to all the other verses that detail well loved lands now lost and out of reach, and all curious vistas that have invoked dim impossible memories of previous visits.

The final sonnet, XXXVI, in the light of this article the somewhat ironically titled "Continuity," is similarly conclusive; although the exact nature of the secret hints, tantalizing clues, and hidden keys remain obscure, Lovecraft finds a balance and a purpose in these veiled signs. While other sonnets have been draped in melancholy and longing, "Continuity" sees the narrator discovering that these mysterious impressions ultimately provide a connection to the cosmos, a sense of being part of "the fix'd mass whose sides the ages are."

Perhaps very tellingly this verse strongly echoes Lovecraft's own words on his writing which I shall quote again here—

> I'm simply casting about for better ways to crystallise and capture certain strong impressions (involving the elements of time, the unknown, cause and effect, fear, scenic and architectural beauty and other ill assorted things) which persist in clamouring for expression."

However "Continuity" gives us reasons why such impressions were so important to capture.

While some have brought madness and horror, others have revealed the wonders of the cosmos. And a handful are somewhat ambiguous—for example although his neighbors are horrified by what they discover John Whateley has summoned out of the nether world, is this rural occultist as terrified as they are by his unearthly visitors? Similarly in "The Window," the masons are horrified by the opening of the portal but the narrator is enraptured. And in "The Bells," is the realization that the phantom tolling is emanating from a sunken city beneath the waves a revelation of horror or wonder? If familiar with the goings-on in Innsmouth, then one may assume this is a dread realization, but it is worth recalling how the end of "The Shadow Over Innsmouth" plays out...

As I hope I have demonstrated, once the artificial categories we use to classify Lovecraft's fiction are stripped away, the arrangement of sonnets in *Fungi from Yuggoth* actually contain considerably more links and continuity than have been previously noted. And while Lovecraft uses a variety of different methods to establish a subtle flow throughout the cycle, striving and yearning for revelation have been the dominant recurrent themes.

Thus sonnets such as XXIII "Mirage" and XXXIV "Recapture" are not as different as at first they may seem: They may be written in different modes and employ dissimilar imagery, but both detail a transcendent experience. As a devotee of weird fiction, Lovecraft understood the pleasure one gains from reading a tale that evokes a sudden and strong fear, and that such states "cut the moment's thongs" in a similar way that a beautiful landscape may induce reveries—both fear and awe may be keys to transcendence.

Before beginning this epic tour of the *Fungi from Yuggoth*, we alluded to the fact that structurally the placement of the poems is telling. And now having seen how Lovecraft has distributed the various sonnets, we see that there is a definite progressive pursuit of themes through the cycle. Wonder and terror play off each other as we tumble through his universe; though some of those who seek to unravel the mysteries of the cosmos may well fall foul of the vast horrors that populate the myriad dimensions and worlds, others will discover marvels to behold.

Taken together these twin strands ultimately resolve into the conclusion of Continuity—indeed if one ventures too far, he or she may be confronted with the final truth of all things, which in Lovecraft's fictional universe is the dread horror that is Azathoth. However, what distinguishes Lovecraft from the hordes of imitators, and indeed many other horror writers, is that the terror isn't simply due to discovering there's a monster behind everything. The real horror is that there is a "god" that created our reality but he is mindless and indifferent. Humanity's fortunes are left to whims of Nyarlathotep.

Reflecting Lovecraft's own rational beliefs, his devotion to science leaving no room for a benevolent god, the nuclear chaos that is the daemon sultan Azathoth is a symbol of the horror of realizing we are adrift in a godless universe and our lives are not only cosmically insignificant, but totally meaningless.

Despite his rationality, though, Lovecraft also clearly felt the lure of spiritual—although he could not countenance a belief in a god; mythology, legend, and arcane still called to him. And in literature, in history, and in his dreams he found a spiritual transcendence of his own devising. It may have been more aesthetic than religious in nature, but his reading of Machen, Blackwood, Dunsany, and Poe, as well as his travels to visit antiquarian buildings and historical sites, opened these personal inner doors.

The close of the cycle seems to suggest that Lovecraft believes it is the taste of the mysteries and not their resolutions that matter. When speaking of these intimations of infinitude in XXVIII—"Expectancy," he remarks that "none gains or guesses what it hints at giving," and as the cycle shows pursuing these strange hints and impressions may bring one to confront the shattering truth of Azathoth. However, in the final two sonnets, we arrive at a balance: one may not ever be able to discover the origin of these mystical impressions that haunt us, the land of lost dreams may remain out of reach, but approached in the right manner the fact that they do move us may provide an anchor in a sea of uncertainty.

The guiding laws that govern our world may be the creation of Azathoth's whims, but we still may meaningfully connect with the cosmos—not all realms are wastelands of horror; there are bright worlds of dreams and vision where beauty and wonder flower. They may not be any cosmic salvation in Lovecraft's cosmology, but there is personal redemption in the understanding that through poetry, fiction, music, and beauty, we may step outside of ourselves and see a wider world of wonders, if only fleetingly.

Jim Moon is a writer, broadcaster, and artist. He assembles annotated and illustrated anthologies of classic weird tales and narrates audiobooks of vintage ghost stories. He also produces the regular podcast Hypnogoria *discussing weird fictions. He is working on a pair of scholarly volumes on M.R. James.*

The Haunter of the Library
What Lovecraft Taught Me

Brad Strickland

When I reached the age of twelve, my parents agreed that I was old enough to go to the library on my own. Extreme nearsightedness and childhood asthma had made me a bookworm, unsuited for baseball or football. Books were my consolation and escape. The problem was getting hold of them.

In Hall County, Georgia, the library at that time was in the basement of the court house near the Gainesville town square. Up until my birthday that year I could talk my dad into driving me in maybe once a month. Being able to go unaccompanied meant more frequent visits.

For me it was close to a two-mile walk each way. My family was too poor for me to have a bike, and anyway, my mother wouldn't have trusted me to ride a bike in city traffic (maybe one car every five minutes) and not get flattened by a chicken truck.

However, walking was safe enough for her to agree. From then on, once a week I'd take the trip into Gainesville, to the library, and then back home. I'd check out four books each time—that was the limit then—and by the following Thursday I'd have read them all and would be ready for more.

Quickly I read through all of the children's-section books on dinosaurs. I remember asking the librarian if I could check out some adult books on paleontology. She had to look the word up and then said she thought I could handle them. The library had several books by Roy Chapman Andrews, and I read them all. In fiction, my tastes ran to mysteries—Agatha Christie, John Dickson Carr, Ellery Queen—and I'd read a few paperbacks, but the library had hardcovers, and once I had permission to look in the adult section, I ripped into these.

And then there was weird fiction, meaning science fiction, fantasy, and horror. I read a lot of Poe, I remember, and Mary Shelley's *Frankenstein* (though I thought the Monster talked too much), and Bram Stoker's *Dracula*. Then one day I discovered *The Omnibus of Science Fiction,* edited by the oddly-named Groff Conklin. It was a fat book, an anthology of forty-three short stories, arranged by topic. The first one in the section on outer space was by a writer whose name I did not know, H.P. Lovecraft. The story was "The Colour Out of Space." It was the first one I read.

And it hooked me.

"West of Arkham, the hills rise wild, and there are valleys with trees no axe has ever cut."

Within a few paragraphs I learned that the countryside was about to be flooded for a new reservoir. As it happened, my grandfather had just had to move because his farm was about to be flooded for Lake Lanier, a new artificial lake and reservoir. I immediately felt a kind of connection to old Ammi Pierce. The narrator turned out to be a young fellow surveying for the new dam and reservoir, and he vividly described coming across a strange patch of ground, a blasted heath. No one wanted to talk about it, the narrator said. It was … *eldritch.*

Lovecraft sent me to the dictionary, and not for the last time. As I read that story, and as I hunted out and read more and more stories by the man, I gained a considerable vocabulary and regretted only that daily life gave me no occasion to use it: *amorphous; antediluvian; charnel; chthonic; cyclopean; daemonic; effulgence; foetid; gibbous; noisome; stygian; tenebrous.* Wouldn't it be cool to remark casually, "This tenebrous evening is practically chthonic!" I never tried. How would you pronounce *chth*?

The grabber of "Colour," though, was what happened: a meteor fell from the sky and somehow … *hatched out,* I suppose … a life-form that seemed merely a shifting color (or colour—for a time I tried to spell things the British way, but my teacher put her foot down) but that somehow fed on life-energy, killing and turning crops gray and brittle, making animals virtually disintegrate, and then, worst of all, going to work on humans whose mind it sapped as it took their living energies and dissolved their flesh.

Though I went on to read most of the stories in the anthology, encountering writers whose work I would later enjoy—Sprague de Camp, Theodore Sturgeon, James Blish, Richard Matheson, Ray Bradbury, John D. MacDonald, and others (it was a boys' game back then, you see)—"The Colour Out of Space" seemed to stick most firmly in my mind.

As mentioned, I returned to the library time after time and read all the Lovecraft I could discover. Usually I had to look in collections, and all too often the same three or four stories would appear in them. Then in a news stand I found a Lancer paperback, *The Dunwich Horror and Others,* that included a slew of familiar and unfamiliar tales: the title story, of course, and "Pickman's Model," "The Rats in the Walls," "The Call of Cthulhu," "The Whisperer in Darkness," "The Shadow Out of Time," and others. I think the book cost all of fifty cents, but I bought it and just knowing it was out there led me to discover yet more paperback collections.

By then I had become a teenager, interested not only in reading but in trying to write. My dad worked in a cotton mill, and in our little town, job opportunities were limited. I knew that, poor though we were, somehow or other I was going to college to find wider horizons. At the age of thirteen I got my first paper route to save money for education. By the time I was fifteen, I also was helping with a milk route and squirreling the funds away. Still, I always had a little cash to buy paperbacks at Uncle Jack's News Stand in downtown Gainesville. Once as I handed him my quarters, Uncle J. himself said to me, "You read the damndest books," and probably I did.

One reason is that somehow or other, without planning it, I had begun to read analytically, watching myself read, and when something surprised or pleased me, I'd ask, *Now, how did the writer do that?* Then I'd re-read to discover the trick. Lovecraft taught me a lesson that perhaps no one else, not Charles Dickens, not William Faulkner, not Virginia Woolf, could have taught me: *Make the reader your partner.*

Lovecraft left things up to the reader's imagination. He could produce an indescribable horror, trusting the reader to imagine just how awful it was. He could write with aplomb of the *thing that could not be,* confident that his reader would conjure up something more shocking and more terrifying than anything that could be pinned down on paper or pictured up on a movie screen.

At the same time I was reading Lovecraft, I was staying up late on Friday nights to see the Big Movie Shocker on Atlanta's WAGA-TV. Hosted by an art-film aficionado, George Ellis—in the guise of clownish "Bestoink Dooley"—this show featured some fine old Universal horror films along with a considerable amount of schlock, from the Karloff *Frankenstein* to something called *Kronos,* about a blocky, hundred-foot-tall metal monster that looked like a metal skyscraper with an observatory dome on the roof pounding along on two short legs and a long cylindrical one that simply pistoned up and down. It was a machine sent by aliens to rob the Earth of energy—sort of a robotic electric vampire, and you know how terrifying that would look.

In short, I liked the films, but none of them ever scared me. I never looked away from a shock moment.

At some point I realized that none of the movies had been based on a Lovecraft story. More, I knew that if one had been, it wouldn't be nearly as scary as the written version— and soon enough, when one came to the local theaters, something featuring the elderly Boris Karloff and entitled *Die, Monster, Die!* I saw why. Though based on "The Colour Out of Space," the film, even with Karloff, was not one-tenth as effective, for one simple reason: We saw the monster.

Implication, Lovecraft had taught me, trumps the explicit. That was a valuable lesson and a critical one for someone who had dreams of writing one day. Of course when I began to come up with an idea for a story, it was, well, eldritch. The notion gestated as I walked my paper route, work that a chimpanzee could probably master if you could teach one to make change. Ghost story, I thought. Set in the South, I thought. Maybe in the Civil War or Reconstruction era, I thought.

Essentially, as I walked the paper route day after day, I told myself the story of a soldier who returns home to Georgia after the end of the Civil War and discovers that he is dead. Well, *presumed* dead, anyway. In his home-town church graveyard are the graves of his parents, and next to them one with a headstone that bears his name. He was reported dead, and…

Twists and plot turns and an ending swirling in mists of stygian gloom came to my mind. I borrowed my older sister's typewriter and with two fingers banged out the story on paper. Stuck for a title, I slapped on two words, "The Grave," not at that time realizing that I was cribbing the title of one of Katherine Anne Porter's finest stories.

Having done that, I sent the story to a magazine—specifically, *Ellery Queen's Mystery Magazine,* which had a "Department of First Stories" and solicited stories from writers who had never before been published. About a year later, the editor, Frederic Dannay, bought my story for one hundred dollars, and some months later it was published in the magazine under the title "The Third Grave," an improvement.

Dannay was half of the team that wrote mysteries as Ellery Queen, and my sale of that story also launched a years-long correspondence with him. He was unfailingly kind and helpful and not at all bothered when I asked him technical questions about writing. He once remarked that he had bought that first story of mine for one reason: "You implied more than you showed."

That was what H.P. Lovecraft had taught me. What is not seen looms larger and has more resonance in the heart than what lies in plain view. The meaning of a story, and the emotions it carries, live in the reader's heart only when the reader becomes a partner with the writer.

When I did get to college, I began to see the same great truth, handled with subtlety and to masterful effect in the writings of the gods of literature. Chaucer knew it, and Dickens, and Austen. So did Shakespeare, so widely encompassing in his understanding and sympathy that *Hamlet* is never the same for any two actors or any two readers. The grand framework of Shakespeare is there ... but to come alive it demands collaboration with a reader or an actor and audience.

The secret is implication, subtlety, and trusting the reader's imagination. It was a great lesson to learn, and in my own writings it has helped me more than anyone can imagine.

So, very belatedly but with full sincerity, thank you, Howard Phillips Lovecraft.

Brad Strickland is the author of more than 75 novels, dozens of short stories, a few poems, and three non-fiction books. He is a former professor of English at the University of North Georgia. He has written and/or performed in adaptations of several H.P. Lovecraft stories for the Atlanta Radio Theatre Company. He writes detective thrillers under the pen name Ken McKea.

An Interview
with Cherie Priest

The following Interview occurred over lunch on April 18, 2013, at Pasha Coffee & Tea, a local, independent coffee house in Chattanooga, TN.

Leverett Butts: So you've interviewed here before?

Cherie Priest: I have. I did a piece for the *Times Free Press* a few months ago.

LB: That's awesome.

CP: It was. When I lived here I couldn't beg, bribe, borrow, not for love or money get anyone to pay any attention to anything I was doing. Apparently, leaving for a few years is what it takes.

LB: Yeah, and a couple of best sellers under your belt.

CP: Technically *Boneshaker* was a best seller but it wasn't; it never broke any lists. It was just kind of a slow burn.

LB: I definitely want to get on tape the story about how you first came across H.P. Lovecraft.

CP: My parents were divorced when I was five. My mom is a fundy.[1] When I'm feeling less charitable I like to say that she's part of an esoterical cult. Which is a slight exaggeration, but only a slight one.

And so, she was really, really locked down and we weren't allowed to have any fiction in the house that wasn't Christian fiction or literature. Like, I checked out some Nancy Drew books from the library, and she threw them away and made me pay the library back with my allowance because I should have known better than to invite the presence of Satan into her home. I wish I was making that up. So my dad figured out that a kind of a loophole was that "literature" meant the author was dead. So, when I was like 11 or 12, he gave me the big Arthur Conan Doyle compendium with the Sherlock Holmes stuff because he knew I liked mysteries. And I read that cover to cover a million times, and then the next year it was Edgar Allan Poe, and then a year or two after that, when I was about 13 or 14, it was Lovecraft. And my mom didn't know who Lovecraft was, like she knew who the other guys were.

But they were kinda arguing about it at some point. She was like well I don't know this one, who is this one? And my dad is slick. Or he certainly thinks he is. To be fair, it's not very hard to be slick when dealing with my mother.

So he tells her, "Well this guy was writing in the 1920s. Like you know, Hemingway and like Steinbeck and those guys."

And my mom is just "Oh, well, it's back in the 20s; they weren't writing bad things back then. I'm sure it will be fine." And she didn't like to read these books, so she never read them herself. Just trusted that they were probably not bad. But, she let me have them and that's how I found them.

LB: I love the idea that Nancy Drew is the daughter of Satan, but H.P. Lovecraft's A-OK.

[both laugh]

CP: No, she knew who Nancy Drew was, and she knew that there were mysteries sometimes, like Scooby Doo, but oh my God, you could not tell her that it was Old Man Winters in a mask. She wouldn't believe you, and she wouldn't watch it to find out. That's what got me. It's like "You won't even check it out to find out."

"No, you're just trying to tempt me."

Eventually I came around to the idea that if your beliefs are so fragile they cannot withstand the barest brush against anything else, that's kind of a problem I think.

Bless her heart. Now we just talk about other things. For a long time when anybody would ask her what her daughters did … my sister was a grant writer for the University of Connecticut, and I was married to a man who worked at Amazon. And sometimes she would say I was a writer and when people would ask what: "You know reviews, and she has a website." We don't talk about it. We find other things to talk about. She's a nice little lady, and she has loosened up over the years. But every now and again, I'll get the big speech about why you won't just write something nice. I don't understand.

LB: Has she read your books?

CP: Oh no she won't. She won't read them at all. She won't have anything to do with them. She won't even have them in the house. For a while she would keep the first couple like between some bibles on a shelf or something.

LB: 'Cause that's the buffer.

CP: Yes. Yes. In case they leap out. But no, she won't have them, and won't let anyone else in the family have them either. I used to send them to my younger cousins and my aunts or whatever, but she made such a stink about it, and gave them such hassle that I quit doing it. It's okay. It's fine. And Dad's my biggest cheerleader. He and my stepmom run around like "Yes, my daughter's a writer! Would you like to see her stuff?"

LB: [laughs] My dad's very similar. I published a collection of short stories, and "Oh Lev, he's published a collection of short stories. He's a writer now." He hasn't read them, but…

CP: No, but he's sure.

LB: He's sure. "I'm sure they're good. I'll read 'em one day."

CP: My dad and stepmom will get around to it eventually. But they're, she teaches nursing and he's a CRNA, and they're kind of busy. But they always do get to it. And I appreciate it.

LB: Do you remember the first H.P. Lovecraft story you read?

CP: Um, I want to say it was "The Rats in the Walls."

I don't remember how they were organized. Anytime I got a compendium, I was just like pick and choose, and the one after that was *The Case of Charles Dexter Ward*.

LB: "Rats in the Walls" was mine as well.

CP: It was kind of accessible. It's shorter. You know, when you're not really sure how you're going to like all the stuff that's in this big, fat book. You know?

LB: That was my first copy. I actually have it. [pulls the book from satchel] It's the first story I think.

CP: I don't remember. It was a similar compendium. But it wasn't that one. Though I do have that one now.

LB: I had heard about him a lot. One of my friends says "Well, you just need to read him."

And I said "What should I start with?"

He goes "Anything. Just pick something."

And I picked that one.

CP: *At the Mountains of Madness*, cause I was like picking longer and longer and longer ones is uh, but it was a really big, fat…

LB: I've not read that one yet.

CP: To describe it makes it sound kind of boring, but it's fascinating, because it's a guy explaining to someone what he has learned by reading some hieroglyphics. And so, he's recounting the history of this war and civilization and race from beyond the stars, etc., etc. etc. But he's really just telling you, and it's kind of like why don't we get to see the battles and the … but no, we just get some guy giving you the jargon and telling you what happened. But it's still fascinating.

LB: What's your favorite Lovecraft story? Or stories?

CP: I don't know. Um, "Rats in the Walls" always has a soft spot in my heart. I really do think it's one of the better ones. It's certainly one of the tightest, most concise complete ones I think, 'cause he tends to leave these things a little open ended. So that's always the one I go back to. I'm actually re-reading *Charles Dexter Ward* right now. I'm only about two-thirds through it. 'Cause a lot of them I haven't read in years and years and years, and right now a project I'm working on is very Lovecraftian, it's basically *Dracula* via Lovecraft. Um, with Lizzie Borden.

LB: Awesome.

CP: Fighting Cthulhu with an axe. But I literally wanted it to be a gothic epistolary, *Dracula* style, but it has to take place a few years before Lovecraft, but I wanted it to be like this is a story that he maybe would have read about in the paper that would have inspired him sort of deal. So, I'm trying to re-familiarize myself with his stuff now.

LB: Okay, you gotta let me know when that gets published.

CP: Sure. It's coming out through Ace next year. It's called *Maplecroft*.[2]

LB: That leads right into the next question: What draws you to Lovecraft? What is it about H.P. Lovecraft's work that you like?

CP: Well, first of all, bless him, he's problematic in a lot of ways.

LB: Oh yeah.

CP: I think ultimately everybody is, and if you find someone who is perfectly unproblematic and loved by everyone, they're doing something wrong. He was a man of his time, and he was difficult. He was afraid of everything. You know, women, black people, Jewish people, you name it, he was afraid of it. And it comes through a lot, so I always find myself kind of disclaiming a little bit, like, you can't take the man out of the work and maybe you shouldn't. But, I was on a panel a few years ago with a handful of other people talking about Lovecraft, and I was the only woman on the panel, which when you're in horror kind of happens. And somebody said, "As a woman don't you find him extremely problematic?" And all I could think of was no, it's hard to take personal.

LB: As a reader I find him problematic sometimes.

CP: As a reader, but as a woman, no, because it really wasn't personal. He was terrified of everything and everyone. He barely left the house. So I always find myself disclaiming when I start talking about the things I do and don't love about him. But I think the core of what I love about him, apart from all that, is that horror typically, and I'm an old gothic, from the horror tradition more than science fiction or steampunk regardless of what I'm known for. So, there is a tendency to over-rely on people making stupid decisions or being weak. And Lovecraft gives you these immensely credible, competent people, but he makes the threat bigger than they are.

And that's far more compelling to me. And I think, you saw it in the slasher movies in the 80's where the teenagers at the summer camp, and they're doing stupid stuff, so when they get hacked to death by Freddie or whatever. I wasn't allowed to watch those movies. And I didn't catch up on very many of them as I got older. But, you're like "Haha, you had that coming."

LB: Yeah.

CP: Yeah. Well, they were stupid they deserved it. But Lovecraft gives you people who make reasonable and informed, intelligent decisions, but they're still fighting something so much bigger than them. And that kind of tension is far more interesting to me. And it's still a problem you have if you're dealing with scary stories or suspense or horror or whatever, you're working a lot with coincidence, with improbable stuff.

'Cause most people if they see a light, a green light, and slime oozing out from under their door, they don't open the door to check it out. You need a good reason for them to check it out. And the good reason can't be because they're dumb. It can't be because, well, they were really high.

There has to be some compelling, credible reason and what they find behind the door has to be bigger and badder and scarier than them, but they need to be prepared to meet it. And still maybe lose. He really set the gold standard for that.

LB: Yeah, he really did. 'Cause I'm reading "The Colour Out of Space" right now, and that is one thing I've noticed is that all of the scientists are making really bad decisions, but it's not because they're stupid.

CP: Yeah, they're working with the information they have at hand, and its literary irony as well. You, as the reader, know that they're doing the wrong thing, but they have no reason to know that they're doing the wrong thing. And you do have these guys who are racist homophobes, misogynist pigs, or whatever. And so obviously I'm not speaking for all womankind right now when I say you don't take it personally, but I think in the bigger picture, he makes these people who are stronger and more capable than he is. And then he puts them into these situations. Because he is not the kind of man who could stride into something like that. He's afraid to open his front door. So he creates these guys. And in the end, maybe they go mad or they're invalids or whatever and they're more like him. But they start out the heroes of their own stories that end poorly for everyone. I think he said somewhere that he wanted to write horror stories that would frighten an atheist.

That's not exactly the quote, but that's the thrust of the quote. I want to write stories that would frighten an atheist. And a lot of horror even now, and certainly Victorian horror, the tradition he's coming out of, really relied very strongly on Christianity, and good versus evil. I mean, look at *Dracula* even. A few years before him.

LB: I think it's important, too, the whole frightening atheists thing I see is separating him a lot, is the fact that there is no good versus evil. We don't even factor into the elder gods' plans.

CP: It's a soulless universe. And the thing that kills me, and I used it in another book later, when I figured it out, one of the things that always ran through these stories for me is how these cults who are worshipping this strange, alien space god … if that exists, you do not want its attention. [laughs] You do not want it to sit up and notice you. You want to be a small and insignificant…

LB: Stay in the middle of the herd. Don't be the outliers.

CP: Exactly. Just no, what is wrong, that is exactly the kind of thing people do. It's a power grab, you know, so I see a lot of that. His stuff feels like wish fulfillment, even as it ends horribly, because he writes these strong, competent, intelligent heroes that he's not.

Still, when the end result is that they've lost all their friends and family and have gone mad and they're living in an attic or whatever. Now they're more like me again, so it's okay.

LB: "It's alright. I could've been that way."

CP: "I could've been that way. That could be how I got like this. Yeah."

LB: It's funny, when you were describing him I was thinking of Norman Bates.

CP: Yeah, kind of.

LB: And I remembered Robert Bloch[3] was one of his buddies.

CP: Yeah, he was one of the Arkham guys.

LB: And I'm wondering, I know Bates is based a lot on Ed Gein, but I'm also starting to see some Lovecraft influence just…

CP: It was his mother and his aunt who raised him, wasn't it? Something like that.

LB: Yep.

CP: So he has these strong female figures who he was deeply devoted to, but he writes these terrible things about women. What a double think you have going on here.

LB: What's interesting too, I've not read *Mountains of Madness* yet, but I was telling a friend of mine, the guy that actually got me into Lovecraft, he said what he likes about the *Mountains of Madness* is you know, everybody talks about what a racist he was, what a misogynist he was, and you can't deny that…

CP: No.

LB: It was there. But he says, you know he did change in later life.

CP: Yeah, and he tried to retract a lot of that. And be like who wants to be judged for opinions they had when they were 19?

LB: Exactly, but my friend says *At the Mountains of Madness* kind of reflects that change to him, because again, I've not read it, but this is just what he said,

CP: It's been several years since I have.

LB: What you have in that story is you've got the aliens, and you've got the humans, and both of them don't understand the other, and if there was any possible way that they could communicate, you get the feeling that story would have ended a lot differently.

So that what you have there isn't that "look at these weird aliens, we're so much better than they are." It's more about the irony of how these two people wind up mutually destroying each other because they don't understand each other.

CP: Yeah, and they can't communicate in any meaningful way. And it seems to me that toward his later material, it becomes less man versus everyone else, and humankind against something bigger.

But, I really kind of wrestled with Lovecraft for a while. Because he is really problematic, I know. I was actually reading something by Caitlín Kiernan on her blog talking about the thought police and how, for her anyway, the idea is that every single person everywhere holds some belief or some problem. Somebody's gonna be problematic for someone else. I defy you to find two people who even agree on the definition of right. 100 percent. And if you take every single person, there's nothing left. There's no one.

But, I've found that I got more out of Lovecraft than I found problematic.

And I grant you that it's a little bit of privileged distance, but it was important to me. And it was something that taught me how to write a scary story. Or gave me a different framework because I didn't like what I was reading. Like, I wanted to love scary stories, but they were so dumb. But then here are smart and scary stories. And yeah, there's some icky stuff in them, but there's icky stuff in everything. I'm gonna mine for gold here. I'll die on that hill if I have to I guess. I cannot deny the impact it's had on me. And obviously what I'm working on now, so.

LB: Here's my last question: How has Lovecraft's work influenced your own writing? Which, you kind of talked about your other novel, the one that you're working on, but has it influenced your other books in any way?

CP: *Fathom* is very Lovecraftian. It was my first starred *Publishers Weekly* review, and nobody read it. [laughs] I could have sold more copies of that book out of a trench coat at the park.

But I like the idea that having intelligent protagonists up against something bigger than them, and in *Fathom* I played with the idea of Lovecraftian cults trying to attract the attention of arcane powers from beyond. Like, "You don't want their attention. Shut up. When you get it, it's gonna go badly for you." I think that's just the way it is.

So I try to goldmine and take the good and run with it, 'cause when Lovecraft was right, he was really, really right, and wrong about a lot of his private beliefs, but right when it came to telling a suspenseful story.

So, that's what I try and take from him.

Cherie Priest is the author of the Eden Moore, Clockwork Century, *and* Cheshire Red Reports *series. She has written 15 novels and novellas set both within and outside these series. Her writing has received the Pacific Northwest Booksellers Association Award and the Locus Award for the Best Science Fiction Novel, among others. She is working on several gothic horror, steampunk, and modern fantasy novels.*

An Interview
with Caitlín R. Kiernan

The following interview was conducted over email in early to mid February 2014.

1. When and how did you discover Lovecraft?

I found him in Trussville, Alabama on a yellow school bus. I was seventeen years old. It was a rainy morning in the spring of 1981, and Lovecraft was lying all alone on an empty seat, in the form of a book from the Birmingham Public Library that someone had accidentally left behind when they got off. It was, in fact, the original 1965 Arkham House edition of *Dagon and Other Macabre Tales*. The black-and-white cover, by Lee Brown Coye (1907–1981), depicts a decrepit, bug-eyed man clad all in rags, a monstrous figure that reminded me at once of Captain Ahab Ceely.[1] The bug-eyed man is wielding a harpoon, which, as one might expect from a decrepit sort of Captain Ahab Ceely, has impaled an albino sperm whale. Turns out, Coye had something of an obsession with *Moby Dick*, and whales are a recurring motif in his artwork. But the man on the book's cover was a giant, by comparison to the whale, which, I'd soon learn, echoes a passage from "Dagon." So, that's when and how I discovered Lovecraft.

2. What was your first Lovecraft story? Why did it make you want to read more of his work?

I can't say for certain which story in *Dagon and Other Macabre Tales* I read first. That was, after all, thirty-three years ago. But I do know that the story from that collection that left the greatest impression on me was "The Hound." Now, it's a terribly overwrought story, and a long, long way from Lovecraft at his best. But it struck a nerve, all the same. It still strikes a nerve. A couple of years back, I wrote a sort of sequel, "Houndwife,"[2] which I think says a lot about how the story has continued to strike those nerves in me down three decades.

3. What is your favorite Lovecraft story? Why?

"The Colour Out of Space" is definitely my favorite. For one thing, it might be his best written story. He has a greater command of his voice here. There's a restraint that, I think, all too often eluded him, and it's the sort of restraint without which weird fiction usually fails. In "The Colour Out of Space," Lovecraft does a superb job of *suggesting* the horrors of the "blasted heath" and the fates of Nahum Gardner and his family, holding back, giving us dreadful hints, but leaving the reader to piece together their own specific images. People often say that suggestion is the key to the success of HPL's handling of the supernatural, but I find that usually that's not true at all. In *At the Mountains of Madness*, for example, there's a clinical, scientific attention to detail. We know *precisely* what his Elder Things looked like. Not so with the alien force that visits the Gardner farm. Indeed, the idea at the heart of the story is an encounter with an extraterrestrial entity that can't be described, *except by analogy.*

And this brings me to another reason I hold the story in such high esteem. This is Lovecraft moving away from Poe and the supernatural and soundly into science fiction. "The Colour Out of Space" is a very important early SF tale, and it's one of the best stories of encounters with an alien Other that has ever been written. This alien *is* alien, ultimately incomprehensible, and there's no familiar, reassuring point of reference for the reader to latch onto. "It was just a colour," we are told. Brilliant. Just brilliant. Also, I would point to Ambrose Bierce's "The Damned Thing" and Algernon Blackwood's "The Willows" as obvious and strong sources of inspiration for this story.[3]

4. How has Lovecraft influenced your own writing? Are there things you have tried to emulate? Are there things you have tried to avoid?

If an author is honest with her- or himself, they have to admit that their voice is a stew. Everything we read—it goes into the pot to one degree or another, consciously or unconsciously. But, then there are the authors whom you fall in love with and, for better or worse, *do* try to emulate. There are certainly authors whose voices I've caught myself trying to ape, from Shirley Jackson to John Steinbeck to Angela Carter, Harlan Ellison to Ray Bradbury to William Gibson. That said, no, I've never tried to actually imitate Lovecraft's style, not even when writing stories set within the so-called Cthulhu mythos. And yet he has been hugely influential on my work. What I've taken away from Lovecraft, what I continue to take away from him—because his writing is a well I go to again and again—is his characterization of the universe as a thing fundamentally inhospitable to the human race, and his understanding that humanity is wholly insignificant in the face of Deep Time and Deep Space.

Caitlín R. Kiernan is the author of several novels including the The Drowning Girl. *Over the last 15 years, her short fiction has been collected in numerous edited collections. She was trained in geology and vertebrate paleontology, and in 1988, she described a new genus and species of mosasaur,* Selmsaurus russelli. *She is working on* Alabaster, *a graphic novel adaptation and expansion of her Dancy Flammarion tales.*

An Interview
with Richard Monaco

The following Interview occurred on the evening of June 4, 2013, on the roof of Richard Monaco's Manhattan apartment building overlooking the Hudson River.

Richard Monaco: Now you gonna ask me these questions, huh?

Leverett Butts: Yeah.

RM: Okay we'll start with H.P. Lovecraft was a really funny looking dude, man.

LB: He really was.

RM: Like, nervous. If I'm sitting in the bar next to him, I'm like, [Monaco feigns looking nervous] "Oh yeah, H.P. how ya doing today?" [laughs] I don't mean to be risible.

LB: Oh, no.

RM: Irisible. Okay, I'm answering questions about something that I know a reasonable amount, but not an enormous amount.

LB: Most of the questions are about your experiences with Lovecraft. When did you first read Lovecraft? How did you first find out about him?

RM: Find out about him? Interesting. Back in the, it was after the Great Flood, but not that near. It's true, I picked up a book. I said what is this, then I read the back, and said ah, that sounds interesting. I like mythos and stuff. So I read one and that was it. I don't remember where or how. It probably was when I was a teenager and it probably was when I'd steal money from my father, who didn't know it. I'd take his coins and go down to 4th Street to the used bookstore, thinking it was okay because I was buying books.

You know, that's how I got punched in the head for it, but when he found out I was buying books, he said "Oh, you were buying books." So he had to forgive me. I wasn't taking it to buy candy or drugs, I was buying books.

But I think it was in that period that I bought one. I said, "Wow, that's sort of interesting." But many years passed before I really read that stuff. I know it was a long time after. Because I remember by the time I read it I said, "Well this guy has stylistic problems and *blah blah blah*. He reminds me of Nathaniel Hawthorne and what's his name? Poe."

Too much language. Not enough image and story. Nevertheless, there was something there that was remarkable.

LB: What do you think that something was?

RM: Uh, first of all, what got me was, like with E.E. Smith and the *Lensman* series.[1] One of the worst writers who ever lived wrote, I don't know, some of the most imaginative and terrific books in some ways. It was terrible execution, but great concept or whatever. So, I enjoyed it. You'd love 'em. So, Lovecraft wasn't as bad as Smith, but the idea was that

I love that Smith. I'm dedicating part of my work I'm doing now to Smith, 'cause I love that scope.

It was the scope. It was the idea that you could create something out of the ground. You know, where you could be in Brooklyn. Brooklyn. Think about that. Red Hook. And you'd experience these amazing events, and that affected me. Affected me tremendously. Yeah, that's great, that's great. It's everywhere. You know it's not just in some, you don't have to go to the South Pole, but they went there, too. That was cool. My favorite book of his I think is the one where they went to the South Pole. *At the Mountains of Madness.*

It's one of my favorites. But the whole idea that he had this underlying thing which was organized and hooked together, that impressed me a lot.

LB: *Mountains of Madness* is cool to me, 'cause you know I'm reading it for the first time…

RM: Really?

LB: And there's not a lick of dialogue; I think there's like one line. But you never notice it. It flows. It may be his best written story.

RM: In some respects it was always my favorite. And maybe that's the reason because I felt like it didn't trip over itself. You didn't have guys saying silly stuff.

Or, you know, worrying about what's his name? *Necronomicon* guy. They'd be talking about him. Yeah, you're better off not talking about him. The Mad Arab. You mention him once and that's good enough. Mad Arab. [laughs]

LB: I like the idea that it can happen anywhere, that New York. You know, a lot of this stuff happens in the wilderness of New England.

RM: Right, and it's waiting.

LB: But it also happens in New York City.

RM: Right. Anywhere. And it's waiting for you. And that's something that I always appreciated, and it affected my own work. I love the idea that you tap into something that's not particular, that's not like you're crazy or you're here or you're there, this stuff is like lurking at the outskirts of your comprehension. Or at least your ability to perceive things.

LB: Do you remember the first story you read?

RM: Uh, that's a good question. I keep thinking…. I think it was *The Call*…?

LB: *The Call of Cthulhu?*

RM: Yeah, "The Call of However You Pronounce It." I never could pronounce it.

LB: You're not supposed to. I found out last week, actually. It's supposed to be word, or letters that add up to approximation of what his voice … what his name sounds like.

RM: So he probably got that idea from who, the Jews. With the Yahweh. Can't say the name of God.

LB: His wife was Jewish, so maybe…

RM: Ah, is that right? I know so little about H.P. Lovecraft it's scary. 'Cause his picture was enough to…

LB: Scare you to death.

RM: [giggles] Okay, he's probably a great guy. Hope I don't have to have dinner with him. It'd be a bit odd. That's interesting. That's interesting, 'cause that idea came to me, I said, "I don't know how to pronounce this name, but I know it's of great significance, so…"

I think that was the first thing I read. Made me a little uneasy.

You know, mildly uneasy.

LB: That's a good book, too because the narrator … nothing ever happens to the narrator. Everything that drives him crazy is just stuff that he reads. He keeps getting more and more removed from the actual horror and just the implication of what happened to these other people that he heard about through other people is enough to just send him to the loony bins.

RM: Right. I think that worked well. I think that's a great technique. As I said, I don't think of him as a marvelous writer, in the sense of his technique and his execution, but his ideas and his vision and all the rest of it carry it. That's why I compare him to E.E. Smith. Although, I think he's better than E.E. Smith. I think my dog has better prose style. But E.E. Smith had that one thing. He had, same thing Lovecraft had which was a vision which was something you can expand on. It goes to the ends of the universe.

LB: Right.

RM: It doesn't matter how he got there.

LB: His style does get better as he goes on. I think *Mountains of Madness* is one of his last stories.

RM: No, I'm saying he wasn't without, I don't think he was without talent at all.

LB: You can actually kind of see it grow.

RM: He was working in that Poe kind of constriction, you know, where they all were getting stuck.

LB: Yeah.

RM: In those days.

LB: All the old British spellings. The o-u-rs instead of just the o-rs. The r-es.

RM: Yeah, and it gets a little ponderous, you know?

LB: How has Lovecraft influenced your own work?

RM: In the sense of scope.

LB: How so?

RM: Because I like the idea in some works of mine. Not all of them. Of having an, like when I'm reworking *Shadow Gold*,[2] of an underlying universal organized set of opposing forces.

LB: Right.

RM: And you got the darkness here, and the light here. Whatever it is, and that kind of thing appealed to me in his work. If I had to read him paragraph by paragraph I'd go yeah, you know, he could use an editor. Really, you know? He really could use an editor.

But where it went was intriguing and fascinating and had a certain amount of power.

LB: I don't know if this was intentional or not, but I remember in your *Parsival* series,[3] I think it's *Blood and Dreams*, there's a scene where they're underground and they start calling all of these things from this, God it's been a couple of years since I read it the last time, but this well or something, but all these

RM: Yeah, the well. At the bottom.

LB: And all these creatures start coming out of the well, and I remember reading that going, that sounds like, a lot like something Lovecraft would write.

RM: That would be a very good example of Lovecraft's influence on me, because yeah sure, that would be…. I wanted to do a Baroque, and it turned out to be a Baroque version of the other books. And the Baroque version would mean exaggerating a lot. Like, exaggerating the monsters and exaggerating the disgusting horror.

Maybe it was the critics who thought I was too horrible. It was so unspeakable that they don't know what to say, but yeah I would definitely think Lovecraft.

I was looking for the monster within the monster. The mystery within the mystery, the thing that comes up out of the ... the thing that scares you to death when you're first waking up and say is it a heart attack or a stiff arm? The older you get, the more you're going to decide that the stiff arm or the strange pain is deadly. You're okay until a certain period of your life, but then a little longer and is this it? Is it time?

It's gotta be. How long can it be put off? What is it? What is it? Oh, heartburn. Thank God.

LB: What's funny is that I didn't notice it the first time I read the *Parsival* books, 'cause I actually discovered your work before I discovered Lovecraft.

RM: Yeah, you read my work as a kid. I remember you telling me that.

LB: Yeah, as a kid.

RM: Scott Thompson[4] told me. Said you'd turn up with stuff in your bag and you'd read it.

LB: Yeah, I carried *Parsival* around.

RM: Mentally unbalanced. Even as a child.

LB: Just in case I decided I wanted to read it again I'd have it. I had it in my bookbag.

RM: Wow. I'm like that with a few books, but not my own.

LB: Yeah, and then in college I discovered Lovecraft, and I went back and re-read the *Parsival* books and that's when I noticed, okay, I see that connection there. I think that may be why I wanted to ask you about Lovecraft.

RM: Well, to the degree that you brought it up, yeah, that's true. That kind of thing always interested me and was something I might go for.

And I just have to keep saying, with the book I'm doing now, you know, that this Lovecraft and Smith. In fact, when you read *Shadow Gold*, and if I am able to finish it properly, you'll find a lot of that. You'll find a lot of Lovecraft type stuff. You'll find a lot of E.E. Smith type stuff.

LB: Tell me more about *Shadow Gold*.

RM: What can I tell ya? The basic idea was I wanted to do a book, and remember this was a long time ago. I don't have any of the impulses now that I had when I started to do that book.

So when I'm reading it now I'm going I see why I did this. Yeah, that's pretty cool. I wouldn't want to do it now. Too much time has passed. I gotta think about other stuff, but within this frame of reference I get it. I loved the Ring Cycle of Wagner. I loved a lot of those myths of that time. As I told you already, I loved Smith and people like Lovecraft.

So, in a funny way I won't want to use that. When I first started writing I think I mentioned, I don't know if I ever said this to you. I know I mentioned it in the memoirs.[5] My first ideas was I loved certain things so much that I wanted to be able myself to do something like that. You know, I loved *Hamlet* when I was a kid. I loved *Bambi*. I loved these things, and I love this science fiction like Smith's stuff, and I want to be able to do them and I said I can't do better than *Hamlet*, but I wanna make these other things like *Hamlet*. Make them better. You know, make them really classy. Make them really kill ya.

You know, and not have cumbersome, stupid characters and ridiculous bad prose like Smith and Lovecraft, so my idea was to bring, in total intensity.

LB: What was Smith's first name?

RM: Edward Elmer Smith. Ph.D. [laughs] In the early days he would always sign it

Ph.D., 'cause he wanted to give him some credibility 'cause he was writing science fiction. He was actually a chemical engineer. Of mediocre attainments. But he was a writer of tremendous, limited imagination.

What do I mean by tremendous, limited imagination? He was using the whole universe, but he had a very narrow way of envisioning the whole universe.

LB: Kind of like Lovecraft.

RM: Yeah! Exactly right. His idea was that you got a guy, he's bigger than you, you find a way to beat him up, then you find a guy bigger than him and you gotta find a way to beat him up and it goes on and on and on till you finally reach the ultimate evil forces of the universe and then you get slightly better guys to beat them up.

He's a Taurus. Taurus is what I am. Tauruses think that *humm boom boom* [punches the air]. In the end, you just get stubborn and you fight it out.

So, I admired that, but that's not all there is. By any means.

LB: I'm trying to … [fiddles with smartphone] I wonder if we could figure out when Lovecraft was born.

RM: Look him up! It's just a matter of record. Born 18 something or other. Had to be.

LB: I'll see what his astrological sign is. That'd be interesting to see, especially for a guy whose whole mythos revolves around the stars being right. Wonder how close his chart will come to his life.

RM: Oh yeah, we could do that. If you were around here for a week, we could do a lot of astrology stuff. One of the most important things in my life is when I discovered that astrology worked and all the implications of it. Which puts an end to nonsense about you're born and you die and you're just a mechanical crap. It's all nonsense. Utter nonsense. You're not an electrical machine full of crap.

LB: I want to say Lovecraft was born in late August.

RM: But you can't tell what somebody is from their birthday alone. You gotta know where the moon and the ascendant is. When and where was Lovecraft born?

LB: August 20, 1890, at around 9:00 a.m. in Providence, RI.

RM: Lemme run his chart and I'll let you know what it says.

An Interpretation of
Lovecraft's Astrological Chart

BY RICHARD MONACO

For the following discussion of H.P. Lovecraft's natal astrological chart we refer readers to basic texts like Sakoian and Acker's *Astrologer's Handbook* or Alan Leo's texts should they wish to confirm the general, accepted definitions of the simple, obvious points we'll make here. The point is just to show how much of what we already know about the man is reflected in his horoscope. There are other things that show up, of course, but we'd need him or maybe his wife to confirm them.

You don't need to be born in the sign to be an Aquarian or any other of the 12. It's a matter of which planets dominate a chart. We're all a mix of elements but some are less mixed than others. HP is essentially an Aquarian which always shows an interest if not an obsession with the odd, the unusual, the advanced, often things like astrology which he had more than a passing acquaintance with (to judge by the stories) as well as fascination with electric phenomena. He has a rising Moon in the 1st house showing the self in a chart, and that object is conjunct (together with) Uranus, the main ruler (dominant influence) in the sign Aquarius. I would expect he had a disproportionately heavy tread, for instance, based on the conjunction.

Jupiter here is in Aquarius; the planet signifies gain, growth, luck and goodwill, among other things. Bear in mind, planets, stars, etc., just *signify*, they don't make things happen with unseen beams of compulsion. They indicate the mechanical unfolding of a lifetime's karma, i.e., cause and effect. They say nothing about creative intelligence, conscience and comprehension: they'll suggest what you look like, how you act and speak and the kinds of things that will happen to you along the way: the mechanical side. In Aquarius, Jupiter shows expansion and profit through unusual (for the times you live in) ideas, freedom of expression with a humanistic bent. Because of its position his home ought to have had many antique and unusual items. Uranus, as ruler of Aquarius, always shows breaking with expected norms of behavior or, as in HP's case, norms of interest and literary expression.

Because his Moon/Uranus conjunct in 1st House is in the sign Libra there's a tendency towards art along with mood fluctuations affecting decision-making. That plus Venus in Libra shows deep love of artistic expression, fairness and law. With Sun in Leo added in he would have been a proud, just fellow. His birth time is probably at least 10 or 15 minutes later than given as he otherwise ought to have been a strikingly good-looking, delicate-featured narcissist. In the past, birth times were routinely rounded-off, so we really have no way of knowing his exact time of birth.

Based on his Venus Mars relationship (with Lusty Leo in the mix) he would have been an expansive, loyal very sensitive lover in keeping with his intense, poetic/highly imaginative sensibility. Wish I could ask his wife. As reflected in his figure she should have been a direct, expansive, up-front probably more traditionally religious than he and not afraid of an argument; the lady was no pushover. This is judged by examining his 7th House which indicates wives, partners, the public, etc.

Richard Monaco was the bestselling author of the Parsival *series and studied musical composition at Columbia University. He wrote screenplays, taught poetry at Columbia, NYU, and Mercy College, and published numerous novels and works of nonfiction. Two of his novels were finalists for the Pulitzer Prize in literature. In addition to writing, he studied and practiced astrology since the 1980s. He passed away in June 2017, and his unfinished novel,* Shadowgold, *is currently being edited for publication.*

Providence After Dark

T.E.D. Klein

A very smart friend of mine, impressively well-read, swears that in his early teenage years his favorite books—in fact, the only books he ever read for pleasure—were paperback novelizations of sci-fi and horror films he'd seen. Not, mind you, the original works on which the films were based; the novelizations, that most scorned of genres.

I mention this to illustrate how lowly, plebeian, in fact downright philistine one's entrance may be to the halls of literature. I'm sure there are professional writers, no doubt a few Ph.D.s as well, who'd prefer to forget that they once cut their teeth on Readers Digest Condensed Books or Classics Illustrated comics. (It's remarkable how often the latter, in my own case, have served as a lifelong substitute for the real thing.)

My earliest encounters with H.P. Lovecraft were just as humble. I wish I could say that I first read him in the celebrated black-bound Arkham House editions that, for those of us of a certain age, are forever identified with his writings, but I didn't discover that series till years later. I was probably in sixth or seventh grade when I first stumbled across a Lovecraft story—two, actually, "The Dunwich Horror" and "The Rats in the Walls"—in the local library's copy of *Great Tales of Terror and the Supernatural,* a mammoth, much-reprinted anthology that has introduced him to generations of new readers; in those days, with mortality unimaginably distant, the fatter a book was, the stronger its appeal.

But what really confirmed Lovecraft's status in my juvenile literary pantheon was a paperback called *The Survivor and Others,* whose cover (from which gazed a scary, scaly monster with, oddly, three nostrils) bore the byline, in large letters, "H.P. Lovecraft" and in smaller, fainter ones, "and August Derleth." In truth the book's contents were almost entirely by Derleth, HPL's most prolific and energetic disciple. After Lovecraft's death in 1937, Derleth had cofounded Arkham House to rescue Lovecraft's work from the pulp magazines where it had originally been published; additionally, he'd taken plot ideas out of the master's commonplace book—sometimes just a single line—and had spun them into stories that I now see were exceedingly mechanical and formulaic. (He also specialized in Sherlock Holmes pastiches.) At the time, though, as a 14-year-old, I paid no attention to the warning at the beginning of *Survivor* that these tales were based upon mere "scattered notes" from HPL and that the results were to be regarded as "a final collaboration, post-mortem." All I knew was that I found the stories thrilling.

So what made me a Lovecraft fan was not even genuine Lovecraft. And aside from those two initial tales in the library anthology, I'm not sure I'd actually read much authentic, unadulterated fiction of his (nor was it yet so widely available) when, in the fall of 1964, I found myself in Providence on the morning before my one and only college interview—for Brown, as it happens: the university, aside from Miskatonic, most closely associated with Lovecraft. (I should add that this connection had very little to do with my choice of schools.) Vaguely aware that he had lived somewhere in the area, I stopped in the college bookstore and asked if it stocked any books by him. It did not; but one of the salespeople, providentially knowledgeable, informed me that that I might find what I wanted downtown, at Dana's Old Corner Book Shop on Weybosset Street. In fact, I was told, Lovecraft himself had actually frequented the shop.

Wasting no time, I dashed down College Hill and visited the place, a little low-ceilinged establishment below sidewalk level that smelled of books new and used; on the wall that lined the steps leading down was a mural of Alice tumbling down the rabbit hole. The proprietor, old white-haired Mr. Dana, confirmed that Lovecraft had indeed been among his customers but admitted he had no particular memories of the man. Still, the store displayed a partial shelf of Arkham House titles, my first encounter with that exotic imprint, and I bought two or three—hardcover volumes that in those days sold for three dollars, five dollars, and six fifty (which struck me as a bit steep). This excursion downtown—followed by a hurried visit to the Lovecraft collection at the John Hay Library up the hill—gave me something to chat about at my interview later that day; the interviewer, I recall, had never heard of Lovecraft, but I expect he was impressed by my enthusiastic geekdom.

In fact, comparatively few people had heard of him then. Providence, like the world at large, is far more conscious of him today, 77 years after his death; Lovecraft is practically a minor industry there now. When I began college there, Lovecraft had been dead for some 28 years. That, too, seems a rather long time, and yet, looking back, it sometimes felt as if I had just missed him. The city has changed considerably since I lived there—it's awfully yuppified these days—and it's lost much of what I once treasured about it, the sense of its being a slightly seedy, slightly sleepy old backwater, albeit one with more than its share of well-preserved Colonial architecture. For Lovecraft, it was always a romantic and magical place; for me as well—partly because this corner of New England seemed so full of history (in contrast to the bland, charmless Long Island suburb where I'd grown up), and partly because Lovecraft's presence seemed to haunt every street.

College Hill, in particular, was filled with Lovecraft connections; he had walked the neighborhood's streets throughout his life, and loved them all, and immortalized them in his stories and letters. Exploring them—occasionally prowling the lanes and alleyways after dark as Lovecraft did, seeking glimpses of what he had called Old Providence—became something of a preoccupation during my four years there. I remember one night, with a friend, suddenly coming upon a little cemetery, its centuries-old tombstones standing out against the lights of the city spread out below; only afterward did I learn that this was St. John's churchyard, where Lovecraft, in a modified sonnet, hints that visitors might spy "amidst these tombs the shade of Poe." (One of HPL's early literary influences, Poe had descended on the neighborhood in 1848 in search of a wife. His name is spelled out in the first letters of each line of Lovecraft's poem.) In my freshman year, I spent an evening in a distant part of the city with Cliff and Muriel Eddy, an elderly couple, sadly impoverished, who, as onetime fellow writers, had been friends of Lovecraft's; in fact, HPL is credited with having "revised," or even rewritten, Eddy's story "The Loved Dead," whose necrophiliac theme had supposedly caused a minor scandal when it appeared in *Weird Tales*. The eighteenth-century house where I lived my senior year—the third floor, which another student and I occupied, contained four fireplaces, including one in the kitchen—stood between the Providence Art Club on one side and the landmark Fleur-de-Lys house on the other; both are mentioned in "The Call of Cthulhu," in which the latter is home to one of the main characters. The so-called Shunned House—today just another piece of desirable East Side real estate—was a couple of blocks away.

Supernatural horror tales, at their best, transform the ordinary world into something scarier, more exciting, more fun; I know that sounds ridiculously simplistic, but I think in essence it's all they should hope to do—to add a little wonder to the world. Lovecraft's tales made living in Providence more fun; and later, during the '80s, when I was spending many a weekend in southern Vermont, that region was likewise enhanced, if a good deal less dramatically, by the fact that he'd used it as the setting for one of his admittedly less successful tales, "The Whisperer in Darkness." I would find myself driving from Brattleboro to New-fane and Townshend on the very same road along the West River that the tale's narrator traveled, and that ordinary scenic journey, and those ordinary, charming, slightly touristy Vermont towns, would seem a shade more magical.

The same is true, to some degree, for all New England—for me, it's all Lovecraft Country. It's not exactly the New England of the guidebooks, the history books, or even the historical novels (endearing though that New England is); rather, it's a more mysterious, more richly atmospheric region that, in Lovecraft's hands, manages to combine the quaint and the cosmic, the specific—specifically named streets, specific actual houses—and the utterly strange. It's a place, as well, where tiny actions can have near-universal significance, where a grubby backwoods hermit can mutter words out of a dusty, worm-eaten old book with earth-shattering consequences, opening the gates to another dimension.

Please understand that, alone, each of those particular elements doesn't seem quite so remarkable; what appeals to me about Lovecraft isn't so much the now-familiar collection of forbidden old books (almost a contradiction in terms, when you think of it) or the menagerie of extradimensional monsters led by that now-practically-iconic winged being with tentacles coming out of its face. What appeals, rather, is the conjunction of such fantastic stuff with staid old New England.

I wish I could say the same for New York, where I live now. Lovecraft spent a couple of years here, during his brief, uncomfortable marriage; he set a few stories here as well. Indeed, every few weeks, when I'm in Brooklyn, I invariably walk past his last local address. Yet somehow the city seems to resist Lovecraftian transformation. Maybe I'm just too old, or perhaps this place is just too busy, too modern, too mired in reality. I can understand why HPL fled back to Providence.

T.E.D. Klein is the author of bestselling horror novel The Ceremonies, *and of the story collection* Dark Gods. *He was the editor of* Twilight Zone *magazine and later of the true-crime monthly* CrimeBeat. *Klein received the World Horror Society's Grand Master award in 2012.*

Notes

History of the *Necronomicon*

1. Shams al-Dīn Abū Al-ʿAbbās Aḥmad Ibn Muḥammad Ibn Khallikān (1211–1282) was a 13th Century Shafiʾi Islamic scholar of Arab or Kurdish origin. Lovecraft mistakenly places him in the 12th century.

2. A lost city, a tribe or an area mentioned in the Quran; some scholars believe this as a geographic location, either a city or an area, though its location is up for debate:anywhere from Alexandria or Damascus to a city which actually moved or a city called Ubar. Others believe it is the name of a tribe, possibly the tribe of ʿĀd, with the pillars referring to tent pillars.

3. *Yog-Sothoth* is an Outer God who is coexistent with all time and space yet locked outside of the universe we inhabit. It knows all and sees all. To worship it may bring knowledge of many things. However, to see it or learn too much about it is to court disaster. Some authors claim that its worship requires a human sacrifice or eternal servitude; *Cthulhu*, one of Lovecraft's Great Old Ones, is a malevolent entity hibernating within an underwater city in the South Pacific called R'lyeh. The imprisoned Cthulhu is apparently the source of constant anxiety for mankind at a subconscious level, and also the subject of worship by a number of human religions While Cthulhu is currently trapped in R'lyeh, it will eventually awaken from its slumber, and return.

4. Michael IV Autoreianos was the Patriarch of Constantinople (the leader of the Eastern Orthodox Church) from 1206 to his death in 1212.

5. Ole Worm (1588–1655), a.k.a. Olaus Wormius, was a Danish physician and antiquary. In medicine, Worm's chief contributions were in embryology, but he was also a collector of early literature in the Scandinavian languages, and wrote a number of treatises on runestones and collected texts that were written in runic.

6. John Dee (1527–1608/9) was a Welsh mathematician, astronomer, astrologer, occultist, and adviser to Queen Elizabeth I. He devoted much of his life to the study of alchemy, divination and Hermetic philosophy.

7. A fictional university possibly modeled on Brown University in Lovecraft's hometown of Prov-idene, RI, though it is placed in the equally fictional town of Arkham, MA (itself based on Salem).

8. A reference to Lovecraft's story "Pickman's Model."

9. Robert William Chambers (1865–1933) was an American artist and fiction writer, best known for his 1895 book of short stories entitled The King In Yellow. The book is named after a fictional play with the same title which recurs as a motif through some of the stories. S.T. Joshi describes the book as a classic in the field of the supernatural. There are ten stories, the first four of which, "The Repairer of Reputations," "The Mask," "In the Court of the Dragon," and "The Yellow Sign," mention The King in Yellow, a forbidden play which induces despair or madness in those who read it. This book was a great influence on Lovecraft's work. In 1927, Lovecraft read The King in Yellow and four years later, included passing references to the book—such as the Lake of Hali and the Yellow Sign—in "The Whisperer in Darkness."

The Call of Cthulhu

1. Algernon Henry Blackwood (1869–1951) was an English short story writer and novelist, one of the most prolific writers of ghost stories in the history of the genre. "The Willows" is one of his best known short stories. Lovecraft considered it to be the finest supernatural tale in English literature.

2. Those who study the systems of esoteric philosophy concerning the mysteries of being and nature, particularly the nature of divinity.

3. A form of sculpture in which a solid piece of material is carved so that objects project from a background.

4. Unpredictable, whimsical, wild, or unusual ideas.

5. *Cubism*: a school of art characterized by the reduction and fragmentation of natural forms into abstract, often geometric structures; *futurism*: an offshoot of cubism that glorified themes associated with the future, including speed, technology, youth, and violence, and objects such as the car, the aeroplane and the industrial city.

6. A style of visual art having the aim of objectively recording experience by a system of fleeting

impressions, especially of natural light effects, in sculpture this achieved by having subjects only partially modeled and surfaces roughened to reflect light unevenly.

7. Formed with large, undressed stones fitted closely together without the use of mortar

8. American Archaeological Society Meeting

9. *William Scott-Elliot* (d. 1930) was a theosophist who elaborated on the idea concept of root races, a concept refering to successive evolutionary stages through which humanity goes in its pilgrimage on our earth each earlier root race appears on a lost continent such as Atlantis. His most notable works were *The Story of Atlantis* (1896) and *The Lost Lemuria* (1904), later combined in 1925 into a single volume called *The Story of Atlantis and the Lost Lemuria.*

10. *Sir James George Frazer* (1854–1941) was a Scottish social anthropologist influential in the modern studies of mythology and comparative religion. His most famous work, *The Golden Bough* (1890), documents and details the similarities among magical and religious beliefs across the globe; *Margaret Alice Murray* (1863–1963) was a prominent English Egyptologist, archaeologist, anthropologist, and folklorist. In her 1921 book, *Witch Cult in Western Europe* she claimed that a common pattern of underground pagan resistance to the Christian Church existed across Europe.

11. Unconventional; bizarre.

12. Someone who loves and understands beauty, art, music, etc.

13. A city in Lebanon and legendary birthplace of Dido.

14. On February 28, 1925 (March 1, universal time), a large area of the northeastern United States and eastern Canada was shaken by a magnitude 7 earthquake. A large portion of New York State experienced intensity 4 effects; lesser intensities were noted south of Albany.

15. Feverish.

16. Extraordinary in size, amount, extent, degree, or force.

17. Latin Christians who lived under the Ottoman Empire and their descendants living in modern Turkey and the Middle East. The term is sometimes used pejoratively to refer to people of mixed Arab and European descent and to Europeans living in the Middle East who have assimilated and adopted local dress and customs.

18. A mollusk characterized by bilateral body symmetry, a prominent head, and a set of arms or tentacles.

19. Eskimos.

20. A supreme eskimo deity who lives in the underworld and is depicted as a large seal, a bear, a warrior or a tiny midget.

21. A natural light display in the sky, especially in the high latitudes (such as Arctic and Antarctic regions).

22. Jean Lafitte (1776–1823) was a French pirate and privateer in the Gulf of Mexico in the early 19th century, who helped Jackson defend New Orleans during the War of 1812.

23. A small-headed drum, usually long and narrow, that is beaten with the hands, usually as a signalling device, most often associated with American Indian and other aboriginal tribes.

24. Having many feet or roots.

25. *Pierre Le Moyne d'Iberville* (1661–1706) was a soldier, ship captain, explorer, and founder of the French colony of Louisiana of New France; *Robert de La Salle* (1643–1687) was a French explorer of the Great Lakes region of the United States and Canada, the Mississippi River, and the Gulf of Mexico who claimed the Mississippi River basin for France.

26. *Sidney Sime* (1867–1941) was an English artist in the late Victorian and succeeding periods, mostly remembered for his fantastic and satirical artwork, especially his story illustrations for Irish author Lord Dunsany, whom Lovecraft noted as a major influence on his own work; *Anthony Angarola* (1893–1929) was an American painter, printmaker, and art instructor whose work focused on people who struggled to adapt to a foreign culture. Both Sime and Angarola were favorite artists of Lovecraft.

27. A drunken, orgiastic, or riotous celebration.

28. Occurring or responding in turns; alternating.

29. Declared.

30. A person of combined European and Native American descent.

31. Showed.

32. Georgian architecture is a subset of Colonial architecture, referring to the architectural style prevalent from 1720 to 1820. It features red-brick masonry with strict symmetry, multipaned, unpaired windows, and a centered panel front door.

33. An artistic movement especially of late 19th-characterized by refined aestheticism, artifice, and the quest for new sensations.

34. Arthur Machen (1863–1947) was a Welsh author and mystic of the 1890s and early 20th century, best known for his supernatural, fantasy, and horror fiction. He was a major influence on Lovecraft's work.

35. Clark Ashton Smith (1893–1961) was an American artist and author of fantasy, horror, and science fiction. As a member of the Lovecraft circle, and a close correspondent with Lovecraft until Lovecraft's death in 1937, Smith's subjects were often fantastic portrayals of cosmic and weird motifs.

36. A set of formal questions put as a test.

37. Reality consists entirely of physical matter that is the sole cause of every possible occurrence, including human thought, feeling, and action.

38. A major seaport in Chile.

39. About 1,300 miles northeast of New Zealand.

40. About 2,200 miles east of New Zealand.

41. Pacific Island workers employed in British colonies, such as British Columbia (Canada), Fiji and Queensland (Australia) in the 19th and early 20th centuries.

42. A sailor or militiaman from the Indian Subcontinent or other countries east of the Cape of Good Hope, employed on European ships from the 16th century until the early 20th century.

43. After the fact.
44. About 3,000 miles eastof New Zealand and about 200 miles southwest of the *Alert's* encounter with the *Emma*.
45. A settlement built on elevated ground.
46. Spectrally.
47. Inconsistently with what is usual, normal, or expected.
48. The quality of being dark, shadowy, or obscure.
49. Swelling or protuberant.
50. Unearthly, strange, and/or supernatural.
51. Vigintillion: in the U.S.: 1 followed by 63 zeros: intheUK: 1 followed by 123 zeros; given Lovecraft's anglophilia, it is reasonable to assume he means the latter figure.
52. *Gibbered*: babbled; *Polypheme*: the Cyclops Odysseus blinds in the *The Odyssey*.
53. Hazily or vaguely.
54. Laughing loudly and convulsively.
55. The deep abyss that, in Greek mythology, is used as a dungeon of torment and suffering for the wicked and as the prison for the Titans.

The Colour Out of Space

1. A symmetrical two-sided roof with two slopes on each side.
2. Lovecraft claimed this reservoir was based on the Scituate Reservoir west of Providence, RI, however, S.T. Joshi suggests it may also be based on the Quabbin Reservoir, construction of which begun in 1926.
3. Grandmothers.
4. Strong contrasts between light and dark, usually bold contrasts affecting a whole composition.
5. Salvator Rosa (1615–1673) was an Italian Baroque painter best known as "unorthodox and extravagant" whose brooding, melancholic landscapes feature haunting ruins.
6. The fictional Miskatonic River flows west-to-east across Massachusetts, originating from springs in the hills west of Dunwich, flowing southeastward through Arkham, and emptying into the sea two miles to the south near the fictional coastal town of Kingsport (roughly where the real-world town of Prides Crossing sits).
7. Trapped gases.
8. A test for the presence of certain metallic elements by observing the colours given to a bead of borax in a loop of platinum wire held in the oxidizing and reducing parts of a Bunsen burner flame.
9. A type of torch utilizing compressed oxyhydrogen gas producing a flame hot enough to melt refractory materials (such as platinum, porcelain, or corundum), valuable tool in several fields of nineteenth and early twentieth century science.
10. An optical device for producing and observing a spectrum of light or radiation.
11. literally "royal water," another name for nitrohydrochloric acid, a highly corrosive mixture of nitric and hydrochloric acids making a fuming yellow or red solution, so called because it can dissolve the "royal" or "noble" metals (gold and platinum).

12. A colorless volatile liquid used frequently as a building block in organic chemistry as well as an industrial and chemical solvent.
13. Unique figures of long nickel-iron crystals, found in the iron meteorites and consisting of fine interleaving of kamacite and taenite bands or ribbons.
14. Of the same or a similar kind or nature.
15. A small globe, esp a drop of liquid.
16. Meteorite.
17. Perennial herbs with showy flowers and often with tufted leaves.
18. Perennial herbaceous plant with flowers that look like white trousers, native to the woods of eastern North America.
19. Perennial herbaceous plant native to eastern North America with yellow and white flowers whose roots contain a blood-red juice.
20. Green vegetation.
21. Foul-smelling.
22. The triangular portions of walls between the edges of dual-pitched roofs.
23. A light farm wagon that has two or more seats and is drawn by two horses.
24. A strong, fould smell.
25. A weather phenomenon in which luminous plasma is created by a coronal discharge from a sharp or pointed object in a strong atmospheric electric field (such as those generated by thunderstorms), often considered a bad omen.
26. A reference to the Holy Spirit descending on the apostles as described in Acts 2:1–31.
27. A stately court dance of the 17th and 18th centuries resembling the minuet.
28. A music compositional technique interspersing the primary diatonic pitches and chords with other pitches of the chromatic scale, in contrast to the major and minor scales.
29. *Cygnus* is a northern constellation lying on the plane of the Milky Way, deriving its name from the Latinized Greek word for swan, which it resembles. It one of the most recognizable constellations of the northern summer and autumn and contains *Deneb*, one of the brightest stars in the night sky and one corner of the Summer Triangle.
30. Frozen.
31. Unfit to be spoken of.

The Dunwich Horror

1. *Gorgons*: In Greek mythology, any of three sisters (Stheno, Euryale, and Medusa)who had hair made of living, venomous snakes, as well as a horrifying visage that turned those who beheld her to stone.; *Hydra*: In Greek mythology, an ancient serpent-like water monster with many heads, if any one head was chopped off, two more grew to replace it; *Chimeras*: In Greek mythology, a monstrous fire-breathing creature composed of three animals: a lion, a snake and a goat; *Harpies*: In Greek mythology, female monsters in the form of birds with human faces, that steal food from their victims while they

are eating and carry evildoers (especially those who have killed their family) to the avenging Furies. *Celeano* is their queen.

2. Charles Lamb (1775–1834) was an English writer and essayist. His essay "Witches and Other Night-Fears," published in 1821, discusses the connection between poetry, dreams, and imagination.

3. *Aylesbury* is a fictional town in north central Massachussetts. The Aylesbury pike connects the town with the fictional Arkham (based on Salem). *Dean's Corners* is another fictional village between Arkham and Aylesbury.

4. A mountain in Midwest Massachussetts near Amherst.

5. Historical records.

6. Aristocratic families permitted to carry a coat of arms.

7. *Voices of Azazel and Buzrael, of Beelzebub and Belial*: With the exception of Buzrael, these are all fallen angels and demons found in the Old Testament. Buzrael, though, is a creation of Lovecraft.

8. Those who study physical geography.

9. Creatures, spirits, angels, or deities in many religions whose responsibility is to escort newly deceased souls to the afterlife.

10. A Native American tribe formerly inhabiting western Massachusetts.

11. Celebrated on February 2, Candlemas celebrates the presentation of the child Jesus, His first entry into the temple; and the purification of the Virgin Mary.

12. A breed of dairy cattle originating from the British Channel Island of Alderney. Such cattle were smaller, more slender boned animals than the cattle of the other Channel Islands and in some ways they were more deer-like than bovine. Their milk was copious and produced very rich butter. The breed has been extinct since 1944.

13. A mound of earth and stones raised over a grave.

14. A common form of wooden siding consisting of long, thin boards.

15. Teaching through a system of regualry questions and answers.

16. Smelling nice.

17. Playful or humorous.

18. In American folklore, the whippoorwill's call is often considered an omen of death.

19. Lammas, meaning "loaf mass," is August 1 and is the festival of the first wheat harvest of the year.

20. Characterized by snoring or heavy breathing.

21. Extensive nowledge acquired from reading.

22. All Saints Day, November 1st.

23. Excessively noisy and unruly laughter.

24. Characterized by trembling fear.

25. Ideal.

26. Inarticulately chattering, babbling.

27. A mountain in the north of Lovecraft's Dreamlands, beyond the Plateau of Leng, on which the Castle of the Great Ones (where reside the gods of Earth).

28. Published in 1894, this novella about a half-human/half demon hybrid, was admired by Love-

craft, and Robert M. Price considers "The Dunwich Horror" an homage to Machen's story.

29. May Eve, or Beltane, falls on April 30th, the night before the first day of summer. This marks the beginning of the pastoral summer season, when livestock are driven out to the summer pastures. Beltane rituals mainly involve the symbolic use of fire and supposedly protect the animals, crops, and people from harm, both natural and supernatural, while also encouraging growth.

30. Roodmas (meaning "cross mass") is held on May 3, and is the celebration of the Feast of the Cross, commemorating the finding of the True Cross in Jerusalem in 355 by Saint Helena.

31. When days and nights are of equivalent length, this happens twice a year: in Spring and Fall

32. Foyer, atrium, or antechamber.

33. Concerning the study of abnormal physiological development.

34. Resembling a net, with criss-crossed veins, fibers, or lines.

35. Having a spotted pattern of large unpigmented (usually white) areas with normally pigmented (usually black) patches.

36. Covered with scales or plates.

37. Having a fringe of hairlike projections.

38. Ringlike.

39. Suborder of reptiles including lizrds, crocodiles, and dinosaurs.

40. Mournful.

41. In the early twentieth-century, a party wire (a.k.a. party line or shared service line) was an arrangement in which two or more customers were connected directly to the same local loop. This meant that if customers tried to use the phone, there was a good chance they would overhear their neighbors' conversations when picking up the receiver and have to wait for the line to clear. Prior to and during World War II in the United States, party wires were the primary way residential subscribers acquired local telephone service.

42. Unstoppable, unchangeable.

43. Islamic.

44. Specialized knowledge or detail that is mysterious to the average person;

45. These are all books, ranging from the 16th to the 19th centuries, exploring cryptography, or the study of codes and secret languages.

46. A midnight meeting of witches to practice witchcraft and sorcery; in the Middle Ages it was supposed to be a demonic orgy, usually associated with seasonal changes.

47. Restlessy.

48. Complete destruction, eradication,

49. The Elder Things were the first extraterrestrial species to come to the Earth, colonizing the planet about one billion years ago, roughly eight feet tall resembling a huge, oval-shaped barrel with starfish-like appendages at both ends. The top appendage was a head adorned with five eyes, five eating tubes, and a set of cilia for seeing in the darkness. The bottom appendage was five-limbed and was used for movement. They also had five evenly

spaced leathery, fan-like retractable wings and five evenly spaced sets of branching tentacles that sprouted from their torsos.

50. Eons; an eon is a geological term equating to half a billion years or more.

51. Remigius is the Latinized pen name for Nicholas Remy (1530–1612), an infamous French judge who presided over witchcraft trials. *Daemonolatreia* is a compendium of information about witchcraft, intended to be used for prosecuting alleged witches.

52. Effectiveness.

53. Car.

54. "The pestilence that walketh in darkness"; "Thou shalt not be afraid for the terror by night; nor for the arrow that flieth by day; Nor the pestilence that walketh in the darkness; nor for the destruction that wasteth at noonday." (Psalm 91:5–6)

55. Grew.

56. Large casks of liquid, primarily applied to alcoholic beverages such as wine, ale, or cider, equivalent to 63 U.S. gallons.

57. Harmonious.

58. Dark and dismal as of the rivers Acheron and Styx in Hades.

The Whisperer in Darkness

1. Known as one of Vermont's most devastating events, the flood of November 2–4, 1927 killed 84 people, including Lt. Governor S. Hollister Jackson and destroyed 1,285 bridges, several miles of roads and railroads, and countless homes and buildings.

2. Layer.

3. *Montpelier*: the capitol of Vermont located in the north-central part of the state. The Winooski River, a tributary of Lake Champlain, flows through the city; *Windham County*: the southeasternmost county of Vermont. Its county seat is Newfane, through which the West River flows; *Caledonia County*: located in the northeast Vermont. The Passumpsic River flows through the county and drains into the Connecticut River. Lyndonville is in the northeast part of the county.

4. A solid figure all plane sections of which are ellipses or circles; a three dimensional oval.

5. The fictitious *Legends of New England*.

6. *Benning Wentworth* (1696–1770) served as as the colonial governor of New Hampshire from 1741 to 1766.

7. A native American tribe that primarily inhabited the Merrimack River valley of present-day New Hampshire and Massachusetts, sometimes called the Merrimack people.

8. *Hurons*: native American tribe indigenous to the St. Lawrence River valley in southeastern Canada and northeastern U.S.; *the Five Nations*: a confederacy of five groups of Iroquois Indians: the Mohawk, Oneida, Onondaga, Cayuga, and Seneca nations originally located in upstate New York.

9. Primitive.

10. People in their 90's.

11. *Fauns*: a class of rural deities represented as men with the ears, horns, tail, and later also the hind legs of a goat; *dryads*: female spirits of nature (nymphs), who preside over the groves and forests; *satyrs*: a class of woodland deities, attendant on Bacchus/Dionysis, appearing as part human, part horse (sometimes part goat), noted for riotousness and lasciviousness; *kallikanzari*: malevolent goblins in Southeastern European and Turkish folklore that dwell underground but come to the surface during the twelve days of Christmas, during which time the sun ceases its seasonal movement.

12. Cave-dwellers.

13. *Mi-Go*: a race of winged fungoid aliens with large claws and heads covered in antennae from the planet Yuggoth, a fictional planet located on the extreme edge of our solar system; Abominable Snow-Men: a.k.a. Yeti, an ape-like being taller than an average human and allegedly inhabits the Himalayan region of Nepal and Tibet.

14. Affirmed earnestly.

15. *Charles Hoy Fort* (1874–1932) was an American writer and researcher into unexplained supernatural phenomena.

16. Engagingly provocative.

17. Esquire: a courtesy title used in the United States largely for lawyers and the United Kingdom for certain members of the gentry.

18. *Sir Edward Burnett Tylor* (1832–1917) was an English anthropologist who studied cultural evolution, explaining long-term change in human sociology through socio-cultural socially rather than biological means; *Sir John Lubbock* (1834–1913) was an English scientist who made significant contributions in archaeology, and ethnographyby positing an evolutionary framework for the accumulated archaeological remains bearing on human beginnings; *Sir James George Frazer* (1854–1941) author of *The Golden Bough*; *Armand de Quatrefrages de Breau* (1810–1892) was a zoologist, anthropologist, and professor of anatomy and ethnology at the Natural History Museum in Paris, who authored a treatise on pygmies that expounded the theory of the polyphyletic origin of man, the idea that man derived from multiple ancestors as opposed to a single ancestor; *Margaret Alice Murray* (1863–1963) was a prominent English Egyptologist, archaeologist, anthropologist, and folklorist; *Henry Fairfield Osborn, Sr.* (1857–1935) was an American geologist, paleontologist, and eugenist who developed the Dawn of Man theory, claiming that man evolved separately from apes and shared no common ancestry with them, and aristogenesis, claiming evolution comes from a creative faculty innate in living matter that anticipates the need for adaptation perfects it in advance; *Sir Arthur Keith* (1866–1955) was a Scottish anatomist and anthropologist and a strong proponent of the Piltdown Man, a paleoanthropological theory based parts of a skull and jawbone, allegedly collected from a gravel pit at Piltdown, East Sussex, England in 1912, that were presented as the fossilized remains of a previously unknown early human. However In 1953, it would be exposed as a hoax; *Marcellin Boule* (1861–

1942) was a French palaeontologist who in 1920 published the first analysis of a complete Neanderthal specimen and was an early sceptic of the Piltdown Man; *Sir Grafton Elliot Smith* (1871–1937) was an Australian-British anatomist and a proponent of the hyperdiffusionist view of prehistory, the idea that all major inventions and all cultures can be traced back to a single culture, in Smith's case, ancient Egypt.

19. "Nothing comes from nothing."

20. The material supposed to fill the region of the universe above the earth.

21. Because of its cool summer climate, New England was often a summer vacation spot, especially for Southerners and city-dwellers in the years before air conditioning.

22. The quality of being strange or odd.

23. *Fallibility*: the abilty to be wrong or false; *mendacity*: untruthfulness.

24. A sign or symbol that directly represents a concept, idea, or thing rather than a word or set of words for it.

25. *Tsathoggua*: creation of Clark Ashton Smith, a Great Old One who, while amorphous, often takes the form of a furry, toad-like being with sleepy eyes and a toothy grin; *Nyarlathotep*: in the Lovecraftian mythos, messenger of the Outer Gods, the Great Old Ones, and the Other Gods. It dwells in a cavern at the center of the earth; *Azathoth*: a.k.a. The Primal Chaos, one of Lovecraft's Outer Gods. Normally a shapeless and chaotic mass, it can take on the form of other beings when summoned; *Hastur*: Great Old One who lives or is imprisoned on a dark star in the constellation of Taurus; *Yian, Leng*: Yian may be the dreadful and forbidden capitol city of the Plateau of Leng; *the Lake of Hali*: Originally created by Robert W. Chambers in his collection *The King in Yellow* and incorporated by Lovecraft into his own mythos, it is a misty lake found near the city of Hastur (whether the city is named after the Great Old One or is its residence is unclear). The mysterious cities of Alar and Carcosa are built on its shores; *Beth-moora*: a fabled city in the story of the same name by Lord Dunsany, one of Lovecraft's greatest influences; *the Yellow Sign* the sign of Hastur the Great Old One and is used by members of his cult to identify one another; *L'mur-Kathulos*: a being associated with League of Hastur that may also be the Atlantean sorcerer of Robert E. Howard's story *Skull-Face*; *Bran*: Bran Mak Morn, last king of the Picts in Robert E. Howard's swords-and-sorcery fiction; *the Magnum Innominandum*: its name is Latin, meaning "Great Not-to-Be-Named." This being is the spawn of Azathoth and is possibly the progenitor of, Yog-Sothoth. It is also associated with Hastur. It is considered to be extremely dangerous to sorcerers, hence its title (meaning not to be summoned or ritually named in an incantation).

26. In many Lovecraft stories, the planet beyond Neptune is Yuggoth. Pluto was discovered in February, 1930 (as Lovecraft was writing this story) and here he seems to equate both planets.

27. A reference to Einstein's theory of relativity.

28. Before the introduction of public bus transportation, it was common for commuters to ride passenger trains even for day trips.

29. The Boston and Maine Railroad, a passenger train line operating in New England from 1836–1983.

30. Novice.

31. Characterized by disgrace or shame.

32. Another equating of Pluto with Yuggoth.

33. Having a secret meaning, mystifying.

34. Daylight Savings Time was enacted in the U.S. as part of the Standard Time Act of 1918, which established standard time zones and set summer DST to begin on March 31, 1918.

35. Located near the southwestern border of New Hampshire and southeastern border of Vermont, location of several Bigfoot sightings.

36. A sudden unpredictable change.

37. *Il Sodoma* (1477–1549) was the name given to Giovanni Antonio Bazzi, an Italian Renaissance painter whose style blended that of the High Renaissance style of early 16th-century Rome with the later Mannerist tradition.

38. Leonardo da Vinci.

39. Magic involving summoning or raising the dead; black magic or witchcraft.

40. Collection.

41. A thin watery or blood-tinged discharge, bile; also ethereal golden fluid that is the blood of the gods and/or immortals.

42. In the Lovecraft mythos, these manuscripts predate the origin of man. The Great Race of Yith is believed to have produced the first five chapters, which, among other things, contain a detailed chronicle of the race's history. They eventually found their way to Hyperborea (a fictional pre-historic land created by Clark Ashton Smith).

43. The present time.

44. *Magellanic Clouds*: two irregular dwarf galaxies visible from the southern hemisphere, which are members of our local group and may be orbiting our Milky Way galaxy; *globular nebulae*: possibly a reference to globular clusters: a spherical collection of stars that orbits a galactic core as a satellite; *allegory of Tao*: Tao, or "the way" is unknowable, thus followers of Tao seek understanding, but never fully achieve it; *Doels*: flesh-eating creatures living in a dark dimension that only mystical voyagers may visit; *Hounds of Tindalos*: Created by Frank Belnap Long, the "hounds" live in our distant past (or possibly another dimension) in the Tindalos, a city made up of corkscrewing towers, but are able to to travel to other places and times when tracking prey. They appear as either black formless shadows or green hairless canines with blue tongues; *Yig*: appearing as a serpent man, a bat-winged oriental dragon, or a giant snake, the Grat Old One Yig is responsible for the creation of reptiles, insects, and allegedly man. Unlike most of its brethren, Yig is often benevolent to man, though also quick to anger.

45. A fever marked by recurring spasms of chills and sweating.

46. In Lovecraft mythos, a pre-human city where the high temple of the Elder God Ulthar sits, also possibly the name of the Mi-Go leader.

47. *Jean Nicolas Arthur Rimbaud* (1854–1891) was a French libertine and poet who prefigured surrealism. *"Paul" Gustave Doré* (1832–1883) was a French artist working primarily with wood engraving. He most known for his illustrations of fantastic or mythological works such as Dante's *Divine Comedy*, Milton's *Paradise Lost*, and Coleridge's *The Rime of the Ancient Mariner*, among many others.

The Shadow Over Innsmouth

1. Jails.
2. Though not named in the texts, Lovecraft's notes reveal the name of the narrator as Robert Olmstead.
3. Newburyport is a small, coastal city in Essex County, Massachusetts, United States, 35 miles (56 km) northeast of Boston. Though Lovecraft mentions it here, it is also the model for Innsmouth.
4. Fictional river in east Massachussetts, based on the Merrimack River.
5. Croesus (595 BC–c. 547 BC) was the king of Lydia from 560 to 547 BC and was renowned for his extravagant wealth.
6. The Danvers State Hospital, a.k.a. The Danvers State Insane Asylum, was a psychiatric hospital located in Danvers, Massachusetts. It opened in 1878 and closed in 1992. Many critics believe it served as Lovecraft's inspiration for the Arkham sanatorium from H.P. Lovecraft's "The Thing on the Doorstep."
7. *Ichthyic*: characteristic of fishes; *batrachian*: characteristic of amphibians, especially frogs and toads.
8. One of the oldest secret societies, Freemasonry dates back to the MiddleAges. It is popularly believed that many if not most of the United States Founding Fathers were Freemasons.
9. Pertaining to the skin.
10. Degeneration theory was a widely influential concept in the social and biological sciences between about 1860 and 1910. In broad terms it theorizes that as races intermix, humanity becomes less complex and differentiated, and more primitive and animalistic. As the nineteenth century progressed, the increasing popularity of "degeneration" reflected an anxious pessimism about the future of European/Western civilization.
11. Plum Island is located off the northeast coast of Massachusetts, north of Cape Ann and is approximately 11 miles long.
12. *hipped roof*: a type of roof where all sides gently slope downwards to the walls; *cupola*: a small, domed structure on top of a building; *widow's walk*: a railed rooftop platform often with a small enclosed cupola frequently found on 19th-century North American coastal houses. The name refers to the wives of seamen, who would watch for their husbands' return, often in vain since many were killed at sea.
13. A bell-tower.
14. small, lightweight, shallow-draft fishing boats, about 16 to 23 feet long with high sides, flat bottoms and sharp bows.

15. Resembling monkeys.
16. April 30th is Beltane, or May Eve, the night before the first day of summer. October 31st is, of course, Halloween, but is is also Samhain, or the festival marking the end of the harvest season and the beginning of winter, the darker half of the year. Both festivals fall relatively halfway between the winter equinox and summer solstice (the point when the earth's access tilts closest to the sun, marking the shift from summer to fall).
17. A reference to Edgar Allan Poe's poem of the same name, which deals with human mortality and the inevitability of death.
18. Upper-class, aristocratic.
19. Ornamental flowe.r gardens having the beds and paths arranged to form patterns.
20. A reference to Edgar Allan Poe's short story of the same name about self-destructive influences and compunctions to do wrong for wrong's sake.
21. Drunken rambling.
22. Self-righteously moralizing.
23. *Othaheite*: the former name of Tahiti, located in the archipelago of the Society Islands in the southern Pacific Ocean; *Ponape*: the former name of Pohnpei, part of the Caroline Islands in the western Pacific Ocean. The ruins are a reference to Nan Madol, a ruined city adjacent to the eastern shore of the island; *Easter Island*: a Polynesian Island in the southeastern Pacific Ocean famous for its 887 extant monumental statues, called moai, which resemble people with overly large heads.
24. A reference to Kanakas, Pacific Island workers employed in British colonies, such as British Columbia (Canada), Fiji and Queensland (Australia) in the 19th and early 20th centuries.
25. A fulling mill is a water mill where wool cloth is fulled, or cleansed, to eliminate oils, dirt, and other impurities, and to thicken it.
26. Drunkard.
27. *Mene, Mene, Tekel, Upharsin*: In the Book of Daniel, these words appear on the wall at a banquet hosted by King Belshazzar as the guests profane the sacred vessels pillaged from the Jerusalem Temple. Daniel interpretes this message to mean that the days of the Babylonian kingdom are "numbered, weighed, and divided." That night, Belshazzar is killed and the Persians sack the capital city.
28. In Freemasonry, a commandery is one of the upper-level administrative bodies. The Calvary Commandery is located in East Providence, RI, and would most likely have been responsible for this particular Masonic Hall.
29. In Lovecraft's mythos, Mother Hydra and Father Dagon are overgrown rulers of the Deep Ones (a race of intelligent ocean-dwelling creatures, roughly humanoid but with an amphibious or fishlike appearance). Together with Cthulhu, they form the triad of gods worshiped by the Deep Ones.
30. "Hail! Hail! Cthulhu dreams! In his house at R'lyeh dead Cthulhu lies dreaming-."
31. Maumee is a suburb of Toledo; however, it is possible that this is a reference to Maumee Valley Hospital's psychiatric unit.

32. A private liberal arts college in Oberlin, Ohio.

33. *Brachiate*: having wildly diverging paired branches; *efflorescence*: flowering.

34. *Pth'thya-l'yi*: The narrator's great-great-grandmother; *Y'ha-nthlei*: the Deep Ones' city off the Coast of Innsmouth beneath Devil's Reef. This is the only named city of Deep Ones in Lovecraft's fiction.

35. A geologic period that began 66 and ended 23.03 million years ago.

36. "Hail R'lyeh! Cthulhu dreams! Hail! Hail!"

Waste Paper

1. "All is laughter, all is dust, all is nothing."

2. A brass horn played much like a kazoo.

3. "(Won't You Come Home) Bill Bailey," originally titled "Bill Bailey, Won't You Please Come Home?" and commonly referred to simply as "Bill Bailey," is a Dixieland and jazz standard published in 1902 and written by Hughie Cannon (1877–1912), an American songwriter and pianist.

4. "When the Whip-Poor-Will Sings, Marguerite" was a popular 1906 song written by C.M. Denison (lyrics) and J. Fred Helf (music).

5. *American Notes for General Circulation* is a travelogue by Charles Dickens published in 1842 detailing his trip to North America from January to June, 1842, where he acted as a critical observer of North American society, almost as if returning a status report on their progress.

6. Possibly a reference to Lovecraft's maternal grandfather, Asaph "Asa" Phillips (1764–1829).

7. A reference to the last line of T.S. Eliot's poem *The Waste Land* (of which Lovecraft's poem is a parody) literally it means "peace, peace, peace" though Eliot translated it as "The Peace which passeth understanding."

8. Written by William Loren Curtiss. In a letter that appears in the March 7, 1914 issue of *All-Story Weekly*, Lovecraft prasies this story as "the best of the two he has contributed" to the magazine.

9. A pulp magazine begun in 1905 (though it did not publish weekly until 1914). Edgar Rice Burroughs was its most famous contributor.

10. A popular song from 1921 by Dorothy Terriss and Julian Robledo.

11. A reference to the first line of one of Lovecraft's earlier poems, "Nemesis."

12. A reference to the first line of *The Iliad* as translated by Alexander Pope (1688–1744).

13. Field Marshal Julian Hedworth George Byng, 1st Viscount Byng of Vimy (1862–1935) was a British Army officer who served as Governor General of Canada from 1921 to 1926. It is the governor-general's duty to act as the monarch's representative and carry out most of the crown's constitutional and ceremonial duties.

14. Possibly a reference to Joseph Miller (1684–1738), a British humourist and the author of *Joe Miller's Jests* (1739), a hugely popular joke book of the 18th century. S.T. Joshi, however, has been unable to verify the existence of an 1847 U.S. edition.

15. *The Conchologist's First Book* (sometimes subtitled with *Or, A System of Testaceous Malacology*) is an illustrated textbook on conchology (the study of mollusks) issued in 1839, 1840, and 1845. Though the book was originally printed under Edgar Allan Poe's name, he wrote just the preface and introduction. He allowed the printer to put his name on the title page for $50 (roughly $1,078 today).

16. George Creel (1876–1953) was an investigative journalist, a politician, and, most famously, the first head of the United States Committee on Public Information, a propaganda organization created by President Woodrow Wilson during World War I.

17. Lovecraft despised Eliot's poetry, *The Waste Land* in particular.

18. William Congreve (1670–1729) was an English dramatist who shaped the English comedy of manners through his brilliant comic dialogue, his satirical portrayal of the war of the sexes, and his ironic scrutiny of the affectations of his age.

19. Governing through lies and misdirection.

20. A reference to Poe's poem "Ulalume."

21. *The History of Tom Jones, a Foundling*, often known simply as *Tom Jones*, is a comic novel by the English playwright and novelist Henry Fielding (1707–1754). Published in 1749, it is one of the earliest English novels.

22. Benny Leonard fought Lew Tendler in the boxing ring twice, July 27, 1922 and a year later on July 23, 1923. It is probably the first match Lovecraft is referencing here.

Fungi from Yuggoth

1. Shaped like a vertical elongated diamond.

2. A disorderly collection.

3. Presumably the *Necronomicon*.

4. The lands of an estate or manor.

5. City in ancient Greece, the site of the tragedy in *Oedipus Rex*.

6. Most of these sonnets were written in late 1929-early 1930; it is possible, then, that the image of Innsmouth here recurs before the events of Lovecraft's "Shadow Over Innsmouth," written in late 1931.

7. Suffering from leprosy, a disease causing scaly skin lesions.

8. *Mongrel throngs*: crowds of mixed-blooded people.

9. One of the twin moons of Yuggoth, it is described as a dark world.

10. *County farm*: short for "county funny farm," the county mental hospital.

11. One of the five cities of the plain of Jordan in *Genesis*, which escaped the fire and brimstone that destroyed Sodom and Gomorrah.

12. Meaning "western land," this may be a reference to a mythical garden in the western corner of the world tended by the Hesperides, nymphs who are the daughters of Hesperus, the evening star.

13. The brightest star in the constellation Piscis Austrinus and one of the brightest stars in the sky.

14. A third moon of Yuggoth covered by fungi and having luminescent clouds obstructing all sunlight.

15. Antarctica, this sonnet foreshadows events in *At the Mountains of Madness*.

16. A flat, elevated region; a plateau or mesa.

17. The part of a bell that hits the inside wall, making the chime.

18. Divided into two equal parts.

19. The other of the twin moons of Yuggoth, Lovecraft gives no description of it.

20. Native peasants or laborers of the middle east.

21. A reference to Azathoth, the idiot god at the center of ultimate chaos.

22. Public ceremonies and splendid displays.

23. Made of no material, insubstantial.

24. A mineral that most often forms as an alteration of calcite, as magnesium replaces much of the calcium in the crystal structure.

25. A fictional planet orbiting five suns millions of light years away from earth, it is in the same part of the night sky as Deneb.

26. Caverns found on Yuggoth's moon, Thog.

27. Blended.

28. Discern.

Supernatural Horror in Literature

1. Expresses earnest disapproval.

2. The basic tenets of Freudian psychoanalysis are that a person's development is determined by events in early childhood; human attitude, mannerism, experience, and thought are largely influenced by unconscious, irrational drives; attempts to bring these drives into awareness meet psychological resistance in the form of defense mechanisms; conflicts between conscious and unconscious, or repressed, material can materialize in the form of mental or emotional disturbances, for example: neurosis, neurotic traits, anxiety, depression etc.; and the liberation from the effects of the unconscious material is achieved through bringing this material into the conscious mind through the skilled guidance of a therapist. Lovecraft was generally scornful of Freud's theories.

3. Of the same age, date, or duration.

4. Intentionally harmful or evil.

5. *Elsie Venner: A Romance of Destiny*, an 1861 novel by American author and physician Oliver Wendell Holmes, Sr. (1809–1894), tells the story of a neurotic young woman whose mother was bitten by a rattlesnake while pregnant, essentially making her daughter half-woman, half-snake; "The Upper Berth" (1886), by the American horror writer, F. Marion Crawford (1854–1909), tells the story of a traveller who books passage on a ship across the Atlantic, and is at first pleased to find he has a stateroom to himself until he discovers it is haunted; "The Monkey's Paw" (1909) by the English writer William Wymark Jacobs (1863–1943) tells of a couple who make three wishes on the paw of a dead monkey that exact a price for interfering with fate.

6. *The Book of Enoch*: a non-canonical ancient composite religious work, ascribed to Enoch, the great-grandfather of Noah, and describes his travels through the heavens; *Claviculae of Solomon*: a book of magic ascribed to King Solomon, probably dates to the 14th or 15th century.

7. A body of mystical Jewish teachings based on an esoteric interpretation of the Hebrew Scriptures.

8. Ancient Germanic or Celtic person.

9. Northern.

10. Aryans (now known as Indo-Europeans) were a people who were said to speak an archaic Indo-European language and who were thought to have settled in prehistoric times in ancient Iran and the northern Indian subcontinent. According to 19th century anthropologists, these light-skinned Aryans invaded and conquered ancient India from the north and their literature, religion, and modes of social organization subsequently shaped the course of Indian culture, particularly the Vedic religion that informed and was eventually superseded by Hinduism. Modern anthropologists no longer accept this theory.

11. The Mongols caused great terror throughout Eurasia during the Mongol Empire invasions of the 13th century.

12. A religious ritual allegedly performed by witches and Satanists characterized by the inversion of the Mass as celebrated by the Roman Catholic Church.

13. *Saint Albertus Magnus*, a.k.a. Saint Albert The Great, (c. 1200–1280) was a Dominican bishop and philosopher best known as a teacher of St. Thomas Aquinas and as a proponent of Aristotelianism at the University of Paris. He established the study of nature as a legitimate science within the Christian tradition; *Raymond Lully*, a.k.a. Ramon Llull (c. 1232–c. 1315) was a Majorcan writer, logician, and philosopher credited with writing the first major work of Catalan literature.

14. *Nostradamus* (1503–1566) was a French apothecary and reputed seer who published collections of prophecies that have since become famous worldwide; *Johannes Trithemius* (1462–1516) was a German Benedictine abbot and a polymath active in the German Renaissance, as a lexicographer, chronicler, cryptographer, and occultist; *John Dee* (1527–1608/9) was a Welsh mathematician, astronomer, astrologer, occultist, and adviser to Queen Elizabeth I. He devoted much of his life to the study of alchemy, divination and Hermetic philosophy; *Robert Fludd* (1574–1637), was a prominent English physician remembered as an astrologer, mathematician, cosmologist, cabbalist, and Rosicrucian apologist.

15. An evil spirit or demon.

16. *Rev. Sabine Baring-Gould* (1834–1924) was an English Anglican priest, hagiographer, antiquarian, novelist and eclectic scholar. His bibliography consists of more than 1240 publications, though this list continues to grow. The work Lovecraft refers to here is *Curious Myths of the Middle Ages* (1866).

17. *Gaius Petronius Arbiter* (c. AD 27–66) was a Roman courtier during the reign of Nero and author

of the *Satyricon*, a satirical novel believed to have been written during the Neronian era. Lovecraft is referring to chapters 61–62 of this book; *Apuleius* (c. 125–c. 180 CE) was a Latin-language prose writer whose most famous work is the novel, the *Metamorphoses*, also called *The Golden Ass*, the only Latin novel that has survived in its entirety, which relates the ludicrous adventures of one Lucius, who experiments with magic and is accidentally turned into a donkey; *Pliny the Younger*, a.k.a. Gaius Plinius Caecilius Secundus (61–c. 113) was a lawyer, author, and magistrate of Ancient Rome. The letter Lovecraft refers to here discusses the existence of ghosts and relates some allegedly true ghost stories; *Phlegon of Tralles* was a Greek writer and freedman of the emperor Hadrian, who lived in the 2nd century AD. His book, *On Wonderful Events*, is a compilation of grotesque, bizarre or sensational anecdotes.

18. King James I was notorious in his hatred and persecution of alleged witches.

19. Daniel Defoe (c. 1660–1731) was an English trader, writer, journalist, pamphleteer, and spy, now most famous for his novel *Robinson Crusoe*.

20. Tobias George Smollett (1721–1771) was a Scottish poet and author. His 1753 novel, *The Adventures of Ferdinand Count Fathom*, tells of an unscrupulous dandy who cheats, swindles and philanders his way across Europe and England.

21. *Ossian* is the narrator and purported author of a cycle of epic poems published by the Scottish poet James Macpherson (1736–1796) from 1760. Macpherson falsely claimed to have collected word-of-mouth material in Scots Gaelic, said to be from ancient sources, and that the work was his translation of that material.

22. Robert Burns (1759–1796) was a Scottish poet and lyricist. "Tam O'Shanter" (1791) is an epic poem describing the escapades of a drunken Scottish farmer.

23. James Hogg (1770–1835) was a Scottish poet and novelist. "Kilmeny" discusses the immortality of maidenhood (purity's power to transport one from the everyday to the marvelous).

24. Gottfried August Bürger (1747–1794) was a German poet. His poem "The Wild Huntsman"tells the story of a legendary evil huntsman doomed to an eternity of being chased by his own hounds. "Lenore" tells of a young girl kidnapped a ghostly rider, posing as her dead lover.

25. Sir Walter Scott (1771–1832) was a Scottish writer, most famous for his novel, *Ivanhoe*, who wrote his own adaptations of these two poems.

26. Horatio Walpole (1717–1797) was an English art historian, man of letters, antiquarian, and politician, famous for his 1764 novel, *The Castle of Otranto*.

27. Anna Laetitia Barbauld, née Aikin (1743–1825) was a prominent English poet, essayist, literary critic, editor, and children's author.

28. Clara Reeve (1729–1807) was an English novelist, best known for *The Old English Baron*.

29. An English author and a pioneer of the Gothic novel whose descriptions of landscapes and long travel scenes is clearly romantic, but whose Gothic quality emerges from the use of supernatural elements.

30. Charles Brockden Brown (1771–1810), an American novelist considered the most important American novelist before James Fenimore Cooper. His most famous novels are often referred to as "gothic" due to their sensational violence, dramatic intensity, and the suggestion of supernatural elements.

31. An English novelist and dramatist, often referred to as "Monk" Lewis, because of the success of his classic Gothic novel, *The Monk*.

32. George Edward Bateman Saintsbury (1845–1933), was an English writer, literary historian, scholar, and critic.

33. Edith Birkhead was a lecturer in English Literature at the University of Bristol and a Noble Fellow at the University of Liverpool. The history Lovecraft refers to is *The Tale of Terror* (1921).

34. William Thomas Beckford (1760–1844) was an English novelist, art collector and patron, critic, travel writer, and sometime politician. His novel, *History of the Caliph Vathek*, was published in French in 1782 and translated to English in1786.

35. Antoine Galland (1646–1715) was a French orientalist and archaeologist, most famous as the first European translator of *One Thousand and One Nights*.

36. William Godwin (1756–1836) was an English journalist, political philosopher and novelist. He was also the father of Mary Shelley, the author of *Frankenstein*.

37. Edward George Earle Lytton Bulwer-Lytton, 1st Baron Lytton PC (1803–1873), was an immensely popular English novelist, poet, playwright, and politician.

38. George William MacArthur Reynolds (1814–1879) was a British author and journalist. *Faust: A Romance of the Secret Tribunals* and was published 1847, and *Wagner, the Wehr-Wolf* was published serially in 1846–7.

39. Mary Shelley, née Wollstonecraft Godwin (1797–1851) was an English novelist, short story writer, dramatist, essayist, biographer, and travel writer, and wife of the Romantic poet and philosopher Percy Bysshe Shelley (1792–1822).

40. Alphonse Louis Constant (1810–1875) was a French occult author and ceremonial magician. Eliphas Lévi, the name under which he published his books, was an attempt to translate his name "Alphonse Louis" into Hebrew.

41. Apollonius of Tyana (c. 15–c. 100 CE) was a Greek philosopher. He has been compared with Jesus of Nazareth by both early Christians and modern writers.

42. *Joseph Thomas Sheridan Le Fanu* (1814–1873) was an Irish writer of Gothic tales and mystery novels and was central to the development of the ghost-story genre in the Victorian era; *Thomas Peckett Prest*, a.k.a. Thomas Preskett Prest (c. 1810–c. 1859) was a British journalist, musician, and prolific producer of penny dreadfuls. He is now remembered as the co-creator (with James Malcolm Rymer) of the

fictional Sweeney Todd, the "demon barber" immortalized in his *The String of Pearls*; *William Wilkie Collins* (1824–1889) was an English novelist, playwright, and author of suspense stories; *Sir Henry Rider Haggard* (1856–1925) was an English writer of adventure novels set in exotic locations, predominantly Africa, and a founder of the Lost World literary genre. His most famous works are *King Solomon's Mines* (1885), which introduced the character of Allain Quatermain (literary precursor to Indiana Jones) and *She* (1887), which introduced Ayesha, the mysterious white queen of a lost African kingdom who reigns as the all-powerful "She-Who-Must-Be-Obeyed"; *Sir Arthur Ignatius Conan Doyle* (1859–1930) was a Scottish physician and writer most noted for his creation of the detective Sherlock Holmes, but was also a prolific writer of fantasy and science fiction; *Herbert George "H.G." Wells* (1866–1946) was a prolific English writer in many genres, but best remembered for his science fiction novels. He shares the title of the father of science fiction Jules Verne (1828–1905) and Hugo Gernsback (1884–1967); *Robert Louis Balfour Stevenson* (1850–1894) was a Scottish novelist, poet, essayist, and travel writer best known for the novels *Treasure Island* (1883), *Kidnapped* (1886), and *Strange Case of Dr Jekyll and Mr Hyde* (1886).

43. Ernst Theodor Wilhelm Hoffmann was a German Romantic author of fantasy and horror whose stories were influential during the 19th century. He is perhaps best known as the author of *The Nutcracker and the Mouse King* (1816), on which the ballet *The Nutcracker* is based.

44. Friedrich Heinrich Karl de la Motte, Baron Fouqué (12 February 1777–23 January 1843) was a German writer of the romantic style. He is most known for his fairy-tale novella *Undine* (1811).

45. Paracelsus, born Philippus Aureolus Theophrastus Bombastus von Hohenheim (1493–1541) was a Swiss German Renaissance physician, botanist, alchemist, astrologer, and general occultist.

46. Johannes Wilhelm Meinhold (1797–1851) was a Pomeranian priest and author.

47. Pierre Jules Théophile Gautier (1811–1872) was a French poet, dramatist, novelist, journalist, and art and literary critic.

48. *"Avatar"* (1856) is a fantasy short story that deals with mind-switching; *"The Foot of the Mummy"* (1840) tells the adventures of a man who purchases the four thousand year old foot of an Egyptian princess; *"Clarimonde"* (1836) is the story of a priest who falls in love with a vampire.

49. Published in 1838, this story relates an imagined romantic incident between Cleopatra VII and Meïamoun, an admirer who spies her bathing.

50. Charles-Marie-Georges Huysmans (1848–1907) was a French novelist who published his works as Joris-Karl Huysmans.

51. Prosper Mérimée (1803–1870) was a French dramatist, historian, archaeologist, and short story writer perhaps best known for his novella *Carmen*, which became the basis of Bizet's opera *Carmen*. "Venus of Ille" (1837) tells the story of a statue of

Venus that comes to life and kills the son of its owner, whom it believes to be its husband.

52. Thomas Moore (1779–1852) was an Irish poet, singer, songwriter, and entertainer. "The Ring" is a ballad relating the tale of a young man who finds himself accidentally wed to a demon.

53. Fitz-James O'Brien (1828–1862) was an Irish-born American writer, some of whose work is often considered a forerunner of today's science fiction. The story Lovecraft references here is "What Was It? A Mystery" (1859) is one of the earliest examples of an invisible antagonist in fiction.

54. French authors Émile Erckmann (1822–1899) and Alexandre Chatrian (1826–1890), nearly all of whose works were jointly written, wrote under the name Erckmann-Chatrian.

55. Jean-Marie-Mathias-Philippe-Auguste, comte de Villiers de l'Isle-Adam (1838–1889) was a French symbolist writer of fantasy, horror, and mystery.

56. Maurice Level (1875–1926), was a French writer of macabre fiction and drama. His works were printed regularly in Paris newspapers and sometimes staged by le Théâtre du Grand-Guignol, a repertory company devoted to melodramatic productions emphasizing blood and gore.

57. *Gustav Meyrink* (1868–1932) was the pseudonym of Gustav Meyer, an Austrian author, novelist, dramatist, and translatormost famous for his novel *The Golem* (1914), which tells the story of a ghetto in Prague haunted by a monster; *Ansky* was the assumed name of Shloyme Zanvl Rappoport (1863–1920), a Russian Jewish author, playwright, researcher of Jewish folklore, polemicist, and cultural and political activist. *The Dybbuk, or Between Two Worlds* (1914) is a play that tells of a young bride possessed by a malicious spirit on the eve of her wedding.

58. Charles Pierre Baudelaire (1821–1867) was a French poet, essayist, art critic, and translator of Edgar Allan Poe.

59. *The Decadents* were an artistic movement especially of late 19th characterized by refined aestheticism, artifice, and the quest for new sensations; *The Symbolists* believed that art should represent absolute truths that could only be described indirectly through metaphor and suggestion, endowing particular images with symbolic meaning.

60. The process of logical thinking.

61. Ernst Theodor Wilhelm Hoffmann.

62. Obsession.

63. Edward John Moreton Drax Plunkett, 18th Baron of Dunsany (1878–1957), an Irish writer most notable for his fantasy tales, one of Lovecraft's great influences.

64. Lovecraft's source for this knowledge is unknown.

65. A reference to the styles of Ann Radcliffe and Matthew Lewis.

66. The Byronic or Romantic hero has been described by the British historian Lord Macauley as "a man proud, moody, cynical, with defiance on his brow, and misery in his heart, a scorner of his kind,

implacable in revenge, yet capable of deep and strong affection."

67. Manfred is the title character of Byron's *Manfred: A Dramatic Poem* (1817) who is tortured by guilt over with the death of his beloved. Throughout the poem he challenges all of the authoritative powers he faces, and chooses death over submitting to the powerful spirits he raises to ask for forgetfulness.

68. Paul Elmer More (1864–1937) was an American journalist, critic, and essayist.

69. Samuel Loveman (1887–1976) was an American poet, critic, and dramatist. He was the basis of Harley Warren in Lovecraft's story "The Statement of Randolf Carter."

70. Dr. Frederic Taber Cooper (1864–1937) was an American writer, and editor of several periodicals such as *The New York Commercial Advertiser*, *The Forum*, and *The New York Globe*.

71. Robert William Chambers (1865–1933) was an American artist and fiction writer, best known for his book of mostly interconnected short stories, *The King in Yellow* (1895).

72. George Louis Palmella Busson du Maurier (1834–1896) was a French-born British cartoonist and author, known for his cartoons in the British humor magazine *Punch* and also for his 1894 novel *Trilby*, which tells of a tone-deaf half–Irish girl working in Paris as an artists' model and laundress.

73. Mary Eleanor Wilkins Freeman (1852–1930) was a prominent 19th-century American author of fiction combining domestic realism with supernaturalism.

74. Irvin Shrewsbury Cobb (1876–1944) was an American humorist, columnist, and author of more than 60 books and 300 short stories.

75. Leonard Lanson Cline (11 May 1893–15/16 January 1929) was an American novelist, poet, short story writer, and journalist.

76. Herbert S. Gorman (1893–1954) was an American writer and literary critic whose 1927 novel, *The Place Called Dagon*, was a likely influence on at least two of Lovecraft's works: "The ShadowOver Innsmouth" and "Dreams in the Witch House."

77. Patrick Lafcadio Hearn (1850–1904) was an international writer, known best for his books about Japan, especially his collections of Japanese legends and ghost stories, such as *Kwaidan: Stories and Studies of Strange Things* (1903).

78. Matthew Phipps Shiell (1865–1947) was a prolific British writer of West Indian descent remembered primarily for supernatural and scientific romances. *The Purple Cloud* (1901) is his most famous and most often reprinted novel.

79. Francis Brett Young (1884–1954) was an English novelist, poet, playwright, and composer. *Cold Harbor* (1924) was a psychological thriller and part of his Mercian series, a series of linked novels set in a loosely fictionalised version of the English West Midlands and Welsh Borders.

80. Walter John de la Mare (1873–1956) was an English poet, short story writer, and novelist probably best remembered for his children's books though he also wrote several psychological horror stories.

81. Edward Frederic Benson (1867–1940) was an English novelist, biographer, memoirist, archaeologist, and short story writer of, among other subjects, ghost stories.

82. Herbert Russell Wakefield (1888–1964) was an English short story writer, novelist, and publisher remembered for his ghost stories.

83. William Hope Hodgson (1877–1918) was an English writer of essays, short fiction, and novels, spanning several overlapping genres including horror, fantastic fiction, and science fiction.

84. *William Carleton* (1794–1869) was an Irish writer and novelist best known for his *Traits and Stories of the Irish Peasantry* (1830) a collection of ethnic sketches of the stereotypical Irishman as well as Irish folklore and legend; *Thomas Crofton Croker* (1798–1854) was an Irish antiquarian known for his book, *Fairy Legends and Traditions of the South of Ireland* (1825); *Jane Francesca Agnes, Lady Wilde* (1821–1896) was an Irish poet who had a special interest in Irish folktales, which she helped to gather; *Douglas Hyde* (1860–1949) was an Irish scholar of the Irish language, the first President of Ireland from 1938 to 1945, a leading figure in the Gaelic revival, and first president of the Gaelic League, one of the most influential cultural organizations in Ireland; *William Butler Yeats* (1865–1939) was an Irish poet and collector of Irish folklore and legends.

85. *Edmund John Millington Synge* (1871–1909) was an Irish playwright, poet, prose writer, travel writer, collector of folklore, and a key figure in the Irish Literary Revival of the early 20th century; *George William Russell* (1867–1935) who wrote under the pseudonym Æ (sometimes written AE or A.E.), was an Irish editor, critic, poet, artistic painter, nationalist, and writer of mysticism; *Isabella Augusta, Lady Gregory* (1852–1932) was an Irish dramatist and folklorist; *Padraic Colum* (1881–1972) was an Irish poet, novelist, dramatist, biographer, playwright, children's author and collector of folklore. He was also a leading figure in the Irish Literary Revival; *James Stephens* (1880–1950) was an Irish novelist, poet, and collector of Irish myths and fairy tales.

86. Also known as ring forts or fairy forts, raths are circular fortified settlements that were mostly built during the Early Middle Ages found in Northern Europe, especially Ireland. Tradition associates their circular remains with fairies, leprechauns, and giants.

87. Literally: Sabbath wine.

88. Montague Rhodes James (1862–1936) was an English author, medieval scholar, and provost of King's College, Cambridge (1905–1918), and of Eton College (1918–1936), mostly remembered for his ghost stories, which are regarded as among the best in the genre.

89. A two-handled onyx cup carved with Dionysiac vignettes and emblems, now conserved at the National Library of France in Paris and at one time believed to have been commissioned by Ptolemy II (309–246 BC), king of Egypt.

The Structure of Lovecraft's Longer Narratives

1. Rpt. In my *H. P. Lovecraft: Four Decades of Criticism* (1980), p. 69.
2. The narrator's cat [ed.].
3. Cf., e.g., Cedric Whitman *Homer and the Homeric Tradition* (1958), Ch. 12. It is interesting to note that Lovecraft, in his juvenile retelling of the *Odyssey* ("The Poem of Ulysses," 1897), simplifies the structure of the epic vastly and narrates the plot strictly chronologically, to the point of omitting entirely the Adventure of Telemachus of Books I–IV.
4. This is not to imply that the tale is necessarily one of Lovecraft's best: indeed, in certain of its philosophical bases, uses of language, and plot elements it is distinctly inferior to many of Lovecraft's longer tales.
5. *Horror!* (1969), p. 268.
6. *Lovecraft: A Biography* (1975), p. 354.
7. "A Literary Copernicus"' rpt. In *H.P. Lovecraft: Four Decades of Criticism*, p. 57.
8. This was suggested to me by Donald R. Burleson [noted horror writer and Lovecraft scholar, ed.].
9. Cf. H.D.F. Kitto, *Greek Tragedy* (1954 ed.), p. 199: "The horrible death of Glauce and Creon is described exhaustively in the terrible style of which Euripedes was such a master. It is sheer Grand Guignol. We have yet seen nothing like it in Greek Tragedy."
10. "Lurking" 232. For a political interpretation of the phrase see Paul Buhle, "Dystopia as Utopia," rpt. In my *H.P. Lovecraft: Four Decades of Criticism*, p. 207.
11. Cf. Fritz Leiber's explanation of this concept in Lovecraft; "A Literary Copernicus"' in my *H.P. Lovecraft: Four Decades of Criticism*, p. 56.
12. *Ibid.*, pp. 56f.
13. *Lovecraft ou du fantastique* (1972), p. 12.
14. *The Notes and Commonplace Book* (1938; rpt. 1978), p. 5.

Cosmic Fear and the Fear of the Lord: Lovecraft's Religious Vision

1. Both of which can be found in S.T. Joshi's *H.P. Lovecraft, Four Decades of Criticism* [ed.].

The Victorian Era's Influence on H.P. Lovecraft

1. Scholars have provided several starting and ending points for the Victorian Era. Some prefer a literal approach and give the reign of Queen Victoria (1837–1901) as the range, while others will reach back to the First Reform Bill in 1832 and forward only to the 1880s (see Altick 1–16). For the purposes of this broad approach to the period, however, we will use the earliest and latest dates, 1832 & 1901, as our chronological bookends.
2. Although the reference certainly did not give the time period its name, it is interesting that one of the more infamous items in Oscar Wilde's *The Picture of Dorian Gray*, one that contributes to the title character's continued moral degeneration, is "a book bound in yellow paper, the cover slightly torn and the edges soiled" (102). Although the work's identity is unclear, many critics believe it to be J.K. Huysman's *Against Nature*, explored later in this essay.
3. Never willing to rest comfortably, Huysmans's narrator also enjoyed collecting not only "artificial flowers aping real ones," but also "natural flowers that would look like fakes" (97). The emphasis on form, on artificiality, however, is still omnipresent.
4. The original structure stood for 6 months, the duration of the Great Exhibition. It was then dismantled and relocated to Penge Common, where it was reassembled and rebuilt in an enlarged form by 1854.

The Internal Continuity of Lovecraft's *Fungi from Yuggoth*

1. It must be noted that this particular era isn't exactly highly popular among readers of poetry these days; not that the Augustans don't still have their aficionados or fail to make it into popular anthologies, but they don't command the same public recognition and affection as the later Romantic Poets. And hence Lovecraft's adoption of the Georgian styles hasn't exactly endeared him to poetry readers—many find the original Augustan poets too structured and overly mannered, never mind Lovecraft's imitations of them.
2. The Thog mentioned in this verse is, one of the twin moons of Yuggoth according Lovecraft.
3. Which would ultimately become the model for these beings in many RPGs and video games.
4. The vast ice entombed horror mentioned at the end of this sonnet is one of Lovecraft's Great Old Ones, Gol-goroth. This particular demon was actually created by Robert E Howard and in his story "The Fishers From Outside," Lin Carter links Howard's stories with this sonnet, claiming that Gol-goroth is entombed in the Antarctic beneath Mount Antarktos.
5. Another name for Azathoth [ed.].
6. It is quite possible that these black-winged, crouching things could very well be the Night-Gaunts from XX.
7. Leng is frequently mentioned in Lovecraft's fiction. However where exactly this mountain fastness is located is unclear—in some tales such as *The Dream-Quest of Unknown Kadath*, it appears to be on the edges of Lovecraft's dream world, but in others such as "The Hound" and "The Call of Cthulhu,"

it would appear to be located somewhere in the Himalayas, an evil counterpart to other unmapped realms like Shambhala or Shangri-la. Seemingly like the Peaks of Thok in XX, Leng appears to exist in both the waking world and the dimension of the Dreamlands.

An Interview with Cherie Priest

1. Religious fundamentalist.
2. Both *Maplecroft* an its sequel, *Chapelwood*, are now available through Ace books.
3. The author of *Psycho.*

An Interview with Caitlín R. Kiernan

1. The antagonist of Melville's novel *Moby Dick.*
2. Published in Sirenia Digest #52, March 2010; reprinted in Black Wings II, 2012; PS Publishing.
3. Lovecraft cites both of these stories as excellent examples of the weird tale in his essay *Supernatural Horror in Literature.*

An Interview with Richard Monaco

1. Edward Elmer Smith, PhD (1890–1965) a.k.a. E.E. Smith, was an early American science fiction author, best known for the *Lensman* series. The Lensman series, which consisted of six books published between 1948 and 1954, was a space opera that followed the adventures of heroes who protected the galaxy from ever more dangerous villains. The series is noted for its internal consistency, long-term story planning, and breathtaking originality of plot and concept.
2. *Shadow Gold* would have been Monaco's tenth novel in the late 1980's, but he found himself unable to complete it. Then it was lost, and found again in 2012. It is currently being revised and edited for publication.
3. Monaco's Parsival series consists of five books: an original trilogy consisting of *Parsival or a Knight's Tale* (1977), *The Grail War* (1979), and *The Final Quest* (1980), as well as two books set in the lost years between *Parsival* and *The Grail War*; *Blood and Dreams* (1985), and more recently, *The Quest for Avalon* (2012).
4. Author of the novel *Young Men Shall See* and childhood friend of Leverett Butts.
5. *No Time Like the Past* is available from Iron Dragon Books.

Works Cited and Select Bibliography

Primary Works

Lovecraft, H.P. *The Ancient Track: The Complete Poetical Works of H.P. Lovecraft.* Ed. S.T. Joshi. New York: Hippocampus, 2013. Print.

_____. *The Annotated Supernatural Horror in Literature.* Ed. S.T. Joshi. New York: Hippocampus, 2012. Print.

_____. *The Fiction: Complete and Unabridged.* New York: Barnes & Noble, 2008.

_____. *H.P. Lovecraft's Collected Fiction: A Variorum Edition.* 3 vols. Ed. S.T. Joshi. New York: Hippocampus, 2015. Print.

_____. *Selected Letters.* 5 vols. Eds. August Derleth & James Turner. Sauk City, WI: Arkham House, 1965–1976.

Lovecraft, H.P., and August Derleth. *The Watchers Out of Time.* New York: Del Rey, 2008.

Lovecraft, H.P., and Others. *The Horror in the Museum.* New York: Del Rey, 2007.

Biographies

de Camp, L. Sprague. *Lovecraft: A Biography.* New York: Doubleday, 1975. Print.

Joshi, S.T. *I Am Providence: The Life and Times of H.P. Lovecraft.* 2 vols. New York: Hippocampus, 2010. Print.

Critical Works, Secondary Sources and Other Works Cited

Altick, Richard. *Victorian People and Ideas.* New York: W.W. Norton, 1973. Print.

Arnold, Matthew. *Culture & Anarchy.* Ed. Samuel Lipman. New Haven: Yale University Press, 1994. Print.

Bacon, Francis. *New Atlantis and the Great Instauration.* Ed. Jerry Weinberger. Illinois: Harlan Davidson, Inc., 1989. Print.

Berman, Marshall. *All That Is Solid Melts into Air: The Experience of Modernity.* 1982. New York: Penguin Books, 1988. Print.

Bryson, Bill. *At Home: A Short History of Private Life.* New York: Doubleday, 2010. Print.

Burleson, Donald R. "The Mythic Hero Archetype in 'The Dunwich Horror.'" *Lovecraft Studies* 4 (Spring 1981): 1–9. Print.

_____. *Lovecraft: Disturbing the Universe.* Lexington: University of Kentucky Press, 1990. Print.

Coleridge, Samuel T. "The Rime of the Ancient Mariner." Poetry Foundation. Web. 15 Sept. 2014.

Davis, Mike, ed. *The Lovecraft EZine.* Mike Davis, Web. 3 Aug. 2014. <http://lovecraftzine.com/>.

Dickens, Charles. *Hard Times.* Ed. Grahame Smith. London: Everyman, 1998. Print.

Evans, Timothy H. "A Last Defense Against the Dark: Folklore, Horror, and the Uses of Tradition in the Works of H.P. Lovecraft." *Journal of Folklore Research* 42.1 (2005): 99–135. Print.

Fanon, Frantz. *Black Skin, White Masks.* 1952. Trans. Charles Lam Markmann. New York: Grove Press, 1967. Print.

García Augustín, Eduardo. "Travelling into the Shadow of Innsmouth." *British and American Studies* 10 (2004): 25–30. Print.

Garofalo, Charles, and Robert M. Price. "Chariots of the Old Ones?" *The Crypt of Cthulhu Archive.* Kevin L. O'Brien, Jan. 2007. Web. 3 Aug. 2014.

Gilmore, Mikal. Introduction. *The Sandman: The Wake*. By Neil Gaiman. New York: DC Comics, 1997. 8–12. Print.

Harms, Daniel. *The Cthulhu Mythos Encyclopedia*. Lake Orion, MI: Elder Signs, 2008. Print.

Harms, Daniel, and John Wisdom Gonce. *The Necronomicon Files: The Truth Behind Lovecraft's Legend*. Boston: Weiser, 2003. Print.

Hillman, Bill. *ERBzine*. Edgar Rice Burroughs Tribute Site. 1996. Web. 21 Sept. 2014.

Hite, Kenneth. *Tour De Lovecraft: The Tales*. Alexandria, VA: Atomic Overmind, 2008. Print.

Houellebecq, Michel. *H.P. Lovecraft: Against the World, Against Life*. Trans. Dorna Khazeni. San Francisco: Believer, 2005. Print.

Houghton, Walter E. *The Victorian Frame of Mind: 1830–1870*. New Haven: Yale University Press, 1985. Print.

Huysmans, J.K. *Against Nature: A New Translation of Á Rebours*. Trans. Robert Baldick. Baltimore: Penguin Books, 1959. Print

Joshi, S. T. *The Evolution of the Weird Tale*. New York: Hippocampus, 2004. Print.

_____. *H.P. Lovecraft, Four Decades of Criticism*. Athens: Ohio University Press, 1980. Print.

_____. *Lovecraft and a World in Transition: Collected Essays on H.P. Lovecraft*. New York: Hippocampus, 2014. Print.

_____. *The Modern Weird Tale*. Jefferson, NC: McFarland, 2001.

_____. *The Weird Tale Arthur Machen, Lord Dunsany, Algernon Blackwood, M.R. James, Ambrose Bierce, H.P. Lovecraft*. Holicong, PA: Wildside, 2003. Print.

_____. *A Weird Writer in Our Midst: Early Criticism of H.P. Lovecraft*. New York: Hippocampus, 2010. Print.

Joshi, S.T., and David E. Schultz. *An H.P. Lovecraft Encyclopedia*. Westport, CT: Greenwood, 2001. Print.

Kimmel, Michael S. *Manhood in America: A Cultural History*. New York: Free Press, 1996. Print.

Lackey, Chris, and Chad Fifer. *The H.P. Lovecraft Literary Podcast*. Podcast.

Loveman, Samuel. "Lovecraft as a Conversationalist," *Fresco*. 8(3), Spring 1958. 34–36. Print

Nietzsche, Friedrich. *Thus Spake Zarathustra*. www.gutenberg.com. Project Gutenberg, 2012. Web. 4 January 2013. Print.

North, Michael, ed. *T.S. Eliot, the Waste Land: A Norton Critical Edition*. New York: W.W. Norton, 2001.

Pearsall, Anthony B. *The Lovecraft Lexicon: A Reader's Guide to Persons, Places and Things in the Tales of H.P. Lovecraft*. Tempe, AZ: New Falcon Publications, 2005. Print.

Penzoldt, Peter. *The Supernatural in Fiction*. Amherst, NY: Prometheus Books, 1965. Print.

Price, Robert M. "Apocalyptic Expectation in 'The Call of Cthulhu'" *The Crypt of Cthulhu Archive*. Kevin L. O'Brien, Jan. 2007. Web. 3 Aug. 2014.

_____. "Cthul—Who?: How Do You Pronounce "Cthulhu"?" *The Crypt of Cthulhu Archive*. Kevin L. O'Brien, Jan. 2007. Web. 3 Aug. 2014.

_____. "Cthulhu and King Kong." *The Crypt of Cthulhu Archive*. Kevin L. O'Brien, Jan. 2007. Web. 3 Aug. 2014.

_____. "Cthulhu Elsewhere in Lovecraft." *The Crypt of Cthulhu Archive*. Kevin L. O'Brien, Jan. 2007. Web. 3 Aug. 2014.

_____. "'Dagon' and 'The Madness From the Sea.'" *The Crypt of Cthulhu Archive*. Kevin L. O'Brien, Jan. 2007. Web. 3 Aug. 2014.

_____. "Demythologizing Cthulhu." *Lovecraft Studies* 8 (Spring 1984): 3–9, 24. Print.

_____. *H.P. Lovecraft and the Cthulhu Mythos*. Mercer Island, WA: Starmont House, 1990. Print.

_____. *The Lovecraft Geek. The Lovecraft EZine*. Podcast.

_____. "Lovecraft's Concept of Blasphemy." *The Crypt of Cthulhu Archive*. Kevin L. O'Brien, Jan. 2007. Web. 3 Aug. 2014.

_____. "The Real Father Dagon." *The Crypt of Cthulhu Archive*. Kevin L. O'Brien, Jan. 2007. Web. 3 Aug. 2014.

_____. "St. Toad's Hagiography." *The Crypt of Cthulhu Archive*. Kevin L. O'Brien, Jan. 2007. Web. 3 Aug. 2014.

_____. "Sea-Monster Reports and the Johansen Narrative." *The Crypt of Cthulhu Archive*. Kevin L. O'Brien, Jan. 2007. Web. 3 Aug. 2014.

Saler, Michael. "Modern Enchantments: The Canny Wonders and Uncanny Others of H.P. Lovecraft." *Space Between: Literature and Culture, 1914-1945* 2.1 (2006): 11–32. Print.

Shreffler, Philip A. *The H.P. Lovecraft Companion*. Westport, CT: Greenwood, 1977. Print.

Smith, Rod. *Traditional Sea Shanties and Sea Songs Lyrics*. Traditional Music Library. Web. 22 Aug. 25. 2014.

Van Hise, James, ed. *The Fantastic Worlds of H.P. Lovecraft*. Yucca Valley, CA: James Van Hise, 1999. Print.

Whitworth, Michael H. Introduction. *Modernism*. Blackwell Guides to Criticism. Malden, MA: Blackwell Publishing, 2007. 3–60. Print.

Wilde, Oscar. *The Picture of Dorian Gray*. Ed. Michael Patrick Gillespie. A Norton Critical Edition. 2nd ed. London: W.W. Norton, 2007. Print.

_____. Preface. *The Picture of Dorian Gray*. Ed. Michael Patrick Gillespie. A Norton Critical Edition. 2nd ed. London: W.W. Norton, 2007. 3–4. Print.

Index